Praise for Michael Bishop's
BRITTLE INNINGS

"*Brittle Innings* is a wonderful conflation of baseball history and horror—and most of the latter not reliant upon the fantastic so much as upon the terrible things that human beings do to one another. Written with the panache that Michael Bishop always dependably delivers."

 —Gregory Frost, author of *The Pure Cold Light*

"Michael Bishop mixes baseball with fantasy and what it means to be human and drives one onto the left-field roof. *Brittle Innings* is anything but brittle. Brilliant might be a better descriptive."

 —Jack McDevitt, author of *Seeker*

"Love, ambition, shame, innocence and experience, mortality and immortality, sex and race—they're all here, in a vivid picture of small town America in the shadow of World War II and the capacity for nobility, and monstrous evil, that it demonstrated. Michael Bishop's great American novel unveils new depths with every reading. See, there is some justice in the world: *Brittle Innings* is back in print."

 —John Kessel, author of *Corrupting Dr. Nice*

"Only a writer as ingenious and skillful as Michael Bishop could stitch the joys of a great baseball story to the mythos of a dark nineteenth-century masterpiece and make the fit appear seamless. An undeniable classic of fantastic literature."

 —Jeffrey Ford, author of *The Physiognomy*

"In some alternate world, *Brittle Innings* is the baseball fantasy movie that everybody's heard of instead of *Field of Dreams*."

 —Gardner Dozois, author of *The Visible Man*

"I first read *Brittle Innings* in 1994, and now in 2012 it's still vivid and real to me, and its wisdom took hold."

 —Gordon Van Gelder, editor of *Fantasy & Science Fiction*

"I've often said that science fiction is the literature of intriguing juxtapositions, and here's a terrific example, luminously combining baseball and . . . well, you'll find out: a homerun of a novel, full of heart and memorable characters, all driven by Bishop's beautiful prose."
  —Robert Sawyer, author of *Triggers*

"Although I've read many fine novels since 1994, this novel remains an all-time favorite. I keep a stash of copies to share with special friends, for this is a book about friendship, dreams, love, and finding one's way in the world—an uplifting story that will make you believe in the goodness of people again. I envy anyone reading it for the first time."
  —Ann VanderMeer, editor of *Best American Fantasy*

"Southern literature has always had healthy doses of the fantastic, steeped in atmosphere. Think Tennessee Williams, Truman Capote, Flannery O'Connor. Michael Bishop stands in such company with this deep, stirring work. It's a Southern Gothic World War Two Baseball Novel, with a twist that you'll never forget."
  —Gregory Benford, author of *Timescape*

"*Brittle Innings* is a wonderful book: knowing, funny, and ultimately moving, with many surprises along the way. Bishop creates a vanished world in vivid and loving detail. I enjoyed it all immensely—and I'm not even a baseball fan!"
  —Nancy Kress, author of *After the Fall, Before the Fall, During the Fall*

"*Brittle Innings* is a richly evocative World War II-era Southern coming-of-age baseball story that's also a worthy sequel to one of the classics of 19th-century literature. I don't know how Michael Bishop wrote this one-of-a-kind masterwork, but I'm sure glad he did. "
  —Andy Duncan, author of *Beluthahatchie*

"*Brittle Innings* is simply one of Michael Bishop's many magnificent novels. His skills, insights, and verbal pleasures should have long ago driven lesser talents into silence."
  —George Zebrowski, author of *Brute Orbits*

"Filled with layered prose that amply rewards discerning readers while never getting in the way of an enthralling story, *Brittle Innings* approaches Great American Novel territory while also serving as a fine sequel to one of speculative fiction's masterpieces. With its unexpected twists and turns and atmospheric details, it is a treasure. "

—Pamela Sargent, author of *The Shore of Women*

"The subject of baseball seems to bring out the best in a novelist—one thinks immediately of W.P. Kinsella's *Shoeless Joe*, Mark Harris's *Bang the Drum Slowly*, and Bernard Malumud's *The Natural*—but *Brittle Innngs* is in a league of its own, burning with a metaphysical audacity to which even Kinsella never aspired. Michael Bishop has blessed his readers with a masterpiece of speculative literature that nourishes the intellect, nurtures the heart, and deserves to remain in print until the last ball game is played on planet Earth."

—James Morrow, author of *Towing Jehovah*

"More than a stylistic tour de force, *Brittle Innings* triumphs on multiple levels of plot, characterization, and theme. Bishop manages a most difficult task: creating a masterpiece of subtlety and character while seducing the reader to turn pages as fast as the eye can absorb its action. Drawing on a passion for baseball, a savor of the gothic, and a piercing poignancy for its two deeply lovable protagonists, *Brittle Innings* embodies my ideal of the Great American Novel."

—Mary A. Turzillo, author of *An Old-Fashioned Martian Girl*

"Told as an extended flashback, [*Brittle Innings*] is drenched in a luminous nostalgia for what amounts to a Golden Age (despite the period's acknowledged defects), a "once upon a time" venue where mythic beings . . . still walked the earth. This Bradburyian evocation of a legendary prelapsarian past is one of the effects SF does all too infrequently, but to which the mode lends itself splendidly in the hands of a master such as Bishop.

—Damien Broderick & Paul Di Filippo, *Science Fiction: The 101 Best Novels* 1985-2010

"There are few books that I can hand to anyone and say, You will love this. *Brittle Innings* is three of them. First it's the story of Danny Boles, a small-town kid with major league dreams, working his way through his first season in Class-C baseball in the 1940s, falling in love and learning that the world is a bit more complicated than he thought. Then it's the story of Jumbo Clerval, and all that has happened to him since we last saw him in a famous 19th-century novel. But the third book is a combination of the two, made of parts that shouldn't work together, but do so beautifully. It's Bishop's most charming novel, featuring two of his most distinctive characters, and their voices will stay with you long after you've finished the book. When you've finished reading it, give it to anyone—and I mean anyone—and they will thank you for it."

    —Daryl Gregory, author of *Raising Stoney Mayhall*

"Bishop's earlier novels . . . earned him recognition as one of the best writers to come out of the science-fiction/fantasy field during the past couple of decades. *Brittle Innings* should secure him recognition as, simply, a truly good American writer."

    —Steven Utley, author of *The Beasts of Love*

"This big, ambitious novel chronicles a minor league pennant race in Georgia in 1943, and creates a South-ful of hilariously vivid . . . characters. You won't soon forget its narrator, feisty Oklahoman Danny Boles, or his mysterious teammate and soulmate Jumbo Hank Clerval, a seemingly superhuman figure around whom Michael Bishop has constructed an ingenious and wonderfully surprising plot."

    —*USA Today*

"Brilliant. One of the best baseball novels this country has ever produced."

    —*The Orlando Sentinel*

"One does not have to know much about baseball to appreciate Bishop's formidable strengths and succumb to his evocation of the old New South, its inflections, its sticky heat, the smell of its dusty ballparks. . . . *Brittle Innings* should secure his recognition as a truly good American writer."

    —*The Austin Chronicle*

"Exciting, precisely rendered and genuinely moving throughout."
—*The San Francisco Chronicle*

"Bishop's mix of the fantastic and the commonplace is so assured . . . may be the first baseball gothic."
—*The Atlanta Journal-Constitution*

"There's nothing everyday about the fiction of Michael Bishop."
—*Atlanta Magazine*

"Resonantly evocative of time and place, with a splendid gallery of characters. . . . Bishop pulls it off brilliantly."
—*Kirkus Reviews*

"Marvelous. . . . Poetic, funny, horrific, and tragic."
—*The Denver Post*

"[A] richly told tale with the full mythic magic of *Field of Dreams*."
—*The Reader's Review*

"Extravagant, powerful, and ultimately . . . moving. . . . All summer in a book."
—*The Detroit Metro Times*

BRITTLE INNINGS

BRITTLE INNINGS

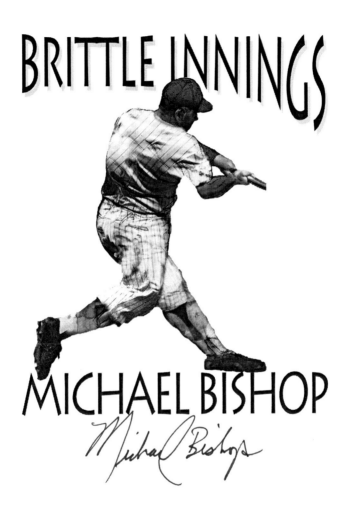

MICHAEL BISHOP

FAIRWOOD PRESS
Bonney Lake, WA

BRITTLE INNINGS

A Fairwood Press Book
August 2012
Copyright © 1994 Michael Bishop

Fairwood Press
21528 104th Street Court East
Bonney Lake, WA   98391
www.fairwoodpress.com

Cover illustration & design by
Paul Swenson

Book design by
Patrick Swenson

Originally published by Bantam Books, May 1994

ISBN13: 978-1-933846-31-6
First Fairwood Press Edition: August 2012
Printed in the United States of America

Brittle Innings:
Outfielders or Outsiders

by Elizabeth Hand

I reviewed Michael Bishop's brilliant, *sui generis* novel *Brittle Innings* when it first appeared in 1994. At that time I wrote, "I wish I'd written it." Rereading it nearly two decades later, I'm even more staggered by Bishop's achievement.

In *Brittle Innings,* Bishop takes on a subject as big and complex and difficult to categorize as the unforgettable Henry "Jumbo" Clerval, the central and most riveting character in a novel that has many: the dark heart of America itself. After a brief preamble, we find ourselves in Tenkiller, Oklahoma, June 1943, embarking on a journey as improbable and absorbing as Huck Finn's, narrated by a character Huck might well have taken up with if he'd found himself playing minor league baseball during the Second World War.

That narrator would be Danny Boles, seventeen and afflicted with a stammer, a talented shortstop with Cherokee blood who's looking to get the hell out of Tenkiller. Danny's age and speech impediment keep him from being cannon fodder, so his chance to get out of Dodge arrives when he's offered a position with the Highbridge (Georgia) Hellbenders, a farm team that prides itself on being the "Terror of the CVL," the Chattahoochee Valley League. The Hellbenders' owner, Jordan "Mister JayMac" McKissic, offers Danny seventy-five-dollars a month, along with room and board, and the golden opportunity to play in

"... a small town league, with a pitiful 'C' training classification, but we make it in spite of the war because we're the hardest-
playing saps anywhere and flat-out beaucoups of fun to watch."

Indeed they are. The Hellbenders lineup reads like the cast list from a lost Damon Runyon sandlot epic: Quip Parris, Clarence "Trapdoor" Evans, Sweet Gus Pettus, Percy "Double" Dunnagin, Junior Heggie. Their rivals in the CVL include the LaGrange Gendarmes, the Marble Springs Seminoles, the Cottonton Boll Weevils, and the Opelika Orphans. Bishop's dialogue throughout is also Runyonesque, in particular the fulsome exhortations of Mister JayMac.

> "Mostly, we've lost to total mediocrities and also-rans. Were I given to worry, I'd be a total ruin. But I've long since taken to heart the scriptural counsel that anxious thought adds not a minute to our lives, and I sleep like a babe in swaddling clothes."
> "Jesus," Hoey said, not exactly reverently.
> "Selah," Mister JayMac said. "I've prayed and I've rounded up these fresh-faced youths."
> "Glory!" Quip Parris said. "What if they're bums, sir?"
> Mister JayMc smiled. "If yall wanted aiggs, would I foist on you scorpions?"

Danny is, for all appearances, one of these fresh-faced youths. But he's now utterly mute, following a violent rape aboard the train from Tenkiller to Highbridge. Still, he's no less a misfit than some of his clowning teammates. And he certainly can't hold a candle to Jumbo Hank Clerval, the booming, seven-foot giant with "a Frenchified accent" who becomes Danny's roommate at the Hellbenders' boarding house. When he first meets Clerval, Danny thinks, "His face was out of alignment somehow, like a pumpkin cut in two and put back together wrong." And, then, a little later:

> His hair was greasy black, with a shock of silver-white in the middle of his lumpy forehead and streaks of nickel-gray around his mangled-looking ears. Cripes, I thought, if you staggered into him in a pitch-black street, the fella'd give you about twelve quick heart attacks. Even the overhead lights and the ragging of his fellow Hellbenders couldn't hide his weirdness. I was ugly, but this guy'd been put together in a meat-packing plant by clumsy blind men.

But Jumbo's a hell of a first baseman, and he has a hell of a story to tell, in the journal he eventually shares with Danny, as the two become friends and confidantes during the Hellbenders' short season under the broiling Georgia sun.

> *At the commencement of my new life, as throughout my old one, bitter cold scant afflicted me. I preferred it to the warmth of summer, responding to it as an assemblage of pistons, flywheels, and cogs respond to lubrication. My chief hindrance lay not in meteorological conditions, but in the body of my dead creator . . .*

It is Michael Bishop's astonishing achievement to braid these two voices seamlessly within one narrative, alternating between Clerval's logbook of his journeys back to what we quaintly call civilization, and Danny's play-by-play account of the Hellbenders barnstorming through the Chattahoochee Valley.

It would have been very easy for such an ambitious and genre-bending work to have ended up as nothing more than an intriguing hybrid, ungainly as Jumbo himself. But in rereading *Brittle Innings* I found myself once again so deeply immersed in Bishop's vision of a lost America that I was startled to look down and realize I was staring at a page. I truly can't recall another book that so beautifully and deftly captures the American home front during World War II.

But for all its exuberance and memorably larger-than-life characters, this isn't a nostalgic evocation of America-at-War. One of the novel's set pieces features a game between the Hellbenders and the Splendid Dominican Touristers, a barnstorming team from the Negro American League, and throughout his novel Bishop doesn't shy away from confronting the rifts between the white players and their black counterparts, in particular the tragic figure of Darius Satterfield.

Baseball may be the playing field on which the exuberant characters of *Brittle Innings* make their bids for sandlot stardom, but this isn't really a novel about outfielders. It's a novel about outsiders: voiceless Danny; doomed Darius; questing, noble Jumbo Clerval, still embarked upon his centuries-long quest to determine where genuine humanity resides: that elusive spark we call a soul. *Brittle Innings* isn't just a great baseball novel, or a great literary novel, or a great science fiction novel. It's a great American novel. And, yes, I wish I'd written it.

BRITTLE INNINGS

PROLOGUE

After pursuing him a week (half my annual vacation from the *Columbus Ledger-Enquirer*), I caught up with Danny Boles on a blustery day in early April at a high school in eastern Alabama. I knew I'd found him because his fabled motor home—he called it Kit Carson, a sly allusion to his job—was parked on the asphalt above the school's ram-shackle athletic complex.

I pulled in next to the RV, climbed out, and peered through the driver's-side window. An empty fast-food sack and an old ruled notebook lay on the front seat. I tried the door. It was locked. From the ball field came the faint chatter of two or three players and a coach's blistering shout, "*Come on, you guys, talk it up!*"

Although not quite five in the afternoon, a twilight chill had begun to creep over the tilled red clay beyond the collapsing rail of the center-field fence. A red-shouldered hawk, hungry or curious, sailed above the clay. I watched it as I heel-walked down the slope looking for Boles.

In that puny weekday crowd, he stood out plainly enough. There were aluminum bleachers on each baseline, but Boles leaned on the fence midway between first base and the right-field foul marker, a metal pole topped by a limp blue pennant. He wore faded dungarees, scuffed loafers, and, as if it were July, a short-sleeved Hawaiian shirt. A wispy-haired and frail-seeming man, Boles rested his arms on the fence and studied the talent on the field. Most folks would have supposed him some player's grandfather.

Aping nonchalance, I strolled past the first-base bleachers, tiptoed around Boles, and took up a place beside him. I hesitated to interrupt his scrutiny of the earnest kids scattered across the field. I also hesitated to confess my real business, for Boles had a reputation as a hater of newshounds.

When that dull half-inning had concluded and the teams began lackadaisically changing places, I said, "Mr. Boles, you're a hard man to track down."

He squinted at me as if I'd jabbed him with a stick.

"If not for your RV," I said, gesturing toward the parking lot, "I might've kept going. This is the umpity-umpth town I've visited in the past five days."

Boles's squint unclenched. His eyes grew a size or two, his irises like tiny pinwheels. April sunlight turned his jug-handle ears translucent. Although it looked as if I could knock him over with a string bean, Boles intimidated me. Why? The sleeves of his flamboyant shirt came down to his elbows, giving him the look of a frail gnome with a bad haircut. Maybe it was his rep that daunted me, or the hint of flint in his close-set eyes.

Almost indifferently, Boles looked away. A between-innings pitching change had taken his attention. A long-armed black kid, with a fullback's thighs, took the mound and hurled incandescent heat during his warm-ups.

Sadly, with a batter at the plate, the kid's performance was high, wide, and ugly. He walked the first two batters to face him, struck out a wild swinger, walked a third kid, struck out a second hitter on a dozen pitches (including several that would have been sure tickets to first if the batter hadn't foul-tipped them), and came irreparably unglued when a blooper to right center rolled to the fence for a bases-clearing double. He shied his next pitch into the hitter's ribs, then stalked around the mound muttering and banging his glove against his thigh.

"If he just had some control," I said.

The manager signaled for the right fielder and the distraught black kid to swap positions.

Only then did Boles look at me again. "*That's where he shoulda been playing to start with. He's a pitcher like the Incredible Hulk's a doily maker.*"

Although his look scalded, Boles's voice unnerved me most. I'd forgotten that several years ago, during an operation for throat cancer, he'd had his vocal cords removed. Today he spoke with the help of an amplifying device, a kind of cordless microphone, held to his throat above the Adam's apple. The sound from the amplifier was intelligible enough, but mechanical in tone. Listening to him, you got the feeling that his rubbery face masked the shiny features and the artificial vocal apparatus of a robot.

"*Who the hell are you, anyway?*"

"Sorry, Mr. Boles." I tried to recover. "A sports writer."

"*Yeah? Who for?*"

"The Columbus papers. Columbus, Georgia."

Boles nodded and pocketed the microphonelike gadget.

"I telephoned your home in Atlanta a few weeks back," I said. "I want to do a major profile. A full-length book. Your wife said she'd relay the message. In the meantime, she advised me to look for you at high school games up and down the Chattahoochee Valley. She said we should have a face-to-face about the feasibility of the project.

"Sir," I added.

Boles put a finger to his lips. In a sudden sweep, he moved it to mine. He wasn't here to jawbone; if I wanted his cooperation, I had better knock off the kibitzing. The scoreboard in left field said that this game was only four innings along. How many innings did high school teams play? Seven? Nine?

Despite a windbreaker and woolen slacks, I had Himalayan-size goosebumps, while Boles, tanned and stringy in his Hawaiian shirt, seemed primed for another four to six innings.

Surprisingly, he lasted only two more feeble ground-outs, then limped away from the fence toward the parking lot, gesturing at me to follow. He didn't look back. Never mind his hitch-along gait, he made good time. At his RV, he keyed open the driver's door.

"The game wasn't over," I said.

He turned around, his amplifier to his Adam's apple. "*At this level, it's not games that matter. It's players. I don't have to wait for meaningless overall outcomes to sort the stumblebums from the racehorses.*" He said outcomes, even with his flat mechanical voice, as if it were a disease. "*Sides, you were getting itchy to leave. Weren't you?*"

"Yessir." It didn't embarrass me to say so. The April twilight had rolled down on us like a corrugated iron door.

Boles said, "*Go around back. I'll open up for you. We'll have us a nip and chew the fat.*"

In less than a minute, he'd admitted me to the boudoir-kitchen-sitting-room of his motor home. We sat across from each other in a cramped table booth that undoubtedly opened out, at night, into a spine-deforming bed. From plastic cups, we sipped Early Times Kentucky whiskey. Kit Carson's interior, redolent of hamburger grease and lime-scented aftershave, felt airtight and stuffy. Its warmth, and that of the booze, made Boles's filmy shirt seem almost practical. I shed my windbreaker.

"*I let you find me,*" Boles said.

"How so?"

"*Usually, on the job, I park this rolling flophouse where the competition aint likely to see it.*"

"The competition?"

"*Other scouts. They know my rep. They figure if I'm tooling around a certain neighborhood, I've scented a prospect, maybe even another MVP.*"

I wasn't above buttering him up. "You've signed over forty big leaguers, haven't you?"

"*Forty-six. So I don't let the competition see* Kit. *I park behind a gym, a dumpster. Sometimes I drive a renter.*"

"You abandon *Kit Carson?*"

"*Else guys'll poach. I'm only out here today*"—waving his cup at the parking lot—"*cause I knew you'd throw in the towel if you didn't find me in a year or two. Right?*"

"Why'd you want me to find you? Are you ready to talk?"

"*I'm ready to retire. Talking may be the way to fatten up the goose that'll let us do it in comfort.*" He smiled. "*Or the only way to clear my head.*"

Boles said he had a story to tell. He just didn't trust himself to tell it like a professional writer would. So he proposed that I ghostwrite it for half any advance monies, plus a seventy-thirty split of all royalties, subsidiary sales, licensing fees, and other incidental income. He had pored over too many rookie contracts not to have acquired an acute business sense. Cannily, he had also checked out my credentials, surveying both my work for the Columbus papers and my profile of the first female National League umpire in a months-old issue of *Sports Illustrated*. His verdict? I was no Shakespeare, but I did okay.

"Mr. Boles, that's nice to hear, but I hadn't planned to do an 'as-told-to' book. I'm an interviewer and an analyst."

"*So interview. So analyze.*"

"Sir, I want to write a book about a major-league scout's life on the road, a book based on firsthand observation."

"*So the goofball who lets you observe him doesn't cut into your profits?*"

"Mr. Boles—"

"*So he doesn't get a damned thing out of it but the pleasure of your company?*"

I held my tongue. I didn't care much for Boles's phrasing, but his assessment of what I hoped for—a book of my own, profits of my own—hit the target dead center.

"No offense, young fella, but your personality lacks the dazzle to make that trade-off work for me."

"Well, there's also glory."

Boles cut his eyes.

"The book I have in mind has the working title *The Good Scout.* You're the good scout. It'll chronicle a full year of your life on the road, scouting for the Atlanta Braves. It'll also—"

"If you did that, traveled with me a year and wrote it all up, you'd deserve the money, all of it. But that aint the book I want to do. Uh-uh." He sloshed himself another finger of Early Times and twisted around to snap on a portable radio balanced on the ledge above our booth. The static-riven broadcast of a ball game gabbled away behind us as we talked. Effortlessly, though, Boles followed the game's progress, even as he outlined his own literary plans and parried my bemused objections.

Other writers, he told me, had produced good stuff—magazine articles, newspaper pieces, even entire books—about major-league scouts, limelight-shunning sandlot prophets who had immeasurably enriched the game. The topic was tried and true, even old hat. I argued that a bang-up writer and a well-chosen scout's signature methods and idiosyncrasies could reinvigorate the topic. Boles shook his head. Yeah, sure, maybe I could do an interesting book, a colorful book, about his career (I'd have to be a droning hack to render his story a total yawn), but it wouldn't be a ground-breaking book, a book resembling nothing else ever published about America's national pastime.

Peeved, I said, "What're you talking about, Mr. Boles? Exactly what do you want me to help you write?"

"Ever hear of the CVL? Of Mr. Jordan McKissic? Of the Highbridge Hell-benders? Of Jumbo Clerval? Of a seventeen-year-old shortstop named Danny Boles?"

Danny Boles, yes. Everything else, no. In fact, everything else in his catalogue had registered as gibberish. Only later was I able to sort out the separate items and give each one a distinct identity. Only later did I learn that CVL stood for Chattahoochee Valley League and that the CVL had a mysterious sub rosa cachet among older Southern sportswriters.

"That's right. Once I was a minor-league shortstop, a real comer in Class C ball. The league I played in lasted six seasons, from 1938 to 1943, and its final season was the only year that young Danny Boles played professionally. That's what I want you to help me write about, sport."

The high-school ball game had ended. The home team had lost. You could hear the away boys monkey-hooting in their dugout. A gaggle of fans filtered into the parking lot, approaching their vehicles and closing in on Boles's motor home. In the greenish glow of the safety lamps that had just fuzzed on, the home team's partisans looked ghoulish: drained and unreal.

I groaned inwardly. Boles wanted me to write about his brief and obscure professional career during World War II. It sounded like a vanity set up. Here he was, arguably the most successful major-league scout ever, but a nagging sense of the illegitimacy of that career made him view his playing days as more bookworthy than his near-mythic accomplishments as a scout. Sad.

Noting my hesitation, Boles tugged one long earlobe. "*I got called up at the end of the '43 season, but an injury, on the very day Mister Jay Mac gave me the good word, kept me from reporting.*"

"An injury?"

"*The Phillies wanted me to take over for them at short, but a spiking . . . Hey, you saw me limp up here from the ball field.*"

I had, but Boles's limp, because he could still locomote with gusto, had struck me as a minor handicap. Besides, no one expected a man his age to be as svelte and rapid as a whippet.

So I'd given no thought to his likely goals before signing on in 1948 as a scout with the Philadelphia Phillies.

"*The importance of that war-year season wasn't what happened to me,*" Boles said, "*so much as it was the fate of my roomy, Jumbo Clerval, and the demise of the whole blamed league. A story unlike any you've ever heard.*"

I'm sorry: I doubted it. I also doubted that the Phillies (in '44, they were renamed, for two unhallowed seasons, the Blue Jays, long before Toronto had a team on which to hang that nickname) had called Boles up to play for them. After all, not many players make it in a single jump from a Class C ball club to a starting job with a team in the Show. Thus I dismissed Boles's claim as unverifiable and unseemly brag.

And he picked up on my skepticism. "*Wonder why I let you find me, sport? I mean, a dozen other pretty good sportswriters've been after me, but I let you track me down. Any idea why?*"

He had me stumped.

"*Cause you byline your stuff Gabe Stewart.*"

"That's my name, Mr. Boles."

"*Danny. It's too tight in here to stand on formalities.*"

"All right. Danny."

"*I chose you because of your name. When the Phillies called me up in '43, a fella named Gabby Stewart was playing short for em. His batting average hung around .200. Not that great a glove man, either. In '44, Freddy Fitzsimmons, the manager, moved him over to third. Stewart upped his average nine or ten points, but the next year he was gone, whether drafted or sent back down to the minors I couldn't say. He never got back to the bigs. Gabby Stewart was my favorite Phillie, though. His weak stick and shaky glove persuaded the front office to give a skinny, big-eared Oklahoma kid a shot. You aint related to the guy, are you?*"

"My first name's Gabriel. Stewart's a pretty common surname."

Boles laughed, silently; he had taken the mike away from his throat. The crow's-feet around his eyes crinkled. His shoulders jogged like the scapulae of a medical skeleton on strings.

Finally, he said, "*First, my book the way I want it done, then yours the way you want it done. You get a split on mine, but yours is all yours, from first pitch to final putout. Deal?*"

"Deal," I said, surprised. How could I do better?

Boles and I shook hands. The ball game on the radio dropped away like a whistling porpoise going under. Over some more Early Times, we agreed on a series of tape-recording sessions. A few days later, fortified by the prospect of a lucrative book contract, I sashayed into my managing editor's office and resigned from the *Ledger-Enquirer*.

1

Way I look at it, minor league ball back then was sort of like B movies. Thrills on the cheap. Cheap buses, cheap hotels, cheap stadiums, cheap seats, cheap equipment, cheap talent.

Cheap-cheap.

Sound like an Easter chick, eh? Or like the mechanical conductor on those subway trains out to Atlanta's airport. What do people call it, a "robot voice"? Yeah, a robot voice. Sorry. Can't help it. At least with this gizmo up to my throat, I have a voice. Couple of long stretches in my life, I *couldn't* talk. Back then, Mama would've reckoned this sci-fi gizmo an honest-to-God miracle. Awful as I sound, she'd've paid money to hear me talk with it.

Oh, yeah: B movies. What I meant was, they were second-line stuff. Not *Gone With the Wind*, not *For Whom the Bell Tolls*, none of that highbrow crap. Sometimes, though, they were fine. Made on the cheap, but not tacky. Monster flicks. Nifty musicals. Gangster shows. You got your money's worth.

Same with an evening at the Highbridge ballpark, McKissic Field, watching the Hellbenders take on the Mudcats or the Boll Weevils. There was a war on. Half of what you wore and three-quarters of what you ate was rationed. Not movies, though, and not ball games. Folks flocked to both for about the same reason—to forget the war, especially the bad or the confusing news, and to have em a bang-up time. To get lost in something besides a muddle of depressing newsprint.

In June of '43, I went into the CVL, the Chattahoochee Valley League, right off my high school team in Tenkiller, Oklahoma, near Tenkiller Lake, in Cherokee County. My county was part of the old Injun Territory set aside by the U. S. Congress for the Cherokees, that Beulahland in eastern Oklahoma the bluecoats herded them to in the winter of 1838 and '39. The Trail of Tears. Anyway, I'm one-eighth or one-sixteenth or one-thirty-secondth Cherokee, some bollixed-up fraction, a kind of Injun octoroon.

Me heading to Georgia from Tenkiller was slogging the Trail of Tears backwards. In more ways than one. I was glad to get out of Oklahoma, to know I'd be pulling down real pay playing on an honest-to-God pro baseball squad down in Highbridge. It beat the stuffing out of pushing a mop in a factory. Or walking into a Jap-infested bunker on the ridge of some steamy coral atoll.

And it beat the fire out of unemployment.

For three years I played ball for the Tenkiller Red Stix, the only team I even tried out for in high school. As a sophomore, I played utility and pinch hit. As a junior, I started.

I idolized Phil Rizzuto, the Yankee shortstop. His first two years with the Yanks were my junior and senior years at Tenkiller High. My teammates called me Scooter because Yankee fans called Rizzuto that. Actually, they called me Sc-Scooter because, if and when I talked, I st-st-stammered.

I could take that. Being called Sc-Scooter, even if it made fun of my handicap, at least showed me the other fellas respected my talent. I hit like Scooter. I fielded like Scooter. I could flat-out play.

What I *hated* was, some of my non-ballplaying school-mates called me Dumbo. To keep from stammering, sometimes I'd just say nothing at all. I'd stare at whoever tried to talk to me. They figured me for a mute; in spitefuller words, a dummy. Also, even before I made the ball team, everyone in Tenkiller had been over to Muskogee or up to Tahlequah to see *Dumbo*, a Disney flick about a pint-sized elephant with humongous ears. Hilarious movie. A scream. And I was the perfect sap to stick a tag like Dumbo on because I couldn't or wouldn't talk and had me this really terrific set of ears. Ha ha. The older I've gotten the more I've sorta grown into them, but as a pimply-faced kid just barely over the puberty line, I looked like a drip.

Back then, kids called nerds drips. A drip equaled a nerd. My schoolmates saw me as the uncrowned king of the drips. The guys, even teammates, pulled gags on me—put horned toads in my locker or cracked raw eggs into my jockstrap. Girls giggled behind their painted fingernails. The one time I nerved up to ask a girl to a dance—a semipretty gal, not the holy homecoming queen—I st-st-stammered like Sylvester the Cat and turned fire-engine red.

"You're sweet," she told me, "but I've got this algebra test to study for." And burst out laughing.

So I wanted out of that hick town. All my problems would go *ffftht!*, like a blown-out match, the instant I left Cherokee County. I'd step into

Arkansas or Texas and turn into Clark Gable. (Or Alan Ladd, who was more my size.)

Talk about a naive fool.

My chance to get out of Tenkiller came from playing shortstop for the Red Stix. All our teams—track, wrestling, basketball—had the nickname Red Stix. We were called after a renegade band of Indians—Creeks, not Cherokees, but the Creeks belonged to the Five Civilized Tribes too—that had fought General Jackson's Tennessee militiamen at Horseshoe Bend, Alabama. The batons our track team used in relays were red, and our baseball team had red bats, even though it was hard to keep them looking decent. The barrel of my bat, for instance, was always flaking paint, letting the grain of the timber show through. I got enough hits, only the handle of my bat would stay ruby-red the entire season.

In the spring of '43, the Red Stix regularly beat up on the squads of surrounding schools, even monster schools with a lot more students. Once we took care of an uppity bunch from Fort Smith, Arkansas. That April and May, scrapping every Tuesday and Saturday afternoon, we went fifteen and three. The folks in Tenkiller loved us. We were local heroes. Nearly every working stiff in town took time off to come to our games, even if they had to make up the lost hours later.

Tenkiller is a typical eastern Oklahoma burg: a grocery, a barber shop, a beautician's, a pharmacy, a seed-and-feed depot, a hardware store, a mechanic or nine. Back then, our chief industry was Deck Glider, Inc. Deck Glider belonged to a Tulsa-based firm called the H. C. Hawkins Company. Before the war, Tenkiller's Deck Glider plant made heavy-duty floor waxers. My mama'd gone to work on its assembly line in the fall of '37. Her moonlighting outside the home irked Daddy so bad, though, it goaded him to walk.

Anyway, after Daddy left, without so much as a fare-thee-well or a forwarding address, Mama had to work to keep us fed. By the time of Pearl Harbor, she'd worked her way up to a line manager's position. Problem was, after FDR declared war on the back-stabbing Nips, the WPB—War Production Board—told us floor waxers didn't contribute to the defense effort. Neither did toasters, vacuum cleaners, coffee makers, vending machines, toothpaste tubes, and lots of other products with metal or plastic in em. So the WPB cut the supply of materials our factory needed to make the Deck Glider. In fact, it was *illegal* to make a floor waxer. You could even get fined for hoarding old toothpaste tubes.

Mama nearlybout panicked. How'd she support us if Deck Glider shut down? Tenkiller didn't offer much in the way of jobs for women. It already had all the carhops, waitresses, switchboard nellies, and secretaries it needed. Besides, any of those jobs would've meant a step down in pay. Mama had monthly house payments to meet. Some men, heads of bigger households than ours, were even scareder than Mama.

Then a section chief from H. C. Hawkins headquarters in Tulsa motored down to soothe everybody's fears. The parent company—old Mr. Hawkins had brains—had arranged some war-production contracts with Uncle Sugar. Deck Glider, Inc., would close for a month to convert its equipment and its assembly lines to the boring of gear housings for antitank guns. No one would get laid off. It might even be necessary to add on to the plant and hire some line workers from out of town. Local builders would have to put up housing for these people. Commuting—even with car pooling and special gas and tire dispensations for defense workers—was unpatriotic.

When Mama told me how the Hawkins Company had saved her job, she cried. "It's gonna be Boomer Sooner around here again, Danny. The armed forces need a *lot* of antitank guns."

But even after Deck Glider geared up for war work, a core of old hands—native Tenkillerites—set up their hours, or traded off with new workers on other shifts, so they could attend Red Stix home games. The plant ran three shifts. It never shut down. Mama worked days, six days a week. Even so, our field had a bleachers section, behind the backstop, for Deck Glider personnel. Despite her shift, Mama never missed a home game or a single hour of paid labor. She traded off or went in early. And Mama was no crazier for the Red Stix than Mr. Neal, the barber, or Tom Davenport, the owner of a wildcat oil company, or anybody else in town. The Red Stix glued that sagebrush community together. Deck Glider and our local churches didn't even come close. . . .

Sunday mornings, New York's Mayor LaGuardia read the funnies to his city's children over the radio. A station in Muskogee picked up this feed and played it for us dumb Okies and Arkies. I heard him once. I knew LaGuardia's kisser from Movietone newsreels. I'd seen him conducting civil defense exercises, supervising air-raid wardens and such. He'd wear a white metal helmet, wave his arms, and carry on, reminding me of Lou Costello, the short funny fella in the Abbott and Costello comedy team. Over the radio, he sounded sort of sissyish. How did a fella who looked and sounded like him get to be mayor of New York? Tenkiller's mayor, Gil Stone, wore yoke-collared shirts, snakeskin boots, and dungarees.

Then I read in the *Tulsa World* that a crew of politicians wanted to halt major-league ball for the duration. LaGuardia got hot about that. He ripped into the jerks: "Our people don't mind being rationed on sugar and shoes, but these men in Washington will have to leave our baseball alone!" Hooray for LaGuardia. A guy who stood up for baseball was defending America better than some hot airbag in Congress, maybe even better than a poor dogface on KP down in Alabama or Missisloppi.

Of course, baseball was my meat and drink. Mayor LaGuardia, even if he looked like Lou Costello, at least read the funnies to kids over the radio and gave the antibaseball nuts what-for. I never stopped to think he had three major-league clubs in his own city, that maybe greenbacks and greed had as much to do with his defense of baseball as a love of the game. Or maybe it was just LaGuardia hanging tight with the Yankees' pinstripe Mafia: DiMaggio, Crosetti, and Rizzuto. Who knows?

Okay, okay. How'd I get from a sagebrush town like Tenkiller to a peanut-growing burg like Highbridge? From the Red Stix to the Hellbenders, a scrappy gang in the low minors? After all, the war emptied the big leagues' farm systems. The Selective Service Acts, a.k.a. the draft, carried off so many able-bodied young guys it nigh-on to wiped out the minors.

For a couple of reasons, though, I was a candidate for a farm club, if the farm clubs survived.

First off, I played crackerjack ball. As Dizzy Dean used to say, "It aint bragging if you can back it up." I could. In the twenty games the Red Stix played that spring—a couple were exhibitions—I made only one official fielding error. Even that boot you could've argued. Our scorekeeper charged it to me on a hard drive I knocked down and scooped to Toby Watersong for a force at second. Toby had to reach a bit, and he dropped the toss. The error could've been mine, it could've been his. But Toby's uncle happened to be keeping score that day. So what? No sweat, I figured. And still do.

You hear a lot about good-field/no-hit players: whizzes at hoovering up grounders and turning double plays, but zilches at the plate. I could hit. That spring I had thirty-six bingers in seventy-five at bats, including a game against a semipro oil-company squad that didn't count in our division standings. A .480 average, seventy points higher than Ted Williams hit when he became the first major leaguer since Rogers Hornsby to pass .400.

I didn't lead the Red Stix in batting, though. Franklin Gooch did. Goochie pitched, played center field, and ran like a scorched jackrabbit. He outhit me by over thirty points. Day after he graduated, he enlisted in the Marines. In June of '45, he died on Okinawa on Kunishi Ridge, shot through the eye by a Jap sniper. I still have the letter Goochie wrote me from the field a month before the sniper got him.

Sorry to stray. But Goochie's story ties in, sort of. The second reason I was a candidate for the minors, gangbuster stats aside, was I wouldn't turn eighteen until after the '43 season. My birthday's in November. Even though I was single and a high-school grad, I wasn't yet draft bait. Even at eighteen, I'd probably end up classified 4-F: unfit to serve.

I had a speech problem. Sometimes, I refused to talk. When I did t-t-talk, I st-stammered. Out would come broken phrases, like bursts from a half-jammed machine gun, then nothing. Sometimes the nothing, even when Coach Brandon yelled at me (maybe especially then), stretched on and on. So I sullened my way through school, eyes peeled and hackles up. Almost every other way, physically, I was normal, but my speech problem gave folks the creeps. If the Army docs didn't find some physical reason for it—a cleft palate was out, and my bruised vocal cords should've healed long ago—Mama figured they'd cull me as a borderline nut case. A GI has to have a voice, if only to yell "Lookit!" when an infiltrator chunks a grenade into a buddy's foxhole.

A third thing put me on the road to Highbridge. A couple that came to all our Red Stix home games was Colonel and Mrs. Clyde Elshtain. The colonel'd retired as an Army supply officer to become a big-shot procurement specialist at Deck Glider, Inc. Mama suspected he may've tugged a few strings to help the Tenkiller factory get its conversion contract. The real baseball fan of the two, though, was the missus, Tulipa Elshtain. Swear to God, that was her name: *Tulipa*. At fifty-something, Miss Tulipa still walked and drawled like a *Gone With the Wind* belle. Even in Oklahoma, she remained a member of the Confederate magic circle. At Red Stix games, though, she'd shed her ladylike ways and whoop and boo like a sailor at a prize fight.

"Come on, Goochie, give us a four-ply wallop! Drop it into the Mississip!"

Miss Tulipa and the colonel took to sitting at the top of the Glide Decker bleachers, next to Mama. At the games, they tried to make Mama—the poor, hard-working, abandoned Mrs. Boles—feel like their pal and rooting partner.

"I'm their pity project," Mama said after they'd started this. "A swell game-day friend, but nobody to invite home."

Colonel Elshtain was management, Mama was labor. Miss Tulipa would climb up into the bleachers wearing lace blouses, peg-topped skirts, and either a velvet beret or a fancy-dan straw hat with peacock feathers. Mama wore coveralls and head scarves.

"*Attaway, Scooter!*" Miss Tulipa would yell. "*Attaway to rap it, punkin!*"

Eventually, the Elshtains *did* ask us to their home, a two-story antebellum job with columns. It'd once been the home of a rich, uprooted Cherokee named Trenton Cass. The Cass Mansion, everybody calls it yet. Mama sported heels, bottled stockings, and her prettiest clingy polka-dot dress. I wore khaki pants, store-bought galluses, and my Sunday tie.

At that special after-church dinner—I can still see it—we had iced-down shrimp for appetizers, bleached asparagus, a rice-and-chicken dish Miss Tulipa called Country Captain, and, for dessert, orange sherbet and blueberries. I don't know where the Elshtains got the fixings or how many ration points it set em back, but a classier meal I'd never had. I wolfed it all, even the asparagus, a la-di-la vegetable I never liked and haven't eaten since. (Babe Ruth said asparagus made his urine stink.) They even had wine, but nobody offered me any.

"You can flat-out play," Miss Tulipa told me over dessert. "How'd you like to help a pro team win a championship?" Her voice was like Coca-Cola: sweet and fizzy, with a sting.

Mama had done most of the talking so far. I looked at her. From the gramophone in the library, just off the dining room, came the scratchy diddle-diddle-diddle of the colonel's chamber music. Like Miles Standish, I tried to speak for myself.

"I wuh . . . I wuh . . ."

"Take your time, Daniel," Miss Tulipa said.

"I want to pl-play in the m-m-majors," I blurted.

Miss Tulipa's smile sparkled like the cut-glass chandelier over the table. "Why, of course you do."

"He's a baby," Mama said. "He needs a honest job of work."

The colonel'd already excused himself and wandered into the library, but Miss Tulipa nodded. "Oaks begin as acorns and major leaguers as sandlot players. What you need, Daniel, is seasoning."

I understood that. Saying I wanted to play in the bigs didn't mean I expected to start there. So I gawped, a drip with a speech problem. My tongue felt like a folded washrag. Mama saw my panic, the Jell-O wobble of my bottom lip.

"You think he's good enough to go pro?"

"Laurel, Laurel dear, he's a *prospect*. Denying him a chance to develop his gifts would be cruel. Suppose DiMaggio had become just another San Francisco fisherman?"

"He'd've been a good one, probably."

"Of course, Laurel. But he'd've labored virtually unseen. The loss to our national heritage, ah, incalculable."

"A lot of ifs and maybes," Mama said. "Why fret it?"

Miss Tulipa shut up for a bit, then said, "Daniel should sign with the Hellbenders in my old hometown. My brother Jordan"—Tulipa said JUR-dun—"will pay him seventy-five dollars a month, twenty-five more than he'd make as a private in the Army. Jordan'll also provide lodging and instruction. This rotten old war has just *decimated* the majors. If he does well, Daniel could be wearing big-league flannels sooner than you think."

Colonel Elshtain, wearing a honest-to-God ascot, wandered back in. "Army pay's gone up. Daniel'd make *sixty* a month, even as a private. And the benefits that accrue as—"

"Please, Clyde. If you're trying to recruit him, remember Daniel's medical condition may preclude his induction."

"He should have no trouble at all shooting a carbine."

"You forget his—his *handicap*."

"Send him to boot camp. To your own Camp Penticuff. The DIs there might well divest him of it."

Miss Tulipa exploded. "How many young men do you want to ship out as cannon fodder? Do you want to be rid of them all?"

"We've more at stake today than a minor league pennant." The colonel's lips had blanched like day-old fish bait.

"Given your patriotic fervor," Miss Tulipa said, "why don't you have your commission reactivated?"

The colonel lifted his chin. "Perhaps I should." He returned to his staticky gramophone, sliding a panel door into place between the library and us. You could still hear his music bumbling up and down the scale, though, like drowsy bees.

"Laurel, what do you think?" Miss Tulipa said, turning on the Suthren belle charm. "Would you allow Daniel to sign with Jordan if Jordan agrees he has the talent?"

"Danny'd be a high-school graduate," Mama said. "He could do whatever he wants."

I struggled to ask the last question I'd ever ask at the Elshtains' table. "Which farm s-s-system?"

"Pardon me?" Miss Tulipa said. "Oh. The farm system. The Hellbenders belong to Philadelphia. Does it matter?"

Not much. So far as I knew, no other organization had even scouted the Red Stix. Even so, the name Philadelphia hit me like a concrete medicine ball. Philadelphia had two big-league clubs, the Athletics in the American League and the Phillies in the National. Both clubs reeked. The Athletics had finished last three straight years and the Phillies five. The Phillies had been the only major league club to lose over a hundred games in '42. If any American city ranked as Loserville, it was Philadelphia.

"Oh," Miss Tulipa said. "Which team there? The Phillies. Your opportunities with the Phils are boundless."

Bingo. I had a better chance of ousting Gabby Stewart at short than I did Rizzuto at that spot with the Yankees or Pee Wee Reese in Brooklyn with the Dodgers. Even so, I'd've almost rather thrown myself into a Japanese POW camp than go to Philadelphia.

Mama and I left the Cass Mansion, and I comforted myself by remembering that in Highbridge, at least, I wouldn't be playing for the Phillies, I'd be playing for the Hellbenders, a team supposedly on the rough-and-tumble rise.

2

Jordan McKissic—Mister JayMac to everyone in Highbridge, as I learned later—came riding into Oklahoma in a Pullman car behind an old steam engine. He planned to watch two Red Stix games, one on a Saturday, one the following Tuesday, and return to Georgia. April of '43, two weeks before the Hellbenders kicked off their regular season. Mister JayMac came by train because the Office of Defense Transportation had nixed pleasure driving. You could legally call a scouting trip business, but patriotic pols—like the scoundrels LaGuardia had lit into in the paper—wouldn't admit pro ball deserved that courtesy.

'Forty-three was the year the ODT forbid major leaguers to go South for spring training. Except for the Cardinals, who practiced in St. Louis, ballplayers had to train east of the Mississip and north of the Potomac and Ohio rivers. Wiseguys called this the Landis-Eastman Line, after Baseball Commissioner Landis and the fella heading up the ODT. Mister JayMac was a mucky-muck on the Hothlepoya County draft board, down in Highbridge. To do his part for national defense, he'd left his Cadillac and colored driver at home and faced the blowing coal dust and the jostling hoi polloi on a passenger train.

In Tenkiller, Mister JayMac stayed in the Cass Mansion. I first laid eyes on him on Saturday, when he climbed into the Deck Glider bleachers with Mama and his hosts. He stood out in that crowd. He was pushing sixty—a couple of years younger than I am now—but tall, fit, and dapper. He wore a striped white dress shirt, old-fashioned pleated linen trousers, and a pair of military-pink suspenders. His hair was iron gray, cut close at temples and neck. A salt-and-peppery forelock fell over his forehead like an owlet's wing. Even from my shortstop position, I could see this terrific blue glint in his eyes: a sharper blue than Miss Tulipa's, like sapphire dust bonded to a couple of zinc-coated war pennies.

From the stands, Mister JayMac watched me. He watched Toby

Watersong, Franklin Gooch, every kid on both teams. Whenever I had the chance, I watched him back. Mister JayMac was the Great Stone Face, perched above the hubbub like a Supreme Court judge, mysterious and cool. Studying.

I had a good game Saturday, thank God, a couple of singles and an unassisted double play at short. Afterwards, I sort of expected Mister JayMac to come down and speak, maybe even to make me a job offer, but he and the Elshtains vanished, off to the Cass Mansion, I guess, without so much as a nod. In the stands, Mama said, Miss Tulipa and the colonel had been as supportive of the team and as complimentary of me as ever, but Mister JayMac had scarcely spoken two words.

"Not my notion of a courtly Suthren gentleman," Mama said. "Eyes like a starved wolf's."

The Red Stix never practiced Sundays, and Mister JayMac didn't attend church with Miss Tulipa and the colonel. Monday, though, he watched us from the stands on the third-base line, taking in our every wind sprint, pepper game, and half-assed batting-practice bunt. I could feel him studying me, intense and chillylike. The process—letting him gander—reminded me of what a beauty-pageant hopeful has to suffer.

During this workout, I muffed a cozy roller at short, then overthrew Jessie Muldrow at first trying to outgun the runner. Bad. Baaad. At the plate, I swung too hard, topping the ball once and popping it up on my second at bat. Rotten. Not even the Phillies would've wanted me. Time I got a third chance to hit, Mister JayMac had vamoosed. I got on base, but with a cheap swinging bunt I legged out from sheer embarrassment. But so what? Mama'd better check with Colonel Elshtain to see if Deck Glider had an assembly-line job for me.

Tuesday afternoon, in a game against Checotah, I forgot the crowd, the bench jockeys in the other dugout, the dogs barking on Cookson Road, everything but the rope-sized seams on every ball floating my way. Don't know why, but the ball looked big as the moon to me. Hitting or fielding, I couldn't miss it. For all the effect he had on me, Mister JayMac—up in our stands—could've been in the Belgian Congo. I played great. Afterwards, the boys from Checotah got on their bus as low and hollowed-out as dogwood stumps.

Mister JayMac didn't speak to me after this game, either. Once we'd put it away, I *did* start thinking about him again, my ticket out of Tenkiller. When he still didn't show up, though, I thought, Nuts to you, mister.

Shortly after supper that evening, Mister JayMac showed up at our stucco house on Cody Street. Five-and-a-half rooms, just big enough for a couch, a pair of beds, a beat-up table, a w.c., and a cheap cathedral radio. It always seemed to smell of hash and eggs.

Mister JayMac didn't reach six feet, but in a buttermilk coat with awning-sized lapels and pockets, he *filled* our house the way a film actor can sometimes glut a whole movie screen. Mama got a chair from the kitchen and made him sit. Didn't want him looming. Then, like two kids in a dentist's waiting room, she and I huddled together on the sofa.

"Ma'am," Mister JayMac said, "I'd like your son to come with me to Highbridge tomorrow." He didn't bother to look at me. He aimed all his magnolia gallantry at Mama. "My club, the Hellbenders, has need of him."

"So do the Red Stix. Plus, Danny's got school to finish."

"Yessum," Mister JayMac said.

"He's been going twelve years, nearly," Mama said. "Why fall shy of a sheepskin by a piddlin two months?"

"Why, indeed? An enlightened attitude," Mister JayMac said.

"He needs his education."

" 'What sculpture is to a block of marble,' " Mister JayMac told Mama, " 'education is to the soul.' Addison."

"Well, Addison spoke true."

"Yes he did," Mister JayMac said. "But there's education and there's education. If Danny doesn't return to Highbridge with me tomorrow, he'll miss the chance to train with us and the opening month of our season." He pulled a string-tied packet from inside his coat. "Here's a contract, Mrs. Boles." He untied the packet and handed an official-looking form with a clip-on to Mama. "Also a check for seventy-five dollars, his first full month's pay." He could've dropped a garter snake down my shirt—that kind of thrill went through me. "But, Mrs. Boles, you must countersign my enabling form and let Danny go back with me." He reached over and tapped the check.

I was a slave who *wanted* to be sold. School was lectures and yawns, girls smirking and wiseacres pulling stupid jokes.

Mama stared down at my clipped-on check. "Coach Brandon says some nigger ballplayers make twice this, maybe."

"That's probably true," Mister JayMac said. "I daresay those players draw better than Danny's likely to jes yet."

"Well, he can't go now anyway," Mama said. "Even when he can, seventy-five won't do. That's coffee-and-cake pay. Danny may jes be starting, but *no* colored boy ought to make more than him."

My mama, the John L. Lewis of ball agents. All she needed was Lewis's eyebrows. Mister JayMac ripped up his check, and I almost swallowed my tongue. Smithereened. My whole career.

"Mrs. Boles, you drive a hard bargain." Mister JayMac took the contract back. "I'll up his pay twenty-five and send yall a new contract. Forget this one. Mr. Boles," finally looking at me, "we'll send you a train ticket. Ride down soon as you've got your diploma, hear?"

I tried to answer. "Yessir," I wanted to say, but it might as well've been the Lord's Prayer in Gullah.

As promised, the revised contract came two weeks later. Mama and I signed it for a notary, with Coach Brandon and the Elshtains as witnesses. Two, three days later, Mr. Ogrodnik announced my good fortune to the student body in the gym. Kids cheered, pretty girls and class-officer types among them. If I'd had the guts, I would have raspberried half the hypocrites there, even though I did like hearing them cheer.

Franklin Gooch said I was a lucky bastard. When we'd won the war, guys like DiMaggio, Williams, and Greenberg would come home and their stay-at-home subs would disappear completely. A real talent, though, would survive.

"You," Goochie said, "are a real talent."

Goochie was already eighteen. Early in '42, his mama's younger brother had been killed on the cruiser *Houston* in the Battle of the Java Sea. Goochie wanted to take a few Jap scalps in the Marines, but he didn't begrudge me my shot at a career in pro ball. Envied me, but didn't call me a feather merchant. He had other kettles of fish to fry. Too bad his goals led him into the hands of a graves-registration crew on Okinawa.

3

Because Tenkiller was a side-track burg, I caught the train in Tahlequah. Mister JayMac had sent me a ticket.

Colonel Elshtain had a C gas-rationing sticker on the divided window of his automobile, supposedly because his job at Deck Glider had such import to the national defense. Actually, I think, he had buddies in the War Department, who knew folks in the Office of Price Administration. Anyway, that C sticker got Colonel Elshtain all the gas he wanted, and he and Miss Tulipa drove Mama and me to the station in Tahlequah in his 1939 Hudson Terraplane. (That car was a picture of chrome and ivory. It even had a radio.) My only luggage was a duffel full of clothes. The handle of my favorite baseball bat—Coach Brandon had given it to me—stuck out of my bag, and my bag rode in the Hudson's trunk. In the back, next to Mama, I felt partly like a rich swell and partly like a murderer riding in style to the gallows.

On the station platform, Mama looked angry enough to spit. In truth, she'd just clamped her lips to keep from crying. I was grateful she was managing so well. No seventeen-year-old kid wants his mama blubbering all over him in public. And that railway depot was crowded. Tahlequah looked like Tulsa.

Recruits in civvies heading for Camp Gruber or Fort Sill. GIs going back to Chaffee, Benning, Polk, or Penticuff after furloughs. Cardboard suitcases and duffels. Parents and girls mingling with the sad-sack soldiers and recruits. All the guys were riding passenger trains, not troop-train expresses, with civilians like me in a near-invisible minority.

Some of the GIs wove back and forth through the redbrick station building. In buddy-buddy groups. Sometimes they'd stop near Mama and me to look me up and down. I was only to scoff at—soldier material like marshmallows are ammo. I could hardly believe I'd have to share a car with these rude and crude dogfaces. The ones with stripes on their sleeves scared the Cherokee piss out of me.

"You puny cur," Mama said, "don't forget to write."

I only stood five-five, but Audie Murphy, who came along later, wound up the war's most decorated soldier, and he was no bruiser either. Me, I was in tiptop trim. If I could play ball in the Chattahoochee heat, why'd so many of these wiseguy doughboys seem to think I couldn't charge into Jap artillery fire? Why'd Mama assume I'd steam into vapor under the Georgia sun and never even send her a postcard?

"I can't watch you leave. Be good. Do good."

A pair of nuns came up, smiling. Only they weren't nuns, but pillow-breasted Red Cross gals in habits and wimples. They had a hospital cart loaded with goodies, like stewardesses on a Delta flight. They took me for a recruit. They wanted to give me magazines, Tootsie Rolls, Lucky Strikes.

"He don't want none," Mama said. "Thank you."

The Red Cross nuns toddled off, but the soldiers nearby didn't. When Mama kissed me on the lips, a good slobbery one, they had a snicker riot. Mama left me with the Elshtains. I hoped the colonel would put the fear of God into those dogfaces by calling them down for crooked gig lines and ungentlemanly public comportment. He didn't, of course. Soldiers on furlough were privileged characters, prodigal sons in gabardine. And rightly so, maybe. They'd sweated out fourteen weeks of basic, and a lot of em, like Goochie, would come home as statistics, battle fatalities, instead of people. Colonel Elshtain understood. He'd served in the Great War, the War to End All Wars, and he understood.

Then the colonel and Miss Tulipa left too, and I was alone with all the trained heroes and smiling Red Cross nuns. A redcap directed us—everybody going my way, at least—to our coaches, and porters with hand trucks stowed our duffels in their proper baggage cars. Anyway, this rail ride from Oklahoma to Georgia gave me a new look at humanity. Time I jumped off that train, I'd've sworn the defense of the United States was in the hands of sadistic cretins. Jerks that shot up colored training camps in New York State and Louisiana. Yahoos that, a couple of months later, danced the hat dance on zoot-suiters in L.A. As a civvie, I felt like soft-shelled predator bait too. Forget that my draft status had everything to do with being seventeen and nothing to do with being afraid. Did a wish to cap off the last year of my childhood playing Class C baseball make me a coward?

They packed us aboard that train like cattle. On a mirror in the John, somebody had taped an "Off the Record" cartoon of a GI in his skivvies standing outside a Pullman lavatory with his shaving gear. He fingers his stubbly jaw. "*Great Scott!*" he barks. "*I must've shaved the guy next to me!*" Every seat in every coach was taken; every aisle was a logjam.

I got up once, and a sergeant took my place. So I squeezed my way through the clicking coaches till I found the only empty seat in the last five Pullmans. I sat next to a PFC whose head looked like the bowling-ball jaw of the guy in the cartoon. A hulk, with a mug like a skinned Pekingese's.

"How you know that seat's not saved?" he asked me.

I wanted to say, "Screw you," but the snarl in the PFC's challenge had taken all my sand away. I hadn't exactly had a quarryful to begin with.

The PFC said, "Nice ears, yokel. Buy em by the yard?"

I went "Duh" like the yokel he'd pegged me and laid a hand on my Adam's apple to indicate my speech problem.

"Tonsillitis?" he said. "Strep throat? You got some kinda contagious damned communicative disease?"

"I have a st-st-stammer."

"You do, huh? And astigmatism too if you couldn't see I was holding this seat for Pumphrey."

"P-P-Pum—?"

"P-P-Pum yourself," he mocked. "What's your name? I'd like to meet your whole yokel cl-cl-clan."

He was probably from a real metropolis like Coffeyville or Enid, but I was a yokel.

"B-B-Boles," I said. "D-D-Danny Boles."

"Where from?"

"Tenkiller, Oklahoma." No stammer. Give me a medal. Send me to radio-announcer's school.

"Well, Boles, ya goddamned Okie, move your skinny ass fore I line it with teeth." The guy bumped me with his elbow. His nose floated in front of me like an elevator button I didn't dare mash. "Hey, you're still in Pumphrey's seat."

"B-but where can I g-g-go?"

He laughed. He couldn't believe me, a kid innocent as bottled water. He put his thumb into my chin dimple, to show he *meant* for me to hop up. I jerked away and stumbled into the aisle—which jostled with foot traffic, landlubbers trying to get their rail legs.

I went enginewards. GIs, recruits, MPs with gunbelts sat jammed into their seats, not one tender female among them. Every car smelled of dried sweat, scorched khaki, cigarette smoke, caked boot polish.

I finally stopped on a platform between two coaches. An accordion-pleated rubber hood was supposed to join the cars (to keep passengers out of the wind and coal dust), but the train people hadn't hooked it up. I rode the coupling. The wind felt good. So did being alone. The countryside had gentle hills, dogwoods and redbuds still showing color in amongst the evergreens. It got prettier the farther from Cherokee County we chugged. Had Congress designated the Injun Territories for their flatness and lack of trees? Probably.

I'd stood there a couple of minutes when a baby-faced GI banged through from the forward car. He scowled and patted his pockets. He shouted, "Got a smoke, buddy?"

"N-no, I d-d-don't."

"Screw you!" he shouted. Did he think I'd mugged a Red Cross lady for her cigarettes, then squirreled away my booty from regular Joes like him? I just stared at him. Maybe a 4-F civilian had snaked his girl, or a recruit had short-sheeted his bunk. Running into such meanness just then felt like having grain alcohol poured into a cut. My stare got harder. I lifted my fists to my ribs. The kid saw them shaking. He spit down at the tracks, easy-like, and returned to the coach he'd come from. That should've boosted my morale. I'd shown my steel and a GI had backed off. Problem was, he'd looked like a Campbell's Soup kid.

In all the wind and clatter, I began to cry. The platform had me for good, then. I couldn't go back in with tears on my face. The GIs would've ridden me all the way to Georgia.

Our train wasn't an express. It crawled through every podunk crossing, rattled to a chain-reaction stop in every town with as many as two letters to its name. Passengers lurched back and forth between coaches, but I clung to the coupling's guard rail and ignored them.

It took an hour and a half to get to Fort Smith and another thirty minutes to pass through Fort Chaffee, the post southeast of it. Recruits off, GIs on. A trackside do-si-do. Finally, we clacked off through Arkansas again.

Later, in the dining car, I sat with three other guys who seemed to be loners too. A swabbie going to Pensacola and two dogfaces. We'd all been strangers, but the other fellas struck up a friendly debate about the credentials (Ol' Diz would've said *differentials*) of the Cards without Enos Country

Slaughter and the Dodgers without Pistol Pete Reiser, who ran full-tilt into outfield walls and knocked himself out.

My kind of debate. Except my vocal cords had a clamp on them. All I could do, like some kind of chimp, was point, nod, grunt, and grin. The other guys—the friendliest servicemen I'd yet bumped into—must've figured me for a runaway from the Oklahoma Institute for Hayseed Dummies. I paid my check and stumbled back to the coupling platform.

And stayed there, where my kidneys began to feel like hip-hugging cocktail shakers. In the fields whipping by, I could make out pole beans, snap beans, alfalfa, cotton. The soil had the richness of devil's food cake. We drove deeper into the unreconstructed South. The air thickened, smells got odder, the unfamiliar crops sort of scared me.

A soldier came out onto my platform. I bent over my rail, but he didn't go away. I could feel his stare seeping through the back of my shirt and up my arms—like kerosene through a pile of rags. Finally, I faced him.

An older guy. Stripes on his sleeves, ribbons on his breast pocket, heavy lips. His coloring reminded me of a slice of Spam. A sergeant. A vet of some combat theater, probably. I relaxed. Battle-tempered noncoms showed themselves hard-noses in training camps, but teddy bears with kids and women and well-meaning civilians.

"Your name Boles?" the sergeant shouted. This scared me, but I nodded. "I'm First Sergeant Pumphrey. Private Overbeck told me about you! Described you to a T! You from Tenkiller, in Oklahoma?"

"Y-y-yessir!" I yelled back. Shaking again, not just from the rattling of the train.

"Sergeant!" he corrected me. "I'm not an officer! I'm not a gentleman! I'm damned sure no egg-sucking sir!"

"N-n-nosir!"

Pumphrey gestured at the train, the flashing rails, the marching ranks of cotton. "This is horseshit! Come on!" He yanked me into the sudden hush of the passenger car.

My ears gulped at the quiet. Pumphrey prodded me down the length of the coach, and then the length of another one, and so on until we reached a car with a lavatory. Pumphrey pushed me inside. Did he have queerish tendencies? Coach Brandon had warned us boys in fifth-period hygiene about that sort of crap, but I still didn't get it. Half our male seniors had thought hygiene was a dirty word.

We had that lavatory almost to ourselves. The only other guy in there had his tailbone on the back edge of a toilet seat, his toes over the seat's front edge and his arms around his knees to keep his shoes from slipping off and jolting him awake. His open mouth hissed softly. Pumphrey ignored him like he would a water stain and backed me up against a sink.

"I know your dad, Boles," he said. "Until two weeks ago we served in the same goddamned support group at an Army airfield in the Aleuts. Ever hear of Otter Point?"

I shook my head.

"It's on Umnak. Cold as a polar bear's prick. Windier than Chicago. Foggier than a dry-ice factory."

I couldn't figure what Pumphrey wanted me to do. He seemed to blame me—or my daddy, if the part about knowing him wasn't a lie or a smokescreen—for the Aleutian weather. His red lips flapped. Threads of spit webbed them.

"Cold, cold, cold," he said. "Oil up there turns to peanut butter. You use blowtorches to thaw your bomber engines. If spray gets on an airplane's windshield, it's like trying to see through a sheet of pebbled glass. One drop of high-octane fuel on your skin—if you're cluck enough to expose it—will lift a blister the size of a walnut. Follow?"

"Y-y-yessir." I didn't, but what the hell?

"I once saw your old man's eyelids freeze shut. In our Quonset, I made him rack out on a cot with his face between the struts and the canvas webbing. Held a hot cup of coffee under his eyes. Kept saying, 'Don't touch yourself. Unless you want to go around with a finger glued to your eyeball forever.' You hear me, kid?"

I nodded. Hard.

"At's how well I knew your papa, Boles," Sergeant Pumphrey said. "You favor him. Grow into those ears, you could almost pass for his natural get."

My daddy, as I recalled him, had been a solid, good-looking man. Leaving aside my athletic ability, no one'd ever accused me of *favoring* him. Not in any physical way. I usually got told I *didn't* resemble my father. And who feels lower than the homely kid of good-looking parents?

Pumphrey let go of my arm and pushed away from me. "Just how much're you like your old man, anyway?"

That seemed a fair moment to beat it. Pumphrey was wound up, pacing and question-posing. I made a break.

Bam! Pumphrey slid between me and the door and nearlybout paddled me slaphappy with his lips.

"Hold it! Dickie Boles's the worst excuse for a soldier—hell, for a human being—I've ever served with. A goldbrick and a back-stabber. Pray God, you take after your mama."

"He ever m-m-mention m-me?" I said.

"I dunno. I guess. Said something once like he may've sired a son. May've. Like if he had, it would've made him a fraternity brother of God's. Otherwise, kid, he was too busy rejigging duty rosters and miscounting ammo shipments to expend the effort."

"He st-still up there?"

"Oh yeah. Oh yeah." Pumphrey sort of giggled. "There's ossifers on Umnak who think he should spend the rest of his natural life at Otter Point. For the sake of everybody down here in the free forty-eight." Pumphrey moved aside again, and I stepped all over myself trying to get out of there.

"Hold it!" He grabbed me, breathing licorice or schnapps, something sweet and foul, into my face. "Not so fast, kiddo!" I felt strangled. What'd the crazy bruiser plan to do? "How much money you got on you, Boles?"

"M-m-money?"

"Yeah, m-m-money. Cash money. Your goddamned dad was all the time borrowing. Wouldn't pay it back, neither. How much you got?"

I'd boarded the train with fifty bucks cash money, half of my first paycheck. I still had whatever I hadn't spent.

Pumphrey spun me, shoved me against the wall, fumbled my billfold out of my hip pocket. Holding me in place, he counted out my money, crammed the bills into his own breast pocket, and flipped the billfold into a lavatory sink.

"You're short. About fifty shy of what your old man owes me, kiddo."

"I'm n-not my father's k-k-keeper."

"Maybe not. But I'm still out half a sawbuck. What're you gonna do about it, kiddo?"

"You're st-st-stealing. You're a d-d-damned th-thief."

"Settling a debt don't work out as theft, prick!" Pumphrey snatched me away from the wall, then slammed me back into it. My lip split. I cried out. "Hush, boy. Accounts still don't tote. We gotta make em tote."

Pumphrey pushed me into the stall next to the sleeping GI's, wedged a hankie into my mouth, and spun me around again. When he yanked my pants down, and my shorts along with them, I finally had a two-bit notion of what he had in mind and lashed back at him with an elbow. He showed me the blade of a pocketknife, told me he'd take my liver by way of my rectum if I gave him any more grief, and bent me over the open commode. What he did then took about two minutes and hurt like fire.

"You *still* owe me," Pumphrey said, yanking my pants back up. "Nine more wouldn't break your daddy and me even."

I'd started to cry.

"Stop it, Boles. Mention this to a soul, and your ass is mine forever."

He left me there. I fetched my billfold, washed my face and hands, and stood at the mirror not recognizing myself. The PFC on the toilet—I could see his awkwardly sprawled body in the mirror—had slept through the whole assault, snoring like an asthmatic sea lion.

4

Some folks find sleeping on a train soothing, like lying under a tin roof with rain chattering down. Not me. The clickety-click of grooved iron wheels sliding on long metal tongues reminds me of an alarm clock ticking. I keep waiting for the bell to go off. I kept waiting for my train to derail.

I was near dead from humiliation, but if an alarm started to clatter, I'd spring up like a jack-in-the-box. (I'd claimed my berth after some soldiers got off at Camp Robinson and some others switched trains in Little Rock.) I drowsed some, but only after crying myself to sleep. Drowsing, I dreamt of my daddy, Richard Oconostota Boles.

My daddy's folks came to Oklahoma—U. S. Injun Territory—with a remnant of the cholera-stricken Cherokees from what's now Pickens County, Georgia. See, I had great-great-great-grandfolks, full-blooded native Americans on Daddy's side, on the Trail of Tears. They wound up in a reservation settlement on the site of the town known today as Checotah.

Mama Laurel was a Norwegian Helvig, a paleface farmer's daughter through and through, but she and Daddy met at a Lutheran church picnic on Tenkiller Lake while he was doing carpentry work for a Wells Fargo agent out of Muskogee. Daddy was nineteen when I was born, seven years younger than Mama. They had a hard go of it. Money stayed tight, and my father had a hurtful weakness for honky-tonking and catting around. Mama excused him because he'd been so young when they married—seventeen, just my age when I left Oklahoma on that train—and because she adored him, never mind he had the brain of a sly ten-year-old and the loving heart of an armadillo.

Daddy played pickup baseball whenever he could, paid good money for bad illegal whiskey, and sparked all the "bad" young gals in and around Muskogee. He built barns, smoke-houses, and graineries for folk, and he learned auto mechanics from a local Pierce Arrow dealer. He loved cars. Well, no, their *motors*—their grease and pistons and belts.

A year before the stock market bottomed out, Daddy drove a trap from farm to farm selling Ful-O-Pep Mash, a chicken feed with cod-liver meal. It was supposed to prime a hen to lay eggs the size of baseballs. Mama said Daddy always held up a real baseball for skeptics, as if the mere sight would convince em. And the first time he drove his trap around hawking Ful-O-Pep, he did okay. Second visit, though, all a farmer had to do was hold one of his runty eggs next to Daddy's baseball and the jig was up. The farmer'd say a sore-armed pitcher might appreciate the egg, but *he* felt cheated. Before long, Daddy quit drumming mash and locked into fixing farm machinery.

Mama had no job then. *I* was her job—a go-go mobile with a PA-system mouth.

Anyway, the market crashed, the Depression struck, and the Great Plains turned into dust sumps. Storms swept down even on our easternmost prairies and the hills around Tenkiller. Spooky roarers. The sun looked like a rusted garbage-can lid behind a big tea-stained curtain. Pure grit flowed through every chink in the shotgun hovel Daddy rented from Mr. Neal on Tenkiller's outskirts, coating every window ledge, shelf, and door lintel. It drifted into ridges under thresholds. Our gums bled. We mined our noses for booger pearls. Jobs dried up even faster than the land. Folks started to move.

On dust-free days, Dickie Boles played ball with me. He taught me how to catch and throw. I'd stand in front of the rear wall of Tenkiller's abandoned icehouse hurling a rubber Spaldeen at it. (One of those hard pink hollow balls city kids used for stickball.) That sucker would bounce back faster than light. I'd field it bare-handed, quick-shift my feet, and snap it back at the bricks as hard as ever I could.

Daddy had me do that until I'd damned near drained off my last kilowatt of kid power. Time I was seven, I could play the bounce-backs for half an hour, bad hops and all, without booting a one or alley-ooping a single throw.

"If you can handle that," Daddy'd say, "you can field em all."

Daddy also taught me to hit. For that, he'd march me into the alley between the Cherokee Feed Store and Schlatt's Small Appliances: Sparrow Alley. The chinks in the upper half of the feed-store wall sheltered hundreds of English sparrows, house sparrows, wrens. A sparrow apartment house. Those birds'd chirp and scold. If you didn't take care, they'd get you with a whitewash bomblet or two.

In our alley games, the pitcher stood halfway along it. The hitter faced him from its streetside mouth, a broom or a mop handle for a bat. Daddy'd start, pitching the Spaldeen underhand. Before too long he'd go to a modified wind-up and a three-quarter delivery. I had to hit as many pitches on a clothesline to dead center as I could. No pulling or pushing the Spaldeen more than a foot or so to either side of my dad. If it hit a wall before getting past him, it was an out. A ricochet beyond him was a hit, though. So were uncaught blue darters up the middle. Rollers counted as fouls, but pop-ups were inning enders even if you'd just come in. A home run had to fly out the far end of Sparrow Alley in the air.

The Boles & Son Jes-for-Fun Oklahoma World See-ries. So Daddy called our games. If a dust squall didn't blow up, we'd play until dark. Usually, Daddy beat me. If I won, I'd strut and preen. I'd brag to Mama. Today I know most of the games I took from Daddy were ones he let me have. Sometimes, though, he'd go on jake-leg binges and play me smashed. I'd beat him easy then, no charity to it.

Down a few runs, he'd lose the ball on purpose or break the broom handle over his knee and call me an upstart snot-nose. I got where I avoided him drunk, even though he was a pretty easy drunk, not a mean one, right up till I took a lead on him and he began to grasp how poorly he was doing, motor skills-wise. Strange to say, after Prohibition had ended just about everywhere but Oklahoma, Daddy swore off drink for a while. Then, when I jumped him at alleyball, he'd laugh and call me "Tenkiller's Ty Cobb."

Dick Boles wasn't Jesus Christ, but recalling him as he'd been when I was small, I couldn't picture him like Sergeant Pumphrey did—as the sorriest man he'd ever had the bad luck to serve with. Until I was eleven or twelve, Dick Boles had been a sockdolager daddy, good as a boy could want.

Lots of people, with the ruin of their farmlands, loaded up their pickups and set out for California's San Joaquin Valley: Okies. Will Rogers said they raised IQ levels in both states. Maybe so. The Boleses didn't go. Daddy liked Oklahoma, and Mama still had kin about—in Muskogee and Tulsa, mostly. Jobs posed a problem, though, and in '35 Daddy disappeared for eight months. Mama knew he wasn't dead because he sent her twenty bucks a month through a cousin in Tahlequah. I attended school by then, and Mama clerked at Rexall.

Turned out, Daddy had upped with the Civilian Conservation Corps. You had to be unmarried to join. Daddy fudged and got in anyway. He spent most of his time planting wind-breaks in Kansas, living in a camp between Coffeyville and Independence. The CCC gave him all his shots, fed him, and worked his tail off. Pay came to forty bucks a month, and, if the dust storms held off, all the fresh air and sunshine he could stand. Daddy snuck away in September, beelining it home. One of his bosses had acted like General Black Jack Pershing—plus, Daddy hadn't been able to tinker with car engines as much as he liked.

In '37 or '38, Deck Glider opened its plant in Tenkiller. Probably Colonel Elshtain's doing, using his connections. A few months later, Mama said good-bye to Rexall's and went on the line at Deck Glider. Her take-home pay doubled. About this time, I guess, Daddy started breaking down into the no-account jerk Pumphrey remembered from Otter Point. He could've had him a job at Deck Glider too, but the very idea of hunching indoors over buffer-brush assemblies made him stir crazy. He figured Mama herself would finally crack and begged her to quit. She wouldn't. He smuggled booze in from Fort Smith, or bought it off local leggers, and got stewed three or four times a week. He and Mama battled. Lots of times, they woke me up screeching like peacocks and shoving chairs around. Mornings, scratches on the floor would shine like yellow paint.

The summer World War Two started in Europe, Daddy cut out again. So what? I asked myself. So what? He hadn't taken me to Sparrow Alley for months. I'd fire bounce-backs at the old icehouse, though, over and over—until my arms felt like window-sash weights. An outlet, you know. Therapy, a shrink today would call it.

Mama and I expected Daddy back at any moment, the way he'd turned up, hungry-puppy-like, after his unhappy stint with the CCC, but as the days wore on and the news from overseas got gloomier, we stopped expecting it. He didn't wire us cash every month, the way he had before, and none of his cousins in the area would admit to having a clue about his whereabouts. Maybe they really didn't, but Mama had her doubts.

In my Pullman berth, though, I dreamt about him.

My Red Stix team has to play a bunch of soldiers on a windy airfield in the Aleutians. Us Tenkillerites have on our regular flannel baseball togs, but the soldiers have dressed for the cold: boots, jackets with hoods, gloves like Army-drab oven mitts. An away game, see? The home team sets the playing conditions. I hop around at short, flapping my arms to keep warm. I hate playing soldiers because they're older and more experienced. And, up in the Aleuts, they get last bat.

Bottom of an inning, pretty far along. Feels like we've played a week. Otter Point two, Tenkiller zero. Except for the screaming wind, my dream's silent. Guys open their mouths, but nothing comes out. I can't tell if the wind's drowning our voices or floating overhead like piano notes at an old Buster Keaton flick.

After a while, I seem to be alone. I've got teammates, but shrouds of fog have swallowed them. They're like ghosts in fuzzy straitjackets, I'm the only Red Stix player with a clear outline or any freedom of movement, the only Red Stix player acting fired up, but I'm . . . well, I'm scared.

When I move, my spikes strike fire—like wading through an ankle-high forest of Fourth of July sparklers. The airfield is a big checkerboard of holey steel mats. The engineers on Umnak have locked the mats together over the tundra as a runway for patched-up Flying Fortresses and Liberators. In newsreels, it's called Marsden matting.

From that point forward, every batted ball comes my way, every chance. Grounders skip at me like lopsided rocks. Pop-ups and liners are worse. Every time I dive or try to set myself, I snag my spikes in the grid and fall. The mats' edges slice me up. My hands bleed, my knees look like tomato pulp.

C-c-come on, you g-guys! I yell. *Ya g-g-gotta h-help me!* The wind blows my words to Siberia. I only hear them because I yelled them into that godawful williwaw.

Hours later, I get the inning's last out and hobble in for my own at bats. The other Red Stix have vanished. I've got to bring us back from what looks like sure defeat—the Umnak bunch must've scored a dozen times in their at bat—but the cold's begun to gnaw into me. My fingers feel carrot-stick brittle. Two or three snap off when I pick up my bat.

I try to dig in against the Otter Point pitcher anyway. He jams me with an inside curve. The ball rotates in like a chunk of packed ice. When I foul it, mostly to protect myself, my thumb shatters. Now I'm holding the bat with one finger and the heel of my hand. How can I drive the ball even if I make contact? The outlook isn't brilliant. I seem to fall apart the piecemeal way icebergs do.

D-D-Daddy! I yell.

The Otter Point pitcher vanishes. So do the guys in Army-green parkas and gutta-percha boots behind him. Just like the Red Stix, gone. I stand at the plate, a perforated steel grid at the end of a steel runway. The runway looks like an ocean, an ocean of Marsden matting. It laps at the foothills of a squat rampart of mountains.

An airplane appears in a mountain notch. As it drops toward the field, its wings rock in the fog. A P-40 Warhawk—like the planes piloted by Chenault and his Flying Tigers, tiger jaws painted on its snout—flies straight at me.

Behind the P-40, lightning splits the sky. Fiery, zigzagging snakes of lightning. A thunderclap bounces the runway's long steel gridwork, the first thing besides the wind I've really heard. More thunderclaps. They back up on one another and blend into one flat murmuring *BOOOOM!* The landing strip buckles in waves. If the P-40 doesn't plow me under, the mats will hurl me down and stamp me like a waffle. But I freeze where I stand. The Warhawk's pilot doesn't drop his landing gear or try to land. He blitzes toward me a few feet above the steel plates, ahead of the crest of their buckle. If he won't pull up, his propellers will dice me for sure.

Then I see the pilot in the cockpit. His face belongs to my father, Richard Oconostota Boles, but a twisted version of the face I remember. His eyes bulge. His lips sneer. His nose lies flat, like a second-rate pug's. Just before he yanks back on his joystick and goes roaring away toward the sea, he gives me a wink; a *wink*, for Christ's sake.

Then the last wave of the Marsden grid drops toward me, clattering. I cross my arms over my head in a stupid attempt to keep the panels from crushing me. The background keen of the wind seems a fit sort of white noise to what's happening. I still can't tell if its keening scours my mouth or comes from it, but so what? It suits our loss. Also, my daddy winked.

I jerked awake. The clicking of the rails echoed in my chest: *clickety-clack, clickety-clack.* Life meant more than baseball. The look on Daddy's face rushing toward me in that P-40 was a look he'd really given me once, right down to the wink. Sitting there, I dredged up that old memory, the whole lousy business.

When I was thirteen, early one A.M., Richard Oconostota Boles and the former Laurel Helvig shouted and scraped chairs around. Again. I'd have to remap the living room in my head to get to the john without stubbing a toe. The shouting never let up. The shouts smeared into an angry howl. Sofa legs scraped, chair legs tap-danced.

Usually when my folks argued, at some point the noise level dropped off. A breather. Not this time. The din got so loud I figured they'd called in a few pals to help them argue. Then, over the raised voices, I heard a storm of flaps and soft collisions—the noise you'd probably get if you set up a huge fan at one end of Sparrow Alley. Had Daddy released a bunch of bats in the front room?

"*Tear up another one, Dickie, and I'll kill you!*"

"*Try it! Jes try it!*"

My leg'd gone to sleep, but I limped into the front room to see the row firsthand. I hoped just a glimpse of me would shame my parents into making up. But I'd walked into a holy mess. Daddy had been playing Jack the Ripper with Mama's *Life* magazines. Black-and-white photos of Hitler, Shirley Temple, Lou Gehrig, and so on shingled the floor. Bedsheet pages. Daddy had torn them out and strewn them. One teetered on a lampshade. Marian Anderson at the Lincoln Memorial dangled from between a pair of Venetian-blind slats. I took in every detail because the room looked like a hand grenade had deranged it.

"See there," Mama said. "You've done woke up Danny."

"Get out of here!" Daddy yelled. "Go back to bed!"

I stood there in my too-short pajama bottoms, and Daddy hurled a rolled-up magazine at me. It opened out and slid to rest at my feet. All the coverless copies of *Life* lay about like stepping-stones to a loony bin.

"Yell at me if you like!" Mama said. "Go ahead! But leave your son be!"

"Mine, is he? Look at him. He don't favor me. He don't favor me a bit."

"What's that supposed to mean?"

"Danny don't look, or do, like I do. Moren likely, some smoothie planted the boy while I was over to Tahlequah trying to make some dough."

"Filth! An adult'd be ashamed to say it."

"I *am* ashamed. My son aint my son. My wife let somebody else spike her." Daddy's high pink color told his drunkenness.

Mama cried, "Lousy redskin scum!" and started for him. A *Life* squirted out from under her. She toppled before she could begin flailing away. Daddy caught her, but yanked her sideways and dumped her on the sofa like a potato sack. She made for him again, cursing and wailing. But Daddy seemed an even worse monster, the way he'd insulted us. I charged, nearly slipping on a photo page. Daddy held me off with one hand. "Lousy redskin scum!" I said. A curse good enough for Mama was fine for me. I started to curse him again when he chopped me in the throat with his hand. I crashed. It felt like he'd knocked my head off. If I looked back, I'd see my body jumping around like a neck-wrung chicken's. I wanted to scream, but couldn't even gargle.

Daddy's bloated face came down for a look-see. "He don't favor me, Laurel. And he don't do like I do, neither."

"Baseball," Mama said from the sofa. "You taught him how to play. He does that the way you do."

"Mebbe so. But it's a trick." Daddy gave me a goatish wink. "Well, you bastid, your mama's secret's safe with me."

He slammed out the door without even scrounging up a change of clothes. Late August, early September, Hitler messing up folks' lives in Europe. You heard about it on the radio. Like a fight between your parents scrawled in letters the size of buildings.

"Dick! Come back!" Mama shouted at Daddy, who'd just said he wasn't. Finally, she realized her boy lay hurt.

My voice box had closed. I sat up amongst black-and-white portraits, still lifes, scenes of war. Except for the mark on my throat, I must've looked more or less okay. When I started breathing again, I was okay. But I didn't talk again for two years. And when I did, I st-st-stammered.

*

On the troop train, I pulled on my clothes and made my way between curtained berths to the coupling where I liked to ride. The shanties of poor white and colored sharecroppers clicked by like old photos, or maybe negatives, of themselves. They looked as empty as I felt. My voice box had closed again. When our locomotive whistled going into the curve on a kudzu-smothered ridge, I tried to mimic it. I tried to scream like that monster two-six-two engine.

Nothing came out.

5

That night between cars lasted forever. I kept expecting Pumphrey to come through. The sun *did* come up, finally, and we rattled into Georgia over the Chattahoochee River and a swaying trestle bridge. The tracks looked like poured mercury. Early June, but already godawful hot. If we stopped in some podunk town or weedy switching yard, gnats and noseeums attacked us in eggbeater tornadoes.

Oklahoma got hot—its dust storms could blast you raw—but Georgia's heat came like the rolling smoke of a junkyard tire fire. Once, its land had been wooded, but loggers and peanut fanners had cut the trees and turned it into a clayey plain. We chugged over it into a sprawl of roadhouses, motor inns, and billboards: Highbridge's outskirts. (Gas rationing had killed most of the inns and roadhouses.) Camp Penticuff lay six or seven miles southeast of town. The Panhandle-Seminole Railway line we'd come in on cut a slant through the post. Civilians got off in town, soldiers kept riding.

Climbing down from the train, I finally saw some of the other nonmilitary types who'd been aboard. They stood in knots on the platform fanning themselves and greeting friends. Don't ask me where they'd hid themselves. I'd seen mostly uniforms aboard—one damned uniform too many. With all the signs around asking you to limit your time in the dining car and to forgive any travel delays, you realized the railroad preferred military cargo to nonessential civs like me.

At Highbridge station, I began to get scared. I'd figured Mister JayMac would meet me, but Mister JayMac was nowhere to be found. Now what? If somebody could've proved to me that Pumphrey had got off in Alabama, I would have ridden on into camp with the dogfaces.

Instead, I wandered into the depot. My duffel saved me. It had a bat—a red bat—poking up through it.

"*Yoobo?*" said a high-pitched voice in the gloom. I looked around, bumpkinlike. Louder, the voice said, "*Yoobo?*" I turned and looked down. There, staring up at me blank-faced out of chocolately eyes, slouched a twelve- or thirteen-year-old urchin, barefoot. He wore a too-big man's shirt and shiny cotton trousers. Little Black Sambo. On top of my manners, I might've called him a colored, or a pickaninny. I only had a few years on him, but at our ages that was a generation. What did he want? A handout? "*You Danny Bo?*" he shouted, like I was deaf as a jackhammer jockey.

Holy cow. Someone in Highbridge—a barefoot nigger kid out of *Uncle Tom's Cabin*—knew my name. Sort of.

"*Yookla.*" He stuck out his hand—to shake, I figured. So I reached to give his hand a pump. His look curled from blankness to suspicion. He didn't pump back. His hand dropped like a slab of raw liver, detouring to my duffel bag, his aim all along. He was my reception committee, sent out by Mister JayMac to fetch me to him. Should I feel honored or snubbed?

"*Cmn,*" he mumbled, then dragged my duffel through the waiting room to the street. Out front, at the curb, hulked a rusty brown-and-white bus, a wingless Flying Fortress. The kid jumped up its steps and disappeared inside.

The bus had some fancy curlicue writing on its side: HIGHBRIDGE HELLBENDERS. Under that, in smaller letters, TERRORS OF THE CVL. On the fender above the front wheel ran a line of script giving the bus's nickname: *The Brown Bomber*.

"Well, Mr. Boles, you riding or admirin?" said a deep voice from the driver's seat. It belonged to a well-built colored in his mid to late twenties. He had one big hand on the steering wheel and one on the door lever. To show him I couldn't talk, I touched my throat and shook my head. I didn't want him, nigger or no, thinking I was stuck up.

"So thoat?" he said. "Damn. A so thoat in summer's bout the wusst."

Uh-uh. I waved off his guess, tapping the end of my tongue with my finger. Passersby gave me looks.

"Git on up here," the driver said. "Keep that up, somebody haw you off to the rubber room."

I climbed aboard. The kid with my duffel had gone all the way to the back. Above a far seat, the top of his head poked up like a nappy black cactus.

"Cain't talk, eh?" the driver said. When I shook my head, he stipulated, "Sit down and lissen, then."

I slid into a seat catawampus to the driver's, sweating so bad I put a Rorschach blot on it. Except for him and my half-pint porter, I had *The Brown Bomber* to myself.

"At boy back there's Euclid," the driver said. "Euclid. Like the Greek geometry man."

Yookla, I thought. Yookla equaled Euclid.

"I'm Darius Satterfield." He drew out the long i in the middle of Darius. "Euclid's my brother. Fo now, Danl, that's bout aw you need to know."

Danl, not Mr. Boles. A true-born white boy might have taken offense, but it never crossed my mind Darius had overstepped his place. Besides, nobody—black, white, or polka dot—had ever called me Mr. Boles.

Darius drove us away from the railway depot. Factories and cars floated by. Giant water oaks and live oaks lined some of the streets. Toward Highbridge's eastern edge, glimpses of pancake-flat land flickered between mill houses and shanties. A few soldiers strolled by, but mostly I saw white civilians—until, at least, we reached a market area where colored women carried baskets of tomatoes, okra, beans, and squash on their heads. Close by, dusty lots had filled up with covered traps, mule-drawn wagons, even a couple of ox carts.

I felt like a visitor to Tanganyika. Darius didn't act as a tour guide, though, and Euclid's head had slumped out of sight. Anyway, everything about Highbridge—part city, part country crossroads—amazed me: the sights, the smells, the people. I was a foreigner.

Even in '43, Highbridge had nearly 10,000 people, with another five or six thousand soldiers, WACs, and support personnel out to Camp Penticuff. The locals, with the war on, made a lot of their money off the doughboys. On Penticuff Strip, which angled southeast from the old business district, there were pawn shops, beer joints, dancehalls, tattoo parlors, even some two-buck-a-tussel cathouses. For jobs, the town had some holdover industries from prewar days: meat-packing plants, textile mills, foundries. The ironworks now made torpedoes, though, and a crate-making factory had started turning out duckboards for trenches and foxholes. Peanuts were the biggest local crop, but cattle, pecans, and cotton weighed in as old reliables too.

On a single ride from the railway depot, you couldn't see everything in Highbridge. If you started regarding it as a sleepy burg, maybe even malaria-ridden, you began to feel superior to it—even if you hailed from a no-account town in Oklahoma. Tenkiller at least qualified as a frontier town, you figured, but Highbridge, even if more like an African colonial outpost, gave itself big-city airs, airs like trying to support a professional ball club.

In about fifteen minutes, Darius pulled the Brown Bomber into a parking lot at McKissic Field. The stadium reared up: tall wooden walls, bleachers like railway trestles, insect-eye lights on poles above the clubhouse and the outfield. Even on the bus, I could hear bats cracking, horsehide popping glove leather, players shouting. Looking at McKissic Field's rickety outside, I figured not even the New York Yankees had a stadium as grand.

"Come see the end of Mister JayMac's morning sweatout," Darius said. I wanted to fetch my duffel from Euclid, thinking I might need my glove, but Darius shook his head. "Naw, naw. Jes you watch today, Danl. Jes be thanking God the *obligation* aint on you to huff it up wi them mens awready out there."

Darius led me through an entrance near the bleachers on the third-base line. We ducked through a low concrete tunnel and broke into the ballpark's summer dazzle.

Grass you wouldn't believe, trim and green, the pride of an eager-beaver team of groundskeepers. Even the ads on the walls seemed magical: signs for local department stores, Octagon Laundry Soap, Obelisk Self-Rising Flour, War Bonds, Old Golds, Shelby Razor Blades, 666 Cold Medicine. Most touted stuff you can't buy now, but, just then, they bamboozled me. I wanted to dash through the outfield grass (me, a shortstop), make leaping grabs against the Feen-A-Mint and the Moroline Petroleum Jelly signs. I wanted to play the caroms off their paint. And right after the game, I'd run downtown to stock up on chewing gum, cola, soap, smokes, you-name-it.

Lord among us, McKissic Field was Heaven!

Never mind no other park in the CVL, except maybe the one in

LaGrange, could stand beside Mister JayMac's place. Never mind how quickly I learned even McKissic Field didn't equal the Land of Beulah. I mean, it had bumps in the infield, shadowy corners where a fielder could get lost, camelback crickets in the showers, and split benches in the bleacher sections. That morning, though, the old stadium dazzled me.

Near the third-base line, Darius hurtled a low wall and ambled onto the infield grass. He picked up a catcher's mitt and waved it at a player lazing around the batting cage. The player—Peter Hay, better known as Haystack, but I didn't know that then—followed him to the bullpen, where Darius squatted and caught Hay's warm-up tosses. After a while, Darius pounded his mitt, asking for more heat; he fired Hay's pitches back harder than Hay'd thrown them. Hay struggled to put more zip into what he was doing. An amazing scene: In a south Georgia ballpark, a black man instructing, even cussing out, an older white player.

"Nigger gave *me* that crap, I'd deball him with a spoon."

Until then, I hadn't seen the rookies—three guys in street clothes—in the stands behind me. The kid who'd just spoken hunched between two others about his age, all of them squinting like moles, each about as nervous and mock-tough as the other two. The one who'd spoken wore caked boots and denim overalls; he had a blacksmith's arms. He also had, several hours ahead of schedule, a five-o'clock shadow.

"Would you let a nigger boss you thataway?" he asked me.

I turned half around. I shrugged.

"You a ballplayer?" he said. "Or jes lost?"

"The nigger brought him," one of the other two guys said. "He cain't be lost."

Both these fellas had on cheap jackets and ties. They were taller than the farm boy; next to him, they looked like *Esquire* models—or like they'd mistaken the day for Sunday and McKissic Field for a concert hall. Their names, I found out later, were Heggie and Dobbs. The farm boy with the stubble was a south Georgia cracker name of Philip Ankers.

"He's ugly, though," Ankers said, looking at me. "Nothing that nigger do or say can stop him being ugly."

Maybe these drips were dogfaces on furlough.

"What's yore name?" Ankers asked.

I patted my throat and gargled a few gargles. For safety's sake, I stayed put, three bleacher rows ahead of him.

"What is it, Rube? Ya swaller a sock? Or ya jes don't know yore name?"

I gave the farm boy a quick up-yours sign, half expecting him and his dime-store clothes-horse buddies to come down and boot the pea-turkey out of me.

But Ankers laughed and said, "Screw ya, Rube." His pals chuckled too. When they started watching the practice again, I edged over a few feet so they wouldn't be right behind me.

From the mound, Mister JayMac hurled batting practice into a chicken-wire cage. Criminy. Mister JayMac had his health, I guess, but the sight of that old guy unleashing strikes on his own players couldn't help but get you. He creaked some (not too much), but the dust on his cuffs and the clay on his shoes didn't faze him. After yanking a swinging strike on a batter, he made the klutz take three laps. No one, Mister JayMac said, should flat-out whiff against him. He wasn't Bob Feller. Or even Lefty Grove. Thing was, though, not many Hellbenders took Mister JayMac to the outfield, and nobody hit one over the wall off him.

At Mister JayMac's orders, players changed in and out, coming in to hit or hustling out to field. Pretty soon, I'd started sizing up the shortstop. The number on his practice flannels, also the team's away uniforms, was seven. I didn't expect to move in on this guy unless he produced nothing but air currents at the plate. He could field, and throw, and think. I reckoned him at least twice my age, mid-thirties, maybe older, gray winking at his temples, cowboy creases from his nose to his lip corners. On every pitch, he crouched so low you wondered if he had the body grease to unravel and make a play. He always did, though, and gracefully: a whangdoodle shortstop.

The other big thing I recall about that practice is how bad the guys playing first base did. Mister JayMac used at least four fellas there, but not one could handle a first baseman's glove. That leather claw gave them fits. One fella, Norm Sudikoff, moved pretty as a gazelle, but usually managed to turn a sure out into a misplay. My pal Goochie would've given all these goons a clinic.

Me, I wished I was six or seven inches taller. Then, if I couldn't beat out Number Seven at short, I might win a starting job from the relay team of jokers yo-yoing in and out at first base. Otherwise, I might spend my whole season on the bench. Growing a half foot fast would help, but I'd do as well to pray for a Hollywood agent to tap me as the next Gary Cooper.

At noon, practice ended. Darius hadn't brought me to McKissic Field so much to watch it as to keep from having to make an extra trip from the players' boardinghouse to the stadium. He'd picked up the other three rookies, Georgia boys all, a couple of hours earlier, when a train from the Atlantic coast had dropped them at Highbridge Station.

Now Darius came over, diamonds winking in the black lamb's wool of his hair, his coffee-colored skin aglow. "Yall go git on the bus. Sit toards the back. The other mens don't like rookies crowding em."

"Who sez?" Ankers said to Darius.

"Ast em," Darius said. "Be my guest. But ast em on the bus, or yall might have to foot it to Mister JayMac's."

Dobbs and Heggie didn't grumble, but Ankers flicked Darius a lightning storm with his eyes.

On the bus, these guys sat a row or two in front of Euclid, now reading a *Plastic Man* comic, but I plonked down next to him, not out of any Eleanor Roosevelt fondness for black folk, but because he had my duffel. He paid me no mind, poring over his comic like it was a book of secret codes.

In about twenty minutes, ballplayers started straggling out and climbing aboard, including Darius. Mister JayMac swung up into the seat back of Darius's. None of his players had tried to sit in it, his reserved spot. They always scattered about here and there, flopping like wore-out bird dogs. Number Seven, the shortstop, came laddering down the aisle and dropped into the long rear seat. He stretched his arms along its back and goggled around.

"Hey, Darius," he said, "who're these handsome cats?" He meant the three new Georgia boys.

"I disremember their names, Mr. Hoey. Course I'm jes a driver, not a traveling secretary."

"Oh now, Darius," the shortstop said, "you're more n a driver, you're a Hellbender institution."

Hands on the wheel, Darius didn't seem to want any of Hoey's soft soap and told him so by clamming up. Of all the men who'd practiced that morning, he was the only one still wearing the clothes he'd worked out in. The top of his head showed in the big rectangular mirror just inside the divided windshield, his hair asparkle with sweat.

Mister JayMac grabbed the pole of the driver's cage and pulled himself up. He sported a string tie and a white linen coat. If we didn't get rolling soon, his ballplayers would start slinging off enough BTUs to give every last joe aboard a drop-dead case of heat prostration.

"Don't yall worry who thesere boys are," he said. "Worry about how piss-poor yall played today." He paused, more for effect than from tiredness. "I could drum up a half dozen 4-Fs in a TB ward who'd look sharper than yall did this morning. So think, gentlemen, on your many personal deficiencies."

You could hear Euclid turning comic-book pages.

"Understand?" Mister JayMac said.

"*Yessir!*" nearly everyone on the Bomber said, like recruits out to Camp Penticuff.

"Meeting in the parlor this evening right after supper," Mister JayMac said. "I want everybody there. Understood?"

"Everybody?" the infielder named Hoey said. "Even Jumbo?"

"I said everybody."

"So why wasn't Jumbo at practice, sir?" Number Seven said. "We could've used him at first. His subs made him look like Nijinski. Compared to those galoots, he *is* Nijinski."

"Take a leap, Buck!" Norm Sudikoff shouted.

"Jumbo Hank Clerval had some personal business in Alabama to attend to," Mister JayMac said. "He'll be at our meeting tonight, Mr. Hoey, never you fear."

Buck Hoey, the shortstop, just wouldn't let up: "*Alabama?* How'd Jumbo get to Alabama?"

"He borrowed my car," Mister JayMac said,

"Your Caddy?" Hoey said. "How'd Jumbo get to be such a privileged character? Going four for four gainst Marble Springs? Shit-a-load, sir, I once hit for the cycle gainst those palookas, and you never loaned me a car. What's Jumbo got anyway? Proof of some kinda draft-board hanky-panky?"

The other men on the Brown Bomber ducked; they cowered in their places. The only soul among us not drawn gut-tight with shock and worry, except maybe Hoey, was Euclid. He was paging through *Plastic Man* for maybe the twentieth time.

"Let it go, Mr. Hoey," Mister JayMac said.

"Jesus," Hoey started. "You'd think the guy was—"

"Let it go."

Hoey let it go. Didn't seem too trodden upon, though. He seemed happy. Mister JayMac sat down. Darius put the bus in gear, and we bumped out of the parking lot onto a boulevard lined with water oaks. Hoey caught my eye and waved at all the browbeaten ballplayers in front of us.

"Ever see such a bunch of pantywaists?" he asked.

I could only look at him. Hoey was the stud I'd have to beat out to become a regular.

Worse luck, he was lean, tough, and not to be messed with.

"S matter with you, kid? Cat got your tongue?"

6

Darius drove us to McKissic House, the team boardinghouse where Mister JayMac, for part of everyone's monthly salary, put up all the single men on his team. In McKissic House, this entire summer, I'd eat my meals and spend my nights when the Hellbenders didn't have an away game.

Cripes, I thought when our bus growled up its semicircular drive. How great, not to have to wear down my shoe leather looking for a place to rent—especially with Camp Penticuff so close and wartime housing so tight that roomers doubling up with relatives or friends matter-of-factly read the obits to get a jump on likely vacancies.

Because Mister JayMac owned a dozen or more old mill houses in the Cotton Creek area of Highbridge, he'd taken that worry off all his players' shoulders. Men with wives and kids in town, I learned later, rented these tarboxes from Mister JayMac for at least six months, April through September, his minimum lease. In October, he'd offer his vacant houses to military transients, but with the stipulation they clear out at the end of March so married Hellbenders could reclaim the premises in time for the new season. In a military town with beaucoups of demand for rental properties, he had a high-handed marketing approach, maybe even a greedy-seeming one, but Mister JayMac didn't care about the money he could make—he could do that renting to either GIs or players—but about the welfare of his immediate employees during each CVL season. So most of us looked at Mister JayMac not as a robber baron but as our very own Daddy Warbucks.

Only two-thirds of the Hellbenders made the trip all the way from McKissic Field to McKissic House. Darius drove first to the Cotton Creek neighborhood, where six men rented houses, and dropped them off. Buck Hoey, the wiseguy shortstop who'd bellyached about the first baseman who hadn't come to practice, hopped down last, near a blue frame house with more shrubs and a prettier paint job than any house around it. When Hoey got off, I relaxed a bit.

As for McKissic House, it hunkered back from Angus Road, on a woodsy stand of acreage on Highbridge's southeastern corner, floating among the magnolias and the leafy pecan trees like a man-of-war. It had cupolas, turrets, gables, a widow's walk, and a pair of outside staircases for fire escapes. It wasn't Tara, though: no columns. Also, Mister JayMac's ancestors had built it after, not before, the War Between the States.

The front half of the house smacked your eyes out. It had a wrap-around porch with fresh-painted balusters and a half dozen or more rocking chairs. It had shutters and a huge oaken door with a stained-glass fanlight above it. It had plum-colored draperies in the windows and umbrella ferns in hanging baskets. The whole place shone white, like some kind of lighter-than-air marble.

Coming around the drive, though, you saw that the back part of McKissic House didn't keep up appearances. No shutters on the sides. In places, boards overlapped on a fallen slant. Paint had cracked or curled or flaked or flat-out vanished. One tricky back wall had a two-tone color, light above and dark below, like an unfinished kitchen cabinet nailed to a barn's weathered side. I still liked what I saw. It outdid any place I'd ever lived. It had such size and so many build-ons I imagined myself prowling through it for weeks, finding hidden passages, secret nooks, the decaying skeletons of roomers who'd lost their way and starved to death. McKissic House spoke to the strangled poet in me, stirring a wormy sort of dread into my blood. Could I last a whole summer in one of its closed-in rooms?

"You new boys," Mister JayMac said from the bus's step well, "make yourselves to home, best yall can. Supper's at five-thirty, team meeting an hour later. Darius'll settle you in. Tomorrow, spot challenges and an intrasquad tussel of big-time importance."

Mister JayMac got off, climbed the wide fan of steps into McKissic House, and went inside. Everybody else but Darius, me, Euclid, and the other three rookies piled out after him.

"Shoo," Darius said. "Kizzy'll give you somethin befo dinner. Yall gots to be hongry."

Ankers, Dobbs, and Heggie got off the bus and jostled up the steps. I held my seat.

Darius said, "You deef as well as dumb?" He regarded me in the rearview.

I shook my head. I thought Darius would coddle me a tad, give me a little encouragement. Instead, he shut the Brown Bomber's door and jammed the bus into gear. He bounced it off the gravel drive, through a lane of pecans and dogwoods, and past one of McKissic House's shabby pine-board fire escapes to the backyard. To keep from cracking my head on the bus's tin ceiling, I hung on for precious life.

Darius braked by a screened-in porch on the side of the house, not far from an old carriage house. The porch's fly-blown screen had tears in it; its splintery steps, just off the kitchen, canted this way and that. The house's rain gutters had rusted through; sections hung loose, like chutes at a gravel quarry. The eaves, if you looked up from under, had neat little holes bored into them, like somebody'd corkscrewed hooks in there, to swing mum or begonia pots from. Carpenter bees had drilled the holes, though, not a flower-mad lodger. The only decorations between the porch and the carriage house were a compost heap, some rusted-out metal pans, and a tractor cannibalized for war scrap.

Through the porch screen, I could see a long row of kitchen windows. Through those windows, the yarny-looking gray head of a colored woman bobbed back and forth behind a counter. The woman's face had caved-in cheeks, bulgy lips and eyes, and a beaklike nose. Her hair had braided rat tails coming down behind her head and over her shoulders to the front, a more squawlike than a mammylike do. From the bus, her head seemed to lack a body; it rolled here and there in the kitchen's steam and clatter.

"Kizzy," Darius said. "She either feed you or use you in a pie. Whynt you see which it gon be today?"

Just then, though, I saw Mister JayMac strolling through a big victory garden toward the old servant quarters behind the main house: a neat little bungalow. It had hydrangea bushes with smoky blue flowers big as cabbages, and a red-tile roof that made it look more Spanish than Suthren.

"Office back there," Darius told me. "Office and bedroom. Him and Miss Giselle got to have they privacy." I watched Mister JayMac amble, thinking Darius might say more, but he added only, "Git out, Danl. Go on. Git."

I stood up. I'd reached my "home." Never mind I had no notion what to do now or even how to make my feet move.

"Holy Jesus," Darius said. He came down the aisle, grabbed my arm, and dragged me off the bus and up the decaying steps into the kitchen. "This young man hongry and speechless," he said. "Feed him, Kizzy, but don't spec no thanks." He slammed on out of the kitchen through a swinging door more like you'd see in a restaurant than in an old Victorian home.

Euclid came through another door from the dining room and the parlor beyond, where Hellbender ballplayers, from kids like me to grizzled codgers like Creighton Nutter, were listening to the news and debating the capture of Attu in the Aleutians.

"Stupid," somebody said. "Shoulda let the Japs have it. Two-bit icy rock aint worth one GI's life, much less five hunnerd's."

"You betcha," a second player said. "Troops up there'd be more use here to home kicking striking miners' butts."

"You don't know squat, Fanning," somebody else said. "My dad mined coal. If not for baseball, the mines'd have me too."

And so on. I remember the argument because my dream of Umnak and the tidal wave of Marsden plates clattering down still sprocketed through my head. I could close my eyes and relive the nightmare in milky black-and-white.

Euclid gave me his *Plastic Man* comic book. He climbed up on a stool next to the wood stove and asked for something to eat. Kizzy poured him a fruit jar of buttermilk and gave him a plate of tomato slices with a crumbly chunk of cornbread.

"Danbo too, Awnt Kiz," he said.

"Whynt you eat in the dining room wi the other mens?" Kizzy asked me. "Got a full spread out there."

I shook my head. They'd ask me questions, just like that farm boy Ankers at McKissic Field had done, and the silence I gave them back would irk or tickle them in troublesome ways.

Kizzy (if she was Euclid's aunt, she had to be Darius's too) had hands like long ash-colored mackerels. She sliced me a chunk of cornbread and sloshed me a glass of buttermilk even bigger than Euclid's fruit jar. I wolfed the cornbread and the buttermilk standing at a dough-rolling counter in the middle of the kitchen, sweating in the heat pouring off the wood stove. The kitchen's wallpaper—calico-gowned ladies and top-hatted men on old-timey bicycles—peeled in strips, steamed away by heat and the fumes from boiling kettles of greens or tea.

"Meetin in parlor, six-thuddy," Euclid said. He put a dollop of strawberry jam on his cornbread and wedged the whole chunk into his mouth. "Yo hea?"

Kizzy gave me all I could eat, including a bowl of greens with some pepper sauce and a piece of cold chicken, and shoved me into the backyard with my comic book and a baseball-sized green apple.

"Iw caw you fo supper," she said.

I sat in the rusty metal seat of the junked tractor reading *Plastic Man* and shooing away noseeums. From the parlor, I could hear dance music on the radio, jokey arguments over a hearts game, a soap opera, more war news. I dozed, tuckered from my train ride. I woke and thumbed back through Euclid's comic. I dozed again. Next time I woke, I got down from the tractor and explored the house's spread-out grounds. I stood clear of the bungalow out back, out of respect for Mister JayMac and Miss Giselle's privacy, and maybe the simple fear he'd shotgun me if I bothered them. Eventually, I dozed off again.

"Danbo," Euclid said. "Suppa."

I didn't want to, but I ate with the other players boarding in McKissic House. Counting me, sixteen fellas crowded the long table. Lon Musselwhite, the team's six-foot-four left fielder and the biggest man in the dining room, had the seat of honor next to the kitchen. (Musselwhite was team captain.) The chair at the table's foot, more a throne than a piece of furniture, stayed empty, even though Kizzy had set it a place. I guessed it was for Mister JayMac, who'd show up when he felt like it. Reese Curriden, the third baseman, and Q. U. Parris, a pitcher nicknamed Quip, served us, toting bowls of vegetables and plates of meat in from the kitchen so Kizzy wouldn't drop dead trying to do everything alone.

"Don't fret," Reese Curriden told us newcomers. "This is just a get-acquainted deal. Yall'll get your shot next week."

"KP," Quip Parris said. He was short, blond as wheat, and triggered like a clock spring. Soon enough, I learned he saw himself as the linchpin of the pitching staff. He hailed from Raleigh, North Carolina. His initials stood for Quintus Uriah, which explains why everybody called him Quip.

With nearly all the food on the table, Musselwhite rapped his spoon against his tea glass and said, "Yall please bow." Everyone bowed. Kizzy came back in with three banana cream pies on a rack of lacquered dowels. She sighed loudly. "Sweet and holy Jesus," Musselwhite said, "thy blessings on the lady that prepared these victuals, the victuals themselves, and all who aim to eat em. Give us strength—also victories over our CVL enemies, as Thou dost give our fighting forces victories over the Nips and Krauts. Amen."

"Amen," said everybody at table.

"Pass them ol field peas," Musselwhite said.

Bowls began shuttling around. Kizzy finally got to squeeze her rack of meringue-topped pies onto the table.

"Okay, fellas," Musselwhite said, "innerduce yourselves." He served himself field peas, tomatoes, fried squash, okra, butter beans, green beans, and mashed potatoes. He grabbed off several biscuits and forked up a breaded pork chop, a slice of ham, a batter-fried chicken breast. I followed suit.

Players introduced themselves. In addition to Reese Curriden and Quip Parris, we heard from Clarence "Trapdoor" Evans, Burt Fanning, Lamar Knowles, Charlie Jorgensen, Sweet Gus Pettus, Vito Mariani, Jerry Wayne Sosebee, Rick Roper, and Percy "Double" Dunnagin. Us newcomers to Highbridge included Philip Ankers, the farm boy who'd called me ugly; Jefferson Dobbs, alias Skinny; and Junior Heggie, shy and decent and maybe a tad smarter than the other two rookies.

Lon Musselwhite pointed his butter knife at me. "Okay, champ, who're you?"

On one of her glide-throughs from the kitchen, Kizzy said, "He don't talk, but you can caw him Danny Bowes."

Boles, I wanted to correct her; *not Bowes*.

"Why the hell don't he talk?" Musselwhite said.

"Maybe he's taken a vow of silence," Vito Mariani said.

"You figure him for another damned Papist?" Musselwhite said. "Uh-uh. He's got Primitive Pentecostal writ all over him."

"Darius told me he's a born-again shortstop," Quip Parris said, "with serious plans to excommunicate Hoey."

"Hallelujah," Lamar Knowles, the second baseman, said; he said it quietlike, but everybody heard him.

"Careful," Rick Roper, a utility player, said. "Heggie may be out for you like Bowes is out for Hoey."

Boles, I thought: *Boles!* I tried to talk. What I got was a loud gargle that shut me up quicker than a right jab to the mouth. I could feel myself reddening, burning like I'd plunged my whole head into a bucket of liniment.

Musselwhite had just started to speak when the biggest, nigh-on to ugliest, man I'd ever seen came lumbering in. He had to stoop to get under the transom between the dining room and the parlor. Like Ankers, he wore overalls. His overalls were the biggest pair I'd ever seen, enough denim to outfit every man jack in an Oklahoma oil field. He also wore a long-sleeved white shirt and a brown cap with a fancy H for Highbridge on it. His face was out of alignment somehow, like a pumpkin cut in two and put back together wrong. It even had the color of a blotchy pumpkin. He looked semi-Oriental. At the corners of his bottom lip, two pale scars rucked up, like lopsided buttons. His eyes brimmed with a yellow goo. He wiped them with the back of one meaty hand, then wiped that hand on his overalls. His bare feet reminded me of gray rubber galoshes, but they were only feet—a Titan's feet, with horny calluses, ropy veins, and ingrown toenails.

The Titan pulled out the thronelike chair at the end of the table and lowered himself into it. Even sitting, he had a good foot on Musselwhite. A helluvan entrance. Ankers, Heggie, and Dobbs had frozen in place, with tea glasses or forks lifted to their mouths. Me too, I guess.

"Gentlemen, meet Jumbo Hank Clerval," Musselwhite said. "Glad you could join us, Jumbo."

"Thank you." The big guy's voice was like a ship's gun booming over deep water.

"Meet the new guys," Musselwhite said. "Ankers, Dobbs, Heggie, and Bowes. Bowes is their silver-tongued spokesman."

"Call him Boles," Parris said. "With an *l*."

"Delighted to meet yall," Jumbo said, glancing at us with what seemed like real curiosity. Despite the *yall*, he had a Frenchified accent, an odd lilt that rode the natural booming of his voice. Jumbo—how else could I think of him?—turned to me. "How do yall like Highbridge, Mr. Boles?"

"Boles aint *my* spokesman," Ankers said. "I am."

"Actually, Mr. Clerval, Danny *cain't* talk," Junior Heggie said, a hiccup in his voice.

Everybody, including Jumbo and me, looked at Junior as if he'd belched at a piano recital. Not that I didn't welcome his explanation; only that, being so bashful, he'd boggled us all just by speaking. "But I'm shore he can play ball," he hurried to add.

"He looks like a player," Jumbo said.

"He looks like a chitlin with ears," Trapdoor Evans said.

I flushed tomato-red again. The whole table, except for Heggie and Jumbo, guffawed. In Jumbo's case, I couldn't tell if he hated jabs at people's looks or if he had the sense of humor of a cast-iron pot. In my view, Evans hadn't meant to hurt me; just to get off a funny saying, a josh.

"Too bad about your disability, Mr. Boles," Jumbo said. "I'm Henry Clerval. Muscles"—he nodded at Lon Musselwhite—"has an imperfect grasp of the etiquette of introductions."

Mariani whistled, meaning, "Boy, he popped you, Muscles," but Jumbo frowned at the other guys' sniggerings.

"You're a big one to talk about *my* imperfect Emily Posts," Musselwhite said. "Coming down here with your cap on. You owe the house kitty a dime, Jumbo."

"A dime!" the ballplayers all cried. "Ante up! Ante up!"

Jumbo's yellow eyes darted. Bare feet were okay at Kizzy's table, I guess, but wearing a cap indoors was a McKissic House no-no. Like you'd been raised in a pigsty. Jumbo yanked it off and pressed it down into his lap, out of sight. His hair was greasy black, with a shock of silver-white in the middle of his lumpy forehead and streaks of nickel-gray around his mangled-looking ears. Cripes, I thought, if you staggered into him on a pitch-black street, the fella'd give you about twelve quick heart attacks. Even the overhead lights and the ragging of his fellow Hellbenders couldn't hide his weirdness. I was ugly, but this guy'd been put together in a meat-packing plant by clumsy blind men.

Everyone called Clerval Jumbo, including Musselwhite, and Musselwhite towered over half the guys on the team. It was scary, those two big palookas sitting there and Jumbo making Musselwhite look like a midget. I wanted to bolt for my room, but I didn't *have* a room yet. About then, a line job at Deck Glider back in Tenkiller didn't seem so bad a fate.

Although I didn't get up and run, I had a devil of a time eating. Not Jumbo. He anted up his dime and dug in, paying no attention to the war talk, baseball gossip, and gripes about wages or family problems going on around him. He asked for, or picked off in the passing, every bowl of vegetables on the table. In fact, he wiped out the mashed potatoes, the field peas, the okra, and the squash. He drank a pitcher of water. He inhaled half a wheel of cornbread and a dozen biscuits. He cut one of Kizzy's banana cream pies in two and knocked back half of it like it was a jigger of hooch. The last to stumble in, he finished chowing down first, then laid his greasy napkin aside and gazed cowlike and content around him.

"Please excuse me," he said to Muscles in his bassoon of a voice.

"You're excused." Musselwhite gnawed on his second or third pork chop. "If there's an excuse for you."

Jumbo said, "Gentlemen," then unfolded upward from his chair. He ducked out clutching his Hellbenders cap and made his way up the foyer staircase. The stairs creaked under him (but not much more than they would've for Junior Heggie or me); and he disappeared, leaving behind a fleet of empty bowls, his own slick china plate, and a table of half-amazed men. Not even the old hands, it hit me, had totally adjusted to either his looks or the shows he put on at mealtimes.

"The Great Thunderfoot," Reese Curriden said.

"Hell, that's Sudikoff," Trapdoor Evans said. "Jumbo's dainty next to Sudikoff. A regular twinkletoes."

Sudikoff, a married fella, wasn't there to defend himself. He was chief backup at first base, though: the graceful lummox who'd tried to fill in for Jumbo at practice.

I can't recall much else about my first sit-down meal in Highbridge, not even if I got a piece of Kizzy's banana cream pie, a treat renowned countywide. Jumbo's performance wiped every later impression of that meal right out of my head.

7

Soon after, every Hellbender, including married fellas from the Cotton Creek district, along with our driver and unofficial team manager, Darius Satterfield, had crowded into the parlor for Mister JayMac's big meeting.

The only person not there to begin with was Jumbo Clerval, who, like Buck Hoey had charged that afternoon, seemed to have a weird privileged-character status. Well, why not? "When does a gorilla show up for dinner?" "Whenever he damn well feels like it."

Anyway, the parlor burst with edgy ballplayers, not counting Jumbo. Sweat ran down my sides. Every face in the room, even with a fan creaking overhead, looked greasily sequin-sprinkled. Chairs, footstools, sofa backs, even the floor—players sat or sprawled on any sort of furniture, or surface, they could find.

In wrinkled seersucker trousers and a sweated-out dress shirt, Mister JayMac had worked his way, along with Darius, to the front of the parlor. Darius set up an easel and a book of flip charts to help Mister JayMac explain the Hellbenders and the CVL to Ankers, Dobbs, Heggie, and me. It meant a tedious rehash for the old hands, but nobody squawked. Not even Buck Hoey, who perched on a sofa back to the rear, an expression on his face like, Hey, what a welcome refresher, we're all so lucky to get the full scoop again.

"Gentlemen, hayseeds, and hangers-on," Mister JayMac said when Darius had his flip charts ready. "As most of yall know, we play a seventy-seven-game season. Today, after a month of what passes for some of yall as top-notch baseball, we're a shabby seven and eight, five games back a the Opelika Orphans, a crew I once wouldn't have reckoned fit to climb a molehill without succumbing to oxygen deprivation. Muscles called them mewling pansies, and we trail them by five. So what does that make us?"

"Pansy chasers," Buck Hoey said.

Nobody laughed. Like Jumbo, though, Buck Hoey seemed to have a special status; he could rag the boss—some—without getting sent to his room. Anyway, I felt again how hard it would be to take his job away. And if I did, the other guys would probably resent my success.

Mister JayMac looked around. "Where's Jumbo? Didn't he make it back for supper?"

"Like the locust made it to Pharaoh's Egypt," Hoey said.

That line *did* get a laugh.

"So where is he now? What the hell's he doing?"

"Conferring with Count Tallywhacker," Hoey said. "That's why it's taking him, uh, so long."

A kind of hesitant edgy laugh this time. Mister JayMac curled his lip the way you would if a whiff of spoiled poultry spilled from your Frigidaire. But he sent Euclid upstairs to fetch Jumbo from his third-floor apartment.

"So *looong*," Hoey said as Euclid went by. This time, half a dozen guys whooped like world-champeen morons.

"Hush," Mister JayMac said. I realized then, or gradually over the next few days, that Mister JayMac never said, "Shut up." I'd heard a lot of "Shut ups" in my short life, so I liked the way he said "Hush" instead.

"Any of yall who've been dogging it'd better look sharp," he said. "We're taking on some young fellas who can *play*. I've seen em. This isn't hearsay, but observed fact."

"High school wonders," Buck Hoey said.

"Perhaps," Mister JayMac said. "But I don't like being tied for fourth place in this league, and I won't allow us to stay in fourth if good alternatives to mediocrity present themselves. Maybe they already have."

Euclid came into the parlor ahead of Jumbo Clerval, who, by the looks of him, had "dressed" for the meeting. He wore a humongous pair of wingtip Florsheims, a pair of patched gray pants, and a shiny black frock coat. Euclid played tug to Jumbo's ocean liner and, as soon as he got the big man among us, tooted on out of the room. Jumbo's head, capless now, spiked up almost to the picture molding. He slouched against the wall, straight across the doorway from Buck Hoey on the broken-backed sofa. It looked as if Mister JayMac might say something to him, bawl him out even, but he didn't. He nodded at us four rookies.

"Yall come up here. I want everybody to see you."

Ankers, Dobbs, Heggie, and I sidled to the front of the room to stand beside the easel. Ankers may've been the only one of us not unsettled by the spotlight. When Mister JayMac introduced us, he stepped out and gave a clasped-hands salute, like a boxer greeting a ringside crowd.

"High school graddyiots," Hoey said.

"Actually, Mr. Ankers has only completed his sophomore year," Mister JayMac said.

The Hellbenders stared at Ankers like he was a sideshow freak. Unless he'd been held back a time or two, he was fifteen years old, a baby with the stubble of a lumberjack.

"All right," Mister JayMac said, "give these fellas a friendly Hellbender hello. Ready? Hip, hip . . ."

"Hooray," the regulars said, without much in it.

Mister JayMac told them to try again. "Hooray!" they said, with maybe an exclamation point. "Again," he said. They did a third cheer so loud it more or less mocked the idea of hip-hip-hooraying. But Mister JayMac nodded and tapped a pointer on the first page of his chart:

CHATTAHOOCHEE VALLEY LEAGUE / CLASS C PROFESSIONALS

"Ever last fella here ought to be reminded how damned lucky yall are to be playing ball," he said. "You could be training as infantry replacements with all the scared puppies out to Camp Penticuff. Or crawling on your guts toward a bunker full of deadeye Jerries or Japs."

"We could all be dead," Hoey said.

"You could indeed!" Mister JayMac roared. "But no, thank God, yall're privileged to be playing baseball, the national pastime, and getting paid for that hardship to boot."

"Some of you guys're getting *paid?*" Hoey said.

"Can it, Hoey," Lon Musselwhite said.

"Major league baseball continues on presidential sufferance and the affections of our war-weary citizens. Minor league ball is wounded. Nationwide, the farm system is down to ten training leagues in only seventy cities, and, as I know from my work on the draft board, Uncle Sam needs even more able-bodied men to defeat the foes of democracy abroad.

"Listen up now," Mister JayMac went on. "The Chattahoochee Valley League, one of the youngest around, is a small-town league, with a pitiful

'C' training classification, but we make it in spite of the war because we're the hardest-playing saps anywhere and flat-out beaucoups of fun to watch. Wouldn't you agree, Mr. Nutter?"

"Yessir." Creighton Nutter was a married relief pitcher, a balding guy in his late thirties.

"In addition," Mister JayMac said, "our eight teams are near to one another. The President and the Office of Price Administration appreciate the fact it doesn't siphon off all that much gas or use up that much tire rubber for one CVL team to travel to another CVL team's field for a three- or four-game series. Jes last year, the Attorney General said the CVL is the only league he's ever visited where the National Anthem plays at the end as well as at the start of every contest. A tribute to our national pride. Let me further remind yall that FDR himself views ballplayers as morale boosters and heroes. I concur. At least the good ones are. The bad ones, on the other hand, are—"

"Traitors." Jumbo's judgment boomed and echoed.

It stopped Mister JayMac for a second. "Near to," he said. "Playing the national pastime bad is like spitting on Old Glory. A sorry bungler may not purposely affront the game, but it's still damnably hard to forgive him."

"Amen," Lon Musselwhite said.

Mister JayMac turned to us rookies. "Mr. Boles, tell us the locations and names of the eight teams in the CVL."

My tongue jumped to the roof of my mouth. My eyes cut around like minnows. The last time I'd been in Mister JayMac's presence, I'd had at least stammering use of my own tongue.

He remembered that.

"Tell us *one* team in the CVL," Mister JayMac said. "*Other than* the Hellbenders."

"Speak up, dummy!" Hoey shouted this out.

Darius, over Mister JayMac's shoulder, said, "The Boles boy is a dummy, sir. Got no voice."

Mister JayMac gave me a put-out look, like he'd asked for swordfish steak and the waiter'd brought him a lousy crawdad. Quick, though, his gaze jumped over to Junior Heggie, and he asked Junior to do the naming I couldn't.

"The Opelika Orphans," Junior Heggie said.

"Well, sure," Mister JayMac said. "Name the other six."

Junior studied his shoes. He came from the other side of the state. It'd've been easier for him to name the last six British prime ministers.

"Darius, the chart," Mister JayMac said. Darius flipped the top sheet over the back of the easel and showed us a new page. General JayMac, an Allied officer in a secret command post, briefing his staff. "All right. Look here." He rapped the chart with the top of a collapsible pool cue:

CHATTAHOOCHEE VALLEY LEAGUE

TOWN	POP.	NICKNAME	STADIUM
		Georgia	
Highbridge	*14,012*	*Hellbenders*	*McKissic Field*
LaGrange	*15,301*	*Gendarmes*	*The Prefectures*
Marble Springs	*8,205*	*Seminoles*	*Seminole Park*
Quitman	*11,153*	*Mockingbirds*	*The Aviary*
		Alabama	
Cottonton	*4,251*	*Boll Weevils*	*The Fields*
Eufaula	*7,908*	*Mudcats*	*Lakeview Park*
Lanett	*6,102*	*Linenmakers*	*Chattahoochee Field*
Opelika	*12,027*	*Orphans*	*Opelika Stadium*

Mister JayMac told us something about each franchise: what big league club it belonged to, its strengths and shortcomings, and why Highbridge, given our talent, should be in first place.

"Gentlemen, it's a minor disgrace that after fifteen games we're tied for fourth behind the Orphans, the Gendarmes, and the Mudcats. It's a *major* disgrace we're tied with that sorry crew from Cottonton. Cottonton! A hole in the road! They've got chickens on Main! I once saw a goat—an *animal*—figure in a call over there!" He banged his pool-cue pointer on the flip chart. It ripped the page listing the CVL's franchises. "Most of the Weevils are ex-semipros off mill teams. They're hacks and mercenaries. It's absurd to be locked in a fourth-place tie with em. Absurd!" The pointer whacked the chart, and all us rookies, except maybe Ankers, flinched.

"Steady down, Mister JayMac," Darius said.

Mister JayMac steadied. He left off being a high-powered general and became instead a low-key explainer—all Darius's doing, as maybe only Junior Heggie and I noticed.

"All right. We've got ex-major leaguers in this room. I want those men to raise their hands."

You'd've figured that with so many old guys on the team, journeymen players sliding into middle age and past, maybe five or six would've had at least a few at bats or some heavy-duty bench time in the bigs. But only two men raised their hands; neither, it did my soul good to see, was Buck Hoey.

"You gentlemen come up here," Mister JayMac said. He tapped the floor, and two fellas I'd've never guessed shuffled to the front of the room. Ex-big leaguers! Even Ankers got excited.

"Huzza!" Hoey called. "Failures! They went up, but they came back down!" Joshing, but not totally. His little barb rang true.

"Failures!" some other guys chanted. "Failures!"

"At least we made it up," Creighton Nutter said,

"I think you made it *all* up. You and Dunnagin's adventures in the bigs're all in your heads." Laughter. Musselwhite was captain, but Hoey did his bit as official team comedian.

"In the record books, you mean," Nutter said.

Nutter and Dunnagin, our former Showmen. Nutter reminded me of the chip-on-his-shoulder second barber in a two-man shop, a fella who argues because he's sick of playing second fiddle. He had acorn-colored skin, which he'd probably got from a north Georgia farmer with Cherokee blood.

Dunnagin was thirty-eight or -nine, a mick with jet-black hair and eyes as blue as core samples of Canadian sky. His upper body said weight lifter; his legs said whooping crane. At practice that morning he'd worn full catcher's gear: chest pad, shin guards, birdcage, the works. Even then I'd noticed his shin guards were wider than his thighs. You expected him to tumble over, like a tower of alphabet blocks with a block too many at the top.

"Tell them who you played for, Mr. Nutter," Mister JayMac said, "and what kind of record you compiled."

"Murder," Hoey said. "Corrupting female minors."

Nutter blew off the kibitzing. "In 1927, I pitched in nineteen games for the Boston Braves. Seventy-six innings."

"Ah, but your *record*," Hoey said. "Tell us your *record*."

Nutter glanced over at Mister JayMac, who gave him a nod. "I was four and seven with two saves. My ERA was . . . 5.09."

Total silence. Hoey may've already known Nutter's record, but most of the other Hellbenders didn't.

"Four and seven," said Vito Mariani, himself a pitcher. "Not so hot. That earned run average aint so hot either."

"Mr. Mariani, you have no ERA in the majors at all," Mister JayMac said. "And there's not another pitcher in Highbridge today with more big-league victories than Mr. Nutter nailed down for the Braves. Give him the respect due him."

Ankers started clapping, the rest of us joined in. Nutter glued his chin to his chest, but smiled an angry-barber smile, like he disagreed with a customer's opinion of the New Deal but didn't want to job his tip by saying so aloud.

"Very well, Mr. Dunnagin," Mister JayMac said, "tell us in what capacity you reached the bigs and how you fared there."

Dunnagin stood like a Marine at parade rest. "I went up as a puling babe with the St. Louis Browns in 1924. I played reserve catcher and pinch hit for all or parts of the next six seasons."

"After which the Browns cut you?" Mister JayMac asked.

"Nosir. In 1929, my pa's business hit an iceberg. I quit the Browns to take care of my folks, God rest them."

Hoey faked playing a violin. Imagine, though. Dunnagin had played in the majors two years before I was born. He'd held on to a Browns roster spot for six years! And the club hadn't dumped him for half-assed play. He'd quit to sweep up the debris of a family disaster. Now, a dozen years down the line, he was trying to earn another berth in the bigs.

"Tell the boys your nickname," Hoey said. His violinist act hadn't made anybody laugh, so he was trying something else.

" 'Double,' " Dunnagin said. "My teammates on the Browns called me Double. In my first-ever at bat, against the Yankees, I slapped a two-bagger off Bullet Joe Bush. The ball scooted into the alley between Witt and Ruth. Well, I thought, I'm on my way. Look out, Cobb. Look out, Ruth and Hornsby."

"Go on, Percy," Hoey said. "Tell em the rest."

"Double worked as a nickname later not because I regularly knocked out two-baggers," Dunnagin said, "but because I had a bad tendency to ground into double plays every time the Browns looked like they might score." He stared past Clerval into the foyer, where a grandfather clock had begun to bong.

"Son, you're modest to a sadistic extreme," Mister JayMac told Dunnagin. "Tell them about your best year."

"I hit .330 in 1926," Dunnagin said, reciting it by rote and looking bored. "In ninety-four at bats, I had two home runs and fourteen doubles. But with more at bats in '27 and '28, my average fell off over sixty points both years."

"Which means he'd've still outhit all but three other Hellbender starters here with us this evening," Mister JayMac said. "A hand for Mr. Dunnagin, please."

This time I led the applause. So what if he'd last put on his catcher's getup for the Browns the year the stock market crashed? We had a near legend for a teammate, a fella who'd once hit over .300 in the bigs.

"With this leadership," Mister JayMac said, "we belong in a tie for fourth about as much as Patton and Montgomery belong in a tie for *anything* with von Arnim and the Eye-talians. (No offense, Mr. Mariani.) So look to these men as inspiration and examples. Thank you, gentlemen."

Nutter and Dunnagin returned to their spots in the parlor. Junior Heggie started to follow, but Mister JayMac halted him with the pointer. "Stay. We're not quite finished. Darius."

He whacked the chart.

Darius folded the franchise sheet over the back of the easel to show us a new page:

CVL STANDINGS
(As of June 3, 1943)

TEAM	WINS	LOSSES	PERC.	GAMES BEHIND
Opelika	12	3	.800	-
LaGrange	10	5	.666	2
Eufaula	9	6	.600	3
HIGHBRIDGE	7	8	.466	5
Cottonton	7	8	.466	5
Quitman	6	9	.400	6
Marble Springs	5	10	.333	7
Lanett	4	11	.266	8

"Remember, gentlemen," Mister JayMac said, "yall haven't even played the Gendarmes or Linenmakers yet—one of the best teams and the absolute sorriest. So, mostly, we've lost to mediocrities and also-rans. Were I given to worry, I'd be a total ruin. But I've long since taken to heart the scriptural counsel that anxious thought adds not a minute to our lives, and I sleep like a babe in swaddling clothes."

"Jesus," Hoey said, not exactly reverently.

"Selah," Mister JayMac said. "I've prayed and I've rounded up these fresh-faced youths."

"Glory!" Quip Parris said. "What if they're bums, sir?"

Mister JayMac smiled. "If yall wanted aiggs, would I foist on you scorpions?"

"Don't like aiggs," Burt Fanning said. No one else said a word.

"And so, gentlemen, I give you Messieurs Ankers, Boles, Heggie, and Dobbs," Mister JayMac said. "They'll no doubt irk a few of yall, but I also expect em to be a hypodermic in this team's draggy ass. Now, give em another Hellbender welcome."

A smattering of claps. Hoey, Jumbo, and Parris didn't clap at all. But this time, Mister JayMac didn't jump all over his men for cold-shouldering us.

He had Darius flip the chart page. Another chart came up. Then another one after that. And so on. A chart showing which CVL teams had ex-big leaguers. A map of Highbridge's business district, another of the part of town called Penticuff Strip, and even one of Camp Penticuff itself, down to parade grounds, dining halls, obstacle courses, and ball fields. Would we all be inducted if we didn't pass muster as Hellbenders? Anyway, Darius kept flipping the charts, and the grandfather clock in the foyer kept bonging out the quarter hours.

Finally, blueprints of every floor of McKissic House.

"Okay," Mister JayMac said. "Who's rooming with whom?"

The boardinghouse had two rooms for ballplayer-lodgers on the first floor, four on the second story, and a sort of garret nook on the third. Us rookies would settle in faster, the theory went, if we each had an old hand for a roommate.

"Sir, don't we need to see who's gonna get cut before we start assigning roommates?" Sweet Gus Pettus said.

Mister JayMac studied Pettus sorrowfully, his head cocked. "To be fair, yes. But I already know who I think'll be gone by tomorrow noon. You, Mr.

Pettus. Also, Charlie Jorgensen, Rick Roper, and Bobby Collum. Mr. Collum rents from me over in Cotton Creek, but all four of yall should be thinking about finding other work and moving out."

"What?" Rick Roper cried. "*What?* Spot challenges tomorrow and you're not even waiting to see how we do?"

"Mr. Roper, you've played seventeen innings at shortstop this year," Mister JayMac said, "but you have three times as many errors as Mr. Hoey, who's played over a hundred. You've fanned every time you've come up to bat."

Roper shut up. You could tell Pettus, Jorgensen, and Collum because they sat like glum statues. Roper went into a pathetic hangdog hunker of his own.

"For room-assignment purposes," Mister JayMac said, "I'm going to assume that tomorrow at this time the four men whose surnames I've called will no longer be around. If any of yall want a head start on a new life, I'll give you your pay and a small severance check. I'm no heartless monster, gentlemen."

"No he aint," Hoey said. "Ask Jumbo. The boss loant him his car."

Mister JayMac looked at Jumbo. "And you, Mr. Clerval, why did I have to send Euclid to fetch you?"

"Sir, I fell asleep. My errand earlier today fatigued me."

"What errand was that?" Hoey asked Jumbo.

"A personal errand. A private matter."

"He got his ashes hauled!" somebody shouted.

"If he did," Hoey said, "it took a dump truck to do it."

"Hush," Mister JayMac said. Nobody did. "Knock it off! We have room assignments to make and swapping out to do."

Heggie, Dobbs, and Ankers got picked for roomies right away, by Knowles, Curriden, and Musselwhite, and the guys identified as culls were thrown out on their ears. No one, though, jumped to take me.

"Dumbo with Jumbo," Buck Hoey said. "A perfect match."

Dumbo. The nickname the smart-alecks back in Tenkiller had hung on me. Hoey was just like the jerk back home who'd offered to buy me a ticket to *Dumbo* because it's "a good idea to stay in touch with your fambly, kid."

Jumbo studied me with his custardy eyes. "Okay," he said. "I agree to take Mr. Boles into my roost."

Jumbo's apartment was the only third-floor room set aside for boarders.

If you could trust Mister JayMac's wall chart, *roost* was a great name for it. Every guy at the meeting looked back and forth between Jumbo and me. Cripes. He was the kind of joker you have bad dreams about, and Mister JayMac was going to let him take me upstairs to his . . . *roost*.

8

I 'd left my duffel and my bat in the kitchen. When I went to get them, Curriden and Parris, on KP that week, followed me in and said I should start scrubbing dishes. I glared. Pro ballplayers, scrubbing dishes? Why couldn't Kizzy do them? Getting thrown into Jumbo Clerval's dutches had soured my mood, but I still couldn't see why Mister JayMac'd pay a skinny old female shine just to cook and slouch around. Hadn't he also hired her as a housekeeper? Why have colored help if your paid white ballplayers had to pitch in to help the help?

Kizzy read my mind. "Danl Bowes, I cooks and cooks. Aint nobody in this house goes hongry. You hongry?"

Nowhere like. If I'd taken another crumb, I'd've burst like a ripened pimple. I shook my head.

"Then you best git it in yo head to hep. Else I'm gone, off to do fo folks what'll preciate it." She poked me with a finger like a voodoo bone. "Hear what I say, Danl Bowes?"

This time I nodded. I heard her.

Parris said, "You run off Kizzy, Boles, you might as well be dead. Word gets round you chased her, you *will* be dead."

"I loves to cook," Kizzy said, "but hates to mess wi the pots and pans, the spills and overbiles that come wi a fixin bringe. When Mister JayMac stole me from Mrs. Lullworth's in 'thuddy-eight, he say I don't have to mess wi aw that truck again. So I won't, Danl Bowes, I gots me options."

"You go on now," Curriden told her. "Quip and me and this rude boy here'll finish up."

Kizzy rinsed—"rinched," she said—her hands off, gathered her stuff up, and limped to the porch door off the kitchen. She sported a flapper's hat from the roaring twenties and a picnic basket-size handbag. She looked back at us. "Mo pie in the Frigidaire. Yall gits hongry, go to it." And she left in a slicked-up Model T, its gas coupons courtesy of Mister JayMac.

"Too damned uppity for her own good, all right," Curriden said when she'd gone. "But who's going to tell her?"

Parris got Junior Heggie to come down to help me scrub pots and towel-dry plates. The sink had been installed for a person no more than five feet tall. I could see why Curriden had wanted to hand the dishwashing chores on to a rookie. It killed me to stoop over that basin, and Curriden had a good half foot on me.

By the time Heggie and I finished, the team meeting had long since broken up. The guys who lived in Cotton Creek—Hoey, Nutter, Sloan, and four others—had ridden back to the old mill district in Mister JayMac's Caddy. He'd chauffeured them himself, eight men packed like sardines into his two-seater, with Hoey, according to one report, perched on Norm Sudikoff's lap like Charlie McCarthy on Edgar Bergen's.

"See there," Parris told me when we'd heard this story, "Hoey's a dummy too."

Jumbo waited in the parlor. Three of Mister JayMac's culls sat with him looking glum and confused. (A fourth, Bob Collum, had returned to Cotton Creek with Hoey and pals, probably to tell his wife some dicey times lay ahead.) When I came in, the culls looked up at me like I was their hangman.

"This way to our room," Jumbo said. He ducked into the foyer and lumbered for the stairs. I wanted to follow him about as much as I wanted rheumatic fever.

One fella got up from the card table he'd been sitting at and stopped me: Roper, a rangy player with eyes like tenpenny nailheads and a foul cigarette stink on his breath. Just then, though, I couldn't put a name to his face. (One convenient thing about being a dummy—you can forget other folks' names without them realizing it.)

Roper dropped a long arm over my shoulder. "If you're any good atall, Boles," he said, talking into my ear, "I'm history. Spot challenges tomorrow, but Mister Jesus JayMac's already throwed me out. I roomed with Muscles, but he's already showing that Ankers kid my half of the premises. Is that fair?"

I couldn't shake my head. Roper's hand'd clamped the back of my neck—it felt like a claw.

"We're subs, scrubs, third-stringers," he said, yanking my head around, to look at Pettus and Jorgensen. "Expendables. You and them other wet-eared recruits have done for us. So I hope yall're worth it, us getting booted." He finally let go.

Pettus and Jorgensen eyed me from the card table. Even before being dropped from the club, they'd been semievicted from their rooms.

Where would Pettus and Jorgensen sleep? On sofas? In musty old chairs? I felt sorry for them. They looked sledgehammered, like heifers about to crash. I didn't feel that sorry for Roper. He wanted to blame me for the whole room-and-roster shuffle, but I felt no guilt—I hadn't bombed Pearl Harbor either.

The real culprit was the war itself. CVL teams made do in '43 with twenty-man rosters; marginal guys over that number had to face the blade. In most CVL towns, a twenty-man roster gave management a payroll that didn't chew up the season's gate. It also squared pretty well with the manpower needs of the Selective Service Acts and each club's search for usable talent.

"Dick Roper's my name," Roper said. "I may have to leave this bunch of shitasses, but yall'll hear from me again."

(Actually, we did. He got drafted later that summer—one of the reasons Mister JayMac released him, I imagine, and fought in Europe with the Ninth Army. Today he's a U. S. Congressman from a district in western Georgia, a born-again shill for the national gun lobby.)

Jumbo came back from the foyer to get me. Roper retreated to the card table and his cast-off buddies. If Jumbo felt sorry for them, he didn't show it. He took my bag—in his hand, it resembled a sack of marbles—and made for the stairs again. Following him, I knew he reared up to seven feet, maybe seven-two. In Tenkiller, I'd never seen anybody even close to that size. Six foot took the cake. In fact, Lon Musselwhite was the biggest man I'd ever seen until Jumbo came along, and I hadn't seen Muscles until just that morning.

Anyway, I had my doubts about soldiering up the stairs behind Jumbo. It reminded me of beanstalk climbing. Fee-fi-fo-fum. The steps creaked. Once we'd reached the second floor and the steps to the third, the house—with its mildewed wainscoting, wavy picture molding, and uneven hardwood floors—

had started to seem as echoey and crooked as a fairy-tale castle.

We finally hit the third floor. A T-shaped hall divided it. We went down the crossbar to the house's southwest side. Jumbo keyed open his door and nodded me in. Not counting the kitchen, this was the hottest room in McKissic House I'd yet visited, the stiflingest by far. Jumbo didn't say two words, just pointed me to the corner under a gable roof. He dragged over a canvas cot for me to stow my gear under and to sleep on: an Army cot, bought or liberated from Camp Penticuff. Jumbo broke it open and set it up for me.

No need for blankets, but I'd've looked with favor on a pillow and a sheet. I didn't relish undressing in front of Jumbo, but because I usually slept in my skivvies, a showdown would eventually come—unless I copped out and slept in my clothes. The heat nixed that notion. My first bad dream, even one of Aleutian snows and icy Marsden matting, would trigger a killing fever attack. But I couldn't tell Jumbo how I felt, what I wanted, why I ached to cry, and he didn't ask. At least my smelly cot sat next to a window and an outside fire escape. But Jumbo'd probably let me camp there because he was too tall to move easily under the gable's ceiling.

Jumbo had a bed with white iron bedposts, two sets of springs laid side by side, and a couple of rectangles of scrap plywood on the springs. The setup didn't look comfy, granted, but it had my cot beat all the way to the nearest mattress factory. Well, okay. Jumbo had let me into his room. He was the landlord, I was the tenant. But why couldn't I have a bed too? After all, McKissic House didn't shelter convicts or street bums.

"You'll adjust," Jumbo said. "After a time, the heat becomes bearable."

Wham! it hit me: my rookie status, the attic room, the hideous galoot I had to live with. I broke down and sobbed, like I had on the train. Anywhere else, with anybody else, I'd've tried to hide how trampled on and scared I felt. Jumbo, though, I let watch.

Then I reached under my cot, pulled my Red Stix bat out of my bag, and stood there glaring and wringing the bat's handle. I didn't plan to clobber Jumbo—he'd've clobbered me back, no doubt—just to squeeze out some sawdust to catch my tears in.

Jumbo had a dust-clogged revolving fan with a metal safety basket. It rested on a pitcher stand between his bed and my cot. He turned the fan toward me and switched it on. It buck-danced around, moving muggy air. If he'd hoped the fan would improve my mood, it didn't.

I continued to cry.

In his frock coat and patched trousers, like a hulking Abe Lincoln in a Mathew Brady photograph, Jumbo sat down on his bed. He didn't seem to be sweating, just steaming comfortably from the inside. He gave off a clayey smell, a smell with a soothing edge to it but also a buzzing persimmonish feel; not a sick-making smell, but a *different* one.

Crying, I noticed Jumbo'd done a few things to make his attic homey. *Semi*homey. Shelves lined the wall behind his bed, pine planks he'd made into a bookcase with the aid of several large cans of Joan of Arc red kidney beans. He'd used these cans the way folks today use cinderblocks, as braces between the shelves. He'd stacked them eight cans high, in three columns, two cans per column between each shelf.

Books glutted the shelves. Over them he had this William Blake reproduction of Adam and Eve being kicked out of Eden by angels with fiery swords. It looked like Jumbo had cut the picture out of a magazine— *Life?*—and glued it to a piece of cardboard with a mat of green construction paper but no glass. Then he'd hooked it on a loop of wire to a nail in the wall.

Anyway, the books, the fan, and the magazine picture didn't do much to hide the fact he lived in a grungy third-story oven. Now I lived in it with him. In the old days, English noblemen with crazy wives or daughters stashed their women in attics like this one and hid the keys in old ships' trunks.

Say something, I thought. Say something, you lummox.

But he didn't. He didn't even shed his stupid coat. He sat there, sorry or maybe embarrassed for me, miffed at himself for agreeing to take me in. I slammed past his bed into the hall, Jumbo didn't try to stop me. Either he didn't care to risk my anger or my leaving didn't exactly crush him.

I stumbled down the stairs. On the second floor, some players, including Heggie and Dobbs, stood around in the hall, the doors to their bedrooms open. I startled them. Sure I did—a nutso-looking kid with a bat trying to find something to break.

Double Dunnagin flapped out of his room in shower thongs and a bathrobe. He copped in a wink how I was primed to let go of my wayward, ornery pain.

"Hey there, Danny. Swell bat."

"Get him off the hall with that thing!" Mariani yelled. "The twerp's gone round it."

Dunnagin came over. He asked to see the bat. I pulled it back, cocking it. Everybody else on the hall—Mariani, Parris, Heggie, Dobbs, Knowles, Curriden—had shut up. Dunnagin kept smiling, kept coming on. He said he understood how arriving in Highbridge on a steamy day and getting paired off with Jumbo could "tetch a fella." He took my elbow, even though I could've knocked his head off with one swing, and steered me into his room. His roomy, a pitcher name of Jerry Wayne Sosebee, bridled to see me.

"For God's sake, Double," he said, "don't bring the crazy kid in here. I'm trying to balance my checkbook."

But Dunnagin, without even wrenching my bat away, had already closed the door. Sosebee stood up. He wore nothing but a pair of khaki boxer shorts and eyed me like I'd brought cholera. His side of the room—a room twice as big as Jumbo's hotbox—boasted photos of family members, pets, a Ford sedan on blocks. He'd papered the wall next to his bed with Varga girl pinups from Esquire. Even half unglued, I ogled them.

"The guy's whackers," Sosebee said.

"Seems healthy enough to me," Dunnagin said.

"Get him out. Jesus H. Christ."

Dunnagin shuffled on a pair of trousers and a T-shirt, flipped Sosebee a salute, and led me down the stairs and out of the house.

Tiptoeing through the rows of a victory garden, he pulled me along by the barrel of my bat. We crossed a stretch of lawn below the garden and Mister JayMac's bungalow and ended up in a gazebo near a good-size pond.

In Tenkiller, the Elshtains had a gazebo. In his carpentry days, my dad'd built a few for townies with big yards and a need to show their money. Down South, gazebos sprout like toadstools. I don't know why. They make little sense—moronic structures with roofs but no walls, more for show than everyday use. But Dunnagin pulled me up the steps of this one and made me put my keister on a bench inside it. I held my bat between my knees, where it jutted up like a bodacious hard-on. Dunnagin laughed. I set it down and rolled it under my bench with my foot.

"Thanks," Dunnagin said. He began to pace. It wasn't quite dark yet. Only a couple of stars twinkled. You could smell these typical Hothlepoya County smells drifting in from town or from the countryside and colliding with each other. One smell was of plowed earth, like rotting burlap. Heavier, though, was the sweet, starchy fragrance from the Goober Pride peanut butter factory. Back then, these stinks haunted Highbridge, especially the trackside factory districts. In residential neighborhoods where Dutch elms, maples, and oaks could filter some of the peanutty stench out of the dead air, it dropped to tolerable levels. Nowadays, I can't catch a whiff of it without thinking first of gazebos and second of Highbridge.

"Don't panic, Danny," Dunnagin said, pacing barefoot in front of me. He had his hands in his back pants pockets. Plenty of room there—he hardly had any fanny at all. "Jumbo hasn't killed anybody yet. He looks like death blown up to dirigible size and painted battleship gray, but, I mean, hey, he's human, isn't he?"

Was he? I didn't know.

"He doesn't have a social knack as well developed as his vocabulary, I admit it, but that shouldn't shake you—you're not exactly a social lion yourself, I wouldn't think, and even Harpo has a bigger vocabulary than you do." He squeezed the bulb of an imaginary airhorn: *Beep, beep.*

"Look," Dunnagin went on, "you should feel flattered he took you. Clerval had the only private room in McKissic House." Dunnagin stopped pacing. I had my eyes on his feet. He didn't start talking again until I raised my sights to his face. "Mister JayMac assigned that attic room to Clerval last year, his first on the club, and I'd've figured him about as ready to take on a roomy as Hitler to show up at a kosher gig in Miami. So you should feel honored. Chosen, even."

My eyes grew hubcap round. I did feel chosen, I just didn't know for what.

"Yeah, he's big. Six-ten, seven, maybe seven-two. Hard to say. He sort of slouches. Taller than Howie Schultz, though. Schultz, the kid who plays first for Brooklyn. Sportswriters call him The Steeple. Got nixed for military service for being too tall. S one reason Mister JayMac hurried to sign Clerval—the Army wouldn't come calling. A better reason is, Clerval's a good country player. A bit slow, not a lot of range, but a champ at digging out bad throws and snagging tosses that'd sail slap over anybody else's head. He's also good at catching darters right back at him and shots down the foul line that might drop in for extra-base hits."

I pulled my bat out from under the bench. I rolled its handle back and forth between my palms.

"Yeah, he can hit. Sort of. Last year his batting average hovered around .220 or so—poor for the minors, fatal for a guy with big-league ambitions. But he's got a scary knack for making the hits he does get count. He's slammed fence busters in spots that'd've killed us if he hadn't come through.

Killed us. So Mister JayMac gave him his own room. He's valuable even if he isn't quite bigs material."

Dunnagin took my bat and sighted along it at the evening star. Then he swung it a few times. Me, I swatted mosquitoes, a swarm from the shallows of Hellbender Pond.

"Here." Dunnagin handed the bat back to me. "Cigarette?" He shook a couple out of his pack, stuck one in my mouth, and lit me up. "Sometimes the smoke'll run the bastards off." He meant the mosquitoes. "Soothe your nerves too."

I took an awkward puff. Back in Tenkiller, Coach Brandon had hated the habit. Called cigarettes wind-robbers. Sharing one with Dunnagin felt a lot like breaking training.

"Old Golds," Dunnagin said. "They got this apple honey stuff in em to keep their tobacco moist."

I couldn't taste any "apple honey," but I kept smoking. In a minute or two, I had a coughing fit. Dunnagin didn't notice.

"Around the loop, players started calling Clerval Jumbo. He tolerates it. Just don't call him Goliath, Behemoth, or Whale. He *hates* Whale. Call him that, it's like you're knocking not only him but all the whales in the seas. Jumbo's okay, though, because it's fairly neutral. It just means he's big, which he'd be a blind fool to deny."

I kept coughing; a fuse sizzled straight down my tongue.

"No idea how old Clerval is," Dunnagin said. "Thirty? Maybe thirty-five or -six. He sometimes limps around like a crip. Other times, he's light on his feet as Astaire. Even DiMaggio'd die for Clerval's swing on his good days. I sure would."

With one hand I smoked. With the other I scratched a mosquito bite on my shin. Blood stained my pants cuff, and flesh rode under my fingernails.

"Did you see him eating tonight?" Dunnagin asked me. "Take a look at him and you'd assume he's a meat-eating barbarian. Nosir. He's a vegetarian, a strict one. Won't touch chicken or eggs. Eats a ton of produce a week, though. And Goober Pride peanut butter. Practice mornings, game days, he devours half a jar. Good thing he's near the source, eh?" Dunnagin rubbed his chin. "Come on. I'll walk you back up. Clerval won't bite. He only bites vegetables."

I let Dunnagin lead me back to the house and up the stairs to Jumbo's room. Dunnagin knocked.

"Hank, is it okay if young Boles here comes back in?"

The door swung open. Jumbo stood framed in it from the chest down. He bent at the knees and peered at us sideways.

"Come in, Mr. Boles."

"See you tomorrow," Dunnagin said. He did a swami's farewell, touching his forehead and chin and rolling his hand over. Then he beat it back down the stairs. Jumbo had changed our room. A divider—a loosely woven grass mat—hung between his bed and my cot. He'd also put a quilt and a feather pillow on my cot and set up his revolving fan at the edge of the grass curtain so that it blew into his half of the room through part of its arc and into my half for the other. It moved hot air around, but also kept mosquitoes from drilling us like Texas oil fields.

"I intend to read a while. Tell me if the lamp disturbs you." Jumbo ducked behind the mat, where his shadow hung, scaring the Tenkiller crap out of me. I sat down on the quilt he'd rustled up and stared at his lumpy silhouette.

Dunnagin's efforts to calm me didn't calm me now I was back in Jumbo's room. I heeled off my shoes thinking he was about to rip down the mat, grab me by the earlobes, and dump me out the window. Jumbo never did that, but sometimes his head would seem to turn my way and stare at me through the weave, his eyes—I imagined—leaking a thin yellow lava.

I lay down in my clothes. Mama Laurel, the Elshtains, Coach Brandon, Franklin Gooch, and everyone else in Tenkiller might as well've rocketed off to Mars. At last I slept. Later, I awoke in darkness. The fan still bumped away, and Jumbo still breathed over its whirr in deep, even gasps. Gasping myself, I went under again. . . .

9

The next morning, I woke before Jumbo. My mouth felt like it'd been emery-boarded and stuffed with cotton balls. (Dunnagin's Old Golds?) The mosquito bites on my ankles and finger joints looked like razor nicks, I'd scratched them so hard. I needed a bath.

I rummaged up a towel and skulked past the mat dividing the room. In the early grayness, Jumbo lay atop his bed-clothes, in extra-large BVDs, a human mountain range—knees, hips, rib cage, shoulders, head. He lay twisted in a way you'd've thought impossible for the human form to get into without permanent damage, but his breathing—gentle, gasping snores—said just the opposite. The ugly galoot'd really gone under.

In sleep, though, Jumbo's ugliness grew uglier. His body parts didn't seem to fit. His stringy-haired block of a noggin didn't belong with the bullish neck and the wide sloping shoulders under it. His proportions were more or less okay, I guess, but the colors and textures of his skin didn't match up the way you'd've expected. It was like someone'd kneaded biscuit dough, cake dough, and a mass of Piedmont clay together without blending them. Even as he snored, Jumbo reminded me of a body, wounded or dead.

In the bathroom, I got presentable. I didn't look in on Jumbo again.

I snuck downstairs to the parlor. Pettus, Jorgensen, and Roper had disappeared.

No one'd removed the easel and its charts. On the easel I saw a map of Penticuff Strip, with all the honky tonks, tattoo dens, and "horizontal refreshment stations" Mister JayMac had declared off-limits to us, saying hidebound morality didn't lead him to discourage us from visiting these dives, only his certainty no Hellbender with any sand could venture over there without getting in a brawl.

"Those Camp Penticuff boys see the Strip as their private party turf," Mister JayMac'd lectured. "Way they see it, any able-bodied male who shows up there in civvies is a pussy-stealing shirker who needs his balls kicked. If you go, don't expect me to foot your hospital bills or your hoosegow bail. I'll cut you loose first. I'll tell your draft boards you're ready for basic training and a quick-march slog into combat. Yall got that?"

"Yessir!" everybody said.

This morning, though, I thought it awfully dumb or awfully thoughtful of him to leave in plain view a map of all the barrel houses and sin cribs we'd do so well to avoid. I stood there in the bad light trying to memorize that map and its prime attractions: The Hot Spot, Corporal John's, The Wing and Thigh, Effie McGee's. I'd worked from the Strip entrance at Market Street to Pawnshop Row, about three quarters along it, when a voice from the dining room whirled me like a caught-out burglar.

"Up so early," Kizzy said, "you can hep me git my breakfuss going, Mister Danl." She waved me toward her with a hand made ghostly by biscuit flour, then banged back through the kitchen door like I'd follow her in on command. Overnight, I'd gone from Mr. Bowes to Mister Danl—a step down, I thought. And why'd she singled me out for KP this morning? Hadn't I done my duty last night?

My gut told me to do what Kizzy asked—I always did what grownups said. But if I'd stayed in my room like all the other slugabeds, I wouldn't've had to make a decision. Kizzy was stiffing me for my Ben Franklin up-and-at-em ethic. Not fair. So I turned again to Darius's map of Penticuff Strip.

The kitchen door swung open. I didn't even look up. With a finger, I traced the distance from GI George's Camera Shop to a dancehall called, I swear to God, the Jitterbuggery.

"Mr. Boles," a drawly female voice said, "Kizzy just asked for your help. Come at once. Please." The "please" was a sop to the fact the speaker and I were both white. Confusion held me a second, then I double-timed it. Just inside the kitchen's doors—boy, it smelled good in there!—the white woman who'd spoken to me was flensing strips from a greasy slab of bacon.

Seeing bacon startled me. Meat rationing'd begun at the end of March, and Mama and I had tried to support the war effort by eating cold cereals. Goochie had called this "gut patriotism." He hated cereals for breakfast, meatless chili for lunch, scrambled eggs for dinner twice a week. At McKissic House, though, no one had to sacrifice much.

"Grease these baking sheets," the white woman said. "Then halve and squeeze those oranges, please. The juicer's over there. At least a pitcher's worth for starters. See if you can't strain out those noxious little seeds. A seed in a glass of orange juice is an irritant and a reproof."

This woman, at fifty-something, looked several years older than my mama. She wore a floral-print dress, all blue and violet, with a clean white apron over it—like a dairy maid or a Swiss nun. Her hair shone whiter and softer than the slab of pork under her hands, but a beautician had cut it like a girl's, swept it up high and drawn it back in wings over her ears, with a cameo clasp at the base of her neck. She had pink lips, dark eyebrows, and eyes like blue aggies. To me, she was . . . the sunrise in an apron.

Don't get me wrong. I didn't develop an instant crush. I just realized a female as striking as this intruder in Kizzy's kitchen was a bird of paradise. She belonged in a storm of biscuit flour about like Vivien Leigh belonged on her knees with a scrub brush in a public John. Just then I didn't know much else about her. Maybe she secretly poisoned hummingbird feeders. One thing for sure—she could boss you like a topkick out to Camp Penticuff.

I started greasing baking sheets while Kizzy measured fresh grounds into a coffee pot the size of a small oil drum. The sun hadn't risen full yet, but the kitchen had already begun to creak and steam. I felt like a galley slave.

"I'm Mrs. McKissic," the white woman told me. "Giselle Crouch McKissic. You may call me, as everyone does, Miss Giselle." She paused in her rapid-fire bacon slicing. "Or could, that is, if you could talk. So you may *think of me* as Miss Giselle. However, you will probably settle on a private name in tune with your own vulgar tastes and biases. I can't prevent that, but it betrays your upbringing, Mr. Boles."

"Mister Danl's a good boy, ma'am. Jes cain't talk."

"I know he can't talk," Miss Giselle said, "but he can think. Not well, necessarily, but freely, unimpeded by any human concern for the feelings of his elders. Muteness affords an awfully convenient armor against self-revelation. Perhaps we should all aspire to it."

"You thinking way too much, ma'am," Kizzy said. "Thisere boy's awright."

"A judgment based on only half a day's experience?"

"Yessum. That's aw I gots."

Miss Giselle said, "Enough greasing, Mr. Boles. Lard and butter are rationed. Do you wish to run us out?" Impossible, I thought. This kitchen seemed to have reserves of everything from tabasco sauce to oatmeal. "To the juice, please. A herd will soon be gathering."

I went to the juicer. It looked like a glass Ku Klux Klan hat, with a moat around it. I halved oranges and mashed out juice. Kizzy hummed radio melodies—"Paper Doll" and "Pistol Packin Mama," not corny spirituals or big-city blues. Miss Giselle cracked eggs into a big mixing bowl and whipped them into a froth with a long-handled spoon.

Darius came in from his room above the carriage house. "Kizzy, Miss Giselle, Mr. Boles." He waited.

"Yes," Miss Giselle said. "You may roust them out."

Darius banged out of the kitchen and into the foyer. "Rise and shine!" He climbed. "Rise and shine, gentlemens. You don't eat now, you don't eat till noon! Rise and shine!" I heard him pounding on doors. "Rise and shine!" He climbed to the third floor. "Don't eat now, you don't eat till noon!"

Somebody yelled, "Damn, man! You're the loudest nigger in the whole brought-low Confederacy!"

It didn't phase Darius. Back on the second floor, he shouted, "Rise and shine!" Reveille at McKissic House. I felt smug about beating this wake-up call, even as I crippled my throwing hand on a juicer spindle and missed my extra winks.

"When you're through there, Mr. Boles," Miss Giselle said, "get out the cereal and sweet milk for Mr. Clerval. He can't abide animal protein."

"He *is* a picky fella," Kizzy said.

"I admire that in him," Miss Giselle said. "It's unusual to find a cogent particularity in any human male."

Darius came back into the kitchen. He took a biscuit from one of the baking sheets Kizzy'd removed from the oven, cut it open, and smeared it with strawberry jam.

Miss Giselle looked on with the sourest expression I'd yet seen on her porcelain-pretty face. "Who said you could have that?"

Darius finished eating and licked his fingertips. "Nobody, ma'am. I'll be eating shortly. Hardly seems a crime to grab a early taste."

Miss Giselle just looked at him.

Darius tightened his jaw. "Sorry, ma'am." He stalked out to the screened-in porch. At its door, he said, "After breakfuss, see me fo practice flannels, Danl. Tell them other new fellas the same." He went on down the steps. The screen door banged to like a mine going off.

10

At practice that morning, I backed up Buck Hoey at shortstop. Heggie backed up Lamar Knowles at second. Skinny Dobbs birddogged Trapdoor Evans in right field. Philip Ankers, who'd probably learned to pitch chunking clods at cows, went down to the bullpen to warm up with our second-string catcher, Nyland "Turkey" Sloan.

"S only me you've got to get by, Dumbo," Hoey said as we stood in the infield watching Mister JayMac hit fungoes to the outfield. I gave Hoey a look. "Roper's gone. Roper, Pettus, Jorgensen—they all took Mister JayMac's offer of back pay, railway tickets, and severance pay. So did Bob Collum. Mister JayMac's savvy. He knows everybody's skills and limitations. Yours too, Dumbo. So I hope he's right."

From right, Dobbs threw one in like a bazooka shot to Dunnagin at home plate—a no-hopper, the kind of dead-on-target throw you don't see twice all year.

"S too soon to showboat, Mr. Dobbs!" Mister JayMac yelled. "You ruin that arm, I'll unsocket the other, jes to keep em a matched set."

"Yessir!" Dobbs yelled back. "Sorry, sir!"

"My wife and Collum's wife're big pals," Hoey said. "Now the Collums're leaving. Looks like Mister JayMac may've guessed right on Dobbs, though. Collum never threw like that. What about you? Did he guess right on you? Or am I gonna send you home with a dent in your cup and mud on your face?"

I pretended to watch the fielders catching and throwing in. In fact, I *did* watch em, them and Mister JayMac.

In refusing to wear baseball duds, Mister JayMac set himself apart from most other managers. He dressed like a man off for a scrambled dog at the corner drug store, casual but neat. Today, he wore beat-up spikes instead of street shoes. The dirt around home was loose, and hitting fungoes from there required purchase.

Seeing Mister JayMac at a flip chart, you'd've figured him for a manager who'd ride the bench with a bourbon bottle in a paper sack. But I'd seen him throwing hard yesterday, and today he was *smacking* the ball. He'd even step in front of his catcher to pick off one-hop throws from the outfield. He liked his players to put out. "Exert!" he'd yell. "Sweat! Dive!" He liked leaping grabs, all-out tumbles, flamethrower pegs to first or home.

Even in his linen pants, dirt spilling from his cuffs, Mister JayMac was something. Trying out for him, I busted my tail. So did Junior at second and Dobbs in right. Not only did we want to earn ourselves starting spots, we also wanted to please—really please—Mister JayMac.

At the three challenge spots, three rookies against three old hands, we had us three battle royals. Mister JayMac tested every pair of rivals, turn by turn. He'd say, "Men on first and third, one out, Boles and Heggie up," or, "Bottom a the ninth, tie score, runner on second, Hoey and Knowles up," toss the ball up, feint one way, and fungo it another, with such a skitter on it you'd be lucky not to catch it in your teeth.

I had my championship year on the Red Stix going for me. Even more important, I had a history of hundreds of thousands of fielded ricochets from the wall of Tenkiller's icehouse. I don't think even Buck Hoey, a career minor leaguer, had handled more chances than me. Eight or nine a game tops it out for a shortstop, with a few hundred to a thousand more chances in spring training. Hoey had talent and more experience in actual game situations, but I had talent too and I'd practiced more—a hundred years as an all-star vet of Ye Olde Icehouse Loop. Off the field, I lacked confidence, but I had so much sass on it, you could've given half of mine to Stepin Fetchit and made him swagger like Mussolini. Swear to God.

Today, back from whatever errand he'd run yesterday, Jumbo *owned* first base. His backup was Norm Sudikoff, a married guy renting one of the boss's Cotton Creek mill houses. Jumbo had Sudikoff behind him all day, but Mister JayMac waved Sudikoff into action only every fourth or fifth time he fungoed to the infield. Mostly, Sudikoff stood twenty yards behind the bag, in foul territory, while Jumbo put on a fielding clinic.

Standing or striding, Jumbo was a disjointed wreck. His shoulders, elbows, knees, and head jutted weirdly. Slouching from here to there, he looked a step away from unhinging and falling apart. His physique and his hitch-along gait gave him a brittle, palsied look.

On the field, though, Jumbo sparkled. He played a deep first base, on the edge of the outfield grass. (Not even Howie Gooch, who'd had better range than any other high school player I'd ever seen, had played so deep.) This gave Jumbo extra time to catch hard-hit shots to either side, even if the pitcher sometimes had to cover the bag for the putout.

Vito Mariani—Speedy himself—fielded the pitcher's spot. Each time Mister JayMac sent a runner to first after rapping out an alley-seeking fungo to Jumbo, Jumbo and Manani would team to nip the runner by a step or two. Red dust would geyser up. My heart would stagger at the sheer loveliness of their execution and the thrill of the race to the bag.

But Jumbo didn't *always* toss to Mariani. Sometimes he'd short-hop the ball, wave Mariani off, and pelt across the bag, all windmilling elbows and knees, before the runner'd even come out of the blocks. He had the headlong out-of-control velocity of a runaway locomotive. Scary.

"He can't walk," Hoey told me after one of these plays, "but he sure can jump and run." Jumbo also had a never-miss lobster pincer in his glove and an arm like a catapult. Once, after Mister JayMac had put an invented runner on third with less than two outs, Jumbo'd almost knocked Dunnagin silly with a blistering throw home.

In the challenges at second and short, Jumbo played no favorites. He'd rumble to the bag, shift instinctively for the throw, and pick it out of the air or scoop it up from the dirt, to hell whether you were vet or rookie. His acrobatics at first made every player throwing to him look like an all-star. Not much got by him.

Sudikoff, by comparison, was a graceful second-rater. He had style around the bag and an easy way of carrying himself, but he'd screw up. Throws in the dirt were his comeuppance—he couldn't come up with them. On some chances, he'd look like a matador doing a cape twirl, nifty and elegant as you please, but the ball'd scoot past him and roll to the seats. Sudikoff put on an *act*, Jumbo a bona fide *show*.

At second, Junior Heggie et Lamar Knowles's lunch. The kid from Valdosta backhanded screamers up the middle, twisted like a gill-hung bass, and threw back over his shoulder without a spike in the ground to push off of or anything but desire on the ball to get it to first. He et Knowles's lunch.

I did okay, but I didn't eat Hoey's lunch. My steadiness had him hassled, though. Mister JayMac'd gone out to Oklahoma to recruit a new shortstop, so Hoey saw himself on his knees under a guillotine blade. If I made a play, he had to. If I knocked a darter out of the air, pounced on it, and got back on my feet to nip the runner, he had to match my heroics. Mostly, he did. But the heat—from the sun, from Mister JayMac—made him snippish and petty. He tried to rag me into misplays. He asked me how far I reckoned beginner's luck would carry a dumb-fart Okie in the CVL. It irked him I couldn't answer. He'd've enjoyed an insult-slinging free-for-all.

"You're a showboat, Dumbo. I'd tell Mister JayMac to stick one in your ear, but that'd be too easy."

Hoey was *scared*. About Dunnagin's age, he'd never spent six minutes, much less six seasons, in the bigs. With time out between '36 and '40 peddling Ohio real estate, his whole career had played out in the minors: the Carolina League, the Southern Association, the Appalachian League, the Sally League. A wife and four pre-Pearl Harbor rug rats had kept him out of the Army, but a smidgen less talent than he needed, or bad luck, had kept him out of the bigs. The worry in Hoey's good-looking mug came through loud and clear. I wanted to outplay the jerk, but I didn't want to unemploy him. How would he tell Mrs. Hoey? How would he feed his rug rats?

"Yall get in here!" shouted Mister JayMac, red-faced and sweaty. He'd soaked his shirt out. His T-shirt showed through like a filmy corset. His trousers were sopped, from waist to thigh, like he'd sat down in a wash tub. We circled him on the infield grass, amazed by his energy, just as he wanted. You had to hand it to him, though. He didn't huddle in the dugout with a jar of white lightning and a hand-held Jesus fan from Stiffslinger & Sons' Christian Mortuary.

"How'd we do?" Reese Curriden said. Curriden'd played third, with relief from Burt Fanning, and he'd done fine. You just had to hope he didn't go down with a sprung hamstring. A pitcher or a utilityman would have to replace him, and no sub could do it. The Hellbenders weren't exactly the Georgia Light and Power Company. Like most other CVL clubs, we had a shortage of utilitymen.

"Better than yesterday," Mister JayMac said. "Yall seem to've remembered what this"—he held up a dirty baseball—"is for, after all. Praise Saint Doubleday."

"Screw Saint Doubleday," Buck Hoey said. "Who's starting where the next time we play for keeps?"

"Whoa," Mister JayMac said. "I got to see how my rookies measure up in the hitting department."

"Look at our box scores," Hoey said. "Check our averages. Knowles and me didn't fall off a milk wagon three hours ago. It's too damned hot for this chickenshit."

"So they say out to Camp Penticuff too," Mister JayMac said. "Except it *isn't*, not for Army recruits. Men's lives hang in the balance. Likewise this team's."

"I meant my chickenshit remark respectfully, sir."

Everybody laughed.

"A queer bit of English on it then," Mister JayMac said.

"Should Trapdoor, Lamar, and I start pounding the pavement for defense jobs and new housing?" Hoey said.

"No one here today's in danger of the ax. Only my next lineup's in doubt. We'll play an exhibition so I can decide."

"*Now?*" Peter Hay said.

The other ballplayers called Hay Haystack. He had yellow hair and waddled like a haywagon. Mister JayMac always had him running, but he could pitch and that kept him on the squad. As soon as he said, "Now?" a half dozen Hellbenders linked arms and spieled:

"Huge Peter Haystack,
Please move your hulk.
Your gut goes by flat car,
Your butt goes by bulk."

Hay just grinned and pounded a fist on Turkey Sloan's head, mashing his cap in.

Sloan had started the chant. He'd got half the team to join in by waving his arms like a chorus leader. Mister JayMac let it happen, seeing it as a tension-breaker.

Turkey Sloan backed Double Dunnagin at catcher and handled most bullpen chores. *Turkey* didn't mean, back then, what it does now—a brainless jerk, like a turkey that lifts its head to watch it rain and ends up drowning. Sloan had got his nickname because he caught, and ballplayers at the turn of the century, thinking home plate looked like a serving plate at Thanksgiving, started calling it the turkey.

Anyway, Sloan had a catcher's body build—big shoulders, big thighs, and a teddy bear's friendly mug. He also had brains. He'd written the "Huge Peter Haystack" rhyme, among others, and the team saw him as its unofficial poet laureate. A weakness for Mother Goose doggerel and a lot of time on his hands had helped him claim the title.

I glanced around.

The only other guy not laughing was Jumbo. He squinted at us like a scowling Jehovah. You figured he'd been born during a Puritan sermon with a dirge as accompaniment. You figured if he ever told a joke, it would start with "Inasmuch as" or something else lawyerly.

"No, Mr. Hay, not now," Mister JayMac said when everybody'd quieted down. "In"—he checked his watch—"forty minutes. Take a break."

Players cheered, like kids let out for recess.

Hoey said, "Hey. Who's gonna be playing who? The regulars versus the rubes?"

"With that breakdown," Mister JayMac said, "some of yall'd have to play yourselves."

"All right, then. Who's pitching for who?"

Mister JayMac held us there on hooks. He didn't want to tip his hand yet.

"Fess up, Mister JayMac," Parris said. "What's forty minutes gonna mean? Announce your pitchers."

"Tell us!" a whole slew of players cried.

Mister JayMac made calming motions. "Easy. Don't herniate yourselves. The rookies and their pals will play behind—"

"Ankers!" Hoey said.

"Astute deduction." Mister JayMac smiled like a kindly grandpa with a bandolier full of machine-gun ammo.

"And who for us?" Hoey said. "Who for us?"

I wanted to know too. Which pitcher, after our break, would I have to step in against? Quip Parris? Nutter, the ex-big leaguer? Mariani? Or Dunnagin's roomy, Jerry Wayne Sosebee? They all looked tough, even the Eye-talian, a 4-F punctured-eardrum.

But Mister JayMac said, "Darius Satterfield."

"You're kidding," Hoey said gleefully.

"Darius Satterfield," Mister JayMac repeated.

Hoey shadow-boxed a tornado of noseeums. "Hot dog!"

Sudikoff, doomed to play with rookies, cried, "Jesus, why you wanna throw that speedballin nigger at these new boys?"

"At *you*, you mean." Even with his spikes in red Georgia clay, Hoey walked on a bed of cumuli, giddy as hell.

Showily, Mister JayMac checked his watch. "Yall're down to thirty-six minutes. Be back at ten-fifteen. Nickel-a-minute fine for latecomers."

"Don't sound so fine to me," Quip Parris said.

"Beat it!" Mister JayMac said.

11

Most Hellbenders stumbled to the clubhouse to shoot a jet from the water cooler up their noses or to lie down on the concrete. Muscles, Curriden, and Charlie Snow, gluttons for punishment, played a game of pepper in some outfield shade.

A small crew—including Junior and Mariani, Junior's new roomy—crossed a tree-lined street to a row of pretty shops. Junior was a rookie too, so I followed these guys. Oaks, elms, and sycamores strained a kind of surf music through their leaves. Behind the shops, you could see folksy neighborhood stuff: tool sheds, a dog house, an automobile up on blocks, a loaded clothes line, lots of victory-garden plots. One garden had a fort of bamboo staves and a web of strings for pole beans to vine around and tomato plants to lean against. The street seemed human, a harbor in Highbridge's angry summer dazzle.

One store in the row was a ma-and-pa grocery. Over its door, a metal sign with glossy red letters as tall as shovel blades said HITCH & SHIRLEEN'S NEIGHBORLY MARKET. Two Coca-Cola ads flanked this sign, and paper scrolls in the windows advertised Fancy Pink Salmon, Dixie Crystals Pure Cane Sugar, and Campbell's Vegetable Soup, for cash plus ration points. Even after the other Hellbenders had gone inside, I stood on the curb. How would I ask for what I wanted? If I pointed, I'd look like a moron or a stuck-up creep.

But, hey, I didn't have two cents on me. Baseball togs don't have change pockets, per se, and I'd left McKissic House outfitted for ball, not a market trip. Four guys came out with Cokes and Twinkies and sat on the curb in shifting patches of shade. Sheepishly, I spiked past them and went inside. Dobbs toasted me with his bottle.

Junior stood next to a gingerbreaded-up cash register flirting with the clerk. My eyes had to adjust. When they did, I looked around. Six double shelves ran front to back. A soft-drink cooler with ice water in the bottom and metal stalls for the bottles stood opposite the cash register. Two creaky overhead fans turned. The store had a pressed-tin ceiling with design squiggles in the stamped-out squares. The smells of damp sawdust and wrapped cold cuts hung in the air. At last, I could see to read a homemade sign nailed to a shelf near the cash register:

PLEASE!!! COUNT YOUR
CHANGE AND EXAMINE
YOUR POINT BOOK
BEFORE LEAVING WITH FOOD ITEMS.
MISTAKES <u>CAN'T</u> BE FIXED
LATER!!!

Every Hellbender player who lodged at McKissic House had given his ration book (War Ration Book Two) to Kizzy, through Mister JayMac, so she could shop for the whole house. Only team members with their own places got to keep their books. So if you wanted a snack, you couldn't buy rationed items. You had to get junk food—soda, cupcakes, and such, from companies that had already justified their sugar allotments—and you bought it with coin, not coins and stamps. But I had no coin, and it looked like all I'd be able to do was shuffle and covet.

"Danny!" Junior Heggie called. "Danny, git yore tail over here and meet this spitfire pixie!"

I angled back to the cash register. The clerk behind it was a girl with a fox's face, reddish-blond hair, and a costume-jewelry cluster, a kind of exploded pearl, on one ear. She wore a khaki shirt with a single set of captain's bars on one collar and a pair of rolled-up blue jeans. She didn't reach five feet. She looked twelve, but the earring and her hipshot stance told you twelve underestimated it. Well, maybe the earring didn't. Girls will do a lot as preteens to make themselves look older, but wearing Papa's shirt isn't usually one of them, so you knew this pixie had a grudge on, a war orphan's crow to pick. Her daddy was overseas, and don't you forget it, buster.

"Who's this?" she said. "Ichabod Crane in a baseball suit?"

"He don't talk," Junior said. "Name's Danny Boles. He's from Oklahoma. Plays a whangdoodle shortstop."

"Whynt you talk, Okie? Explain yoresef."

The sunburn from our workout probably hid my blush.

Junior got mad. "You half-wit! I said he don't talk, and he don't. It's an affliction. Leave him be."

"Folks come in here to buy junk, not to sashay about going, 'Mmmm,'" she said, mocking an uppity window shopper.

"You deaf?" Heggie said. "He *cain't* talk. I done told you."

"Take your Twinkie, son, and put it where your mama won't ever find it." A genteel little piece, passing out Suthren hospitality.

Junior like to gagged. We had our speechlessness in common.

"What a man," the girl said. "Absodamnlutely flusterated if a female don't drop down P.D.Q. to kiss his shoe." She looked at me. Her next words weren't so smart-alecky. "Like a person who cain't talk, cain't talk. Like yo're no different from a box of laundry soap."

"I didn't say he wasn't no different from a box of laundry soap," Junior said. "I uz jes trying to—"

"For sweet pity's sake," the girl cried, "will you have the decency to hush? Yo're a disgrace to yore sex—a ballplayer's commonest failing."

Creighton Nutter came back into the store. He grabbed a pack of cigarettes, the last pack of Regents, and paid the girl from a coin pouch looped through his belt. Junior muttered something—*bitch*, I think—and brushed past Nutter onto the sidewalk, as flusterated as the girl had accused.

"Ah, you're being neighborly again here at your Neighborly Market," Nutter said. "Swell."

"Mister Creighton, take a leap," she said.

"She can't stand ballplayers," Nutter told me. "Or thinks she can't. In her view, we should all be in the Army."

"Not you," she said. "Yo're too old. You'd git ten jokers round you and blow em all up by accydent."

"Miss Pharram," Nutter said, "allow me to present to you Danny Boles. Mr. Boles, the fair Miss Phoebe Pharram."

"You think I want to know this skinny pill?" Phoebe said.

"Calm down," Nutter said. He yanked the pull on his Regents, tapped out a cigarette, and lit up. Smoke whirled away in the downdraft from an overhead fan. "Phoebe here is Mister JayMac's great niece, daughter of his late brother Jude's child, LaRaina. Hitch and Shirleen are her paternal grandparents, and by a special arrangement with the team, their Neighborly Market allows us Hellbenders to buy on credit. Get what you want and Phoebe will record your purchases in a ledger set aside for us." He took a deep drag on his cigarette, blew the smoke at Phoebe, and elbowed out, letting the screen slam like the neck-snapper on a mouse trap.

"I hate the name Phoebe!" Phoebe yelled after him. "I pee on it!" Somebody on the sidewalk giggled. "I hate all first and last names that start with the same letters!"

I stood there awed, drinking her in.

"Call me Skeeter," she told me. "I hate the name Phoebe, and I shore as Shirleen don't answer to bitch."

Of course, I would think of her then and always as Phoebe. Skeeter cut this feisty little girl down to something you went to a lot of trouble to swat. Besides, back then, girls who talked like Phoebe were about as plentiful as cow bells in an Episcopal choir.

"Cripes, Ichabod." My admiration chapped her. "Bring me somepin to write up in this ledger. Or clear out."

I hustled to get an orange soda from the cooler and a Baby Ruth from the candy aisle. I brought them over to Phoebe, who turned to take inventory of the cough-drop boxes, poker chips, and clip combs on the shelf behind her. I rolled the bottom of my soda bottle on the glass countertop.

"Yeh?" she said, not looking around.

I waited. Phoebe ignored me. I fidgeted. It might be nearly time for our practice to resume. I used my soda bottle like a bell clapper, ringing it against the fancy metal register. She spun around. Her eyes, a marbly grayish green, jumped like hard-thrown jewels.

"Watch it, Ichabod." She came to the counter, grabbed my drink and candy bar, pulled a book out from under the counter, and wrote down all the needed info—everything but my name. She'd heard my name twice, but'd already forgotten it. She saw me looking, waiting for her to finish up.

"Okay," she said. "What gives here, Ichabod?"

I pounded my fist on the countertop. Phoebe blinked. Her face turned fish-belly pale, then her eyes flared again. Even an Army .45 wouldn't have scared her for long. It embarrassed her not to remember my name, though, and I couldn't tell her because . . . well. Mexican standoff.

I charged around the counter, yanked the "Big Red" Parker Duofold pen from her, and bent over the ledger to scribble my own name in. The Duofold was a clumsy near-antique, and I wrote my John Hancock just like Hancock, *big*: DANIEL HELVIG BOLES. Then I went back out front, grabbed a pack of Camels, and had Phoebe add them to my tab. Rustled some matchbooks from a box, took my soda bottle by the neck, scooped up my Baby Ruth, and headed out the door afraid I might drop something and wind up looking a cluck.

"Hey, wait a sec." I stopped and looked back at Phoebe. "Sorry I called you Ichabod. Nobody likes a name dropped on em like a peed-on blanket."

She had that right. I banged outside and sat down on the curb next to Nutter, now puffing away like a factory.

"Camels," Nutter said, seeing my pack. " 'They don't tire my taste. They're easy on my *throat*. They suit me to a *T*.' If we smoked sandpaper dust, their ads would say the same thing."

I drank my orange soda, I ate my candy bar, I smoked a Camel. I thought I heard an adult—Hitch? Shirleen?—talking to Phoebe. Good. A high-strung gal that age didn't need to be tending a whole store all by herself. Wasn't safe.

.

12

Darius'd driven us all to practice that morning in the Brown Bomber, then disappeared. Now he showed up in spikes, knickers, and a long-johnish jersey that didn't hide the ropy muscles in his upper body. His arms looked like weight-lifting eels. He snapped off warm-up tosses to Dunnagin.

Now, even in Tenkiller I'd heard of Satchel Paige. By '43, five years before he joined the majors with the Cleveland Indians, Paige was already a legend—for pitching in the Negro leagues and on barnstorming tours. Folks said he threw an *invisible* fastball. Paige would sometimes call in his fielders and retire the opposing side on strikeouts. No one'd ever come closer to unhittableness than Satchel Paige. A Negro sports-writer in Kansas City had called his right arm a "bronze sling-shot."

Other black ballplayers had talents like Paige's, but Paige had charisma and got the ink, so far as any colored player got it back then. And so you've never heard of Hilton Smith, a hurler for the Kansas City Monarchs who—from '40 to '46—may've been the greatest pitcher in the world. In '41, Stan Musial and Johnny Mize hit against Smith in an exhibition—*tried* to hit against him—and both claimed never to've seen a better curve.

Darius Satterfield, who couldn't play in the CVL because his skin shaded out too dark, had downhome Satchel Paige-Hilton Smith stuff, an eye-boggling arsenal of pitches. Just watching him warm up, I knew I'd never faced anyone like him. No one. Darius threw like a kicking mule or a jinking hare, depending on the need, but was the only player on the field Mister JayMac didn't call mister.

Several Hellbenders had trouble with Darius's role—not his bus driving, or bag toting, or his trainer's work on sore arms and legs (good nigger work, with tradition behind it). What bothered some of the fellas—not Hoey, though, or Dunnagin, or most of the starters, whether Dixie-born or imports like me—was *playing ball* with him. As if the ball flying from Darius's hand to their bats or gloves would weave a bit of Africa into their own skins.

The most sickening get-that-nigger-off-the-field cry-babies on our team were Trapdoor Evans, Jerry Wayne Sosebee, Norm Sudikoff, Turkey Sloan (a little surprisingly), and, it turned out, Philip Ankers. They wanted Darius for a pack mule, not a teammate, and all that kept them from niggering him to death or threatening to bolt to a team with a "real white man" for a manager was Mister JayMac himself. He'd outright bench them. He'd let them know any traitor to the Hellbenders would never play in Alabama or Georgia again, if he could help it. In fact, if the troublemakers were young and fit, Mister JayMac would threaten them back, usually with pulling strings to put them into uniforms, so they could go after Nips and Huns instead of Negro Americans.

Dixie had laws against blacks and whites playing each other in organized sports. Laws that prevented all-star squads of colored barnstormers from showing up in small Alabama and Georgia towns and challenging the local white heroes, something they did profitably in Wyoming, say, or Kansas. First, they'd've had no place to stay, except in Negro homes or their own touring cars. Second, it'd've bruised the whiteys' egos to get skinned by coons in front of their neighbors. Third, everybody—whites and coloreds alike—seemed to understand if white folks let down their guard in something as human as baseball, they might drop it elsewhere too.

Black ballplayers played in the South for professional clubs in Atlanta, Memphis, Birmingham, and Jacksonville, and on Army teams on posts like Fort Benning, Fort Stuart, and Camp Penticuff. But even on these bases, they played other coloreds. Forget the war. Never mind that Americans of every shade wore one-color-fits-all khaki. Whites would go see blacks play each other because they put on a bang-up show, but at Atlanta's Ponce de Leon Park, whites bought tickets at separate entrances and sat in bleacher sections off limits to the nigger hoi polloi.

Darius didn't play in the CVL, but he sure as heck took part in practices and intrasquad games at McKissic Field. He served as a lieutenant commander to Mister JayMac, except he didn't very often come up and tell you to do something. He sort of *hinted* you should do it. He asked if you wanted *help* getting a hitch out of your swing or a sad double clutch out of your throws to first. Mostly, Darius kept his mouth shut and taught by showing. Usually, when he led a practice, everyone accepted the sham that even though Mister JayMac had deputized Darius as his stand-in, he *could have* tapped almost anybody else on the squad.

Anyway, Mister JayMac had ordered a scrimmage, first stringers versus recruits and scrubs, and Darius had drawn the pitching start for the regulars. The regulars also got to be home team. Us rookies and scrubs had to use the visitors' dugout and give up the advantage of last at-bats. I didn't like it, but so what?

Creighton Nutter pulled me into our dugout, where Mister JayMac had tacked up lineups for both teams. Nutter'd been appointed our manager. Mister JayMac would run the A squad. He seemed to want us underdogs in a snugged-up croker sack from the get-go. Nutter studied our lineup. By rights he should've drawn up our batting order, but Mister JayMac had done it for him.

"Damn," Nutter said. "We've got two pitchers at players' spots and a baby on the mound. Thank God for empty bleachers."

I read the lineup too. Mister JayMac had me batting first. I wouldn't get to watch another hitter against Darius before I had to face him myself.

"Get on up here, Mr. Boles!" Mister JayMac yelled. He wore a chest protector and a mask, ready to ump as well as to manage. That seemed unfair, but when he sent Parris, one of our boys, out to call the bases, I relaxed a little.

I rummaged up my Red Stix bat, crossed to the batter's box, swung it a few times. Its barrel shone red in the sun.

"You drop that thing in a vat of Mercurochrome, Dumbo?" Hoey yelled from short.

At third Curriden gave an egg-sucking grin. "My pecker's about that color when it gets angry."

"And you *wish* it was that big," Dunnagin said from his crouch behind the plate. A bit more hoohah over my imported timber before Mister JayMac snarled, "Batter up!"

I dug in against Darius with a catch in my heartbeat. My first pitch in my first at-bat as a hired pro. It came out of Darius's shoulder-dipping windup so hard I hardly even saw it. I just heard it go *thwaap!* in Dunnagin's mitt.

"Strike one, Mr. Boles," Mister JayMac said.

Hoey and the other infielders chattered away, badmouthing me: "You couldn't hit the floor if you fell off a stepladder, Boles!" "Cmon, Dumbo, make like the Dorsey brothers and swing!" "Whassa madder, rookie? All the blood in you go into that stupid bat!"

Darius got me on four pitches, two quick strikes (the second one swinging), a teaser high for a ball, and a peppy slider on the outside corner I lunged at like a beginner with a bayonet. I jammed my bat into the ground to keep from eating a pound of red Georgia clay.

The jeering stopped: I was history.

Junior and Dobbs went down too, Junior on an excuse-me nibbler back to Darius, Skinny on three air-pummeling cuts that would've unsocketed almost anybody else's shoulder. Seven pitches and side out. Things looked bleak for us Mudville boys.

"Pingless wonders," Muscles said, trotting in from left after tossing his glove down. "Way to go, Darius."

Philip Ankers took the mound for us, the B squad. A fifteen-year-old hurling against good journeymen players and cagey retreads. Nobody on A squad was less than thirty but Knowles, a twenty-something 4-F with the same million-dollar problem that'd kept both Mariani and Frank "I'll Never Smile Again" Sinatra out of the Army, a punctured eardrum. But Ankers *looked* older than Knowles, with his greasy beard and the body of a pit bull.

In his first time out, Ankers had to face Hoey, Charlie Snow, and Muscles. He looked to have just two pitches: a fastball and a fadeaway. Today you'd call a fadeaway a screwball or a scroogie, and it's not usually a pitch high schoolers master. Somehow, Ankers had. He'd start it off like a speedball, but finger-lip it. Just as it got to a righthand hitter it jerked in and dropped away. With that pitch, he made Hoey and Snow look like amateur-night contestants. They both rolled out to the infield. Musselwhite, though, muscled one to the right-field wall for a triple because Ankers slipped up and threw him a fastball low and inside. Muscles batted left, and that was the perfect pitch for him to cream. Ankers learned from his mistake. From then on, he threw nothing but fadeaways and teaser fastballs.

Jumbo was batting cleanup, but Jumbo couldn't clean Muscles off third. Ankers kamikazied him with dipsy-doodle junk, mostly fadeaway variations. Jumbo took a couple, fouled off a couple, and ended up missing a pitch—like Muscles, he batted left—that tailed away to the outside corner. This swing dumped him on his rear, a fall that seemed to shake the whole infield. I thought it might take a crane to hoist him up again, but he rolled over to all fours and got slowly to his feet.

The game went on like that. Darius made us B-squad boys look like stooges; Ankers wriggled out of every potential trap with a killer fadeaway. In fact, by the fourth inning, Sloan'd started calling him Fadeaway. It stuck. Ankers became Fadeway for ever after.

Goose eggs stacked up. Noon yawned like an oven. Each time Ankers escaped another A-squad wrecking crew with his shutout unblemished, Mister JayMac waved his regulars onto the field and yelled *"Batter up!"* at us scrubs. He looked to be steam-cleaning his gear from the inside out.

"We won't git no rest," Norm Sudikoff griped, "till the bastid has him a five-alawm heat stroke."

I wondered about that. Should a rookie like Ankers pitch more than five hard-throwing innings? Come our next CVL game, would us Hellbenders have the bounce of boiled spaghetti? And how many times would Darius make me look like a fool? Coming to my third at bat in the top of the seventh, I'd struck out swinging and a second time counting the stitches on a goofer that'd dropped through the strike zone.

Now I felt semipanicked. Guessing what Darius planned to throw would pickle your brain. Because you couldn't guess, you had to watch and react. So far I'd watched and reacted a lot less well than I'd just watched.

"It's the old red-stick wagger," Hoey welcomed me. "Wave that baton, maestro. Conduct yourself back to the bench."

I dug in. Darius threw me some chin music for a ball, but the pitch did what he wanted, moved me off the plate. Next, a curve on the outside corner, just beyond my swing, for a called strike. I edged up a little. The next pitch jammed me, a hundred-mile-an-hour bullet. I swung in self-defense. The ball hit my bat handle and nubbed out between Hoey and Curriden on a half dozen skittering hops.

Contact! On my follow-through, the bat's barrel had splintered like kindling, helicoptered into the outfield, and landed on the grass. My broken bat had gone farther than the ball. I ran with five inches of bat handle in my fist. My hands and forearms stung from the vibes. Hoey made a grab in the hole and threw off-balance to Jumbo. Parris, umpiring at first, signaled me safe, and not one A-squad player yelped, not even Hoey.

Darius came down off the mound and ambled over to take Jumbo's flip-back. "Danl," he said, about twenty feet away, "I reckon you could outrun the word God."

It took me a minute, standing there winded, to realize he'd complimented me.

But not much happened after my scratch hit. Junior struck out, and Dobbs blooped one to Knowles at second.

Sudikoff came up. He had bulk, but Darius owned him. If I wanted to get around the bases, I'd have to shove myself along and hope a passed ball, a wild pitch, or an error on an infield grounder assisted me. But despite his praise, Darius didn't seem to think I'd steal. He pitched from a full wind-up, not a stretch. It worked because, after his second pitch to Junior, he whipped the return throw from Dunnagin over to Jumbo and nearlybout picked me off.

On his first pitch to Sudikoff, though, I got a decent lead and broke for second the moment Darius twisted into his wind-up. Bless his heart, Sudikoff lunged at an obvious ball, missing it by a foot or better, to help me out, and I did a quick down-and-up slide into second, where Hoey knelt for a throw that never came.

I'd stolen on Darius, not Dunnagin, and when Darius had the ball again, he walked over and peered at me like I was a channel cat with legs.

"Like I say," he said.

On his next offering to Sudikoff, I edged off second and darted for third as soon as his motion home committed him to throw. I *barreled*. Sudikoff laid off a low fastball—he'd already swung at one for me—and Dunnagin, uncoiling from his crouch, leapt in front of the plate and fired the ball to Curriden at third.

All my B-squad teammates popped up from our bench to watch me slide. The peg from home had me nailed, but my toe hooking the corner of the base got under Curriden's tag.

Nutter, coaching third, gave the safe sign. Mister JayMac, out from behind the plate, agreed. A cheer went up from the B-squad bench, the A-squad boys groaned.

Darius sashayed over, loosy-goosy, to get the ball from Reese Curriden. He gave me a smirk. The smirk didn't seem to be *at* me, though, but *for* me. "G, O, D," Darius said. From then on, he pitched from the stretch. I'd've been nuts to try to steal home on him, or on a catcher as smart as Dunnagin. Anyway, I had no chance. Darius got Sudikoff on strikes, the third one a swing a herd of chiropractors could've retired to Bermuda on.

Sudikoff flung his bat away. "Pesky damned nigger."

Darius had to've heard him, but he strolled to the A-squad dugout with his back straight and his head up and spoke not a word.

Just about then, I saw somebody in the bleachers behind our dugout: Phoebe Pharram, Mister JayMac's great-niece.

My first thought—pretending not to see her—was, Did she see my hit?

Did she see me steal second? Did she see me slide into third like the great Mike "King" Kelly?

Dumb. Phoebe was jail bait and blood kin to my boss. Why in Cupid's name would she take a bead on me anyway? "Ichabod," she'd called me—the high-pockets drip in an old American short story. Besides being a drip, I couldn't talk. For God's sake, my nickname was Dumbo.

The game goose-egged on.

But in the bottom of the eighth, Jumbo rainbowed one off Fadeaway over the right-field wall, and Fadeaway fell apart, yielding four more quick runs on a series of walks and hits, including a triple by Darius.

Fadeaway slapped his glove against his leg. His face got this weird stove-in look. He began blubbering. Mister JayMac went out to the mound.

"That hulksome galoot!" Fadeaway nodded in at Jumbo. "Him and that biggity *damned* nigger!"

"Shut up and sit down." Mister JayMac put Quip Parris in for Fadeaway. Parris retired the next three batters. Darius trotted home on Hoey's sacrifice fly, though, and at the end of eight full innings the score stood six to zip.

That was the final score, although in the top of the ninth I sent Charlie Snow to the wall for a long out, the best hit ball of the game against Darius.

At the end, Darius shone with sweat. It encased and oiled him. I could see him pitching another nine, eighteen, maybe even twenty-seven innings—without grouse or twinge. Darius shone like a jewel.

13

In the clubhouse, Mister JayMac gave Junior, Fadeaway, Dobbs, and me our own lockers. Mine had belonged to Bob Collum, a popular player axed along with Sweet Gus Pettus, Roper, and Jorgensen. We peeled off the faded masking tape marked with their names and stuck on new strips marked with ours. My locker hunched between Curriden's and Jumbo's. Curriden sat next to me removing stirrup socks, then skinning out of his clay-stained sanitaries. Jumbo had flat-out disappeared.

"You did good out there, Dumbo," Curriden said. "A leg hit and a liner to the wall."

I nodded my thanks, silently damning Hoey for hanging that nickname on me again.

"Darius no-hit yall except for that legger," Curriden said, "so you were the B boys' heavy artillery today."

I grinned, sort of, and took off my sweat-sopped shirt. Behind us, a shower ran. Dunnagin stood in it singing "I'm Getting Tired So I Can Sleep," crooning in a tenor better than half your big-band soloists'. It echoed out to us prettier than a clarinet.

"No one wants to bat against Darius," Curriden said. "If he uz white and his manager let him pitch every other day, he'd win thirty-five games a year in the CVL. Forty. And you, a bony little dink, lined out to Snow up against the Feen-A-Mint sign. That makes you bout the hittingest thing, ever, against Darius, Dumbo. No crap."

I looked around. Had Darius and Jumbo gone back to McKissic House in their uniforms? Cripes. Sweaty flannels weigh a ton. And the smell . . .

Curriden stood up buck naked. "Darius showers on the visitors' side— else he'd have to wait for us to finish up in here."

I tapped Jumbo's locker.

"Jumbo?" Curriden said. "Keeps an extra glove in there. Some sanitaries. Cept for that, he don't use it at all. Won't shower here. Foots it back to McKissic House."

"There's something wrong with him," Turkey Sloan said from Fadeaway's bench. "He's different from the rest of us." Sloan looked at me. "Till you come along, sweet cheeks, none of us but him had a private room."

Something wrong with him? Like what?

"I reckon he was born with some oddball deformity," Sloan said, like he'd just read my mind.

"Or it's a war injury," Hoey said. "From the last war. A problem like that guy in the Hemingway book had."

"The Germans blew his pecker off?" Parris said. "Naw, the poor guy's an auto-wreck victim—that's my theory."

There was an empty lapse in the guessing. Hoey seized Parris and knuckled the crown of his head. "Your theory makes me feel like a heartless jerk."

Parris weaseled away. "People should feel like what they are—so they don't wake up thinking they're Albert Schweitzer. Or Jack Benny."

"'*Oh, Rochester,*'" someone said, mimicking Benny's radio voice: "'*Oh, Rochester.*'"

In a gravelly copy of the voice of the colored fella that played Rochester, somebody else said, "'*Yes, boss?*'"

This back-and-forth went on all around me. I couldn't get into it. Even if I could've talked, I'd've felt too much like the new kid in the neighborhood.

I went to the farthest spigot in the shower room and faced into it so the other guys in there could see only my skinny backside and jutting ears.

"Listen, Okie," Mariani said. "Don't drop the soap. You bend down to fetch it, Norman there starts to get ideas."

"Screw you, wop," Sudikoff said.

"Baby, don't you wish," Mariani said.

Don't drop the soap. I flash-backed on Pumphrey and the lavatory on the troop train. Really quickly, I finished showering, dressed, and scrammed.

Outside, I walked under a bleacher section, part of the concession area behind home plate—a cave for hot-dog stands and program hawkers. Shady. Semicool. All around me, support girders, chain-link gates, and cubbyholes for vendors.

Then I saw Phoebe—beside an aquarium in the main gangway. Coming through the turnstiles from the parking lot, you got funneled past this tank, a yard long and two feet tall, mounted on a belt-high base. Phoebe had climbed to the tank's rim on a set of movable wooden steps.

"Hello, Daniel Helvig Boles." Her voice echoed.

I lifted my hand: How, squaw. Did Mister JayMac use tropical fish to homify his ballpark?

Did Phoebe have to feed them?

"Cmere, Boles." She waved me towards her. "I don't bite. If yo're careful, neither does Homer."

I walked over. Even without a stool, I stood about as high as she did. Water in the tank. A gravel bottom. A thin strip of sunken wood. Some ferns, like seaweed on stalks, poking up from the gravel, hula-dancing in the currents.

"You met Homer yet, Boles?"

I shook my head.

"Well, *look*," she said. "Looking's how you meet him. I won't pull him out for you to shake his iddy-biddy hand."

I bent. I stared. The narrow strip of bark hovering above the sand, floating in the tank's thready green murk, had eyes. One end of the mystery thing resembled a tail.

"There," Phoebe said. "You've just met Homer."

I kept staring at the critter. It really did look like a piece of bark. With legs. With eyes. Like sombody'd epoxied it out of sycamore cork and pecan twigs.

"Donchu even know what Homer *is*, Boles?"

I just kept staring at him. It. Whatever it was. I might not know much, but a lunk who tipped his ignorance to a girl was doomed to regret it.

"You *don't* know what Homer is," Phoebe accused.

I tapped my head to show her I'd already safely stored the information. I was a walking Smithsonian Institution.

"Horsefeathers. You don't know squonk, do you, Dumbo?"

Dumbo! I'd rather she called me Ichabod. If she said it again, I'd strangle her.

"Homer's yore stupid team's mascot, stupid. A hellbender. You ever heard of a hellbender, Okie boy?"

Phoebe Pharram seemed to want to show me up, like some pitchers will taunt a patsy they've just struck out. I stood a frog's hair away from dumping her into the tank.

"I'll bet you think a hellbender's a damned soul who breaks alla Mr. Pitchfork's rules," Phoebe said.

I stared at her, one eye starting to tic.

"A hell*bender*. Git it?"

I banged the tank with my fist and headed for the parking lot.

"Hang on, Boles!" she called. "I don't mean nothing, talking this way. Mostly, it's other folks giving *me* what-for, not vicy-versy. Mostly, I jes give back what I've awready got. Gits to be a habit. When somebody cain't or won't talk, I imagine em giving me what-for before it's even come. Then I give em it back thout em ever giving it to me to begin with. You git me?"

Funny enough, I did. The explanation almost made sense. I walked back to look at Homer again. My jug ears were reflected in the tank's glass, but Phoebe kept talking. My looks, or my lack of them, hadn't scared her off.

"A hellbender's a quatic salamander," she said. "I found this un in a creek when I uz nine. Uncle JayMac gave me a dollar for it and put it here in McKissic Field when Highbridge entered the CVL. I feed Homer, change his water out, tote him home when the season's over. Got a table in my bedroom for his tank. During ball season, though, I keep a typewriter on it and write letters to homesick sojers."

How thoughty and patriotic. FDR, or *Mrs.* FDR, should give you a medal, Phoebe.

"A corporal and two PFCs have awready proposed to me. They think I'm older. I sorta let em spose it. My letters read pretty passionate, I guess."

The knuckleheaded hussy. I'd've laughed, but she had no more sense of humor about herself than I did about me. We both had the teenage disease of raging self-solemnity.

"Baseball's a mug's game," Phoebe lectured me. "Sometimes it's jes not very nice. Yall do things in front of a thousand folks I wouldn't do alone in my own bedroom."

One minute she admitted writing "pretty passionate" letters to servicemen and the next she suggested it embarrassed her to see a ballplayer setting his jock straight.

"We do have *one* thing in common," Phoebe said.

Okay, I thought. Don't keep me in suspense.

"Good reasons for not being in the military—I'm a woman, and yo're, well, yo're a dummy."

Yeah. I put my hands behind my ears and made em flap like a flying elephant's.

"Anyway, if you didn't have yore . . . problem, you'd join the Army. Wouldn't you?"

Hmmmm. In another five and a half months, I'd be eligible for the draft. Maybe my dummyhood was a ploy I'd come up with, subconsciously, to sidestep induction.

Dunnagin walked up behind us from the clubhouse. "You're right, Phoeb. I know I'd rather be out killing Nips than chasing a CVL pennant. It burdens my mind, getting left out of all the fun."

"Yo're old, Dunnagin," Phoebe said. "But not so all-fired old you couldn't enlist." She looked more or less pleased to see him.

"If only you knew," Dunnagin said. "Methuselah's got nothing on me. If I don't make it back to the bigs this year, my career's over. I'll be yesterday's papers."

"You'd be doing more for the Uncle Sam in the Army. And more for yoresef."

"I'm boosting civilian morale," Dunnagin said. "I'm boosting *player* morale. They see me on the field, they think anybody can do it. They go home fortified and hopeful."

"Shame on you," Phoebe said.

Dunnagin didn't look too abashed. "Danny, the *Bomber*'s about to leave. Hustle it up."

I nodded, and Dunnagin wandered away.

Phoebe came down off the stair step. In the tank, Homer wriggled, stirring the murk—the first time I'd seen him look like anything other than a spongy piece of bark. Hooray. No ball team wants a dead or paralyzed critter for its mascot.

"Go git yore bus," Phoebe said. "Yo're keeping a slew of folks stewing in a real pressure cooker."

I did a two-fingered salute.

"You do play a whangdoodle shortstop," she said. "And you can run like a autumn crop fire."

Unexpected praise. But I still wanted to add, Did you know I can outrun the word God? A local authority told me so today.

My speech problem, thank the Lord, kept my mouth shut.

14

On my second evening in McKissic House, I tried to delay entering the hole I shared with Jumbo. Its heat and the idea of huddling on the other side of his throat-tickling grass mat while he slept or read—well, why bother going up? I couldn't talk to him, of course, and the curtain he'd hung between us said he didn't much care. Thank God. Maybe he'd taken me on as a roommate *because* I couldn't talk.

Back from practice, I washed dishes, sat next to some guys playing hearts, and listened to dance-band music and news reports on the old cathedral Philco. John L. Lewis, said H. V. Kaltenborn, had taken his soft-coal miners out on a strike that had patriots gnashing their teeth. Up in Alaska, the Army'd finished mopping up Jap resistance on Attu, and the Eleventh Air Force kept on bombing the hell out of Kiska. Not caring for cards, I worked on a jigsaw puzzle—the Eiffel Tower—while listening to the radio. Nobody bothered me.

Finally, I had to go up. McKissic House had an eleven o'clock curfew. Rest and regular hours guarded Mister JayMac's investment in us. He'd fine you for missing curfew.

Anyway, Jumbo lay stretched out on his bed reading. He'd tied back the grass mat divider so a breeze from the window could reach him, if a breeze ever blew up. His fan bumped and shimmied like a stripper in a whalebone corset. From the door I could see into the whole room. What I saw flabbergasted me.

Jumbo had put a big bronze vase of cut flowers—hydrangeas, snowballs, Queen Anne's lace—on the floor next to my cot. The flowers helped. Except for the labels on the cans of his Joan of Arc red kidney beans, the room didn't boast much color. The flowers livened the place up. I saw Jumbo look up at me—even in that heat, his eyes made me shiver—and started to walk over to my cot. Jumbo lifted his hand.

"You played well this morning."

I ducked my head. He'd played well too. He'd knocked a heavy balata ball out of McKissic Field and fielded like a man with some kind of magnet for horsehides sewn into his glove. But his looks made me think of the other players' guesses about him. Of injury, pain, and death. Up close, I had an *aversion* to his looks. Well, I was no prize myself.

My reaction to Jumbo reminded me of my reaction as a twelve-year-old to my best friend in Tenkiller after he'd had a sledding accident. My friend's name was Kenneth Ward—Kenny for short. One snowy winter, Kenny'd cracked up on a Northern Flyer going over a ledge into a sink hole lined with briars. He dropped ten or twelve feet. The briars ripped and scraped him like so many darning needles wrapped in wet cotton. The plunge knocked Kenny out. He concussed. It took three of us to rescue him, and we may've hurt him even more pulling him up through all those white brambles to the edge of the drop-off. Kenny's dad got there somehow and hurried him to the emergency room at the Cherokee County hospital. I didn't visit Kenny in the hospital, but I saw him several days later at the Wards' little house in Tenkiller.

Kenny didn't look like Kenny. He looked like . . . I don't know, the victim of a thousand wasp stings. Or a pit-bull attack. He had two puffy black eyes (actually, more red and purple than black), an out-of-kilter nose, and a set of lips more like an albino channel cat's. Kenny's looks scared and confused me. Away from his house, I started to think I hadn't seen Kenny at all. Instead, I'd called on something strange, ugly, and maybe a quarter dead planted in the Wards' house by UFO people. I didn't go again. Even when Kenny got over his injuries and began looking like the buck-toothed kid I'd once known, a weirdness between us—disgust on his part, shame on mine—kept us from getting friendly again.

Jumbo made me feel the way Kenny, with his nose whacked askew and his eyes in bruised pouches, had made me feel.

"Last night," Jumbo said, "I was, ah, less than friendly."

Uh-uh. I pointed at myself, meaning he'd behaved more or less okay but I'd acted like a total jerk.

A lie.

Because he'd acted at least as jerky as I had, not speaking more than three sentences all evening and dividing his digs the way small-town Suthren doctors once split their waiting rooms into a half for coloreds and a half for whites.

"I hung that"—Jumbo nodded at the mat rucked up against one wall—
"assuming you'd prefer a little privacy to no barrier at all." Jumbo grimaced.
He made a face. And he could make a face, a spasm of cheek and forehead
muscles.

"Forgive. I seldom talk. U. S. slang confounds me. All my speech
originates in the written word." He gestured at his book shelves. "My tastes
run to philosophy, science, religion, medicine, Victorian novels, and current
events. And my tastes inevitably influence my diction."

Wow. An attack—for Jumbo, anyway—of verbal diarrhea. It embarrassed
him. He rubbed his hands like a man trying to coax blood into frost-bitten
fingertips.

"To you, the mat must have appeared a method of exclusion, not a
courtesy."

I stayed mute, of course.

"If you want privacy, pull the mat out from the wall. If not, leave it." He
looked me in the eye. "At certain points, whatever your state of mind, I'll
draw the mat. Please don't view my doing so as a sign of pique or ill favor. I
sometimes require solitude."

I nodded. Okay. Understood.

"And you have my standing consent to draw the mat whenever you wish.
Would you care to do so now?"

Not really. Outside of Dunnagin's counsel in the gazebo, no other talk I'd
had in Georgia had lasted so long or promised so much. On the other hand, I
couldn't add much to it. So I started toward my cot again, and Jumbo halted
me again.

"You've lost a button," he said. "Give me your shirt."

I undid the buttons I had, gave him my shirt, and sat down on my cot.
Jumbo took a needle, thread, and a carved ivory button box from one of his
shelves and sewed on the new button in five minutes. You'd've thought his
sausage-size fingers would've made the task hard for him, but he did it like
a pro, quick and neat.

"Here," he said, holding up the shirt. It danced like a flag in the breeze
from his fan, dropped like a windsock on a calm morning, then danced again.
Fetching my shirt, I noticed the grooves, calluses, dents, and scars in the
ends of Jumbo's fingers. The skin looked dead at the tips, white or yellowish,
with whorls of brown or feverish pink on their inner pads. The clay-and-
persimmon smell came off him in ripples. Near to, his eyes were like peeled

orange slices with the membranes still on. It was my lost friend Kenny Ward all over again.

On the floor by Jumbo's headboard sat a cardboard box full of old—but not too dirty—baseballs. Most used balls in those days ended up in the servicemen's Baseball Equipment Fund so the men at military posts here and overseas could play ball for training purposes or to relax. Even I knew that. The Baseball Equipment Fund was a big patriotic deal. So this box of balls struck me as suspiciously like hoarding. What did Jumbo plan to do with them? The team had all the baseballs it needed, and none of this battered bunch looked fit to plump out a scarecrow with, much less to toss or fungo around.

Jumbo reached down and grabbed a ball. He inserted his fingernails into its split seam and peeled its more or less glossy cover off. He dropped its balata core back into the box and spread the leather cover open on his knee. He rubbed the cover with his thumb, as if to work out its only visible stain and make it spotless again, then flip-flopped the spread cover and rubbed its other side.

"They lived once," he said. "Think of it—these skins, once the hides of tall and powerful animals." He stopped rubbing and laid the split jacket on top of the other baseballs in the box, the way you or I would return a silver dollar to a display of rare coins.

That chilled me. I slipped my shirt on.

Jumbo said, "May I call you Daniel rather than Mr. Boles?"

I hesitated a second before nodding.

"Then you may call me—you may think of me—as Henry. Two men lodging together in such intimacy shouldn't have to stand on oppressive formalities."

I figured just the opposite, but what could I do? Jumbo had some age on me and deserved a little respect. He stuck out his hand to seal our bargain. I took it with as much zeal as I'd grab a hot wire.

"Daniel, know me from henceforth as Henry." His hand felt cold and dry, spongy and hard—like sliding your palm into the grip of a solid-rubber statue.

Henry didn't strike me as a suitable name for a power-hitting ballplayer. *Hank* did, like in Hank Greenberg, but Jumbo hadn't asked me to call him Hank.

"A moment yet. I have a small present for you, Daniel." From under his pillow, he took two notebooks and a handful of pencils snugged together with a rubber band. One notebook you could've used in school, a fat thing the size of a Leo Tolstoy novel. The other, a little bigger than a deck of cards, you could carry around in a pocket. One of the pencils, already sharpened, had a pocket clip on it. Jumbo dumped this caboodle into my hands.

"Should you wish to converse with me," he said, "simply write in the smaller notebook, tear out that page, and hand it over. I will respond as its substance dictates."

I hammocked Jumbo's gifts in my shirt tail and duck-walked to my cot, where I spilled them all out.

"The larger notebook you may use as a journal," Jumbo said, "chronicling your exploits throughout the remainder of the season."

Hey, I'd graduated. Why would I want to scribble rehashes of ballgames in a notebook? It was the thought that counted, I guessed, but I'd've been happier with a candy bar or a risque pulp magazine. In the next moment, though, I started thinking I might *enjoy* keeping a record of my days in Highbridge. I didn't plan to live in Georgia, after all, and one day I might like having a memory token of my minor league career here.

Jumbo, however spooky his looks or weird-sounding his talk, had begun to treat me like a roomy, not just a pestiferous kid Mister JayMac'd dumped on him. Probably, my play at McKissic Field had turned him around. What did that say for his scale of values? If I'd played lousy, would he've gone on treating me like a cockroach? But, hundreds of miles from Tenkiller, Oklahoma, I rejoiced in his turnaround, whatever'd caused it.

I fell asleep in my clothes, with my notebooks and pencils nearby and Jumbo reading Wendell L. Willkie's *One World*.

When I woke up, darkness everywhere.

Jumbo had pulled his woven-grass mat into place between us. I could smell it. I could also smell the gritty perfume of the hydrangeas in their bronze vase. I undressed and lay down again. Jumbo's snores wheezed above the whirr of the fan, and our grass divider swayed.

15

Mister JayMac called our first Friday home game against Lanett Scrap Metal Collection Drive Night. Every kid under eighteen who brought a pound of scrap metal—a shovel blade, a bag of spent cartridges, a hoard of old soup cans—got in free. Ushers collected the scrap, and businessmen-volunteers turned it over to the War Production Board.

Anyway, the stands rocked, a lot of the crowd teenagers or soldiers from Camp Penticuff. It being wartime, GIs got in for half price, paying fifty cents for baseline seats and watching the skirts closer than they did the game. Milt Frye, the PA announcer, told us attendance stood at over three thousand, a better than decent turnout even if beaucoups of our admissions had "paid" for their seats with scrap metal.

CVL teams staged most games on weekends. Sometimes you'd have a series start on Thursday or Wednesday evening, but you could always count on open Mondays and Tuesdays, as travel days or as make-up days for rainouts.

In the clubhouse, Mister JayMac announced his starting lineup. Not a rookie in it. Junior, Skinny, and I would ride the bench until somebody got hurt or one of us was needed for strategic reasons. Fadeaway wouldn't play at all—Mister JayMac planned to start him on Sunday.

"That's just two days' rest," Fadeaway said.

Everybody gaped like he'd just decided not to join the bucket brigade at an orphanage fire.

"Way I figure it, it's three," Mister JayMac said. "Hell, son, you're fifteen, aren't you?"

"Yessir."

"Then your recovery time for both pitching and screwing's bout as fast as it'll ever be, and I didn't recruit you to screw. You gonna pitch when I ask you to or jes when you feel like it?"

"When you ast me to."

"Good," Mister JayMac said. "Stop pouting."

Twilight crept over the field. The electric pole lights came on, bright as day. That summer, no one worried about a Nazi U-boat swimming up the Chattahoochee to knock out a riverside shipyard or a lone supply barge. Under the lights, McKissic Field looked like a wonderland: green grass, shiny signs, the gauzy ghosts of cigar and cigarette smoke curling everywhere. Even the tiresome smell of burnt peanuts couldn't douse my wonder. When Mrs. Harry Atwill, the organist, played "Take Me Out to the Ball Game," I got shivers. It seemed the sky would split open, like a milkweed pod, and an air force of seraphim drift down to mingle with the crowd like Mardi Gras partiers.

Creighton Nutter pitched that night, and if he hadn't had his stuff, Highbridge would've lost. Our regulars played like cripples. They missed signs, booted grounders, misplayed easy flies, overthrew cutoff men, and so on. In the fourth inning, our fans began to catcall us. They singled out Trapdoor Evans for abuse after he turned a basket catch into a thump to the groin that left him writhing on the grass. Charlie Snow dashed over from center to pick up the ball and throw it in.

"*Ball-less Evans!*" a row of soldiers chanted. "*Ball-less Evans!*"

Over the PA system, Milt Frye said, "Steady now, folks. Your management has great regard for our military, but we won't tolerate smut from any quarter."

"*Ball-less, ball-less, ball-less Evans!*" the GIs chanted. Frye's scolding didn't faze them a bit, and when he barked, "Those persisting in immature hooliganism, even men in uniform, will be removed," a whole row of them turned towards the press box and shot it a rippling sequence of birds that would've won a drill competition at Camp Penticuff. But, truth to tell, no spectacle was grosser that night than our Hellbender regulars. Even folks with kids had more kindly feelings for the GIs than they did for our stumblebums.

Going into our final at bat, after playing like blind men, we were down just one run. Nutter'd kept us in it, pitching smart and refusing to rattle even when his fielders performed like dancing hippos. The shock of the night—a blow to Mister JayMac's strategy of letting us humiliate ourselves at home—came when we somehow won the game, three to two.

It wasn't pretty. Or just. But so what?

The win put us at eight-and-eight on the season. Opelika, Eufaula, and Cottonton lost that same night—to Quitman, Marble Springs, and LaGrange respectively—so we picked up a full game on both the Orphans and the Mudcats and broke a fourth-place tie with the Boll Weevils. But it still teed me Mister JayMac had held us rookies out, especially with his starters sucking wind like they had.

"What would our starters have to do to git the boss to give us new boys a chanst?" Junior asked Skinny Dobbs.

"Lose," Skinny said. "Them buggers got to lose."

Actually, Skinny'd got that wrong. We played our next game against Lanett at five on Saturday afternoon. The league's schedule makers had decreed a number of twilight weekend games, to go on without lights. A nagging drought'd dogged the South for years, crimping its ability to make electric power. Day and twilight games eased demand. That was good. War plants—shipyards, torpedo factories, assembly lines—had to run around the clock. You could squeeze a whole game in between five and sunset, if you didn't go to extra innings.

Anyway, just before we dressed out for the second game in the Lanett series, Darius came into the locker room and read the lineup to us:

"Batting first, playing shortstop, Danl Boles. . . ." He went on from there, but the only other items to get my interest came in the seventh and eighth spots, where Junior and Skinny would bat, Junior playing second base and Skinny taking over from Trapdoor Evans in right.

"Is this a joke?" Buck Hoey asked Darius. "I hit one for three last night. Nobody else did better."

"Mr. Curriden did," Darius said. "If you hadn't walked up his backside on that pop-up, he mighta done even better. That knot on yo fohead go down yet?"

"Easy, Darius," Hoey said. "You're treading thin ice."

Darius rubbed his oxford's toe across the concrete floor. "Aint no ice in here atall. Was, you could put it on that knot you got."

"Read it again," Junior said.

So Darius read the afternoon's starting lineup again. My body began to hum, like a tuning fork. Saturday, June 5th, 1943. Soon, I'd actually start at short on a pro ball club.

"I can't believe Mister JayMac wants me on the bench," Hoey said. "I've got a nine-game hitting streak going."

Darius popped the lineup card with his knuckles. "Nothing here say the change got to last fo awways, Mr. Hoey."

That drilled a nerve with me. If I booted a chance, or fanned with runners in scoring position, Hoey'd most likely have his job back tomorrow.

"So whatn hell we sposed to *do*?" Evans asked Darius.

"How bout rest?" Darius said. "Seems logical to me."

"The hell with that," Hoey said.

"Well, capn, Mister JayMac wants you to coach first."

Vito Mariani was scheduled to pitch. "Buck up, Buck. I'll set em down so fast you won't have enough bench time to rub the nap off your pants."

Darius left. Hoey stared at the floor. Knowles, the deposed second baseman, went over to Junior and put a hand on his shoulder.

"Tear em up, kid," he said.

The game wasn't a laugher, but the Linenmakers never really got close either. Kitchen Fats for Victory Night followed Friday's Scrap Metal Collection Night, and although nobody got in free for bringing in hamburger grease or bacon drippings, Milt Frye and three usherettes saw to it every fan who turned in a can of solidified fat got his or her name put in a drum for a drawing during the seventh-inning stretch. Top prize was a weekend for two in Atlanta, with a room at the Ponce de Leon Hotel. Anyway, the drawing seemed to mean as much to the civilians in the stands as the ball game did.

You could *smell* the rancid kitchen fats everyone'd brought in. The idea was that munitions factories would melt down the drippings to extract their glycerin, then use it to make bombs or howitzer shells. Kitchen Fats for Victory. After the war, though, I heard we'd used it to make soap. Dirty dogfaces have low morale, and the services needed our kitchen fats for soap. But asking civilians to turn in fats for soap didn't sound romantic. Or sanitary. So the government told the public our used grease would go to make devices for blowing people up, and *wham!* the home front got with the program.

Anyway, I went three for four. A squib behind second base was my first safe bingle in money ball. A row of GIs gave me a standing O—out of sheer relief the Hellbenders wouldn't stink worse than the stadium did, like we had last night. They loved it I could put wood on the ball.

Hoey, coaching first, sauntered over to me as I returned to the bag after making my turn. The center fielder'd just faked a throw behind me, a threat I hadn't much credited.

"Don't let the cheers go to your head. Those guys'd cheer a little old lady tripping on a popcorn box."

I watched Charlie Snow, a super hitter, settle in and tap his spikes with a Louisville Slugger he'd lathed into the shape of a skinny champagne bottle.

"Me, I'd be *ashamed* to reach base with a dying gull like the one you goofy-bunted out there," Hoey said.

I shrugged. My batting average was a perfect thousand—at least for now.

"Watch O'Connor's pick-off move. Get tagged out here and you might as well've gone down swinging."

"Back in the coach's box," the umpire Happy Polidori told Hoey, "and leave the poor kid be."

"Up yours, Polidori. It's my *job* to give advice to kids with marshmallows for brains."

"Move it," Polidori said. "Your body, not your mouth."

With no go-ahead from anyone, I stole second on O'Connor's first pitch. The GIs came to their feet, whooping. Lanett's catcher didn't even try to throw me out. I lifted a hand to Hoey—to show him I hadn't hurt myself, not to mock him—but he kicked up a cloud of red dirt, p.o.'d.

Snow hit a long single to right. I came home. The whole rest of the game went like that. We ended up winning eight to three—no laugher, as I say, but no knuckle-whitener either. My other two hits were a bunt toward first and a high bounder off the pitcher's rubber. Hoey badmouthed them too, calling them luck, saying the next time I went to church I should drop a C-note in the plate. It almost, not quite, *relieved* me when the Linenmaker right fielder ran down my longest clout of the day and webbed it against the Belk-Gallant sign for the game's second-to-last out.

Hoey applauded this catch. He liked seeing me robbed of a four-for-four outing on a ball I'd flat-out creamed.

At shortstop, though, I did manage a perfect day. Despite his earlier brag, Mariani didn't pitch well. Junior and I consistently got him out of jams by turning double plays or knocking down potential RBI rollers. On our double plays, we clicked like castanets.

"For the fourth time today," Milt Frye told us all, "your double-play combo was Boles-to-Heggie-to-Clerval, tying a team record set back in '39."

Whistles, applause, foot-stomping. Mrs. Atwill swung into an up-tempo version of "I Get a Kick Out of You."

"Danny Boles hails from Tenkiller, Oklahoma," Frye said. Then, stretching it: "Boy's got a few quarts of Cherokee blood, making him the first uprooted Injun to find his way back South on the Trail of Cheers." Frye said

Junior Heggie, a Georgia boy from Valdosta, deserved some applause too, and Hoey's spit probably turned to battery acid in his mouth.

After the game, a scratchy recording of the National Anthem blasted through the speakers. I stood on our dugout's top step with my cap over my heart listening to the boozy chorusing of our remaining fans. Mister JayMac had to order the field lamps snuffed to get them to leave.

In the clubhouse, Lamar Knowles told Junior and me if we kept it up, Boles-to-Heggie-to-Clerval would become as famous in the CVL as Tinker-to-Evers-to-Chance was in the bigs. He wasn't kissing tail either—he meant it. Junior'd taken his starting job, and Knowles could've moped or cried beginner's luck, but he didn't. My respect for him hitched right up the pole.

After we'd showered, Mister JayMac came in and said the most important thing about the evening's game wasn't breaking in some jittery rookies or tying the old club double-play mark, but that for the first time since our season opener on May the 7th, the Hellbenders had a *winning* record.

"Tonight, gentlemen, we stand nine and eight. That's good: a winning percentage of about .530. But it won't take this or any other pennant. Beat these loom-operating yokels one more time, tomorrow, and we'll head down to Quitman on Wednesday to pluck the Mockingbirds three out of three. Opelika lost again tonight, and LaGrange is in another extra-innings brawl with Cottonton.

"Keep scratching and clawing, gentlemen. By the end of August, we should be at the king-rooster top of the whole CVL cock pile."

Everybody slapped backs and hurrahed.

Hoey said, "Who starts at short tomorrow?"

That turned our jazz-band parade through an empty swimming pool into echoey silence.

Mister JayMac said, "Given our performance in our past two games, who do *you* think should start tomorrow?"

"Given my performance over the past *sixteen* games, I don't think that's a fair question. Sir."

"Perhaps we should *vote* on our lineups every day. Ask team members to judge the fairness of my decrees."

Hoey shut up. He could win this debate only with a pistol or a hypnotist's help. Everyone but Evans, Sloan, and a couple of others wanted him to clam up. He'd turned our victory party into a nitpicky postmortem.

"Good," Mister JayMac said. "Curfew tonight's one A.M. No, to hell with that. Be in bed by midnight and sleep late tomorrow." He left.

Oh yeah. In that night's game, Jumbo didn't have a hit, but he'd sucked up every chance at first smarter than a Hoover and played his monster heart out. So if Buck Hoey was ammonia under our noses, Jumbo was honeysuckle and mint.

1 6

That night—three or four in the morning—I had a powerful urge to pee. Kizzy'd set metal pitchers of lemonade all over the parlor after our game, and I'd drunk gallons of it. I'd sweated away a lot, but about a quart still ached for release, so I got up, tiptoed past Jumbo's bed, and bumbled down the hall to the third-floor john. Weird thing: When I got there, light showed in the cracks around the door, the knob wouldn't turn, and I could hear a rough drizzle on tin.

It wasn't Jumbo. He'd been in bed, a forbidding ridge of lumps and gulleys wheezing dreamily. Somebody from downstairs had come upstairs. Why? Had Sosebee organized a crap shoot up here? It teed me off. Where'd this Hellbender palooka get off hijacking our shower?

My bladder was a pulled-pin bomblet. I needed relief. I didn't have time for the jerk in the shower to finish up, towel down, and let me in. I'd flood the hall first. I looked for alternatives: open windows, flower pots, umbrella stands. But nothing presented itself. I had just one option, to creep downstairs and check out the bathroom on Dunnagin, Junior, and everybody else's floor. So down I went. Each step on that narrow staircase threatened to trigger me. If I went off, I'd turn the steps into a waterfall and drown my teammates in their beds—everyone in McKissic House but Jumbo and the skinnydipper in our shower.

I kept my bladder dammed and reached the second floor. Nobody was in its bathroom. Nobody. I dashed in and drained off my pain. My *physical* pain. It still irked me some unknown soul had stolen our bathroom. The one down here had four times the square footage and more soap and toilet paper. Why would another lodger sneak upstairs to ours?

For privacy, maybe. Somebody on the second floor didn't want spectators while he showered.

I started back upstairs. As I groped my way up, somebody else groped down, and I froze at the bottom of the chute. The person coming down looked suspiciously—deliciously—like a woman. By the glow of an electric sconce on the wall, I could see that although the woman had some age on her—late thirties, early forties—she was a looker, maybe even something of a vamp.

She had on a towel. Anyway, she *sort of* had it on.

Obviously, she hadn't expected to meet anyone. She didn't scram, though. She cocked her head and smiled, her strawberry hair pulled back from her forehead and swept over her shoulder in a damp strand. She clutched that strand and kept her towel from slipping with the same hand, her left. I know it was her left because she had a wedding band on it.

"Mr. Boles—our brand-new whangdoodle shortstop."

My shorts covered more than a bathing suit would've, but I blushed. If I'd rubbed myself with horse liniment, I couldn't have felt any hotter or glowed any brighter.

"Relax, kiddo. I'll let you by." The woman laughed. "Two ships passing in a tight." She pressed herself, towel and all, against the wall. "Climb on past, handsome."

I climbed with my head down. Shadows moved around us, but the amber sconce gave the woman's shins, arms, and breastbone the gleam of knife blades. Head high, I'd've stared straight up her towel into the valley of the shadow. As I climbed, I quaked. Stand me, any day, in the batter's box against a guy with a ninety-miles-per-hour speedball.

On the very same step as the woman, I brushed her hand and something damp landed on my instep. Her towel had fallen. I reached down to get it. My brain had shut off. My bumpkinish chivalric instincts had kicked in. When I straightened again, I was gazing on her nakedness, breathing the scented glycerin of Palmolive. I froze. I got dizzy. I felt like a statue on a revolving lazy Susan.

"Thanks." She didn't hurry to rewrap. "Preciate it."

I shut my eyes and dropped to my knees. In a darkness of my own concoction, I walked on them to the top of the stairs. When I got there and nerved up to look back down, the woman'd started moving again. The towel wrapped her from midback to just below the pretty half moons of her fanny. I peeked. When she reached the second floor and angled out of sight, I crept back down and peeked again. She sashayed to a room at the far end of the hall and tapped on the door. Curriden opened it and pulled her inside.

Skinny Dobbs roomed with Curriden. Did this woman whore for a living? Had Curriden and Skinny hired her for an orgy? Did an early morning of sweaty sex qualify as an orgy if more than two folks got in on it? Hold it. Maybe Curriden and the woman were secretly married. Bingo. The woman'd worn a ring. She looked *about* the right age to be Curriden's old lady. But if so, why didn't they live in Cotton Creek like all the other married Hellbender couples?

As I watched, the woman came out of Curriden's room wearing a polka-dot white-on-red dress and a big wheel-brimmed hat with ribbons. She had a straw handbag. She toted her high heels by their straps. She ran on her toes to the other staircase and tripped down its steps. She'd vamoosed before I could draw any conclusions except she was stunning and really knew how to wear clothes. (She also knew how *not* to wear them.) And she knew I played a "whangdoodle shortstop." That gave me pause—not that she liked my play, but the phrase itself.

I didn't move. Mostly, I didn't move. An old friend found the door of my shorts and poked his head through for a one-eyed look around. I was about to ease my old pal when Skinny Dobbs came up the main staircase shuffling like a drunk. He crossed to his and Curriden's room. He didn't have a hangover, he just hadn't slept much. My old pal collapsed in wrinkles. On her way out, Curriden's wife had probably told Dobbs, sleeping on a parlor sofa, he could slink back to his room—her and Reese's conjugal visit was over.

I crept back upstairs, with a side trip to the steamed-up john, and sacked out again. Didn't get much shuteye, though. I kept seeing that lady jaybird-nude on the stairs.

The CVL, I learned, had started playing Sunday games in its very first season. People called Dixie the Bible Belt. Even at midweek, street preachers in Highbridge could work up a powerful rant and a healthy amening crowd. Nobody opposed Sunday baseball, though. It took place *after* church and ranked right up there with God, flag, motherhood, and hunting.

Fadeaway Ankers started the final game of our series against Lanett— on either two or three days' rest, depending on whether you figured it like Fadeaway or Mister JayMac. During his warm-ups, he grinned and preened and threw screaming BBs, like he enjoyed being out there, which, I guess, he did. He wanted his first Linenmaker hitter bad as a starveling bluetick wants its next soup bone. And he struck him out.

Mister JayMac had tapped me, Junior, and Skinny to start too. Unofficially, it was Rookies' Day. Officially, it was War Bonds Day.

In the outfield, groundskeepers had hung War Bonds banners over some of the biggest signboards, with the okay of the companies whose ads they hid:

IT'S TEN MINUTES TO MIDNIGHT!
WAKE UP, AMERICANS. . . .
YOUR COUNTRY'S MOST FATEFUL HOUR IS NEAR!
DON'T BE TIGHTER WITH YOUR MONEY THAN
WITH THE LIVES OF YOUR SONS!

MONEY TO PAY FOR THE WAR, YES;
BUT NONE AT ALL FOR FRILLS IN THE
CIVIL OPERATIONS OF ANY OF OUR GOVERNING BODIES.
THAT IS THE EDICT OF THE AMERICAN PEOPLE.

Neither Skinny nor Curriden looked at full speed. Even though Curriden hadn't gotten up for church, he could barely haul his ass around. That gal in the towel might as well've strapped an icebox to his back, he had so little vim. Skinny looked sharper; he could run and throw. Sometimes, though, he stopped dead and opened his eyes so wide he seemed to be trying to breathe through his eyeballs.

"What ails you two?" Mister JayMac asked after our second at bat. "Yall stay up last night herding woolyboogers? I swan, Mr. Curriden, with some rouge on your cheeks, you'd look like a dead man." He put Hoey at third for Curriden and Evans into right for Skinny.

When he did, Hoey said, "Why don't you move Dumbo over to third and let me pick up where I left off Friday? Sir."

Mister JayMac just looked at him, his eyes as dead blue as an old lady's hair rinse. From then on, though, Hoey played next to me at Curriden's spot, never making an error. None of the right-handed Linenmakers could pull Fadeaway's scroogie, and none of their lefties ever hit to third.

The game was a walkover. I rapped my first extra-base hit, a triple off the EDICT OF THE AMERICAN PEOPLE banner, and a single too. Every other Hellbender, Hoey and Evans excepted, got good wood too, and when Fadeaway finished pitching the sixth, Mister JayMac lifted him for Sosebee.

"That's plumb stupid!" Fadeaway shouted in the dugout when he realized what'd happened. "I got a three-hitter going!"

"Relax, Mr. Ankers," Mister JayMac said. "All you can do if you stay in is lose it."

"My daddy taught me to finish what I start."

Parris said, "He shoulda taught you a little respect for—"

Mister JayMac made a hush-up gesture at Parris. "You like to finish what you start, Mr. Ankers?"

"Damn right!"

"Then I want you to know you started *six innings*. You've jes finished em. A helluva fine job you did for us too, start to finish."

Fadeaway looked confused, a bird dog thrown off the scent. Then Mister JayMac's "reasoning" sunk in, and he bought it, the whole bolt. He strolled along the bench and sat down next to Haystack with a hambone-licking smirk on his face.

"You won't lose," Haystack said. "You'll either win or get a no-decision if Sosebee fucks up. You're sitting pretty."

"I don't sit no other way," Fadeaway said.

Sosebee's stuff didn't sizzle, but the Linenmakers couldn't hit a raindrop in a south Georgia thunderstorm. At game's end, the scoreboard read 13-0. The crowd whooped so loud we could hardly hear the recording of the National Anthem.

Afterwards, Mister JayMac cornered me in the dugout. "You youngsters've come along jes fine, Mr. Boles. My sister Tulipa is a bred-in-the-bone baseball gal, but she never scouted me a kid worth leftover pot liquor till she stumbled on you. You're hitting .750 after two games, and you play short as good as anybody, including Ligonier Hoey." Ligonier was Buck Hoey's real first name—he came from a town in Pennsylvania called Ligonier. So, of course, he went by Buck.

"Grab a shower and meet me under the grandstand in your street togs," Mister JayMac said. "Dinner's on me tonight."

Why not Fadeaway, Junior, and Skinny too? I thought. Why not Jumbo, for that matter? He'd had another long home run and another errorless day at first. Did proving the shrewdness of Miss Tulipa's judgment entitle you to dine every Sunday evening with the boss?

I met Mister JayMac in the concessions area. He stood next to Homer's tank, talking to two people—females?—half-hidden by girder shadows. One of the females, I saw, was Phoebe. The other had to be her mama, the daughter of Mister JayMac's dead brother. Made sense, I guess, but my heart double-clutched—I hadn't seen Phoebe at any of our recent games—and my hands turned cold as ice tongs.

"Ah, Mr. Boles!" Mister JayMac shouted. "Got some ladies here I'd like you to meet!"

I sauntered over. Phoebe was Phoebe, of course—but tonight she had on a dress instead of blue jeans, and a pair of tiny gold earrings instead of one gaudy exploded pearl. In her open-toed heels and her wide-brimmed straw hat, she looked like a miniature woman. Her mother . . . well, I reddened. My eyes glanced down to flit over the candy wrappers and dirty popcorn around the base of the aquarium.

"Mrs. Luther Pharram, better known around here as LaRaina, and her lovely daughter Phoebe," Mister JayMac said. "Ladies, Mr. Daniel Boles—Mr. Boles, Mrs. Pharram and Phoebe."

Not too long ago, LaRaina Pharram and I had bumped into each other between the second and third floors at McKissic House, only she'd worn a towel and I'd worn shorts and an all-over blush. My blush'd come back, prickly as radioactive shellac. Miss LaRaina, despite the damage she'd wreaked on Curriden and Skinny, looked bright-eyed and amused. Every time I glanced up, she gave me a batted eyelash—mockery—and a smile halfway between a grin and a pout.

We have a secret, her grin-pout said. Aren't you glad you can't tell my uncle? "Sorry, Uncle JayMac," LaRaina Pharram said aloud, "but I can't call this handsome fella *Mr.* Boles."

Handsome! More mockery. I wanted not to like this woman—she had a husband overseas, she'd spent the night playing slip-skins with a ballplayer, she'd gotten a big kick out of my embarrassment, and now she was making mock of me—but I still felt more or less kindly toward her.

Mister JayMac said Miss LaRaina could call me Daniel, if she liked, but he'd stick to Mr. Boles.

"My, such a fuddy-duddy," Miss LaRaina said.

Phoebe'd picked up on my jitters, and my behavior struck her as rude or immature. Her pretty lips seemed to've wrapped themselves around a sour lemon drop.

"So how's Miss Giselle?" she suddenly piped, then went back to sucking her make-believe candy.

"Fine," Mister JayMac said. "Now. Where would you gals advise taking our hero for a victory supper?"

"Ast him where he'd like to go," Phoebe said.

Mister JayMac said, "But he's ignorant of his choices."

"Ast him what he'd like to eat," Phoebe said. "American, Eye-talian, Chinese."

Mister JayMac lifted an eyebrow at me. At that moment, I had all the appetite of a spooked cat. I was trying to adjust to Miss LaRaina's presence and cooling down from nine innings of sticky twilight baseball.

"The Live Oak Tea Room at the Oglethorpe," Miss LaRaina suggested.

Phoebe looked at me. "Thass a nice place."

"The Linenmakers booked rooms at the Oglethorpe," Mister JayMac said. "The tea room's going to swarm with em."

Miss LaRaina smiled at her uncle. "I know."

Mister JayMac's jaw tightened. "Have a care," he said. "For decency. For your daughter."

"Phoebe's not likely to put the mash on a Linenmaker. She hates ballplayers."

"Not awluvem," Phoebe said.

You could've fooled me. The pinched V between her eyebrows and the pucker of her mouth didn't say fondness, not in any language I knew.

"The Oglethorpe Tea Room is out," Mister JayMac said.

"Corporal John's over on Penticuff Strip?" Miss LaRaina said. "It's got an attractive clientele."

"Absolutely not."

"A joke. It's closed today anyway. Sunday sure limits a body's choices here in Highbridge."

Mister JayMac herded us into the parking lot, where Darius had pulled the Caddy as close as he could to the main gate, given the fans still about. Darkness had just begun to settle, and several groups of people smoked and gabbed in the parking lot. Dance music drifted from a radio through an open car window. Artie Shaw, Benny Goodman, Glenn Miller.

Before we could get in the Caddy, a hefty man in overalls and a frowzy woman in a print dress came over. Their clothes seemed to have as much dust as cotton in them.

"Jordan McKissic?" the man said. "Thass you, aint it?"

"It is. How may I help you?"

"Show him, Sue Beth."

The woman—Sue Beth—pushed a paper under Mister JayMac's nose. He retreated a step.

"S from the War Department," the man said. "Hit us a coupla days back. It's our Donnie."

"He aint coming home," the woman said. "He done got kilt in North Africa."

"I'm sorry," Mister JayMac said. "A terrible thing."

"You oughta be," the woman said. "You done for him. You took him when he coulda had him—*shoulda* had him—a heping-job zemption. Eyetalians didn't kill our Donny. You did it with a stinkin fountain pen."

Mister JayMac said, "Please, folks, tell me yall's names."

"The Crawfords," the man said. "Ira and Sue Beth. Little people, ordinary folk. *Ordinary!*" Crawford didn't exactly shout, but his kettle-drum voice carried. Some loitering fans began ambling towards us.

"Donnie never shoulda gone!" Sue Beth Crawford did shout. "And you damn-all know it too!"

"Mrs. Crawford, God bless your martyred son," Mister JayMac said. "I'm sorry every American boy who dies has to make that sacrifice."

"Yessir," Ira Crawford said. "But the draft board had its quota to fill so you thew our innosunt young un in."

"Every boy in the hopper's innocent in one way or another. Thank God we don't yet have an army of criminals and cynics."

"Yore precious ballplayers don't go!" Crawford accused.

"Not one Hellbender comes from here," Mister JayMac said. "They're too young or old, or their local draft boards exempted them. I pulled no strings for any player."

"Mebbe you did, mebbe you didn't," Ira Crawford said. "But you cain't say the same bout thatere black nigger. How come he aint on bivouac someres?"

Darius heard this—he had to've—but he opened the Caddy's rear door and helped Phoebe and Miss LaRaina in.

"Mr. Crawford, federal law forbids inducting Negroes in greater numbers than they appear in the general population. Hothlepoya County has almost as many coloreds as whites so we take more than most boards, but a limit exists."

"Hog slop," Ira Crawford said.

"Look, even if we loaded the Army with coloreds, they'd end up in service units—the quartermaster corps and such. They probably wouldn't fight and die like you and the missus seem to want em to."

Near the big Caddy, you could've heard a cricket poot. Sue Beth started to cry, Ira cursed. They joined hands and walked back through the dusty lot to a dented Ford pickup loaded down with feed sacks.

"I *am* sorry about your son!" Mister JayMac called out.

"I bet," said somebody unseeable in the crowd.

The Crawfords slammed opposite doors and rattled away in their spavined pickup.

"Git in, sir," Darius said. "I'll drive yall to the Royal." He meant the Royal Hotel, a place with a restaurant supposedly even better than the Oglethorpe's.

Off we rode. Mister JayMac sat next to Darius, brooding. Miss LaRaina jabbered away, happy that the Hellbenders had won and made a move in the standings.

17

In the Chamberlain's room at the Royal Hotel, we all had prime rib—except Darius, who ate beef soup and French bread in the kitchen. (Judging by the fruity smell on his breath after, he'd also tossed back some of the house wine.) Mister JayMac's mood improved. Miss LaRaina was his "date." Phoebe, going by age and seating arrangements, was mine.

Talk ran from baseball to a possible invasion of Sicily to Phoebe's plans for her senior year at Watson High. I learned that in Georgia the senior year was only a student's eleventh of public schooling. (Not until after the war did Georgia create a twelfth year.) That made me—next to crackers Ankers, Heggie, and Dobbs—nearlybout a college man.

"S a bother you cain't talk," Phoebe finally said to me. "You shore this condition aint some sort of numbskull play for sympathy?"

"Be nice, Phoeb," Miss LaRaina said. "And purge yourself, please, of those irritating *cain'ts* and *aints*."

"I cain't," Phoebe said. "It aint in the cards. And I'm bout as nice as Mr. Boles deserves."

Mister JayMac changed the subject. "You talked when I met you. You stammered, but you talked. What happened?"

"Smart, Uncle JayMac," Miss LaRaina said. "You've asked him to tell you what rendered him speechless."

"Taint a silly thing to ast if he's faking," Phoebe said. "It makes tons a sense."

I'd've liked to tell Mister JayMac that what'd struck me dumb was seeing Miss LaRaina jaybird nude on the stairs, but that sequence of events didn't exactly gibe. Everyone stared at me, though, like I *might* talk; and if my tongue'd worked, I'd've given them the Gettysburg Address just to be polite. In fact, I tried to talk: a gargle, a gag, a hack.

Which disgusted Phoebe. "Dogs," she said.

In my inside jacket pocket I had the small notebook Jumbo'd given me. I pulled it out. Mister JayMac saw me patting my pockets for something to write with and reached me his fountain pen. (The one he'd used on Donnie Crawford's draft papers?)

I opened my notebook and thought. What could I tell these people? I couldn't tell them about Sergeant Pumphrey. Hell, I couldn't even *think* about that. I probably didn't *think* about it. I had no mental picture of Pumphrey at all—the man didn't exist for me in Highbridge.

So I printed: *On the train from Tenkiller I had a bad dream. My daddy flew at me in a plane. A long metal runway rolled at me and knocked me down. When I woke up I couldn't talk.* I tore out the sheet of paper and passed it across the table to Mister JayMac.

"Some dream," he said.

"Read it to us," Miss LaRaina said, and he did.

"Gimme," Phoebe said. Mister JayMac handed the ripped-out page to her, and she read it aloud right after him, making my dream sound like a comedy film. "Then it aint physical," she said. "It's jes head-stuff. If you wanted to bad enough, you could talk."

I took the page away from Phoebe, flipped it over, and printed: *It wasn't head stuff once. My daddy smacked me in the throat when I was 12. Took me 2 yrs to learn to talk again.*

I gave the page to Mister JayMac, who read it aloud for Phoebe and Miss LaRaina. From then on, that's how I talked, scribbling my messages and passing them on to Mister JayMac to read out.

"Your daddy must've been a prince," Miss LaRaina said.

I loved him. He taught me how to play ball.

"A man who teaches his boy to play ball cain't be a total jackass, can he, Uncle Jay?" Phoebe said.

"I know your opinion of baseball players, child," Mister JayMac said. "How do you want me to interpret your question?"

"No sarcasm meant," Phoebe said. "Not a hair."

"There *are* nicer words than jackass," Miss LaRaina told Phoebe.

"Like prince," Phoebe said. "I spose."

Miss LaRaina gave Phoebe a razor-sharp stare, then turned to me again. "Is your daddy still alive? If so, where is he?"

Alive. A guy on the train (Pumphrey! I refused to think) *said he's in Alaska working on planes.*

"Working on them or flying them?" Miss LaRaina said. "In your dream, you saw him flying a plane."

But I'd written what I meant. I nodded at Mister JayMac, and he read my last message again. Forget that in my dream Dick Boles had flown a P-40 Warhawk. I wrote:

I dreamed baseball on a steel runway—in the Alooshans. Me vs. a air force ground crew. Baseball in the snow.

"Well, it guv you laryngitis," Phoebe said.

"Young Mr. Boles lives, breathes, and dreams baseball," Mister JayMac told the women.

Miss LaRaina leaned over the linen-and-lace tablecloth: "You share a room with Jumbo Hank Clerval, I've been told. How do you like that? What kind of man is he?"

A big man. I like it fine.

Phoebe and Mister JayMac laughed. Miss LaRaina, though, kept studying me, like I knew more than I'd written.

"Mama, Mr. Clerval's a big, smart man," Phoebe said. "He reads books and wallops long homers. What else do you need to know? *Why* do you think you need to know it?"

"Mr. Clerval incites curiosity," Miss LaRaina said to me. "He has mystery. He's also—well, hideous, one could say."

"A man has awful little control over the face God chooses to bestow upon him," Mister JayMac said.

"Neither does a woman," Miss LaRaina said. "Which doesn't stop her from trying." She kept looking at me. I had the key, she seemed to think, to the mystery of Jumbo Hank Clerval. I could make use of what I knew to reveal him to her. Except I couldn't. I still didn't know what made Fadeaway Ankers tick, much less my brooding highbrow galoot of a roomy.

Politely I wrote: *He's a vejiterran. He snores. He gave me this notebook.* (Vejiterran—like he came from Vejiterra, a planet in some flaky Flash Gordon universe.)

Mister JayMac, Miss LaRaina, and Phoebe all laughed, and I got self-conscious about my spelling and my sloppy printing. I decided to sit tight as Tarbaby from then on—nothing out of my mouth, nothing more from Mister JayMac's pen. I passed it back to him. Miss LaRaina didn't notice.

"How do you suppose it'd feel to kiss him?" she said.

Phoebe moved like somebody'd shot a jolt of current through her. Our silverware jumped, our glasses shook. Phoebe's face turned red. Anger? Shame? A cocktail of them both?

"Mama!" she cried. "That's vile!"

"Why? Because Mr. Clerval doesn't resemble Clark Gable?"

Phoebe looked down. "No, Mama. You've a husband in Europe in the war."

"Goodness, girl, I was speaking hypothetically. Don't blow a gasket. Tell me, Daniel: Is it wrong for a married woman to ask a hypothetical question about kissing another man?"

Mister JayMac said, "I'd venture, LaRaina, that it's not so much wrong as unwise. Thought precedes action."

"In many cases, it follows. I speak from both experience and observation," Miss LaRaina said.

"Scuse me," Phoebe said. She got up—she almost knocked her chair over—and wove her way through a jungle of fancy-set tables to the restroom. The Chamberlain's Room had filled with customers. The noise level was so high you could've raved on about bomber production in Marietta without drawing a warning from a plainclothes OSI man. During the war, you expected such crowds. Movie theaters, bistros, and restaurants ran at full throttle. People had money, and worries to chase.

"Phoeb's awfully touchy this evening," Miss LaRaina said. She lit a cigarette.

"She loves her daddy," Mister JayMac said.

"So do I." The smoke around Miss LaRaina's face and shoulders swirled dreamily. It made her green eyes look shady and then as bright and hard as holly leaves.

"Yes," Mister JayMac said, "but do you stay busy enough?"

That got Miss LaRaina's goat. "My lord, Uncle, I'm still the secretary of the Officers' Wives' Club at Camp Penticuff. I chair two different fund-raising committees of the Highbridge Women's Club. I helped organize your last three war drives at the ballpark. I read books. I go to movies. I write Luther cheerful letters. I'm also a *mother*."

"I haven't forgotten. You shouldn't either."

Miss LaRaina blew out a stream of smoke like a genie from an Arabian lamp. Get me out of here, I wished. My fidgets pulled Miss LaRaina's attention.

"Your all-knowing boss thinks I'm a neglectful mother, Daniel."

"No, LaRaina," Mister JayMac said. "It's just that—"

She cut him off. "Actually, he fears I may be a . . . a *bad example*. Is that it, Uncle?"

"The times're out of joint, LaRaina. The climate's at once permissive and judgmental. For your sake, as well as Phoebe's, you should try to hold your reputation as wife and mother above reproach."

"Ah," Miss LaRaina said. "Caesar's wife."

"If the analogy fits."

" 'Do as I say and not as I do.'" Miss LaRaina stubbed out her quarter-smoked cigarette in an ashtray, grinding it like a woman with a grudge.

"LaRaina," Mister JayMac said.

"He hates it. I'm often as enamored—hypothetically—of the players he imports as he is. What can I say, Daniel? I like men. I'm young yet. All my hormones work."

"You've said a good deal too much." Mister JayMac didn't raise his voice: he might have just said, *It's raining out.*

"Uncle Jay understands hormones," Miss LaRaina said. "Even though he was born during the Trojan War, his flare up in all their ancient splendor at least twice a week."

I wanted out of there bad. A spaniel that strays into a family argument gets its butt kicked.

Darius dropped off Miss LaRaina and Phoebe at their house in Cotton Creek and drove Mister JayMac and me home to McKissic House.

I felt nothing but relief getting back upstairs with Jumbo, even in our stifling attic room.

"Good evening," he said, then went back to reading Willkie's *One World*. Because he'd nearlybout finished it, he didn't say another word to me until bedtime.

"Good night, Daniel."

Believe me, I'd appreciated his silence up till then.

18

In the second week of June, we went on the road against Quitman and Marble Springs and played good ball.

We didn't sweep either series, though. That next Saturday, we split a doubleheader against the Seminoles, losing the opener on a squeeze bunt RBI in the bottom of the twelfth. Talk about peeved! We revved for revenge in the so-called nightcap (so-called because the sun never had a chance to set) and shellacked them three to zip in about ninety minutes. We got some nutritious shuteye that night and ambushed the poor saps again on Sunday.

At the end of my first road trip, we had fourteen wins and ten losses. Because Opelika and LaGrange had been playing like drunken Looney Tune characters, the pennant race tightened. We had a homestand against Eufaula and a big road trip against the Orphans and the Gendarmes scheduled at the end of the next week. I got a glow on thinking about it. Wins in those games could say a lot about that summer's final standings.

Now, some pro leagues, including the Negro bigs, liked to play a split season because they always had more personnel changes than the two white major loops. At summer's end, they had two pennant winners, a first- and a second-half champeen, and a playoff to decide the overall victor. Mister JayMac's wartime philosophy—and he had a lot of say in the CVL—was simple: Since no team'd get more than a half dozen new guys once play started, we should pull one hard-fought season with the guys on board. If one team ran away with it, attendance might falter, but that summer we had balance at the top and lots of jockeying around during the dog-day swelter. So the fans never jumped ship. Even bunglers like the Boll Weevils, the Linenmakers, and the Quitman Mockingbirds drew crowds when Highbridge and the other top teams came to town.

On the road, we traveled in the *Bomber*, with Darius at the wheel and Mister JayMac in the catbird seat behind him. In other towns, the boss depended on taxies for transportation, or obliging locals with cars, or his own sore feet. But because he had a lot of friends around south Georgia, you seldom saw him walking. Sometimes he'd hijack the *Bomber*. Ration stamps for gas never posed him a problem.

Hellbender players didn't stay in motor courts or hotels—with the exception, of course, of Hank Clerval. Jumbo wanted lodgings in commercial hostelries, and he got his way because, well, he could play. Also, he cowed even Mister JayMac, who still didn't care for Jumbo's taste for private rooms—his arrangements with locals to board his players were thriftier than running a hotel tab. I benefited from Jumbo's stand because I got to stay with him in hotels. Or I *guess* I did. Maybe I just lost my chance to meet some charming folks. But whether in Highbridge, Quitman, or Marble Springs, where we shared a beat-up cabin in a motor court near Seminole Park, I often felt like a cockroach, a bug underfoot. Jumbo seemed more at home in these places than I did.

With a draw on my first paycheck (I never told anybody a soldier on the train had stolen my money), I'd bought a used radio, but Jumbo didn't like me to play it, not even to catch up on war news. He preferred books to radio programs. He thought war, even news about it, "uncivilized." When I turned on my set in our motel, he clomped around his mat and clicked it off, the scars at his lip corners glowing like coals.

"The hostilities of nations revolt me. They prey upon and increase the petty insecurities of men."

Unlike baseball, I thought.

But, hey, what a speech. Jumbo belonged in politics. He should run for dogcatcher. If he nixed public appearances and ran a radio campaign, he might even win.

I sat there on my cot, scared and angry. Couldn't he've just asked me to turn the radio down? Somehow, though, he picked up on how bad he'd browned me off.

"I'm a pacifist, Daniel. Even had I not been too tall for the services, conscience would have required me to resist my own induction. Frankly, I would have run away."

This speech didn't bleach the blackness out of my mood. At my first team meeting, he'd labeled bad ballplayers traitors. Now he was talking lily-livered trash.

"My only citizenship, if I possess one, is Swiss. In both war and peace,

Switzerland remains neutral." Jumbo lumbered back to his bed. Outside, a thousand cicadas whirred.

Bus trips aboard the *Bomber* would fag you out faster than a boulder-pushing contest. The speed limit was thirty-five miles per hour. That turned a trip to Cottonton, our farthest pull, into a five-hour fatigue fest. Mister JayMac tried to avoid travel on game days, but if we had two series on the same road trip, he couldn't arrange off-day travel. Usually, though, CVL schedule makers set it up so back-to-back away series occurred against teams just two or three hours apart. On my first road trip, we lost to Quitman on Friday night and left town at nine the next day to get to Marble Springs by noon, two hours before the twin bill we split there. The ride had drained us. We did great not to drop both games.

If you began fresh and had a cloud cover, the bus rides could be a hoot. Sosebee played guitar, Fanning harmonica, and just about everybody else could mouth a Kleenex-and-comb kazoo or drum a seat back. Dunnagin and several other guys sang. Darius told funny courting stories, on himself, his buddies, or players no longer with the team, tales that skirted sleaze by zeroing in on his heroes' hopes, then ticking off all their missed connections and comeuppances. We'd fall out laughing, but not Old Stoneface, Darius. His singing voice, though, was a frog's croak, and the only musical instrument he really knew how to play was the *Brown Bomber*'s clutch.

Riding back to Highbridge, Mister JayMac always made us review our games. With a score book open on his seat, he'd defend or apologize for so-so plays, and ask us all to analyze our botches. We'd also discuss opposing hitters—how we'd got them out, how to retire them in future games.

"Play better," Sloan always said. "Jes play better."

"Gentlemen, we play better by practicing," Mister JayMac said. "By thinking about what we've done that didn't work. By reviewing from all sides what actually may."

"Thinking too much'll kill you faster than a jilted honey with a Smith and Wesson," Charlie Snow said. Snow had the best ballplaying instincts on the club. He flowed from one spot to another and hit with the grace of an otter sliding off a rock.

"Think *beforehand*," Mister JayMac said. "Not during. Most bush leaguers never go up cause they don't want to put in the *before* and *after* work necessary to improve."

"Other clubs don't do this," Fanning said. "They use bus trips to cool down and have some fun."

"*Good* teams do it," Mister JayMac said. "Who among yall wants to copy the Boll Weevils?"

Darius said, "The K. C. Monarchs do it. The Birmingham Barons do it." Colored clubs, both of them.

"Yeah," said Sloan. "And look where *they* are. Right at the tippy top of the baseball world."

Anyway, Mister JayMac guided us through that three-game skull session for better than an hour. He asked Fadeaway to explain why he'd slacked off towards the end of Sunday's game.

He told Evans to get Snow to teach him how to bunt.

"I *know* how to bunt. I jes didn't get it done Sunday."

"Then you *don't* know how to bunt. All you can do is fake the stance and pop out backwards."

"Fine him!" Hoey shouted from a seat or two behind Jumbo and me. "Fine the sorry peckerwood!"

The *Bomber* rolled past drought-stricken cattle pastures and peanut fields, rattling like a gypsy's wagon. Most of us had pushed our windows up, and the air blowing through still had a vague morning coolness.

Lon Musselwhite lurched up the aisle. "Hear ye! Hear ye! The Rolling Assizes of the Hellbender Bureau of CVL Justice is now in session! The Honorable Judge Lionel K. Musselwhite presiding."

"Lionel?" Skinny said. "His name's *Lionel?*"

"Baseball-Latin for Muscles," Hoey said.

Almost everybody else clapped or stamped. Muscles held up his hand. Darius glanced back and cried, "Stop! Yall gon bust the bottom outta this boat!" That helped some. So did Mister JayMac lifting his hands and making stifle-it gestures.

But the hubbub went on, and the *Bomber* did seem about ready to burst open and spill us onto the blacktop. In the pasture whipping past, moon-faced cows watched us go by.

Muscles said, "Sergeant-at-Arms Clerval, *ten-HUT!*"

Jumbo got up, his head turtle-ducked to keep from scraping the ceiling.

"Sergeant-at-Arms Clerval, remove from this assembly anyone whose behavior upsets the scales of justice," Muscles said. "Toss em out a window."

"Yessir." Jumbo didn't smile. Even in his clumsy stoop, he towered like a grizzly. It was half a joke and half a real threat. When everyone got quiet, he sat back down.

Muscles said, "Mr. Evans, a party of some probity and maybe even of unimpeachable expertise has accused you of—"

"Brown noser!" Hoey shouted.

Muscles ignored him. "—a demonstrated ignorance of the art of bunting. How do you plead?"

"Give him a defense attorney!" Quip Parris said.

"Turkey Sloan," Evans said. "Give me Turkey."

"Nyland Sloan, the court hereby appoints you to defend the incompetent accused," Muscles said. "Mr. Dunnagin, you must prosecute."

Sloan traded places with Fanning so he could talk with Evans, and Muscles asked anyone willing to witness to say so. Sosebee, Fanning, and Sudikoff agreed to testify for Evans; Nutter, Curriden, Hoey, and Snow to speak against.

"How does your client plead?" Muscles asked Sloan.

Sloan stood up and said, "Your Honor, Mr. Evans thinks these whole proceedings reek vilely of kangaroo dung. The fix is in. A skinny kid from Brunswick"—he meant Dobbs—"grabbed his starting role thout so much as a by-your-leave n—"

"A *by-your-leave?*" Mister JayMac roared. "Mr. Dobbs beat Mr. Evans like a drum! What's this *by-your-leave* folderol?"

"Sorry, Mister JayMac," Sloan said. "Just a formal legal way of speaking. It don't mean pig tracks, actually."

"Then you admit it's a lie," Mister JayMac said.

"Sir, you're out of order," Muscles said. "Mr. Sloan, how does your useless scumbag of a client plead?"

"*Objection!*" Evans said.

"Shut up," Muscles said. "I mean, 'Hush.' Overruled. I can't say anything objectionable. I'm the judge."

Sloan stretched out one arm and cleared his throat:

> "The question is, Can Trapdoor bunt?
> Does he know how, or is it a stunt
> When he assumes the stance and then
> Allows the ball to bruise his shin

Or bounce off his bat like popping corn?
Does he deserve our ruth or scorn?"

"For Christ's sake, Turkey, how're you pleading the sap?" Hoey said. "We aint got time for the goddamn *Iliad*."

Sloan blinked and continued:

"Is a player who cannot bunt
A guilty lout or a innosunt
Victim of our expectations?
Blame we him or those cruel matrons
Who sewed the ball to such a trim
Its twisting seams bamboozled him,
Causing him to look a lout
By poking it up, for an out?
So how pleads Evans this fine day?
Like this: *Nolo contendere*."

"Okay," Muscles said. "Mr. Evans, I hereby fine you two bits and sentence you to practice bunting with Mr. Snow."

"Wait a sec," Hoey said. "Don't I get to present my testimony against the bastid?"

"Yeah," Curriden said. "What about Nutter and me? Evans can't bunt any bettern he can fart 'America the Beautiful.'"

"He doesn't say otherwise," Muscles said. "I've assessed the fine and stated the penalty. Case closed. Court continues in session, however. Next case!"

The *Brown Bomber* groaned along, belching and smoking. Nobody said anything. I looked out the window. A line of oaks or elms split one of the rising pastures. Their branches dripped with Spanish moss. Red-winged blackbirds perched on the weeds in the roadside ditch; puzzled cattle looked out from hardwood clumps along the pasture ridge. Despite the bus's growling, I felt nearly peaceful enough to fall asleep.

"Cmon, you guys," Muscles said. "Next case!"

Jerry Wayne Sosebee stood up. "Awright." He swallowed. "I accuse Jumbo and young Boles there of hoodwinking the boss. He gives em special road privileges that hurt team morale and affect how we play."

A flight of locusts wheeled through my gut. The bus went quiet as a morgue.

Mister JayMac turned in his seat. "*Hoodwinked?*"

Only Hoey got a kick out of Sosebee's accusation. "Jerry Wayne thinks Dumbo and Jumbo mumbo-jumboed you, sir."

A couple of players sniggered. Guys with sense, though, hung on bent tenterhooks and bided their time.

"Do you really believe a speechless flea like Mr. Boles could hoodwink me into anything, Mr. Sosebee?" Mister JayMac said.

"Sir, I jes don't believe Mr. Boles cain't talk. I think he could if he tried."

"Case thown out," Muscles said. "Mr. Sosebee has based his accusation on ill will and prejudice. Therefore—"

"No, no," Mister JayMac said. "I assume Mr. Sosebee plans to *demonstrate* how Messieurs Clerval and Boles hoodwinked me?"

"Well, mebbe Dumbo didn't," Sosebee said. "He's jes flying on Jumbo's coattails."

"You excuse Mr. Boles from your accusation?" Muscles said.

"Yeah, sure. I mean, the real favorite in this business is ol Goliath there."

"And you see yourself as David?" Mister JayMac said.

"Nosir. Well, mebbe," Sosebee said. "Jumbo needs to be brought down, though. Somebody has to do it."

"Brought down? From what?" Mister JayMac said. "Leading us in home runs and RBIs? Playing his bag bettern any other first baseman in the league?"

"Taking advantage and stirring up ill will," Sosebee said.

"You must be talking about yourself, Jerry Wayne," said Lamar Knowles. Wow. Knowles never came down on anybody. If you pulled a merkle, he'd sidle over and tell you to forget it.

Jumbo stood up. "I confront my accuser."

Sosebee's jowly gills went ashy-gray, but he kept facing Jumbo across five seat backs. He didn't sit.

"Mr. Sosebee must speak for others too," Jumbo said. "How many agree that Mr. JayMac's kindnesses to me have undone your good will or degraded the quality of your play?"

No one answered.

"A fair question," Mister JayMac said. "Do any of you play sloppy ball because Jumbo gets commercial rooms on the road?"

"I resent the special treatment," Trapdoor Evans allowed. "I don't play any worse for it, though."

"It'd be hard for you to play any worse than you did this past weekend," Buck Hoey said.

"An honest admission," Mister JayMac said. "Give credit."

That remark—praise instead of a lynching—opened some more guys' mouths. Sloan, Sudikoff, and Fanning all spoke up—not malcontents, exactly, but ballplayers who always looked outside themselves for Christs to hang on trees.

Jumbo said, "Last year I lodged alone, both in Highbridge and on the road. By nature I'm a solitary person, and Mister JayMac saw that I could tolerate the compelled camaraderie of our sport, or of any joint human enterprise, for only so long. I did not *demand* this favor. I asked it humbly and received it most gratefully."

"He speaks true," Mister JayMac said.

Sosebee kept standing: Jumbo was answering his charge. He looked less hepped than before, though. His skin had turned ashy-gray. Sweat showed in loops under the arms of his shirt.

"I would have agreed to the lodgings that Mister JayMac arranges for us," Jumbo said, "except that small children and a great many female adults find mine a fearsome presence. I also discomfit not a few men. I didn't wish to test the hospitality of Mister JayMac's host families by presenting myself to them as a guest. I had no wish to burden them."

"He still speaks true," Mister JayMac said.

"Once last year, I might add, an innkeeper in Eufaula refused me a room because my appearance . . . offended him. I made no clamor. I simply went elsewhere."

"So why'd you accept Dumbo as a roomy this season?" Jerry Wayne Sosebee asked.

"It was time," Jumbo said.

"And Dumbo's as close to nobody as Jumbo could get without taking nobody," Hoey said.

"I assure Mr. Sosebee that Daniel cannot talk," Jumbo said, "but I reject the slur that his inability to speak renders him a cipher."

"Translation!" Hoey shouted. "Translation, please!"

Jumbo put one big raw hand on his chest. "Mr. Sosebee, if you still feel that I must relinquish the privileges I enjoy, I have a compact to propose. A *deal*."

"What deal?" Sosebee said.

"I will come down to the second floor of McKissic House if you will take me as your roommate."

Sosebee looked at Jumbo, then at Mister JayMac. No one wanted to give him any help. "Never mind," he said. "Forget it." He lowered himself back to his seat. Either he or the seat cushion sighed like a bellows.

"Mr. Sosebee," Muscles said, "the court fines you two bits for trying to initiate a meritless proceeding. Case closed! Court adjourned!"

So ended that morning's Rolling Assizes.

Forty minutes later, we hit the outskirts of Highbridge, gagged on the sweet stinks of the Goober Pride peanut butter factory, and waved at a gaggle of colored young uns waving like mad at us. Their heroes had come home.

19

Halfway through June, I'd played in—actually played in—seven straight games. Hoey got into our games, if he got in at all, as a pinch hitter or a late-innings sub. On my first road trip, I'd had two off games in a row, the loss on Friday night to Quitman and the loss of the twin-bill opener against Marble Springs on Saturday afternoon. Mister JayMac put Hoey in for me in the seventh inning of the loss to the Seminoles, but I felt sure he hadn't won the job back. And he hadn't. I played every inning of our next two games, strong wins, and got more hits than any other Hellbender but Charlie Snow, who'd slipped into such a groove that his bat fired off hits with the lickety-split golly-wow of a machine-gun.

Hoey didn't cotton to my success, but he did stop hazing me as a flash-in-the-pan. He had to. My stats were radioactive. Of course, my statistics didn't stay that bright all season—nobody's could've—but they told every skeptic I could play. In the long run, I'd even help the bench riders, malcontents, and jerks who didn't like me.

Up to a point, anyway.

Hoey's living arrangements made it hard to read his changing feelings about me. He had a wife, a family, a house of his own. At our workouts he gave me tips—how to set up against certain hitters, how to flip the ball to Junior to speed his crossover pivot on double plays, how to drag bunt for a safety instead of just a sacrifice. He didn't teach me like a man voluntarily passing on these skills—more like somebody with six months to live tying a ribbon round his life. Did he badmouth me at home? His kids didn't act like he did. They didn't blink at me like I was messy roadkill, a polecat, say, or an armadillo.

Back from that first road trip, I sat down to write Mama a letter and to send her some money. (Jumbo was reading.) I ought to've written her sooner, but how could I say a soldier'd buggered me and I'd gone dummy again? Long-distance calls were out (Uncle Sam asked you to keep the lines open for servicemen and emergency messages), and I didn't relish trying to explain my roomy was an ogre of a pacifist.

My first letter home:

> Dear Mama,
>
> Sorry not to write before now but Im fine. You know that already I think. If my train had recked or somebody had killed me in ball practice by mistake youdve got a telegram saying I was dead. I know you havent. People here seem nice, more or less. My roomate reads alot. Im batting over 500 and starting nearlybout every game. Hows work? Use this money for yourself. Next time I write Ill send more.
>
> Love, Danny

I'd already had three letters from Mama, one mailed the day I left Tenkiller. It came the day we squeaked by Lanett, three to two. Everyone boarding in McKissic House got mail in care of its Angus Road address, but Miss Giselle sorted through it and slipped the right letters into the right cubby-holes at our post-office wall in the foyer. Mama's letters—she never wrote more than a page—made me homesick and kept me going at the same time. I sent her clippings, to make up for the fact my notes never ran longer than a Listerine label.

One of Mama's letters—I still have them—complained about a recent act of Congress:

> Those co-kniving gasbags in Washington have done come up with a legal crime called PAY AS YOU GO. They ask your boss to figure about how much you would owe in taxes at the end of a year, and they order him to hold back enough each month to cover it. It'll tell in our paychecks, this BILL will. Money I used to get won't be there any more. They say its to keep us from feeling poleaxt come taxing time, but why let these THIEVES IN SUITS fiddle with our pay, just to keep us working fokes "ahead of the game"? It's butt-in-skee, if you ask me, uppity and dictatorlike. Watch out, Danny, their going to get you to. Old FDR turns redder every year. By the time this DAMN WAR ends, look for a Hammer & Cycle right in the middle of the Stars & Stripes.

In mid-June, we had a four-day layoff between our win over the Seminoles in Marble Springs and our first home game with the Eufaula Mudcats on Friday. A part of one of those days we used to travel, but the other three, Tuesday through Thursday, felt like holidays. Practice in the A.M.'s at McKissic Field, then drowsy hot afternoons and radio-filled evenings.

Junior taught me to play poker, and he, Fadeaway, Skinny, and I would lock up in cutthroat five-card stud, with piles of buttons (supplied by Kizzy) for chips and pitchers of lemonade for refreshment (likewise). If a game seemed about to turn into a fistfight, Miss Giselle'd threaten us with fines or room arrest. She seldom had to threaten twice. Once, though, Skinny accused Fadeaway of palming an ace and left the table to find a bat to rehabilitate Fadeaway with. Miss Giselle grabbed Skinny on his way back into the parlor, wrassled the bat away from him, and sent him upstairs.

Several of the older Hellbenders worked at defense jobs on a part-time basis, punching in from one to three times a week in the early afternoons of days we didn't have games or mandatory team meetings. They'd pull eight-hour second shifts and get back to their homes or to McKissic House around midnight, limp as boiled asparagus and almost as pale. Moonlighters included Muscles, Curriden, Hay, Nutter, Sudikoff, and Dunnagin. They had special arrangements with either the local torpedo factory, Foremost Forge, or our duck-board manufacturer, Highbridge Box & Crate. Mister JayMac pulled a double handful of strings for them—not to keep them out of the draft, as Ira Crawford had accused, but to find them war work that didn't interfere with their ballplaying.

Anyway, when I learned about these set-your-own-hours defense jobs, I understood why nobody at Monday morning's Rolling Assizes had seconded Sosebee's charge Jumbo'd received special treatment. Every Hellbender got special treatment. Some looked a little more equal than others in getting it, but hardly anybody had to poach his own eggs—if you know what I mean. Players in the bigs and even a few blue-chip Negro stars might make more money than we did, but Highbridge had earned itself a dead-on nickname: Sittin' Pretty City.

It did surprise me nobody'd reraised the point about Mister JayMac's loaning Jumbo his Caddy. Loaning a car was personal . . . in a way flexing your long-term political clout could never be. Loaning your car meant you trusted the loanee. If he didn't qualify for gas stamps, you even had to bend or play peekaboo with the law.

On Thursday, Jumbo borrowed Mister JayMac's Cadillac again, and Mister JayMac lent it to him. At two in the afternoon, the Caddy's keys changed hands in the parlor, just as Fadeaway, Junior, Skinny, and I were about to start another poker marathon.

"Home before dark," Mister JayMac told Jumbo. "We've got the Mudcats tomorrow. You'll need some rest." And he stalked on out of the house.

Jumbo squeezed the car keys in his fist and lumbered up the stairs towards our room. I deserted my poker buddies to go after him, but Jumbo took two or three steps at a time and got there ahead of me. Inside, he stood holding the box of used baseballs I'd always wondered about.

"I have a sick relative in Alabama," he said. "I meant to take these to him on my last trip, but, well . . ."

Your sick relative likes old baseballs? I thought.

"A project," Jumbo said, hefting the box. The lumps on his face flushed, then faded to their old chalky hues at different speeds. "Excuse me, Daniel." I got out of his way.

Jumbo carried the box downstairs, put it into the back seat of Mister JayMac's Caddy, and drove away. His body seemed to fill the front seat, like a Thanksgiving Day float.

He got back about five hours later, looking empty-eyed and blue. He went straight upstairs and lay down. I carried him some iced tea and a pan of vegetables, but found him lying in a kind of trance, not quite sleeping but not quite keyed to the outer world either. He didn't eat or drink a thing.

Jumbo seemed okay again in the morning. (At breakfast, he wolfed down fruit, pancakes, and juice.) But *I'd* had a hard night. My weird-ass roomy'd lain only feet away with his eyes like yellow slits and his meaty paws squeezing the coverlet. I stumbled around all morning like a codeine junkie. My first game against Eufaula loomed.

Damn you, Jumbo, I thought, I'm gonna play like a zombie.

Well, I did. The Mudcats finned us. They just cut us up. We lost that Friday, nine to one. Mister JayMac cleared the bench looking for somebody who could do even a splinter's worth of damage against their pitcher, Jimmy Becker. Nobody could. By the seventh inning, even Muscles and Charlie Snow'd come to the bench, replaced by Burt Fanning, a *utilityman*, and Quip Parris, a *pitcher*. Hoey'd gone in for me at short, Knowles'd taken Junior's place at second. Our fans had set up catcalling clubs or gone home in a snit.

"Fair-weather friends," Muscles said.

"They're entitled," Snow said. "They don't pay their money to watch us crap our pants."

Snow, I noticed, had a strange purple bruise on the inside of his forearm, maybe from running into the wall in the third inning for a home run that'd barely cleared—a long, fragile injury, like a lavender-blue snake with a fringe of back hairs and another of veiny feet. For some reason, I reached over and touched it. Lightly. He pulled back so quick you'd've thought I'd jabbed him with a cattle prod.

"Lay off, Boles."

What the devil. Snow ranked with Musselwhite, Curriden, Nutter, and Dunnagin as one of the Hellbenders' toughest characters. In Army uniforms, I sometimes thought, those five guys could easily chase the Huns out of North Africa.

I don't know where I got the grit, but I pulled Snow's hand towards me the better to see his snake bruise. Boy, he must've really collided with that headache-powder sign out there. Snow seldom hit the wall. Even right up against it, he always timed his leap to avoid rebounding in a drop-dead roll. No mad Pete Reiser heroics for Snow. He didn't need em. He always got a good jump on long flies and measured his distances.

"It's not from today," Snow told me, a little friendlier. "And it aint as bad as it looks. Let go."

I let go.

"My male kin have always bruised easy. Stupid, but it kept me out of the Army, bruising easy. So I'm careful. Mostly."

"If you bruise that easy, Charlie," Muscles said, "you're an idiot to play ball."

"At least I don't box."

Mister JayMac walked by. "Anybody who plays like Charlie—Mr. Snow—would be an idiot *not* to play." He strolled on past, pacing, flusterated, out of sorts.

Snow, I learned, wore a strip of sponge in the palm of his fielder's glove. He also wore hip pads, cloth cushions inside his shoes, sliding pads, and a sleeveless jersey under his flannel shirt—all to help prevent bruising. People thought of Snow as stocky because, dressed like that, he *looked* stocky. Out of uniform, though, he wasn't much thicker in the chest and butt than Dobbs or me. Batting hurt him more than any other part of the game. The shock to his hands and forearms when he banged out another hit would always raise a bruise. He worked to reduce the harm by growing calluses on his palms and trying to smack every pitch on the bat's sweet spot.

A pox on us, we also blew the second game of our four-game series with Eufaula, the opener of Saturday's twin bill. Between games, Mister JayMac said, "Win-win, lose-lose, win-win, lose-lose! Damn the pattern yall've fallen into!"

"We got a win-win coming tonight and tomorrow," Hoey said. "Want us to break the pattern?"

"Ha ha," said Mister JayMac. "Not until we get to Opelika on Wednesday."

Funny thing, we *didn't* break our pattern. We beat Eufaula in Saturday's nightcap and again on Sunday afternoon. Then, in Opelika, we lost two straight to the Orphans (with no parent club in the bigs and no home field until 1941, they'd played every game up till then as roadies, or "orphans"), then beat em in the nightcap of a rare Thursday-evening twin bill.

The next night, in LaGrange against the Gendarmes, we broke our two-up, two-down jig by *losing*. That made us seventeen and fifteen on the season, and nine and seven for June—a winning record, but only just.

"God!" Mister JayMac exploded after the loss. "That gets yall out of your rut—it puts us in a hole instead."

The two weekend series against Opelika and LaGrange, our biggest CVL rivals, could've given us momentum. Instead, we lost each series two games to one and slunk home to change our splints and savor the home cooking of the fans at McKissic Field.

20

O n the Monday before a trip to Opelika and LaGrange, Jumbo came upstairs to find me writing down my stats from the Eufaula series and weighing them against my teammates'. It embarrassed me for him to see me doing this—I still had a sky-high batting average and came down harder on my teammates than on myself. I couldn't quibble with Jumbo's stats, though. He'd played great on the road—my notebook said so.

"Daniel."

I slammed my notebook shut on my knees.

"Some of my library books fall due this week. Go with me to return them." Jumbo packed a laundry bag with books.

I turned an imaginary steering wheel. Would we drive? Jumbo smiled, sort of, and walked two fingers over the quilt on his mattress. Uh-uh, I thought.

"Please come. The heat here's barbarous and the light at your cot poor."

The heat everywhere in Highbridge was barbarous—unless you went to a refrigerated movie or the bowling alley. A walk to the library in Alligator Park would push our temperatures to sunstroke levels. On the other hand, an invite from Jumbo came round about as often as Halley's comet.

"I'll help you acquire a library card," Jumbo said. "I'm on very good terms with Mrs. Hocking, the librarian."

I agreed to go. And, yes, we walked.

In the farmer's market, people shouted at Jumbo: "Way to gig them

Mudcats, Jumbo!" and "Hit me a rainmaker gainst them lousy Gendarmes!" And so on.

An Eye-talian-looking man at a produce stall asked Jumbo to autograph one of his watermelons with a grease pencil. He took my signature on a big yellow squash, but only after Jumbo told him my batting average and sold me as a future big leaguer.

Three colored boys—one turned out to be Euclid—dogged our heels all the way to the edge of Alligator Park, where Negroes seemed to be forbidden unless they were using hedge clippers or pushing a pram with a pink-skinned kid in it.

The Alligator Park branch of the Highbridge library system was a red brick building not far from the church Mister JayMac, Miss Giselle, and a few of the Hellbenders sometimes attended. It had a pot-bellied white portico and windows separated by rose trellises or well-trimmed snowball shrubs. In Tenkiller, this branch would've held every book in town—maybe the whole county—with space left over for a LaSalle showroom.

Mrs. Hocking surprised me too. She didn't have blue hair or a squint or blocky black shoes with ankle straps. She had a pretty face, a plumpish body with flying-squirrel flaps on her upper arms, and a smile that made my own mouth muscles ache. I guessed her age as fifty-plus. She greeted Jumbo like he was an electrocuted loved one brought back to life—I mean, she was overjoyed.

"It's so good to see you, Mr. Clerval! One of the titles you asked me to put on reserve has just come in! Now I won't have to send you a postal notice!"

Despite being on very good terms with Mrs. Hocking, Jumbo looked startled. He unpacked his books on the central desk and kept his mouth shut, a rebuke for all the fuss.

Mrs. Hocking's young assistant hovered at the far end of the desk, eyeballing Jumbo and me the way she would've a pair of prison escapees.

"But you've only had these books out once!" Mrs. Hocking thumbed through her card bin. "You could have renewed them!"

"Yessum," Jumbo said. "But to what end?"

"Why, to give yourself time to read them all."

"I have read them all."

"Oh. Then you're a truly resourceful reader. You must have *formidable* powers of concentration."

"Which of my reserve titles has come in?"

"Why, uh, this one, Mr. Clerval." Mrs. Hocking picked a small book out of a nearby stacking cart. "It's very popular just now. Mr. Salmon, its last reader, checked it out two days ago and brought it back just this morning. Perhaps you and he should meet. You have much in common, including—"

"Please, Mrs. Hocking, hold it for me here until I've made my other selections."

"Of course. Pleased to. Let me know if Margaret or I can be of any further assistance."

"My friend Daniel would like his own card."

"All right. Does he reside in Highbridge or in Hothlepoya County?"

"Like me, he's a Hellbender," Jumbo said. "His stay here will certainly outlast August,"

"Then he's *not* a resident?"

"His mailing address, like mine, is McKissic House on Angus Road. For the next two and half months."

"Yes, but, it appears that—"

"What length of residency entitles one to a card?" Jumbo's voice boomed through the building. Folks in the stacks looked over at us. A little boy grabbed his mother's skirts.

"What we must do is issue a temporary card," Mrs. Hocking said gaily. "If Margaret lists you as one local reference, Mr. Clerval, whom may we designate as the other?"

"Mr. Jordan McKissic."

"Certainly. Very good. Here, Margaret. Help this young man fill out the application. Begin with his name and—"

"His name is Daniel Boles," Jumbo said, already turning toward the nonfiction shelves. "B-O-L-E-S. Complete the form as far as possible without us."

"Of course. Of course." Mrs. Hocking waved us away. "Browse to your hearts' content."

In the philosophy and psychology sections, Jumbo put his hands on my shoulders and tried to whisper:

"Inside, Daniel, Mrs. Hocking feels much as her assistant Margaret does— unquiet, frightened. I realize that now. Her overfriendliness shows the truth. She hopes to hide from both me and herself the extent to which I repel her."

Uh-uh. Jumbo needed to believe Mrs. Hocking actually did like him for himself.

"I'm correct in this," he whispered. "From her behavior, I should have deduced her attitude before." He let go of me to prowl the stacks, mouthing titles and authors' names, tiptoeing around other patrons like a gigantic reshelver.

With our arms full of books, we returned to the main desk and spilled them out like hodcarriers dumping bricks. Mrs. Hocking added Jumbo's reserve book to the pile, and I completed the card application her assistant had started.

"Isn't that more than ten?" Mrs. Hocking stamped away.

"Eleven, with the reserve book," Jumbo said. "But you may put that one on Daniel's card."

"I'm afraid we—" Mrs. Hocking started to say. "Very good," she said instead. "Daniel may even benefit from reading it, should you finish it quickly enough to pass it on, Mr. Clerval." She bustled and stamped. "Good day, gentlemen. Give our rivals in your baseball matches glorious what-for."

"Thanks," Jumbo said. "You're more than kind." He shoved our loot into his satchel and led me out the door.

Outside, I looked at him with real disappointment. He'd just called Mrs. Hocking "more than kind." But if he'd sized her up correctly in the stacks, that was a lie.

"She *desires* to be a friend," Jumbo replied to my look, "even if the natural impulse to that state eludes her. I spoke to her desire, not to the canker of her predisposition."

That had a highfalutin ring to it, but it nailed me anyway. If Jumbo wanted to fledge Mrs. Hocking's better angel, he rquired leave to appeal to it.

At the farmer's market, we bought pears from a pavilion vendor and sat on the concrete platform to eat them. Stacks of produce—turnip greens, unshucked early corn, plump tomatoes in bushel baskets—more or less hid us from autograph seekers. I ate my pear first, then took my notebook from my shirt pocket and wrote out a question:

What book did you reserve?

Jumbo dug through his bag and found it. He dropped it into my lap. I wiped my sticky hands on my pants so I could handle the volume: *On Being a Real Person* by Harry Emerson Fosdick, a self-help thing by this famous New York clergyman.

"'The central business of every human being is to be a real person,'" Jumbo said. "Mr. Fosdick's opening sentence."

Back then, Fosdick's line didn't impress me at all. All I could think of was *Fearless Fosdick*, the cartoon detective Al Capp had created in *Li'l Abner* to send up *Dick Tracy*. Fearless Fosdick strolled around with bullet-hole windows in him—they never seemed to bother him much. Anyway, I imagined this Harry Emerson Fosdick guy sitting at his typewriter with bullet holes in him, banging out *On Being a Real Person* despite looking like a wounded cartoon character himself.

I wrote *Fearless Fosdick?* on a notebook page and handed it to Jumbo, whose expression reminded me of the look you see on a baby's face when it's trying to load up a diaper.

"I believe this Mr. Fosdick"—he tapped the book—"is more fearless than most acknowledge. It takes . . . balls to write a treatise on achieving authentic identity."

We set out again for McKissic House. I carried the book bag, and Jumbo walked along reading Fosdick's best-seller. In his hands, it looked no bigger than a matchbook.

21

In Tenkiller, Mama'd practically had to drive a steam shovel into my bedroom in the mornings to chase me out of bed and off to school. In Highbridge, though, I loved the morning, especially the early morning. I got up before Darius prowled through calling, "Rise and shine!" I woke to some strange internal chime, and I *moved*. Maybe I just wanted to scrub my face and pull on my clothes without Jumbo's spooky yellow eyes tracking the whole business. Maybe I just wanted to escape the killer summer heat in the brief moments before the milk wagons clattered.

Anyway, on the Tuesday morning of our road trip to Opelika, I crept downstairs and smelled bacon frying, biscuits baking, oranges set out to be halved and squoze. Kizzy'd taken over the kitchen already. With her spoons, whisks, and wood-stoked ovens, she was scraping the last fresh edge off the morning. A small price to pay—the mean-as-a-rattler heat would stick its fangs into us by ten or eleven, anyway. I sat on a stool next to Kizzy's biscuit-making counter and claimed dibs on the first biscuit out.

"Don't jes set, Mister Danny." Kizzy mopped her forehead with the back of one hand. "Miss Giselle comes, you gon find yosef to work mighty quick."

Phaugh. Kizzy liked me. Over the past weeks, we'd become good buddies. I helped her mornings, even before Darius came in from the carriage house or Miss Giselle from the bungalow. My dummyhood may've played a part in our friendship too. Kizzy used me as a tattletale-safe soundingboard. I didn't echo. I absorbed.

With one flour-dusted oven mitt and a knotty black forearm, Kizzy fetched her first biscuit tray out and banged it down. "Go on. Burn yo greedy fingers gitting it." I obeyed, right down to getting burned, but juggling that first biscuit made me happy. The sky hadn't even begun to redden, and I had me an edible treasure.

"Eat it fast n do the jooz, or Miss Giselle's gon have yo haid. Mine too." Kizzy bustled in her easy way.

I broke the biscuit into crumbly halves and dawdled over it as long as I could, chewing and chewing.

"You think Miss Giselle's a hard woman with a tart tongue. She do sometimes seem hard, but the mens in this house—even Darius, who can fill her with vinegar jes by walking by—they done become her chirren. She's like that nussry-rhyme woman and her shoe. Don't know what to do, cep feed em n boss em, to show how happy she is she got em."

Happy, I thought. Miss Giselle happy? She didn't much act it. She acted like Mister JayMac'd gone off to the employment bureau and invited a dozen hungry people to come home with him as guests.

"Got no womb chirren," Kizzy said. "Not having none, being ever bairnless, it put her bitter. It slapt her ever-other-day mean. Under that burden, she is downright *happy* for a houseful of ballplayers."

While Kizzy talked, I halved the oranges and ground them on the fluted glass dunce cap of the juicer.

"When Miss Giselle looks yall dagger eyes and snaps her beak like a swamp tuttle," Kizzy said, "it aint so much yall she's mad at. It's things, things in genl. And it don't hep Mister JayMac don't brim with husbandly lovingkindness like he should. It don't hep none he sometimes—"

The outer porch door banged, and Kizzy cut off her spiel like a butcher chopping the end off a butt roast. A good thing. Miss Giselle herself swept in, her face on, her hair just so. A looker in spite of crow's feet, a rumpled cotton dress, her beat-up work shoes.

"Kizzy, you got any people in Detroit?"

"Mawning, ma'am," Kizzy said. "How you feeling today?"

"You had some kin who took off north once. Where did they eventually settle, Kizzy? Detroit?"

"Chicago, ma'am. Some in Philadelphia."

"The coloreds in Detroit have all gone crazy. Radio says it's chaos there. A riot. Buildings and automobiles afire."

"Mercy, but they aint any Lorrowses doing it," Kizzy said, "less it's a bunch I never met up with."

"You'd think this war would be enough mayhem for anyone," Miss Giselle said. "You wouldn't imagine people would go out of their way to add to it with riots in their own cities. How would you feel if a policeman told you your own child was dead as a result? It must be terrible, learning a son in uniform has lost his life. How much worse to discover the bloodshed has occurred on American streets, at the hands of people with whom your child had no quarrel."

"Folks bout everwhere prone to quarrel," Kizzy said.

Miss Giselle cast an eye on Kizzy. "As *you* are prone to quarrel with *me*?"

"Nome. Breakfuss aint done yet."

"Tell me why your people've gone crazy this way. A few days ago it was Beaumont, Texas. Now it's Detroit. Where'll it be tomorrow? Have yall decided to work for Hitler and the Japanese on the *inside*!"

"Ma'am, it *aint* my people," Kizzy said. "Far's I know, never been no insanity atall in us Lorrowses."

Miss Giselle paced between the sink cabinets and the long center counter. "Do you like working here, Kizzy?"

"I didn't, I'd be gone. I got me my options."

"Have you ever heard of the Eleanor Clubs? Do you know what they are? Do you belong to one? Do you intend to join one?" Miss Giselle grabbed a halved orange and ran her tongue around its inner peel. "I won't fire you if you do. Or taint your references. But I regard the Eleanor Clubs as a treason on a par with the chaos taking place in Detroit."

"When I got time to blong to a club?" Kizzy said. "Full Gospel Holdiness Church bout my only one."

"You've never heard of the Eleanor Clubs?"

"Eleanor?" Kizzy said. "Mrs. Roosevelt?"

"She may be the First Lady, but the rebellion she foments among poor women of color deluded into thinking they're preyed upon by their bosses—well, that borders on apostasy."

"Yessum," Kizzy said.

"Do I prey upon you, Kizzy?" Miss Giselle said. "Do I exploit you any worse than the great and wonderful Mr. Jordan McKissic does Yours Truly, his wife and galley slave?"

"I don't blong to no Eleanor Club, Miss Giselle. I don't even like clubs. Most of em's got dues."

"Or committees," Miss Giselle said. She stopped pacing. She perched herself on the stool where I'd eaten Kizzy's first biscuit of the morning. "So Mrs. Dittrich's girl Janet didn't leave her at the urging of a local unit of the Eleanors?"

"Ma'am, Janet's done gone to work fo Fomost Foge fo twelve dollahs a week. Missus Dittrich guv her three."

"Is everything in our life money? Money or sex? What's become of loyalty? devotion? faithfulness? *I'd* like to know."

"Don't know," Kizzy said, "but peoples tell me it's a free country and trains run both ways."

You'd've thought Miss Giselle might have bristled at that—a remark so uppity—but she laughed. She got down from the stool, tied on a smudged gingham apron, and pitched in with the breakfast preparations. In the dining room, I laid the table. As I did, I could hear her and Kizzy babbling away, more like sisters than a hoity-toity employer and her downtrodden cook.

I was back in the kitchen when Darius straggled in from his apartment over the bus barn. He had an alarm clock out there, an old metal bonger that rattled him awake at six or so. But alarm clocks'd grown scarce by mid 1943, so many folks junked them during scrap drives and so few companies still made them. Which was why Darius had become a roving human alarm clock for McKissic House's boarders.

"Rise and shine," he mumbled, entering from the porch. "Flash them brushed-up ivories, folks." Sleepy banter, but a kind of tucked-under grumbling too.

Miss Giselle'd treated Darius pretty well since we'd been back in Highbridge, but she turned on him now faster than a rabid birddog. "I'll have no more of your rackety wake-ups around here," she said. "I mean it, Darius. I'm sick of the noise and your idiot cheeriness."

"I never meant em to be lullabyes."

"Don't do it anymore."

Darius pulled in his chin. "Wake the boarders up?"

"Go shouting through the house like a fishmonger. I *hate* it. I totally *despise* it."

"How'd you like me to git everbody up?"

"Walk up the stairs. Knock on each door. Announce in a low and civil tone that it's nearly time to eat. Understand?"

"Yessum. Simple directions in simple English. That'll do it fo me awmost ever time."

"Leave those biscuits alone!" Miss Giselle snapped. "And never mind your piddlin ritual this morning. Today, Mr. Boles will do it for you."

"He can knock, ma'am, but he cain't talk. I'd be pleased to truck upstairs with him to hep."

"Then you'll be damned before you're pleased, Darius. I want you out of this house until Kizzy calls you back to eat. For now, Mr. Boles must do the best he can with his knuckles and his youthful imagination. Out, please."

Darius left, head up. Kizzy kept mum.

The use I put my imagination to was climbing to the third floor and waking Jumbo first. I scribbled him a note about what Miss Giselle wanted me to do, and he lumbered from room to room with me. I'd knock, and he'd say, "Breakfast. Rise and shine. Don't compel us to come in after you." No one stayed too long in bed after hearing him say that.

At breakfast itself, Mister JayMac put in an appearance. A show of solidarity with his players before a big road trip to Opelika and LaGrange. He didn't sit at the head or foot of the table—Muscles and Jumbo had those spots—but squoze in between Vito Mariani and me like any other journeyman 'Bender.

Funny thing, though—Miss Giselle did him the V.I.P. honor of bringing him his own humongous platter, with three cigarlike sausages, a steaming dipper scoop of cheese grits, and a puffy cream-colored omelet, like the sort of pale-yellow cravat you'd rent from a tuxedo shop. At first I thought, Well, I guess a guy can take this I'm-just-a-regular-Joe stuff too far. Except Mister JayMac scowled when his wife put that platter down, like he figured she meant to make him look bad—uppish and scornful—with such showboaty favoritism.

"What'd you put in this highfalutin aigg?" he asked before Miss Giselle could get back to the kitchen.

"Ham, diced bell pepper, tomato, onions, a dash of tabasco sauce." Miss Giselle cocked her head. "Why?"

"The green's bell peppers?"

"It is. Did you think I'd chopped the bitterest dandelion stems I could find into it?"

"Nome, not really. Thing is, Darius don't much care for bell peppers, honey."

Miss Giselle crossed her arms. "But I made that for you, Jay."

"Well, who ast you to? I eat what the boys eat. So take this masterpiece omelet to Darius. He can eat around the pesky peppers."

Darius took breakfast at a junk counter on the screened-in porch—out of the kitchen, out of the dining room, out of the way. And he was out there now, finishing up.

"He won't want it," Miss Giselle said. "He's already eaten enough for three normal men."

"Take it to him anyway. Let him decide. I can't abide special treatment."

"Well, I won't take it to him, Jay, for I can't abide abuse or humiliation. And I *won't* abide them."

For the next few seconds, all anyone could hear was forks scraping china and Muscles glugging back his juice.

"This food can't go to waste," Mister JayMac finally said. "Take it to Darius."

Miss Giselle closed her eyes, hugged herself, and swayed, like a grieving mama at a funeral. Her posture—and her sudden silence—gave everybody an even bigger discomfort than her and Mister JayMac's arguing had. So I pushed back my chair, picked up the ritzy breakfast, and headed for the kitchen with it—my stab at doing my blessed best as a peacemaker.

Behind me, I heard Jumbo say, "I'll walk Miss Giselle back to your house, sir."

"You do that," Mister JayMac said.

On the screened porch, I set Mister JayMac's breakfast in front of Darius, who'd already eaten several biscuits and a couple of fried sunny-side-uppers. He gave me a wary sidelong look, but pulled the plate to him and dug in. Just then, Jumbo ducked into view with Miss Giselle on his arm and Miss Giselle in some sort of glassy-eyed trance.

"An apt diversion," Jumbo told me. "You cerebrate as well off the field as on." He helped Miss Giselle down the rickety porch steps and through the dewy victory garden to the bungalow out back. They made an odd pair, those two. Of course, Jumbo and *anybody* made a freakish twosome.

I slouched back to the dining room.

22

On the way to Opelika on Wednesday, the *Brown Bomber* had a blowout, and Jumbo bruised his thighs supporting the bus's front bumper when the jack slipped. We lost our game against the Orphans that night and split with them in a doubleheader on the following day.

As we rolled into LaGrange on Friday, the air had a silken, sluggish feel. Its taste, falling from a sky more dirty-cream than blue, had a heavy rain tang. You don't forget that taste, its dust-laying potential grabs you even at the crazy-making height of a drought.

"Bless it," Mister JayMac said, "I don't *want* a rainout."

"Sir, if we uz primed to lose again, it'd be a blessing," Fanning said. "For everbody."

Mister JayMac whirled on him. "If us losing tonight would guarantee bumper crops, I'd still rather win and swallow the consequences than lose this one and wax fat!"

Darius and a few of us others dragged suitcases and duffels out of the Bomber's luggage bins and passed them around to the guys they belonged to. Some Hellbenders walked to the houses of their host families. Others got picked up in fancy cars and driven there.

Jumbo and I, like Mutt-and-Jeff drummers, hiked through town to the Lafayette Hotel. The desk clerk wore a white shirt and the kimono-swirled vest of a blackjack dealer. He had an Army recruit's haircut, though, and didn't at first answer Jumbo's questions about our reservations because we'd spooked him barging in. New there, he had a nellyboyish way about him that may've explained how he'd sidestepped the draft.

"Cler-VALL," he said at length, paging through his register. "Cler-VALL, -VALL, -VALL. Mmmmmm. That's French, isn't it?"

"With one -*vall*, it could be," Jumbo said. "My father hailed from Switzerland." The boom in his voice startled the clerk crapless all over again.

"Oh, yes," he managed. "Yall're ballplayers. Hellbenders, no less. Room 322. Mr. Suiter has you down for three nights."

"Key, please," Jumbo said.

"Do you play when it rains?" the clerk asked. "Or is that, ah, football?"

"Football," Jumbo said.

"Then yall may get a rest this weekend. Storms're coming—tonight, tomorrow, who knows? Swell view of Lafayette Square from the third floor. Hope yall enjoy."

We trudged the stairs because the elevator didn't work. Our room had two single beds, a chest of drawers with a metal basin and a china pitcher on top of it, and ugly water-stained wallpaper: chrysanthemums, over and over.

As per usual, Jumbo dragged a length of clothesline from his suitcase and rigged a curtain out of it and the grass mat he'd also packed. Ouch. I thought we'd built an iffy sort of bond, a truce with doorways in it. For now, though, he didn't draw the mat across its string.

Instead, he dumped his books onto the tufted bedspread of the bed nearer the door, then lined the books by height along the baseboard there. He'd finished *On Being a Real Person* our first night in Opelika. Now, he eeny-meeny-minied his books and wound up with Saroyan's *The Human Comedy*. He lowered himself to his bed, twanged the bedsprings getting comfortable, and flapped the cover open.

Me, I lay down for a nap.

While Jumbo read, I felt the lonely afternoon grumbles of thunder tremble my blood and tug at the horizons. I slept, but the thunder seemed even closer than Jumbo's raspy breathing, proof Mister JayMac's dreaded rainout had marched to the very edge of town.

"Let's go." Jumbo's hand shook me. I jarred awake, muzzy and sweat-doused, thinking I'd lain down in Tenkiller and awakened to a loudspeaker broadcasting tornado news. Jumbo's yellow eyes bored a hole in my heart and dripped the tough waxy fact of LaGrange into it.

Home was far away.

Two hours before game time, Jumbo and I suited up in the hotel and strolled to the ballpark in our street shoes, our spikes slung around our necks like ice skates. Folks boggled at us, but we ignored their boggling. Most knew a Gendarme-Hellbender showdown loomed, and some recognized Jumbo from last year's games.

By the weekend of our first series with the Gendarmes, every smart fan in the Chattahoochee Valley knew this year's flag belonged to Highbridge, LaGrange, or Opelika. Eufaula, despite splitting a four-game series with us a week ago, had had a rotten month. Now LaGrange and Opelika shared first place with identical eighteen-and-thirteen records. We were a game back, at seventeen and fourteen.

Nothing unusual about the tightness of the race or the fever in the streets—banners in store windows, rosin-potato vendors in front of the stadium peddling spuds from iron cauldrons black as pitch. One man'd parked his jalopy pickup out front, with a tailgate sign reading *UN-BRELLAS—50 Sents* and rifle stacks of umbrellas—rough-carved handles, polka-dot fabric panels—in its load bed.

"Git you a un-brella!" he yelled from the pickup. "Git ready for a Dixie dirtsoaker! Buy from me!"

A guard let Jumbo and me in through a player gate, and we walked to the visitors' quarters. You felt like a hometowner in that locker room, though. It had benches the color of ripe wheat, spanking-new lockers, and shower fixtures as coppery bright as new-minted pennies. No stale sweat smell. No mildew or fust. (The toilet stalls had doors!)

Jumbo and I put on our spikes and finally wound up in the outfield. A few early-bird fans gave us thumbs-down signs and catcalled. Loosening up, I admired the clean dark-green fence panels, the press box behind home plate, the light batteries set around us like humongous electric sunflowers.

Jumbo and I played long toss, throwing pop-ups that seemed ready to vanish into the blue at the heart of the surrounding cloud attack. Thunder went on mumbling. Polka-dot umbrellas sprouted around us like toadstools, the air smelled *moist*, the temperature dropped into the low eighties.

Mister JayMac showed up a half hour before game time and hit us infield.

"Pray for a rainout!" a fan shouted. "You suckers!"

Mister JayMac called all his starters in. He gave Little Cuke Gordon, the head umpire, his lineup card. He told us to come out swinging against Sundog Billy Wallace—because "If you cannonade Sundog early, he'll buckle."

"He's greatly chasable," Mister JayMac said. "The longer he hangs around, though, the guttier he feels. You'll have to skin Satan to uproot him."

Unexpected trouble with the PA system, or scoreboard crew, or something. Emmett Strock, the Gendarme manager, came over to tell Mister JayMac it might be another twenty minutes before Little Cuke could shout, "Play ball!" Would we like to take a few more minutes of infield?

"Criminy," Mister JayMac said. "What a charade. Anybody wants more warm-up time, hit the field!"

Junior and I sprinted out. Curriden ambled over to third, a papa dog behind his puppies. Dunnagin trotted to the plate to catch in, and Darius, to the surprise of the whole crowd, followed him over to rap out fungoes. Jumbo didn't take first, though. He sent Sudikoff out and vanished into the dugout. I figured he didn't feel too well himself, a result of Tuesday's accident and a big dip in the barometer reading.

Even so, Junior and I gave the crowd an eyeful, pirouetting around second, and Jumbo's weird disappearance slipped from our minds.

"Five minutes to game time!" Little Cuke Gordon shouted to both benches. "No more delays!"

We trotted in. The Gendarmes trotted out. Jumbo wasn't in our dugout, he'd up and melted on us. If he didn't show up before Wallace threw his first pitch, we'd have to pinch hit for him, losing him for the entire game. Mister JayMac grabbed me and wrung my arm like a wet shirt sleeve.

"Find Clerval. He's batting fifth, so hurry!"

I knew my way around the Prefecture about as well as I did King Tut's tomb, and in that stadium, in my Highbridge uniform, I felt about as welcome as a colored at a cross burning. Jumbo wasn't in the locker room. I banged out into a hallway leading to the concession stands and ticketstiles. I spike-walked through these areas, but still no Jumbo.

The Gendarmes got their balky PA system working—if it'd ever balked. A voice like a woodwind reed began to announce the starting lineups. Jiminy! What if I didn't make it back before Wallace stepped to the rubber? Mister JayMac'd lose *two* prime players to the same damnfool wild-goose chase.

Behind a hotdog booth, I climbed a ladder towards the top of the grandstands and the press box. Up there, I'd be able to scan every inch of the stadium. Climbing in spikes scared me—they kept slipping off or catching on the ladder rungs—but I monkeyed up em as fast as I could. The evening sky opened out, and the alleyway under me narrowed like a pit.

Once on the roof, an acre of salty gravel stuck in asphalt, I didn't have to scan anything. Jumbo stood near the pole of the central battery of lights. Behind him, thunderheads reared against a pink wash of sky, like trout blood thinned in a basin of water. Charged dust hung in the air, the streaks of hanging dust like a battle line of angels. Take away the thunderheads, though, and the dark hadn't begun to settle yet; meanwhile, the breeze skating across the mock-beach of the roof carried on it the smells of old bark and minty pigleaf.

Jumbo had his back to this wind, his hair lifted and flew. He'd spread his arms, like an angel on the brink of soaring, or like somebody crucified.

Somewhere, a groundskeeper yanked a switch.

All the lamps above Jumbo, eye after stinging eye, leapt on. Facets. Dozens of facets. They mirror-blazed like the compound eyes of a giant dragonfly. Brilliant. The blaze left me with shivering mother-of-pearl oyster shells at the back of my walloped eyeholes.

It seeped into me again—*sight*—in a slow-motion flash. But, lordy, Jumbo: His eyes turned silver. Then copper. Then gold. Then glassy amber, like a startled cat's. His body jerked, rejerked, and jitterbugged without a single motion of either foot—like he'd convulsed from the knees up. His arms stiffened and flopped, and did it again, the way a man in the chair at Reidsville would twitch when our paid executioner got the go-ahead and slapped him a scorching jolt.

Thunders cracked over the stadium. People gasped a long "*Ooooooh*," crooning their amaze over a fireworks show. Then, whatever'd happened to Jumbo—his rooftop recharging—stopped happening. It cycled itself through. It ended and let him go, and Jumbo lurched a stagger step towards me. And another. I wanted to scuttle crabwise back over the roof and down. But I leaned into the wind, grabbed the front of Jumbo's shirt, and yanked him step by step to the ladder.

I waved Jumbo onto it. Its tubes shifted as soon as he'd climbed on. Him first, me second. Me going first would've been too much like Jack rushing in terror down the beanstalk ahead of the giant. What if Jumbo slipped? Falling, he'd strip me off too and ride me to a screaming marriage with the concrete. So Jumbo went first, and I pecked along after him, spiking his head softly every time he froze up.

Anyway, we made it down and clattered into our dugout only moments before Little Cuke Gordon cried, "Play ball, dammit!"

Mister JayMac had me leading off again, so I hurried to set myself in the batter's box, still juiced from my escapade and stunned weak-kneed by the nearness of disqualification. Then Sundog Billy did ego surgery on me with his major league curve, striking me out on five pitches.

The storm—with all its rumblesome witchery—divided and drifted in lightning-figured banks around the Prefecture. Like the Red Sea parting. A miracle of sorts.

With that split storm chewing at the town's edges, Jumbo played like a man on fire, his best game so far on this road trip: a pair of solo shots and a two-bagger off the right-field wall. But, Jumbo's blasts aside, we blew that game and wound up two full games behind the Gendarmes, with no report yet on how Opelika had fared.

In the clubhouse, Mister JayMac said we *had* to win both Saturday's and Sunday's games. If we did, we'd leave town tied with the Gendarmes for first. If we split them, we'd gain no ground. And if we lost em both . . .

Me, I *really* had the blues. Despite everybody-but-Jumbo's dead bats, we'd gone into the last half-inning locked at two all. Then, with two outs and a chance at an extra at-bat, I'd pumped a throw over Jumbo, sending three guys in the stands bailing for cover. My error let Fat Boy Fortenberry, a pinch hitter, score the winning run from second. *Fortenberry!* With his love handles, basset-hound gait, and asthma wheeze.

Hoey came over to console me: "Couldn't cut the mustard, could you, Dumbo? Shows what you're really made of—Twinkie filling."

I shucked my gear and ducked into the shower room. Jumbo scrammed, and no one under the spigots said "Boo!" to me. As I dressed, the only guys to say, "Don't worry bout it, you'll pop em tomorrow," were Knowles and Dunnagin.

Dunnagin gripped my shoulder as I buttoned my shirt. "If we'd put a few runs up, one flubbed throw wouldn't've meant *nada*. This bunch still owes you. Boot away five or six more, and Hoey *might* have a case."

I footed it alone from the stadium to the Lafayette. The storms that'd missed the city had regrouped. You heard them bellyaching above the copses of magnolias and yaupon holly southwest of the ballpark. Sheet and candlewick lightning flickered on the diamond-cut tops of those trees. Snaky cloud tentacles reached into the sky over LaGrange and fanned long fringes of blackness into the gaps behind them.

Even before I'd turned onto the square facing our hotel, it'd begun to rain. It bucketed down.

Upstairs in room 322, Jumbo sprawled on the floor, doing Army-style crossover toe touches. The room had a thin carpet, and it and every other piece of fiber near him, including the mat he'd strung, reeked with his body odor. Why the exercise? He'd just played every inning of a killer game.

Jumbo nodded at me, but kept working. "I'm discharging an excess of energy. Otherwise, I won't be able to sleep." Then he stopped. "You're drenched, Daniel."

I sneezed. Outside, heaven's waterworks emptied into the gutters. I shed my clothes, dried myself, and wrapped a bed sheet around me. I took down the grass mat dividing our room, rolled it up, slid it under Jumbo's bed, and flopped down on my own. I faced away, clenching like a rolypoly. For the first time since Tenkiller, I shivered with cold, not fear.

Jumbo didn't say anything. After a while, he got up and shuffled down the hall to the men's bath. When he returned, he shut the light and lay down on the other bed—without a word, but also without trying to hang his curtain again.

23

The rain hung on all that night and all the next day, but bad weather didn't much bug Jumbo. He had his books and took a reminiscing kind of pleasure in the storm. Me, I wanted to ask the Lafayette's other guests to join me in breaking up our room furniture. The nearer game time drew on the harder the drilling rain fell. Jumbo and I peered into Lafayette Square from our third-story lookout. The elms, the azaleas, and the statue of the square's namesake seemed on the verge of melting into the Piedmont aquifer.

At four o'clock, a desk clerk—not the one who'd signed us in—brought word of the game's cancellation. Mister JayMac had signed the message. He'd added we should eat well, hoard our strength, and get ready for two games on Sunday.

Never mind Mister JayMac's instructions. Jumbo didn't eat or sleep. He looked out the window, paced, or read. Between four-thirty and five, I took a nap, a nap clabbered with war dreams (insects stinging; bullets snapping past), dreams born of the rain's fizz and snap. When I woke, Jumbo said, "Hello," and held up a book—not *The Human Comedy*, or *It Is Later Than You Think*, but the Harry Emerson Fosdick he'd finished reading in Opelika.

"Listen," he said: " 'A constructive faith is the supreme organizer of life, and, lacking it, like Humpty-Dumpty we fall and break to pieces, and the wonder is—' "

I sat up the better to hear him read.

" '—and the wonder is whether all the king's horses and all the king's men can ever put us together again.' " Jumbo's lemon-drop eyeballs rolled up into his forehead, leaving his sockets empty-windowed and spooksome. Blank of eye, he said, "Neither a king nor his horsemen first put us together. We should hardly expect them to reassemble us when the world has destroyed us." His eyes clicked back. If only they'd seemed to belong to him, their reappearance might have steadied me. They *didn't*, though, and if not for the clattering downpour and the shaming sadness of Jumbo's words, I'd've bolted.

"Perhaps I'll take more pleasure in Mr. Smith's *Life in a Putty Knife Factory*," Jumbo said. He reached over (the galoot had to've been double-, maybe triple-jointed) and chose another title from his row of books. Just as he'd thumbed the book open, there came a rapping at our door: *Tap, tappa, tap tap . . . tap tap.* You know, *Shave and a haircut, two bits.*

"YES?" Jumbo boomed.

That gave the knocker a start. "Uh . . . Western Union."

"YES?" Jumbo boomed again.

"Delivery for, uh, ah, it says here, 'Mr. Daniel Boles, shortstop of the Highbridge Hellbenders.'"

I hunched my neck. I'd never had a Western Union delivery in my life.

"Maybe it's the bigs, Daniel," Jumbo said. "Maybe Mr. Cox of the Phillies has had his scouts observing you."

Then those scouts'd seen me throw away last night's game. Jumbo'd go up before me, even with his drag-ass base-running.

"WHOM IS THE MESSAGE FROM?" Jumbo said.

"Mrs. Laurel Boles," the messenger in the hall said, "of, uh, cripes, I don't know, somewhere in Oklahoma."

Jumbo lifted an eyebrow. "Your mother, Daniel?"

I'd already started for the door. Mama wrote, but never telephoned or sent packages—she was too frugal.

The joe in the hall didn't look like a Western Union guy. In fact, it was the clerk who'd checked us in. I reached for my delivery, whatever it was.

"Not so fast," he said, a hand behind his back. The other clutched a sheet of onion-skin paper, which he lifted to chest level. "I must read this to you—a singing telegram that isn't sung."

He read it in a snotty sing-song, though:

> "My dear darling Daniel,
> My dear dummy child,
> When out in your flannels,
> Don't throw it wild.

> "I like the ball white, son.
> Why did you soil it?
> What the 'Benders had won,
> You flushed down the toilet.

"Your shame like your words, lad,
Must stick in your throat.
So to cuddle at night, kid,
You've got . . . MY GOAT!"

Here the clerk pulled a stuffed toy goat, with a furry chin beard, from behind his back and thrust it at me. "Telegram's signed, 'Laurel Boles, your loving mother,'" the clerk said. "Evening."

And before Jumbo could ask him who'd put him up to such a crappy stunt, he tossed his message down and scrammed. I turned and flung that goat at the wall. It burst a belly seam and spilled some stuffing. One of its horns twiddled out of true and flopped like a bird dog's ear.

I walked to the window, grabbed the curtains, and began to cry like the rain. Jumbo stepped off his bed, with a rustle of ticking and a drum-brush creak of the springs, and towered at my back. He had no more notion what to do or say than I did. All I knew was, my .432 batting average and my prestidigitation at shortstop didn't amount to a phony two-bit piece if I was homesick and crammed to my eyeteeth with fury. So Jumbo did something to distract me. He turned me around.

"Turkey Sloan," he said. "Turkey Sloan probably wrote the ditty read to us by that . . . by that shitass impersonator of a Western Union man. Who helped Sloan?"

Buck Hoey, I thought, my comforter in the locker room.

"Buck Hoey," Jumbo guessed. "Evans, Sosebee, and Sudikoff: malcontents, troublemakers."

I'd known Hoey was my enemy, but it despunked me to hear a whole list of fellas who wanted to tire-iron me.

Jumbo read this news in my eyes. "Laugh at them. Laugh *with* them. Their playfulness"—he nodded at the poem— "may ride on spite, but it yet remains playfulness." He picked up and looked at the poem. "This has some crude wit, Daniel." He handed it to me.

I read it twice, memorizing it against my will, then tore it into confetti and hurled the pieces at Jumbo. He blinked in the face of my conniption, as one scalelike flake landed on and hung from his eyelid.

"Daniel," he said. "Daniel."

He may've meant to calm me, or to chide, but the weirdness of my name on his lips, the puzzle of what it told, lifted my hackles the way the stadium lights had cable-jumped him. I could feel my skin glowing. I reached down and picked up the stuffed goat that'd bounced off the wall. Hissing, I got my fingers into its split seam and gutted it. I popped its eye buttons, dehorned it, twisted its tail off, mangle-snapped its legs. Stuffing flew around us like the insulation blown from an attic when a devil wind's sprung its roof. Anyway, Sloan and Hoey's goat lay here and there in pieces, although I still had its whitish silver pelt in my hands. I knelt on the floor, gasping and hammering my fist.

Jumbo pinched my shoulders and drew me to my feet. His hands fumbled at my shirt, setting it straight, giving me an Army gig line.

"Let's talk to that unprincipled clerk." I let him guide me through the door and down the stairs. At the registration desk, the clerk sat listening to a radio. When he saw Jumbo and me marching towards him, his face seemed to pull across his cheekbones; he looked embalmed and rouged. He clicked off the radio like a man caught lollygagging.

"Who hired you to play a Western Union man?" Jumbo asked.

"That's private information." The clerk squirmed.

"No law protects mischief makers. Your allegiance has a vile monetary cast."

"Loyalty to those who pay you isn't a crime. Usually, it's what they pay you *for*."

"To how many buyers do you extend your loyalty?"

"That's no business of yours either." Squirming more.

"But if I paid you for it, it could be, yes?" Jumbo closed the Lafayette's counter book and leaned over it on one muscular forearm. "YES?"

The clerk pulled back. "What'd you have in mind?"

"NOTHING!!!" Jumbo boomed. "We *know* who paid you. Why should we bribe you for information already in our possession?"

"Bribe me? Listen—"

"LaGrange has a movie theater?" Jumbo cut him off in the shank of his huff. "We need the diversion of a film."

"A movie theater?" The clerk was confused.

"I know your city supports at least one."

"We have three. The Roxy's nearest, just down the street."

"When does its next feature presentation begin?"

"Seven thirty," the clerk said, and Jumbo turned me towards the Lafayette's revolving door.

"But it's Saturday, right? The fourth Saturday of the month?"

"Yes," Jumbo said.

"Then yall can't go there tonight. You wouldn't *want* to."

"I beg your pardon."

"Fourth Saturday of the month. It's nigger night at the Roxy, place'll be crawling with em."

"I beg your pardon."

"Well, the rain could hold a few of em out. But it's finally stopping"—he nodded at the lobby's only window—"and you'd have to declare martial law to keep em out after a day as dull as this un. Why don't yall try the Cairo or the Pastime? They have colored-only balconies, but yall wouldn't run slam into the foppery of nigger night."

"My profoundest secret"—Jumbo leaned into the clerk's face—"is that I am an *honorary* nigger."

"A what?"

"And Daniel, whom others paid you to mock, cares less for his seatmates' color than for the quality of the film."

"Okay." The clerk produced a copy of the LaGrange Daily News. "At the Cairo, *Reveille with Beverly*. At the Pastime, a Mickey Rooney thing. At the Roxy, a triple bill yall wouldn't care to—"

"Hush," Jumbo said.

"Yessir," the clerk said.

And after a quick bite to eat in the nearby Magnolia Café, Jumbo and I hit the sidewalk, not in a downpour but a tingly drizzle, and walked through the early twilight to the Roxy for a triple feature of some sort.

24

It was nigger night at the Roxy for sure. Even the rain couldn't spoil these folks' Saturday evening. They'd turned out in chattering, straggle-in mobs. Groups of them clogged the sidewalk under the marquee and stretched around the corner from the box-office window.

One double file hugged the Roxy's brick wall in a futile effort to keep the drizzle from beading their hair or soaking their out-for-fun finery. They couldn't go to the ballpark to watch their Gendarmes bruise the Hellbenders again, but they could catch a delicious scream fest—three classic chillers for the price of one—here at the Roxy. The storm had no power to chain them in their mill houses.

The Roxy'd thrown LaGrange's coloreds—and any other soul open-minded enough to wait for a ticket—a horror festival. The marquee told the story:

FRANKENSTEIN
BRIDE OF FRANKENSTEIN
SON OF FRANKENSTEIN
* * *

Boris Karloff as the Bogeyman to End All Bogeymen

When Jumbo saw the marquee and realized what he'd let himself in for, he had second thoughts. He mumbled something kindly about *Reveille with Beverly*. But I wanted this triple feature. I'd never seen a one of these films (even though I'd read Mary Shelley's *Frankenstein* in high school), and I hoped the films would shear my mind away from dumbass thoughts of getting back at Hoey and his pals.

We finally reached the ticket window, and I handed in my money. Jumbo pushed up right behind me.

"If you haven't already seen *Frankenstein*," he said, "you may find it a . . . a primitive dramatic vehicle."

Did he want to talk me out of seeing it? The white girl in the booth, with her hair in a kind of mesh oriole's nest, said, "Ticket money, sir." Jumbo paid her and shoved behind me into the salty popcorn smells of the lobby.

In its crush, he said, "*Bride of Frankenstein* surpasses in quality the film to which it is the sequel, and *Son of Frankenstein* features Karloff's last essayal of the role that made him famous and a good performance by Bela Lugosi as Ygor. Should we stay for all three, however, we'll violate curfew."

Jumbo stood out like an ostrich in a parade of penguins. His whisper boomed above even the feisty talk of those black folks, and some of them looked at him like he'd arrived aboard an ambulance.

At the refreshment stand, I nodded at the Coca-Cola toggle and the glassed-in popcorn popper next to it. Soon as I had my stuff, Jumbo marched me towards the screening room. The seats there'd begun to fill. Folks surged through the lobby and into the auditorium. We slipped in at the back, after two thirds of the crowd'd already gone in, and found seats against the rear wall, under the projection booth. Bodies crammed every nook, teenagers eeled up and down the aisles searching for friends or showing themselves off, and the hoots and cat-calls didn't fade away until the house lights dimmed.

The curtains over the screen, the royal-purple one and the see-through job behind it, purred aside. Coming attractions, newsreels (mostly war stuff), and a Popeye cartoon that prodded the crowd to talk-back applause.

Then *Frankenstein*, with an opening scene—Latin mumblings, peasant faces in a cemetery—that really did slap a chill on everyone's high spirits. Except for the projector purr and the film's sound track, all you could hear now were creaking seats, nervous titters, and coughs. Bodies dug up, hanged murderers cut down, the theft of an ABNORMAL brain by the doctor's stupid helper. Halfway along, the crowd'd really gotten into it. Squeals, shrieks, laughter. Some folks stood up to yell at or plead with the actors on screen.

"Come on now," a man told the monster, "you don't want to do that. Uh-uh. Gon bring you nuthin but misery."

"Vile!" somebody else said. "He *so* vile!"

"Lawd, cain't you see he didn't mean it?"

"Naw, naw, naw. Go back! Go back!"

The longer I sat there the queerer I began to feel. I kept sneaking peaks at Jumbo, who sat rigor-mortis still. He didn't much favor Karloff playing Dr. Frankenstein's critter, or else Karloff's goose-stepping monster didn't exactly favor Jumbo, but you'd've had to be blind not to see a likeness—the lumpish blocks of their heads, the bearishness of their bodies. Still, Jumbo had a suppleness lacking in the other, a sad lopsided quirk of face that made Karloff's monster look regular, even handsome, by comparison. There was a mechanical, a *robot*like, quality to the screen thing Jumbo didn't have. He sometimes lumbered and wrenched, but when he did, it was more like a hurt beast than a broken robot. Anyway, Jumbo's resemblance to the made-up Karloff didn't scare me—it embarrassed me into a fever. Even the Roxy's "iceberg air" didn't help. How must Jumbo feel, towering there marble hard as the Lincoln memorial, hands clutched like gauntlets to his knees?

He must've had an inkling half the people there, including his own roomy, 'd already compared him in their minds to the bogeyman on screen. And the inkling could have come from a lifetime of overheard slurs and otherwise hard-to-account-for snubbings. I knew such stuff myself.

Three quarters or more through it, I dropped the thread of *Frankenstein*. It had no music score, and every little gasp or cushion creak—when folks weren't sassing the Karloff monster or arguing amongst themselves— slammed me back to the iceberg there-and-then and the sting of my own embarrassment. Lots of scenes limped along on talk.

But near the end, when the villagers torched the old mill and the monster appeared to burn with it, I found the thread again. I forgot about Jumbo and watched. A respectfulness like awe fixed the audience in a hurricane light, centering us in the hush of its eye. Pity for the monster, and relief it wouldn't rampage again in this picture, and dread in knowing that, like Christ in a bad suit, it would rise again. To take a wife. The sequel was already spooled.

"Let's go." For the first time since we'd claimed our seats, Jumbo tried to get up. I put both hands on his chest and held him in it. The clock on the square hadn't chimed nine yet. Even Jumbo couldn't be that keen on *Life in a Putty-Knife Factory*. Groaning, he sank back.

During intermission, folks headed for the lobby to stock up on jujube beads, soda, chewing gum. With the houselights on, they saw Jumbo's head lolling against the back wall, his eyes squinting like a big iguana's. They slowed to ogle him or sped up to get past quick.

Whispers and nudgings cycloned around us, and two or three more seats in our area wound up empty.

"S a publicity gimmick," somebody said.

"S a wounded sojer, home from the war."

"Naw, it's that Hellbender first baseman who poked him a coupla long uns lass night."

"Ugh. Somebody done beat him silly with a ugly stick."

The houselights blinked, signaling the second show. Fewer people came back in, and the empty seats around us multiplied. Jumbo slid down and down, like he hoped to disappear into the spilled Coke gleaming on the floor like gummy blood.

Bride of Frankenstein began with its loud rum-ta-ta-tum-tum score—music-box tinklings during the opening with Mary Shelley and the bozos made up like Byron and Percy, and mad flourishes every time the monster staggered on or Colin Clive as Dr. F. had another headache. By the time Clive got Elsa Lanchester, with her Harpo Marx hairdo, jump-started, Jumbo's head was no higher over his seat back than mine was over mine. His knees rose out of the chop of the Franz Waxman's score like islands. It hurt to see him cramped, but with its cockeyed sets and its skinny Dr. Praetorius, this movie had its points. How could I leave until the whole silly show'd unsprocketed?

Bride ended. The houselights came up again. A moviegoer on his way to the lobby stopped and pointed a shaky finger at Jumbo. "You don't blong here. Yo're a demon from the crypts and gallows." The man reeked of a bad peach wine. "Begone, Satan, you damn viper!"

"Shhh," somebody said.

"Don't yall shush me. This man aint a man, he a debil, got him a snake for a tail."

"Ol man, you drunk! Ol man, you a fool!"

"He's a white debil. Don't blong here, don't blong noeres but Hell." He looked back at Jumbo. "Begone, you damn viper!"

Two white high school boys seized the man and frog-marched him out of the theater. Jumbo hugged himself and stared up at the star-sprinkled ceiling. One of the kid bouncers came back and peered down the row at him.

"Sorry bout that, sir. You awright?"

"Sticks and stones," Jumbo said.

"We screen for carriers, but some of these jigs're jes lousy boozehounds." He saluted. "Enjoy the last show, sir."

"What time is it?"

The bouncer shot his cuff to check his watch, an old one with a radium-painted dial.

"Ten-twenty," he said. "Zat awright?" (Did he plan to have the Roxy dragged by tractor into another time zone if the hour didn't suit us?)

"Thank you," Jumbo said, and the kid left. "Daniel, Mister JayMac's curfew—"

The houselights dimmed again. The opening credits for *Son of Frankenstein* began to roll. I put my hand on Jumbo's arm—humor me a little longer, I was begging him.

Next to and in front of us, more empty seats. Only three other people still sat on our row.

Basil Rathbone played Wolfgang Frankenstein, son of the maker of the first picture's monster. In one scene, Lugosi as Ygor takes Rathbone to the monster's sleeping body.

"*Cannot be destroyed. Cannot die. Your father made him live for always,*" Ygor said. "*Now he's sick. . . .*"

Jumbo moaned.

"*You mean to imply that that is my brother?*" Rathbone asks as they stand over Karloff in his sheepskin vest.

"*But his mother was lightning,*" Lugosi says.

Jumbo's knees thumped the seat back in front of him. He struggled up like a gorilla trying to burst a steamer crate. "What've these celluloid nightmares to do with you?" he boomed at everyone who'd cranked around to look at him.

"Can that yammering!" somebody shouted back.

"One more damn drunk," somebody else said. "A black un and a white un, bofe trouble."

The ushers showed up again—startled to find Jumbo, a giant shadow with his head just below the projector window, at the center of the commotion, railing at the film on screen and the blameless folks who'd paid their hard-got money to see it. I tried to lever Jumbo back down.

"Fie on these blood wallows!" he shouted. "These hymns to corruption! My patience exhausts itself!"

The ushers exchanged a look. Who'd move first to give him the old heave-ho? Thank God, Jumbo hadn't gone off on an all-out woozy tear yet. He saw the worried boys.

"No need to oust me bodily," he told them. "My friend and I are leaving."

"Good riddance," somebody several rows up said. "Sho hope we can git on wi our blood waller in peace."

Jumbo edged aislewards, pulling me with him and apologizing to anyone near enough to hear. A third of the remaining audience clapped when he opened the door to the lobby. That hurt him. Through two whole films, he'd behaved himself. Not until a drunk'd called him a "damn ol viper," not until the pressure of Mister JayMac's curfew began niggling him, and not until a slew of scenes into the third movie had he stood up to protest the mayhem and the morbid stuff.

Now his fellow moviegoers—some of em, anyway—applauded his exit. The unfairness of that slapped him like a gas-soaked rag. Out in the lobby, I watched shock and hurt ripple over his face in frame-by-frame waves. Rage shook him. He let go of me and turned back towards the theater—to tear out a seat by its floor bolts and hurl it with a roar into the crowd?

"He's completely superhuman!" Wolf Frankenstein would say. *"The entire structure of the blood is quite different from that of a normal human being!"*

"Come on," one of the ushers said. "You don't wanna let a bunch of niggers git under your skin."

"You do, they'll shore change its color for you," the other usher said. And both ushers laughed.

Jumbo's rage drained away. He didn't rip up a seat. He growled and swung his arm in a tired wave. He left the hall again and paced the foyer, where the coming-attraction posters shone in glass boxes.

Together we walked through the muggy air to our hotel. Jumbo stooped as he slouched, but his size still suggested Karloff's killer hobgoblin. On my first day in Highbridge, I'd figured him for a giant in coveralls. Now, shook up by three movies and the superstitious venom of a wino, I wondered if he was even human.

Back in our room, I went to bed under his chilly stare, but tonight it seemed one more penalty, along with Sloan's fake telegram and Hoey's stuffed goat, for throwing away the first game of our first series against the Gendarmes.

I couldn't sleep. From the creakings of his bedsprings and his moans, I assumed Jumbo couldn't either. He'd said nothing on our walk back from the Roxy and nothing since we'd settled in. A fly on the wall would've had a devil of a time figuring out which of us was the dummy. I'd stopped believing that he might strangle me in my bed, but I hated thinking that at the Roxy's triple bill we'd become unmoored from each other, shoved apart like two boats on a vast, poisoned lake.

Jumbo made a noise like a cow getting sidetracked in the middle of a low and ending with a snork. I rolled over and switched on my bedside lamp. Shadows leapt onto the walls. Jumbo'd heard me, but he lay facing away, a one-man mountain range. I got out of bed and found my message notebook. With a pencil I printed out a question, two questions, three:

Where are you from? Really?

Do you have any living kin?

Did you ever have an accident that caused you to look the way you do now?

I took the notebook around Jumbo's bed and held it so he could read my questions, which he did. Still lying on his side, he crooked his finger for my pencil and notebook, took them from me, and printed:

Too many places to list.

No.

Only my "birth."

He gave the notebook back to me and closed his eyes. I sat down on my bed and read his answers over and over again, like he'd written them in an alphabet with hundreds and hundreds of meanings in every letter. *Too many places to list*, *No*, and *Only my "birth,"* I figured, put into code his whole mysterious biography. Why had he put *birth* in quotation marks? After our evening together, I was afraid I knew.

25

Mister JayMac dropped by our room at eight the next morning to tell us the Gendarmes' owner, Mr. John Sayigh, wanted to play a doubleheader that afternoon to make up for yesterday's rainout. The weather report—sunny with high cumulus—promised us a shot at it.

"What of the field?" Jumbo asked.

"The groundskeepers got a tarp over the infield on Friday night. Outfield's pretty squishy, though, and it'll take some doing to firm up some spots where the tarp didn't do its job. Mr. Sayigh suggests volunteers from both our clubs show up at the park within the next hour or so to tackle the drying-out."

"Yessir."

"Begging your pardons, but both you fellas look like you could use some drying out too. Didn't go honky-tonking last night, did you? A little arm-wrasslin with John Barleycorn?"

"We went to a movie," Jumbo said.

Three movies, I thought.

Mister JayMac turned to me. "Didn't you sleep? You look about as peakéd as I've ever seen you."

"He'll look swell after some labor on Mr. Sayigh's field," Jumbo said.

"Let me stress," said Mister JayMac, frown lines between his eyes, "that neither Mr. Sayigh nor I expect anyone to work who'd rather idle the morning away or go to worship services. In fact, if you don't want to assist with field repairs, I'd like yall to come with me to church."

"We'll assist," Jumbo said.

"All right. If everything goes well, today's opener will start at two. The Gendarmes' front office plans to announce the time over the radio and pass out flyers to folks leaving church. I expect a good crowd."

"Yessir," Jumbo said.

I found the empty hide of the stuffed goat the desk clerk'd brought me yesterday and handed it to Mister JayMac.

"What's this?" he said.

"A toy," Jumbo said. "Please return it to Mr. Hoey, who must have sent it to our room in an unfortunate mix-up."

"Looks a little the worse for wear," Mister JayMac said. It did. That goat was dishrag-limp. Mister JayMac turned the empty skin over in his hands and said good-bye. I halted him again and gave him the goat's picked-off eye buttons. Mister JayMac wrinkled his forehead and left.

Jumbo and I suited out in our flannels, splurged on a taxi, and rode to the Prefecture. True to Mister JayMac's word, a half dozen groundskeepers'd beaten us to the task. With rakes, brooms, zinc buckets, wooden drags, and burlap bags of sand or sawdust, they struggled to repair the field. Jumbo and I went to work with three other Hellbenders—Dunnagin, Knowles, and Sudikoff—and maybe ten of the Gendarmes. Most of the guys treated this shit detail as a party, cracking wise and singing in rounds. It went okay.

Nowadays, you've got beaucoups of ways to dry out a field. You can sprinkle this more or less new-fangled chemical product called Diamond Dry around and let it absorb the water. You can vacuum up standing puddles with a machine. Or pour gasoline on the wet spots, flip a match in, and boil some of the moisture away. (Course, you can also burn down your ballpark.) Hell, nowadays you can hire a helicopter to hover over the swamp like a flying blow-dryer.

Back then, though, nobody'd heard of Diamond Dry or outdoor vacuums. Because of rationing and the hazard to your stands, no one would've thought of using gasoline. Helicopters? Ha! Not until '39 did Sikorsky—first name, Igor—make one of those ungainly contraptions fly.

So you used other methods. You helped your groundskeepers by wielding brooms to spread the water out, by forming bucket brigades to scoop it up and dump it elsewhere, and by digging runoff trenches. That Sunday morning, some of us swept, some of us bailed, some of us scattered sawdust or hay around. By noon, Jumbo and I'd burnt our energy reserves down to fumes, but our labors guaranteed a game or two that afternoon, and the wives of some of the Gendarme players brought us a covered-dish dinner. Jumbo ate for the first time since his rooftop juicing on Friday night: creamed sweet corn, snap beans, yellow-squash casserole, tomato slices, popcorn okra, and creamed potatoes. The food was lukewarm, the women'd toted it so far, but it tasted like manna to me, even the meat dishes Jumbo wouldn't let himself touch.

That afternoon, our restoking didn't seem to help that much—not at first, anyway. Jumbo and I played like kittens overdosed on catnip. Ordinarily, Mariani pitched like a street fighter, nicking the edges of home plate, stalking around the mound with his teeth gritted and his eyes afire, throwing heat when the batter expected finesse, and vice versa. None of these tactics worked for Mariani in the opener. The Gendarmes boarded him like fleas on a long-haired spaniel, then roughed up Parris and Hay in relief roles. We lost the opener, six to two, and fell two games behind LaGrange. Another loss'd shake us hard. It could take two weeks, even a full month, to regain the ground we'd given up, if we could regain it at all.

Gendarme fans, especially the coloreds in the outfield bleachers, carried on like their boys'd already snatched the CVL pennant out of Mister JayMac's pocket. I felt sure that some of the raucous crew at last night's monster flicks were tap-dancing and thigh-slapping out there.

In the dugout between games, Hoey sidled up and sat down next to me. He popped me with some sort of rag, then dropped it over my thigh and leaned back.

"Hear you got a telegram from Mama yesterday."

The rag on my thigh was the toy goat I'd gutted.

"Hearing from Mama didn't inspire you to new heights of glory on the ball field today, Dumbo."

I flipped the fake goat skin out onto the infield grass.

"Looky there—flies almost as well as your namesake, don't it?" Hoey squeezed my knee. "Maybe Mama's words weren't meant to inspire, maybe they were meant to *sting*."

"Lay off the boy," Double Dunnagin said.

Hoey ignored him. "You were a regular sojer boy up at the plate in that last one."

If I hadn't gone aught for three, with a deliberate walk in the eighth to load the bases and set up a rally-killing double play, I might've figured his remark for praise. What it meant was, I'd stood in the batter's box like a soldier at attention, never taking my bat off my shoulder. It never crossed Hoey's mind—or Sloan's, or Evans's, or Sosebee's—he and his wiseacre chums had slid a banana peel under my confidence.

Mister JayMac came into the dugout. "This game's do or die. And I don't expect Darius to drive a load of stiffs back to Highbridge. Yall follow?"

"Yessir," four or five guys more or less mumbled.

"In the debacle jes past," Mister JayMac said, "yall played worse n I ever thought you could. Play up to your potential, not down to your shortcomings, and we'll escape with our limbs intact and our hopes alive. Need I say more?"

"NOSIR!" most of the team shouted.

"All right. I'm deferring here and now to Darius, who has some interesting intelligence for you."

"Nother nigger nugget," Fadeaway told Sosebee. Mister JayMac didn't hear. Otherwise, Fadeaway would've spent the evening hand-washing our jocks.

"Gundy's pitching this game," Darius told us, sitting on the dugout ledge with his hands hanging between his legs like dark plumb bobs. He avoided eye contact. "I've seen him pitch befo, and I've watched his warm-ups."

Where, I suddenly wondered, had Darius spent the night? In the *Brown*

Bomber? At a cousin's or an in-law's somewhere in or around LaGrange? I couldn't have told you.

"Gundy tips his curve," Darius said.

"Tips it?" Sloan said. "My, my. Usually, you've got to be in the batter's box to tip one. Gundy must be faster than the word God to tip one of his own pitches."

"Mr. Sloan, that's enough," Mister JayMac said.

"Gundy *telegraphs* his curve." Darius looked Sloan in the eye, and Sloan started picking lint off his sleeve. "He'll thow you a fastball, a change, or a knuckler out of his glove—ever time, no surprises. You got to figure which it is as it's riding in. I cain't hep you there. But if you cain't tell a knuckler's dip-dip-shimmy-shimmy from a fastball's straight-in zip, they's eye doctors you should visit."

"Unless you're a pitcher," Hoey said. "Nothing scares a hitter worse than a half-blind moundsman."

Darius smiled. "True nough. But Gundy's curve, now—he's gon tip you to it sho as sunrise, gon take the ball to a place back of and under his right butt cheek and twiddle it there till he's got his grip. If Gundy drops his ball hand behind him, yall're gon see a curve—ever time."

"That could be a ruse," Nutter said. "When he goes back to his glove for the windup, he could regrip. A hitter thinking curve and lunging at something else would look a fool."

"Mr. Nutter, you've been to the bigs," Darius said. "You know sech things. Gundy aint been up and most prolly never gon to be. In this business, he's as perdictable as a hell-fire sermon, and nobody on the Darmes, not even Mr. Strock, has had the sense to cotch him out on it yet n jerk him straight."

"Anything else, Darius," Mister JayMac said.

"Nosir. Important thing is, study where his ball hand goes fo he winds, then cat-pounce any curve in the zone." He slipped off the dugout ledge and glided away.

If any other CVL team had had a colored scout, management would've milked him of his skinny and passed it on without telling where it'd come from. Mister JayMac took another tack, whether from social conscience or from some sort of weird snag Darius had him in, I couldn't say just then.

Fadeaway pitched the second game. He blanked the Gendarmes through six, using a fadeaway and a perky fastball to bumfuzzle Mr. Strock's gang and keep the homies solemn as a surgeon at a recent patient's burial. Meanwhile, the rest of us teed off on Gundy's telegraphed curve. We also managed to decipher most of his other pitches before they reached the plate.

Gundy, shell-shocked to near zombiehood after less than four innings, trudged to the showers to a concert of boos. We picked up on his reliever where we'd finished with Gundy, the rhythm of hitting in us like a boogie-woogie tune, the Darmes' dashed hopes—for a sweep—making them more stumblebummish the longer the game went on.

Even the run they got in the seventh, a rain-bringing Ed Bantling pop-up the wind pushed into the right-field stands, didn't set them afire. His homer struck even Bantling as flukish. He trotted to second backwards, watching the ball rise and rise, in unreal stages, like a Ping-Pong ball on an air-hose jet, until it finally stopped bounding higher and fell on a sudden slant into the bleachers. As he crossed the plate, Bantling had begun to laugh, but more like a soldier who's dodged a bullet than one who's just lobbed a mortar right on the enemy.

And for good reason too. We beat LaGrange thirteen to one and saved ourselves the embarrassment of going home on a losing streak.

26

Jumbo and I spent one more night in the Lafayette Hotel. He slept like a dead man, hardly breathing or moving. Despite my bad night the night before, the day's excitement—along with a nagging fidgetiness about those three Karloff flicks—had me keyed so tight I couldn't unwind. I flopped around like an epileptic, then got up and paced, mentally replaying every inning of Sunday's second game.

Well, why not? My play in that game qualified as one of my best performances yet. No errors, an unassisted double play, and five hits in six plate appearances, with a double down the line, and four runs scored. Hoey hadn't congratulated me, though. He'd spent the afternoon either riding the bench or squatting in a coach's box glumly clapping his hands. Once, I'd seen him and Turkey Sloan with their heads together in the dugout. Plotting their next toy purchase? Writing another rhymed telegram? How, I wondered, had I managed to make such an enemy of the guy? How could I turn him from a menace into a friend, or at least a neutral?

Around three in the morning, I stopped pacing and looked at Jumbo. He worried me too. A few hours ago he'd powered two Roric Gundy curves and a low-and-away fastball from Gundy's reliever out of the Prefecture. Those shots'd given him five home runs for the series, tying a CVL record held by a former Opelika Orphan now in the Marines. This morning, though, he seemed a coma victim, too fagged to've performed the feats just listed.

I leaned over him. The quarter moons of orangish-yellow under his lids looked sicklier than usual. I picked up his clammy wrist. I guess he had a pulse, but maybe I'd plugged into the throbbing feedback of my own. The pale light leaking into our room from the streetlamps outside gave Jumbo's still body a gorgeous creepiness. I returned to my bed and sat there watching him. A little later, I eased over onto my side and fell asleep.

Jumbo woke me before dawn, and the Hellbenders assembled in the Prefecture's parking lot around eight to board the team bus and return to Highbridge.

Riding home, I stayed awake, jostled by the lurch and sway of the *Bomber's* worn-out chassis and picked at more or less good-naturedly by my teammates. On Highbridge's northwestern outskirts, though, I slumped against my window and escaped into a dream-addled sleep....

"*—more in tarnation could you want?*"

"*A life, Mister JayMac. My own life.*"

Voices—two voices—dragged me wincing and blinking out of the pit of my stupor. I lay on the split upholstery of one of the *Brown Bomber's* rearmost seats. Jumbo had deserted me. As quietly as I could, I peeked over the back of the seat in front of mine. Every Hellbender, not just Jumbo, had left the *Bomber*—some time ago if the absence of travel kits, ball gloves, and snack wrappers meant anything.

In fact, the darkness of the bus's interior, the coolness of its metal floor, and the murky shade surrounding our bus told me Darius'd driven it into the garage of the buggy house beside McKissic House. Now, he and Mister JayMac faced each other across its aisle up front. Neither knew I was still aboard.

Maybe I should've coughed or sashayed nonchalantly up the aisle, but it shamed me to've fallen so hard asleep I hadn't noticed our arrival or heard Jumbo, Junior, Dunnagin, and all the others getting off. More than likely, they'd crept off the bus as tiptoey as elves, just to see how I'd react to waking up alone after they'd all gone inside.

Anyway, instead of showing myself, I hunched down out of sight and held my breath.

"You have a life here," Mister JayMac said. "You have a damn fine life here. Even an enviable one, I'd say."

"You might believe that," Darius said, "but I cain't."

"Would you rather be in an all-Negro unit in New Guinea building runways and taking atabrine to stave off malaria?"

"Nosir, I'd rather—"

"That stuff makes your ears ring. Turns the whites of your eyes custard-yaller. You'd *have* to take it, though, because the Army's precious *quinine* supplies go to their All-American Caucasian boys."

"Mebbe they'd give me half atabrine and half quinine. Jes one ear'd ring, jes one eye turn yaller."

Mister JayMac didn't seem to hear Darius's reply. He said, "Or how'd you like to be in a colored regiment pick-axing away at the Alcan Highway in subzero temperatures?"

"I know a man doing that. He's proud to do it, he can pint to that road and say he holp to build it."

"He's got a frozen tail, trench foot, and frost bite. I kept you out of that. Saved your hide for better things."

"Leastwise, for *other* things."

I pulled myself up again and peered over the seat. Mister JayMac had a flask of whiskey and a brown ceramic coffee mug. Darius had a mug. Mister JayMac tilted his flask and shared out generous sloshes of liquor. Its yeasty sweet-tart smell filled the bus.

They'd already shared at least a mug each. Knee to knee up there, they seemed close to exploding. Only Mister JayMac's bosshood and Darius's role as a black hired hand kept them from pitching into donnybrook. The wrong word, the sass of an eye, or one more slug of hooch might yet shove them to it.

"Doesn't playing baseball beat the likely alternatives?"

"I don't play baseball. I drive a bus. I step n fetch."

"Nobody but you and me may know it, but you're a grand sight more than a glorified chauffeur and houseboy. You're the de facto assistant manager of a contending CVL baseball team."

"De facto," Darius said.

"It means—"

"I know what it means. Hardly means doosquiddy. Means I'm a nigger with a big-shot friend."

Mister JayMac sipped at his mug. After a while, he said, "A life? A life you say. What does *that* mean? Just what do you want that the world—this world, not some pie-in-the-sky pipedream—is ever gonna let you have?"

"A tryout with the Atlanta Black Crackers. Or the Kansas City Monarchs. Or the Jacksonville Red Caps."

"Are you asking my *permission* to leave Highbridge to play with some run-on-a-shoestring colored squad?"

Darius stared out the window over Mister JayMac's head, at a rotting harness on the wall of the old buggy house.

"If you leave," Mister JayMac said, "I'll see to it your number comes up. I'll see to it you get tracked down fast and straightaway inducted."

"That'd be bettern this glorified chauffeur and houseboy job I got now," Darius said.

"*Assistant manager!*" Mister JayMac stood up and purposely sloshed the whiskey in his mug on the *Bomber's* steering wheel. He didn't let go of his mug, but only because he'd tangled his middle finger through its handle. "The only colored assistant manager of a pro white ball club in the whole United States, south or north, east or west, de facto or otherwise, and you want to play with a bunch of unlettered darkies who never know from year to year how many games their season's gonna have or even if their ballclub's got the financial stuffing to last a month. Right?"

"I want to play where the Powers That Be gon let me, Mister JayMac. That's all."

"*I* let you, I let you when I can. But, Darius, I'll see you in battle dress before I'll let you sign with an uppish bunch of Ethiops who're just as lief to file for bankruptcy as to play ten games back to back. How does Private Satterfield grab you?"

"Fine."

"Fine? What do you mean, fine?"

"If I cain't play baseball, how bout gitting me sent to the Tuskegee Army

Airfield? Or to Shorter Field? Or mebbe to Dale Mabry Field down to Tallahassee?"

Mister JayMac laughed. "Got your sights set high, don't you? Well, hear the straight skinny, Darius. The only place monkeys get to fly in combat is in *The Wizard of Oz*."

Darius chug-a-lugged his whiskey and gave his mug to Mister JayMac, who set it and his own mug on the dash. He looked ready to climb down and stalk to the house. Darius got up and swung himself into the driver's seat. He gripped the wheel, then lifted his fingers from the wet-paint tackiness of the heavy liquor coating it.

"What you forgit, Mister JayMac, is monkeys come in more colors than one. Some got two-toned souls."

Mister JayMac slammed his hand down on the dashboard. The mugs there jumped, but didn't fall or break.

"Darius, don't leave."

Darius took his handkerchief and wiped the steering wheel, then his hands. "A different color monkey probably wouldn't want to."

"Don't," Mister JayMac said. Did he mean don't leave or don't talk that way or both? Darius stayed mum. Mister JayMac banged the door open, leapt out, and strode through the sawdust and pulverized shell litter on the floor.

I ducked to keep him from seeing me as he came past the bus's rear. Behind me, he creaked the tin-plated door open and eased through this crack into the yard. The door rattled shut again, but the light that'd fanned in, a burst of white-orange sunlight and a storm of dancing motes, told me I hadn't slept the whole day away.

Darius kept sitting behind the wheel. I couldn't get off without him seeing me, and the talk I'd overheard didn't incline me to show myself. Mister JayMac'd call me a filthy sneak, and Darius'd take me for a whitebread spy. So I lay low and waited for Darius to move.

Problem was, my pocketknife slipped from my pants and hit the floor with an echoey clunk and a metallic bang. It hit on its end, then toppled over on its side. *Clunk-bang!*

"Who's back there?" Darius said.

I bit my bottom lip.

"Mice? Nazis? Cmon out, whoever you are."

I sat up. Darius stared at me in the slanted rectangle of the rearview.

"Jumping Jesus," he said. "What're you doing back there, Danny boy?"

My shrug didn't explain much, I guess.

"Git," Darius said. "Leave me be."

I picked up my pocketknife and other gear, and pussy-footed up the aisle, half expecting Darius to swat all my stuff out of my hands, push me down, and tell me how only creeps did what I'd just done. He kept sitting, though. He didn't look at me, not even a glance in the rearview.

I got off the bus. Its baggage holders stood empty. Jumbo must've carried my bag upstairs. He must've enlisted everyone else's help—everyone's but Mister JayMac's and Darius's—to play a joke on me. Ha ha. As I left the garage, Darius stayed slouched behind the steering wheel: hollow-eyed, hair-trigger, mute.

27

That evening, after dinner, a rap on our door. The room seemed smaller than usual because, during our road trip, a carpenter had put together a bed for me, with a headboard and sliding storage drawers under the mattress—my belated due as a Hellbender.

Anyway, the rapping startled us because we hadn't heard anything, no tattle-tale creak of steps or floorboards. We *should've* heard something: I sat scribbling a letter to Mama Laurel, while Jumbo, despite hating most war-related stuff, read *Burma Surgeon*—because, as he put it, "Colonel Seagrave devotes himself to healing, not destruction." Finally, though, we did hear.

Jumbo opened the door without getting up or losing his place. Kizzy Lorrows, a brown gnome of a long-haired Seminole woman. Her arms had flour on them, a rime like the gritty blow on a plum. So did half her forehead. She wiped her hands on her apron and pointed into the room at me.

"Danl, you got a telephone caw. Long distance. Better git yosef downstairs licky-spiddle."

"That would be senseless," Jumbo said. "Senseless."

"His mama wants to talk to him. She don't know his tongue stove up. *He ain* told her."

I stood up. I shook my head. Mama didn't like the phone, but I should've guessed she'd eventually ring up to hear me stammer.

Well, eventually'd come, and Kizzy dismissed my head shakes with a floppy-wristed wave.

"Ever minute you tarry you toss good money at them telephone folks. Cmon, honey boy."

"I'll speak for him," Jumbo said. He got up and nodded at me. Kizzy barely reached his waist.

I grabbed notebook and pencil and hurried after them, my heart cinched and a-gallop. Kizzy let us run ahead of her down the two staircases to the foyer where a box-and-cradle phone hung on the wall. Jumbo had to bend over to use it. (Kizzy'd used a stool.)

"Mrs. Boles, I'm your son's roommate, Henry Clerval," Jumbo told my mother. "Daniel is fine."

Tell her I have larinjitus, I scribbled in my notebook.

"Except, I'm sorry to inform you, he's contracted a severe case of laryngitis," Jumbo said. "Otherwise, his strength and vigor put the rest of us to shame."

Kizzy gave us both a scornful squint and strutted back to the kitchen, swinging her arms like a Munchkin. The parlor and game room were empty. Most of the other boarders had gone over to McKissic Field for a community softball tournament.

I wrote, *Say its temporary say its from cheering to hard.*

"Yessum. We won the last game of an otherwise frustrating road trip. Daniel played well." He covered the mouthpiece. "Wherefore . . . why this subterfuge? Why not the truth?"

Upset her, I wrote. *She'd want to come down here.*

"When?" Jumbo said. "Why, quite recently." He covered the mouthpiece again. "Under the aspect of eternity," he told me, then spoke into the mouthpiece again: "Yessum, he plays hard, eats well, and sleeps a sufficiency."

Mama said something.

"Yessum, plenty of sleep. Plenty."

I held up a new message: *Say Ill call later say Im writing a letter.* That last told the holy truth. No one could call me a neglectful son.

Jumbo gagged the mouthpiece with his hand. "She wishes to talk to you."
I shook my head. Jumbo slapped me with a look. "Yessum, he still has the
use of his ears. No, no infection. No ear ache. A moment." He passed me the
tubelike earpiece. Static hissed at me, rough electrical surf.

"*Danny?*" Mama said from hundreds of miles away. "*Danny?*"

Jumbo leaned into the tuliplike cup of a speaker. "He's listening, Mrs.
Boles."

"*Danny . . . I miss . . . I miss you.*"

"And he you in return, Mrs. Boles," Jumbo said.

"*Thank you, Mr. Clerver,*" Mama said. "*Danny, Colonel and Mrs. Elshtain
got plans to visit Highbridge this weekend. Come Sunday, it's the Fourth. They'll
want to see you. I'm sending you a little something by way of Miss Tulipa. Look
for it.*"

"Yessum," Jumbo said. "He will."

"*Bye. Love ya. Bye now. Bye,*" Mama said, her voice lost in the screak and
gabble of the line.

Jumbo took the earpiece from me and cradled it. "Lying to a devoted
parent robs one of the regard of honest men. Perhaps you have cause, perhaps
you do not."

And if I dont, I wrote, *Im no longer a REAL PERSON???*

"Cut to the quick." Jumbo trudged across the foyer to the stairs, then
went up, his body windowed between the balusters like a person caught in
the frames of a film strip. Like the creature in the Frankenstein movies.

Anyway, I didn't want to go upstairs with Jumbo—not yet, at least. He'd
helped me with the telephone call, but he'd also accused me of lying, of not
being a REAL PERSON. To hell with him, let him go.

Tardily, I followed Kizzy into the kitchen. At her center island, she stood
rolling out dough for a huge blackberry and dewberry cobbler.

"Yo mama sweet to caw you, Danl. Course, mamas aint got much chice
but to worry bout they chirren—s bred in, like a quail dog's urge to pint."

Kizzy'd stayed late. Sometimes she did. The kitchen of McKissic House
(so long as she didn't have to scrub pots or throw-mop the linoleum) gave
her a sharper sense of home, I figured, than the four-room box of shingles,
tarpaper, and sheet metal, over by Penticuff Strip, where she lived. Her
"chirren"—Muscles said she had seven—had all grown up and married. All
but a no-account son or two had moved away, to Atlanta or Chicago, and
these homeboys, depending on how you viewed the matter, either didn't

torment Kizzy any longer or flat-out ignored her. Kizzy's husband, a man she still called Oliver Bob, had died during the corn harvest of '21, under a buckboard driven by a rattlesnake-mean white farmer.

I lit into scrubbing a pot tonight's KP squad had left in the sink. I plunged into that pot up to my elbows. Above the sink, I could look through both a rippled window pane and the torn mesh of the screened-in porch.

Through them I saw the carriage house. An ivory trellis guided a strangle of rose vines up it to a raised window with a crooked jamb and two broken shutters. Darius slept there, over a storage room for ball equipment, over the garage where the Brown Bomber ticked and simmered. What did Darius do up there when he couldn't sleep—when the call of another life clanged inside him like a fire alarm?

Kizzy said, "I told you Miss Giselle's got no chirren. That's true. She don't. Cain't have none. Once, thuddy-fo, thuddy-five years ago, she and Mister JayMac did have a chile. Come to em dumpling-fat, pink as a fresh red wriggler. But it took Miss Giselle bettern a day to have her, and when the baby do come, the secundines—what my mama cawed the foller-long—didn't want to foller."

I revved my elbow, but kept my ear cocked to Kizzy's story. She'd begun it soon as she'd noticed me peering through the honeysuckle-loaded gloom at Darius's window.

"The secundines, the afterbirth, it had to git clear. Somebody had to fetch it, not fo the bairn so much as fo Miss Giselle. That baby was turned jes fine, but Miss Giselle had her a fever skin, a shiny jacket o birth sweat. She got fluster-brained. She magined she was heping her daddy tree a possum over by Cotton Creek n likewise trying to hush this pair of hollering dogs.

" 'Quiet!' she'd caw. 'Quiet, Cherie! Quiet, Smut!' Then she'd go, 'Shoot that night rat, Daddy! Please, you gots to shoot it!' I didn't midwife in them days, but Dr. Sellers had me there wi Mister JayMac to hold Miss Giselle down. We pinned her, held her to, like hired mens at pig-sticking time. She thrished n thrashed, but we held er. Pritty soon, her cries got real groany, and her eyes rolled back, white as hard-biled eggs n jes as blind.

" 'I've got to fetch that afterbirth,' Dr. Sellers told Mister JayMac. 'Cain't leave it in er like a rag in a pendix hole.' He scrubbed his hands with lye soap n rinched em real good in grain alcohol, then set down twix the missus's legs to pick at the blood organ what wouldn't come of itsef. He fished for that broke-up thing n got it out in pieces over a battle o three, mebbe fo hours.

" 'Doc,' Mister JayMac say, 'you're damn like to kill er.' "

" 'Not if you hush up n set that lamp where it jes might do some good,' Dr. Sellers say.

"Way it look at fust, baby gon live, but Miss Giselle bout set for morticianizing n hymns. Dr. Sellers had dug in her deep and she was weak. It happened reversed around, though. That fat n wriggly gal baby took sick n went down like a orphan calf. She jes skinnied off n died. Mister JayMac cussed the doctor, flung some ol crockery bout, carried on like Job hissef. Miss Giselle, though, she *improved*, bloomed n flourished right up to the pint Mister JayMac had to say they gal baby gone.

"Don't think she flew off like Mister JayMac. Uh-uh. Aw by hissef, he's upsot nough fo a whole family. Miss Giselle withered into her own quiet woman grief, but she didn't go down, didn't pitch over broke. Not at fust, anyhow. Then her bosoms flooded, like she'd had these kicking twins stead of a gal baby awready dead. Had so much milk she leaked into her bedclothes, her nightdresses, day clothes too. Mister JayMac tol Dr. Sellers to *do* something. If he don't, he gon pay.

"So Dr. Sellers hopped. He sweet-talked, soothed, and nigh on to comfort-coddled Miss Giselle, who lapsed anyways, turning back to fever sweats. With her mind on Canaan, her bosoms made even mo milk. Dr. Sellers tol Mister JayMac her problem wi the placenter gon to steal any chanst fo other young uns, no matter what he try, no matter how hot Mister JayMac's temper biles. Mister JayMac didn't rant or nothing, jes ast the doctor to ease Miss Giselle's bosom flow n bring her on back from her addlement.

"Anyhow, Dr. Sellers reckoned he could try whatever, now things gone so bad n Mister JayMac so deep in his melancholy. And what he did was, he brought these two hongry bluetick puppies in and put em at Miss Giselle's bosoms. These pups had freckle bellies n snouts so squashed they looked like ugly ol men. When the doctor stuck em to Miss Giselle's teats to draw off her milk, they scrumbled n rooted n tormented that po fevered woman something furious.

"Mister JayMac come home. He heard pups whining and his missus yipping pitiful under the nick o they milk teeth. He bulged right in n slung the doctor to the flo. Gashed him from chin to ear, used his belt to do it. Thew that man out the house, down the steps. Dr. Sellers moved off to Alabama— Fairhope, I think. Miss Giselle, she stayed wounded. Couldn't have no other baby, gal or manchile. Never understood fo the longest how she'd come to git sech scratches n pricks round her bosoms."

The inside of my pot shone like a cannon bore. My hands ached from the scouring I'd given it.

"That's a Highbridge story. A Mister JayMac n Miss Giselle story. I didn't work fo them then, but I heard that story quick nough afterwards. Miss Giselle was among the last to hear, and she's mebbe never gon stop suffering from what that fool doctor done after her gal baby born, then again after the po thing passed."

Crickets chatted and whistled on the screened-in porch. Outside, fireflies bobbed, turning their flashlights on and off. One lit up at the sill of Darius's window, rose a foot or so, and got blotted out by the brighter light coming from the room behind it. Darius crossed in front of the window. For a second or less, the firefly scorched a point into his dark form. Kizzy stood at my side, both of us gawping at the buggy house, straining our vision through the screen. Honeysuckle leaked its easy smell into the yard, and the night hung down around us black as overripe muscadines.

"That Darius," Kizzy said. "He's jes ashes n wormwood to Miss Giselle."

I looked at Kizzy.

"Why?" she said. "Cause he's Mister JayMac's oldest living chile."

28

The next day, after a light workout at the ballpark, Jumbo borrowed Mister JayMac's Caddy—he did get perks no one else did—and drove off into Alabama again. Why? He had no living kin there, although he'd lied about that before (if he wasn't lying now), and even a quick trip over and back could leave you panting. On a steamy Georgia day, I'd've rather played some more ball than go for a ride in a blazing-hot auto.

Upstairs, I had lots to mull. Mama'd nearly found out I'd slid back into dummyhood again. To muddy the waters more, the Elshtains would arrive this weekend to visit the McKissics, and they'd easily discover what I'd tried to hide from my mama over the phone. Mama would find out from the Elshtains later, and although she might see, and even forgive, my lie as an attempt to spare her pain, she might also decide I should come home to Tenkiller for treatment and TLC.

I didn't want to leave Highbridge. Despite the South's summer swelter, the torments Buck Hoey and friends had aimed at me, and a roommate big enough to scare a Marine, I'd begun to adjust. To the weird rituals of McKissic House. To my role on the team. I liked playing ball for the Hellbenders. I didn't want to return to the mile-long apron strings and the boredom of my life in dust-bowl Oklahoma. I loved Mama Laurel, sure, but I'd truly begun scrapping for my manhood—a sense of my stand-alone self—in the CVL.

While Jumbo prowled the oiled and gravel byways of Alabama, I had nothing to do. A few guys had gone to their part-time jobs at Foremost Forge or Highbridge Box & Crate. A few others had caught a trolley uptown to a matinee, and everybody else'd settled in to nap, play cards, or letter-write. I'd mailed Mama a letter just that morning. Cards, with no cricket chirps or dance-band music to play by, appealed to me about as much as a swig of bicarbonate.

Upstairs, I had idle hands. So I fired up a cigarette, crossed my arms, and rocked on my heels like a tough in a gangster show. Humphrey Bogart? George Brent? Lloyd Nolan? I had to've looked like one of em, right?

By degrees, though, I ambled across the room to Jumbo's space: his humongous bed, his pine-plank-and-tin-can bookcase, his bedside washstand and lamp table. I stood there puffing my Old Gold and eyeballing all this stuff. The book shelves I'd examined before. Along with new library books, they held poetry, novels, philosophy, history, and religious texts, many old and some in French or German.

I walked around the bed, sat down on it by the bookcase, and opened something in French by a woman named Christine de Pisan. The book's paper smelled like dried beetle wings—dusty sharp, I mean—and sour ink. I couldn't decode a word, once past stuff like *le* and *la* and *amour*. It all just stymied me. So I shut old Christine and stuck her back in the bookcase. Something—boredom, curiosity—made me look back between my legs. Up under Jumbo's bed I saw crammed what looked like a small boat, a kind of Eskimo canoe.

Yeah, a *kayak!*

I dragged the skin-covered frame out from under the twin plyboards Jumbo slept on. There was barely room for it in the space between bed and bookcase. I had to turn it longways and straddle it. It hadn't slid all that easily either, probably because Jumbo'd loaded it with stuff through its central manhole. Dustbunnies furred its sides.

The first thing I found in the cockpit was the mat he'd hung as a curtain until my angry fit in LaGrange. He'd folded it five or six times and stuffed it down into the manhole as a plug. I pulled it out and looked under it. There sat a loose bag of animal hides, tied at the neck with cords of sinew and knotted with little ivory beads. It smelled fusty-funny, in a way I can't describe.

No matter how I resisted, that bag felt like a dare, a dare to look inside it. Pulling a kayak out from under a bed hadn't struck me as prying, but removing that folded mat had inched me towards a bad self-feeling, and the bag posed an even harder test of my honor. I'd stooped, so to speak, to snoopery, and Mama hadn't raised me to pry. But Jumbo needed unlocking worse than his bag did; maybe untying it would open him too.

Inside the bag, I found a journal bound in split and marbled leather, with a bundle of ribbon-tied letters between its last page and its back cover. The letter sheaf had the bulk of a small book. I studied it closely, but didn't unknot the ribbon. The paper felt brittle, crisp as fallen leaves—I feared I might crumble some pages. At last, I withdrew the top letter, eased it from its envelope, and unfolded the first of four or five thin pages.

The handwriting—with all its squiggles, smudges, and such—was in English, not some unspeakable foreign lingo. The first letter, addressed to an English woman, was dated "December 11th, 1798." It said, "You will rejoice to hear that no disaster has accompanied the commencement of an enterprise which you have regarded with such evil forebodings." It took a minute to decipher that sentence, but once I'd figured it out, I read it again and went on to the rest.

The writer was a young "naval adventurer," the captain of an English merchant ship sailing from a Russian port towards the North Pole. The man called himself Robert Walton, and he stupidly reckoned the polar cap a "country of eternal light," despite the ice plains his ship would have to navigate to reach it. The English woman he wrote was his sister, Mrs. Saville.

In his fourth letter, which turned into a log of shipboard events, he said he and his men had seen a "sledge" on the ice. A manlike giant had mushed his dog team beyond them, out of telescope range. "This appearance," Walton wrote his sister, "excited our unqualified wonder." I guess so.

Anyway, his mention of a giant made me think Jumbo'd hidden the letters because they reported on his ancestors. I figured Walton had seen an early forebear of Jumbo's on the sled, maybe Great-great-grandfather Clerval.

After four of Walton's letters, I reached the opening of the life story of a fevered European rescued from the ice by Walton's sailors. Walton had acted as this man's secretary, writing down all he said, so even though you got the guy's whole personal history, you got it in Walton's handwriting. "I am by birth a Genevese," the man told him, "and my family is one of the most distinguished of that republic." Of course, I didn't care rip about his la-di-da family.

So I refolded the letters and tied them up again with a ribbon such as could've decorated a ball gown for Napoleon's Josephine. I was about to jam this sheaf into the journal or log that'd held them, and to stuff the log back into the funny skin bag, and the funny skin bag back into the kayak—when a powerful urge to check out the log overcame me and I thumbed it open at the beginning:

Here I commence a new life. In the wretchedness of the candle-end of my former existence, I hoped only to die. So far into the maw of ruthlessness and depravity had I fallen, albeit at the heartless prodding of my maker, that I now despised myself as the world did. I ached for death, for the surcease of unappealable extinction, and hopefully I commended my spirit to that bleak demesne.

Of a sudden, after who knows how long or wherefore my unwelcome reprieve, I breathe again. My damaged heart thumps in the cave of my chest. My frozen limbs stir. My eyes, moments ago eclipsed by a primordial dark, lift into focus the Arctic stars and the sapphirine ice of a world that yesterday, or centuries past, I all too gladly fled and foreswore. Today, like Christendom's fabled Son of Man, I am resurrected.

This entry had no date, but it looked—old. It sounded old too. Reading it over, I could hear Jumbo speaking. So I also imagined him, once upon a time, writing them in a fancy hand—in English. He'd shaped his words a lot like Walton's, almost like he'd used Walton's for a model.

I carried Jumbo's log to the school desk at the head of my new bed, where I started copying Jumbo's story into my bigger notebook. It seemed important to do this—the most important thing I could do to keep Jumbo whole in my mind while I cut him open and laid him out like a lab frog in my crabbed copybook hand:

In homage to the merchant captain who set down in its entirety the story of my tormented maker, I indite in English this account of my final days as his creature. Of my new life subsequent to a perplexing resuscitation I also write. English leaps as readily to my brain, and thence to my hand, as does French. Did my brain once belong to a native of Albion? Whatever the case, I commence my new life with the fresh mental perspective afforded by the tongue of Marlowe, Shakespeare, and Milton.

What I now recollect of my old life is that after fleeing the ship on which had died the author at once of my being and its wretchedness, I could not steel myself to follow Frankenstein into the all-consuming abyss. Nay, I could not slay that which he had animated. Although I had promised Walton, in our unplanned meeting over my father's corpse, that I would annihilate myself in flames, I temporized. I discovered excuses to sustain my body, that great puppet of patchwork flesh that hauled about the ice my anguish-freighted soul; and with my body, my consciousness.

As I delayed, the weather grew ever more vicious and storm-racked. The northern lights faded behind a veil of tattered and then granitic clouds, from which snow whirled in turbulent blizzards and beneath which the oceans turned to entrapping rock. Walton and his crew could not break their vessel from this white prison, nor did the storms or cold relent to hearten, with even a feeble glimmering of escape, these unhappy men. By mid-October, all aboard the Caliban, *Walton's ship, had perished, frozen, starved, or been slain; previously, however, the captain had bent himself to copying every single word of every unsent letter to his sister, as if this obsessive activity would both warm his bones and free the fast-held* Caliban *from the ice.*

During the winter onslaught, I huddled with my sledge against the elements. I gathered about me my dogs. Around us, I erected a crude but fanciful fortification of ice. Inside the eye-stabbing brightness of this shelter, a dome on the groaning floes, I watched with pitiless interest the decline of my dogs, so cruelly deranged in their discomfort and hunger. They snarled at and bit one another, gnashing their teeth in fury, so that to prevent a massacre among them, I throttled the instigators, as I had throttled the foremost loved ones of my creator.

Even with their insulating fur, the dogs withstood the Arctic cold less well than I, for the howling of the gales invigorated me. Indeed, the continuous whipping of snow and pelletlike surface ice across that desert served only to confirm in me my decision to live.

Frankenstein, in assembling me from the bloodless leftovers of corpses, had unwittingly inured me to the depredations of polar cold. My dogs, however, suffered from it, turning on one another in terrifying fits of rapaciousness. In those same days, I so far forsook my preference for fruits, berries, and nuts that I ate the flesh of one of my animals. Later I distributed a moiety of its substance to the starved survivors.

At the end of these storms, I released from my pitted icehouse the only three dogs yet alive. With cries and menacing gestures, I chased them across that wasteland. They did not understand this eviction. Indeed, one dog sought to recover my affections with a fawning crawl and much ingratiating tail-wagging. At last, though, my unappeasable hostility conveyed itself to this animal and its four-legged comrades: with a barrage of ice missiles I induced them to retreat.

If I could not die on a self-made funeral pile, perhaps I could take my life by striding over the floes to the pole itself. Unlike Walton, I had no expectation of encountering there an eye of balmy warmth, but rather a ravaging cyclone of such sharp cold that, in the space between heartbeats, it would annihilate me. Hoping for such a fate, I set off from my ice shelter in what I assumed the correct direction. Above me, the sky burned like an alarming white mirror.

At length I spied at some distance the shroud of ropes and canvas that tented an ice-locked ship. I recognized this vessel as the Caliban. What other vessel, at this bleak time of year, had ventured so far into the Arctic wastes? Whether the storm had disoriented me or some inner compass had guided my steps mockingly towards my maker's wooden tomb, I know not. I knew only that I must complete my unplanned trek and board the ship. I did so with a curiosity greater than my revulsion at the thought of again exposing myself to human enmity.

I need not have trepidated. Every person aboard Walton's ship, as earlier noted, had died of hunger, frost, or intestine violence among the crew. The Caliban entombed not only Frankenstein, but also Walton and his sailors. I trod, then, a ship of death, and only the decay-postponing stewardship of the cold kept the odours of rot from checking my headlong inspection of the vessel.

Frankenstein, I should remark, had known a death-sleep longer than that of any other soul on the Caliban. I had no difficulty locating either him or Walton, however, for at some point in their ordeal the most vengefully inclined sailors, *perhaps thinking to defile the bodies of those to whom they attributed the full burthen of their predicament, had brought the two men—one dead, one presumably yet alive—abovedecks. Here they had lashed them back to back to the forward mast. Here Walton had died, his body so disposed that he might gaze impotently upon the unfolding mutiny. My creator, meanwhile, faced the blankness of the northern sea, his eyes cracked like small glass balls, his lips the silver-blue of oiled metal. I had slain before, but never had I witnessed at one moment, among creatures purportedly rational, such desolation and carnage, nor had the terrible melancholy of this scene devolved wholly from the blows of wind and frost. Dogs and men, it occurred to me, shared a desperation-fed savagery.*

Mayhap I laughed.

Abovedecks and below, I explored the Caliban. *After hurriedly perusing and securing for myself both the packet of letters that Walton had written his sister and the copy that he had made, I returned to the bow mast and cut down the author of my grotesque form and so of my pariahhood. Frankenstein's skin had pulled tight to his bones. His limbs had less pliancy than wood, not because rigor mortis had untowardly persisted but rather because the fluids of life had frozen in his veins. In this way was my maker rendered a macabre monument to his own vanity and hardness of heart. There on the deck, I kneaded him into a parody of flexibility. Then I threw him over my shoulder like a sack of meal and quitted the* Caliban, *leaping to the ice from a height that would have staggered a being of merely human parentage.*

I stopped copying. If Jumbo had written this sensational stuff, he was laying claim to a sideways sort of kinship to a European scientist named . . . well, Frankenstein. He'd also confessed to an unspecified murder or murders: "*I had slain before.*" That thrilled me. I mean, it'd taken me nearly a month to persuade myself Jumbo, despite his size and looks, meant no one, least of all me, any harm. And now I'd just read four words in his own hand that shot down all my hard-earned notions of his harmlessness.

I lit a cigarette. The butts of a couple of others lay smoldering in the ashtray on my desk. My tongue tasted like a charred wedge of bologna.

Then a calming thought occurred, a thought that made more sense than tagging Jumbo the mad golem of an eighteenth-century anatomy student and chemist by the name of Frankenstein: Jumbo was writing a book, a novel. His bulk and his lopsided face had led him to see himself in Karloff's screen monster—which he really didn't much resemble—and to write an original story featuring himself in the monster's role. That theory tied up a few of my frayed nerves.

I went back to reading and copying:

With Frankenstein's corpse as freight, I struck out from Walton's ship towards the south. In the long dusk at that latitude, directions were hard to verify. Still, both the rush of ice-capped sea currents and the benison of fuller sunlight told me that I had intuited my course aright. Even the lovely gyre-making of a raptor, shadowed on the snow, seemed to approve my migration route. Oddly, I had no idea what my destination must be or why I had undertaken this grueling journey; a month or more ago, I had thought to end all my journeyings in the swift uprush of a funeral blaze.

Almost insensate, I trudged the whiteness. I steered by the low-riding sun on a southeasterly oblique that at length brought me off the ice onto a vast range of undulant snow. I scarcely paused, either to moisten my parched lips or to poke beneath the glacial crust for a root or tuber with which to propitiate the gods of hunger. Whenever I chanced near crude fishing villages or inland settlements, I took pains to avoid confrontation with the inhabitants. I fled men as the tundra wolf does.

Indeed, I had for companions on one leg of my journey a pack of wolves. They trailed alongside, eager for me to stumble under the dead Frankenstein and so succumb to their fangs. Once, half exasperated, half exultant, I stooped and compacted a missile of ice. Immediately, I dispersed the pack by hurling this frozen shot into its ranks. It slew—yea, nearly decapitated—one lean but shaggy animal, the example of whose demise vividly impressed itself upon the others.

One morning, after a rare surrender to the call of sleep, I awoke to find myself and the inert nearby form of my creator surrounded by reindeer. These lithe beasts browsed that terrain as if he and I had inextricably melded with it. No alarm, or even skittishness, did we provoke in them, not even when I arose from my bed of snow and once more lay my father's corpse over my shoulder. For miles, it seemed, I trudged with these deer, migrant with them, a fallen seraph among the ice waste's ghostly kine.

An unexpected change in the weather at last effected our separation from the herd. A wind of gale proportions blasted ice grains across the snowscape. I howled into this howling. Land forms but an arm's length away shewed as blurred geometries. I flailed at them, for I wished both contact and certainty. Between the roaring gusts, I sometimes thought I saw fantastic cliffs, as white as milk and evanescent as truth.

At length I came to those ill-seen ramparts. Like a thousand panpipes the storm whistled, even as snow sleeted in interthreaded sheets. A channel in the rock led me blindly upwards. Had I known the precariousness of my ascent, with a corpse as entrammeling cargo, I would have thrown myself upon the nearest rock face and clung to it like an apperceptive lichen. Fortunately perhaps, I had no such understanding of the danger and so proceeded with the singlemindedness of a zealot.

It would have eased my task to drop Frankenstein and struggle on alone, but a stubborn scrupulosity prevented me; a perversity, many might accuse, for at some point on my trek I had resolved to recompense myself upon this man, who had so aggrieved and hurt me, by tearing his heart from his breast. I intended to feed that cold organ, piece by bitter piece, to the hawks of the Kara Sea, and no hardship met on my way could turn me from this aim.

The passion of my will notwithstanding, I weakened. The wind's howling, combined with the unrelenting sting of ice and blasted rock, vitiated my strength. Fatigue came. In time, groping along a narrow ice ledge, I chanced upon a crevasse, a doorway into shelter. I crawled in, dragging my passenger with me. Here I obtained to a peacefulness in which I had nearly lost faith. Here, indeed, I slept.

Let me rather indite that like a peltless bear, I hibernated. How long I lay thus stupefied, wrapped about my sire's body, I cannot tell. Somewhere in that sleep, I drifted so near the ivory reef of extinction that I dreamt myself moored to it. The deepest flint of my awareness now took as dead the foundered body that it had once animated. That iota's last spark guttered towards darkness. Insofar as consciousness remained to me, it exulted in the nearness of its extinguishment.

Time passed. More time succeeded to this. Then, to my initial dismay and bewilderment, my shelter's roof fell in—clamourously, precipitously—and a myriad spectacular figures of lightning revived me to the long heartache of the world. Precisely how this revival occurred, I cannot relate. Why it should have happened capsulates a mystery even more recondite. Lightning, thunder, biting sleet—meteorological phenomena seldom seen in train—assaulted my cavern, quickening in me the blood-borne engines of life. Although Frankenstein, my author, of course continued dead, I had reluctantly arisen. The outcome of this fleer at mortality lay hidden in the ice rains of the night and the unforeseeable weathers of tomorrow. . . .

I'd been copying Jumbo's words—if they were his words—for nearly three hours. Boy, could he spin it out! His story had a raw power. So did his old-timey sentences. I stopped at "unforeseeable weathers of tomorrow" because those words ended the first section of his journal. Thumbing ahead, the less I thought it all an opera-sized fiction and the more I figured it a record of a man's—an artificial person's—long and peculiar life.

In fact, the next section of the journal had a title, "From Remorse to Self-Respect: My Second Life."

By now I'd smoked seven cigarettes and sweated through my T-shirt. Jumbo didn't just look like a monster, the victim of a crazed pituitary—he *was* a monster, the handmade stepson of a scientist whose name had become a synonym for . . . well, for Hollywood jeepery-creepery. Mister JayMac had given me to room with an inhuman critter who'd killed, cursed life, and stalked his shook-up maker to a packet ship in the Barents Sea. I was *living with* the thing!

Suddenly, in that hot attic: an icicle to the heart.

I heard Jumbo on the stairs. Despite his size, he didn't have a heavy footfall, but the steps from the second floor to the third, if hit just right (or just wrong), creaked like a mast rigging, and Jumbo sometimes hit them so as to warn me he was on his way. Pretty thoughty. He didn't want to catch me whacking off to a Varga girl, I guess. Or maybe he just hoped I'd reverse the favor. Anyway, I should've hurried to slide his stolen letters back into his journal, and his journal back into the bag, and the bag back into his kayak, and the kayak back under his bed, so he wouldn't catch me snooping.

But I didn't. A funny feeling grabbed me, and I convinced myself my snooping didn't weigh a sou against the cruddy deception he'd worked on my teammates and me. Especially me. He'd tried to pass as a human being—*On Being a Real Person*, what a joke!—when he actually had blood lines similar to a can of Spam's.

I put his letters in the journal, his log in the leather bag, and his bag in the kayak, but I left the kayak out from under the bed, a slap at his dishonesty.

Jumbo came in. "Hello, Daniel. It's infernally hot up here. Why aren't you—?" He saw the kayak. He saw that I hadn't even bothered to replug its manhole with his grass mat, and he shot me a look. I shot it right back, cheeky as rip, condemning him for a liar.

Jumbo sighed and removed his ivory-tied leather bag from the kayak. He eased his marbled log book out of the bag. The letters fell out. The looseness of the ribbon holding them together—it unraveled as they fell—told Jumbo what he wanted to know: I'd eyeballed the contents. He made no move to pick up the letters.

Instead, he opened the log. He held it in one hand, like a hymnal, and licked his index finger so he could page through it. He turned three or four pages. He squinted at the book's gutter, sniffed it, and made a face—which was sort of like Quasimodo pulling on a Halloween mask. Then puffed into the log and blew a scatter of cigarette ashes at me.

He knew. I knew. We both knew.

"Ah," Jumbo said. He sat down on the edge of his bed and stared past me out the window.

Maybe I should've run for cover. An inhuman fiend had caught me red-handed—well, pink-handed—rummaging through his stuff. It stood to reason he'd want to wreak bone-crushing havoc on my person.

I couldn't get scared. I'd lived with Jumbo a month. I'd trusted him enough as a teammate to make dozens of long throws across the infield to him. I'd eaten with him and listened to his manateelike gasps as he slept. He was my roomy. Besides, the idea of an inhuman fiend compiling private papers sort of contradicted itself. Most inhuman fiends don't write memoirs. If they do—*Mein Kampf*, say, or *The Enemy Within*—they don't often refer to themselves as fiends, demons, abominations, ogres, or wretches.

"You made excellent use of your afternoon, I see." Jumbo put his log on his knees and flipped on through it. "You don't disappoint me. I had hoped your curiosity would prompt you to this. Like nearly everyone else, Daniel, I yearn for a kindred spirit. A friend."

Pardon me? Had Jumbo just implied that because I'd snooped on him, he'd now regard me as a friend?

"I *wanted* you to find the kayak," he said. "And hoped that it would lead you to examine it further, even to the point of unloading it. I feared only that a superstitious scruple would prevent you from ransacking my belongings for their secrets."

A scruple like honesty?

"Your activity this afternoon greatly relieves me. Now I don't have to hide my origins or lie about myself. Thank you, Daniel, for having more curiosity than character."

You're welcome, I thought.

Was Jumbo pummeling me with sarcasms? He didn't seem to be. He tapped the log in his lap. "How far did you read?"

I shrugged.

Jumbo set the log aside and stood. "The Karloff festival in LaGrange was a lucky event. Despite the pain those films often give me, I took you because I'd decided—*almost* decided—to reveal my true identity to you. The *Frankenstein* trilogy highlights the similarities and the differences, of bearing and behavior, between Karloff's impersonation of a monster and my daily burlesque of a human being. On line there, I almost lost my nerve and tried to dissuade you from going in, but, happily, you insisted. My nerve failed me again inside the theater, but you prevailed there too. Tell me, then—did those films in any way prompt today's meddling?"

I shrugged again.

But Jumbo had neared the truth. Since attending the Roxy, I'd allowed all my shapeless doubts about him to gel into one fat suspicion.

He paced. "Those movies corrupt events more accurately portrayed in the epistolary writings of Robert Walton." He picked up the letters from the floor and went on pacing. "The world knows these events, however, as the first novel of Mary Wollstonecraft Shelley, wife of the English poet, Percy Bysshe Shelley. Daniel, have you ever read the text published as her novel *Frankenstein*?" I felt like I was listening to several different radios at the same time: too much information raining down. "*Have you?*" For the first time since returning to our room, Jumbo scared me.

I nodded because I had.

"Excellent. You apprehend that I am the ogre whose origins receive such injudicious, even libelous, treatment in the first Karloff film." He shook the letters. "The fiend whose true history discloses itself here. Did you peruse these pages or only my journal?"

I nodded at the journal on his bed. I couldn't explain that I'd skimmed Walton's first four letters before . . . well, copying out the opening entry in his log.

"Before you question me, read these letters," Jumbo said. "*All* of them." He placed them on my desk, on the notebook I'd been using when I first heard his footsteps.

I picked up the letters.

Jumbo went to his bookcase and took out a stained volume. "Or reread this. Its text more or less duplicates the texts of Walton's letters. Where they diverge, the letters represent the more accurate transcription of events." He gave me the book and took the letters away. "But read the book. Its type is easier on the eye than Walton's cursive."

Jumbo tied his letters up again and placed them, along with his journal, into the beaded leather bag. He put the bag in the kayak and the mat into its cockpit, shoved the loaded kayak back under his bed, and abruptly left the room.

29

Reading a book on the sneak has a lot more allure than getting it thrown at you as an assignment. *Oliver Twist* as a book-report chore will bore you to lip drool. The same pages sampled in the library stacks will rev up your mind and carry you faster than a bullet train to a new world. I'd enjoyed reading Jumbo's log. Whether I'd like rereading *Frankenstein* on his outright command was a moot question. I had half a mind to throw his plump little book out the window.

But I started it and ran headlong into the blah-blah-blahs that'd almost stopped me dead in my tracks in high school, junk like "diffusing a perpetual splendor," "the inestimable benefit which I shall confer on all mankind," "under your gentle and feminine fosterage," and so on.

Luckily, the writer—Mary Shelley, Robert Walton, whoever—finally rolled out the cannons and calliopes, adrenaline-rousing stuff about whale-fishers, Russia, dog sledges, and a creature of "gigantic stature" out on the ice—sections that reminded me of Jumbo's own log, of course, and even of his highfalutin style, but that riveted me to my chair anyway.

Pretty soon, I'd reached Victor Frankenstein's account of trying to build a creature "about eight feet in height, and proportionately large." It got to be evening. Jumbo came in and put a cake pan of vegetables and a fork in front of me.

"Eat," he said.

I noticed that Jumbo's face—yellow cheeks, watery eyes, bluish black lips—squared with the book's first description of the monster. But I kept reading and ate without looking at the cake pan or tasting what Kizzy'd fixed.

I read all night. Jumbo may've walked the grounds or dozed on a parlor sofa. Who knows? Around four in the morning, he poked his head back in just as the fiend in *Frankenstein* says, "Polluted by crimes and torn by the bitterest remorse, where can I find rest but in death?"

Yeah, where? I motioned Jumbo in and read the story's last three paragraphs.

"Well?" he said.

I tossed the book back and paced the room with my hands in my back pockets. I must've looked a little like the tormented anatomy student at the height of his project: eyes red-rimmed, hair sweaty, hands as fluttery as quail.

Jumbo had evolved out of the body and the personality of a patchwork thing gimmicked into life by Victor Frankenstein. In the account said to be Mrs. Shelley's, Jumbo'd had no name, just *creature, monster, fiend,* or *demon,* and nobody but nobody called him *mister* or *sir.* Henry Clerval, the name Jumbo used today, had once belonged to Frankenstein's best friend, another of Jumbo's early murder victims. So you had to believe he'd killed, or caused to die, at least five people, including the man who'd created him, and the friend named Clerval.

Thing is, despite Jumbo's journal and his looks, I still didn't quite buy that he was *the* monster. My mind's eye kept casting back to that ship caught in the ice of the Barents Sea, but the off-chance that Hoey and his pals were trying to con me kept me from tumbling brain over butt to its "truth."

"I asked you to read my story," Jumbo said, "because you would understand that the crimes of my youth have had no sequel in this epoch of my life. I require an ally, Daniel."

I rubbed my upper arms like somebody trying to stay warm in a meat locker. Every lobe of my brain felt more tightly stuffed than a butterball turkey.

"Practice in four hours," Jumbo said. "Perhaps we should sleep." He stretched out on his bed and, in thirty seconds or less, began to snort and wheeze.

My questions sorted themselves into a long, worry-laden file. In Mrs. Shelley's doctored transcription of the deathbed confession of Dr. Frankenstein, his creature had been a true monster: eight feet tall. Nobody could look at him without cringing or picking up a stick. "No mortal could support the horror of that countenance," Frankenstein had said, "a thing such as even Dante could not have conceived." Which mostly proves Dante never visited Dixie: Jumbo had a fair claim on ugliness, but if you looked, he wasn't much grottier than some of the folks prowling Kmart of an evening.

Other questions?

Well, the fiend in the "novel" has the agility and stamina of an Olympic athlete. Once, like an ape with vernier jets, he shinnies straight up the face of a small mountain. Jumbo had the upper-body look of a gorilla, but his bad legs wouldn't let him scale a cliff that fast.

I also had to wonder again about Jumbo's age. If he and the monster in Mrs. Shelley's "novel" were one and the same, what had my roommate been doing for the past century and a half? No one that big could hide very long, at least not in a city or a town, and I couldn't imagine how he'd ended up playing ball in Highbridge.

Finally, how did Jumbo feel about himself and everything that'd happened to him? Dr. Frankenstein couldn't tolerate his critter's looks. He'd skedaddled soon after mumbo-jumboing awake the graveyard parts he'd used to model the thing. If you bought this *Frankenstein* foofaraw, Jumbo didn't actually rate, biologically, as the doctor's get—but the doctor'd made him, and if you give something life, you're responsible for helping it out, right? Laws exist against running out on your kids, even against sitting on an alimony check. So Dr. F. doesn't stack up too well against your basic alimony jumper, some of whom have pretty good reasons for missing payments, and a lot of whom love their kids even if they can't pay. But old Dr. F. turned his back on his son—sorry, his creature—then lied to him and tore apart the cut-and-paste Eve beast he'd promised to build him as a way of making up for his fatherly shortcomings.

As Jumbo slept, I mulled this stuff. I hiked around the room too keyed up to lie down and rest from nearly ten hours of straight reading. Even in his reddest-eyed condition, Jumbo's daddy didn't have much on me . . . .

At practice that morning, Jumbo, Muscles, and I all played like sleepwalkers. My backasswardsness—once, a double-play toss from Junior bounced off my left tit—all went back to my rereading of *Frankenstein*. Jumbo's slipshod play had a like explanation. He'd stayed out of our room to let me read.

But Musselwhite's lousy play puzzled me—till I saw LaRaina Pharram sitting next to Phoebe in the left-field bleachers. Miss LaRaina wore a dress of orange, red, and white, like a lion leaping into a sunset full of cockatoos. She gave Muscles the eye and shifted around so her easel-splash dress whipped about her calves and pulled tight across her thighs. No wonder Muscles couldn't motor. He'd probably been busier last night than I had.

"Oh, puh-*leeze!*" Phoebe said a few minutes into this show. "Act yore age, Mama!"

"Mind how you talk," Miss LaRaina said amiably.

Phoebe got up and stalked all the way from the bleachers to the Hellbender dugout. After talking to Phoebe, Mister JayMac stood on the dugout step and yelled, "LaRaina, go home! You're distracting the troops!"

"Could've fooled me," Miss LaRaina yelled back. "A flat Coke's got more fizz than this sorry crew!" But after blowing a kiss off her palm at Muscles (to Reese Curriden's chagrin), she seized her pocketbook and sashayed out of view.

Finally, Mister JayMac whistled us in. "Yall stink today," he said. "I doubt you could field a tumbleweed with a tennis net. A few of yall need deodorizing worsen the Highbridge sewage-treatment plant. Go home. Tomorrow's another day, but it'd better be bettern this one or I'll sell yall to Johnny Sayigh and move to Cuba." He stomped off.

After practice, Phoebe met Jumbo and me in the parking lot at the *Brown Bomber*. She had on overalls, bebop shoes, and a floppy short-sleeved shirt that made her arms look as snappable as day-lily stalks.

"Come to dinner with Mama and me on Friday after the Marble Springs game," she said. "Mama said I could ask."

The invitation surprised me. It confused me a little too. I held the back of my hand to Jumbo's stomach to ask if Phoebe meant him too.

Phoebe blushed. "I was asking you, Danny," she said. "It, well, it wouldn't . . ." She stared at her bebops.

From the bus, a rude farting sound and ugly laughter.

Jumbo said, "It wouldn't look good for a bachelor to visit your house while your father's still abroad."

"Her daddy's not a broad!" Turkey Sloan shouted out the nearest window. "He's a captain!"

"Will you come?" Phoebe asked me.

Ack. I'd already had one dinner with Phoebe and her mama, and it hadn't exactly gone down like an oyster on a slide of bourbon. Also, when Miss LaRaina wondered what kissing Jumbo would be like, Phoebe'd said, "*Mama, that's vile!*" But what, when she'd cried that, had worried her more—the health of her folks' marriage or the foulness of Jumbo's looks? She'd really broadcast mixed signals on that one.

"Accept her invitation," Jumbo said.

Miss LaRaina, at the curb in a gray '38 Pontiac, mashed her horn—once, twice. Phoebe peered at me, half pleading but more than a smidgen peeved.

"He accepts," Jumbo said. "Don't you, Daniel?" His hand seized the back of my skull. Out of Phoebe's view, he pushed my head forwards and, with a yank on my hair, tugged it back to upright. Then he let go.

"After Friday's game then," Phoebe said. "We'll give you a ride soon's you've showered." She sort of skipped towards her mama's smoky old Pontiac.

The *Bomber* carried us Hellbenders back to McKissic House. A crew of them razzed me about Phoebe, but Darius kept as quiet as a gambler computing blackjack odds.

30

Here." Jumbo put his journal on my desk. "You've copied the first part of my log in your own hand." He put my notebook down beside the log. "Continue. Act as my amanuensis, and copy the rest. One day, you can corroborate a story few would otherwise believe."

Seeing the log and my notebook together embarrassed me, but I opened them and began reading the log where I'd left off, at Jumbo's resurrection in the ice cave. With his blessing, I copied this new material as I read.

From Remorse to Self-Respect:
My Second Life

At the commencement of my new life, as throughout my old one, bitter cold scant afflicted me. I preferred it to the warmth of summer, responding to it as an assemblage of pistons, flywheels, and cogs responds to lubrication. My chief hindrance lay not in meteorological conditions, but in the body of my dead creator. I felt an obligation to keep it with me as both a macabre talisman and a relic of loathsome veneration. Wheresoever I ventured, I carried Frankenstein with me, initially slung over my shoulder or under my arm, but later arrayed on a sledge dressed with evergreen boughs, a rude travois, that I fastened by a barken harness to my waist and pulled, as a bride goes before her wedding train. Unlike a bride, I sought to deflect attention from my passage and so invariably travelled by night, frequently through thick forests or over rugged terrain. More than once, after a violent spill, I had to retrieve my passenger and lash him more firmly to his carrier.

What thoughts I had—what overriding goal—I cannot fully recall. I understood, I think, that in my second advent I had no more hope of gathering companions or of confounding likely foes than I had known in the unholy year of my first reign. Thus, I wandered the most remote and desolate places of Siberia, eschewing any human contact but availing myself of every chance to study the habits of the strange beings whose lands I traipsed.

As a result, having first mastered a language by eavesdropping on another drilling in French, I quite early added to my repertoire not only English and German, but also the curious Hyperborean tongues of the Kets, the Yukaghirs, the Luorawetians, and the Gilyaks. To these I added the dialects of other peoples scattered about the fjords and inlets of the Arctic Circle, not excluding the two chief dialects of the Innuits, or Esquimaux, across the Chukchi Sea in North America.

During one blizzard I took shelter in a hovel roofed with tundra blocks, chinked with peat moss, and protected on the northeast by gnarled cedars. In the dugout's only room, the skeleton of a Cossack trapper, who had starved to death, kept me grinning company. I grew fonder of this mute lodger than I had ever been of Frankenstein, for I had no memory of abuse at his hands or of contumely from his lips. The corpses got on well, however, and I rejoiced in their undemonstrative friendship. Neither protested when I took the hovel's only table as my desk.

Soon afterwards, I coaxed a corroded lamp into operation with oil from a covered bucket. With sufficient light to work by, I began to indite in my counterfeit of Walton's cursive the texts of his epistles to Mrs. Saville. As an icy northern siroc keened over the dugout, I scribbled for hours without respite.

Occasionally I paused to replenish the oil in my lamp or my paper from the stores of the Caliban. *Several times, aghast at the indiscriminate rapaciousness of my hunger, I made a meal of stringy dried meat—fish, fowl, or mammal, I neither knew nor cared—purloined from a smokehouse earlier in my travels. Insofar as I knew diurnality, I finished my copy in six or seven days and slumped across the table in a stupor of exhaustion.*

Why such fever-blighted labour? Unless I discharged the obligations of my previous life, I felt, I could never turn the promise of my new incarnation to aught but catastrophe. That way I had already journeyed. I owed the ghost of Captain Walton my gratitude. In trying to tell his sister Mrs. Saville of his activities, he had set down in all its grisly particulars the tale of my creation. He had also left a chronicle of my rejection and my subsequent career as a pitiless Fury. This record of my dashed hopes and my shameful crimes would henceforth lesson me. My debt to Walton for producing it demanded that I repay him by sending to Mrs. Saville the letters, or legible copies of the letters, comprising that tale. Thus I had determined in the first lucid moments after my lightning-prodded rebirth. Perhaps selfishly, I had also resolved to claim the original documents as my own.

Dispatching even my copies of these epistles to Mrs. Saville proved a formidable undertaking. I had sheltered miles from human habitation. No post-road or port was readily accessible. However, the unfortunate Cossack who had excavated the dugout had situated it near a river that hastened turbulently beneath a skin of ice to a bay on the Siberian Sea. With difficulty, I followed this frozen waterway to a bayside settlement, hauling on my travois my desiccated and indurate creator.

This settlement harboured between two glacial cliffs near the cold sea's jewel-green waters. On the western escarpment, I took up my observations of the mercantile activity below. At night I prowled like a phantom among the rude shops and barracks fronting the water. During my reconnoiterings, I heard a bearded Ket in sealskin leggings call the village Janalach.

A Russian vessel lay at anchor in the bay. Fully rigged and masted, its sails were furled in horizontal cocoons. It had wintered in Janalach. Its captain and sailors patiently awaited the brief Siberian summer and the short-lived retreat of the ice. Cossack seamen and Yakut nomads conferred amid the mud- and slush-defiled streets with Yukaghir traders, a polyglot scene both festive and fraught with disaccord. The sun's wan eye had thawed not only the harbour ice but also the heretofore frozen hatreds and cupidities of all those gathered there. I witnessed quarrels, cozenings, fisticuffs, and sanguinary mayhem. That Frankenstein had viewed my behaviour as singular and tantamount to depraved began to impress me as a provincial narrowness of vision. Had he never remarked the reprehensible doings of his own kind?

Soon I became aware that a speculator of Scottish descent had voyaged aboard the Russian ship, the Tamyr Princess, *to this bleak coast. The Cossack sailors called him Angus Ross, pronouncing his family name* Roos, *as if he had ties to their motherland more binding than the crassly mercantile. They also chaffed him about his ruddy face and his unruly muttonchop whiskers. Ross habitually answered with a swearing surliness that they rightly took as bluster. His Russian was of the inept pidgen variety that provoked further ridicule and general merriment. The sailors, it seemed, viewed him as their mascot. He got on better with the Yukaghirs in Janalach than did most of the Russians, however, and, despite his brusqueness, rarely fell into a serious quarrel with anyone.*

I once ventured close enough to witness Ross's dealings with a Yaket clansman working a movable forge in the lean-to of a smithy. The smith converted various metal articles supplied by the sailors—belt buckles, fish hooks, hatch rings, and so forth—into cooking wares and weapons for his tribespeople, trading animals skins and trinkets for the wherewithal of his craft.

Ross bartered crisply with the Yaket for a set of small metal polar bears. The smith would accept nothing for them, as, I surmised, Ross had known from the outset of their negotiations, but the old pistol wedged in his belt. The works of the pistol had long since rusted, and its trigger would not pull. At last, however, the men made their trade, whereupon the Yaket stoked the engine of his forge and proceeded to work from the flintlock's barrel a handsome tobacco pipe. Ross watched the process (as did I, albeit clandestinely), with evident appreciation of the smith's handiwork. Soon, after all, the nomad who acquired the pipe must return to Janalach for tobacco.

Upon quitting the lean-to, Ross walked to a set-apart jumble of boulders near the water. To gloat, perhaps, over his booty, he disposed himself on a rock and arranged his iron figurines upon it between his legs, as a child would deploy a regiment of tin soldiers. I approached Ross from behind, covered his mouth and muttonchops, and impelled him irresistibly to his back; his toys fell like dominos. Ross essayed a scream, which my hand muffled. Additionally, the backwards force I imparted to his chin warned that further struggle would snap his neck. I regretted the subterfuge, but deemed it necessary to quiet him. He subsided beneath me, the horror engendered by my countenance evident in the wildness of his eyes.

"*When do you return to your own country?*" *I asked Ross in English.*

"*What manner of creature are you?*" *he replied, when I provisionally unstopped his mouth. "Why this attack?*"

"*Because only you among all those gathered here speaks the language in which I now address you,*" *I said.*

"*Then for the first time I curse my birthplace,*" *Ross whispered. "Pray, let me go.*"

"*When do you next plan to visit your homeland?*"

"*In the fall,*" *Ross said. "As soon after the* Tamyr Princess *has put in at Murmansk as I may book passage.*"

"*Passage to where?*" *I asked.*

"*I have family in Kirkcaldy upon whom I have not laid eyes in five years,*" *he said. "I pray that I am not to be denied a chance to see them again, ever.*"

"*I wish you no harm, Angus Ross of Kirkcaldy. Rather, I desire from you a not unreasonable boon.*"

"*I am at your service.*" *At this confession, I smiled, perhaps for the first time since my rebirth; the Scot drew away from my smile as if from an unsheathed dagger. "Pray, sir, tell me what you would have me do.*"

"*First, Mr. Ross, what I ask, I ask for another's sake. Also, I have waylaid you as I have because I well know the hateful, even violent response that my unforeseen appearance among your kind everywhere excites.*"

Through gritted teeth Ross said, "That I understand."

I released him. He made no move to bolt, and I put a finger to my lips. "Know," *I whispered, "that once you leave here, sworn to secrecy about both your charge and its author, I have no power to guarantee your faithfulness to it. Should you abandon the task, you need fear neither my following curse nor the eternal prospect of retribution. What I ask, I trust you to do from a sense of honour.*"

"*A mighty trust,*" *said Ross, whether to commend or belittle it I could not tell. He deposited his figurines in a bag of waterproof fishskin. I, in turn, took from my pocket the letters that I wanted Ross to deliver to Mrs. Saville. I outlined for him his charge and gave him the packet. Although I could hardly enforce his compliance, I asked that he refrain from trumpeting any word of our talk or even of his unexpected meeting with me here in Janalach.*

"*But who are you?*" *Ross asked. "Aye, what are you?*"

"*Because you have agreed to carry these letters, I give you leave to read them,*" *I said. "They explain, not always fairly or compassionately, what I do not choose to reiterate on this dreary shore. Fare thee well, Mr. Ross. I thank you in advance for the brave accomplishment of your errand." With that, I leapt away into a nearby crevice and scaled its chimney, for atop the cliff I had hidden my sire in a fortress of glacial debris.*

Ross, I observed, stood rooted to the spot where I had accosted him. Had he imagined my unlikely manifestation? At length the packet in his hands persuaded him otherwise, and he ambled bemusedly back into the company of men.

As I learned years later, Ross fulfilled his humanitarian charge. The letters entrusted to him—nay, my copies of those letters—he delivered to Mrs. Saville, a neighbour of the Godwins in Holburn, on his trip home to Kirkcaldy. Later, in a quest for solace, Mrs. Saville passed them along to a member of that family, either to peruse and destroy or to bring out under the imprimatur of M. J. Godwin & Co.

Ross had told Walton's sister that he had received the copied letters from a giant much resembling the creature delineated therein. Mrs. Saville, knowing the handwriting for a good but imperfect forgery of her brother's, rejected the Scotsman's tale and his letters as a cruel hoax. She had long ago deduced, and resigned herself to the fact, of Captain Walton's death. For his part, William Godwin, author of Enquiry Concerning Political Justice *and the novel* Caleb Williams, *could not steel himself either to destroy or to publish the peculiar manuscript passed along to him by his second wife, the erstwhile Mary Jane Clairmont.*

Almost by default, the letters fell into the keeping of the adolescent Mary Wollstonecraft Godwin, a young woman of enormous wit, independence, and energy. She regarded Walton's letters as a cabalistic document of Promethean consequence. Even before her "elopement" to the Continent with the married poet, Percy Bysshe Shelley, in the summer of 1814, she had struggled to shape a readable story from these materials. Almost four years later, having reworked and abridged my copies of the letters, Mary allowed them, with more revisions by her husband, to appear anonymously in three small volumes from the little-regarded publishing house of Lackington, Hughes, Harding, Mavor, & Jones.

Some literary historians have contended that this "novel" burst upon the world without an acknowledged author because Mrs. Shelley feared either that reviewers would never believe a woman her age the originator of such a brutal and abhorrent tale or that her notoriety as a wanton and unorthodox, even anarchic, female would poison its reception and sales. I offer a simpler reason for the absence of the author's name from the title page: Mrs. Shelley, though she introduced certain clarifying changes into the manuscript, neither conceived the story nor wrote it. The text of Frankenstein *indisputably reveals its author to be the late Robert Walton. On the other hand, because that text consists largely of my creator's partisan recitation of his own biography, even Walton deserves little credit beyond that due any conscientious scribe or amanuensis. In a sense, the book's title simultaneously reveals its author. Why, then, would a person of Mrs. Shelley's talent and probity wish to recommend herself as the fountainhead of this monstrous story?*

Initially, of course, she did not. Later, however, when the book created a nationwide stir, prompting a writer in Blackwood's *to put forward his sincere wishes for the putative author's "future happiness," thereby forgiving Mrs. Shelley her unconventional past, it became harder to insist upon her role as an editor and ever more tempting to embrace the work as wholly the product of her own philosophical musings and storytelling proclivities. In 1831, this temptation led her to elaborate upon her husband's mood-setting fiction of the ghost-story-writing competition at the Villa Diodati in the summer of 1816. Further, she irrevocably acknowledged authorship of* Frankenstein *by allowing the publishers of the revised edition of 1832 to feature prominently on its title page her name. Perhaps the fact that in the fourteen years between the two editions she had published three novels of her own, along with many accomplished incidental writings, effectively obscured for her the actual genesis of the work. Mrs. Shelley suffered much in her heroic life, from the high-minded betrayals of her most cherished loved ones as well as from the untimely deaths of her husband and all but one of her children. Thus, I do not anathematise her for claiming unassisted creatorship of the one title—*The Last Man, *fine as it is, does not qualify—that enrolled her among the immortals.*

Quitting Janalach, I blessedly had no foreknowledge of the events that would carry my distorted biography to the world. I wished only to atone for the crimes of my past life and to discover in my second incarnation a place of at least marginal acceptance. The necessity to hide, to make certain salubrious changes in myself as well as discreet contacts among the tribespeople of the ice coasts and the taiga, required discipline and fortitude. I hiked east, sustaining myself on lichens, bog moss, and the leaves and spring fruit of several different kinds of stunted shrubs. I made skis of larchwood and built myself a movable blind of mammoth bones and evergreen foliage. The blind enabled me to skirt the encampments of nomads, and the fluid edges of reindeer herds, without betraying to either man or beast my presence in or near their environs.

After several months' travel and the overmastering of many hardships, however, two Chukchi hunters caught me traversing a barren expanse of tundra and let fly at me from their compound bows a barrage of arrows. That I dragged a travois and attired myself as a human being enraged rather than conciliated them.

I had trespassed their demesne, and my size convicted me as a likely scourge of their hunting grounds.

Two arrows struck home, their walrus–ivory points embedding themselves in my flesh, one above my hip and the other in my calf. I roared bitterly. I menaced the bowmen with broad semaphoring gestures. Uncowed, they muttered unintelligibly, perhaps disappointedly, before retreating out of sight beyond a fluted sastruga.

Thus abandoned, I sought to minister to my wounds. I snapped off the arrow shafts and removed my leggings to expose the embedded points. In this half-naked state, I would have presented a prodigiously vulnerable target, had my Chukchi tormentors returned with reinforcements. I made haste, then, to dislodge the ivory barbs with the tip of a skinning knife. The pain was slight, but a copious oozing of pale blood accompanied this surgery. With spruce resin and rags I dressed my wounds. Then, lame and sore, I drew on my leggings and retreated several miles to an orphaned copse of cedars. Therein I erected a hut of branches and sailcloth in which to mull my outcast state and to recoup my vigour.

This recoupment, although at the time I hardly knew it, protracted into a hibernation akin to my death sleep in the ice cavern far to the west. A blizzard stormed and departed. The twilit autumn turned to night. I may have had some imperfect consciousness of time's passage, but in my womblike shelter, the lashing of the sleet, the lamentations of the wind, and the brittle starlight strewn above the grove chimed in me as inward rather than outer phenomena. In my stupefaction I reposed much as a salmon, stunned by the cuff of a bear and twitching on a rock, would nonetheless intuit its fate.

Eventually, I awoke to ice, snow, and uncouth Aeolian music. My wounds had healed. Revitalised, I fought clear of my wintry entombment and journeyed again towards the utopia of my innocent fancy . . . .

At dinner, Curriden griped Kizzy'd put baking soda instead of baking powder into her biscuits. (Or vice versa.) They looked like "baby cow flops" and tasted like "carbon-paper ashes."

"Mrs. Lorrows has had an off day," Jumbo defended her.

"Uh-uh," Kizzy said. "But I sometimes has a turrible day when the likes of yall jabbers yo ugly spite."

"Mr. Curriden has had an off day too," Jumbo said.

"These biscuits could drop an ox," Curriden said. "From the inside or out, eaten or thrown."

"From here on out, Mister Reese," Kizzy said, pointing a witchy finger at him, "pray God I don't pyson yo tea."

I scrambled back upstairs to find my place in Jumbo's log, and the argument in the kitchen—the feud—got louder. Soon, though, I was hip-deep in Jumbo's autobiography, and the noisy dipsy-do downstairs might as well've originated in Zanzibar. I no longer heard it.

3 1

My Second Life (Continued)

I nitially without aim or plan, I wandered the coldest and least-known wildernesses of Siberia, from its northernmost bays to the sparse taiga forests of the Kolyma Mountains, and many other remote locales besides. Why did I live?

At length I found reasons: to atone for the murders I had committed as Frankenstein's outcast get; to discover a suitable resting place for my late progenitor; to enter human society as a worthy and productive citizen.

Vain hopes!

The cold agreed with me, as I have said, and I had little trouble sustaining myself even on thin soups of such despised vegetable matter as lichens, bark, evergreen needles, moss, and the tubercules and roots of many an unprepossessing shrub. As one item in my continuing penance, I had resolved never to eat flesh again, and had perfectly heeded this self-commandment. Other opportunities for atonement seldom arose, however, and I began to sink into a lonely despondency inimical to my most basic goals.

The body of my creator ever posed a difficulty, acting as an impediment to my travels, aimless though they were. By now, it had suffered much from exposure to the elements and from fluctuations of temperature. Frankenstein's once handsome face, albeit pallid from inward struggle and his final illness, now resembled that of a tortoise. His nose suggested a beak, his mouth a V-shaped scar, his throat a desiccated wattle. During a brief period of inattention, I had allowed a magpie *to pluck out one of his frozen eyeballs; the other had oozed away over days of blinding—nor do I use the word in jest—sunshine.*

Owing to the ambient cold (unremitting but for these bright interludes), the decay process in him advanced by staggers. Although his body never emitted an insupportable odour, only on the iciest days was it altogether free of a sickly perfume. At such times, his limbs had the hardness of gun barrels; at the Siberian summer's height, however, they flopped like a rag doll's and by such movements wafted their attenuated stench.

"Oh, Frankenstein!" I once apostrophised him. "Is this how I honour you? Is this how I justify myself in your sightless gaze?"

As both thinking creature and nomad, I lacked direction. The place most likely to accept and hallow my progenitor's bones, the city of Geneva, stood leagues and leagues away. I had no idea how many. It might as well have nestled in a lunar vale, for how, without divine aid, could I reach either Switzerland or the moon?

Often I thought to slip my burden and to pay homage to my maker by setting out his remains on some wind-blown promontory, where eagles or wolves could reverence his spirit through the machinery of their appetites. Frankenstein had loved the Alps, their glacial majesty and their vistas of desolate loveliness. In my creator's belated obsequies, could not the icescapes and mountains of eastern Siberia serve as either emblems or proxies of the Alps? Although I hoped so, the strictness of my call to atonement argued the reverse.

At length, however, I discovered for him on an inlet of the Chukchi Sea a temporary resting place, a grotto of stone which I further concealed with driftwood and glacial rubbish, where I could safely cache his body during my rambles afield. By this expedient, I preserved not only that which persisted of his corpse, but also my freedom as a moral agent.

Why, my hypothetical reader may inquire, did I remain in the Siberian wilderness without soliciting the companionship of men? In one regard, the question is foolish, for my treatment by the human species, from Victor Frankenstein himself to the Chukchi bowmen of a more recent encounter, had little inclined me to trust it. In another regard, however, the question demands an answer, for I had fixed as one of my goals my own domestication and socialisation. The process could not fulfill itself if, confining my rambles to remote wastelands, I shunned even the most glancing impingement on members of my creator's race.

Nothing had occurred, I understood, to render my physique or my hideous facial features less alarming to human beings. Indeed, these attributes had turned even Frankenstein against me. His genius had succumbed to his weakness of soul; he had repudiated me almost in the instant of my first emergence into consciousness. I still had a powerful recollection of that moment: the chemical-stained hands of my maker and the flicker of ineffable disgust in his eyes. Unhappily, my deformed countenance, still provoking fear, would prevent others from compassionating me. Even had my face shone as comely as Apollo's, my great size would always speak to the timid or the wary my undeniable potential for inflicting ruin. The universal policy of men towards me, then, had founded itself on either flight or preemptive recourse to a garbled Golden Rule, namely, Do unto Frankenstein's creature what it unquestionably purposes for thee.

Therefore, I practised and took pride in caution. I inwardly celebrated my ability, honed in Switzerland and the Orkneys, to come within a whisper of my human prey without alerting it, or others, to my menacing proximity. Now, however, I intended no threat. I told myself that my stealthiness facilitated observation when, in fact, it had become habitual, a means whereby I evaded natural human commerce and further inured myself to solitude. Intellectual diversion—be it reading, games, debate, or philosophical contemplations—had completely fled my world; day by day, I devolved toward the instinctive mindlessness of the timber wolf or the snow owl.

A fortuitous encounter, involving no human beings at all, put a halt to this bestial slide. As aimlessly I worked my way along the icy palisades on the Bering Strait, I heard the clamorous voices of mating walruses. This passionate baying, at once like the barking of dogs and the squealing of swine, echoed from the cliffside rocks. I sought its source. Before long, I had clambered to a throne of barnacled granite downwind from the sea beasts' rookery.

From this perch, I had a hidden view of the harem and of the sultanic male treading a young female. He bellowed his triumphant ecstasy. His lovemaking impressed me with both its ardour and its violence, for it hardly seemed that the pinned sultana could derive any pleasure from her paramour's coercive affections. On the other hand, she may have relished her role as his and the other females' cynosure; thus, she periodically barked her doubtful rapture. The females unoccupied with either procreation or the establishment of a pecking hierarchy tended their wet-eyed pups.

All this I absorbed with the greatest curiosity, irritation, and excitement. Shamefacedly, I confess that I considered attempting to cuckold the bull with one of his concubines. The feat struck me as possible but riskful: I might incur a tusk wound. If his massiveness were any trustworthy measure, however, the king walrus must weigh five times as much as I. Thus, he had not my nimbleness or speed, and the rookery was large. An ingenious rogue might well swyve a lady or two at sufficient distance from him to escape either interruption or injury.

I seriously entertained this notion, unnatural as my maker or his murdered bride would have adjudged it, because the yearning in my loins had produced a persistent tumidity; I ached with bittersweet excruciations impossible to describe. At last (appalled by the image of myself in coitus with a bewhiskered, legless, fish-eating sloth), I foreswore the temptation and spilled my lavalike seed on a rock.

Call me Onan.

My lust momentarily deflected, I took more acute note of the walrus society apart from the rutting couple. It charmed and enchanted me. The mothers and their pups displayed a sweet, reciprocal affection, the beholding of which retrieved and intensified the rage I had felt in the Orkney Islands at my creator's destruction of the female companion he had promised to make for me. Like nearly every other sentient being, I had known loneliness well ahead of lust. My desire for friendship, the consoling warmth of a propinquitous body, antedated and so took precedence over the mating urge. With the mothers and pups of this rookery at least, a kindred longing had found at once its natural outlet and its satisfaction. I envied the affectionate creatures.

In my envy, my rage subsided. Frankenstein was dead. How, then, expect him to build me a wife? Furthermore, as I must soon or late acknowledge, no one else could accomplish that same miracle. I must abandon by degrees my self-exile and seek a female companion among the children of men. Or, given the vast unlikelihood of success in that endeavour, I must embrace self-control and reform my character. These changes, I hoped, would lubricate my introduction into the human community. As part of it, my gentleness and honesty established, I might draw to me the companion of all my longings. Or I might not. In either event, I had determined to quit the wilds and to embark upon a career as a devout philanthropist.

I owed this turnabout to a revelation on the edge of a breeding ground of walruses. Perhaps I had shamed myself there, but I had also come into harmony with the repressed aspirations of my higher nature. Who can condemn me? Who can demand more?

The sequent era of my life became the happiest I have yet known. As it unfolded, I lacked the inclination to chronicle even its chief events. Thus, I seldom wrote here of either the people or the quotidian occupations that persuaded me I had found my niche in human society. In truth, what I did write I long ago ripped from this log and sank in a polar-bear skull in Kotzebue Sound, as latter-day Alaskans now call the inlet. I here reprise this part of my earthly career, in an abridgement painful to indite, to shew the connection between my early resurrection self and the semireclusive citizen I later became.

For sixty or seventy years, I dwelt with a small population of alternately maritime and inland Innuit, a people whom the Cossacks and other Europeans call Esquimaux. I reached them by stealing an oomiak, or whaleboat, from a trading outpost on the easternmost tip of the Chukchi Peninsula and sailing it across miles of open water in the Bering Strait to an icy spit near present-day Shishmaref. My creator, exhumed from his grotto on the eastern side, sailed with me, but his limited contributions to our crossing scarcely warrant inscribing him on the manifest as a crewman.

Once across, I hiked westward, dragging my maker on yet another travois, until chancing upon a village near a river southeast of a vast inlet. I had skirted many such villages, but this one recommended itself to me by the cleanliness and symmetry of its houses, fish-drying stands, and sled racks, and by the animation and good humour of its people.

Let me call the village Oongpek for the snowy-owl totem displayed on its chief kazgi, *or men's lodge, and the people themselves the Oongpekmut after the name of their village. I have no wish to identify more specifically either the place or its inhabitants, who numbered about forty persons and comprised five or six families related by consanguinity or marriage. Oongpek, I determined, would well serve as my adoptive homeplace, and after many a careful survey of the village, I strove to insinuate myself into it as an ally and denizen.*

The Oongpekmut at first regarded me with a suspicion as relentless as that of the Chukchi hunters who had wounded me in Siberia. Dread commingled with this suspicion. The villagers beheld me as if I were an evil spirit given form and substance. I had appeared to them with my travois behind me, and the corpse upon it little advanced my cause. Although I addressed them in Yoopik, their own tongue, pledging to add to their food stores and to protect them from enemies, whether animal or human, my friendly overtures foundered on their startlement and disbelief. I wanted companions, and a place of only moderate esteem in their collective. At length, however, my evident docility and their mounting impatience with my presence gave them courage, and they chased me away with harpoons and clubs.

Insofar as I could do so, I altered my appearance to approximate more closely their own. I cut my hair at the nape and around the ears to resemble the bowl-like coiffures of the men. I perforated my lower face at each lip corner to make possible the insertion of labrets, stone or ivory ornaments curiously evocative of walrus tusks. I made my labrets of creek stones and wore them daily until I could tolerate their chaffing and pull. I retailored my overshirt, leggings, and boots after the local masculine fashion. I made toys of spruce or willow wood for the village children, storyknives for the girls and carven animals for the boys.

On my next visit to Oongpek, I left my dead creator in a tree and appeared to the villagers gift-laden and familiarly dressed. I placed my gifts at Oongpek's edge and danced in the succulent summer grass a modest dance of appeasement and petition. I meantime chanted the conciliatory words of a song of my own authorship. The children greatly desired to collect their bribes, and some of the younger adults seemed to look upon my renewed overtures with favour, if not with unmitigated delight. The village angalgook, *or medicine man, who wore as an amulet the mummified remains of a human infant, reviled me as a trickster, an evil bear in the guise of a deranged giant. Two well-respected hunters concurred in supposing it unsafe to allow me any nearer approach. Indeed, the Oongpekmut hectically debated the nature of my identity, agreeing only that trusting my words might invite general destruction.*

Asvek, the medicine man, claimed that his counterpart in a distant village had sent me to forestall an attack of the Oongpekmut upon that village. The other angalgook's people had abducted a local woman in a raid, owing to an ancient feud, and so Asvek contended that the enemy shaman had transformed a diseased bear into the hideous spirit oracle that sought now to deceive Oongpek's people. After this pronouncement, no one could concede that I might mean my words or that I had come to them free of my imperfect disguise as a man. Once again, then, the villagers whose companionship I desired drove me away.

I persevered. As shortly after my creation I had done with the De Lacey family in Switzerland, I became the secret benefactor of this group of Innuit. I did them various unsolicited kindnesses, from providing them with plant food—at best, a marginal part of their diet—to repairing their fishing nets and sealskin boats. Later, I rescued a small child who had wandered unattended into a kenneling area and fallen between the paws of a hungry sledge dog. Braving the possibility of another attack, I walked the child back into the village to her sisters and cousins. When I passed the smiling child into their care, I reiterated to them and several nearby adults my kindly feelings and my honourable intentions towards all the

Oongpekmut. I also disclosed myself as the mysterious benefactor about whom much superstitious speculation had arisen.

By degrees, then, these words and acts brought me into the compass of local regard, including even that of the shaman Asvek. I was allowed to stay for longer and longer periods. When I explained that the corpse I had brought with me belonged to my maker—not my father, as they first wished to interpret my words, but one who had alchemically fashioned me from potions, powders, and revitalised flesh—Asvek and the other Oongpek elders expressed relief as well as astonishment. If the man who had made me lay dead, then I was undoubtedly not the handiwork of a living enemy: I had power over my creator, rather than he over me, and that power I could use, as I had repeatedly sworn to do, on behalf of Oongpek. It also cheered the villagers to note that the mummified Frankenstein little resembled his walking creation.

That I had kept his body with me for a trek of thousands of miles, however, struck these Innuit as a risible indulgence. The devotion I showed his corpse impressed them as eccentric, if not unhealthy, for they mused but little on the afterlife, in which they believed implicitly, and sometimes disposed of their dead by leaving them out for wolves. This method obviated any excavation of the frozen tundra and declared to the animal world their feelings of sacred fellowship. It nonetheless appalled me. I much preferred the alternative method of bidding farewell practised by most of the Oongpekmut; namely, the scaffolding of the deceased on platforms in the woods, the bodies wrapped in skins and joined on their death journeys by such favourite belongings as kayaks, bolas, harpoons, and sled frames.

Beyond the letters I had taken off the Caliban, I had few of my creator's personal effects. Indeed, on the Chukchi Peninsula he had lost even his eyes. When I found that ravens, owls, or bears might yet eat the dead laid out on platforms, I rejected even that option for Frankenstein. Together, however, the Oongpekmut and I hit upon a method for sanctifying his body that offended neither their sensibilities nor mine. We lacquered him from head to foot with an ointment of seal oil and evergreen resin and sewed him into a caribou hide. This funeral package we carried many leagues to a Stygian chamber in a volcanic cave, outside of which we chanted songs of praise, farewell, and godspeed.

This duty accomplished, I assimilated myself with the aid of my hosts into Oongpek's enjoyable round of days. I relaxed my vegetarianism virtually to the point of denying it, nor do I see how I could have remained among these Esquimaux—the word means "eaters of meat"—without adopting this immemorial component of their behaviour. On the grounds of necessity, I forgave myself, for the Innuit had *no formal agriculture and thus no ready way to accommodate the rare visitor who spurned their wonted diet.*

Further, and additional balm to my conscience, these Oongpekmut sang or prayed to the creatures they hunted, using them with the utmost esteem, if not actual reverence, and so ritually abstracted their meat-eating from the profane practises of Europeans.

As I had early sworn to do, I dedicated myself to the welfare of Oongpek and strove diligently on its behalf as hunter, fisherman, kayak wright, net mender, arrow fletcher, and guardian, I thereby obtained the respect and admiration of my adoptive villagers. With them I knew a contentment that had once seemed as ungraspable as frostfire.

Owing to my size, the people called me Takooka, grizzly bear. Because I religiously declined to shew myself either to Innuit visitors or to any white-skinned trader or surveyor, they also called me Inyookootuk, the Hiding Man. And because I reminded some villagers of a mythical creature, the worm man, that had lived when beasts could change at will into people, others addressed me as Tisikpook. Takooka was by far the most common of my appellatives, but I answered to them all. Indeed, I delighted in the fact that I, a creature once either nameless or marked out exclusively by deprecatory epithets, now had more names than any of my fellows.

In time I became such a stalwart Oongpekmut that no one complained of or saw as improper my dalliance with one of the village's unattached women, a small, sturdy person with strong hands and eyes like sparkling stars. Owing to the redness agleam in her hair, the people called her Kariak, or red fox, and she never shied from my attentions. I lay with her, took her to wife, and established with her in a sod house with whalebone roof joists our own domicile. My brother-in-law had wanted us to move into a house with his family, but his wife had argued with considerable justice that a man of my size needed more room. Kariak concurred, and I excavated our new house, with the aid of many other Oongpekmut, to accommodate just the two of us, with room for additional sleeping benches for the children we purposed. I loved this woman, and she in turn loved me, taking a perverse joy in the fact that to make me a parka, or a set of leggings, or a pair of boots, required twice as many caribou skins as any other male Oongpekmut needed for those items.

Our great love notwithstanding, my union with Kariak proved the groundlessness of one of my creator's bleakest fears. His chief ethical concern in crafting me a bride—indeed, his rationale for tearing my intended companion to pieces before animating her—was that together we might propagate a race of "devils." This conjectural species, Frankenstein believed, would turn its perfidious energies to the indiscriminate elimination of humanity. He need not have feared. Kariak and I conceived no children. Our clanspeople at first attributed this failure to her, for the Innuit suppose infertility a female imperfection—-unless someone can shew that a malignant shaman has thrown a spell or that the seed of another man could quicken the childless woman's womb. Kariak and I had no conspicuous ill-wishers, however, and although Esquimaux husbands sometimes invite male visitors to enjoy, as a form of hospitality, the bodies of their wives, never did I consent to this custom, so possessive was my love and so vehement my uxoriousness. In truth, only in these traits did I offend the Oongpekmut, but they overlooked my shortcomings on account of the services I daily rendered. Further, Oongpik had acquired a reputation as impervious to attack, evil spells, and famine. If anyone begrudged my possessive behaviour, it was Kariak.

Saying so, I acknowledge, may appear to convict my wife of a fickle heart, perhaps even of faithlessness, but the charge dies aborning. Among the Innuit, children confer status and security. They greatly bless their parents, at first with the flattering exactions of their dependency and later with the active succour of their hands. In hunting, fishing, cooking, sewing, bow-making, and a hundred other enterprises, they make their value plain. It therefore bruised Kariak's heart to continue childless, and the gibes of her distaff kindred, as perfunctory and mild as they were, grew ever more difficult to bear. She had already suffered many jocose insults, a few of which had nonetheless stung, for marrying so grotesque an interloper, even if I had proved a beneficent influence on the community as a whole. Abruptly, then, Kariak began to badger me to offer her to kinsmen visiting from elsewhere, as a sign of my full adoption of Innuit ways and of my unimpeachable cordiality.

Again and again, I declined. Instead, I carved from ivory a doll-child only slightly bigger than my hand, as a petition to the inyua, or spirits, and as a charm. This doll Kariak and I dressed and tended as if it were a living infant, feeding it forest celery, wild potatoes, and even a delicacy of porcupine, crushed salmonberries, and seal oil known as agoutak. None of these ministrations served to impregnate Kariak, however, and her unhappiness grew. Once I arrived home from an expedition for snowshoe hare (during which these creatures had moved about as thick as tomcod in the brush) to find that she had broken our doll-child and thrown it onto a midden. I bent to nuzzle her red-tinged hair, but she pushed me away and wept copiously.

A few days later, three seal hunters from Shishmaref, one a kinsman of Asvek, came to Oongpek for a visit. Kariak asked me to permit at least one of them to lodge with us during their stay.

I refused. I did not wish to share my wife with anyone, much less any of these laughing strangers; further, I intended to absent myself from the village for the whole of their visit. I would play Inyookootuk, the Hiding Man, by retreating to the woods. It would mock propriety for Kariak to entertain a male visitor in our house during my absence, which Asvek or Kegloonek, a respected elder, would impute to my desire to lay out a pattern of game snares.

As soon as she understood my intentions, Kariak moved out of our lodge, dry-eyed in her leaving, and crossed the Oongpek commons to the house of her sister's husband. Here, I learned upon my return, she entertained the most dashing member of the Shishmaref party, a full-faced young hunter with happy-dancing eyes. She then departed with him for the coast. Nine moons later, on a night of popping ice sleeves and wolf-cry winds, Kariak brought into the circle of another clan a baby boy with eyes greatly like his father's. Weeks later this news reached my brother-in-law, and everyone in Oongpek understood what it signified: I, Takooka, was sterile, and Kariak, my erstwhile wife, had endured the malediction "barren," even if often hurled in jest, for my pride's sake.

Oddly, the happiness that her kinspeople now felt for Kariak overrode any resentment of me for the injustice—in which, in fact, many of them had conspired— that I had done her. No one sought either to punish me for humiliating her or to taunt me for my infecundity.

I remained among the Oongpekmut as a bachelor in the clan of my departed wife. Another in my place might have suffered a diminishment of status, but I had qualities that offset my shame. No other local woman wanted me for a husband, but I did not lack for willing lovers.

Two years later, Kariak returned with her new husband and her bright-eyed son for a visit. At the urging of Kasgoolik, the husband, I lay again with my first and last heartmate, and, at the moment of our little dying, laughed heartily in her small embrace. The bittersweetness of this possession without possession prevented me from accepting any further invitations from Kasgoolik during their visit; and when Kariak and her family, after a week's sojourn, returned to his village, I never saw her more.

Oh, Frankenstein (I often thereafter lamented), for this you destroyed my first bride, that I might not sire upon her a race of Titanic murderers.

But suppose, fiend, that your seed had in fact impregnated a female made after your own pattern? (I have imagined my maker replying). That was hardly a chance in which I could easily, if ever, acquiesce.

My stay among the Oongpekmut, happy but for the loss of Kariak, lengthened into decades. I heard of troubles elsewhere—most notably, between the Azyagmut and the Cossacks at Fort Saint Michael—but my people eschewed active dealings with outsiders and so escaped the anxiety and the physical harm of these periodic upheavals. I heard, too, of the smallpox epidemic that had swept through many Innuit villages, killing hundreds, but the disease never reached our village, and the only Oongpekmut to die of it contracted the pox on a visit to Egavik, on Norton Sound, and died there, far from home.

By and large, I still declined to appear to anyone other than my own clanspeople, especially Europeans, whom I could trust only to imprecate and abuse me, had they the means to do so. When a small team of white doctors came to Oongpek to vaccinate our people against the pox, I removed myself from the village and stayed away until it had completed its program and departed. When traders arrived, I fled.

However, in more than one disagreement with nearby Innuit, I effected an outcome both just and favourable to Oongpek simply by shewing myself to our would-be adversaries, as the Philistines had no doubt employed Goliath until his fatal contretemps with David. In this way, as well as in the faithfulness of my service to my clans people, I attained to an almost legendary status among the Esquimaux of my circumscribed region.

"The Hiding Man, Inyookootuk, lives in Oongpek," hunters would say. "He is a man. He is a bear. He can change back and forth like inyua from the ice days."

As the years flew, I observed the effects of time on my clanspeople and friends. Asvek died.

Asvek's wife died. The chief Kegloonek died. Other villagers advanced from youth or middle age into senescence and death. I, on the other hand, did not, but remained, as I always had, a giant of a certain established maturity, ill-featured but neither decrepit nor wizened. Kariak's parents died. Kariak's brother drowned in a whaling accident involving an oomiak and a wayward harpoon line. Seal hunters and salmon fishers of the age group that had initiated and taught me fell one by one—like leaves in autumn—to accident, disease, and age.

That I appeared immune to these natural depredations, continuing youthful in my hideousness, did not go unremarked. Many Oongpekmut, especially those of generations subsequent to mine, regarded my persistence among them as uncanny, perhaps even malignantly so. I watched in dismay as they ineluctably withdrew from me their trust and affections. No one used me ill or commanded me to quit the village, but I soon perceived that what had hitherto existed between me and the industrious Oongpekmut could not last.

Further, I could no longer tolerate the cold as well as I once had; each succeeding winter seemed to add to the ice in my veins, to diminish my ability to warm myself when blizzards raged and the urine in our collection barrels froze into amber stelea. On my sleeping platform, at the height of the blasting siroc, I dreamt of sunshine, unruffled water, and lizards basking. These images won my reverence even though I could scarcely conceive their origin.

One day an old man calling himself Kasgoolik appeared in our village. He had journeyed many difficult leagues by dog sledge to tell me something. At length I realised that he was the husband of my former consort, Kariak.

Kariak, he said, had died.

Inconsolable in his reemergent grief, he wept to relay this message, which struck me with the accreting weight of an avalanche. I, too, wished to weep—to pound my head on the frozen earth, to rend my garments like a Hebrew. Instead, I sought to console Kasgoolik, who, knowing that I had loved Kariak unflaggingly, with a devotion equal to his own, had travelled all this way to share his grief.

How strange, he observed, that over forty-five years had passed since Kariak had shared a household with me here in Oongpek. Why, their own first son had vanished nearly thirteen winters ago, carried out to sea on an ice floe and never seen anywhere near his village again.

This intelligence also desolated me, as if a child of my own loins had disappeared.

A month later I abandoned Oongpek. If I could not die, then I had "world enough and time" to drink the indilute elixir of life. After one brief stop, I directed my steps southwards, slowly but inexorably out of the Alaskan mists.

32

After reading Jumbo's story, I couldn't much concentrate on baseball. No, that's wrong. I *dived* into baseball like a guy with money worries dives into suicide, to escape what's about to overwhelm him. I played pretty good in our next five games, but their details come back to me only if I check a box score. On the afternoon of our second game against the Seminoles, I tried to return Jumbo his log. I'd had all the lousy copying work I wanted for a while.

"Keep it, Daniel." He stuck his log into the hold of my school desk. "Learn all you can about me."

I shook my head, but Jumbo leaned his knuckles on my desk and held its lid in place. Meanwhile, I thought: I don't want to know any more about you, I already know too much.

"Copy out the rest of my memoir," Jumbo said. "Gradually, over our remaining season."

Jumbo wanted me for a confessor as well as a friend. A dummy, after all, has a few things in common with a priest—for starters, you can tell either one the worst about yourself with no fear they'll yak it all over town.

Anyway, we beat Marble Springs that Thursday and then again on the Friday evening Jumbo gave me his "resurrection memoir." The box scores say I played fine: no errors in either game, five hits in eight at-bats, six RBIs. The same box scores say Jumbo, although a defensive hero, went aught for seven, with a rally-killing roller to the Seminole first baseman on Thursday and a base-running blunder on Friday after reaching first on a walk. Fortunately, Heggie, Snow, Muscles, and I took up the hitting slack. Maybe Jumbo's uncertainty about what to expect of me, now I knew his amazing personal history, had nagged him, a blackberry seed under the gum.

After Friday's game—the better of my two sockdolager nights—I was supposed to go to Miss LaRaina and Phoebe's for dinner. In front of every rabbit-eared Hellbender aboard the *Brown Bomber*, Phoebe had invited me.

In a way, it qualified as a date, a *real* date—unlike the dinner at the Royal Hotel with Mister JayMac and the Pharram women.

Anyway, as soon as I'd showered, Curriden, Mariani, and a couple of others—none known to me as an enemy—congratulated me on my game. Curriden had a brown paper sack in one hand and a grin on his handsome kisser. As I knotted my tie, he pushed me down onto a bench and eased in beside me.

"Know what this is, Boles?" He wagged his paper sack under my nose. I shook my head. "Well, have a look." He peeled the sides of the sack down to reveal a flask-sized bottle of sloe gin. "And have you a drink too."

"He's underage," Mariani said.

"Yeah and Rita Hayworth's a Campfire Girl." Curriden pressed his ruby-colored liquor on me again. "Didn't you see how he played?"

I took the sack, but twisted the top closed around its neck. Mister JayMac allowed only rubbing alcohol in the locker room.

"Country's in a whiskey drought," Curriden said. "You almost got to be wearing khaki to find a goddamn beer. This stuff's rare as radium. Take a swig."

"You deserve it," Charlie Snow said. "It aint cheap stuff either, like Old Spud or hanky-filtered Vitalis."

Snow's good word did it for me. If he thought I deserved a snort, I probably did. I peeled the paper down, twisted the cap off, and sipped. My lips began to tingle, but I liked the stuff well enough to take an even bigger hit, which made even the doubtful Mariani say, "Atta way to do er, kid!"

I recrimped the sack and gave the bottle back to Curriden, my mouth still atingle with the furry bittersweetness of sloe berries. A fire ran from my tongue to my gut.

"You're eating with the Pharram ladies tonight, right? Yeah, well," Curriden said, "you've got to give em an hour or so to get set. Meantime, come along with Quip and Vito and me on a little victory jaunt."

Phoebe'd said to meet her under the grandstand after the game so Curriden's plans seemed wrong to me—but maybe he knew something I didn't.

"It's okay, Dum—uh, Danny. We'll get you to the Pharram place in a hour. Drop you right at their door. Taxi ride's on me—my gift for what you've helped us do, kid." He looked at the eight or nine Hellbenders still in the locker room. "We're four games over .500!" he shouted. "Thanks to Dumbo and his hustlin rookie pals!"

I blushed and took another slug of Curriden's contraband firewater.

"Look, Reese," Parris said. "Same damn color as your gin."

My color stayed high. The furry tingle in my mouth caught an elevator and rode to my brain. I wasn't drunk, but I was already close to tipsy. Even so, when Curriden, Parris, and Mariani whisked me out to the parking lot, skirting the area where Phoebe'd planned to meet me, it felt WRONG. Sure, Curriden'd never had it in for me, and it did seem logical Phoebe'd need some time after the game to get ready. But these rascals had *kidnapped* me.

Parris and Mariani had me wedged between them in the back seat of a red-and-white taxi. Curriden sat up front, playing fingertip drumrolls on the dash and giving directions. "The Strip," I heard him say. "The Wing and Thigh." The stadium sank away behind us like a three-masted ship going under the concealing arc of the world.

The streets boogie-woogied with energy. News of our win had run through tony white and run-down colored neighborhoods alike. Our driver, a horse-faced black man, yelled out the window at some of his friends on a street corner: "Gang way! Got me some mighty Hellbenders hyeah! Gang way, yall!"

"Hush that," Curriden said. "We're incognito tonight."

What you really mean, I thought, is, it'd embarrass us all to the bottoms of our pocketbooks if Mister JayMac learned of our destination and slapped us all with fines. The tingle in my brain shredded into a dozen throbbing aches.

We drove past the farmer's market and crossed the tracks between the business district to the north and the neon-lit part of Penticuff Strip to the south. Our driver hung a right on the eastern side of the tracks. The alley straight ahead—a tunnel of jazzy electric signs and uniformed GIs—opened out like a Mardi Gras party.

"Jesus, lookit all the sojers," Mariani said.

Parris said, "Be nice to em and they'll let you live."

The driver dropped us off in front of an eatery serving fried chicken and cole slaw: The Wing & Thigh. In its window someone'd pasted up movie posters and flyers recruiting farm workers—volunteers—for the fall harvest. Curriden led me, Mariani, and Parris into The Wing & Thigh.

The place had the length and width of two or three railway coaches, with a counter down one side and ten or twelve tables against the facing wall. In the back, through the smoke eeling over the tables, a shaky staircase rose to a rickety landing; below it, a red EXIT sign glowed over the beaded curtain in the door there. A jukebox blared Bing Crosby's "White Christmas," but the smells of boiled turnip greens, pepper sauce, and frying chicken didn't much remind me of yuletide fixings. It was July, even if just barely.

"Don't you want a piece?" Curriden asked me.

Nope. In another hour, I'd be eating with the Pharrams.

"Well, I do," Curriden said. "Order up, Vito." He handed Mariani a fiver—Diamond Jim Brady tipping the doorman. "Order us three he-man plates, with cole slaw, chips, and iced tea, and give me my change when I get back."

"Where you goin?" Parris asked. His sing-song suggested he already knew. "To get Danny *his* piece?"

Curriden grabbed my shirt front and pulled me through that beer-sloshed alley, with its stink of vinegar and fry scald, towards the staircase. GIs looked up from their tables, and some of the gals eating chicken with them, as silk-gussied a bunch as I'd ever seen, their fingers shiny with joint fat, winked at me or reached out to pinch my flank. Mama would've called em hussies, and I already had a hunch—*just* a hunch—how The Wing & Thigh had got its name.

Beyond the door at the top of the landing was another set of stairs, flush with the outside rear wall, that climbed to an access hall right over The Wing & Thigh's kitchen and serving area. In that hallway, Curriden and I came to a desk manned—*womanned*, I mean—by a female in an ivory dress with a push-up bodice and an oval cutout that showed her belly button. Don't ask me to describe her face.

"Do for you gennelmen?" she said.

"For Danny Boy here," Curriden said, "my little brother."

To the woman's right, some paired hooks with number tags on them—like you'd see in a barber shop—ran on a strip of fluted molding nailed up at shoulder height. Each pair of hooks had a woman's name over it, but four of the names had tags reading "Not Available" on them.

"Flossie, Jordan Kaye, Roberta, Sabrina, and Irene are all in this evening," the woman said.

"Give him Sabrina," Curriden said.

"Here." The woman handed him No. 26 from the "take" hook under Sabrina's name. "Payment, please." Curriden paid. "Now yall may go down the hall to wait."

So Curriden and I wove our way down the long corridor. It was furnished with four scummy fish tanks on hospital carts, calendar paintings of old plantation houses, and a worn strip of plum-colored rug. We passed several doors and entered a waiting room—a holding tank, more like—with folding chairs and a low table stacked with magazines.

Three soldiers sat in this room. No one talked or read a magazine. Two GIs looked bored. One had a nervous jiggle in his leg. Curriden and I sat down next to him. This PFC had a rash of razor nicks under his receding chin. He cut his eyes at us, then smiled real big.

"Gonna wear her out. Gonna do my steel-driving level best to split er clean in two."

The corporal sitting next to him said, "Be lucky he don't pop a knee before he gets in there."

"Ha ha," said the PFC. "What a kidder."

Just then, it sledgehammered me I'd come to a *brothel*—I mean, I'd taken in all the accouterments, but now I understood Curriden meant to see me through a rite of passage. He caught me by the shirt and pulled me back down.

Down the hall, a door opened across from one of the fish tanks; a man in khaki strolled towards me to the waiting room, looked in at the five of us, and said, "Number twenty-five for Sabrina. Lady says she's off at nine, whether her trick is or not." He checked his watch. "I got eight till."

"Sabrina," the PFC said. "Whoa, that's me!" He flashed his tag and stood up. For the first time since we'd entered, the floor stopped vibrating. "I'll do her three times in eight minutes. She'll be hanging on for dear life."

Curriden grabbed the guy's number and gave him a wadded-up dollar bill. "Pick a gal who don't get off till later. Life's too short to rush things."

"Hey, gimme my number!"

"Uh-uh." Curriden tipped him back into his chair with a soft three-fingered push and led me down the hall to Sabrina. The GI didn't follow us—he had an extra buck and more sense than to mess with a guy as big and built as Curriden.

In the bulb-lit fish tank across from Sabrina's room—all the light in the hall came from these tanks, dapples of cool aquamarine on the walls and floor—the fish swam in hypnotized and hypnotizing schools: fish with stripes or spots, fish with lacy wedding-gown fins and tails, fish with see-through skins and bones aglow like tiny Christmas trees.

Curriden knocked, the door opened. Out of the corner of my eye I saw a brunette, pale-skinned woman about my own height wearing a yoke-collared shirt with a Johnny Mack Brown bib and pearly buttons for a housecoat. Under that shirt, legs like pruning shears. Red-orange polish on her toe-nails.

Curriden gave her extra money. "Sabrina, Danny Boles. Danny, Sabrina Loveburn. Vito, Quip, and I'll be downstairs eating, kid. Have you a time."

"I'm off at nine," Sabrina said as Curriden walked away.

"Not for what I just gave you, hon. Sides, he's like to go off fastern a firecracker. Have a heart,"

"Come in, then," Miss Loveburn said.

I stared at her toenails and might not've moved at all if a clatter of shoes on the stairs and a barrage of male voices hadn't goosed me to it. Just as a gang of four soldiers burst through the door at the end of the hall, I stepped into Miss Loveburn's room. She shut the door. The GIs knocked on every door in the hall, including hers.

"So yo're a ballplayer," she said. "One that don't talk." Curriden had told her, maybe even before we showed up.

I didn't even try to answer. Her room had a low, narrow bed—more like a couch with no back or arms—a folding chair, a pole lamp, and a door across from the one I'd entered by. Like prairie dogs, the ladies of The Wing & Thigh had at least two exits from their burrows.

Over Miss Loveburn's bed hung a glossy oil portrait of a Tahitian or a Samoan maiden in a sarong, with one brown breast showing. The sun going down behind her had exactly the same plump roundness as her nude breast.

Miss Loveburn's violet eyes halted their gaze at the top of my skin. She was semipretty, with the looks of a pissed-off school teacher. If she hadn't been birthday-suit-skinny under her Johnny Mack Brown shirt, I could've imagined her sitting tight-kneed in a Baptist church pew.

"Give me ballplayers over sojers," she said. "Especially if they've just played a game. Not too many of yall pass up a shower afterwards. A GI, though, you never know about. Some come in smelling like cologne factories, some like geedee goat stalls, pardon my French. If they've scrubbed with a clean washrag, yo're lucky—s bout the best you can hope for, barring a campwide flu and the weekend off."

Miss Loveburn let her gaze drill into my skin. "Cmere. This aint something you can do by phone." She shook her head. "If you don't talk, of course, bout the only thing you can do by phone is dial it, right? Or listen maybe. You look like a decent nough listener. Cmere. Lemme smell ya."

All her talk'd taken most of the scare out of Miss Sabrina Loveburn. I went to her. She put her hands on my shoulders and sniffed me under the chin and around the ears, a dog going over its owner's trouser legs after a cat's been by. While she smelled me, I sniffed her hair—wavy burn-brown wool. It smelt of cigarette smoke and talc. I liked it.

"Not bad," Miss Loveburn said. "Kinda little kiddyish." She went from my ears to my breastbone and from there over to my arm pit, sniffing from one spot to another. "Shower or no, yo're starting to get a smidgen ripe about here." She slipped her hands under my arms and stood straight up. "What do I expect, huh? A young he-fella collidin wi the climate. S okay, though. You'll do."

She sniffed my mouth. "Smoke already, huh? Shouldn't." She lifted my lip, to let the air polish my canines. "Turn these pearlies yeller. Least you don't chew. Got a little hunger on yore breath, though. You hungry?"

I had a dinner date, but Miss Loveburn wouldn't let go of my shoulders.

"Turnabout," she said. "You say what swampy perfumes come off me bout now. Fair's fair."

To oblige, I smelt her forehead and eyebrows: talc, stale smoke, woman sweat, the oils of long-gone lovers. All pretty faint, nothing too foul. But from the room—from her bed—a rancider smell fanned out: sweat, stained linens, downstairs cooking.

"But you cain't say, can you? Never met a dummy before—not sure I believe in em. Lemme see. Open." She prised up my lip again and got me to open wide, then loosened the knot on my tie and peered into my mouth. "Relax. This is okay. You aint a gift horse, are you? Given who paid, I'm liker to qualify. No looking in *mine*, though. Fair's fair, but smart's smart and wise is wise." She put the tip of one finger on my tongue. "Lips okay. Tongue okay." She probed with a finger. I had to warn myself not to chomp down. "Throat okay. Vocal cords, ah, ah, open, keep it open, ah, I cain't even *see* em. Someone cut em out? Yank em like burnt-through wiring?"

I shook my head.

"Then why this speechlessness, honey? It don't become a young man of yore achievements." Miss Loveburn walked me to the bed, where she tugged me to a sitting position on her right hand. Sitting, she lost the coverage till then afforded by the tail of her shirt. I saw the smooth white cables of her thighs, the dark bird-nest tangle at their join. I could feel her warmth. Until that moment, nothing about The Wing & Thigh as a fancy house or Sabrina

Loveburn as one of its women had brought me anywhere near horniness, but I reached it sitting there, and she noticed.

"Spare me yore flusterment, Danny. I've raised the dead. For feisty young rams like you, all I've got to do's *breathe*. Anyhow, nothing happens till I say the word." I put my hand on Miss Loveburn's beautiful knee. I leaned into her and nibbled her throat. "Tonight, Danny boy, yore Open Sesame aint Reese's money or any ol guppy nibbles. You gotta say, 'Love ya, hon,' or 'Shut my mouf.' Otherwise, it's no go. I don't sell to crips—one-arms, hair-lips, dummies—as Reese hissef knows. So tell me you love me, Danl."

Ooooi. Mama, God, and the please-and-thank-you morality of Tenkiller meant about as much to me just then as the prose on a mattress tag. I wanted Miss Loveburn under me, her cowboy shirt hiked to her greyhound-lean rib cage, her legs slicing me into smaller and smaller satisfied pieces.

I love you, I whispered. (I could whisper—Pumphrey hadn't stolen my ability to whisper.)

"Loud-talk it!" Miss Loveburn said. "Say it right out!"

But to do that, I needed a diagram of all the fleshy parts in my throat and instructions for making them twang.

"Shore it's a lie. If you loved me, I'd get me to a nunnery. But you have to say it—*somethin*—to show I aint laying down for a draft-dodging crip. Got that?"

I got it okay, but no matter how hard I tried—curling my tongue, gulping air—I managed only voiceless stammers.

"Uh-uh. That won't do."

I kept trying, straining like a cur with a bone in its throat. A Nazi would've taken pity; a Jap, even. Finally I stopped trying, shoved Miss Loveburn over, and wedged one knee between her legs. Did it count as rape if you tried to have your way with an ass-for-hire who'd taken money and then set conditions that had nothing to do with her price or the exact bedroom yahoo level she'd tolerate?

"Stop it, Danl! I'm warning you!"

She raised a knee into my crotch, hard, but the slam was a billiard kiss off one ball. To keep her from using her knee again, I rolled my hips and pubic bone down on her and smoodged a hungry kiss over her lips, chin, and jaw.

Then a boulder fell out of the sky and crushed the back of my skull into a backasswards sort of headache powder.

33

I woke up alone. A folded hand towel cushioned my head, and the weapon Miss Loveburn'd used to brain me—a glass ash tray with a Wing & Thigh decal inside it—rested on my chest like some kind of weird volume knob. I turned it with one shaky hand; pain boomed inside my head from ear to ear.

Somebody'd moved me from Miss Loveburn's cubicle to a low couch in a hallway almost exactly like the one with the fish tanks and calendar paintings—except it had only a bare wood floor and exposed ductwork under its ceiling. I sat up and looked around. The doors along this corridor hinted it ran parallel to the one down the *other* side of The Wing & Thigh's horizontal-refreshment boxes. I could hear some refreshment going on— thumps, moans, happy cries—beyond the door at the foot of my couch.

"How you feelin, sweety?" A fortyish woman dressed like a USO hostess—stylish, proper—touched the lump on the back of my head. "You look right chipper, considerin."

I winced away. The hurt and bafflement on my face kicked her into den-mother mode. She said her girls—as well trained in self-defense as in bedroom arts—reserved force as an option if impatient Johns tried to "git tough."

"Gitting tough undercuts the agreement freely agreed to by both parties with the exchange of our standard fee," she said. "You tried to git tough. Sabrina could've had you dumped in the alley, but it hurt her to think of sech a dummy tenderfoot coming to out back. So you got to sleep off yore mickey"—she nodded at my ashtray—"righ chere, sweety."

Five doors away, a beefy-faced man leaned against the wall with his arms crossed and his biceps agleam. He gave me a chin dip and a smile more sorrowful than mean.

"I'm Fidelia Florida Foxworthy," the woman said. "Sabrina had some business to tend to elsewhere. We couldn't leave you where you was layin, sweety, cause Mamie had to take over in there. And we couldn't take you down to yore pals cause it's not smart to show off a client with a head knot. So Burley"—she nodded at the bouncer—"told yore pals you'd had sech a fine time with Sabby, you wanted to try out another gal or two at yore own expense."

This story panicked me. I brought my wrist up to my ear like a man listening to a watch ticking.

"I don't wear one either," Miss Fidelia said. "Burley, what time you got?"

The bouncer checked his watch. "Quawduhaffatin." His voice rolled like a tidal wave of honey.

My God, I'd missed dinner with Phoebe and her mama! I likely didn't even have Curriden and his buddies waiting for me. Worse, unless you had an extension from Mister JayMac, curfew on the night before a game was eleven. I'd never get to the Pharrams' to apologize and back to McKissic House before the clock bonged eleven and my transportation—taxi, hay wagon, bike—turned into a pumpkin!

I grabbed the nearest door knob and tried to yank open the door attached to it. The door wouldn't yank.

"Cain't go in there, sweety," Miss Fidelia said. "Mamie's working. They're all working. Or better be."

I jumped onto the couch, hurried over it, stepped down, and wiggled the next door knob on the row of cubicles. It didn't budge either. I dashed to the next door and rattled its knob.

"Burley! Burley, stop him!" Miss Fidelia cried.

Burley came pelting down the hall after me, Jell-O-wobbly love handles rolling faster than his voice had. I'd just about used up all available knobs before one turned, a door clicked open, and, falling down, I barged into the cubicle behind it, landing crash on a rope rug and scrambling back up as Burley grabbed the door and hit his ear on the jamb when his grip on the knob reversed his momentum.

On the bed in this room, I just had time to see a Wing & Thigh gal in a halter top and denim cutoffs using her lipstick tube to transform her client's moony white butt into a winking Popeye the Sailor. My entrance put an end to this end-directed artwork. The girl screamed and sidearmed her lipstick tube at me. Her John's Popeye the Sailor face rolled over, popping his Fighting Red cock and balls, color by Tussey Cosmetics, into view along with his face. His eyes bugged out round and white as his ass cheeks, then narrowed again.

Burley collided with the girl in the halter top as I yanked the far door open and careened into a fish tank on a hospital cart. The cart rolled a foot or two, but caught on the rug and bucked to a halt. The tank kept going. It crashed down, shattering and spilling ten gallons of algae-ridden liquid murk and two pounds of tropical fish. The rug acted like a blotter, and the beached fish hiccupped along its waterlogged strip like a silver conga line.

"Stop, you damned liddle peckerwood!" Burley shouted.

I hopscotched over the crumpled aquarium tank, the fish, the broken glass, beelining it towards the doorkeeper's desk and the door to freedom.

"What the hell!" shouted the victim of Popeye interruptus in the hanky-panky cubicle. "What the fuckin hell!"

I squeezed past the doorkeeper and double-timed it down the stairs. At the landing below Miss Fidelia's cathouse proper (or improper), I had a choice. I could go through the lefthand door into the eatery, or I could xylophone down the stairs into a storage room with an exit on a service alley. I chose the door back inside—safety in numbers.

But witnesses or no, Burley clattered into The Wing & Thigh in pursuit. Four dogfaces had chosen that moment to come up the same stairs. I slipped between or edged around them all, then sprinted down the row of crowded tables to the one where I hoped Curriden and friends would still sit sucking marrow from their chicken bones. Ha. I should have hoped Tojo would yield his imperial forces to me personally.

"Grab that peckerwood!" Burley shouted, jiggling through the crush. "Thatun wid the goddamn ears!"

A GI on the first floor caught me by the forearm. "Where you goin, Dumbo?" He'd thought up this nickname for me all by himself.

Burley barreled up and knocked the dogface loopy with a pudgy elbow. "Thanks, Mac." He took my neck tie in his fist. "Moron's in my custiddy now. You can toodle-oo."

Phoebe'd hate me forever. I'd never make curfew. Hell, my life could peter out in a trash-filled alley. Burley began to drag me towards the rear. Folks waved bye-bye as he hauled me past, a guy putting the come-along on a scared terrier.

"Please be so kind as to unhand my friend."

Burley and I turned around. Jumbo stood in the middle of the place in his Abraham Lincoln frock coat and a pair of black trousers large enough to outfit three or four regulation-size groomsmen. His face would've stopped

Big Ben. It blanched the lip rouge of a half dozen females and sucked in the cheeks of a whole platoon of doughboys.

"Who the hell're you?" Burley didn't quail—I'll give him that—but his voice pitched itself oddly high.

"Henry," Jumbo said. "Henry Clerval."

"Henry," Burley said. "Oh, Henry."

"Careful, fella," a GI told Burley. "S Hank Clerval, the best first baseman in the CVL." He said this with such respect that CVL almost seemed a vowelless code for Clerval, like YHWH is for Jehovah.

"I don't watch it," Burley said. "Baseball."

"Well, he could crack you like an aigg," the GI said. "He inhales pickaninnies for breakfuss."

"That last is a damnable lie," Jumbo said.

"Sorry," the GI said. "Swear to God, sir, I'm sorry."

"Henry," Burley mused. "A simpering Henry."

"Let go of Daniel," Jumbo said, but Burley kept his grip on my tie, which snaked over my shoulder, pulling my head towards him on a hurtful cant. "What has he done to incur your anger or to warrant punishment?"

The question stumped Burley for a moment. All I'd tried to do was take what Curriden'd paid for (now, though, the memory of my attack on Miss Loveburn filled me with self-shudders) and then flee The Wing & Thigh upon learning the time: attempted rape and a missed dinner engagement.

"He . . . he broke a fish tank," Burley said.

"You were taking him back upstairs to mend it?"

"No, I was hauling him out back to kick his scrawny ass," Burley said. "Does the peckerwood look like a tank mender?"

"I would think your boss happier with financial restitution than with an injured customer, a lawsuit, and a court order closing this establishment as a leach upon both the pocketbook and the morality of the American soldier."

Burley had a brain. He let go of my tie, and I walked with as much dignity as I could muster to Jumbo's side.

"Henry is an honorable name," he said. "Men of the stature of Adams, Longfellow, and Ford have worn it. Another Clerval, an altogether admirable gentleman, gave it to me. Don't mock or disparage the name Henry."

"Nosir," Burley said seriously. "I won't."

Jumbo—no, Henry—took his wallet from his coat and counted out ten bills. He handed them to me. I gave them to Burley.

"Is the sum sufficient to replace your broken tank and to restock it with fish?" Henry asked.

"Yessir. You want a receipt?"

"No, thank you. These people here"—he gestured at the crowd around us—"will attest to the mutual acceptability of Daniel's payment. I may assume that, mayn't I?"

"Shore," several chippies and GIs chorused: "You bet."

Jumbo—no, *Henry!*—guided me outside, where Highbridge's nightly ripoff of Mardi Gras partied past, soldiers on the prowl, hookers come-hithering, con artists flim-flamming, and MPs (the dogfaces called them Miserable Pricks) strutting like tinpot dictators.

A taxi stood at the curb. Henry put me into it and told the driver, "McKissic House." We rode. "How did I find you?" he asked as the neon tide of Penticuff Strip lapped the cab's windshield. "Well, Mr. Curriden and his friends arrived back at the boardinghouse without you, after I'd heard that you'd left the stadium in their company. Phoebe telephoned to say you hadn't yet arrived at her house. One by one, I accosted all three gentlemen last seen with you. Mr. Curriden laughed. Mr. Parris said you'd slipped away from them early in the evening. Mr. Mariani confessed the ulterior motive behind your expedition and told me where they had abandoned you."

Abandoned me? Curriden and his pals had deliberately run out on me?

Henry put a hand on my knee. "So how does it feel to have shed your innocence?" His fingers dug into my knee, nearly to the point of making me scream, then let go.

"I'm sorry," he said. "Others plotted your filthy quest. They victimized you, Daniel, denying you your humanity and also your autonomy as a sentient creature." About when I thought he'd let me off the hook, he grabbed my leg again. "But you—at length, Daniel, *you*—took part in your own abasement. What does autonomy mean if not self-sponsorship in the moral arena?"

I deserved the scolding. Sort of. For a few raw seconds up there in The Wing & Thigh, I'd become an animal; not so much for wanting my libido scratched—hell, that was natural—as for using force to bully my chosen scratcher. I'd put the screws on Sabrina Loveburn to get her to put the screw on me.

Funny thing. Sitting in that cab and listening to Henry's harangue, I knew I'd sinned against Miss Loveburn and deserved my ashtray braining. But I resented her for trying to make me talk and then reneging on her contract with Curriden. (You pays your money, you gets your goods.) Shame and bitterness, warring tides.

"Young Miss Pharram says you stood her up," Henry went on. "As you might well anticipate, she is wounded, confused, and resentful." (That made two of us, but Phoebe wasn't to blame for my state of mind, as I was for hers.) "How do you suppose Miss LaRaina, given Phoebe's wretchedness, must feel? Equally wretched, of course. Equally ill-used."

Away from Penticuff Strip, our cab bumped over the tracks dividing Highbridge. The smell of decaying horse and mule droppings swirled around us, along with the stink of a faraway paper mill and the floating scorch of peanuts from the Goober Pride factory. The streets beyond the tracks wore their late-night shadows like tank camouflage, and the folks creeping among the dapples—no matter their race—reminded me of enemy snipers.

"Discomfiting Miss LaRaina was Mr. Curriden's principal goal," Henry told me, his eyes straight ahead. "He harbors no ill will towards you. He may've actually supposed a paid visit to The Wing and Thigh would reward you tangibly for your play for the Hellbenders. On the other hand, he felt no compunction about using you as a pawn in his scheme to hurt Miss LaRaina by hurting her daughter. That the enterprise might injure you and colossally grieve Miss Phoebe meant nothing to him, beyond the turmoil it would inflict on Miss LaRaina. I liked Mr. Curriden before this. Tonight, however, his name fills the rift in my heart with salt and ashes."

Henry sat mute until our cab turned onto Angus Road.

"The joke on Mr. Curriden is that his spitefulness ranks him in my estimation below such louts as Messieurs Hoey, Sloan, Sosebee, Sudikoff, and Evans. For all their bigotry, they attack directly those who shame or offend them, not blameless third parties with whom they have no quarrel." A moment later, he said, "The shameless louse."

Our cabby drove us right up to the columned front porch of McKissic House. Lights shone in windows upstairs and down, but you still got the feeling that, because we'd arrived a little after Mister JayMac's official curfew, the house would devour us as soon as we entered.

Henry paid the taxi fare and tipped the cabby. He more or less frog-marched me up the steps. At the door into the foyer, he stopped and stared down at me.

"You owe me a sawbuck for that fish tank, Daniel—one debt I don't intend to forgive."

I had no trouble with that. I had the money. Besides, my mind had flown back to a moment in The Wing & Thigh. The face of the man with the Popeye-the-Sailor lipstick cartoon on his keister was a face I knew. *What the hell! What the fuckin' hell!* Even the guy's jangly voice had a familiar edge to it. But where had I met him, and why would he want Popeye's homely mug scribbled on his butt?

"Do you hear me?" Henry said.

I nodded, and we went inside.

34

Miss Tulipa and Colonel Elshtain'd arrived in their Hudson Terraplane on Friday afternoon, too late to come to the game against the Seminoles. Miss Giselle had met them and welcomed them into her and Mister JayMac's bungalow. Their dust-covered vehicle, its tire treads caked with red mud from an Alabama creek bottom, hunkered in front of the place.

"Daniel, you're looking fit as a soldier," Miss Tulipa said in the gazebo near Hellbender Pond. "Isn't he, Clyde?"

"Yes," the colonel said. "He should *be* a soldier."

After breakfast, Darius had fetched me to the gazebo as a neutral meeting spot. The Elshtains hadn't wanted to intrude on the players' lodgings, and no player, Darius said, had set foot in Mister JayMac's house since its construction in the first year of CVL play—not even such suspected favorites as Hoey, Muscles, Snow, or my illustrious roomy, Jumbo Clerval.

Not Jumbo, I'd wanted to tell Darius: *Henry.*

"Your mama would beam to see you doing so well," Miss Tulipa said. "How's your laryngitis?"

To that point, I'd got by with nods and head shakes, grins and foot-shuffling. Shy fellas aren't expected to talk much. Now, though, I had to continue my charade or fess up through a note or sign language. A bad case of laryngitis could dog you for quite a while, couldn't it? I rubbed my throat and sadly shook my head.

"*Pobrecito,*" Miss Tulipa said. "What a trial for you."

"I doubt it's that vast a trial," Colonel Elshtain said. "You're simply imagining yourself in the lad's predicament."

Miss Tulipa looked the colonel hard in the eye. "At the moment, dear, I'm imagining *you* in his predicament."

"If you successfully wish laryngitis on me, Tulipa, we'll have a damnably hard time singing 'Row, Row, Row Your Boat' in rounds on our drive home."

That made Tulipa smile. "Clyde, go get Daniel's gift from his mother from the car, would you?"

Colonel Elshtain clicked his heels—sarcastically?—and left to do as bid.

"Your mama misses you hugely," Miss Tulipa said. And then: "*Good heavens!*" A truly bizarre shape had begun to glide out of a tree-lined inlet of Hellbender Pond, and she put a hand to her heart like a movie actress who's supposed to've seen a ghost or a moody mental figment of some sort. Then I reduced the shape on the pond to something familiar.

On a page from the little notebook I carried, I printed, *Its just Henry my roomate in his kyyak.*

Henry paddled his kayak out of the inlet towards us. His upper body came out of its manhole like a smokestack on an ocean liner. He almost seemed to be *wearing* the kayak, and it sat so low in the pond, with mosquitoes and noseeums haloing him, you feared it about to swamp or roll. It didn't, and Henry dipped his double-bladed paddle this way and that with the same hefty grace he swung a clutch of bats in the on-deck circle. He nodded—but didn't wave or smile—as the kayak slid by. Then he sculled it towards the far shore and headed into a flock of domestic ducks paddling out to meet him. He balanced his paddle on the prow and bombarded the ducks with handfuls of old cornbread.

Miss Tulipa couldn't get over the sight. "That's one of those, uh, Eskimo-ish boats, isn't it?"

I nodded, then tapped a cigarette out of my pack. Before thinking to offer Miss Tulipa one, I'd already lit up. She stared dazedly across the water like a whaler's wife yearning after her long-gone hubby—then looked back at me with a funny goggle of disappointment.

"Good Lord, Daniel, what're you doing?"

I wanted to say, *If I'm old enough to earn my own money, I'm old enough to smoke*, but my youth wasn't Miss Tulipa's primary objection. She snatched the cigarette, flipped it to the gazebo's decking, and ground it out with the toe of an ankle-strap Wedgie.

"You must have mayonnaise for brains, and it's gone bad in the sun. Nobody with laryngitis has any more business smoking than a TB patient. Do you intend to grow polyps on your vocal cords? To make your condition chronic?"

It's already chronic, I thought, but I acted contrite and sheepishly shook my head.

Colonel Elshtain returned from the Hudson with my gift from Mama. She'd wrapped it in birthday paper, but the gift's shape told me it was either 1) a fishing pole, 2) an ax handle, or 3) a baseball bat. If pressed to guess, I'd've marked 3) with the smart-alecky confidence of a guy with a crib sheet.

In fact, Mama *had* sent me a bat, another Red Stix model. I peeled it free of its paper and swung it a few times. Swinging it gave me a peculiar heart twinge.

"Coach Brandon wanted you to have it," Miss Tulipa said. "He gave it to your mama as soon as he learned you never got to use the first one in a real CVL game." With a tender smugness, Miss Tulipa watched me swing the red stick. "Doesn't Daniel look like a hitter, Clyde?"

"He *is* a hitter—his average proves it. But what he most looks like to me is a combat infantryman."

"Behave yourself, Clyde."

Out on the water, a duck settled on Henry's shoulder. He fed it by hand. The ducks on the pond flapped and quacked like unbribed city councilmen.

"We look forward to seeing you play at shortstop." Miss Tulipa stepped inside the arc of my biggest swing and kissed me on the forehead. "That's from your mama."

A clatter arose from the pond. Two or three of Henry's ducks, including a green-capped mallard, beat their way aboard the kayak and assaulted Henry himself.

"Don't be greedy!" he yelled. "*Monsters!*"

The mallard got to Henry's head and began to tread him with the zest of a feathered Romeo. In self-defense, Henry knocked the mallard into a side-spin, grabbed his paddle, and purposely rolled his kayak. The ducks scattered, veering off towards the far shore or gooney-bird-walking the ruffled cocoa scum to what their BB-shot brains assumed a safe distance. Henry, with pure upper-body strength and the torque on his paddle, righted the kayak in a fountain of glittery spray.

Impressive. Colonel Elshtain gave Henry a half-bow and very lightly applauded his feat.

"Care to join me?" Henry called, hair and face dripping and the kayak itself streaming.

"Only as spectators this afternoon!" the colonel shouted back.

"Ah, but the water wonderfully refreshes one on a day of such oppressive heat." Henry paddled towards the chokegrass and red-clover lawn stretching from the gazebo to the water.

"This afternoon," Miss Tulipa said to me, "get a hit or two for your dear friends from Tenkiller." That request made, she and the colonel retreated to their sister-in-law's house before Henry could reach the shore.

35

The game that Saturday, the first of a three-game series with Opelika, started at five. A Fourth of July twin bill, with a barbecue in the parking lot as a special attraction, would conclude the series on Sunday. Anyway, after beaching his kayak and upending it on a pair of sawhorses near the buggy house, Henry dressed out and walked with me to McKissic Field about three hours in advance of the game.

Already, three funeral-home tents covered the barbecue pits dug on the south side of the stadium. At least a dozen workers—some black, some white—stoked the pits with hickory, oak, and charcoal. Meantime, the headless carcasses of three slick porkers sizzled in the pits, and a smell a thousand times more tempting than the one from Goober Pride rose above the canopies and the gunk-encrusted Brunswick-stew pots.

"Yankee Doodle Dandy," Henry said. "Unfortunately, I've never been able to abide pork."

Maybe so, I thought, but when you were with the Oongpekmut, you ate walrus, seal, sea lion, and beluga flesh. None of that fishy offal could've smelt half as good as our barbecue.

The closer we got to the stadium, though, the odder Mister JayMac's preparations for the Fourth began to seem. Carpenters had built ramps from the parking lot to the concessions area and from there to the box seats behind our dugout. Just out of Tenkiller, Oklahoma, I'd never seen a boardwalk in my life—rickety piers didn't convey the same flavor—but, looking back, I'd say these ramps had a lot in common with a promenade among the dunes at a beach resort. Mister JayMac's workers had used sheets of plywood instead of abutting planks, though, and the crowd's footfalls echoed like the hooves of cattle. Is this a ballpark or a lumberyard? I wondered as Henry and I entered. You could still hear hammering, and the whole deal seemed such a helter-skelter rush job that it mystified—and irritated—almost everybody.

Mister JayMac met us near the batting cage.

"What's going on?" Henry asked, nodding at the ramps and at the place where the carpenters had built a barricade and hung a sign: NO UNAUTHORIZED PERSONS BEYOND THIS POINT.

"Temporary renovations," Mister JayMac said.

"Why would you wish to renovate temporarily, sir?"

"That's none of your damned business."

Henry looked stricken. "Pardon me," he said sincerely.

"Loose lips sink ships," Mister JayMac said. He rolled out the bromide as a kind of half-assed apology, but quickly turned on me. "Well, I see Tulipa's given you your bat, Mr. Boles. And a handsome, gaudy piece of timber it is. Too bad you won't have a chance to break it in today."

My surprise showed on my face.

"Put it in that rack," Mister JayMac said, pointing to the dugout. When I'd racked my bat, he said, "And put your fanny to that plank."

I sat down.

Henry, embarrassed for me, trotted out to right field to play long toss with Knowles.

"You don't play today, Mr. Boles," Mister JayMac continued, coming into the dugout. "You broke curfew. You pulled a jilt on my grandniece, who went to no little trouble to fix you dinner. Breaking curfew gets you benched.

Jilting Phoeb earns you my contempt. Have you two strong words to say in your own pitiful defense?"

I shook my head.

"Good. Because even if you could say it, Mr. Boles, I wouldn't care a good rip to hear it. Care to know the *third* reason you've forfeited a chance to play before Tulipa and her husband, folks who'd carry eye-witness word of your exploits to your mother?"

I just stared.

"No, I don't imagine you would. Nonetheless, Mr. Boles, you shall know it. In company with three men who should know better, and who therefore bear a greater culpability for this transgression than you, you did visit a section of Highbridge off-limits to every Hellbender."

I just stared.

"Mr. Curriden will not start at third today, nor come in at any time as a substitute. Mr. Parris won't pitch today, either as starter or reliever. Nor will Mr. Mariani. Four players out, owing to the reckless egotism of a man I trusted and the sheeplike complicity of his stooges in crime. I begin to see how a hateful guttersnipe with a Charlie Chaplin mustache could seduce even the nation of Goethe."

I lowered my head and shifted my butt.

"At four o'clock, Phoebe will be across the street at Hitch and Shirleen's. Go see her. Find a way to excuse yourself and make her feel a bit better, then return to watch your teammates play one of the CVL's three best clubs—even if they must do it with sixteen men instead of twenty."

Mister JayMac handed me a lineup. He had Buck Hoey at short, Junior Heggie at third for Curriden, and Lamar Knowles at second for Junior. His starting pitcher—a bigger surprise than his substitutions and position shifts—was Pete Haystack Hay ("His butt goes by bulk"), who ordinarily came in as a late-inning fireman because his lack of stamina after eight or nine batters disqualified him as a starter. Sosebee and Nutter would have to carry the load when Hay surrendered to the hook; we had no other pitchers available because Ankers was scheduled to pitch Sunday.

"Uncle Jay said you'd slither over," Phoebe said when I went to see her. "I figgered you'd sooner answer a altar call buck-naked, but, glory be, here you are."

Because of the pending game, Hitch & Shirleen's Neighborly Market had more than its usual share of customers. Hitch had hightailed it somewhere, but Shirleen was showing an old woman how to use her ration book, and a crew of burrheaded kids hung over the edge of the drink cooler like maybe it held a school of bait minnows. Phoebe and I would've had more privacy in the grandstands across the street. Literally.

"Well, Ichabod, s good to know you didn't jes skip town," Phoebe said for the entire premises to hear. "Sorry. I say Ichabod? I meant Boles. I git em mixed up sometimes, Boles n Ichabod, they sound so much alike." Before I could react in any way to that, Phoebe spoke to the kids at the soft-drink box: "Yall git you a soda or drop that lid! Yo're letting the cool out, wasting juice!"

The kids dropped the lid—*wham!*—and filed past me out the door. One little boy gave my ball uniform a quick second look, but the sight of it conjured no lasting magic for him.

I went to the glass countertop, my ear lobes as angry as infected tonsils, to make peace with Phoebe. She, though, had no hankering for easy terms.

"Don't stand there. I'm gonna have to ring something up. Yo're blocking my register." I took a step back. "Lord, boy, why're you wearing them spikes? Think it's hunky-dory to pock-mark our noleum?" The Neighborly Market's only linoleum ran between the shelf aisles; the heavy-traffic area next to the register and the drink cooler was unpainted concrete. "Take em off, Boles." I'd never taken my ball shoes off in the market, and I'd visited it almost a dozen times since my first visit. "I'm not kidding, Boles."

So I leaned into the counter and took off my spikes. This dropped me a half inch or so, but it still didn't let Phoebe stand nose to nose with me, more like nose to Adam's apple. On the other hand, emotionally I'd stepped into a trench and she'd climbed onto an awards stand. The cold concrete bit through my sanitaries.

"Go to the milk locker." Phoebe nodded towards the rear of the register aisle. "Go on. I mean it." I padded down the aisle to the milk locker. "Open it." I did. "Yore supper's on the shelf next to the aiggs. Take it out and bring it up here." I saw a white china plate covered with wax paper, tied like a Christmas package with a cross of twine. I took the plate out of the locker and returned to the front counter with it. "They's you a stool right there," Phoebe said, nodding at a stool behind the counter, down from the register. "Set down there and eat. I hate for you to have to miss yore supper. Go on. I aint kidding. What I fixed for you last night, Boles, is too good to waste."

I squeezed into the behind-the-counter space and sat down on the stool. Phoebe slapped a tin fork onto the countertop and roughly rang up the groceries of a woman who eyed me like I'd just answered an altar call naked. I untied the string holding the wax paper on the plate and found myself staring at a cold fried-chicken breast, a scoop of cold, semifurry mashed potatoes, and twenty or so green beans wearing sleeves of milky grease.

"Eat," Phoebe said. "Eat."

I picked up the fork.

"Oh, I suppose you want something to drink. Mrs. Nagy, would you git Boles here a strawberry soda. He don't really like em much, but neither do I." Mrs. Nagy fetched me a soda from the cooler. "Pop its cap off for him, please." Mrs. Nagy obliged, using her wet hand and sliding it across to me like a bomb needing quick disposal. Phoebe sacked her purchases, and Mrs. Nagy skedaddled with a scowl.

"Now eat," Phoebe said.

The chicken had meatiness and taste. I like cold chicken. But the potatoes gagged me the way whipped clay would've, and the green beans, under all their grease, had more strings than a textile loom. I forced beans and potatoes down, string by string and lump by lump. The soda helped.

"Now tell me you liked it," Phoebe said.

I nodded that I had. In the case of the chicken, at least, I didn't nod a lie. Phoebe took my fork and plate away from me and stowed them on a shelf at my back.

"Now say yo're sorry, and mean it down to yore toe bones."

I nodded my agreement to this too.

"That jes don't git it." Phoebe put a stubby pencil and a used envelope in front of me. "Tell me right."

I wrote on the envelope back: *Phoebe I'm sorry. Really.*

"Tell me you won't pull that kind of jackass stunt again."

I scrawled, *It wont happen again—promise promise promise!* She took the envelope and read the message—a couple of times, a half dozen. Pretty soon she was staring through the words to her own disappointment and humiliation of the night before. A glazed-over sort of trance.

"Okay," she said, snapping back. "Pology accepted."

I breathed again, but the meal she'd fixed for me rested in my stomach like a bag of fractured bricks.

"Gramma Shirleen," Phoebe called, "cmup here n tell this whangdoodle shortstop he aint God's gift to Highbridge! Fore his head grows so big it swallows his ears!"

36

We lost Saturday's game against Opelika. Buck Hoey didn't get a hit. Junior, at third, made two errors throwing the ball all that unaccustomed way across the infield. Pete Hay pitched six innings, but left trailing the Orphans five to aught, with the visitors playing too heads-up for us to creep back into it.

"Criminy!" Curriden shouted from the dugout when Junior made his second error. "*Think!* This aint the lousy sand-lots!"

"Wish *you'd* thought before your little trip to Penticuff Strip last night." Mister JayMac passed in front of Curriden, who promptly shut up.

Opelika's at-bat went on and on. When we finally got our third out, Mister JayMac eased over and put a hand on my knee. "A fine thing for Colonel Elshtain and my sister to see on one of their rare visits to Georgia. Another loss to Opelika and a sorry-ass performance to boot. Tomorrow, Mr. Boles, you'll start both games at short. Plan on leading us to an uplifting Fourth of July victory. I won't have Tulipa telling your mama that her son, owing to his bad judgment and selfishness, spent Independence Day in a state of bench bondage."

"*Two* uplifting victories," Darius said from his perch down the bench. "Cain't let these fellas settle for jes one, sir."

"Absolutely not." Mister JayMac seemed almost cheery, like he'd *expected* us to lose this one, like losing it would keep us from losing on the Fourth. He clapped his hands in a boosterly way as the Hellbenders dragged in for another go at the Orphan pitcher, Lester Affleck.

Henry was hitless in three at-bats, with a strikeout and two pop-ups to the second baseman. Leading off the inning, he cracked another pop-up, this one foul. It splintered his bat and drifted into the crowd for strike one. Henry gave the bat a flip, caught it by the barrel, and banged its knob on home plate. You could hear the hollow twang, like a chord on a bamboo harp, all over the stadium. He tossed the broken bat to Euclid and trudged over to us for a new one.

Because of my benching, Miss Tulipa still hadn't seen my new Red Stix model do a lick of work in the CVL. I unracked Mama's gift, via Coach Brandon and the Elshtains, and carried it to Henry. He took it with a brain-dead look of distracted raptness and gave it a swing.

"Lord God," Turkey Sloan said, "what you doing with that bloody toothpick, Jumbo?"

Henry turned his gaze on me. "I could break it too." I shrugged. At least the Elshtains wouldn't have to wait until tomorrow to see their gift in action.

In the batter's box again, Henry threatened Lester Affleck with my Red Stix timber. The crowd, and every Orphan sub in Opelika's dugout, scoffed, cracking wise or booing. Henry *did* look like a country doctor with a tongue depressor dipped in off-color gentian violet. That was okay. I still expected him to silence the scoffers with a wrist-flick home run, just like in a movie. He didn't, though. He struck out on the next two pitches, badly missing a pair of changeups and almost losing his footing both times.

"Hey, Jumbo, nex time git you a telephone pole!" a soldier in the stands shouted.

Henry returned to the dugout and handed me my bat. "It may have bowed today, but it is still unbloodied. To you, then, I leave its successful initiation tomorrow."

Thanks a lot, I thought.

In any case, Affleck finished with a shutout, only one of three games all year in which we failed to score.

"Yall come out tomorrow for a big Independence Day to-do here at McKissic Field," PA announcer Milt Frye urged what was left of our crowd. "Two games for the price of one. Barbecue on the grounds. At least one win or your money back. If we take em both, free prizes for everyone leaving after the second game. We've also got a War Bond rally, some down-home gospel singing, and a Big Surprise. Yall be here now!" Frye might've gone on another three minutes, but somebody tracked a needle on our scratchy

78 RPM of "The Star-Spangled Banner," and the blare of the anthem shut him up.

When I left that evening, a group of carpenters had come back in to work on their mysterious system of ramps.

Along with most of my fellow boarders, I ate a light supper in McKissic House, then retired to the front porch to take the breeze. Mister JayMac and Miss Giselle drove by in their Caddy with Colonel and Mrs. Elshtain, going to a dinner engagement somewhere out of town. It sort of scalded me, but also sort of relieved me, that they hadn't asked me along.

Upstairs in my room—Henry had clean-up duties—I copied out some more of Henry's journal. These sections summarized his journey away from Alaska and his ten-to-fifteen-year ramble through the American Northwest. In Washington State, Oregon, and Idaho, he pretty much weaned himself away from meat eating to a diet of carrots, tubers, greens, berries, and nuts. He hid from men, though, and haunted the woods.

Here's one passage:

Even in my estrangement from the friendlier aspects of humanity, in the Cascades I often knew a melancholy joy. One afternoon, I experienced it while seated on a boulder overlooking a creek picketed by trees and curtained on either side by leaf mulch and moss. The plangent gurgling of the water and the azure brilliance of the sky combined to inspirit me—to such a degree that I broke into one of the festival chants of the Oongpekmut.

I do not sing well. My voice has such a barbaric timbre that it may discomfit even me. On this afternoon, however, my chant poured forth like a nightingale's warble. Although the birds themselves fell silent and insects ceased to chirr, I adjudged it as melodious as the nightingale's—wrongly, of course.

Two warriors stepped from the shrubbery beyond the streambed and shot at me with bows. Although the banal repetitiveness of man's aggression towards me had become highly predictable, this attack took me by surprise. Would my author's race always greet my appearance with hostility and violence? Europeans, Asians, Siberians, Anglo-Saxons—even Innuit unfamiliar to me—all reacted as if I posed a danger requiring swift eradication. My attackers, whose arrows flew wide or rebounded from my granite throne, wore the dress of the Sahaptin group of North American Indians: Cayuse, Pahuse, or Wallawalla. I identified them by their vestments and, when they audibly conferred, by certain quirks of their Penutian-derived tongue.

As my shock quitted me, I struggled to my feet to expel a roar of warning and reproach. The leather-clad indigenes withdrew behind a wall of huckleberry bushes.

I roared again.

Fulminating thus, I leapt from my boulder into the verdant ground-cover only a short dash from their conference place. This tactic—advance rather than retreat—bemused and affrighted the warlike indigenes.

"Sasquatch!" one of them cried.

They fled, ripping through the foliage and calling out, as if to unseen confederates, "Sasquatch! Sasquatch!"

Thereafter, apprised anew of my seemingly irrevocable pariahhood, I again took care to avoid betraying my presence either to the natives of the region or to the disregardant Anglo-Saxon invaders. I nonetheless continued to reconnoiter the villages and towns of both groups. How often I heard the alien shibboleth "Sasquatch!" on their lips, uniting these foes in their fear and misapprehension of me. Thus, in my retreat from Oongpek and my subsequent stay in the Pacific Northwest, I became a legend, which had its origin and growth in a mortifying lie.

Henry came into our room a few minutes after I'd read this passage. He liked me copying his journal. Although he'd gone kayaking in front of the Elshtains, I seemed to be the only soul in Highbridge—or anywhere—who understood exactly what that kayak meant in the tangled weave of his life. Or, as he liked to call it, his second life.

To everyone else, Henry presented the kayak as a hobby, a sportsman's hobby, and they bought this explanation the way they bought Henry himself, as a one-in-a-million fella with a talent for ballplaying and a caboodle of crotchets. You ignored these last, though, because, on the ball field, he produced.

Henry, alias Jumbo, towered over Muscles, but he didn't scrape eight feet, as his creator'd written in the account published anonymously by Mrs. Shelley in 1818 and released thirteen years later with an introduction in which she claimed authorship herself. I mean, a galoot eight feet tall would scare anyone, especially, I thought, folks of a stature akin to, or even smaller than, my own. With that thought in mind, I got out my notebook and wrote:

Youre not as tall as Dr. F. says he made you. Why not.

The surprise of the day—a bigger surprise than having Mister JayMac bench me—occurred just then. Henry began to tug on the shoulder straps of the Extra Large overalls he'd worn to dinner, and his overalls collected in a starchy blue-and-white puddle at his ankles.

I had never seen Henry drop trou before; neither, so far as I knew, had anybody else on the Hellbenders. On road trips, when he and I shared a room, he vanished into the lavatory to change clothes or doused or draped off every glimmer of light. In McKissic House, in temperatures that'd've floored a camel, he slept in loose pajama bottoms and kept a sheet up to his chin. The modesty of Hank Clerval would've gotten high marks from a Baptist preacher's missus.

Now, though, Henry stood there in baggy boxers, dingy white skivvies, polka dots in a Dalmatian scatter from hip to fly. He backed up, dragging his overalls, and sat on his bed facing me. He stuck out his oakish legs—gray, purple, yellow, beige, so many colors they reminded me of a fleshy quilt. Pale scars ran in puckered bands around his lower calves, a band to each leg. Had Henry once worn anklets of barbed wire as a scourge, the way monks'd worn hair shirts or bankers and car salesmen wear neck ties? I stared at Henry's legs. No wonder he didn't shower with us, no wonder he sometimes hobbled like a crip.

"My pain receptors operate imperfectly, Daniel," he said. "Or, let me rather say, those triggering bodily—as opposed to emotional—pain function unreliably. I decided to use this truth about myself to my advantage. In a remote section of the Ozarks, during Mr. Cleveland's second presidency, I thought to make myself less fearsome. If my height affrighted people, I would reduce it. If my flesh's grisly damask caused distaste or consternation, I would seek a remedy for my complexion."

Henry leaned forward and gripped his ankles. He looked like a giant being potty trained—Goliath's kid, maybe, or Paul Bunyan's.

"Of all peoples, only the Oongpekmut had accepted me as one of them. Winning their trust had taken more effort than I ever wanted to expend again. I wanted permanent cures, alterations in my bodily self that would ease my absorption into any human community I hopefully approached."

Henry reached into the drift of his overalls, untied his shoes, and heeled them off. Kicking away shoes and overalls together, he sat there in his too-small cotton stockings.

"With great quantities of gin, a kitchen knife, and a hacksaw, I removed foot-long sections from the lower leg bones my creator had scavenged from either a charnel house or an abattoir. Among my father's effects on the *Caliban* had been a small notebook detailing many of the surgical procedures he had employed to build, albeit not to animate, me. This miniature treatise I had read and reread on my journey from the Barents Sea to the Chukchi Peninsula, and then again at intervals during my stay among my woman Kariak's Innuit—to the point of total familiarity and intuitive comprehension.

"Armed with this information, I had little trouble cutting and then reconnecting the appropriate bones. At the summer solstice, with much trepidation I shortened my left leg. After that autoexcision, I performed a similar medial amputation on my right leg"—Henry touched the white scar—"about two weeks later. By my creator's design, I bleed enough to cleanse my wounds, but not so profusely as to deprive me of recuperative vigor. Thus, though at first unable to ramble abroad or to limp from one spot to another in my cave, I healed in the time I had privately allotted; that is to say, within three months, or by the autumnal equinox.

"This was an idyllic time for me, Daniel. In the early phases of my recovery, I had access to a storehouse of nuts, tubers, and dried fruits that I had laid by before abridging my height. I lay on my back in the cave, near a long-abandoned mill, and wrote poetry in my head or tried to solve self-posed geometric or mathematical enigmas. I resisted the urge to sing. Because I had foresightfully equipped my cave with rope ladders and wooden travel rods, I could hand-over-hand from one spot to another without putting any but a therapeutic stress on my lower extremities. This same system took on added import in the rehabilitation process, and it was not long before I again mastered the rudiments of walking.

"My self-surgery left me awkward afoot, but less alarmingly a giant when I crashed about upright. During the latter part of my healing, again ambulatory, I tested myself outdoors. I gathered mockernuts; inhaled the aroma of hand-crushed hickory leaves; and saw mergansers, crimson-headed canvas-backs, and delicate wood ducks scull the September skies. Life apart from man seemed an unutterable gift. Ahead, however, lay autumn's drear gales and the winter's enfortressing cold, a time that I bleakly awaited.

"Indeed, I often thought of insinuating myself into a human community as accepting as Kariak's people had been. I trimmed my hair. I mixed many natural unguents, to repair the twisted lumpiness and hideous variegation of my complexion. I measured my progress in a shaving-mirror shard that I had found. In it, I saw that my lotions and poultices had turned my patchy skin an even pinkish gray. I could pass, I believed, for an ugly, lame Caucasian. No fastidious American woman would want me for a mate, but so long as I could chastely associate with talented men and women of goodwill, I could endure this lack of intimacy with a sympathetic female.

"Over the years, Daniel, I've endured, accommodating myself to a strenuous celibacy. It has proved less difficult than I feared. The years leach one—even a creature doomed, as I am, to a contingent immortality—of desire. A further mitigating factor is my sterility. I neither gainsay nor scorn the allure of erotic pleasure, but, for me, coitus sans any procreative potential loses some of its relevance, and so also its allure, and likewise its power to tempt. No longer do I blaze like a furnace. I don't need women to fuel me. Thus, my capacities for a higher passion channel into three sustaining reservoirs: atonement, human companionship, and baseball."

Baseball I got. Companionship I had a glimmering of. But atonement swept past like water in a spillway. Henry stood up. His sutured calves drew my gaze as surely as would've a starlet's gams.

"I've revealed these signs of my self-mutilation, Daniel, to impress upon you the length to which loneliness and a need to belong once drove me. I do not regret having performed my surgery, but I do regret the evidence of it. The scars don't pain me in a physical sense, but the mere sight of them lays a bruise on my heart. I entreat you then to look away."

"Look away."

I looked away. Henry gathered up his overalls and scooped himself back into them. I didn't see him do this—I heard the rustle of denim and the muffled clicks of brass snaps.

37

On Sunday morning, when the *Brown Bomber* pulled into the parking lot at McKissic Field, the stadium and its barbecue pits had the look of a birthday bash in a military zone. Lots of Highbridgers had paraded off to church, but many hadn't. We Hellbenders, Mister JayMac's public piety aside, fell into the second group. We'd substituted a talk by Colonel Elshtain and some prayers on our bus ride for attendance at an honest-to-God worship service. Anyway, at the field, we saw folks standing in queue for the barbecue (which wouldn't be served until one), vendors peddling all kinds of gewgaws, and several soldiers in battle dress standing guard along a cordoned lane through the lot to the place where Darius always parked.

As soon as we'd stopped, Mister JayMac spoke to us from the front: "President Roosevelt has spent the last two days at the Little White House in Warm Springs. Given the demands of the war, this's been a hard time for him to get out of Washington—except for shipboard conferences with the rulers of our allies or his battle commanders. For reasons I don't think require an explanation"—Mister JayMac wiped the back of his neck with a handkerchief—"the President only rarely visits Georgia at the height of summer. He came for one day in August five years ago; usually, however, he confines his expeditions down here to the spring or fall. His presence this Fourth of July weekend bespeaks his strength as a man and his integrity as a patriot. It honors every soul born or resident in the South."

"Holy cow!" Trapdoor Evans blurted. "That goddamn polio's not going to be at our games today, is he?"

Colonel Elshtain stood. "He'll be here for at least one of your games and maybe both. I'd suggest a more respectful form of address than 'that goddamn polio'—should you have occasion, gentlemen, to meet him."

"How about 'Your Highness'?" Buck Hoey said.

"Criminy," Muscles said. "We have to win. If we lose, we'll shame ourselves in front of the President of the United States."

"Losing won't shame you," Colonel Elshtain said. "Cracks like 'that goddamn polio' and 'How about "Your Highness"?' will far more effectively do that. Whether you personally find the man now in office an ornament to or a blot upon that position, it nonetheless remains that...."

And blahblah, blahblahblah.

A couple of seats up from me, Turkey Sloan raised his hand.

"What is it, Mr. Sloan?" Mister JayMac said.

Sloan stood up. "Not too long ago, sir, I wrote a tribute to the Leader of the Free World, his administration, and the first family. To settle Colonel Elshtain's doubts about Hellbender loyalty, I'd like your permission for me, Mr. Hoey, Mr. Evans, and Mr. Sosebee to recite it for him."

"How long's this gonna take?" Mister JayMac said.

"Not even a minute," Sloan said. "Sir, you know I always write tight."

"You do everything tight," Hoey said.

"If you're going to do this, Mr. Sloan, proceed," Mister JayMac said. "It's too hot to dawdle till Halloween in this four-wheeled inferno."

Sloan made a humming sound, like a music teacher blowing on a pitch pipe. His pals stood up, at smirky attention. " 'The Battle Hymn of the Repugnant' by Nyland Sloan, as performed by the author and his Disgusting Associates." In the farce that followed, Sloan recited the first two lines of each stanza of his "tribute," while Hoey, Evans, and Sosebee joined on every third-line chorus:

> "Tip your fez
> To the Prez?
> *Shout, 'Glory Hallelujah!'*

> "Whose New Deal'll
> Make you squeal?
> *Why, Frankie Rooz-ah-velt-ah's!*

> "Cordell Hull
> Is a cull
> *Who'll downright coldly screw yah!*

> "Eleanor
> We deplore.
> *Hey, buddy, what's it to yah?*

"We regret
Eliot,
Their sorry naval joon-yah!

"Let's debar
FDR!
Make flea-bit Fala Pooh-Bah!"

Taking the whistles and applause, Sloan and his Disgusting Associates bowed to this side and that. (Fala was Roosevelt's Scotty dog and traveling buddy, a regular Fido Firstus.) Henry and I stamped and clapped along with the others. The colonel sank into his seat like a punctured bounce-back toy, rigidly facing front.

Mister JayMac shook his head and shooed us off the bus. "Beat it, yall! Quicktime!"

We filed down the aisle stamping our feet. As we jostled along, every player but me chanted "*Shout, 'Glory Hallelujah!'*" or "*Make flea-bit Fala Pooh-Bah!*"

Mariani pitched the first game, and I started at short. Pregame ceremonies included a War Bonds spiel by a wounded vet, Mister JayMac's welcome, and the colored accordionist Graham Jackson playing "The Star-Spangled Banner" as a black choir, dressed in phony plantation garb, sang the lyrics.

The President and his party hadn't arrived yet; and few folks in the stands understood we expected such a distinguished visitor and sports fan, one of the men who'd kept pro baseball from shutting down for the war. Still, Mister JayMac refused to delay the doubleheader's start.

Bottom of the first, I poked one down the right-field line with my new Red Stix bat. It felt good, that double, almost like it wiped from my past everything that'd happened on Friday night: my gin binge, the trip to The Wing & Thigh, my no-show at Phoebe's house, and Henry's cavalry-to-the-rescue routine. Charlie Snow drove me home with a single up the middle. In our first at-bat, in fact, we sent another six men to the plate and scored two more runs.

Between innings, I heard sirens screaming just outside the stadium. They came closer and closer, eking up higher in pitch and volume until yard dogs began to howl and many people in the stands covered their ears.

"Ladies and gentlemen," Frye announced over the PA system, "it's the one hundred and sixty-seventh anniversary of this great nation, but the first time ever that the President of the United States has attended a baseball game in Highbridge or any other CVL city. All rise!" As if FDR was a judge and McKissic Field a courtroom.

I'd already made my way to my shortstop position. When our old military-band recording of the National Anthem began to play, I didn't have to rise. The fans, though, buckled upward en masse, craning their necks trying to catch sight of the most famous man—forget John D. Rockefeller or Clark Gable—in the whole United States. The sirens outside the stadium stopped about the time the anthem's rockets began to glare red and its bombs to burst in air.

Then, because the President hadn't made his entrance by song's end, Frye played it again. And a third time, with folks forgetting proper hand-over-heart protocol, before a guard of uniformed Marines and helmeted soldiers marched in over the brand-new ramp system. Behind them, some wheelchair outriders in suits appeared at the top of a plywood slope. They ushered in the waving President, a man until then bashful of exposing himself in such an "unmanly" state. On that Fourth, though, he rode, head high, to the caged box seat behind our dugout. Once the military guard had peeled off, in fact, I could see the Prez as well as, or better than, anybody else in the park.

I couldn't believe it. Me, a kid from nowhere, standing maybe fifty yards from the only three-term chief executive in the history of our land. My nape hairs did the Wave decades before that cheer even got invented.

Know what kept rippling through my gray matter, though? *He didn't see my first hit. What if I don't get another?*

Except for the smudges under his eyes and the dents in his cheeks, Mr. Roosevelt looked spiffy, a lot like Francis X. Bushman or some other silent-screen actor. Cool white linen suit, dapper straw snapbrim, fluffy polka-dot bow tie.

Someone had rigged a microphone at chest height—for a fella in a wheelchair, that is—and the President's primary pusher—a Secret Service agent?—slipped him up to it. Ballplayers and fans alike had started cheering. The cheering swelled until it swamped the "home of the brave" finale of "The Star-Spangled Banner." The Prez met the hullabaloo with head nods, his arms in the air like those of some raptured Holy Roller, his smile as wide as Tennessee.

The President's "private" box filled up: military guards and Secret Service men, a bigwig or two from FDR's staff, and, to my hefty surprise, Colonel and Mrs. Elshtain, Miss Giselle, and LaRaina and Phoebe Pharram. In his shirt sleeves, Mister JayMac himself climbed up on our dugout's tarpapered roof and walked over to the Chief to shake his hand and welcome him to Highbridge.

Amid this tumult, Colonel Elshtain stood in the box rocking up and back on his toes and smirking like a Siamese with a goldfish tail showing between its lips. No wonder "The Battle Hymn of the Repugnant" hadn't amused him.

The cheering didn't die. Coloreds and whites alike cheered FDR, the coloreds from the bleachers seats or in their spots as groundskeepers, custodians, and snack vendors. A few people—mostly women—cried. The war'd turned FDR into a god for many folks, even conservative whites. The blacks liked him because his missus spoke out for fairness and entertained Negro leaders in the White House.

The President quieted us with some calm-down hand gestures and an attempt to use the mike: "Ladies and gentlemen, if you please . . ." That wide chin-up smile again. "By gosh, this is a splendid reception, and I'm delighted to be here. Indeed, my apologies for interrupting your game, coming in like the imperial Caliph of Baghdad. Goodness knows, today we celebrate American independence, not the bondage of our national pastime to my holiday travel schedule."

He talked on like that for a minute and then gave up the mike to Mister JayMac, who summoned Graham Jackson and the plantation singers—favorites of FDR's from his stays at Cason Callaway's Blue Springs—back to perform "The Star-Spangled Banner" again. That made five times we'd heard it in forty minutes, but our fans shouted "Play ball!" afterwards as loudly as they had every other time.

Mr. Roosevelt bumped up to the mike again: "Later today, ask your neighbors if they heard about the accident here at McKissic Field. When they say, 'I'm afraid I haven't,' tell em, 'An Opelika player leaned on his bat so long waiting for the game to resume that termites ate the handle out and he fell and broke his back.'" The President threw back his head and guffawed, then leaned again into the mike: "I love it! Don't you just love it!" They surely did. We all did. Even the Orphans broke up, slapping one another on the back and catcalling Max Delaney, the hitter in the on-deck circle.

"If Delaney had an ounce of sense, he'd fall down and grab his back," Curriden told me. "But the palooka aint got roach shit for brains."

The Orphan manager, Lou Ed Dew, tried to convince Happy Polidori, the plate umpire, to scrap the first inning and start us over again. He seemed to think the CVL rule book forbid the playing of anything but a full nine-inning game after "The Star-Spangled Banner." I edged closer to the Orphan dugout to pick up the details of this bizarre squabble.

"I don't recollect that rule, Lou Ed," Polidori said.

"It's in there," Lou Ed Dew said. "I'm pritty shore. I'd bet money. I think I would."

"Would you be as certain if the Orphans'd scored three runs in the first instead of the other way round?"

"Shore. Shore I would."

"That'd be about the foolishest rule ever devised by man then," Polidori said. "A team could hire a band to play the 'Banner' ever time its boys had a bad inning out to field and guv up a run or six. I mean, musicians for the Boll Weevils or the Linenmakers could get rich."

"Check the book, Polidori. Check the book!"

"I don't have to." Polidori lowered his mask and walked away from Lou Ed Dew. "*Play ball!* I mean, *Resume play!*"

Dunnagin took a fresh ball from Polidori and trotted with it over to Mr. Roosevelt's box. "Sir, would you be willing to throw out the"—he pretended to count in his head—"the sixth or seventh ball of this game?"

"Would I?" FDR said. "By gosh, Mr. Dunnagin, I'd regard it as churlish—a missed opportunity—to refuse."

Dunnagin flipped the ball to Mister JayMac and backed up about twenty paces. Mister JayMac handed the President the horsehide, and FDR rubbed it up like a New Englander shaping a snowball. He winked over one shoulder at Miss Giselle, then tossed the ball to Dunnagin, who reacted like the Prez had set his palm on fire. Then he thrust the ball up in the air. Our fans cheered their noggins off again. The organist cranked up a rowdy version—a *really* rowdy version—of "There'll Be a Hot Time in the Old Town Tonight."

"Thow it to your pitcher," Polidori told Dunnagin.

"This baby's going home with me," Dunnagin said. "One day a kid of mine might like to have it."

"The league'll have to fine you for misappropriating CVL property," Polidori said. "The league'll—"

"Screw the league," Dunnagin said. "Toss Mariani a fresh ball, Mr. Ump."

The game did resume. We Hellbenders played inspiredly, in the field and up to bat. I had two more hits in our opener, neither for extra bases, and fielded like FDR's predecessor in office, a Hoover: *thwup, thwup, thwup!* I just sucked em up and howitzered em over to Henry.

It wasn't close, but the President enjoyed himself. He knew Mister JayMac and Miss Giselle, he knew the Elshtains, he had field-level box seats behind the dugout. He had a Co-Cola, a bag of peanuts, and another Co-Cola. I wouldn't swear to it, but he may've doctored that second Coke with a tot of something spiritous. A regular fella, for a Harvard man and a three-term president. It was pretty much a wonderwork I played as decent as I did, I spent so much time eyeing him sidelong and watching in literal dumfoundment how sprightly and pretty Miss Giselle—with her belief in, and hatred of, the so-called Eleanor Clubs—looked bantering with him.

In the bottom of the eighth, Henry, with only one hit to that point, polewhacked a curve off the fourth Orphan pitcher: a flabbergasting blast that cleared the outfield wall, the bleacher seats behind the wall, the parking lot outside, maybe even the Panhandle-Seminole Railway tracks slashing southeast to Camp Penticuff. People stood up to watch the ball soar. In the brief silence that fell over nearly every onlooker there, FDR's high-tone tenor sounded in his open mike and vibrated in every speaker on the field:

"Swear to God, Clyde, that's the most monsterish home run I've ever seen! Who is that fella?"

"Jumbo!" the crowd answered. "Jumbo! Jumbo! Jumbo!"

Henry trotted the bases, running on stems he'd hack-sawed a foot shorter during the second presidency of Cleveland, listing in his trot like a man on a unicycle.

"Well, Jumbo my chum, congratulations," said the President, this time deliberately using the mike. "I haven't seen a shot carry that far since the U.S.S. *Enterprise* showed off her guns for me."

Laughter. Applause. Henry crossed the plate, circled back to our dugout, and tipped his cap to Mr. Roosevelt.

At some point during the twin bill's intermission, FDR and his friends pulled out and rumbled over our highway of ramps to the parking lot. People saw him leaving, of course, but the Fourth of July hoopla on the field—an Army glee club, a quilt raffle—more or less covered his exit.

"I didn't realize he couldn't walk," Sudikoff said between the two games.

"He can," Nutter said. "With braces. But nobody wants to clack as far as he would've had to in a set of leg braces."

"I jes never realized," Sudikoff said.

"You weren't supposed to," Nutter told him.

We took the second game too, although this one evolved into a pitching duel between Fadeaway Ankers and a clever ex-major leaguer known as Smiley Clough. The game ended three to one. Lou Ed Dew probably wished Mr. Roosevelt had watched it instead of our scalp-em-bald romp in the opener. Aboard the Brown Bomber, riding back to McKissic House, I kept hearing FDR say, "*Swear to God, Clyde, that's the most monsterish home run I've ever seen!*" You could tell from that remark how he'd become president; he just had an instinct about him.

38

Angus Road and the McKissic House estate had guards—Camp Penticuff MPs and specially assigned soldiers in battle dress— posted all around them.

Darius drove us past this armed picket line and up the curving drive to the boardinghouse, then along the grassy track between the boardinghouse and the wood-shingled carriage house, then past that garage straight down the clovery slope towards Hellbender Pond. Every player on the team was aboard the bus, not just McKissic House tenants.

The pond's grassy bank boasted three open-sided tents with striped roofs and several trestle-legged picnic tables set out under them. A bank of big electric fans, powered by a noisy gas-powered generator, flanked the tents to keep us picnickers cool and mosquito-free. FDR and his party had already claimed one of these tents, and Marines or a Secret Service detail had furnished it with dining-room chairs and the back seat of the President's touring car, which they'd removed and set in front of a table draped with a linen cloth and laid with china and crystalware.

Kizzy and a rail-thin part-time butler had put out barbecue and Brunswick stew from the pits at the ball field—also cole slaw, pickles, olives, deviled eggs, and suchlike fixings—but *not* on FDR's table. He had a basket packed with fried chicken, California wine, and French bread. He didn't like the vinegary tang of Suthren-style barbecue.

Darius parked not far from the tents, but kept his hand on the door lever, holding us in. "Yall knew Mister JayMac had a to-do planned out here. He jes didn't know if the President tended to stay fo it. Looks like he has. Last thing Mister JayMac told me, if Mister Franklin stayed, was to ast yall to behave yosefs and do ol Highbridge proud."

Fadeaway Ankers said, "What'd do ol Highbridge proud is not to have a uppity woolhead telling grown white men what to do. Jesus."

Wham. Everybody on the Bomber went tight-jawed. Darius'd spoken by way of the rearview, about as boy-humble as he had it in him to be. Now he cut his eyes to one side, and all the rest of us Hellbenders could see of him in the mirror was the top of his head.

"As good as you throw," Charlie Snow told Fadeaway, "you still aint made it to grown yet. And Darius wasn't *telling* nobody nothing, he was passing a message."

You expected Charlie Snow to field his center-field spot like a two-legged whitetail and to clutch-hit the team out of jams, but you didn't expect him to open his mouth a passel, and ordinarily he obliged your expectations.

"I jes chunked a three-hitter at Opelika," Fadeaway said. "How much more *grown* can a fella git?"

"Arm's mature," Snow said. "Head's a baby."

Muscles got up. "And the rest of us're *tired* of listening to this hoo-hah. Let's party with the President. Just mind your p's and q's, dammit!"

Darius levered the door open, and we began filing off the bus.

Off the Bomber, we edged towards the tents. Nobody had the nerve or the bumpkin grace to angle towards FDR's roadster sofa and Park Avenue table setting, though. At the same time, no one could resist glancing over that way and trying to imagine what the President of the United States had to discuss with the McKissics, the Elshtains, or Miss LaRaina and Phoebe.

Once or twice, the Great Man smiled and nodded or wagged his cigarette holder in a folksy greeting.

As Fadeaway sauntered around the Bomber's nose with Evans and Sosebee, Darius put a hand on his shoulder. When he saw who'd touched him, Fadeaway's nose wrinkled, and he triggered himself for curses, maybe even fisticuffs.

"Tell me what you think woolhead means." Darius's voice wasn't much below its normal volume, but the generator and the box fans kept the other picnickers from hearing.

"Lemme tell you what uppity means," Fadeaway said. "You could learn two new words jes by looking in a mirror."

"I know more words than you got memories," Darius said. "What woolhead means, *Mister* Ankers, is you aint got the belly to speak out nigger, or the class to call my name."

Quickly and quietly, Sosebee grabbed Fadeaway's arms from behind. "Easy, kid. Remember who-all's here."

"Remember this instead," Darius said. "If it got figgered on sense and soundness stead of what it is, you'd come up the biggest nigger in town. Watch I don't whup yo red ass black." He stood glaring at Fadeaway when most folks, delivered of such a squelch, would've swaggered away.

Henry leaned over his shoulder. "Enough, Mr. Satterfield. This is no time for a physical collision."

"Sho," Darius said. "Clision time jes never quite comes round, do it?" He pocketed his hands, backed away from the players stalled in front of the Bomber, and hiked up the slope to his apartment.

"Hey!" Kizzy called from one of the tents. "You, Darius, don't you want no victuals?"

He just kept walking.

"Uppity nigger," Fadeaway said under his breath.

Henry and I and the other Hellbenders ate. The family men had their families there, and more than a few—Buck Hoey and his boys, Charlie Snow and his childless wife, Turkey Sloan and his freckle-faced teenage daughter— ventured out on the pond in johnboats to fish.

At Mister JayMac's prompting, Henry removed his kayak from the sawhorses near the buggy house, fetched it down to the pond under one arm, and demonstrated for the President how a man his size—the swatter of a "monsterish" home run—could paddle to and fro among the anglers' boats with hardly a telltale ripple and not even one fish-disturbing splash. By this time, Mister JayMac'd coaxed me into the heart of FDR's picnic circle, with the Elshtains, the Pharram females, and a few fussy suit types from D.C. All eyes followed Henry's silken progress over the pond's cocoa scum.

"Astonishing so large a man can move with that agility," FDR said. "How'd he come by the kayak?"

"He says he built it," Mister JayMac said. "And I've no cause to doubt him. Look how he handles it."

"Indeed, if I could handle Congress half so well, I'd sleep more and haggle less with the likes of Senator George. God knows, I envy Mr. Clerval's finesse with the big stick, whether a ball bat or a kayak paddle."

Mr. Roosevelt had plenty of finesse with words. I milled about close enough to his car-seat divan to catch a lot of what he said, but the Elshtains and Miss LaRaina monopolized the time he didn't give to the McKissics.

I marveled at Miss Giselle. With a glint in her eye, she watched Henry kayak and chatted with the President. How could she lap Mr. Roosevelt in such honey-tongued politeness when his wife's Christian name gagged her like ammonia ice?

"It's my view Mussolini's doomed," Colonel Elshtain broke into their stateside chitchat. "Even he must know it. The air strike on Rome last month had to've told him so."

"Il Duce's an evil man," Miss Giselle said, "but must we destroy the Holy See to uproot him? Is it necessary, sir, to bomb to rubble both the Vatican and the monuments of Rome to unseat this petty despot?"

"Not at all," FDR said. "Nor shall we do so. I've urged the Vatican to try to get him to declare Rome an open city—to remove all military bases and personnel in and about Rome to the countryside, and to desist from using the city's railroad facilities as reprovisioning conduits for either Hitler's boys or the Italian infantry. If Benito listens to reason, Rome survives unscathed. If not, well, to my mind there's not one Roman statue or one relic in the Vatican worth the blood of a single American soldier."

Phoebe pulled me away from the presidential divan. We stalked along the pond, under the long banana-green fingers of a weeping willow, and through a hand-grenade scatter of cones from a magnolia tree farther up the bank. A quartet of Hellbenders—Sosebee, Dunnagin, Hay, and

Parris—crooned "The Music Goes Round and Round," "If I Didn't Care," and "Making Whoopee," among other corny numbers, a capella. The clang of horseshoes in a pair of facing pits near the buggy house echoed like anchors bumping a ship's hull.

"Bravo!" the President cried after one of the quartet's songs. "Splendid, gentlemen!"

"I guess he's all right," Phoebe said, nodding downslope at the President's tent. "For a New York swank."

He seemed all right to me. I didn't know you could, or even should, try to find fault with the President. Which was why Sloan's snotty poem aboard the Bomber had made such an impression on me. To me, FDR was like a king. For the biggest part of my life, no one else had held his office.

"I know where you went the other night when you didn't show up for dinner," Phoebe said. "Penticuff Strip."

I looked at my shoes. Her great-uncle knew where I'd spent Friday evening. So did most of my teammates. At a picnic, you just naturally overheard allegations, brags, gossip.

"Actually, it uz worse than that," Phoebe said. "The Wing and Thigh, a chicken place n chippy house."

The quartet crooning for FDR had just eased in to "Making Whoopee," a wink-and-slink version with lots of eye rolling and so on. I turned red from Phoebe's remark and from the risqué gist of the song. What'd Phoebe know about a chippy house, for God's sake? For that matter, what did I?

"You lose your cherry?"

I looked at her like she'd asked me if I'd been conceived and delivered a bastard.

"I ast, Did some low woman on the Strip git yore cherry?"

The urge hit me to walk away. But a sudden and ripening hunch that walking away would cut me off from Phoebe forever reversed it. I had to answer her, and answer straight, so I shook my head, thankful my dummyhood spared me the mess—and also the tail-tucking—of going into detail.

"You swear?"

I nodded. Curriden's money'd bought me nothing but a knot on the head and a broken chain of shameful memories.

"If that's true, Daniel Boles, you better kiss me."

It'd been true my whole acne-plagued adolescence, but no young female'd ever hinted that my intact cherry entitled me to a Public Display of

Affection. Well, semipublic: the branches of that magnolia half-hid us from the merrymakers by the pond.

Phoebe put her hands on my skinny flanks and reached up on her toes to give me a kiss. I bent to get it. It tasted a little like barbecue sauce and Nehi creme soda, but more like the kitten breath and the dreamful hunger of a fifteen-year-old girl with more heart than slickness. I liked that kiss. It fed, or seemed to feed, almost all of Phoebe into me, the fizzy soda of her hunger, her mouth, her eyes, her breast buds, her armpits, even the commonplace mystery of her sex. I grabbed her and drove the kiss on—harder, more acrid-sweet, ever more puzzlesome to us both.

Tiptoe to keep it going, Phoebe snapped off a blue-darter of a fart. The kickback shoved her teeth into mine with a lightninglike click. The kiss ended then, but I'd lived years since it began, and that little poot, instead of rendering our kiss vile or comical, opened the moment out for me in a funny way. It was like Phoebe'd handed me her diary or walked into my bedroom without a stitch of clothing. I felt singled out, honored, and it befuddled me—expelled me back into the numbing hurly-burly of my Hellbender teammates—when she broke free and hugged herself.

"What you gonna do? That goopy Brunswick stew. I eat two spoonfuls and *that* happens."

I moved to comfort her—not that she needed comforting, more like distracting—and to thieve another kiss. But Mister JayMac, or somebody else with a gale-force pucker, whistled, and Phoebe dragged me by the hand out from under the magnolia's brittle awning into the spread-out bruise of a Fourth of July sunset.

"Yall get down here!" Mister JayMac called. "Pronto!"

The President's flunkies, and some ballplayers, had packed his touring car, reinstalling the back seat so he and his party could return to Warm Springs for the night. Next day, he'd fly to Washington to jump back into harness as commander-in-chief; then, the coming Friday, while the Hellbenders played the first of a four-game set against the Linenmakers, U.S. and British paratroopers would jump into Sicily to lay the groundwork for an Allied invasion of Italy.

Side by side—but not hand in hand—Phoebe and I ambled downslope to the President's open-topped car. Motorcycles straddled by MPs already flanked it, and soldiers in helmets and battle fatigues—right out of a *March of Time* newsreel—held sentinel posts all along a snaky line from the pond to McKissic House to Angus Road. The Elshtains, Miss LaRaina, and the McKissics stood beside the car speaking their good-byes.

Below one of the tents, near the water, a fistfight broke out. Ballplayers and MPs rushed toward the mayhem. Grown men shouted like hooligans. Kids on the grounds hurried to find a sane adult to shield them from whatever'd begun to happen. The two men fighting locked each other around the neck and bent at the waist like recruits doing a peculiar type of calisthenics. They grappled, they fell down, they thrashed like freshly dug earthworms.

"Bust his lip for him, Muscles!"

"Come on, Reese!"

"Hit him! Hit him! *Hit him!*"

The grapplers—Musselwhite and Curriden—got to their feet again, staggered to the pond's verge, toppled, rolled into the water, came back up streaming and sputtering and wrestling, a pair of our best players—fellas right up there with Snow and Clerval—acting like infantile yahoos. The splashing and cursing continued so long and loud it even began to embarrass the President's security people, who'd positioned themselves around his touring car like bank guards around a Wells Fargo wagon. At last, four MPs slogged into the water to put an end to the fracas. One of them, for his trouble, caught a knee in the groin, and the rest went into a domino drop that prompted even some of their buddies to hoohah.

"Hey!" Turkey Sloan shouted. "You're scaring the fish!"

Henry appeared in the hullabaloo near the water. Chinese lanterns strung among the tents flickered in a breeze-blown dance behind him. He elbowed his way to the pond's edge, waded in like Gulliver, and collared Muscles and Curriden without getting pulled to his knees himself. He dragged the lummoxes to shore, one to a hand, like a fisher bringing in a pair of salmon-freighted nets. He kept coming in with them until, side by side on their hands and knees, they gasped on the grass just below the farthest tent.

"There are combats enough about this planet," Henry said. "Doesn't the significance of this occasion"—gesturing toward FDR—"inspire you to at least a mean civility? I am shamed for every Hellbender here."

Curriden and Muscles gasped and sputtered.

Beside FDR's car, Mister JayMac said, "Sir, he speaks for me too. I hope you'll forgive—"

"Forget it, Jay," Mr. Roosevelt said. "Boys will be boys. High spirits and high stakes are a volatile mix, eh? We're all susceptible to a bout of intemperance these days."

"They're out of Wednesday's game against Cottonton," Mister JayMac said.

"Not on my account, I hope. I'm inclined to believe their infra-dig donnybrook reflects a long and vexing day. Go easy. Roll out the velvet."

"They're suspended. You wouldn't hang a medal around an erring battle captain's neck either, sir."

"Hear, hear," Colonel Elshtain said.

FDR laughed. Surprisingly, he caught sight of Phoebe and me. "Ah, Miss Pharram, Mr. Boles, fine evening for a stroll. I bid you a pleasant farewell."

Colonel Elshtain said, "Mr. President, if you would." He and Miss Tulipa traded a look. FDR regarded me like I was a kid hospitalized with tuberculosis. My stomach did a sudden trout flop. My fingers chilled blue.

"You played sharp as a blade today, Daniel," Mr. Roosevelt told me. "And I surmise you've a splendid future."

I offered a strangled croak, trying not to look like a dumb orangutan.

"It's all right. Your friends have told me of your handicap. Please regard it as a species of bond between us, different as our individual problems may appear." FDR nodded at the colonel. "Very well. Let him in. I'm not going to do this in front of an admiring bog."

Let who in? Do what in front of whom?

Colonel Elshtain opened the car's rear door and nodded me in. "The President has something to tell you, Daniel. Ride to the front gate with him."

Me? I hung there doubt-riddled and confused.

"Go on," Phoebe said. "He won't bite."

FDR thought that hilarious. "What big teeth I have, he's thinking. What a set of choppers. Well, Miss Pharram's right—I hardly ever bite a potential Democratic voter." He sobered pretty quick. "Hop in, Daniel."

With everyone looking—even Muscles and Curriden, both like unrecognizable bog monsters—I climbed in next to FDR, behind a black chauffeur and a Secret Service agent dressed to the Beau Brummel nines. The President gave me a nod, and we drove up the slope past Darius's apartment and McKissic House and down one leg of the circular drive to Angus Road. Fireflies winked as we purred through the summer evening.

"Colonel Elshtain asked me to break this news to you as a favor for past services skillfully rendered," the President said. "He seemed to think its coming from me might soften it. I doubt that. All I can do is leaven the inevitable pain with an expression of our nation's sincerest gratitude."

Inevitable pain? What the hell?

The President fished a piece of paper—a telegram?—from an inside pocket of his linen coat. "My goodness, that's clumsy. Forgive me." He opened the paper out and studied it for a moment. "Daniel, your father died in the Aleutian Islands, on the sixteenth of June, not too long after the Fourth Infantry had retaken Attu from the Japanese. He'd flown to Attu with some Eleventh Air Force personnel from Umnak; they arrived in the wake of mopping-up exercises, and on an expedition of some sort to the interior, your father, Richard Oconostota Boles, and four other brave Americans died." The President handed me the telegram. "That presents the unadorned facts, Daniel. The details I have from Colonel Elshtain, who himself has them from an officer in Graves Registration with the Alaska Command. In any event, your father died an honorable death in the service of his country."

I held the telegram. We'd reached the front gate. The limousine, with its escort vehicles and outriders, stopped and idled. A mockingbird meowed from a pine across the road. I saw myself receiving this sorry news like somebody watching a film might follow an overhead shot of a motorcade and eavesdrop on the mutterings of a make-believe president. But FDR sat close enough to touch, and the crumbs from a loaf of French bread had funneled together in a fold of the removable seat's dove-gray upholstery.

"I hear your parents lived apart these past few years," FDR said. "On the other hand, a child's affection for a parent seldom dies utterly after an estrangement, and I imagine—indeed, I hope—you still recall your father with a measure of fondness. I'm deeply honored, and likewise deeply sorry, to be the messenger of your pain."

I couldn't cry. You don't sob—not, at least, if you're a seventeen-year-old pro ballplayer—in the presence of Franklin Delano Roosevelt. The gist of what he'd said didn't corkscrew immediately into me anyway, and memories of my dad crowded fast and thick. I gave the Prez a nod, opened my door, and got out.

"A lift back up to the house?" he said.

I shook my head. My surroundings had gone all blurry and foreign, I could've been standing on a twilit African mud flat.

"A privilege to've made your acquaintance, Daniel."

I nodded and then turned and trudged back up the lawn towards

McKissic House. FDR and his crew processed off the grounds, into the honeysuckle drench of the evening.

Phoebe met me halfway, on a dead run. I handed her the telegram. She didn't read it. Someone'd already told her what it said. She lifted her hands. She walked in a half circle. She threw herself at me, like I was a tackling dummy, and clung to me in a glut of rainy griefs. I hugged her back.

"Phoebe," I said.

39

More than a month had passed between my buggery by Pumphrey and word of Richard Oconostota Boles's death. Call that month a fugue of dummyhood. No one in Highbridge, except Mister JayMac, had known me as anything other than a mute. So it sometimes seemed to me, and probably to others, my affliction had existed from childhood and would go into the grave with me . . . to everlasting muteness. Ha.

On the other hand, just getting Phoebe's name out didn't open the door for a whole stifled dictionary of yawps. My old friend the stammer rode half the words I did say, maybe more. Besides, I'd cast off the habit of talking. Silence seemed easier sometimes, nobler others, and sometimes just happily worrisome for the persnickety folks who wanted either answers or explanations out of me. If my tongue didn't hurry to comply with the speech signals from Language Central, well, I didn't sweat it. People talk too much anyhow. I prove that with my throat mike and these damned interviews.

"Danny can talk," Phoebe announced, leading me back to the others. "He said my name."

Miss Tulipa hugged me. Miss LaRaina hugged me. Kizzy appeared and rocked me to and fro with her forehead hard on my breastbone. Even Miss

Giselle clocked in with a flurry of shoulder pats. Mister JayMac, the colonel, and the Hellbenders haunted the edges of my loss like clueless border guards.

"Such a trauma," Miss Tulipa said. "Such a trauma to overcome your laryngitis."

"You gots to be strong," Kizzy said, her braids like spun-metal snakes in my hands. "Mr. Roozerfeld never told you that sad news to have you go lint-simple, Danny Bowes."

I pushed Kizzy far enough back to gaze into her face. "I d-d-don't c-care. I'm gl-glad my d-d-daddy's dead."

"A kid of the new school," Hoey said from nearby. "A real lover of the fifth commandment."

I found Hoey's silhouette among all the others and glared at him. "Sc-scr-screw you." Nobody whooped or laughed. In those days, you didn't talk dirty in the presence of ladies, even if one was a woman of color and another had at best only a slippery claim on the title. So my retort to Hoey shocked the fellas as much as it did the gathered womenfolk, my champions and my comforters. Maybe only Phoebe appreciated the hassled defiance of it, and maybe she shouldn't have. Everyone made allowances, though—not counting Hoey, I guess—and I got back to my room without being tarred and feathered.

Upstairs, Henry let me be. Huddled on my bed with our basket fan chasing fever chills down my arms and legs, I told myself even doing his duty to God and country hadn't saved my father from hellfire. Anyone could reckon why. He deserved it, frying forever. He'd hurt Mama bad and nearlybout destroyed me, skipping out. He deserved a million-year broil in Beelzebub's furnace.

Then I remembered Tenkiller's abandoned icehouse, and Sparrow Alley, and the Boles & Son Jes-for-Fun Oklahoma World See-ries, and the sump of my bitterness started to evaporate. Did Satan grant pardons? Reprieves? Weekend furloughs?

The Hellbenders' record on July 5, 1943, was twenty-two wins, seventeen losses; we'd played one game past the season's official midpoint. We'd split our last six games with Opelika, who still had a game or two on us, the result of a fast getaway in May. And the Gendarmes, who'd beaten us two out of three in an away series at the end of June, still led the league.

In a meeting on Tuesday afternoon, Mister JayMac assessed the situation and told us what to do to ready ourselves for a successful stretch run: "Tomorrow morning, gentlemen, we go on the road to play the Boll Weevils and the Linenmakers. The next week they come here. These fellas play baseball like the Flying Tigers dance *Swan Lake*. If they beat us, we'll deserve our enmirement in third or fourth place. Yesterday we whipped Lou Ed Dew's hotshot Orphans twice. Congratulations. I heartily thank God you didn't disappoint Mr. Roosevelt, gentlemen."

"Thank God we didn't disappoint you," Buck Hoey said.

"Amen!" amen'd a chorus of Hellbenders.

"But this is no time to suppose that jes because we've got our percherons harnessed and our wagon on track, we're going to roll over everybody else like they were dust chickens. Uh-uh. So I am deeply perturbed that Mr. Curriden and Mr. Musselwhite, team *heroes*, elected by their off-the-field performance last night to sit out Wednesday's contest against the Boll Weevils. Their absence from the lineup—nor do I mean to disparage or demoralize their replacements—could well cost us that game and deny us the psychological momentum to make the entire road trip a success. The rest of yall will jes have to gird up your loins in resolute and selfless compensation."

"Why don't you jes let em play?" Norm Sudikoff said. "It was only a kind of tiff."

"A *tiff*? Howso a *tiff*, Mr. Sudikoff?"

"I mean, it looked like a all-out war, but only cuz they're such bruisers to begin with. A ant boxin another ant don't quake the ground like a couple of rhinos would. So, you know, jes let em play on Wednesday."

Mister JayMac stared at Sudikoff the way a rube at a county fair ogles the bearded lady, wonderingly. "If I had the guts, Mr. Sudikoff, I'd bench them both for the whole road trip and leave them here to do scut work. But I lack em, I lack the necessary sand."

"Well, sir, they'd probably only fight if you left em here without any supervision," Sudikoff said.

"My rationale for taking them with us, Mr. Sudikoff—"

"Sir?"

"Hush, please. I've got something important to do here." He looked at me. "Gentlemen, let me reintroduce you to Daniel Boles. Mr. Boles, please rise."

I stood up.

"Would you like to greet your teammates?"

"Huh-hello," I said.

Henry and Double Dunnagin led the room in a rapid clatter of applause. I smiled and bowed.

Cottonton's ballpark, The Fields, looked like what the locals had named it, a big seashell fan of graded earth with no fences, no lights, no grass, and no clear-cut boundary with the cotton-growing acreage next to it. The Boll Weevils had a chicken-wire backstop, termite-gnawed bleachers along the baselines, and a shingled crate on telephone-pole pilings for a press box. As Mister JayMac had said in my first team meeting in Highbridge, a live goat'd once figured in a close decision at third. Even in Oklahoma, I'd seen boondocky high schools with better facilities than the Weevils had.

But sometimes they drew decent crowds—from whistle-stop and cotton-ginning communities all over the county. You could get four or five hundred people in the stands, even on a week night: farmers, railroad workers, gin operators, feed-and-seed merchants, beauticians, kids. Clem Eggling, a gin operator with a thousand acres of prime Alabama farmland, owned the club and at age forty-six still sometimes caught the opening game of a twin bill. He made his money scrimping on groundskeeping costs, salaries, and ballpark goodies. Watery lemonade, boiled eggs, and culled peanuts dominated the items at his refreshment stands, and you couldn't get ice—shaved, cubed, or melting—unless you hauled it in yourself in an expensive refrigerated truck.

On Wednesday, with Muscles and Curriden out, we lost to the lowly Weevils by six runs. Hoey took Curriden's spot at third, and Evans and Fanning subbed about four innings each in left field for Musselwhite. They fielded their places okay, but every Hellbender except Charlie Snow had forgotten how to hit, and the loss, again except for Snow's bang-up play, qualified as a *dis*concerted team effort. Hard to say if Miss LaRaina's rivals in the lineup would've made a whit of difference. The Boll Weevil's pitcher, Hub Sisti, had us muttering to ourselves all evening.

In Cottonton, Henry and I stayed in a truckstop court called Edweena's Comfy Cabins. If Cottonton'd ever had a hotel for farm-equipment suppliers and haberdashery drummers, it'd long since closed. Edweena's Comfy Cabins got our business by default. Mister JayMac seldom had us leave Highbridge for an away series against the Weevils until the morning of our first game.

That strategy ran the risk of a forfeit, if the *Brown Bomber*'s transmission dropped out, but it cut back our dependence on local lodgings. Henry and I had our ready-made digs, of course, but Cottonton natives willing to house enemy ballplayers didn't run that deep or that trustworthy. Mister JayMac had to squeeze eighteen guys into three semi-friendly houses, and on our last road trip there in '43, he negotiated the use of an empty jail cell, a bus-station pew at Harshanay Drugs, and two more Comfy Cabins—to keep from returning to the home of Weevils fans upset by our one-sided romps over every Cottonton hurler but Hub Sisti.

Darius remained the odd man out. He knew coloreds in other CVL towns, but didn't seem to know any here. He could've had a black family put him up a night or two just by asking. Darius had a certain status. Driving the *Bomber*, doing for twenty or so ballplayers, made him a figure of some glamour. But Darius wouldn't play on his league connections. Wouldn't sweet-talk, trash-talk, or kowtow. Wouldn't even ask outright and humbly, one downtrodden colored to another, for a cleanly place to lay his head. Pride and a festering resentment of Mister JayMac stymied him.

Not long after Hub Sisti'd shut us out, I stood in the open door of the Comfy Cabin called Gladiola Delight ruing my third hitless game in twenty-four starts. You could smell the DDT on the cotton plants across the road, and the used-washcloth odor of the linens in Gladiola Delight. Other Comfy Cabins were named Begonia Bliss, Daisy Dream, Marigold Manor, and Chrysanthemum Heaven. They all looked and smelled the same, though, and the only flowers in their rotting window boxes were dandelions and morning glories.

As I stood there, the *Bomber* growled past on the blacktop from The Fields, where we'd played our last two innings in the dusk. It headed into the empty landscape north of town.

"D-Darius," I said.

"Looking for a place to sleep unmolested," Henry said from behind a book. "The poor slob." That was Henry's shaky grasp of American slang. He meant *fella*, or *bugger*, or *joe*, not *slob*, but I knew that.

"Back l-l-later." Before Henry could call out a question, I'd trotted to the blacktop. I hiked along it in the dark behind the twin embers of the bus's taillights. Darius drove slow, maybe to keep a redneck cop from halting him, maybe to give himself a better chance to find a hidden parking place for the night—so those taillights stayed visible for a long time. I followed them easily. I lost ground, of course, but the road's straightness kept the bus in view. Sometimes I could even hear its gears shifting, a sound like rocks bumping down a metal chute.

A mosquito came out of the cotton after me. Two or three damn mosquitoes. A blood-sucking *platoon* of em. Water lay oily in one shadowy ditch, a breeding ground. The blacktop gave way to gravel. The bigger pieces of gravel—fist-sized rocks—threw me off-stride. I had to find a tire rut and walk in it like a man in a narrow trench. Off to the west, the long charcoal profile of some eroded hills told me I hadn't walked into the unbounded landscape of a nightmare. And a glance to my rear revealed the untidy lamp-lit boxes of Edweena's Comfy Cabins. I could go back if I had to.

Suddenly, the *Brown Bomber*'s twin taillights jinked out of view and its hippoish side appeared in silhouette: a black rectangle with windows into a bigger blackness. Sound of rocks sliding on tin. The bus's nose, behind its headlights, kept moving downward until a berm of earth and night had eaten the lights and swallowed the entire bus. Now I had no floating embers to follow and no sure way to recognize Darius's turnoff when I came to it.

I kept walking. The DDT smell and the edgeless blackness all around me made me think I'd traipsed into the limbo where sick or worried people go when they filch a wink or two of shuteye from their pain. Nowhere. I groped along, though, and came to the side road, a dirt trail, where Darius'd vanished. Every step down this trail sent a lightning bolt up my spine. Shrubbery clustered near, and some sort of tree, an orphan plum or holly, grew up from the inlet of a cotton field, shielding most of the Bomber but its hood. I'd've never found the bus at the bottom of this cut without tracking it from my cabin's very doorstep. I went up to the *Bomber* and banged on its side.

Behind me, a revolver's hammer clicked. A gun barrel poked me in the neck.

"Tell me fast what the hell you want."

"Darius." (No stammer.)

"Jesus, Danl, that you?" The pistol barrel stopped poking me. "Man, you coulda got kilt. What you *doing* here?"

After saying his name, I couldn't get another clear word out. Darius cursed and forced me up into the bus, its engine still cooling, popping and ticking. He prodded me down the main aisle to the long seat at the back.

"This spot's yo favorite. Anyway, it's somebody's. Sit."

Somehow, in that blackness, Darius seemed solider than me. I was a ghost, my skin and bones leached out and water-thin. Without his hand around my upper arm, I'd've vaporized into the stars like a pale gas.

"Sorry bout the gun. I uz taking a leak when you hit the road and come slapping down. Nigh on to scairt the piss back into me, white boy."

That was funny, I guess, but I couldn't laugh. Darius showed me his piece again, a snub-nose with a mother-of-pearl handle. He held it not to threaten, but to let me admire the way it shone in the cloudy starlight slanting in.

"They come to neck-burn me, Danl, well, I send a few on ahead befo I have to tap-dance air." He pocketed the revolver in his khaki work pants. "Whatn hell you want?"

"You sl-sleep here?"

"On the *Bomber*? Sho. Better than a Comfy Cabin any day but Christmas. Plenty of beds to pick from. No loud radios playing. Hot and hot running breezes. Yeah, I sleep here."

"Out in the c-country?"

"I like my privacy."

"What about over in Quitman? Or L-Lanett?"

"What are you anyways, official Hellbender bed-checker? Or you jes want to thow yo pity at me?"

My tongue rolled up behind my top front teeth and stuck like a wet cabbage leaf.

"Suppose I thow it back, Danl? Daddy dead. Yo mouth don't work. Rooming with old Mumbo-Jumbo Clerval. How you like *my* pity dript on you like sorghum?"

Not much. Turnabout maybe represented fair play, but it mocked my Christian concern for Darius by putting my own dumb mug in the mirror he held up. He hummed something bluesy and reached a paper sack out from under our seat. The sack held a bottle. Pray God it isn't sloe gin, I thought.

Darius swigged, wiped his mouth, and offered me a pull. It stank like sour-mash whiskey, the cheapest and strongest kind. I shook my head.

"Lissen, Danl. In every CVL city but Cottonton, I know womens. Who give me rest, and take it too, and give it back again. Only in this redneck town do I got to park in the boonies to nab my Z's. Some ways, though, it's a relief. It's peaceful." He swigged again. "The part that aint, aint got nothing to do with where I sleep. It got to do with how I live. Only times I live jes like I want, I'm sleeping, and where I do it don't strip it down to"—jabbing his chin at the snow-blanket mirage of the nearby cotton—"to that, to what you can see out a window or pint to on a map."

I said, "Y-yeah," and got up. Darius didn't try to stop me. I'd trespassed his private property, even if it moved with him like a dusty turtle shell.

"Better foot it back. I done found my spot, and toting you back's like to stir some pleecemans to hassle me out of here."

I laddered up the aisle, plucking each seat back to keep from falling over.

"Shhhhhhh," Darius shushed me. Loud.

Did he really think Clem Eggling or some other clay-footed rube out here in deepest Alabamastan was going to hear me? I glanced back through the gloom. Darius toasted me with his bottle and canted his head to one side.

"Look down. And hush yo plinking. You gon wake the boy."

I looked. A good-size bundle lay on a seat about midway along the bus, a lumpy smudge on the cushion. It breathed. I squatted for a closer study: Euclid, Darius's half brother and our sometime batboy, depending on if the away park in question would let him fetch for us. Ordinarily, Mister JayMac made him stay in Highbridge. The only way I could imagine him getting to Cottonton was by stowing away in the luggage bin. Tonight, Euclid slept like a rain-ripened bag of concrete mix, heavy and hard.

"Tuckered," Darius said. "Prostrated by his ride over."

No kidding. But Euclid's being huddled there cheered me. Darius had some company, a pick-me-up warmer than his whiskey and not quite so dire as his handgun.

"Anything happen to me," Darius said, "that boy got to git past it to his own tomorry. Remind him a that, Danl."

Remind him? What could happen to Darius? He could drink himself to a retching stupor. He could use his pistol to take a core sample of his own gray matter. That scared me—not the first notion, but the second. A barn owl hooted from somewhere off-road, and the tremolo of its call echoed through the bus like a sighing brake. How could I leave?

"Go on. You done misunderstood me. I'm okay. Got me no-hitters to thow, homers to knock. Jes cain't figger out where. Anyways, git!" I climbed down into the velvety dust.

Darius slid over to an open window and peered out at me.

"Quip hadn't no sass on his speedball tonight. Too bad. Mine a turned them Weevil bats to dick sponge. Everybody knows it, but aint nobody gon let it happen."

"G-g-good night," I said.

Darius had parked behind a full-blown holly. The needle tips of its glossy leaves pricked me as I squeezed past it to the path up to the main road. A bauble of moon-varnished blood erupted on one thumb, and I sucked it as I walked.

Darius didn't shoot himself or Euclid. He didn't drive the Bomber off to Birmingham to cadge a tryout with the Black Barons or to Moton Field near Tuskegee in hopes of becoming a replacement flyer in the air squadron commanded by Benjamin O. Davis, Jr. He showed up at The Fields the next afternoon at three and spent about twenty minutes briefing our regulars on how to hit the Boll Weevil starting hurler's best pitch, a forkball. We hit it. We hit it so often Eggling yanked the guy by the fourth.

After that, all the homies in Cottonton's open-sided flea box hung around less to root on their Boll Weevils than to watch our starters, even Curriden and Musselwhite, put on a power-hitting show that made their fielders wish Eggling had anted up enough cash money for a fence—to spare them the shame of chasing down balls that in any other CVL park would've been ground-rule home runs. To compensate, they started playing deeper and deeper, but guys like Junior, Skinny, Dunnagin, Snow, and me countered by dropping Texas leaguers in front of them like mortar shells.

We whipped Cottonton by fourteen runs, to achieve a split, and drove to Lanett the next morning for a four-game weekend series—with Euclid out of the luggage bin and in a front seat across from Mister JayMac. (He got chewed out for stowing away, though—*royally* chewed out.) At Chattahoochee Field, the Linenmakers, even though last in league standings, played us tough as cross-tie spikes. We split with them too, winning on Friday night, dropping both ends of a Saturday twin bill, and nosing by them on Sunday on Henry's home run, his twenty-eighth of the season, twelve more than the next guy, Lon Musselwhite, a teammate, and Ed Bantling, the Gendarme catcher.

Mister JayMac publicly thanked Henry during one of our Rolling Assizes for salvaging the road trip. Even so, he had Muscles fine every relief pitcher, pinch hitter, and starter who'd contributed to Saturday's fiasco against Lanett. The only Hellbenders to escape fines were Snow, Nutter, Dobbs, and Henry. Even the Honorable Judge Lionel K. Musselwhite had to dig into his coin purse for a quarter, for turning a long fly ball into a triple by overrunning it and denting a signboard.

"Needless and catastrophic showboating," prosecutor Buck Hoey called the play. "You let in two runs and bunged up your shoulder to boot. The captain ought to set us something other than a bad example." You got the idea Hoey was disguising a reference to the dustup on Hellbender Pond between Muscles and Curriden. Anyway, nobody on the *Bomber* voted for clemency.

Darius didn't say two words from his seat up front, and I couldn't help wondering what kind of fine he'd draw for packing a concealed pistol. More than a quarter, I'd bet. In some places down here, he could've wound up decorating a tree just for leaving his fly at half-mast.

40

On Tuesday evening, the bigs played their first-ever night all-star game. Everyone in McKissic House heard the broadcast from Philadelphia over our cathedral Philco. Worldwide, U.S. servicemen listened with us over shortwave radios. Actually, Henry opted out of our party, the only resident Hellbender not on hand. He'd trudged upstairs to read, saying, "Baseball is not my entire life. In any case, at breakfast Mr. Mariani will recount every pitch and putout."

I missed Henry's being there. Dunnagin sat on a folding chair next to me, but he and Creighton Nutter, who'd come over from Cotton Creek, picked at each other through the whole damn game. As an ex-Brownie, Dunnagin wanted the American League to win, while Nutter, an ex-Brave, rooted like crazy for Johnny Vander Meer and the senior-circuit Nats. Most of the rest of us, chattel of the Phutile Phillies, automatically sided with Nutter against Dunnagin. Vander Meer and Vince DiMaggio played like shining princes for their squad, but when the Americans won it five to three, Dunnagin danced around the parlor on his spindly gams. Darius spent the entire game leaning in the door to the dining room, but vanished a split second after the last broadcast play.

When I went up to tell Henry the outcome, he lay face down on his bed, softly wheezing away.

At Wednesday morning's optional workout at McKissic Field, a major from the camp and a colored guy in a bottlefly-green jacket came onto the field just as I started to enter the batting cage. The major, a young guy with a razor slit of a mouth, put his hand on my arm.

"Excuse me, kid," he said. "I'm Major Adrian Dexter. This is Mr. Cozy Bissonette."

I stared. That kid business burned me off. Major Dexter looked about twenty-six. Besides, visitors, outside of family and invited guests, had no standing ticket to our workouts.

"A stadium guard let us in," Major Dexter said, nodding at the entrance tunnel. "We have an appointment." I still didn't speak. "With Mr. Jordan McKissic, the owner and manager." He pronounced the first name like the river—not JUR-dan, the way locals did. "Could you direct us to him, please?"

"We'd be decidedly grateful," Cozy Bissonette said.

"C-cmon." I led them to our dugout, where Mister JayMac sat with Darius, strategizing for our next away series.

Darius looked up, and he and Mr. Bissonette each did a funny click thing with their eyes—almost a shutter snap, like a photographer catching a big-deal event and not just another family-album head shot. Major Dexter and Mister JayMac didn't see it, and I couldn't read it. It didn't work only on the level of one colored greeting another, though; it also involved the sort of flash conspiracy that can happen between any two like-thinking persons, whoever they are. It scared me.

"Are we early?" Major Dexter said. "We could always—"

"Fine," Mister JayMac said. "I'll jes be a moment."

I stayed there in the dugout, cat-curious and vexed, hoping to learn something.

"Go hit," Mister JayMac told me. "I'll handle the coaching details. You jes do what you're paid for." He gave me a face smile, with nothing but distracted cogitation behind it. I spike-walked back out to the batting cage.

That evening, Mister JayMac held a team meeting in the parlor. No flip charts. No recruits to introduce. No rules to review. Of the Cotton Creek bunch, Snow and Nutter seldom griped about anything, but Hoey, Sloan, Hay, and Sudikoff waltzed in bellyaching, having earlier supposed they'd have the whole day to themselves. They put a lid on their bile pot when they saw Mister JayMac impatiently pacing the hardwood.

"This shouldn't take too long," he said. "We've got a vote to take."

"I vote no," Hoey said. "Whatever it is."

" 'Be it resolved,' " Dunnagin said, " 'that we refrain from castrating Buck Hoey the next time he fans with men on base.' "

Even Hoey laughed. (*Henry* only smiled, but, given it was Henry, count it a laugh.)

"This shouldn't take long unless every one of yall insists on auditioning for *The Grape Nuts Hour*," Mister JayMac said.

We ditched our smirks. Darius, I noticed, leaned exactly where he'd leaned during the all-star game.

"This morning, the business manager of a barnstorming club of Negro ballplayers, the Splendid Dominican Touristers, and an Army major from the—"

"Whoa," Hoey said. "The *who*?"

"The Splendid Dominican Touristers. Some Negro leaguers under a rubric de guerre, so to speak."

"Sounds like an order of stuck-up traveling monks," Turkey Sloan said.

"Shut up, Sloan," Vito Mariani said.

Before an argument could break out, Mister JayMac said, "Hush." Everybody hushed. "The Negro American League—the Black Barons from over to Birmingham, the Memphis Red Sox, the Cincinnati Clowns, and so on—well, gas rationing's hit these clubs hard. They've done finished a full split season. Their teams only had to play thirty games to qualify for the Negro World Series. Anyway, Mr. Cozy Bissonette of Kansas City, Missouri, has assembled a group from some of the NAL's better players, and he's seeking exhibition opponents in advance of the club's official formation in Atlanta early next week."

"And the coon wants to play us?" Jerry Wayne Sosebee said.

Darius had his arms folded and his gaze fixed on a knot-hole in the floor's oak planking. Sosebee didn't see him, though; Darius was invisible to Sosebee.

"What about this Army major?" Muscles asked Mister JayMac.

"Major Dexter. First Battalion, Camp Penticuff Special Training Regiment. He wants to sponsor a contest between Mr. Bissonette's all-stars and us, a morale booster to kick off the club's barnstorming tour."

"Sir, Georgia law doesn't allow whites and coloreds to play pro ball against each other in public," Sloan said.

"That's why, if yall vote to do it, we'd do it out to Camp Penticuff, where it wouldn't be so public. For the biggest part, our spectators would be the Negro GIs of the two Special Training battalions out there."

"Jesus," Sosebee said.

"What's in it for us?" That was Reese Curriden. Sometimes you could hear pocket change in his chuckles.

"The Army, Major Dexter says, has offered a payment of five hundred dollars to each club, to divvy however we choose."

"Twenty-five bucks apiece!" Quip Parris cried happily.

"I vote yes," Hoey said. "Whichever way we divvy it."

"I'd recommend returning the money as a contribution to the war effort," Mister JayMac said.

"Except like that," Hoey said. "What are we anyway, a pack of no-account field hands?"

"Tote that bat, lift that base," Sloan said.

"What will the Dominican Jigaboos—sorry, *Touristers*—do with their five hundred?" Sosebee asked.

"I don't know," Mister JayMac said. "Keep it, I imagine. They've got big expenses, their players need the money."

"*I* need the money," Hoey said. "Ever try to feed four house apes on a hundred-plus a month?"

"Hoey's making a hundred-*plus* a month?" Musselwhite's eyes went round, like such a salary staggered him.

"Hold it," Sosebee said. "You want us to play a bunch of jigs—uh, *coloreds*—in front of a bunch of coloreds, and to do it for nuthin?"

"For the morale of the recruits," Mister JayMac said. "For the joy of it. To face a squad of unknown players as good as, if not a smidgen better than, ourselves."

Trapdoor Evans said, "They could ever one of em out-play me from here to Timbuctoo, sir, but they's still no way—no way in hell—it'd make a one of em *bettern* me."

"You said it," Sudikoff said.

"Who plans to suit up for this Mr. Bossy Nut fella on his Splendid Dominican so-and-so's?"

Curriden asked. "A whole club of Negro League all-stars?"

"No," Mister JayMac said. "Jes better-than-most journeymen players. Yall won't have to face the likes of Satchel Paige, Josh Gibson, or Cool Papa Bell."

"Who?" Fadeaway Ankers said.

"But never you fear, these barnstormers'll make LaGrange's Gendarmes look like beginning Little Leaguers."

Henry spoke up from the back of the room. "When would we play them, if we played?"

"Good question," Mister JayMac said. "Two Tuesdays from now, the twenty-seventh of July. The only time our schedule permits."

"No peace for the pooped," Muscles said. "Couldn't this screw our shot at the pennant, Mister JayMac?"

"One game? Maybe. But only if Mr. Clerval has a heart attack walloping one to the Canary Islands."

"Let's v-v-vote," I said.

"I don't play coloreds," Fadeaway said. "*Teams* of em."

"Me either," Evans said.

"Ditto," Sloan said. "To do great on a jig hunt, / Wear chocolate pigment / Exactly like the jig's. / Me, I'd rather forfeit a shot at the Bigs."

"Thank you, Mr. Longfellow," Mister JayMac said. "That's three outright nays, I take it. Any more?"

"Here," Sudikoff said. "No!"

"And here," Sosebee said. "No!"

"Last chance," Mister JayMac said. "Five nays to what I guess is fifteen unvoiced ayes."

"I abstain," Pete Hay said.

"What a pussy," Mariani said.

"What do you mean, a pussy?" Hay said.

"A fence sitter's got no balls," Mariani said.

"Hush," Mister JayMac said. "I'd hoped for unanimity in this vote. *Virtual* unanimity. But when a quarter of you have reservations about the appropriateness of this game, it gives me pause. I wonder about the commitment of the nay-sayers to play their hardest."

"Cripes, sir," Sloan said. "Don't try to blackmail an aye out of us with this commitment guff. I mean, we—"

"Yall're scairt you'll git whupped," Darius said.

Every head in the room turned towards him. He lifted his gaze from the floor and drilled Sloan with it.

"Ten dollars to every No sez them Dominicans'll smack yall like a baby's butt. *If* you got the grit to play em."

"You aint got fifty bucks to bet," Trapdoor Evans said. "You aint got *ten* to bet *me*."

Darius strode like a crop fire up to Mister JayMac. "Give me fifty, sir. Gainst my nex draw."

Mister JayMac took a money clip from his seersucker jacket, peeled off five tens, and slapped them into Darius's palm.

Darius walked through the crowded parlor to Henry and gave him the five tens. "Mister Henry, hold this please. If yall vote it unanimous to play Mr. Cozy's boys, the bet's on. Yall win, I pay. Hellbenders lose, like yall gon to, I git ten each from Mr. Ankers, Mr. Sloan, Mr. Sudikoff, Mr. Sosebee, and the bettern-anybody-colored Mr. Evans."

One by one, the nay-sayers changed their nays to ayes and walked over to Henry to give him either a ten-spot or a signed IOU; then they returned to their places. Henry arranged the wager money in his billfold and then slid the billfold into his frock coat. Jumbo Hank Clerval, reluctant bookie.

"I want in," Hay said. "I vote nay too."

"You abstained," Mister JayMac said. "Election's over. I don't hold with gambling, especially for players. Except this is gonna be an *un*official exhibition, I'd veto it here too."

"You're a paragon, sir," Buck Hoey said.

Mister JayMac ignored him. "Our next vote's on the Army's lump-sum payment. Do we return it, or do yall divvy it mongst yourselves?"

Uh-oh. Which way did you jump on this one? Patriotism or self-interest?

Curriden said, "Look. We'll support the war effort by playing a game for Camp Penticuff's darky recruits." He looked at Darius. "Aint that enough? Do we have to fork over our pay too? Bet you a pork side, Mr. Cozy's boys keep theirs."

"I don't care what yall do with yo money," Darius said.

"We should keep it," Hoey said.

Sloan and friends also voted to keep and divvy the Army's payment, and almost everyone else, including Snow and Nutter, fell in line. Even Henry voted with the mercenary majority, a surprise to me because he had his secret atonement agenda to fulfill and I thought he'd go for the sacrifice. Then I heard his reason.

"If we return our fee to the Army," he said, "they may use it to purchase weaponry and ordnance."

"So?" said Sudikoff.

"I abhor the making and distribution of implements that in any wise maim or kill," Henry said.

That kind of talk didn't go during the war. It *really* didn't go in the South. Hitler wanted a hiding, and the Japs deserved any swift-kick comeuppance American determination and know-how could give them. The parlor lapsed into a silence broken only by mumbles.

"If that's how folks'll read us taking the Army's money," Charlie Snow finally said, "I vote to give it back."

"Jumbo's a crank on that point," Muscles said. "Nobody'll read it that way."

"The greater shame," Henry said.

In the end, of course, we voted to keep and divvy. Only Lamar Knowles and Dunnagin voted to return their pay to the government. Me, I went with the majority, but I can't say if my reasons were more like Curriden's or Henry's. Of all the Hellbenders there, only Mister JayMac and Darius had failed to vote on the two issues before us. Anyway, the meeting started to break up.

"Hold it!" Mister JayMac jammed his hands into the pockets of his seersucker coat, stretching it out of true. "I should tell yall, the nature of this exhibition contest offers me some managerial latitude I don't have in the CVL."

What the hell did that mean?

"I plan to start Darius on the mound."

That news goosed the gee-whilikers out of us. Should we hurrah or squawk? Trapdoor Evans said, "Jesus, sir, he could queer the game a-purpose jes to take Turkey and my and these other saps' money."

"It's more than that," Muscles said. "If we win, and if Darius finishes the game for us, them colored recruits—and all the Splendiferous Whozits—will say it was because one of their own was throwing for us."

"That's precisely the point," Mister JayMac said.

"Why?" Muscles said. "Why?"

Mister JayMac looked over at Darius and winked: an open wink, like an open letter. Darius glanced off, the hinges in his jaw bulging.

"And if we lose," Muscles said, "it'll all come down to us not backing our pitcher—in their eyes, I mean. In their eyes, we'll either ride Darius's arm to a win or jap him with sloppy backup and weak-sister hitting."

"And if we lose," Evans said, "Darius picks our pockets."

"I don't want to pitch this one," Darius said. "Give me some respect, sir. Gimme some respect."

Mister JayMac spoke to everybody: "Those who watch us and those who compete against us will judge each player on his own performance. Remember that. End of meeting."

41

That same week, we had two home games against Lanett and three against Cottonton. We won the first four, but dropped our Sunday finale to the Weevils by a single run. Hub Sisti pitched against us, and Muscles afterwards claimed Sisti had Vander Meer blood, even if his name sounded Eye-talian.

The night before, I'd eaten dinner at the Pharram house in Cotton Creek, a clapboard box with blue shutters, porcelain knickknacks in the open boxes of its wooden porch columns, and an old-fashioned swing on the porch itself. Miss LaRaina and Phoebe had lived in the officers' housing out to Camp Penticuff before Captain Pharram's assignment overseas, but now they rented this place from Mister JayMac. Unless they'd done an all-out tidy-up for me, the Pharram women seemed to keep that house as trim and eye-fetching as a Fabergé egg.

All in all, a nice date. Phoebe had given me a rain check for the night Curriden abducted me to The Wing & Thigh. She fixed exactly what she'd fixed then: fried chicken, snap beans, mashed potatoes. Only this time, I got to eat it hot, all of it.

"More tea?" Phoebe said. "More biscuits?"

"Sh-sure," I said.

"I'm so proud you can talk," Miss LaRaina said. "I feared yall's babies wouldn't be able to." Phoebe folded her napkin and retreated head-up to the kitchen. "A joke. And the girl flies to Tokyo."

Phoebe returned, opened out her napkin, and laid it across her lap. "Mama, heredity don't work that way. Acquired traits don't pass. Don't hammer us with nonsense."

Miss LaRaina flicked her fingers at her plate and made mouth noises like bomb explosions. Phoebe pretended her mama didn't exist.

"I forgot yore tea," she told me formally. "I forgot yore biscuits." She went to get them.

The next night, Phoebe and I rode into town to see Abbott and Costello in *Hit the Ice* at the Exotic and almost laughed our fannies off. On the taxi ride home, I wanted to smooch her silly, to spaniel-crawl her tit-wren body, but the driver kept checking out the rearview and blithering about that afternoon's loss to Hub Sisti.

In Cotton Creek, I asked him to wait and walked Phoebe to her doorstep.

There, under the whorly pecan boughs, we kissed for the first time since Mr. Roosevelt's visit, pushing in to each other. We took so long about it the cabby gave a crabby beep on his horn.

His meter kept clicking the coins in my pocket into his, of course, but he wanted sleep worse than he did a fat fare.

Phoebe broke from me. "Gnight, Danny."

I smiled.

"What is it?" she asked me.

"This time you didn't f-fart."

"This time I didn't eat no Brunswick stew," she said, like that put me in my place. She banged through the screen door. On the porch, a skinny shadow, she hunched her shoulders and gave me a finger-wave toodle-do.

*

Phoebe might like me, but Hoey didn't. He didn't try to disguise his feelings—from me, his teammates, or his wife. He didn't like it I'd "stolen" his position. (Who would?) He didn't like my looks. (Neither did I, but the willingness of Henry, Kizzy, and the Pharrams to tolerate em had almost broken me of cringing away from mirrors.) And he really didn't like me doing so well at bat and in the field—because he, Turkey, and Trapdoor couldn't go on accusing me of being a fuckup and a goat. I led every 'Bender but Snow in batting, and Snow led the CVL. With my lead-off slot and on-base percentage, I'd've probably led the league in runs scored except for missing the season's first fifteen games.

Hoey didn't hit or field that badly, but had serious weaknesses in some fundamentals: executing the hit-and-run, bunting, flipping underhand to second on double-play chances, and, if coaching, keeping his signals straight. Nowhere, though, was there a feistier wiseacre in baseball, except for the Dodgers' Leo Durocher, and most Highbridgers would have bet on Hoey in a dirt-kicking and insult-flinging contest between the two. I would have.

Hoey'd dodged the Army because his status as a father put him in the sixth lowest draft category: *Married Men With Children But Without a Contributing Job*. Three of his kids—Matt, Carolyn, and Ted—had come before Pearl Harbor. His age, thirty-five or so, and some stress-related back twinges had also played a part in saving him from an infantry platoon. Linda Jane, Hoey's Alabama-born wife, and all four kids, including a toddler named (hold on) *Danny*, came out to nearly every home game. Hoey always worked his two older boys into warm-up pepper games, which made you think Uncle Sam'd done right allowing him to stay home to help raise his brood.

Matt and Ted, about ten and seven I'd guess, didn't seem to hate my guts. Much as he disliked me, Hoey hadn't spoon-fed his bitterness into his sons' gap-toothed mouths. They let me hit them pepper fungoes. More than once, they waved to me from the grandstand when they caught my eye at shortstop. (Linda Jane, on the other hand, always wrinkled up her nose at me like she'd chanced upon some supermessy roadkill, a polecat, say, or an armadillo.) Early on, it'd impressed the boys I couldn't talk; and it tickled them, every day I played, that their baby brother and I had the same first name. So they never tossed any smart-ass digs my way.

In fact, after our Saturday doubleheader against the Boll Weevils, Matt jumped onto the field from the Hoeys' box seats and sprinted out to see me.

I mean, that humdinger of a kid *intercepted* me. He stuck a program and a pencil under my nose.

"Sign it, wouldja, Mr. Boles? Yo're the best danged *liddle* 'Bender they's ever been!"

"Teddy!" his mother called from her box. "Teddy, you git on back up here!"

"I wisht I could play like you. I wisht I could." I took his program and began to write my name across the top of it. Buck Hoey slipped in next to his son and yanked the program away.

"Leave him be, Ted. He's wore out."

"Won't hurt him to write his name, Pa," Teddy said. "I got bout ever other 'Bender's graph. I need Mr. Boles's to have em aw."

"You don't need a fritty thing, snip," Hoey said.

"Look, Pa. He don't mind."

I'd yanked the program back to resume scrawling DANNY BOLES on it.

"You back-talking me, Ted? You defying my say-so?"

"Nosir, I'm ony asting him to—"

"Well, *don't!* You hear me! DON'T!" Hoey reclaimed the program and tore it to bits. "Stop that nancy-boy bawling, Ted! STOP IT!" He grabbed Ted's upper arm and jerked him this way and that trying to make him stop crying, which worked about as well as kicking a dog draws it to you. Teddy got louder—not defying Hoey, just giving in to his hurt—and Hoey boxed his ear: wham! wham! wham! wham! *WHAM!*

Henry caught Buck Hoey's wrist and twisted it back on him. "You don't wish to do that," he said. "You fail to project the psychological repercussions."

"Are you my lousy self-appointed bug doctor?" Hoey shook off Henry's grip and stepped sideways to slap Ted again. Then he back-pedaled to the dugout, scolding Ted and loudly cussing out Henry and me. Ted's ear blazed like a night-light, carbuncle red, and the hand print throbbing on his face made him look like a war-painted Comanche.

Henry knelt to comfort Ted as I stood there, eyes closed, a cascade of old *Life* magazine covers rampaging on the screen of my memory.

Anyway, the deeper into July we went, the more time Hoey spent riding the bench or pacing his coaching box. Me, I played every game day, and I played in overdrive. I dove for grounders, stole bases, chased down pop-up fouls behind third, ran out bunts, legged long singles into doubles, and bowled over or slid under catchers twice my size on shallow sacrifice flies. I wore out my uniform pants, four pairs of sanitary stockings, and, in an away series against Marble Springs, my baseball shoes.

After hook-sliding around the Seminole shortstop's tag and asking for time, I got up to find the toe spikes on my shoe torn from the sole and a gaping rip in the side panel. The other shoe looked almost as bad. I could never run on those dislodged spikes. Two steps would sprain my ankle or twist a knee. I showed the base umpire, Jake Schact. Mister JayMac came out to assess the damage, and the Seminole crowd booed as he crossed the infield in his street clothes and again when Hoey trotted over from the first-base coaching box to make it a three-party powwow.

"Don't put on a stall," Schact told Mister JayMac.

"Who's stalling? We're out of shoes."

"*'Use it up, wear it out, make it do, or do without'*"—a wartime motto that Schact quoted. "And hurry it up."

Unless you had an illegal hoard, there was no sure or cheap way to replace rationed items, and Uncle Sam rationed shoes, even baseball shoes. We might've had an extra pair in my size in Highbridge, but in Marble Springs the spare-pair cupboard stood Mother Hubbard bare. Mister JayMac looked hard at my shoes and then just that hard at Hoey's.

"What size do you wear, Mr. Boles?"

"N-n-nines."

"And you, Mr. Hoey?"

"Criminy," Hoey said. "Jesus."

"What size?"

"Nines." (The kind of confession you get from a fella when you put him in a room with a blackjack crew.)

"Give him yours, Mr. Hoey."

"Here?"

"Here and now."

Hoey sat on one half of the bag removing his spikes. I sat on the other half unstringing mine.

"Should I give him my jock too?"

"Please, Mr. Hoey. Don't provoke a display of female ardor beyond your capacity to quench."

The Seminole crowd whooped like picture-show Indians, ready for the game to resume. Hoey, though, had to walk back to the coaching box in his stirrup socks and clay-stained sanitaries. Between innings, he put on a pair of street shoes. It took me a week to find my own replacements, though, and for that week, Hoey wore a pair of boot-blacked slippers. From a distance, they looked like the real things and kept fans from ragging him, but this episode, on top of everything else, guaranteed I'd stay at the top of Hoey's shit list forever.

Thank God Phoebe cared for me. Thank God I had Henry for a protector.

42

My Second Life (continued)

. . . I heard shouts, laughter, and a mechanical sort of hooting. Together, these noises enticed me from the woods, where I had made a shelter of evergreen boughs, and onto the verge of an open field. Here I saw a great many men standing about in like-tailored coveralls and startling red blouses, the blouses identical but for the different numerals in white on their backs. One player, running towards me to retrieve a spherical object struck over his head, showed across the front of his crimson blouse the word POINSETT. He and his comrades, each with this same designation on their chests, had embarked upon a sporting contest against some green-clad men wearing across their shirts the epithet BRAGGADOCIO.

From considerably greater distances, I had seen, and given a prudent berth, games of this raucous sort before. The Caucasian natives of the continental hinterlands—by now I had made my way to northeastern Arkansas—called their pastime "base ball," but it had affinities to ball-and-stick children's games that I had encountered everywhere from Switzerland to eastern Siberia. The rural version of this sport fascinated me, less for its regulated intricacies than for its ability to assemble and amuse many diverse persons.

In any event, I emerged from the woods.

On the outskirts of Poinsett, Arkansas, a hundred or more spectators had gathered about the ill-marked field (known locally as the Strawberry Diggings) on foot, in mule- or ox-drawn wagons, in surreys, and even in self-propelled "Model T's." The drivers of these last vehicles, sometimes called automobiles and sometimes Fords, would pull their movable windshields down to preserve the glass from balls bludgeoned foul by the teams' various batsmen.

Whenever those watching approved a development in the game, the spectators on foot or in wagons would whistle, cheer, applaud, and stamp their feet. Those in Model T's would sound the signalling devices in their conveyances to produce a festive cacophony. Perhaps this continual hubbub should have warned me off; instead, it drew me, as a lamp does a moth.

The ball being pursued by the unsuspecting Poinsett outfielder rolled to my feet. I stooped to pick it up and greatly agitated the man. His eyes, under the narrow bill of a striped cap, grew wide, then hard. I tossed the ball to him. He caught it in a thin glove from which the tips of his naked fingers protruded like pale sausages. The cheers and honking from the devotees swelled in volume and in anxiousness. "Thanks," said the man. Turning, he threw the ball in a low arc to a teammate at one congested corner of the "diamond." This disciplined heave and its skillful reception by a teammate excited the local enthusiasts to even louder approbation. I moved back into the shelter of the woods—to watch the remainder of the contest from this vantage, without detection by the spectators or further intrusion of myself into the game.

Afterwards, the man to whom I had tossed the ball ventured alone to the edge of the evergreen stand. "Sir," he said, "if still here, please shew yourself." I did, but my fulfillment of his request evoked his silent wariness. He had above-average height and strength, but I stood three hands taller and cast him in darkling shadow. "Don't be afraid," I said. "I intend neither you nor your friends any harm." These words clearly ameliorated his mood. He slipped from out my shadow and appraised me with a look of most welcome sympathy.

"That out you he'ped me git," he said in his rude dialect, "was shore a big un. Jes' then, Mister, the game teetered more t'ards them than us, but Flexner's tag at third settled them Braggadocio's boys' hash and skinned us through the tight. So thanks again. 'Thout yore he'p, I'd'a lost two weeks' wages at Griscom's dentistry office to Bruno Shaler."

"It was my pleasure," said I, and the timbre of my voice occasioned him another instant of unease. He quickly recovered and questioned me on my knowledge of base ball and my best self-assessment of my playing skills. I owned that my knowledge derived solely from observation; further, any talent I might possess was that of an awkward tyro.

"If you could hit jes' a quarter lick yore size, you could take the Poinsett Redbirds to a state championship," he said. *"How'd you like a weekday job at Griscom's? Let me th'ow you a few and see what befaws, aw right?"*

The name of this outfielder and dentistry-office factotum was Jimmy Brawley. Jimmy proceeded to test my abilities and to lesson me in the rudiments of the pastime and sport to which he devoted most of his Saturday and Sunday afternoons. When he experimentally pitched to me, at first lobbing the ball, then hurling it with an uncouth ferocity, I excited his admiration by launching seven of these latter pitches almost to the trees. My bat was a modified wagon tongue that Jimmy had held back for me from the equipment of his departed companions. He also had a leather-wrapped india-rubber ball that he delivered from a slat laid down as the pitcher's mark. Finally, I propelled the ball into the very treetops of the woods wherein I had sheltered, and neither Jimmy nor I could recover it.

My impromptu tryout ended on that account, but Jimmy wrung from me through importunate flattery a commitment to appear in the Diggings for a weekday-evening practice.

"Tomorrow," said he.

"Perhaps. I hardly trust my base-ball instincts, nor yet, Mr. Brawley,   my—"

"Jimmy," he told me. *"None of that'ere mister rig-a-roo. Makes me sound I'm awready a laid-out stiff."*

"Nor, Jimmy, do I trust my ability to secure favour equal to your own among your colleagues and supporters. It has ever been thus with me. I offend by my appearance. I go down to dust an outcast because my body incites not only revulsion but also a wholly unwarranted fear."

"If you pound 'er to the treetops wunst or twyst a game, Sonny Man, you could look like a shaved-butt coyote and nobody roundabouts Poinsett'd give a stale tea cake."

For nearly a week, I remained unperceived in the pine stand. At night, however, I betook myself to the diamond on the Strawberry Diggings with a burlap sack of pine cones and a stout bough with which to launch them. For hours I practiced. The flanged configuration of the surface of the cones, along with their relative lack of density, prevented me from propelling them far beyond the fan of the infield, but the persistence with which I drilled instilled in me, over time, great confidence. I decided to accept Jimmy's challenge.

When I first shewed myself to the Poinsett Redbirds on a practice day, Jimmy introduced me to the players and to their manager, Almont Rattigan. Against even the team's best hurler, I batted very well, but fielded so ineffectually that Rattigan *despaired of ever employing me, because of the liability I would pose on defense. The less kind or more ignorant Redbird players referred to me as Flatfoot, Lame Ox, Dropper, and Stoopnot. Mr. Rattigan advised me to quit base ball for coal mining, but Poinsett had no mines.*

Jimmy sought virtually alone to retrieve me from incompetence afield and disfavor among his teammates. With old leather-wrapped balls, then with a crate of mail-order Spaldeens, he tried my limited skills and augmented them through repetition until only my lameness debarred me from excellence as a fielder. This handicap—the consequence, I knew, of my own efforts to humanise my monstrous physique—I overcame through application, diligence, and a style of chicanery in my self-positioning that the other Redbird fielders later strove to emulate themselves. When I could find no one with whom to practise, Jimmy advised, I should take myself to the vacant lot behind Criscom's dentistry office and catapult a Spaldeen at its foundation for as long as I could catch the rebounds. So much did I improve, through devotion to this regimen, that within a week Rattigan had fitted me with an outsized uniform and deployed me in vital town-team contests against Lepanto and Frye's Mill. . . .

From before the Great War to the acme of the American Depression, I changed my residence at least once a year. I eschewed a permanent home and also the inevitability of my neighbours' snoopery for a transient life and the qualified privacy that mobility affords. I played town-team ball in Tennessee, Mississippi, Louisiana, Missouri, Kentucky, Alabama, Texas, and Florida's panhandle. I chose towns far enough apart from one another to prevent old acquaintances or teammates from a prior affiliation from chancing upon me. At intervals, I curtailed my participation for a year, two years, perhaps even three, though I honed my skills even during these sabbaticals. Some towns, when I played, gave me a monthly stipend—$30 was the most munificent—and a sinecure such as sidewalk sweeping or crate handling that did not monopolise my evenings or weekends. I purposely shunned human entanglements, such as that I had enjoyed with Kariak in Oongpek, and behaved myself both on and off the field with as much sobriety and honour as I could, given the transient nature of my allegiances and my wish to hold myself emotionally aloof from my teammates, as well as from the communities that supported us.

Why did I live? In the middle 1930s, with bread lines commonplace and unemployment an evil contagion in even the remotest hamlets, I no longer regarded my absorption into human society as a productive citizen as my primary aim. Playing ball, I realised, had become an end in itself, not a means of such absorption.

What now infused meaning into my days, whether in Donigal, Missouri, or in Hurricane, Alabama, derived less from tiresome social intercourse than from the galvanising physical sensations of hitting a ball hard and far, and of throwing it with exactitude. Once I had wanted a spiritual sharer, but now, drunk with the restored robustness of my borrowed body, I wanted only faceless teammates and unending occasions to exercise my intellectual and animal faculties playing baseball. . . .

In the summer of 1940, I had a janitorial sinecure with a school in Hurricane, up the Tensaw River from Mobile Bay, and the guarantee of at least two town-team games a weekend. The part-owner of a minor-league club in Mobile itself, having heard of my batting prowess, sought me out. Despite the evident distress that my appearance caused him, he bestowed many flowery compliments and offered money, women, and alcohol as inducements to leave the Hurricane Hurricanes in favour of the Mobile Tarpons. Because I had no use for these offers and hated his protestations of high esteem, I declined. He departed from me both confounded by my gentlemanly refusals of his overtures and angry with me for seeing through his dissimulations.

Soon thereafter, Mr. Jordan McKissic of the Highbridge Hellbenders of the Chattahoochee Valley League came to watch me play. A teammate told me of his presence in the stands and informed me heatedly that only an "addlepate" would decline a second invitation to a higher level of play. He seemed sensible of the townwide conviction that although I had graciously shown my loyalty to the Hurricane nine, I had also manifested irrefutable proof of my foolish lack of self-regard. Should I reject another attractive offer, he supposed, every other member of our club would inherit the taint of my simplicity, and the name Hurricaner would soon stand synonymous with ninny, simpleton, or dolt. I ignored this counsel and performed as I always performed; that is to say, with intensity, diligence, and positivity. Indeed, I led the Hurricane Hurricanes to victory.

Afterwards, Mr. McKissic and I conferred. He did not recoil from me. His smile had no falsity, his words no ulteriority. His offer of a regular emolument, along with room and board, veiled no improper inducements or counterweights. His proposal tempted me, but the glare of playing in a larger city, with a major-league affiliate, subverted even the happy impression that Mr., McKissic's sincere demeanour and speech had forged. Neither riches nor glory held any irresistible allure for me; I could fulfill my inbred need for athletic self-expression in an unfenced meadow as well as in a lighted stadium.

"I disagree," said Mr. McKissic. "You'll never realise your full capacities as an

athlete until you play against men as good as, or perhaps even better than, you. A home run against Joe Blow of the Fairhope Shrimpers proves a good deal less than does a home run against Sundog Billy Wallace of the Gendarmes. By the same token, a home run against Billy pales next to one off Rapid Robert Feller of the Cleveland Indians."

This line of argument found a sympathetic resonance in me. "Then, sir," I said, "I should try to play for a nine that periodically meets Mr. Feller's club."

"But the only way to reach such a nine, Mr. Clerval, is through a training league such as the CVL."

To what summit of expertise could I aspire? Glory, although some may dispute this assertion, did not beckon me. Rather, curiosity about the range of my talents filled my thoughts, calling me to some practical resolution of the question. In this way, Mr. McKissic nearly secured my defection to the Hellbenders. Mulling a host of maddening factors, I said nothing, inadvertently prejudicing him to conclude that I would respond negatively.

"Tell me what you want, Mr. Clerval," said he. "If it isn't against my principles or terribly outlandish, I just might give it to you."

I catalogued and sorted through my wants. It scarcely took a minute, but this minute protracted Mr. McKissic's anxiety to the full extent of its elasticity.

"For pity's sake, Mr. Clerval, say something!"

"Occasional use of your automobile and instruction in its operation," said I.

"My automobile? And lessons in how to drive it?"

"Just so," I said. "Those are my conditions."

"All right. Done."

But I finished that season with the Hurricanes, as I had earlier pledged to do, and soon forgot the compensatory pledges of the Hellbenders' owner.

The following summer, though I greatly wanted to play, I determined that my small fame in the Mobile Bay area had so far overthrown my anonymity that I must resign for a time from public view to reestablish it. I did so, passing the time through closeted reading and contemplation.

In early July, I relocated to eastern Alabama. There I apprenticed to a laconic and seldom occupied blacksmith who understood that the automobile had long since rung the death-knell of his profession. In any event, he led me to proficiency in horseshoe making and harness repair while I educated him in the esoteric niceties of scrimshaw painting and the making of fishing nets from the sinew strands of whitetail deer. On December 7th, the Japanese executed a disabling strike on the Pacific fleet of the United States, and my mentor, against my ardent counsel, quit Skipperville to enlist in the Army at Fort Benning, Georgia.

For three and a half months, I oversaw the daily trade of my departed teacher's blacksmith enterprise. My income supported me in austere comfort. With it, I rented an upstairs room in a shabby antebellum home belonging to an eccentric widow. Miss Rosalind, as the townspeople knew her, smoked Cuban cheroots, raised hairless chihuahua dogs, and wore jumpsuits adorned with sequins. She viewed me as excellent company, not as a grotesque curiosity. Indeed, she so heavily freighted my leisure, of which I had a severe plenty, with such meandering local genealogies and such mazy accounts of her dogs' ills and achievements that upon occasion I would have preferred to be shot. Moreover, the fumes from her cheroots pervaded my clothing, begot in me migraines of excruciating tenacity, and called forth my tears. (This liquid Miss Rosalind always misconstrued as a sign of my tender heart.) Often, then, I felt indentured less to my smithery than to my landlady.

In April, Mr. Jordan McKissic and his wife, Miss Giselle, stopped in a handsome automobile outside the dingy garage in which I laboured. A player of his, a young man recently taken into the Navy, hailed from Skipperville, and the player's mother's epistolary accounts of the giant who had moved to town to assume the blacksmithery of Millard Goodsell had come to Mr. McKissic's attention via the low route of boardinghouse gossip. After a visit to his wife's cousin in Brundide, he had driven to Skipperoille seeking to learn the truth of this gossip and the exact identity of the blacksmith's apprentice.

"Ah, Mr. Clerval, it's you," said he. "I renew my offer of almost two years ago. Don't immediately say no. With a war on, baseball at the training level needs an infusion of fresh talent—or the return of competent old talent—merely to survive."

He continued in this vein, appealing to my love of the sport, and stressing what he regarded as my unsatisfactory present circumstances, to finagle my consent. At length his words merely clanged, for the lack of useful blacksmith work and the dubious benediction of Miss Rosalind's society had predisposed me to accept his offer. He may not have noted this pliability in me, however, for I stood in the crepuscular gloom of my garage like a yoked ox, a harness over my shoulders and a bellows in one hand, a figure of almost Satanic apostasy and discouragement.

Then, Miss Giselle made a self-effacing appearance in the doorway, a spectre of sunshine and organdy. She much resembled Elizabeth Lavenza Frankenstein, the bride of my creator, as Elizabeth might have come to look had I not slain her for my own revengeful purposes in the freshness of her young womanhood. Miss Giselle's eyes had not yet adjusted to the dinginess of the garage; she had no cause to fall back in dismay at the sight of an ogre of my bulk and hideousness; but, as her *pupils contracted, it seemed that she adjusted without strain or upset not only to the twilight in my unkempt shop but also to the parodic human creature trapped in its gloom.*

"Jordan, I see you've found him," said she. "Will it be much longer? The sun's ferociously hot."

"I'll be along shortly," said Mr. McKissic with a curtness I had never heard from him before. "Go back to the car." He somewhat relented. "Or stand under that sycamore." He nodded towards it. "Mr. Clerval and I have an item or two more to discuss."

"Mr. Clerval," said the woman, although her husband had offered no formal introduction.

"Ma'am," said I, inclining my head.

She withdrew, leaving me stunned with reminiscences; and Mr. McKissic returned to his needless suasions, for, by now, I had determined to give Miss Rosalind notice. Mr. McKissic nonetheless reiterated his various incentives, including the many chances I would have to try myself against redoubtable competitors.

"Thank you," said I.

"Anything else, Mr. Clerval?" asked Mr. McKissic.

"The occasional use of an auto," said I. "And driving lessons."

"Yes. I'd forgotten. But never fear, you've got it. Report to spring training as soon as you can."

"Yes, sir."

And so began the latest chapter in the long chronology of my second life, a tale whose theme remains occluded to its hero and whose end is not yet told. . . .

43

On Tuesday, July 27, the ball field at Camp Penticuff basked red and dusty in the sun. We rode out to it in the Bomber, dressed out in our flannels, more anxious than we'd admit about taking on these Negro barnstormers in front of a hopped-up crowd of colored GIs. We'd just come off a five-game road trip (three wins, two losses), and the Mockingbirds and the Gendarmes would play us three games each at home towards the end of the week. I had the impression, jouncing past the stripped-down barracks and the parched parade grounds, that Muscles, Hoey, Dunnagin, and some of the other Hellbender vets felt we'd bitten off a chaw big enough to choke us.

The stands out here already teemed with khaki-clad black soldiers. They sat or stood in the main grandstand behind the backstop or on portable metal bleachers a maintenance unit had set up beforehand. The sun blazed, slapping the whole sports and training complex like a huge catfish bladder on an unseen stick. The very air seemed to stretch out and pop under the blows. The Bomber pulled up, after the Splendid Dominicans had already arrived, to some ear-splitting whistles.

"Bout damn time!" yelled somebody sun-sore and antsy.

We parked behind a fleet of ten- or twelve-year-old Buick touring cars, dented and furred with rust; and the Splendid Dominicans ran out onto the field. Until we'd showed, they'd apparently spent their time mingling with the troops: boosting morale. Learning that about em lowered ours. It implied the Dominicans ("These guys're Dominicans like I'm a Hawaiian," said Turkey Sloan) hadn't felt obliged to warm up in advance of our arrival. Two seconds after hitting the field, though, they had a ball whipping around the horn like men born in spikes and caps. I watched them from the Bomber while, outside the fence around the park, Mister JayMac and Darius shook hands with Mr. Cozy Bissonette and Major Dexter.

Inside the bus, Fadeaway said, "Cottonton all over again—no dugouts.

We'll bake in this sorry-ass sun." He had bench time ahead of him, and I almost sympathized. Almost.

In baggy white flannels—shirts with numbers whip-stitched to their backs and the letters SDT sewn to their chests—the Splendid Dominicans didn't seem much like black supermen. Like us, they had guys built like fire hydrants, flag poles, or haystacks. This one could've pruned Azalea hedges in Alligator Park, that one could've tonged blocks of ice at the cold plant. No doubt, though, that Cozy Bissonette's ragtag bunch could hit and hustle.

"All right," Mister JayMac said from up front. "Pile off."

"Criminy, we'll slide out on our own sweat," Parris said.

We got up and pushed through the aisle, looking for relief—from the heat, from our nerves, from the suspense of taking on these colored unknowns, who, in their own cities, had even more fans than we did in Highbridge.

I saw a few white faces—brass and senior NCOs, company commanders and cowcatcher-jawed topkicks. But the faces of the Negro GIs outnumbered the pasty or sunburnt faces among them fifty-to-one. A dark sea in the stands: beige, caramel, chestnut, shiny bruise-black. Even at a military post deep in the heart of Dixie, those hundreds of young Negro men shook me to my boots. What if they all got loose and we had to wade through their strutting tide?

Darius touched my arm and urged me through a gate onto the field. "See?" he asked. (Or was it "Sea," like in "body of water"?) When I glanced at him over my shoulder, he gave me an unreadable smile.

The field had a press box, a platform on stilts that may've sometimes served as a reviewing stand. A goofy-looking white lieutenant in wire-rimmed glasses sat behind a microphone on the platform. His welcome blared out at us from metal speakers mounted on creosoted poles.

"Men of the First and Second Battalions of the Special Training Regiment of Camp Penticuff, Georgia," he said, echoes from the speakers overlapping and blurring, "give a soldierly hello to the fine ball clubs that've come out here today to entertain you—our sister community's Highbridge Hellbenders of the Chattahoochee Valley League, and the Splendid Dominican Touristers, some talented barnstormers from the Negro American League! Let em hear you, men!"

A tumult of claps and gospel shouts. The lieutenant broke into it to read lineups, ours first, and each Hellbender player trotted out to line up between second and third base. Oddly enough, the GIs of the Special Training Regiment made as much racket for us as our own fans in Highbridge would've.

Then the lieutenant read the starters for Mr. Bissonette's glorified pickup squad. "Batting in the lead-off spot and playing second base, Terris 'Slag Iron' Smith!" If that ball field'd had a roof, those colored soldiers would've blown it into the Gulf of Mexico. Slag Iron Smith could've been every last one of em's favorite cousin.

I recall the name of every other Dominican Tourister the lieutenant said, each with a road alias cornier by several degrees than any of ours—Rufus "Pepperpot" Cole, Luis "Gumbo" Garcia, Hosea "The Gator" Partlow. Each of their guys got a send-off Highbridge fans would've reserved for a regiment of heroes. Don't think it wasn't intimidating either.

The Army appointed umpires. No big deal? Ordinarily, maybe not, but Major Dexter'd asked a Negro captain from a Negro tanker unit to call balls and strikes, and a black NCO from his own battalion to patrol the bases. You'd've thought, gauging these appointments by the reactions of our biggest in-house bigots, he'd asked Attila the Hun and Vlad the Impaler to do it. Even Mister JayMac, seeing these men on the field, felt it incumbent upon himself to buttonhole Major Dexter and argue for one white ump—on the grounds we'd made dozens of courtly concessions to Mr. Cozy's boys already, including playing them at all, meeting them in front of their enlisted cousins, and using a CVL rest day to come out here.

Neither Mister JayMac nor Major Dexter would allow himself the pleasure of ranting or kicking dirt—but the argument drug on. Both teams went to their benches, and the GIs began to get restless. They swayed on their seats and sang out ad-lib Jody chants:

> "Left, right, left, right, march yo ass.
> All that glitters must be brass!

> "Left my home in Tennessee.
> Ever DI looks de same to me!

> "Why you fellas has to stall?
> We come out to watch some ball!

"Jody, Jody, see me sweat.
My po body got a liquid debt!

"Count yo fingers, count yo toes.
Be a year fo one team scohs!"

During these chants, the Dominicans retook the field, but without a ball. They *pretended* to have one, though. Their pitcher—Turtlemouth Thomas Clark, a crafty s.o.b. once the game got clocking—went into this showboaty boa-constrictor windup and let absolutely nothing fly. A Dominican at the plate with a bat took a swing as broad as Turtlemouth's windup and drove that whistling air ball into right for a make-believe single.

By this time, the crowd'd stopped chanting. You could even hear the *thwock!* the bat made hitting the ball. (The catcher'd made it, sticking a finger into his cheek and popping it out like a champagne cork.) Anyway, as the batter ran to first, the right fielder scooped up the ghost liner on two invisible hops and fired absolutely nothing to the shortstop covering second. This man looked the runner back to first, walked the nothing in his hands a few steps towards the mound, and flipped it to old Turtlemouth.

"Hell're they doing?" Fadeaway said, not trusting his eyes.

"Shadow ball," Dunnagin told him. "Watch."

The next batter took a couple of pitches, on both of which Turtlemouth wound himself tighter than the rubber band on a model airplane's propeller. The batter banged his third pitch—*thwock!*—an air-ball knuckler, to the shortstop, Pepperpot Cole. Cole flung himself down, trapped absolutely nothing under his scrap of a glove, retrieved it, and zipped it to the second baseman, Slag Iron Smith, who caught this nothing at belt height. The runner from first tried to take Smith out of the play, but Slag Iron pivoted, leapt like a deer, and threw absolutely nothing to first.

A peg in the dirt. The first baseman yanked it out of the dust like a man cracking a whip, and spun around to call the batter out as the runner somersaulted over the bag. Then the first baseman started the ghost ball around the horn in honor of the phantom double play.

The GIs loved it. You'd've figured them at a county-fair strip show, they whooped so shrill and sassy.

"Hard to make that kinda stuff look real," Dunnagin said. "You've got to have your timing down."

Mister JayMac finally got the Negro captain assigned to home plate moved to the base paths, along with the black DI from the First Battalion of the Special Training Unit. The major himself went behind the plate. That way, the foul lines had an ump each. If a wronged Hellbender needed to dispute a call at the plate, he wouldn't have to test the will of a racial and social inferior. Mister JayMac, as I heard later, had used "whitemail" to get his way—he'd threatened to take us Hellbenders home.

Another problem remained. Which team qualified as visitors and which as homies? Mister JayMac wanted the advantage of last bats. So did Mister Cozy. They both went out to Major Dexter—sweating in his chest protector, birdcage, and shin guards—to present their cases. Mister JayMac said no team named Dominican Touristers could be a home team, barnstormers were visitors by definition, and Camp Penticuff lay within hailing distance of Highbridge. Thus, the Hellbenders, even in our away flannels, deserved home-field advantage.

Mister Cozy said this exhibition had begun in his head, his Dominicans had reached the ball field first, and if either team had the local crowd on its side, well . . .

"Flip a coin," Mister JayMac said.

"Okay by me," Mister Cozy said. "Do it."

Major Dexter flipped a coin, it landed tails, and the Splendid Dominicans took the field with last bats in their baggy pockets and grins on their faces.

"Please stand for the National Anthem," said the lieutenant at the press-box mike. Camp Penticuff's flag pole, with the Stars and Stripes hanging limp in the sultry afternoon, grew out of a pile of stones on a hillock two parade grounds beyond the left-field fence. We flapped our caps over our hearts, and a black trumpeter with one stripe on his sleeve marched up into the press box and blew the clearest "Star-Spangled Banner" I'd ever heard, a cross between high-church music and Harry James. As soon as he hit those "home of the brave" notes, the GIs started a cheer that echoed in chilling sweeps to the barracks, the PX, the main gate.

I dug into the batter's box while this unnerving roar went on. Turtlemouth Clark looked past me for his catcher's sign like I wasn't there. My Red Stix bat caught some libel from the crowd—"Hey, you gon hit with a Tootsie Pop stick?" "Boy from Californy, got him a bitty redwood bat."—but Mister Cozy's boys didn't blink. I could've walked up there with a blue shillelagh without goading them to curl a lip. No more shadow ball, the life-or-death horsehide only.

Turtlemouth Clark wound up—except now, he hardly had a windup at all, just a quick pat-a-cake at his chest with glove and ball. Out of this business, he attacked me with sidearm smoke. His pitch had me looking for a doorway in the clay, to escape having a Fearless Fosdick hole drilled through me. I leapt at least four feet backwards.

"*Steeeeeee-rike!*" Major Dexter cried.

The Special Training soldiers laughed a load of wrinkles into their khakis. But I deserved it. I reset myself with a throb in my head and crushed chili peppers in my cheeks.

"Mebbe you'll see the nex one," the catcher said.

Before Turtlemouth could go into his stingy game windup, I called time and walked aside.

"Batter up," Major Dexter said. "*Now!*"

I stepped back in. Turtlemouth struck me out, but put a couple of Band-Aids on my stigma by also whiffing Charlie Snow and Lon Musselwhite—to the noisy delight of the troops. Snow made him unleash seven pitches before chasing a sidearm change, but Muscles, like me, took three wild cuts at three stuttering speedballs and slunk back to the dugout mumbling about the legality of Turtlemouth's delivery.

When Darius took the mound for us, a murmur spiced with a few profanities lapped the stands. If Darius heard, he made no sign, just cycled through his warm-up tosses to Dunnagin, then stepped back to let us infielders throw the ball around. Once in the field, Darius didn't give a cucumber pip what color his opponents were; he wanted them out, the scairter the better, his whole devotion to the uniform on his back. In this case, our dingy Hellbender ash-browns.

In the bottom of the first, Darius matched Turtlemouth's strikeout feat, and we had us a pitched battle—literally—of K's and O's, connipted hitters tossing away their bats after fruitless trips to the box.

Oh, a couple of fellas hit the ball. Charlie Snow tagged one on a pearl-bright clothesline right to the center fielder, and Henry cracked a pop-up that Turtlemouth himself, waving everybody else off, caught at shoe-top height from a ridiculous outhouse squat, a basket catch two inches from the ground. The crowd gobbled up this showboating like peanuts.

In the top of the fourth, I drew a walk—the first hitter on either team to reach base. It seemed near lunatic, but I wondered if Turtlemouth had put me on on purpose, just to wake the crowd. The four balls he'd shown me had all thwapped in too high to hit, too high even to lunge for.

Buck Hoey, in his boot-blackened bedroom slippers, left his coaching box to talk to me.

"What'd you do to deserve a free pass? Promise to suck him off after the game?"

"Up yours," I said as plainly as I could.

"Think you can steal on the shine, Dumbo? We need a runner in scoring position."

Sure I did. I always thought so.

"Play ball," said the colored officer umpiring first.

Hoey ignored him. "Try to draw a throw. See what kind of move to first he's got. Then watch for a pitchout. Waxahachie Beckland has the second best slingshot on this club."

Waxahachie Beckland was the catcher, Turtlemouth's battery mate. Hoey wanted me to measure my lead against both men and mind my p's and q's. He sashayed back into his coaching box.

I drew one throw from Turtlemouth. He had only a so-so pickoff move. (Or he *showed* me only a so-so pickoff move.) I got back to first a full second ahead of his toss. On his first throw to the plate, though, Turtlemouth pitched out to Beckland. If I'd broken for second, Beckland would've gunned me down by a yard or more.

"Way to go, Dumbo," Hoey said. "Watch em again."

I felt pretty smug about drawing a throw from Turtlemouth and then hoodwinking him and his catcher into pitching out to Snow. They expected me to steal. Mister Cozy and his boys had done their homework; they knew I could outrun the word God, they respected my foot speed. I lengthened my lead, feinting once or twice with my upper body.

Turtlemouth showed me the whites of his eyes, but didn't tumble to my feints. He threw to the plate again, another pitchout. I strolled back to first and kicked the bag. The Dominican battery mates looked like fools. They'd risked two straight pitchouts, for nothing. Even worse, from their point of view, they'd run the count on Charlie Snow, the best hitter in the CVL, to two and zero. Only a madman deliberately put himself in the hole with Snow at bat and me on base.

As I took my fourth lead of this at-bat, Hoey caught my eye. Behind his hand, he mouthed, *Go.* He also cradled his left elbow, our sign to steal. Turtlemouth, he obviously figured, had to throw Snow a strike to keep from moving within a ball of walking him. He and Beckland wouldn't dare pitch out again.

So, of course, they did.

I had a decent jump on Turtlemouth and second base looked stepping-stone close. Before I could belly-slide into it, though, Slag Iron Smith leapt in front of me, caught Beckland's stinger from home, and let me tag myself out coming head-first into his floppy cold cut of a glove.

Three straight pitchouts. Stupid. Except their strategy nailed me dead. On the other hand, Charlie Snow, too surprised to try to queer Beckland's throw by swinging at the last one, now had three balls on him. Maybe the Dominicans' ruse *hadn't* worked—not, at least, as slick as they'd've liked.

Forget that.

Cool as ice, Turtlemouth worked the count to three balls and two strikes, then erased Snow on a nibbler back to the mound. He humiliated Muscles with another strikeout and slouched off the field to a standing O.

In the bottom of the sixth, Darius gave up the first two hits of the Camp Penticuff exhibition, back-to-back singles to Gator Partlow and Waxahachie Beckland. Nobody out. Partlow at third, Beckland at first.

"Push done come to shove, eh?" Fadeaway shouted from the bench. "Time to make sure us crackers don't win our money."

Mister JayMac went over to Fadeaway and spoke to him.

"Made it look good as you could for as long as you could, I guess!" Fadeaway shouted around the boss.

Mister JayMac got right in front of Fadeaway and quietly chewed the kid from Sea Island to Pensacola. Fadeaway shut up, and Mister JayMac sat back down again.

Darius struck out the third Dominican batter. The fourth hit a grounder to Junior, who snapped it to me for the force at second. I dragged my foot over the bag and threw to Henry at first. We got the runner there by half a step, and the double play wiped out the run that would've scored from third if my throw had hit Henry's mitt a fraction of a second later.

On his way in to the bench, Darius collected the game ball from Henry and ambled straight to Fadeaway. Mister JayMac hurried to interpose himself, but Darius stepped around him and slapped the ball into Fadeaway's chest.

"You thow, boy. Save yo precious wager."

"Darius, I'll pull you when it's time," Mister JayMac said.

"I'm sittin," Darius said. "I jes guv yall six of the best I got. Let this eggsuck boy carry yall from here."

"Neither of you has a thing to say about it," Mister JayMac said. "Darius, you pitch."

"Nosir. I'm gone."

Major Dexter waddled over in his umpire's gear. "They need that ball for warm-ups. Toss it back out, please."

Fadeaway tossed the ball to Turtlemouth Clark. Then he sat back down, his eyes on the clayey dust between his shoes.

Mister JayMac grabbed Darius's shirt. "This club belongs to me—you pitch because I say you do, nigger!" Despite the crowd noise, everyone on our bench heard this. Mister JayMac heard it himself and looked around.

"So *much* belongs to you," Darius said distinctly.

"I'm sorry," Mister JayMac said. "You've held these fellas in check the whole way. Keep on doing it."

"Nosir. I brung yall as far as I can." Darius stripped to his ribbed gray undershirt and dropped his Hellbenders blouse into Fadeaway's lap. Fadeaway pushed it into the dirt, like he would've a grungy dishrag.

"Damn it," Mister JayMac whispered to himself.

Darius walked through a gate and between a pair of bleacher sections towards the *Brown Bomber*. The soldiers in the stands watched him go with the same sledgehammered curiosity felt by us Hellbenders. Some of the GIs hollered, "Way to sling that baby!" or "Hallelujah!"

Darius raised one arm and held it over his head until he'd disappeared from view.

"Batter up!" Major Dexter yelled. "We need a batter!"

In the top of the seventh, Henry jacked Turtlemouth's first pitch so far over the right-field fence that everyone—*everyone*—stood up to watch it arc off into infinity.

"*Ooooiiiuuuweeoo!*" went Lamar Knowles. "Never seen nobody but Jumbo pole em like that!"

His amazed jubilation didn't extend to the troops. They admired the crunch of Henry's home run, but not Turtlemouth blowing his shutout or yielding a crucial run this late in the game. In any case, Turtlemouth wiped his forehead and mowed down—like a man with a Gatling gun—Reese Curriden, Junior Heggie, and Double Dunnagin.

In the bottom of the inning, Fadeaway swaggered out to pitch. A few disgruntled GIs shot him the razz. They sensed he might have rabbit ears and got on him like cats on a camel cricket: "Fade away, Fadeaway! Oh, fade away, please today, oh, faded ofay, Fadeaway!" And so on. Fadeaway adjusted. He left off strutting and buckled down. In his first inning of work, he allowed one solid single but emerged unscored-on and quietly cocky. It had taken me six innings to get the strut he'd picked up facing only four Dominican hitters.

In the top of the eighth, Skinny Dobbs, Fadeaway Ankers, and I came up against Turtlemouth—Skinny and I for only the third time, Fadeaway for his first. Skinny and Fadeaway lined and struck out respectively, and Henry stopped me as I started up to the plate.

"I know what you should do," he said.

"Yeah. H-h-hit it where they aint."

He took me by the shoulders, gently. "Bunt."

"B-b-bunt?"

"Push it down the third-base line, Daniel. Mr. Clark has a weakness fielding bunts."

"H-h-how do you kn-know?"

"Mr. Clark has an inner-ear problem. I read it in a Negro paper from Birmingham."

"Inner-ear problem?"

"If you push the ball down the line, Mr. Clark will lose his balance trying to retrieve it. With your speed, Daniel, you'll have a hit."

I had no quarrel with Henry's suggestion. In my two at bats, I'd fanned and reached base on a strategic charity ticket. This time, then, I squared around, into the blazing sweep of Turtlemouth's sidearm curve, and, yielding with the pitch, let the ball plunk off my bat and sprinted.

To improve your chances of legging out a doubtful hit, you lower your head and dig. As Satchel Paige said, you don't look back; either somebody might be gaining on you or you've stolen a second or two from your ultimate time. God save my soul, but I peeked to see how Turtlemouth'd attacked my bunt. When I did, I saw him grab for the ball, wheel around his outstretched arm like a besotted maypole dancer, and topple into the dirt. He underhanded a throw to first as he fell, but the ball—by now I was digging again, burning jet fuel—sailed on him, and his wild throw got me all the way to second.

Turtlemouth, walking back to the mound, paused to consider me on second. He sneezed and rubbed his nose. "Done got there so fast you guv me pneumonia." He got back into his stance and toed the rubber from a stretch.

Snow brought me home with a double to the right-field gap, making the score two to nothing. Muscles stranded Snow with a wing-shot gull to the left fielder, and the rest of us trotted back out to defend our lead against the cream of Mister Cozy's batting order. The afternoon's fractured dazzle hung on us like warm honey, golden and clingy.

44

Despite the sunshine, and the peanut scorch drifting over us from town, the rest of that game played out like a wine drunk—some kind of drunk, with the slide-show lurchiness of a bad dream. At shortstop, I watched it all happen, my mouth full of worry flannel.

In the bottom of the eighth, the first bat showed up. I don't mean baseball bat either. I mean *living* bat, a flying varmint with tattered wings. Against the rinsed blue of the sky, it seemed so humdrum, as it dive-bombed the field and swerved up from a thousand near collisions, that most of us mistook it for a bird—if we mistook it for anything other than a scudding magnolia leaf. Then more such wheeling varmints swept into view, and I wondered if a pigeon breeder on the roof of a nearby barracks had emptied his dovecotes. But the varmints got thicker and noisier, breaking into squadrons and chirping like airborne crickets, and I knew them for bats, several pesky flights of them. They stirred more breeze than the day did, zooming from the stands to the outfield, and from the fences to the stands, pip-pip-pipping so damned tinnily I started thinking of them as . . . as pip-squeaks.

In the black half of the eighth, the Dominicans sent up first baseman Gumbo Garcia, center fielder Tommy Christmas, and right fielder Gator Partlow. Fadeaway walked Garcia. The bats blew back and forth overhead like curls of newspaper char from summer's own chimney. Fadeaway punched Christmas a ticket to first, just like he had Garcia.

Major Dexter's GIs began to sway and foot-stamp.

Fadeaway struck out Partlow on a slider-slider-speedball setup, and Dunnagin jumped out from behind his third swing and snapped off a bullet to Henry that nailed Tommy Christmas two feet off the bag. Christmas died on his knees, ducking all the stooping bats a-twitter over the field.

The GIs went as dead as a knobbed-off radio station.

Now the Dominicans had two outs and only the melon-footed and heavy-ribbed Garcia still on second. Fadeaway walked third baseman Judd Davies.

"Buckle down!" shouted Mister JayMac, really hacked.

Fadeaway may've tried, but on his first pitch to Oscar Wall, the left fielder, Wall reached back, his front leg off the ground, and clobbered Fadeaway's best scroogie an Alabama ton. He almost seemed to hit it one-handed—his left hand swept away from the bat handle on his follow-through, while the ball itself hurtled up and away, into a cloud of dive-bombing bats.

I could imagine Fadeaway praying, Dear God, let it hit one of them varmints. I prayed too. Only a lucky midair intercept would prevent Wall's blast from carrying to the fence and tying us at two apiece. And if it *cleared* the fence, the Dominicans would likely beat us.

The ball didn't de-head one damned bat. It flew through them, towards Charlie Snow, on a hard, low arc. They veered away from it like they'd've dodged any other flying predator, by sonar and stunt-flying. Snow ran under the ever-shifting cloud with his back to the ball, the way DiMaggio and later Mays did, thinking to turn at the last instant and pincer-snatch it.

But the bats broke his concentration. He looked back for the drive too soon and had to dig out again at a hard lope. Everyone could see he'd locked into a collision course with the fence. As the ball dropped, Snow sensed the fence coming. He tried to save his body and make the catch at the same time.

He hurtled, a leg-high effort to hit the fence's cap rail with the edge of his shoe, grab the ball at belt height behind him, and spring to the grass with his bones unbroken and Darius and Fadeaway's shutout intact. But his spikes, or the fence, or a crazy skew on Wall's plummeting drive did him in. A spike snagged. He didn't bounce off the fence but somersaulted over it, the ball going with him. When he didn't get up right away, something scary uncurled in my gut.

"Thass a home run," one of the colored umps said. "He made the catch all right, but his feet never come down fair."

Garcia, Davies, and Wall all went round the bases. That made the score three to two, the Dominicans' way. Major Dexter signaled as much.

I began running towards center. So did a bunch of others. Snow still hadn't untangled from the heap he'd made beyond the fence, and both Muscles and Skinny, our other two out-fielders, clambered over it to see about him. From my lungs to my guts, I had a splintery ache, big as a two-by-four. Beside the chain link in center, I knelt with it, a sinner behind a grid, to ask Muscles how it fared with the beautiful Charlie Snow.

"S bad." Muscles had grit in his voice, the first rubbings from a square of sandpaper. "S real bad."

"Throw it in," Snow said from Shangri-La, somewhere out of this atmosphere. "Hold the sucker to three."

"Just you hush," Muscles told him. "S too late for that."

"Yeah," said Snow sweetly. "I know." Heaped there, he hemorrhaged. The wound at his ankle bled like gangbusters. Muscles tried to tourniquet it with his shirt, which seeped through crimson-brown and reeked of sweat and redness in a combo I never want to smell again. The bats peeled off towards their attics. So'd their shadows, moving us out from under an afghan of shifting dapples into a cruel flat burn of sunlight.

Someone—Mister JayMac? Major Dexter?—called for a medic and an ambulance. Gawkers of every stripe and hue appeared.

"Jesus Lord, he's bleeding to death!" Muscles shouted.

"Hang on, Ch-Charlie," I told Snow through the fence.

No ambulance came, but Camp Penticuff's CO, General Gordon Holway, pulled up in a command car with the words THE OLD MAN stenciled on his door over a five-pointed white star. General Holway vaulted out and hustled over to the bleeding Snow.

Go there, do this, call for that, he barked to soldiers and ballplayers alike, and the way guys hurried to do what he said made me feel a little better. By this time, Mister JayMac'd reached Snow too. He stood beside me, his throat pulsing above me like a turkey gobbler's wattles.

"Hemophiliac!" he said. "Yall've got to do something for him damned quick."

"*What?*" General Holway squinted up at Mister JayMac out of eyes as narrow and blue as trout gills.

"He's a bleeder," Mister JayMac said. "A mildly afflicted bleeder, but a bleeder. His blood don't clot like it ought."

General Holway stood up. "A bleeder? And he plays ball? You let him?"

"I have to," Snow said through papery lips. "Aint nothing for me but to play."

Henry came up to me and did a side-saddle leap over the fence. He gathered the damaged Charlie Snow into his arms.

"Hospital? Infirmary? Where may we take him?"

"S dangerous to do it that way," somebody said. "The poor bloke needs a litter and a couple of corpsmen."

"It's dangerous to let him lie," Henry said.

"Put him in my car," General Holway said. "Let's move it!"

General Holway, his chauffeur, and Henry all got into the command car, Henry in the back with Snow propped like a smashed doll in the crook of his arm. Off they bounded towards the administrative and services area, a complex of two-story wooden buildings spaced out in rectangles, every building and every street block a twin of all the others.

The chauffeur played the command car's Klaxon, sounding its raucous bleat every twenty-five yards or so. The rest of us stood back and watched— Hellbenders, Splendid Dominicans, and some of the GIs in Major Dexter's Special Training units, a poleaxed crew of gawkers.

Major Dexter approached Mister JayMac. "Your fellas have one more out to get and at least one more trip into town, sir."

"Game's over," Mister JayMac said.

"Why?" Fadeaway Ankers puled, dragging the word out. "You put me in to finish this thang, didn't you?"

"You've jes finished."

"Then Mister Cozy's team wins," Major Dexter said. "Five full innings are a legal game. This one's nearly gone eight."

"This game warnt legal to begin with," Fadeaway said. "We had to sneak out here jes to start it."

Mister JayMac said, "Hush, boy-o," like a groom gentling a high-strung horse. Then, in the crush of bodies by the fence, he found Mr. Cozy Bissonette and stuck out his hand to him. "A hard-fought game, sir. Your men have skill and moxie. Please tell Mr. Clark and Mr. Wall, in particular, how much their play impressed us."

"Preciate that," Mister Cozy said. "Yo center fielder gon come round n play for yall again real soon."

"He's most likely going to die," Mister JayMac said.

Mister Cozy dropped his gaze. "Then God rest his soul, and God bless yall for letting us play with such a man."

Out there at the fence, us Hellbenders shook hands with Splendid Dominican Touristers, and vice versa. Fadeaway and a few others didn't like it much, but the disrespect finishing out would've showed Charlie Snow was plain even to them and so they finally shut up.

The Dominicans took their win with gravity. One of em—Tommy Christmas, I think—said to me, "You mighta got us, one mo inning. You sholy might," and strolled back to the stands with Partlow and Davies, marveling at the grit of Snow's effort to chase down through a canopy of bats Oscar Wall's tremendous knock to center.

When it was announced over the PA system the Dominicans'd won, the troops whooped and jitterbugged in the bleachers. I didn't fault em. In the lingo of deeds, their champions had proclaimed their honor.

45

Mister JayMac wanted Darius to drive us to the infirmary, but he was nowhere to be found. So Major Dexter, who'd finally shed his umpire's gear, offered to drive us around the field and through the T-square grids of the camp's Quartermasters' 700-series buildings to the infirmary.

"I can't leave Darius out here," Mister JayMac told Major Dexter. "Yall wouldn't enlist him, would you?"

"This is a training camp, not a recruitment station."

"I know what it is, Major. I asked if somebody out here'd accept his papers and put him in uniform."

"Not if you don't want us to, Mr. McKissic."

"Well I don't."

"Then you've nothing to worry about, sir."

"If yall find him out here later, will you truss him up and hold him till I can fetch him home?"

"Yessir."

"Well you'd better."

Major Dexter climbed aboard the *Brown Bomber* and took us on a quick rickety jaunt to the infirmary.

The infirmary looked like every other bleached crackerbox structure at the camp, except it had a concrete loading dock for ambulances and supply trucks. It roosted across the road from an asphalt lot next to the Quartermaster Depot. When we arrived, Henry stood under the dock's shake-shingled awning staring across the road at ten columns of ten men each standing in that lot in rubber sheaths—sacks, I guess—as smooth as lamb's skin but as black as auto tires.

An NCO in a wide-brimmed hat stood in front of this whacko detail (buckra and buffalo together, whites and blacks, but more paleskins than coloreds) shouting, "Hop it, gentlemen, hop it!" so the bodies in those sacks pogoed with a floppy sighing sound—like the painful inflation of a hundred huge balloons with a hundred wheezing bicycle pumps. I beheld this show in rubbernecking disbelief.

General Holway's command car had apparently come and gone, and when the *Bomber* pulled into the ambulance dock, Henry paid us no heed. He kept staring across the road, at the encondomed GIs hopping there like big vulcanized fleas. Or maybe he was staring beyond them, to the ball field where Charlie Snow'd leapt, snarled his spikes, and crumpled headlong. In fact, Henry didn't give a cold hoot about the jumpingjacks across "K" Street. Mister JayMac rushed past Henry into the infirmary to see about his center fielder.

Muscles asked Major Dexter, "What in Uncle Sam's army's going on over there—a punishment detail?"

"Nosir, they're volunteers."

"For what, sunstroke?"

"Nosir, a Quartermaster experiment to test the resistance of GI clothing to the natural corrosives in human sweat. Our men in Alaska, the Pacific, North Africa, even here at home, need reliable clothes, and our scientists need reliable data."

"Lord God," Muscles said, "they'll fall out in this heat."

"They'll fall out only when they've received the order to fall out," Major Dexter said.

"I meant they'll *faint*." Muscles replied. "They won't need an order to do it. No wonder yall've stuck em across from the infirmary—save you a few steps."

"Mr. Musselwhite, they're wearing shorts in those sacks, just their skivvies, not full battle dress."

"I don't follow this, Major, not atall."

"We're collecting sweat. The sweat that pools in those sacks we gather into vials. Later, we apply it—the sweat, I mean—to the various fabrics proposed for use in GI clothing. The Quartermaster Corps' scientists measure its effects on the fabrics in question."

I wondered what the hell Mister JayMac'd found out about Snow, and just then he came out of the infirmary with a major in a white coat. Mister JayMac and the major spoke to Henry on the emergency platform. After they'd talked, Mister JayMac slumped against the wall and put his face in his hands. Henry came to the bus. He placed his hands on its roof, just above the door, and arched his body over the gap between the bus and the concrete platform.

When Major Dexter levered open its door, Henry spoke so we all could hear. "Mr. Snow has just passed." (*Passed*.) Then Henry sort of hung there, bridging the *Bomber* to the squat ashen building in which our dead teammate lay.

Charlie Snow, R.I.P.

"It would've pissed him off to've quit with a whole inning left to go," Turkey Sloan said.

"Anyone here who thinks they know exactly how Charlie felt and thought doesn't know the first thing," Muscles said. "Anyway, we have to do what our own consciences say, not what we think the dead would have us do."

"Spose they overlap?" Buck Hoey said.

Henry shoved himself away from the bus, strode across the dock to Mister JayMac, and led him into the infirmary, into the cheapjack corridors of Snow's last passage. I began to cry.

Across the road, the NCO directing the volunteer jumping jacks in their rubber sacks shouted, ". . . two, three, *halt!*" All the paid perspirers stopped on cue; four or five of em dropped to the asphalt from fatigue or fever.

"Rise from your knees and hoist your sack along with you!" the NCO shouted. "Don't spill a drop!"

The sergeant's voice rang in me the way my mother's or FDR's or Jimmy Durante's would—I recognized it. It had the familiarity of a sadistic high school teacher's. The sergeant pulled his hat off, wiped his neck and forehead, and pivoted towards the *Bomber* with a heated, curious face, amazed that till now he hadn't even noticed our bus.

I recognized the topkick. I'd seen him—briefly—in an upstairs cubicle of The Wing & Thigh on Penticuff Strip, the startled mug of a guy caught out on secret holiday. I'd seen that face somewhere else too—namely, aboard the train that'd brought me from Tenkiller to Highbridge. The face belonged to my ravager in the Pullman car lavatory, Sergeant Pumphrey. I got on my knees on my seat and stuck my head through the window facing the parking lot.

"You filthy bugger!" I cried. "You filthy damn bugger!" No stammer, just outrage.

"For mercy's sake, Boles, mind your manners," Curriden said. "We're guests out here."

"You thief!" I shouted. "You p-p-pervert!"

A hundred dripping men in a hundred rubber sacks looked from Pumphrey to the *Brown Bomber* and back again. Pumphrey, DI hat in hand, gaped at me hanging out my window, nothing in his flat muddy eyes but bewilderment and a dull lack of awareness. He just didn't know me, either from the train or from The Wing & Thigh.

"P-P-Pumphrey, you sh-sh-shitass, you owe me f-f-f-fifty b-bucks!" I shouted at him. "You owe me . . ." Because I didn't know how to figure the finer, or cruder, points of his debt, I couldn't say what he owed. I finished, "*Pumphrey, you owe me!*"

Pumphrey put his hat back on and adjusted its chin strap. He pointed a finger at me. "Go easy, kiddo. Wrought up that way, you run a real ugly mouth."

But I'd abandoned the window. I hurried up the *Bomber*'s aisle and out its open door. No one had the sense or the speed to stop me. I rounded the bus's front end, trotted across "K" Street, and got right in Pumphrey's face. He'd magically conjured, or freed from a canvas belt, a weapon—a billy or a swagger stick—and as I neared him, I eyed that stick as a part of the man needing amputation.

"Fifty dollars!" I screeched. "Fifty dollars and my voice back!"

"Your voice back?" Pumphrey spread his arms, crouched, and waggled his swagger stick. I had the feeling everybody near enough to see me had begun to think me utterly deranged. "You stole my voice," I ranted. "You poked it down so f-f-f-far I can't find it. Give me back my voice!" I feinted this way and that, and Pumphrey moved in agitated reaction to my feints, his baton swinging like a hand-held mine detector.

"This kid's nutso," Pumphrey told his troops. "Totally nutso."

I liked him thinking so. I rushed him, grabbed his baton, and yanked. Pumphrey clung hard to the stick, but my tugging laid him out in a full belly sprawl, one arm towards me as his last prideful link to the baton.

I skipped backwards. With each skip, I'd kick Pumphrey in the chin with the toe of my baseball shoe. A few GIs gasped, but most whistled and whooped. "My voice, yall're my v-voice!" I yelled. I dragged Pumphrey towards me, I shook him like a dog with a fetch stick clamped in its jaws.

The sweat gatherers cheered. Every time Pumphrey got a hand or a knee under him, I stretched him out with another savage jerk, and the sweaty GIs shouted like one happy person. If my well-timed jerks didn't keep him down, I'd jump in and kick him in the throat. The troops cheered these kicks even more loudly than they did my stick-twisting and towing.

All of this'd happened so fast the Hellbenders hadn't had a chance to drag me off. But now Curriden cried, "Boles, you're gonna get every last one of us tossed in the stockade!" He was out of the bus, ten feet behind me—with another five or six players behind him for emotional bracing. "Jeez, kid, *stop it!*"

But the dogfaces'd shifted into root-for-the-upstart mode, whistling shrilly and grunting. I dodged my teammates and dragged Pumphrey in elbow-scraping zigzags. He flinched his head from side to side to escape my baby kicks. I spat at him, hawking up bile. He was my prom partner, this decorated s.o.b. with the chevrons on his sleeves, and I could've danced all afternoon with him. Pumphrey stopped me, though. He let go.

I scuttled backwards a few steps and crashed down on my butt. The sweat collectors gasped, then guffawed. Such fickle fans. Such readiness to turn. I had the swagger stick, but Pumphrey leapt forward and flung the heel of his fist into my mouth. Hoey, of all people, scrambled between Pumphrey and me, and Curriden saved my skull by grabbing my arm and slinging me behind him like a sack of onions. The other Hellbenders passed me along from one to the other until a good fifteen yards and four or five teammates separated me from the bloodied Pumphrey.

"That boy has a canary circus in his head," Pumphrey said. "He wants his kidneys pulled out through his dick."

"You took my voice!" I told Pumphrey from behind Dunnagin.

"What does that mean? Listen at you, punk. You're loudern a cannon crump and you say I took your voice."

"My voice and f-fifty goddamn b-b-bucks."

"He's tetched. One daft sumbitch."

"No I'm not," I said. "*I'm Popeye the Sailor Man. I'm strong to the finish, cause I eat my spinach. I'm P-P-Popeye the Sailor Man.*'"

"*'Toot-toot,'*" said Turkey Sloan.

Pumphrey looked dazed, sledgehammered almost.

"Tenkiller," I said. "*Tenkiller!*" I swung from Dunnagin to Nutter to Muscles to Curriden, the better to see Pumphrey's face, the face from the train, the face from the cathouse. The muscles in his face worked from anger to emptiness to puffy chagrin. "If you don't have my money," I said, "take back what you said about my f-f-father."

Pumphrey back-pedaled. "The boy's fevered. Get him to a medic," nodding at the infirmary, "fore somebody hotter-headed than me grabs up a .45 and plugs him."

"I'll shoot you first!" I yelled at Pumphrey, pointing my index finger and cocking my thumb. "*Bang!*"

The dogfaces hopped into a kind of formation while my pals nudged me away from another face-off with Pumphrey, working me around the *Bomber*'s nose and back inside. They pushed me into a seat on the infirmary side. Curriden wedged in next to me, forcing me into a scrunch over the tire well.

"We're damned lucky MPs didn't show up and run us in as goldbricking troublemakers," he said.

"Miserable pricks," I said.

"What in hell got into you? The logjam break? You talked damned near as much as Kaltenborn."

Henry and Mister JayMac came out of the infirmary and reboarded the *Bomber*. Mister JayMac faced us from upfront, while across "K" Street a hundred human sausages, black sack after black sack, hippity-hopped off the oiled lot and up a wooden ramp into the Quartermaster Depot.

Mister JayMac took off his jacket, showing us a dress shirt blotched with heat sweat, grief sweat, anxiety sweat.

"Charlie Snow died in there. He didn't want to, no more than you or I would, but he played every day knowing it could happen and taking as much care as he could not to let it. His luck—usually he had God's own guardian-angelic grace—well, his luck took the day off. It decamped with Darius. We've lost Mr. Snow, and the squeeze in my guts tells me Darius has also cut his ties to us. It suggests to me, gentlemen, that—"

"Darius aint dead, is he?" Trapdoor Evans said.

"No," Mister JayMac said. "He's jes absconded, high-tailed it who knows where."

"Then he could come back," Evans said. "Charlie won't. He aint got the option. So I don't know whyn hell you got to cry over Darius atall. It's Charlie that died, sir, and it uz Charlie carrying us to another CVL pennant."

"True enough," Mister JayMac said. Then he said, "Endicott Mortuary in Highbridge will pick up Mr. Snow's body later today and prepare it for burial at noon Thursday, five hours before the second game of our Quitman homestand. Mr. Musselwhite will move to center. Mr. Evans, you'll start in left until I decide you need spelling or outright replacement. I expect everybody aboard this bus, not counting Major Dexter, to be at both the funeral and the interment. Henry will drive us home. Complete silence, please, till we get there."

46

Quitman's Mockingbirds hit Highbridge for a three-game series, one game an evening from Wednesday through Friday. The day after Darius left, the day after we lost to Mister Cozy's gang, the day after Charlie Snow died out to Camp Penticuff, the Mockingbirds flew in our faces for nine straight innings. Hit after merciless hit. Slash-and-burn base running that bled our will and gave our fed-up fans so many chances to catcall that fatigue set in. Eventually, any stray breeze creaking through the bleachers made more noise than our fans.

In fact, in the middle of the seventh, when Milt Frye asked for "yore prayers in memory of the brilliant Charlie Snow," the stadium went stone dead. None of our fans had known until then he'd died; their earlier calls to put him into the game, given Trapdoor's play, had made perfect sense. Now a silence like surrender took hold. We'd dropped several runs behind, our star had mysteriously "passed on," and a mood of such cobalt blueness had hit our dugout we all felt sick to heart.

Our loss to the Mockingbirds, we learned the next morning, had dropped us three games behind the LaGrange Gendarmes, who'd beaten Marble Springs on the road. The Gendarmes would roll into town Saturday for a double-header, and a singleton on Sunday afternoon. If we lost another game or two to losers like the patched-together 'Birds, the Gendarmes might haul down 1943's CVL pennant before we could gear back up to stop em.

On Thursday, every Hellbender on the roster attended Charlie Snow's funeral at the Alligator Park Methodist Church. Local fans overran the lawn. Most couldn't get inside because pews were reserved for team members, their families, and a perfumed army of Snow's female cousins, who'd just arrived from Richland, Georgia, his hometown. Even a few Mockingbirds, admirers of Snow's style, showed up, and Mister JayMac, who'd put together and was maybe even paying for Snow's obsequies, showed these 'Birds to some ladder-back chairs behind the main body of pews.

Besides the big female cousins (blonde middle-aged women in veils and pastel print dresses), the only other relative there to mourn Charlie Snow was his wife, Vera Jo, an ex-cocktail waitress he'd married in Cheyenne, Wyoming, in 1931. They had no kids. After the service, I heard the weeping Vera Jo tell Miss Giselle, who'd snugged Vera Jo up next to her for the walk to the cemetery, that Charlie'd refused to let her have a baby for fear it'd come a hemophiliac boy. Bleeders, he'd felt, had too briary a path to walk in this life; he couldn't see helping to bring another one into it.

"I ast him, 'Charlie, would you trade all you've got in the way of love and talent for everlasting nothingness?' But he said, 'I'm here; I have to make do. The never-was aint, and don't. Why take the never-was and afflict it?' He couldn't see no other side. Now I wish I'd had me a whole troop of little bleeders to ease the long nevermore he's gone off to."

Vera Jo wept, Miss Giselle hugged her, and the cemetery, set about with water oaks, sycamores, and pecan trees, filled nigh to overflowing with repiners.

Muscles, Curriden, Sosebee, Hay, Sudikoff, and Dunnagin lowered Charlie Snow's casket into the grave on harnesses of fresh yellow rope. The preacher held his Bible over his head and spoke a final benediction. The crowd broke up and threaded back into the sweltering daylight beyond the cemetery. Henry and I, who'd stood poker-spined near the pecan grove behind Snow's burial plot, likewise started to leave.

"Psssssst," hissed the pecan grove. "Psssssst."

We turned, Henry and I. A shadow in amongst the dog-eared green whorls of the hanging pecan branches beckoned to us, pulling back as it did. Park gardeners had carpeted the grove with pine straw and trenched it with banks of white violets and carefully pruned blackberry hedges, a retreat for the sorrowful. Some anonymous soul'd even placed some slab benches in there for the bereaved to perch their tails on.

Anyway, the crouched shadow in that chapel of pecan-bough whorls beckoned to us again.

"It's Darius," I told Henry in pure amaze.

We crept away from the other departing mourners through a break in the pecan grove. Darius, wary as a fox, had gone even deeper into it, at last turning himself at bay alongside the scabby bole of a tree not much thicker through the trunk than he was through the chest. Beside that pecan, he raised a hand to halt us.

"Yall sit right there," he said. "Pretend to rest." He meant on a moss-grown bench. Henry and I sat down on it.

"Where've you b-been?" I asked.

Darius, maybe ten feet away, laid his cheek against the scabbed bark of the pecan. He hugged it like a person. "I've done signed on with Mister Cozy and the Splendid Dominicans," he said. "We play in Lake City tomorrow. Next summer I could be wi the Memphis Red Sox or the KayCee Monarchs. Playing, Mister Henry—not jes driving a bus. Playing."

"Mister JayMac will find you," Henry said.

"Why? Why'd he want to do that? Sides, I'm gon change my name and play a lot more spots than jes pitcher."

"What about Euclid?" Henry said.

The question gave Darius pause. Me too. I hadn't even thought of Euclid, Darius's supposed little brother, and his'd been the first Hellbender face I'd seen upon arriving in town. Home games, Euclid acted as our bat boy, the only Negro kid in that position in the league. He didn't go on the road with us (not counting his stowaway trip to Cottonton) because Mister JayMac had no control over his treatment in other cities. Euclid had a regular presence around McKissic Field, though, and split his time between Darius's apartment and a trim little house near the farmer's market where his mother—Darius's mother, the onetime brown-sugar fancy woman of Mister JayMac—lived.

But Euclid had no McKissic blood in his veins. His mama, Detta Rae Satterfield, had conceived him with an official of the Railway Porters' Union from Atlanta, a man as long gone from Detta Rae as Darius's daddy and not a whit more missed. Just in her forties at Euclid's making, she'd planned the child as the apple of her early dotage—but the manchild's inbred rambunctiousness wearied her, and she'd begged both Darius and Mister JayMac to take him off, to act as stopgap providers and sponsors. They had more or less agreed, with the understanding Darius would do the biggest part of the guardian work.

"Euclid's got his mama," Darius said. "Got Mister JayMac and a house full of white big brothers."

"Have you told him you're leaving?"

"Lord, Mister Henry, I haven't had a chance. He's gon be awright, though, if he jes git told I'm out there pitchin and hittin. You see him, Mister Henry, tell him that. Let him know I aint gone off to dodge him, I'm doing it to grab my life back from the ol McKissic yoke."

"I'll tell him," Henry said. "Now, though, that yoke will rest even more heavily on him."

"He's awready got a yoke—his black hide—he won't shuck off this side of dying," Darius said.

A brown thrasher rattled about in the underbrush five or six feet from Darius, fluffing out the flecked white vest of its chest and tossing twigs and pine straw around.

"I'm deeply sorry bout Mr. Snow," Darius said. "He wasn't no showboat. He had this easy stillness that spoke straight through everbody else's jive and moonshine. That's why I come here today. To say good-bye—to Mr. Snow and likewise to yall, if I could manage it."

"You m-managed," I said.

"Some stuff awready packed in a bag on my closet shef," Darius said.

"Mister Henry, could you fetch it out here after yall's game tonight and set it on that bench? You could, I'd pick it up round midnight."

"Is your apartment locked?"

"Nosir. Aint never been."

"Then I'll do it," Henry said. "But what impels you to venture forth from McKissic House now?"

Darius seemed surprised. "Why, Mister Cozy ast me, he's giving me a chanst at something I awways wanted a chanst at."

"But you could've taken flight long ago."

The interlocked wheels of the pecan leaves above Darius winched his gaze upwards. He searched all that lacy green for an answer. Then he squatted and trailed his fingers in the pine-straw mulch lapping his shoes. The sheer worn-outness of his hunker got to me.

"Better late than no time," he finally said, peering at us up from under. "But why now? Good question, Mister Henry. I think it's cause my life's done crept into its brittlest part, like unto them innings when the whole thing could go either way—depending on jes when the crucial bonecrack happen, and to who. I awmost waited past the snappin point. Mebbe I did. But if I beat it now, mebbe I'll git past my brittle innings and play on through to a stretch that'll heal me, that won't jes shake me down to splinters and shards." Then he sounded angry and near tearful at once: "Don't give me no grief for coming so tardy to a notice of how damn feeble and rickety I'd got. Jes *don't*. I'm moving now, aint I? Ain't I laying grease in my joints, oiling up for tomorry?"

Henry said, "So it would appear."

"Then don't yall chide me for what I cain't nowise fix."

"Darius, we don't," I said.

"And fetch me that suitcase, hear? They's cash money in it, some clothes, a packet of eelskins." *Eelskins?*

"Have no fear," Henry said. "The deed is accomplished."

"One other thing," Darius said. "You still holding them fifty dollars what got bet on our game out to Penticuff, Mister Henry?"

"I believe I am," Henry said, surprised.

"Well, I won that bet. I heard it said so over them PA speakers round the field. Anyhow, I could use the money."

Henry took his wallet from inside his jacket.

"Don't open it," Darius said. "I could use it, but seeing how that game ended, hexed by them damn bats and dimmed by Mr. Snow's dying, I cain't take it. Give it to Mr. Snow's missus. Say it's a token from a admirer."

"Very well," Henry said. "I will."

"God bless yall. And bye."

Darius saluted and backed off. He rattled the underbrush—the blackberry vines, the pine straw, the tiny white violets—less noisily than the pesky brown thrasher still goofing around in there.

47

Laying Charlie Snow to rest did something kindlesome for us Hellbenders. We won that evening's game against Quitman. We won it big, about as big as they'd beaten us the night before. Win one for the Gipper—except Mister JayMac never trotted out a phony-baloney Knute Rockne ploy like that; he simply said our whole season would fall in ruins if we gave away any more games to outright inferiors, namely, Quitman, Lanett, Marble Springs, and Cottonton.

After the game, back at McKissic House, Henry sent me over to Darius's apartment to get Darius's suitcase. He figured he'd have a harder time than me sneaking down two flights of stairs and over the crushed seashells in the *Brown Bomber*'s garage to pull off our mission. This wasn't a con on his part, just smart planning, but I still resented having to do myself what Henry had promised Darius in the cemetery. So I snuck with a foolish what-the-hell orneriness.

I clomped up the stairs in the garage and twisted the knob on the door at the top of the landing. The *Bomber* slept below me like a hibernating metal bear. The apartment door creaked ajar, and I pushed my way inside. I couldn't turn on a lamp for fear someone in McKissic House would notice, and I hadn't had the wit to bring along a flashlight. I ran smack into a wicker rocker, cursed like crazy, and wound up with a small welt on my knee. I felt my way from the chair to a tomato-crate table and from there to another door.

I'd come to a bathroom, with a commode and a bowl-sized sink with naked pipes. I waved my hand until it brushed a string, which I pulled. A light bulb popped on, lifting sink, toilet, and water-stained walls into the glare of old porcelain and scabby green paint.

A pair of mahogany-colored cockroaches scuttled.

I backed out and pulled the door to. A yellow crack showed from floor to lintel. I could navigate by the pale seepage without much fear someone outside would spy the light and sprint upstairs to waylay me.

The main living area—with a bed, the rocker, a metal stool, a pair of upturned crates, and a cardboard chifforobe—had only one true closet. Darius's suitcase lay in it on a shelf two feet above my head. Worse, the case's handle faced the rear wall. I dragged the stool over and climbed up on it on my knees to reach the suitcase.

"*Whachu doin?*"

I swung around. The stool's slippery seat almost launched me to the floor. I grabbed the doorjamb and hung on. Then I spotted Euclid. Euclid lay on the bed, propped on one elbow in his Hellbenders uniform—capless, shoeless, goggle-eyed. He'd scared the holy bejabbers out of me.

"Whachu doin, Danny Bowes?"

"Cr-crimmy, Euclid."

He just stared. Why hadn't he greeted or jumped me at the very beginning? I felt like a burglar.

For the past two evenings at the ballpark, Euclid had served as bat boy, never once asking why Darius'd disappeared or where he'd gone. But Euclid seldom had much to say. He racked bats, toted balls, chased down nearby fouls, and guarded the team's equipment and medical supplies. He lurked like a ghost at the murky edges of our sight. He'd get Technicolor real only when Sosebee and Evans threw tizzies when they fanned or muffed a fielding chance. They'd lambaste Euclid for screwing with their equipment or for getting between them and a kickable canvas bag at the height of their fury.

"What're you d-doing here, Euclid?"

"I ast you fuss."

"Yeah, you did." I swung around on my knees toward the closet shelf. "D-Darius sent me for this." Reaching for the suitcase, I explained what'd happened at Camp Penticuff—an away game despite the camp's nearness and thus a day off for Euclid—and in the cemetery after Charlie Snow's funeral. I unwedged the suitcase and stepped off the stool. I walked to the bed and set the case down at Euclid's gamy feet.

"Lemme take it him," he said.

"It's heavy."

"Ain so heaby. N I sho nough strawn."

"Okay. If you really don't m-mind."

Euclid didn't mind. What I saw as a crushing chore, he saw as a privilege, an adventure. He put on some grungy sneakers, hoisted the suitcase off the bed, and led me out of the room to the landing.

Down the steps he lurched, through the hydrangea and azalea shrubs next to the buggy house, both hands on the suitcase's plastic handle and his feet as wide apart as those of a man swinging an ax. It'd take him forty minutes, if not longer, to make it to Alligator Park, but he'd get there, sparing me and Henry the trip and giving Darius the chance to tell him good-bye in person.

Back in McKissic House, I told Henry of our good fortune. He lay aside a copy of Reinhold Niebuhr's *The Nature and Destiny of Man* and studied me like I'd strangled a baby with its own burp cloth. "He'll beseech Mr. Satterfield to take him along, Daniel, and Mr. Satterfield will be obliged to refuse the boy."

"Not n-n-necessarily."

"I would wager a month's remuneration." Henry rose on his legs with an *"Oof!"* and a sigh. "And when he comes back, he'll be angry or inconsolable."

"Somebody had to go."

Henry shuffled to our open window and ducked through it to the awningless fire stairs. He sat on the top step, a shoulder against the wall, and stared across the silvery okra stalks, elephant-eared squash plants, pole beans, and tomato vines in the victory garden between McKissic House and Mister JayMac and Miss Giselle's Spanish-style bungalow. His presence out there, bookless and mum, hurled waves of reproach back at me through the dingy clapboards—but I didn't much care.

I went to bed.

Two or three hours later, I awoke to house-settling noises and the scarflike strokings of a midsummer breeze. Something—anxiety, instinct—made me lift my head. Even in the dark I could tell Henry hadn't reentered the room. The window still gaped open. I tried to see through it to the fire stairs, but all that swung into focus was shaggy black treetops and a milky freckling of stars. No Henry.

"Henry?" I said. "Henry?"

Maybe he'd squeezed back inside earlier and gone down the hall to the lavatory. Not likely, though; his book stood tented on his bed just where he'd left it, I crawled to the foot of my bed and peered out the window.

After a while, I stepped through the window in my skivvies and stood there gazing on the litter below (empty paint cans, a shiny old wash basin, cigarette packages, candy-bar wrappers, a set of rusty bicycle pedals) and at the plants (sun-flowers, morning glories, pokeweed, mimosa fronds) sprouting from the debris or hugging the house's foundation. No Henry.

Briefly, I was tempted to climb onto the upper railing of the fire stairs and leap out into the night like a Mexican cliff diver. I resisted the urge—it wasn't hard—and monkeyed my way back inside for a smoke.

Henry didn't come back and didn't come back. I stubbed out my cigarette and lay down again. Next thing I knew, dawn—or something pretty close to it—had skinned up to my pillow. My eyelids sprang open, and I kipped over to the window.

Three or four steps below me, Henry sat with his head down and his shoulders bent over his knees. I drummed the sill. He turned his head to track my drumming. For some reason, he'd set up a turtledovish coo that shook his lips and the cordlike wattles of his throat. "Henry, where you been all n-night?"

"Here. Taking the air."

A lie. *A lie!* Which, just then, seemed a shiftier and more insulting concealment than the whole screwy rigmarole of the kayak, the journal, and the Robert Walton letters. Why would Henry lie to me?

You h-haven't either, I stated to say, stammering even in my thoughts. But a long, pale, ratlike snout twisted out of Henry's bosom and I couldn't stammer a word.

The snout belonged to a possum. Henry had a full-grown possum in his lap. I climbed out to see it better, and Henry leaned back to oblige me.

The possum didn't appreciate my visit. It showed me its sharp little teeth, like a cat silently hissing. Its ears looked like grayish black leaves that a hungry caterpillar'd notched, its tail like a hard white rubber cable smudged with pencil erasures. It had black or white whiskers bristling from its snout, even from beside its beady black eyes. It would've won a beauty contest only if the judges included several other possums, and maybe not even then.

"Possums are st-stupid," I said. "Brains the size of p-potato bugs." I took another step or two down. The possum showed me its teeth again.

"Perhaps a little larger than that," Henry said.

I waved my hand at the possum. It flinched away, its pink ball of a nose wrinkling in anger or fear. Henry stroked its back and made the same cooing noises I'd heard from bed. His concern for the beast irked me. I reached out and flicked it on the nose.

"Daniel!"

The possum flinched and jumped from Henry's lap. It scurried down the steps to escape me, but its short legs and the gaps between the steps combined to send it scooting out of control. For a second or so, I feared it'd shoot out into the dark and drop like a furry bomb into the rubbish and weeds—but after it'd bounced three or four steps, its head and forelegs wedged between two balusters and its pink finger-claws went to work to pull it through the gap and back onto the next step down. From there, it waddled all the way down and off into the cover of our victory garden.

"You might have killed her," Henry said.

"You lied to me. You weren't s-sitting here all night. You couldn't have b-b-been."

"I took a walk around Hellbender Pond. I met Pearl. I brought her up here with me to enjoy the view."

"P-Pearl?"

"The poor creature whose life you placed in jeopardy. She had babies—pups—kittens—whatever one calls the offspring of that marsupial. You placed them all in jeopardy."

"I didn't see any b-b-babies, Henry."

"Still, she has five or six. They ride in her pouch. That belly-flop may have injured or killed them." He climbed to the window and ducked through it like King Kong squeezing through a slit in a detergent box.

Henry's anger kept me from asking him more about his lie. Surely it hadn't taken him all night to walk around the pond and bring a possum up the fire stairs. But, if it had, I'd called him a liar and shown myself a scapegoating petty brute.

Later that day, before our final game with Quitman, Mister JayMac came into the dining room. He had poor Euclid with him, a scared ragamuffin in a one-armed headlock, and he addressed us with the kid helpless in front of him. With his free hand, Mister JayMac knuckled Euclid's hair . . . softly. You got the feeling, though, that a sudden move from Euclid would turn that soft touch into a hurtful grind.

"Darius has been gone for almost three days," Mister JayMac said. "Have any of yall laid eyes on him since Tuesday?"

I glanced down the table to where Henry sat, a mound of squash, collards, fried eggplant slices, and popcorn okra piled on his dinner platter. He caught my glance and barely visibly shook his head.

"How bout Euclid there?" Sosebee asked. "Does that little picaroon know anything?"

"Claims he doesn't," Mister JayMac said. "Could be lying. But for now I'm not asking Euclid, I'm asking yall."

"Darius don't check in and out with us," Trapdoor Evans said. "Why should we know moren the boy?"

"All right, then," Mister JayMac said. "From this moment on, I regard Darius Satterfield as AWOL."

"As what?" Fadeaway Ankers said.

"Absent without leave," Muscles said. "AWOL."

"As if our team were like unto the Army?" Henry said *Army* the way a Holy Roller would say *Episcopalian.*

"Insofar as I require that sort of dedication, yes," Mister JayMac said. "Furthermore, it appears Darius has deserted us."

"Which reminds me." Fadeaway looked at Henry. "You've still got our bet money, Jumbo. We'd like it back."

"You lost the wager. The money is no longer yours."

"Well, it was *never* yours, Jumbo. So pass it on back to us fellas it rightfully belonged to."

"You lost the wager," Henry repeated. "The money shall go to Charlie Snow's widow."

"On whose authority did you decide that?" Mister JayMac said. "Vera Jo's being well taken care of, I can assure you."

On whose authority? I looked at Henry again. Would he confess we'd spoken to Darius after he funeral yesterday?

"Do you believe, sir, that the funds of a lost wager should go back into the pockets of those who haughtily wagered them? I do not, even as I deplore the impulse to gamble."

Mister JayMac looked stymied. When Euclid began to fidget, he pulled his forearm tighter under Euclid's chin, and the boy steadied down again. "How many of yall object to giving the fifty to Mrs. Snow?"

"Jeez," Fadeaway said. "I shore aint crazy bout it."

"Okay by me," Evans said sullenly.

Jerry Wayne Sosebee said, "Let her have it. A widow's a widow. Bible says to care for em."

"I'll give the money to her." Henry didn't specify how or when, but nobody thought to call him on that because when Henry gave his word, you could trust him on it—which made me recall, and regret again, the possum-on-the-steps business.

Mister JayMac let go of Euclid, who rubbed his neck. "Eyes out for Darius. Anybody sees him, let me know. Meanwhile, I've put a new lock on his apartment. Somebody, possibly even Darius himself, visited the place last night and made off with some of his belongings. Euclid says it wasn't him. Anyway, yall stay out of there. It's off-limits."

Just like The Wing & Thigh, I thought.

"If he's not at his mama's, Euclid can sleep on the kitchen porch. Show him some courtesy when he's out there."

"Will do," Muscles said, speaking as our captain.

"LaGrange beat the Seminoles again last night," Mister JayMac said, changing the subject. "We're still three back. We've got to beat Quitman again to make our weekend series against the Gendarmes profitable—to rebound completely from our deficit."

"N I go?" Euclid said.

Mister JayMac waved at him like he would've a buzzing June bug, and Euclid banged into the kitchen. The balloon of worry inside me deflated a little; I could breathe again. Euclid, pressed hard enough, might've spilled the news of my midnight visit to the buggy-house apartment.

"Any yall looked at our schedule beyond this weekend?"

"We play LaGrange again next week, sir," Muscles said. "Two games away before we hit Cottonton for three more."

"If we lose to the 'Birds tonight and play like slew-foots against the Gendarmes, we could be eight or nine games out of first by Thursday night—with less than a month to play."

"Accentuate the positive, sir," Muscles advised. "We also play the Gendarmes our last three homies of the season."

"If we're down eight or nine by Friday night, that last series won't mean mouse-scat, Mr. Musselwhite."

"Nosir, I guess not." Everybody sat quiet while we mulled the crucialness of our next few games—*crunch time*, today's sports hacks would call it.

Then Muscles said, "We're sure going to miss Charlie, Mister JayMac."

"If you're alibing in advance, you'd better—"

"I try *not* to alibi," Muscles said, barb-sharp. "Alibi or no alibi, we're going to miss Charlie a lot."

"We've got a roster spot to fill," Dunnagin said. "We can't play our next dozen or so games with nineteen guys when LaGrange and everybody else have twenty."

"I'm working on that." Mister JayMac banged through the door into the kitchen. The rest of us went gratefully back to eating, and Kizzy came in with three hot peach pies on a big lacquered dowel rack.

We beat Quitman again. Henry hit two glowing, cometlike homers, but I had a measly single in five plate appearances and didn't score a run.

That night, Henry heard me crying and sat up. "You did well, Daniel. Not once did you strike out. The Hellbenders won. No need for tears."

"S nothing to do with the d-d-damned game."

"Then what provokes this despondency? Mr. Snow's death? Mr. Satterfield's departure? Euclid's bereavement?"

Who wouldn't've been depressed? I sure had causes enough.

"Tell me," Henry prompted.

"My f-f-father," I said. And that was so. Partly so, anyway. Maybe more than partly.

48

Next morning, early, I sloughed downstairs and sat in a rocker on the porch facing Angus Road—to take the air and clear the dustbunnies out of my head. The lawn lay fresh-mown and dewy. A gray catbird tiptoed over the clippings looking for crickets, grubs, earthworms. I'd watched it for maybe ten minutes, occasional jays or mockingbirds swooping down to inspect the lawn too, when a figure on a bicycle came through the gate and pedaled up the drive towards McKissic House.

The rider wore a split-seam khaki skirt, bobby sox, and a pair of black and white shoes that kids after the war called squad cars. She stood off her seat to get more traction, and her bike squeaked and clattered, swaying from side to side like a boat in a heavy chop. The rider on that contraption was Phoebe. She dropped her bike like a hot rivet and bounded up the porch steps.

"Danny, you seen Miss LaRaina?"

The question—at six-thirty in the morning, even a Saturday morning—seemed damned abrupt.

"My mother," she added.

I'd known what she meant, I just hadn't expected to speak to anyone so early. I shook my head.

"Does that mean you aint seen her or you don't think she's here or you jes don't plan to talk to me?"

"I haven't s-seen her."

"Ya think she's here?"

"I don't know."

"Listen. She hadn't come home by the time I went to bed last night, and she wasn't to home this morning either. Her bed leaves me clueless cause she hardly ever makes it anyways."

The tic under Phoebe's bloodshot eye took me aback.

"Think she took the starch out of Musselwhite last night? Or Curriden? Or whoever the hell happened to ask her home?"

"I don't know."

Phoebe paced the high concrete. I'd seen her upset before, but never this unhinged. She stopped, hands on hips.

"Well, should I go in there yelling 'Mama, oh Mama, please come home'?"

"You'd probably jes sc-scare up a few guys in their sk-skivvies."

"Oh joy. Smelly men in their dingy unmentionables."

"We all sh-shower, Phoebe."

Phoebe cocked her head funny. "You didn't talk to me at Mr. Snow's funeral—not even a piddlin 'Hi!'"

"I *nodded* at you. It was a f-funeral, not a ice-cream social."

"You know, you were a damn sight sweeter when you couldn't talk—pliter, more charmin."

"Phieuw!"

Phoebe ignored my disgust. "So you don't think it'd do for me to stomp upstairs calling for my mama?"

"Nome, I don't."

Suddenly—really suddenly—Phoebe knelt in front of me and gripped my thighs with her small, tough-looking hands. "Take me off from here, Danny. Carry me home."

So I did. I pedaled that doddery bike with Phoebe perched shakily on its handlebars, her dress yanked up to her sunny red knees. Not once in the whole trip did I put my fanny to the bike's liver-shaped and liver-tinted seat cushion, but we never spilled, and Phoebe invited me in for a Co-Cola.

"No thanks. I haven't had br-breakfast." Nervous, I wanted to get back.

"Spose I said a *cherry* Coke, Danny? Would a cherry Coke make you forgit Kizzy's cantaloupes n biscuits?"

Somehow, coaxed along, I wound up in the living room of the Pharrams' boxy little rental house. I knew—as well as, if not better than, Phoebe did herself—she was playing me like a gill-snagged trout, but neither of us knew when she'd yanked or where I'd land. We looked at each other a minute.

Then, like a kid at a pool getting rid of her coverup, Phoebe took off her blouse, showing me a bra—a *brassiere!*—more like a thin bandage than the double-barrelled slingshot I'd've expected. She looked frail, wounded almost, in that bandanna, sort of like the piper kid in that famous painting of a Revolutionary War fife-and-drum group. Then Phoebe's hands fidgeted behind her back, and the bandage fell away. At least three guys on the Hellbenders—Fanning, Sudikoff, and Hay—had bigger bosoms than Phoebe, but the sight of hers—pear-shaped and jaunty—awed me the way a sunset would a man healed late in life of blindness.

Phoebe took my hand and led me to her bedroom, where her bed, unlike her mama's, had a made-up spread and a pretty folded quilt across its foot. She turned the spread all the way back, the pears on her chest hardly growing even when she leaned over to turn it. But how blessed I felt looking at em.

"Now you," said Phoebe, facing me straight on.

"What do you w-want to d-d-do?"

"Jes what they do at The Wing n Thigh." She thought a moment. "With lusty passion."

"We're not m-married. And I thought you wanted a s-s-sojer to, uh, d-do you first."

"*Married!* I bet most human sex's got zero to do with that n not much with love. A place like The Wing n Thigh tells me so. And so does my ever-lovin mama, thout sayin a word." Phoebe's voice softened. "I care for you, boy. S no fault of yores you aint a sojer. Take off yore shirt."

I did. My chest caved to the breastbone, gooseflesh broke out on me like prickly heat.

"More," Phoebe said. "Yore turn to keep it goin. If you care for me too."

There was a desk beside Phoebe's truckle bed, with an old Royal typewriter on it and a photograph of Captain Luther Trent Pharram in his uniform and service cap. I sat down in the desk chair so I couldn't see the ferret-eyed captain, and I untied my shoes. Not much is more ridiculous-looking than a grown man with his shoes on and his pants around his ankles. As I heeled off my shoes, Phoebe headed doorwards in her squad cars.

"Where you going?"

"For a French letter, Danny. Mama keeps em in a drawer by her bed."

"I d-don't read French."

"Goodness, you won't—parlay vooz—have to. Be skinny by the time I git back. Even with Miss LaRaina in heat half the damn time, we prolly aint got all day."

Not much of what Phoebe'd just said made a hoohah of sense to me. French letter. Parlay vooz. Besides, I was skinny even when I wasn't. I recalled from Tenkiller creek dipping just what she had meant to imply, though, and shed my pants and undershorts. For the looks of it, more than anything else, I also rolled down and ditched my socks.

When Phoebe returned, she wore nothing but a pair of satiny green panties. She hardly had any more hips than I did, but I thought her sexier than a thousand Venuses on a thousand pearly half shells. A bird and her bush are worth two out of hand. Me, I cupped my hands over my lap. That wasn't hard because I wasn't either. So far, the circumstances of our tryst—the early hour, the unfamiliar bedroom, the funny out-of-whackness of Phoebe's behavior—had flustered more than aroused me. I kept waiting for an ashtray to bang down on my head.

"I may look right boyish, Daniel, but I already work like a woman. You gonna have to put this on."

"What?"

"The French letter." She held up a bronze packet about the size of a fifty-cent piece, only thicker. Straight off, I knew what it was. We had them in Oklahoma too.

"That's a rubber."

"Yeah, well, that's a right tatty name for it. But call it how you like, you still got to put it on."

For the first time since this whole freaky episode began, I blushed. The blush scalded me down from my ears, face, and throat, to my chest, upper arms, and belly, like a head-first dunk in a turpentine bath. I didn't move.

Phoebe said, "You want to do this or not?"

"I d-dunno. D-d-do you?"

"Why in a pig's eye you spose I had you bike me home? Whym I standing her nearlybout birthday new?"

"Phoebe, I dunno."

My reply teed her off, but she didn't back down an inch from the vengeance she had in mind. (Not a vengeance *on* me, now, but *through* me.) She curled her finger into the waist band of her panties, rolled them down her hips and legs, and stepped clear. I stared. No weedy triangle between her legs, just a crooked, reddish diamond with pale flesh showing around it so the tuft itself stood out in relief—as pretty, and as damaged-looking, as a Special Service Force patch with a bunch of pulled threads. I stared at it, trembling.

"Show me," she said. "It's not fair for this to work jes one way."

I moved my hands. Phoebe knelt with the rubber, which she'd popped from its case. I wasn't feeling horny, though, just bossed and misplaced. Phoebe examined me, tilting her head to one side and then the other.

"No offense, Danl, but they sort of remind me o turkey wattles—the beak n the wattles, you know."

I looked: veiny pink wattles and a small spongy beak. My groin hair was lighter and sparser than Phoebe's, my bashful equipment as useless as a tissue-paper doorknob. Never in my life had I felt so exposed and ashamed.

"Howm I going to git this on you? It's sorta like wrapping a pipe cleaner with a rubber band." Phoebe touched. "Oh!" she said, "lookit the little booger grow."

We wound up on her bed. We worked to fit, then to please each other the way grownups're supposed to do. Phoebe's body resisted even though she tried to make it stop. Her face—her damped lips, her wide eyes—showed the strain of her fight. I fought too—to stay off the crushable basket of her ribs, to stay hard, to slide in her dryness, to keep from running away.

"Why do people do this?" Phoebe said.

"To make other people," I said. (Just then, I couldn't imagine pleasure entering the equation.)

"I'd as lief adopt. Or . . . or die childless."

A breeze drifting through the room dried the sweat on my fanny. I shivered, and shivered again.

"*Don't!*" Phoebe cried. Then: "There's got to be a better way. Ungh. To make other people. Ungh. Got to. *Unnggh!*"

I came, not very pleasingly for Phoebe, or me, or the venerable name of screwing in general. I hadn't had a more interesting morning before breakfast since arriving in Highbridge, or maybe since my own original birthday, granted—but interesting isn't the same as delightful, and I wondered if maybe Henry's creator hadn't hit upon something smart and useful after all, in sexless parenthood.

Phoebe sort of slipped away from the kiss I tried to plant on her cold forehead. I got up, gathered my clothes, and went into the bathroom to lose the drooping rubber, scrub myself up, and get dressed again. When I returned to Phoebe's bedroom, she lay right where I'd left her—except she'd pulled the sheet over her bosoms and masked her eyes with one freckled forearm. Why hadn't we set each other smoldering? You usually get some smoke, maybe even a fire, when you rub two sticks together.

"Okay," she said, not looking at me. "Now tell *everbody*. Ever Hellbender, ever rival player, ever idjit fan."

"I won't tell anybody."

Phoebe sat up, keeping herself covered. "I'm *telling* you to tell, Danny. I *want* you to."

"Gentlemen d-d-don't."

"Crap-doodle. Gentlemen don't eat at The Wing n Thigh."

"I d-didn't either." Phoebe and I'd bumped into different dead ends of the same alley maze. "Besides, Mister JayMac'd k-k-kill me, Phoeb."

"Tote yore sorry sef out of here, you mollycoddle! Git! I hope I never see you—or another slimy willie—long's I live!" She didn't cry, but her bottom lip pooched out and rolled over on itself like a chimpanzee's.

I turned, walked through the house, and yanked open the screen door giving onto the porch.

"You drip!" Phoebe yelled after me. "Tell em all—tell everbody—how you come over n jazzed me!"

I lurched on outside and kicked Phoebe's bike. Then I walked back to McKissic House through Cotton Creek, past a corner of Alligator Park and then row after row of stalls at the barely stirring farmer's market.

49

That Saturday afternoon we had a doubleheader against the Gendarmes, with one game to follow on Sunday, and a two-game series to begin on Wednesday in LaGrange. Five games in seven days against the league leaders, with no more crack at catching them until a three-game homestand at the fag end of August.

"It's do or die," Vito Mariani said before Saturday's opener.

" 'Do or die,' " Turkey Sloan mocked. " 'Do or die.' Lordy, s that the Eye-talian gift of gab?"

"It *is* do-or-die time," Mariani said. "We lose even one today, Turkey, we make up no ground at all."

"You just can't inspire these downhome worldlies with clichés—with bromides and bushwah."

"I shouldn't have to inspire em at all," Mariani said. "That's Mister JayMac's job. But he aint even here."

" 'Do or die.' " Turkey Sloan shook his head. "Gentlemen, forgive poor Vito. He should've said—he *could've* said—'Excel or expire,' 'Put up or perish,' or 'Suck it in or succumb,' but all that twitched his low-grade dago brain was 'Do or die.' "

"Shut up, Sloan," Creighton Nutter said, "or I'll dock you a day's pay for pointless jibber-jabber."

Not *hush*, but *shut up*. Mister JayMac'd left town to find a replacement for Charlie Snow. In his absence, by decree and appointment, Nutter was acting Hellbender manager—with full power to play us where he liked, use his own dugout strategies, and, if needed, fine our bunglers, layabouts, and hooligans. Sloan shut up. He knew Nutter'd gig him in a minute.

Well, whether you like Mariani's "Do or die" or Sloan's "Suck it in or succumb," we lost our opener to the Gendarmes and dropped four games off the pace. Roric Gundy pitched nine innings for our visitors, yielding just three hits and one run. He no longer telegraphed his curveball—someone'd finally set him wise to the telltale flaw in his windup. I struck out twice, remembering Phoebe nude on her knees and her parting cry, *"Tell everbody how you come over here and jazzed me!"*

With Jerry Wayne Sosebee on the mound and better hitting, we won the afternoon's second game and finished three games back, just where we'd begun it. We'd missed Charlie Snow, though—his whip-quick wrists, his reliability at the plate. I also missed seeing either Phoebe or Miss LaRaina in the stands. Had they ducked out on me at this bend in the season? Or galloped off into the boonies with Mister JayMac on his hush-hush, do-or-die talent search?

On Sunday, ten minutes before game time, Mister JayMac showed up in our dugout with Snow's replacement: a thin, pale, twenty-five- or -six-year-old named Worthy Bebout. Bebout had eyes like a Weimaraner's, hair about that sickly color, and a hand shake as firm as boiled elbow macaroni.

His arms hung too far out of his sleeves, and his pants ended too high on his legs, leaving his stirrup socks and sannies exposed and giving him the look of a fannyless stork.

"Mr. Bebout hails from Wedowee, Alabama," Mister JayMac told us. "Played semipro ball with Ipenson Textiles out of Phenix City."

At Mister JayMac's urging, Bebout came along the bench to shake hands. ("Ol pasta grip," Sloan called him later.) He mumbled his hellos, then sat in the dugout's farthest corner, his knees and shoulders twisted in and his pale face as empty and deadpan as a new-bought skillet.

"How come he's not in the m-military?" I asked Henry.

Henry shrugged, but most of us thought Bebout had finagled—or, worse, maybe even deserved—an NP, or "neuropsychiatric," rejection. He gave off the waves of a serious crazy.

Probably because Mister JayMac was still pulling strings to have him enrolled as a CVL player, Bebout didn't start our Sunday afternoon game against the Gendarmes. Four innings along, though, Mister JayMac got a go-ahead from the three-man commission that ran the league (just as Mister JayMac, by wile, guile, and noblesse oblige, wanted it to); and he pinch-hit Bebout for Trapdoor Evans at the first chance.

The score stood at two each. Bebout responded by swinging so hard at three straight Dink Dewhurst curveballs he almost wrapped himself around his bat. The crowd booed, but Bebout just unwrapped himself and shuffled back to the dug-out wearing a quirky smile. With nearly every other Hellbender watching, Bebout dipped a pinch of snuff from the tin in his back pocket, sucked it into his mouth, and rubbed his upper gum with the first joint of his pinky.

The game went on. In the seventh, Bebout made two super catches, a shoestring grab and a last-second leap-and-snatch to prevent a Gendarme extra-baser off the Feen-A-Mint sign. A couple of minutes later, several of us clustered around him in the dugout to congratulate him.

"S okay," Bebout said, refreshing his dip from the snuff tin that'd made a raised circle on his hip pocket.

As Skinny stood in to bat, Junior Heggie sat down next to me. "Ever dip snuff, Danl?"

I shook my head. I was a smoker.

"You ever start, don't bum a pinch from Bebout there."

"Why not? He t-tight with it?"

"Oh no, he'd give you some all right, but the screwball dips dirt," he said. "That lil tin in his pocket's brimful of loose Wedowee dirt! *Dirt*, by damn!"

Dobbs singled. Quip Parris fanned. I drew a walk. Worthy Bebout came up behind me in Charlie Snow's old batting slot. The fans cheered him for the catches he'd made, but set themselves for his second CVL at-bat with show-me furrows on their brows. No one could forget his debut as a hitter: three torso-twisting swings and no contact.

On Dewhurst's first pitch, Bebout rippled again. Twirled, dropped his bat, fell on home plate. A groan went up. This at-bat looked so much like his first one it gave us a powerful sense of déjà vu. Bebout got up, though, and spanked the next pitch—a rolling curve—into the left-field bleachers, and we went on to defeat the Gendarmes five to two, winning the series and moving within two games of first place. So what if Bebout had celebrated his homer by *skipping* around the bases?

In the clubhouse afterwards, Junior asked Bebout why he dipped dirt.

Bebout took his snuff tin, screwed off the top, and studied its contents— rich black Alabama soil—like he expected to find fishing crickets in it.

"It's Wedowee loam. Bacca gives you gum rot. Sides, a fella knows you got dirt in yore snuff tin, he aint keen to borry it. Mazes me."

"What does?" I said.

"Fellas who aint afeared to slide in dirt act like it's gunpowder when it comes to dippin it."

Back at McKissic House, Mister JayMac met in the parlor with Worthy Bebout and all fourteen of his current boarders. He had to find a room for the new kid. Problem was, every room on every floor already had at least two guys in it, overcozylike.

"Any yall willing to triple up?" Mister JayMac said.

The parlor scarcely breathed.

"I cain't have a room to mysef?" Bebout said.

"Think you're so hotshot you deserve one?" Evans asked him.

"Nosir. Got habits could conflick with whosoever gits put with me."

"Like what?" Curriden said. "You eat live roosters?"

"Nosir. I read my Testaments. I speak to my voices. I talk to my dead brother Woodrow."

"Cripes," Curriden said.

"Jes give me a pup tent outside," Bebout suggested.

And until he devised his own indoor answer to the problem, the pup-tent solution actually went into effect. He slept on the lawn in a tent from Sunday, August 1, to Thursday, August 12 (minus five days on the road in the homes of some of Mister JayMac's friends). Then he moved into quarters unlike those of anybody else lodging in McKissic House.

Before that meeting ended, though, he asked Mister JayMac where we'd stowed his "dip fixings."

"Kitchen porch. Nobody here'll disturb em."

Later, fetching a colander for Kizzy, I saw those fixings: a taped cardboard box full of ordinary-looking but fine-grained dirt. On the sides of this box, with a black Crayola, someone had crookedly printed

WEDOWEE SNUFF.

50

Early in August, Lamar Knowles knocked on Henry's and my door. Henry had missed breakfast and lay in bed, face down, one arm hanging off the mattress. As soon as Lamar saw Henry, he apologized and tried to retreat. He had that morning's issue of the *Highbridge Herald* rolled up in one hand, and he bopped himself in the forehead with it for coming up so early.

"C-cmon in," I said. "It's not early, Henry st-stayed out awful late, that's all." I dragged him in and sat him at my desk; I plopped down on my bed. Fan noise had covered Lamar's entrance. It would've taken a cattle prod to goad Henry awake, and I told Lamar so. That news seemed to reassure him. He opened out his newspaper.

"You try to keep up with our parent club?" he asked.

"The Phutile Phillies?"

"Yessir. No other."

"Only to n-n-notice they aint doing so great."

"Well, on Sunday, their owner-president, Mr. Cox, canned Bucky Harris as manager and hired Freddie Fitzsimmons. Take a look." He passed me the sports page.

I read the story. The Phillies had dropped to seventh in the National League standings. This lurch towards the cellar had so irked William D. Cox he'd given the press an eight-page statement accusing Bucky Harris of calling his players "those jerks" and writing them off as losers. Harris had learned of the statement on Sunday evening. On Monday he said if anybody in the Phillies organization qualified as a jerk, it was Cox: " 'And he's an all-American jerk. If I had said any of those things,'" the *Herald* quoted Harris, and Lamar read out loud, " 'I certainly would be the first to admit them.'"

"Whaddaya think?" Lamar said.

I shrugged. "B-b-business as usual."

Lamar tapped my knee. "Mebbe so, but the way you and Jumbo been playing, it could mean a heckuva break for yall."

"No way," I said.

"Sure. Look, the Phils' first baseman and shortstop aint playing worth used ration stamps. In fact, Harris kept switching out different guys at those spots. It could happen, you and your roomy getting a call-up."

"It could n-n-*not* happen too. Or it could h-h-happen to Henry and not to m-me."

"Or vice versa. I don't say this to amp up the pressure, Danny, jes to remind you your play here has *two* goals, winning us the pennant and training yourself for the bigs. Don't forget that second one, kid." When Lamar offered me the paper, I shook my head. "Fitzsimmons might ask the Phils to call yall as replacements for Jimmy Wasdell and Gabby Stewart."

"Charlie Brewster plays short for the Phillies too," I said. "So does Babe Dahlgren."

"Yeah, but Stewart and Brewster'll be lucky to hit .220 together. Dahlgren plays more first base, subbing for Wasdell, than shortstop. He could use yall's help."

Going up to the bigs from a Class C club seemed about as likely as Hitler catching the Holy Spirit and joining the Pentecostals.

"Even if it happened," Lamar said, "you could end up warming the bench like I do now, or gitting two or three starts in throw-away games towards the end of the season. Still, those games could set yall for starters' roles next year, specially if this stupid war's still on."

"I hope it aint."

"Well, if it happens, yall'll deserve it." Lamar blushed. "It'd tickle me silly." He stood up and laid the *Herald* sports page on my desk. "Show that to ol Jumbo Hank. Tell him what I said. If he ever wakes up."

Later, I showed Henry the paper and told him what Lamar'd told me, that the Phillies' new manager, Freddie Fitzsimmons, might try to call us up. Henry read the story. His licorice-whip lips curled into a smile. He slapped his craggy knees.

"Wouldn't that be delicious?"

If I'd ever doubted Henry's desire to leap from the CVL to the neon glare of the majors, his behavior now made me see how deeply he'd planted the roots of his hopes. Maybe Lamar'd known Henry better than I had.

On Wednesday night, we played the Gendarmes the opener of a two-game series in the Prefecture. Strock started Sundog Billy Wallace, the ace of his staff, and Sundog Billy, on better than four days' rest, hurled a flawed masterpiece.

I say flawed because the umping team, with Happy Polidori over at first, blew call after call in the Gendarmes' favor. If a break could go to the homies, Polidori and his crew made sure it did. During the middle-fifth changeover, a bunch of us discussed the situation.

"These officials will home-cook the flesh off our bones," Henry said. "We will disintegrate in their pressure cooker."

"Hit one out to dead center, Jumbo," Muscles said. "No way they can overrule that kind of shot."

"Don't bet on it," Hoey said. "Plate ump's likely to say he stepped out of the batter's box."

"Knock off the alibiing," Mister JayMac said from the dugout's edge, "especially before these guys've beaten you."

"These guys?" Hoey said. "You mean the Gendarmes or the umps?"

"Hush, Mr. Hoey. We'll win or lose this one based on what we do on the field, not on the umpires' whims."

"Trout tripe," Hoey said. "Mr. Sayigh's promised Polidori and his pal a pipe-job from his lovely A-rab daughters if they trip us up this evening."

Mister JayMac jabbed a finger. "Knock it off. You impugn a friend, slander his kids, defame the character of CVL officials, and degrade yourself. Enough."

"Yessir," Hoey said sarcastically.

Creighton Nutter's pitching kept us in it until the seventh. In the top of that inning, I came up with Skinny Dobbs on first—he'd drawn Sundog Billy's only walk of the evening—and one out. I laid down a bunt, dropping it off my Red Stix bat as pretty as a biscuit and about as frisky. Ed Bantling scrambled out from behind the plate, Wallace off the mound, and Binkie Lister in from third. Although Lister made the play, his throw to first baseman Harvey Coombs got there a full second too late to turn my infield hit into just another well-placed sacrifice.

Polidori blew the call. Trumpeted it. Tuba'd it. Thumbed me out. Claimed I'd jumped *over* the bag. Shoot, I'd banged my ankle hitting it.

Hoey, coaching first, exploded. Tore into Polidori like a terrier into a rat's nest. Jigged before him like a runamok Osterizer. It was like he'd forgotten, now I had my voice back, I could gripe for myself. Then Hoey flat-handed Polidori in the chest and staggered him.

"YOU'RE OUTTA HERE!" Polidori shouted, a hand on his heart.

Hoey wouldn't leave. He'd gone flaming bonkers. He cursed and snarled, edging around like a cougar on uppers. Nobody—I mean, *nobody*—could slow his het-up prowl. The crowd leapt to its feet. When they booed, their boos fell like ton upon ton of flapping canvas. It scared me pissless.

Fans started hurling sample jars of Burma-Shave onto the field, heaving the bulk of these samples towards first base. Just before the game, a pair of fast-talking drummers had passed out the samples to every adult male coming in. Now, those jars rained down like porcelain hail. One jar clipped Hoey on the arm. Polidori, Coombs, and I backed deeper into the outfield. Hoey followed after—not to escape the barrage but to keep cursing the hapless Happy Polidori, for the jar that had hit him had no more effect than a poppy seed.

The PA announcer scolded the crowd. The police threatened arrests. In the outfield, Hoey continued to fume and storm. Finally, Mister JayMac sent Muscles, Curriden, Fanning, and Sudikoff out there—at some peril, for the crowd started catcalling—to subdue Hoey and drag him, thrashing and frothing, if need be, into the clubhouse. This took several minutes because Hoey tried to elude our press-gang, meanwhile heaping dogshit on Polidori's pedigree.

"You ignorant dago!" Hoey dodged Mister JayMac's posse. "Your mama bore you purblind on muscatel!"

"You bigot!" Polidori cried. "You froggy bilge mucker!"

Muscles tackled Hoey behind second base. The crowd cheered. Curriden, Fanning, and the others picked him up and, with Muscles gripping his belt, littered him back towards our dugout like a battlefield casualty. I scurried along behind them: Polidori had called me out and wouldn't change his mind—not in front of these fans, not after blotting up so much of Hoey's abuse.

Once the cops, the PA announcer, and our rescue squad had restored some order, and the groundskeepers had a wheel-barrow full of Burma-Shave jars, Sundog Billy struck out Heggie to squelch our "rally." Nutter shut down the 'Darmes after a lead-off single in the bottom half of the inning, and so on and so on, until the bottom of the ninth, with the score locked at two apiece and half the citizenry of LaGrange trying to deafen us with cowbells.

"To hell wi the Hellbenders! To hell with em all! Tonight they go down! Tonight they do fall!"

I felt nose high to a tic's rump. All the vocal scorn had begun to get even to Nutter. Veteran or no, he could sense the rising heat. He threw two wild pitches in a row and walked the Gendarme shortstop Tucker DeShong. Bang! Mister JayMac lifted Nutter for Vito Mariani, who got the next two batters to pop up. One more out and we went into extra innings.

Cliff Nugent, LaGrange's center fielder and best clutch hitter, came up. Mariani got two strikes on him and wasted two pitches trying to sucker him into a strikeout. His fifth pitch, a curve, broke on the outer edge of the plate—too close for a man with a couple of strikes to let go by—and Nugent drove it on a dying clothesline into the right-field corner. *Foul.* Six inches foul. Maybe a foot.

Happy Polidori watched the ball sail over his head and skid on the divoted turf. He faced second base and chopped his right arm down to signal the drive fair. Nugent sped up again, rounded first, and churned for second. Skinny Dobbs couldn't believe the call, but he chased down the ball, which'd already caromed off the fence in foul territory, and tried to throw it home to keep DeShong from scoring. The throw reached Dunnagin on three feeble hops, too late, and the stands swayed like racketing freight cars.

"*Mais oui!*" chanted the crowd: "*But yes!*"

The Gendarmes had beaten us by a run and stretched their lead to three full games.

Polidori'd blown the most crucial call in the entire ballgame. Mister JayMac couldn't protest it because a hundred or more people had jumped the fences to pound their heroes on the backs, and Polidori and his fellow ump had already hurried off the field.

In the clubhouse, Mister JayMac paced a strip of concrete like a badger.

"Home cooking!" Buck Hoey shouted. Because he'd showered after his ejection, he wore civvies, like Mister JayMac. Turkey Sloan'd already given him the partisan Hellbender take on Polidori's gaffe.

"They stole this one!" somebody yelled.

"Bastids ambushed us!"

"They bought Polidori's ass, thass what! They bought it!"

"*YALL HUSH!*" Mister JayMac cried.

We hushed. Mister JayMac had his chin on his breast-bone and his hands fisted in the pockets of his pants. He'd stopped pacing, but one leg jiggled, like the leg of a hound agitated by a belly rub.

"I don't think Mr. Polidori japped us once this evening—till that call on Mr. Nugent's liner to right."

"He had it in for us all evenin, sir!" Curriden said.

"I asked neither your nor anyone else's opinion."

Curriden shut his eyes. All of us wanted to denounce the one-sided calls and the unruly crowd. Hometowning hurt. It'd cost us an important game. But we stood in our sweaty smelly funk waiting for the Word.

"Mr. Polidori made beaucoups of mistakes," Mister JayMac said, "but all but the last one stemmed, I believe, from misapprehension and the bullying of the crowd—which, let me remind you, pays its money to supply that ingredient. Rafe Polidori knows his business. Under ordinary circumstances—"

"Mister JayMac," Muscles said. "Sir, I—"

An upraised hand cut him off. "—he calls em as he sees em, and he usually sees them pretty well. Tonight, gentlemen, what we witnessed in the bottom of the ninth did not signal any blatant Gendarme bribery, but

Mr. Polidori's personal response to the shenanigans of Ligonier Hoey two innings earlier."

"Sir—"

"Don't interrupt, Hoey." (Not "Mr. Hoey," just "Hoey.") "Mr. Polidori should be an impartial ajudicator on the ball field, but, like all of us, he consists of flesh, blood, and certain deep-seated prejudices bespeaking the imperfection of his humanity. What was brittle in him snapped when you baited him beyond his God-given level of tolerance."

"You're blaming me for the bastid's call?"

"For precipitating it. Yes I do. Your actions in our half of the seventh stank on ice."

"I was standing up for Dumbo here. For the Hellbenders."

"You like to got Mr. Boles conked with a shave-cream jar and the game ruled a Helbender forfeit. Mr. Boles escaped a concussion, thank God, but your team, I remind you, lost."

Nobody spoke.

"Stay tonight and tomorrow with the family putting you up, but don't report to the Prefecture tomorrow. Read a magazine. Listen to the radio. Don't show up here. Stay away."

"Am I suspended?"

"Let me think on that." Mister JayMac looked us square in the eyes. "Go on and shower."

Bebout offered Hoey a pinch of Wedowee snuff, to cheer him up, but Hoey knocked Bebout's tin to the floor.

On Thursday night, without Hoey, we beat LaGrange seven to one behind the pitching of Fadeaway Ankers. The next day we traveled to Cottonton, where we swept a three-game series from the Boll Weevils. Meanwhile, the Gendarmes lost two of three to Opelika, sending us home tied for first with them.

We had almost four full days of rest before our next home game—against the Eufaula Mudcats. During that time, Mister JayMac got busy, mostly over the telephone. On Thursday, Henry took me aside in the parlor to spell out the latest personnel developments as transmitted over the club grapevine.

"Mister JayMac received permission from the Phillies to trade Mr. Hoey," Henry said. "He has done so."

"Tr-trade Buck Hoey? Where'll he g-go?"

"Scuttlebutt"—Henry was proud of this word—""Scuttlebutt has it that the Gendarmes have bought him for a handsome sum of cash and a utility player."

I had a sudden edgy heart thrill. Buck Hoey, gone! The last guy on the club who still called me Dumbo, the only one who remembered—who held a grudge about—the incident that'd resulted in him wearing boot-blacked carpet slippers for a few days. Why, though, had Mister JayMac traded him to a team in a nip-and-tuck pennant race against us?

"Because Mr. Sayigh offered him the most lucrative return on his property," Henry said.

I wondered about Hoey's family and their rented house. What would happen to Linda Jane? To Matt, Carolyn, Ted, and Danny, my accidental namesake?

"As a concession to the hardship spawned by this trade," Henry told me, "the Hoeys and their children may stay in their dwelling rent-free until September. Mister JayMac proffered Mr. Hoey this compact, and Mr. Hoey took it, albeit bitterly."

"If he's a Gendarme, he c-can't live in Highbridge."

"A gravel-quarry owner in LaGrange who admires Mr. Hoey's aggressive style has refurbished a shotgun hovel only blocks from the Prefecture. Mr. Hoey will dwell there rent-free."

During my talk with Henry, I'd heard a muffled hammering and some other peculiar noises. Suddenly, Worthy Bebout stood in the parlor, a carpenter's belt cocked on his hips.

"Think Mrs. Hoey'd like a man around the house while her hubby's living away?"

We stared at Bebout, like he'd just asked our opinion of baby eating or nude evangelism. "I mean nuthm smutty. Jes thought she might want to rent the bed space and cook me some meals while our season lasts."

"Mrs. Hoey likely doesn't have any b-bed space," I said. "The Hoeys got f-four younguns."

"Then I reckon I aint been wasting my time." Bebout picked up a rucksack next to a parlor sofa. "Come see."

McKissic House had a storm and potato cellar you reached through a door set under the staircase to the second floor. Bebout'd spent his morning down there transforming one end of that clayey hole into a bed chamber.

Seeing it, Henry and I understood why he'd asked about boarding with the Hoeys. A Spanish dungeon would've been cheerier.

"Sorta pneumonia-y," I said.

"Sorta buggy too." Bebout yanked the overhead bulb so it threw a splash of light into one corner. Camelback crickets clung to the pocked clay wall and sproinged around the floor. A row of blackened canning jars sparkled on a plank shelf at shin height. The jars held gloopy sludge. I began to quease.

Henry and I beat it out of there as fast as politeness would let us. In the parlor we found Kizzy sprawled in a cushy chair, the hem of her dress hammocked between her legs and a mortuary fan tick-tocking away in her hand. She *never* used the parlor. She hardly ever sat down.

"Kizzy, you s-sick?" I asked her.

"I zausted, that's what I am. Used out. Nigger-weary."

"But why?"

"Bless you, Mister Danny, cause I aint got no hep. Look like the McKissics trying to chase me into a tirement home. Wunst upon a time, I could count on Miss Giselle hauling herself over here to hep do breakfuss. No mo. She aint showed here five days running, and the ony scuse she got is, the heat done prostrate her. Like it's a *e*-lixir to me."

Henry said, "Mrs. Lorrows, you could recruit some of us to help." He kept glancing into the foyer, though, like expecting Bebout to trudge into view with a dug-up cadaver.

"I awready gots me two of you ballplayers a week, but this week's two is good-fo-nuthin clumses."

I looked at Henry. "We c-could help, c-couldn't we?" I *liked* to cook. Mixing up biscuit dough reminded me of arts and crafts in grade school back in Tenkiller.

But Henry'd already turned away. "I must borrow Mister JayMac's automobile. I must take a trip." He waved good-bye with a stiff flapping motion and lurched through the dining room on his way to the McKissics' bungalow.

"Darius was mo hep than Miss Giselle ever knew," Kizzy said. "I sho do miss him."

51

Hoey's replacement from the Gendarmes—I never did learn how much cash money Mr. Sayigh had to ante up too—arrived on the Friday before our weekend homestand against Eufaula. Friday the thirteenth, a bad-omen day . . . if you bought into such malarkey. The replacement player turned out to be Wilbur "Fat Boy" Fortenberry, a bookend, physique-wise, for Pete "Haystack" Hay. Mister JayMac introduced him to us at a breakfast I'd helped Kizzy fix.

"Say it aint so," Quip Parris said. "The *Brown Bomber*'s gonna need a new pair of shocks."

"Don't fry no mo chicken fo dinner!" Muscles shouted at the kitchen. "Take Fat Boy here out to the nearest hen coop and let him inhale—at'll save everybody time!"

But Fortenberry had only one plump biscuit and two slotted spoonfuls of yellow scrambled eggs before bidding us farewell and riding out to Cotton Creek with Mister JayMac. He had a family—a roly-poly wife and two Fortenberry doughboys—and Mister JayMac had arranged for him to rent Charlie and Vera Jo Snow's old house.

Henry said not a word, either during Fortenberry's debut or afterwards when Muscles second-guessed adding a thirty-year-old tub of bear grease to our roster. Henry had veered off into Cloud-cuckoo-land, like he hadn't come all the way back from Alabama yet. His business over there yesterday had somehow stalled his swim through the summer. Or else Friday the Thirteenths didn't agree with him.

Anyway, I spent the morning after Fortenberry's arrival washing dishes with Sosebee and Fanning and cleaning snap beans for the pregame meal we'd eat at two. Kizzy worked nonstop to turn out this ritual feast. Even married Hellbenders had invitations, although usually only Sudikoff and Hay bothered to come. Mister JayMac almost always ate with us too, but after helping the Fortenberrys settle in, he'd posted home to see about the heat-fatigued Miss Giselle.

Even with Mister JayMac absent, the dining room was louder than a party suite in the Tower of Babel. Pork chops, chicken, country-fried steak. A dozen different vegetables. Four kinds of pies. Given the direction of the wind—south-by-southeast—every person in town must've had a saliva buildup.

Suddenly Phoebe burst through the kitchen's swinging door. I hadn't seen her for nearly two weeks, and some of the words she'd spoken then still chimed like breaking soda bottles in my memory: "*I hope I never see you—or another slimy willie—long as I live!*" (Just for instance.)

My appetite died. My inner organs blended themselves into an ebony glop like that trapped in the storm cellar's canning jars. Phoebe probably hadn't come to testify to my tenderness as a lover. I didn't know why she'd come, but her presence—to one side of Muscles's head-of-the-table spot—put everybody, me especially, on notice that our meal would cause bigger problems than gas and oversnug belts. She let Muscles finish saying grace, bless her, and Muscles offered her his chair.

"No thank you. I've done et. Go on, Muscles, sit back down, okay?" She waited, arms behind her back, until Muscles obeyed her. Dishes began to pass, serving spoons to unload, silverware to glitter. Phoebe wouldn't meet my eye, or I wouldn't meet hers, each of us glancing away whenever the other made a feint at contact.

"Well, Missy, what can we do for you?" Muscles said.

"Stay away from my mama. Let her be the decent person she was till Daddy went overseas."

That riveted everybody's attention. Silverware stopped clinking, and the radio in the parlor—tuned to a soap opera—sounded a couple of knob twists louder than it had a second ago. Embarrassment settled like a clammy rubber sheet.

"War's a horrible thing," Muscles said—consolingly, I guess.

"Men are horrible things," Phoebe said.

"Careful, mouthy girl," Evans said. "What's a titwren of a piece like you know about men anyways?"

"Moren you'd ever figger, Mr. Evans."

Oh God, I thought, she's come over here to tell everybody about our Saturday-morning folly. She wants Mister JayMac to drop me in creosote, roll me in feathers, and send me back to Oklahoma hanging upside-down from a cane pole.

"Like mother like daughter." Evans lipped an ugly sneer.

Reese Curriden cracked Evans in the mouth with his elbow. Then he took Evans backwards to the floor, choking him, his thumbs like screw-bolts under Evans's jaw. Five or six guys stood up, but Henry and I stayed seated, benumbed or maybe just too confused to act. Evans, flat on his back in the toppled chair, waved his hands at his shoulders to show he gave up. Curriden let go just as Muscles was about to drag him off.

"I say, 'Men're horrible things,' and yall jump like red-neck crackers to prove it," Phoebe said.

Evans stayed mute this time. So did everybody else, and Phoebe walked from Muscles at the table's head to Henry at its foot, without seeming to care she had interrupted an important pregame energy-stoker. Some of our fellas—Bebout, Fadeaway, Sosebee—dug in and ate, but most of us waited for a payoff, a backfire loud enough to call Mister JayMac. Phoebe's eyebrows sparkled with sweat. Her skin shone like a swimmer's.

"How many of yall've cuckolded my daddy?" she said.

Fadeaway lifted his head. "Cold-cocked your daddy?"

"Cuckolded," Dunnagin told him.

"S what I said, cold-cocked." Fadeaway spoke around a mouthful of greens. "How many of us've knocked her daddy's lights out? Her question don't make sense."

"How many of yall've *slept* with my mama. You Waycross boys got cow flops for brains, Mr. Ankers?"

Fadeaway started to rise, but Curriden rose with him, and Fadeaway dropped back into his chair again.

"Gimme a show of hands," Phoebe said. "All yall who're guilty as scarlet sin, raise em high."

"Phoebe," Muscles said, "this is a bad idea, child. I've had some damned bad uns myself, and I know."

Phoebe jumped all over Muscles. "You could start everbody off, Mr. Musselwhite. Whynt you lift yore own hand first? A team capn should set a zample."

"Phoebe, I—"

"Put your damned ol hand up, Lon K. Musselwhite! You think I want this to take thole rotten weekend?"

Muscles raised his hand. He didn't do it halfway either. He stuck his arm straight up, a macelike fist bristling at the end. He kept a grum face too. When nobody else at table did anything, Phoebe turned to Reese Curriden.

"You too. You don't think everbody down at Hellbender Pond on the Fourth figgered you and Mr. Musselwhite was tusseling over spare ribs, do you? Git yore hand up.

"Phoebe, a hand in the air here's sort of like crowing in the rooster room," Curriden said.

"Yo're *proud* of screwing my mama? Of doing dirt to a sojer overseas?"

"Well, Phoebe, some of us're just called to a different set of arms."

Evans guffawed. A few other he-manly Hellbenders—Fanning, Parris, Mariani, Fadeaway—giggled like Camp Fire girls walking by a cherub statue. My queasiness took on a lumpy sharpness, ice cubes shifting in a plastic bag.

"If you aint ashamed, raise yore disgusting hand!" Phoebe stabbed a potato with a serving fork and held it over her head, meaning, Git em up, git em up, git em up.

Slowly, Curriden raised his hand. Now he and Muscles made a leery pair, the only two players ready—sort of—to admit they'd abetted Miss LaRaina in her infidelities.

"Who else?" Phoebe said. "Phoebe sees all, Phoebe knows all. Fess up while it'll still git you right with God n me." No one joined the hands-up club. "All right, Mr. Musselwhite. All right, Mr. Curriden. I forgive yall, you sneaky sonsabitches."

Forgiveness did it. Suddenly, Dunnagin, Sosebee, and Parris raised their hands, Parris several beats slower than the other two. Five out of fifteen men, a third of the Hellbenders in McKissic House.

"Swell," Phoebe said. "Any more?"

"Miss LaRaina put the mash on me last season," Sosebee said. "Before yore daddy'd even got his tail out of town."

"For God's sake, Jerry Wayne, shut up," Dunnagin said.

But Phoebe'd already walked around Henry and laid a hand on his shoulder. Her hand looked like a doily draped over the crown of an armoire. When Muscles disgustedly lowered his arm, so did the other four men. Phoebe didn't care.

"Hey, Mr. Clerval, didn't Mama vamp you into her bed too? Men's big as you jes seem to pull her, automatic-like."

"Then she musta run up on Quip there in the dark," Worthy Bebout said.

"Can it," Muscles told Bebout, pretty mildly.

Henry's blotchy face crawled with embarrassment. "I have always treated your mother with courtesy, Miss Pharram. And she has always reciprocated, in word and deed, my regard for her. I decry this depreciation of her character."

"Bushwa n Burma-Shave, Mr. Clerval. Why do you lie to me? Yo're her latest throb."

Henry scraped his chair back and stood up. Phoebe's hand slipped from his shoulder like a wind-nudged scarf. "I rarely lie," he said. "Nor do I now. Mrs. Pharram and I have never been paramours. Such allegations wound her more deeply than they ever could me; I resent them unequivocally on her behalf. Excuse me. I can hardly eat under these conditions." He left the dining room and trudged upstairs. Noisily.

Phoebe sat down in his chair without trying to pull it back up to the table. Her feet didn't reach the floor. "So which one of yall's seeing my mama now? Or is it one of them rotten creeps out to Cotton Creek?"

"Phoebe, your mama's got standards," Muscles said. "She never messes with married men. That reduces the possibility she'll hurt anyone but herself and her . . . her friend."

"Whatm I, Mr. Musselwhite? A hank of hair? And what's my daddy, cannon fodder?"

Kizzy came in. I had the feeling she'd heard everything and bided her time until a chance to play peacemaker came up.

"Hush now, Skeeter. They gon hear you aw the way over to the farmer's market. Let the mens eat. Come in here with me and have some coconut cream pie." She eased Phoebe out of Henry's chair and stepped her back towards the kitchen, hugging Phoebe to her with a flour-dusted arm.

"I don't *like* coconut," Phoebe said. "I told you that bout a zillion times, Kizzy. A zillion n one."

"Then don't eat it. Have a slice of my apple instead."

At the door, Phoebe made Kizzy halt. She turned back towards the table and pierced me with a glittering, green-eyed stare. "Did you tell em, Danny? Did you make shore ever last one of em knew?"

I couldn't speak.

"Knock it off, Phoeb," Muscles said. "This is crap."

"What's to t-t-tell?" I said. "There's nothing to tell."

Phoebe's eyes seemed to pinwheel a question at me, then a look of understanding, and finally a thank-you—or, at least, a grudging smile.

Kizzy banged her hip into the swinging door and more or less dragged Phoebe through it into a realm of wood-stove heat and Kizzy-made delectables.

52

E ufaula had a decent ball club. Early in the season the Mudcats'd climbed to second on several occasions, jockeying with Opelika and LaGrange for the league lead. They always played us tough, especially when Zaron Childs pitched for them. That Friday evening Childs shut us out on a two-hitter, yielding safeties only to Bebout and to Norm Sudikoff as a pinch hitter. Milt Frye announced the Gendarmes had routed the Mockingbirds over to Quitman. Their win dropped us one game off the pace, with ten games remaining.

In the clubhouse, after Mister JayMac had praised Childs for his pitching and retreated to the ticket office, Curriden groused, "Childs threw great, but Mister JayMac's great-niece softened us up for the bastid at dinner."

"Don't blame Phoebe," Muscles said. "We stunk."

"Look who got our hits—Bebout, who didn't know what she was talking about, and Sudikoff, who wasn't there to hear. Sidewinder Childs didn't beat us. Phoebe Pharram did."

"It's a poor sort of man who can't overcome some vexatious talk to play up to his capabilities," Henry told Curriden.

"Listen to Mr. Zero-for-Four," Curriden said. "And didn't that little gal's 'vexatious talk' chase you clean off?"

"Can it," Lamar Knowles said. "The game's over."

For some reason, everybody canned it. We all showered and dressed in a starched and testy silence.

On Saturday afternoon, calmer and better rested, we drubbed the Mudcats with a barrage of extra-base hits and a sideshow of stolen bases. Meanwhile, the Mockingbirds beat the Gendarmes. These results locked us and the 'Darmes in another first-place tie, our second of the month. We just had to keep the heat on Emmett Strock and his gang.

Eufaula's manager, Grover Traffley, worked to stymie our momentum. He called on Zaron Childs, on one day's rest, to face us again. Childs yielded nine hits, but only three runs, and the Mudcats beat us by scraping up a patchy rally in the top of the ninth and holding us scoreless in our final at bat. Naturally, the Gendarmes beat the 'Birds again, and we fell a game off the lead with eight games left, our last three a shoot-em-up showdown at McKissic Field.

Henry went out the window. He figured me dead to the world, but I heard him. The heat had come down so pitiless on Highbridge that, before lying down, I'd yanked my sheets off my bed, carried them down the hall, and soaked them in cold water in the shower stall. Then I'd spread them on my mattress, stripped naked, and stretched out on them across from our fan. Doing all that had miffed Henry, but he'd've never admitted it, even if I'd driven bamboo slivers under his fingernails. Me, I didn't care. Somehow or other, I had to get cool.

Anyway, I heard him when he went out. Without even trying, a galoot Henry's size could make a window-sash weight bump in its groove. He took up so much space that, when he left, you felt a Henry-shaped pocket in the air. I sat up, my chest already dry as talc, my backside still damp from the clammy sheets.

Had Pearl the opossum come back? I crept over and peered out. Henry'd already reached the fire stairs' second-floor landing. I ducked back inside and pulled on a pair of jeans, nearly zippering my cock in my rush to dog him.

"It aint Pearl," I told myself on the fire stairs. "Not even Henry'd give up this much sleep to befriend a possum." A judgment I right quick proved.

Henry'd angled off into the pole-bean rows making up one corner of the victory garden between McKissic House and the bungalow behind it. I crept barefooted down the fire stairs and over the grass after him. A craggy chunk of moon silvered the garden, and Henry's head and chest poked up so high I could see him picking his way even among the curling vines. Although he'd sworn a few days back he seldom lied, I knew he'd lied to me at least once. Also, his old impersonation of a human being was a Big Lie, one he ached to make true.

Anyway, creeping through velvety squash leaves, I half expected Miss LaRaina to spring up like Ruth amid the corn, a gleaner of leftover male hungers come to feed not only her weird Elimelech's appetite but also her own. So it dumfounded me when the voice I heard talking to Henry belonged not to Phoebe's wayward mama, but to Mister JayMac's porcelain-pretty wife, Miss Giselle.

"Why here?" she said. "Darius's old apartment would've been more private." Leaves hid the woman from me, but even lying belly down with my cheek on a root-laced mass of clay, I knew her voice.

"Just so." Henry's voice was a gentle bassoon. "Discovery there would mean disgrace for us. Discovery here would afford us yet some hope of preserving our reputations."

"But it isn't very amenable to . . . to play." Miss Giselle laughed, girlishly. I couldn't remember hearing her laugh before, and the feel of it sent a troop of caterpillars marching pleasantly down my spine.

"Giselle, we mustn't proceed on this precipitant course."

"How you talk. I love how you talk." In fact, Henry's protest tickled the stew out of Miss Giselle. She laughed harder, pulling herself to Henry's chest. "You sound like somebody out of a Brontë book."

"On the road, I have few other—"

"Shhh. You can find a happier line to jilt me with than, 'We mustn't proceed on this precipitant course.' How about 'To go on as we have would be curtains for us both'?" She laughed again, but I didn't know why.

"It's scaring me, this series of trysts," Henry said. "We expose to heartbreak even those from whom we hide."

"Hide? Who's hiding?"

"Don't torment me. Neither tease nor quibble."

For a moment, Miss Giselle and Henry stopped talking. I heard them hug, her crinoline against his T-shirt, and wriggled to see past the squash leaves and coiling bean vines to their meeting place—but with no luck.

Then Miss Giselle said, "Come with me, big fella," chuckling, and I heard them rustling through the garden again. I rose to my knees and crawled hard myself. They went even faster, rattling foliage and snapping stalks, so I penguin-waddled after.

Following them got trickier the farther into the garden we went. Tomato plants and other knee-high crops began to replace the beans and walls of tasseled sweet corn that'd shielded me earlier. I could see better, but so could my prey and then—*whoosh!*—the stalks in the next garden section got taller, a copse of leafy half-pikes. The lovers vanished into it like Hansel and Gretel into an enchanted wood. Henry sank beneath the okra stalks, and Miss Giselle eased into his lap.

"And why have *you* led *me* here?" Henry said.

"To rekindle your ardor," Miss Giselle said. "Forget all musts and shoulds. Behold the okra and read my mind."

I edged nearer. The okra leaves shivered. The gouged profile of the moon spilled a soft pewter on their stalks and seamed pods. The pods stood up or out, like tapered hard-ons. If leprechauns could reach the height and hot-bloodedness of men, this was how their members would look in the real world: a forest of tender, silver-green pricks.

"Long have I desired to free myself of animal compulsion," Henry said. "Until you, I believed I had."

"Well, I want to enslave myself to it. Don't let cowardly scruple send me back to my dry, dry marriage."

"You seek revenge for infidelity and neglect?"

"Well, sure. But more of what I want has to do with . . . holding and being held. Riding your body to places I didn't believe I could visit anymore."

"I am a monster. A freak. The caprice of a tortured man's vanity."

"Henry, you're beautiful."

"I should offer you that homage."

"Holding me, you do. I feel it from the inside out."

"Even when I cry, '*Kariak!*'"

"Cry what you like. I can't reproach a man whose emotional faithfulness to his only wife has outlasted her death."

"No. But we must end this deceit, this betrayal of Mister JayMac and our better selves."

"This sweet deceit. Call it sweet."

"Don't torment me. Neither tease nor quibble."

"Shhhh. Look here." Miss Giselle grabbed an okra stalk.

"Don't. It will produce an insupportable itch." He meant that the prickly hairs on the okra pods would.

"I have you for that. Here." Miss Giselle snapped off a pod several inches long. "This one should have been picked already. They're tenderest—unlike you—when smaller. See. This one has a horny rind."

Henry flung the pod away. It whirled through the okra forest and struck me on the neck.

I touched my grated skin and lay flatter.

"Do you like gumbo?" Miss Giselle said. "The clear sweet ooze of the pod? The way it thickens and quickens?" Sitting on Henry's knee, she kissed him on the forehead.

"But we make nothing together," Henry whispered. "I have lifeless seed and you a desolated womb."

"We make each other happy." Miss Giselle's hands clutched his shoulders and her hips rose and fell to an unforced rhythm.

I lay on the blush-fed thumping of my heart.

"*GOD!*" Henry shouted, a thunderclap. I expected McKissic House to empty, our teammates to come pouring out to see what'd happened. I didn't dare move. After a time, Henry and Miss Giselle moved again, crinoline on cotton. I hugged the earth.

"Take me to Darius's old place. You can't leave me now."

"But the possibilities of discovery, scandal, disgrace—"

"Now, Henry. *Now!*"

Henry gathered up Miss Giselle. He carried her through the okra, tomatoes, squash, beans, sweet peas, cucumbers, and corn towards the Bomber's garage and the room above it where Miss Giselle's faithless husband's bastard son had lived and grieved the biggest part of his resentful adulthood.

As soon as they'd gone, I crept quietly back to McKissic House.

Two hours later Henry came to bed. I pretended sleep. He pretended to believe it. But for an hour or more, he sat on his mattress with his arms around his knees, a gray hulk in our cramped and steamy room.

53

Playing ball, you forgot the war. Riding the *Brown Bomber*, you read the papers or talked about it. The fact my dad had died in the Aleutians made me listen up to any news from the Alaskan theater.

On a road trip to Lanett, I read a story in the *Highbridge Herald* about Allied forces invading the island of Kiska, only to find—after taking beaucoups of casualties in the bedlam and fog—the Japs had already evacuated it. In other words, we'd defeated an enemy no longer there. The press called it the "blunder at Kiska." Nobody could figure out how, or when, the Japs'd managed to pull their otherwise doomed troops off the island. I showed this story to Henry, who'd been riding with his head lolling against the window and his hands twitching in his lap. He read it and handed the paper back.

"Stupid," I said. "We let em get away."

"The resourcefulness of the Japanese spared thousands from the maw of death. Why do you long to glut it?"

"They're Japs, Henry—bloodthirsty, conniving m-monkeys."

"A few may deserve your censure. Many do not. War homogenizes the good and the bad. I can only applaud those who escaped. Had the Allies shown a like wit, resisting panic and withholding their fire, no one would have died."

"That's crap," I said. "The Japs left mines and b-booby traps behind." The newspaper said over a hundred men on the destroyer *Abner Read* were hurt or drowned when their ship hit a mine. How could Henry side with the lousy Japs?

Henry said nothing.

Dunnagin leaned over our seat back. "How'd they manage to get away so clean? The Japs?"

"Aleutian fogs swirl and deceive," Henry said. "The Japanese used them, and the capriciousness of fate, to avert many deaths."

"You mean they got lucky," Dunnagin said.

"Perhaps everyone got lucky."

"Cept them poor guys on the *Abner Read* and the d-dogfaces blown to sm-smithereens by b-b-booby traps!"

Henry grunted. The war that had once appalled, now just seemed to bore him. He let his head loll against the window again, where it was buffeted by Sudikoff's herky-jerky driving and maybe by troubling thoughts of Miss Giselle. No wonder he couldn't hold the war on a front burner.

Three seats ahead of us, Bebout leapt up and had some sort of weird schizo fit. Waving one arm, he baptized everyone around him with spastic finger flicks, like a holy-roller on speed.

"Norman!" he yelled. "NORMAN!"

Sudikoff was driving. "What?" he shouted back. "*What?*"

Bebout went into a long nonsensical spiel about the angel Gabriel and his brother Woodrow and who-knows-what-else? I'd never heard anything like it.

Sudikoff said, "Cain't yall git that joker to shuddup? If you don't, I'm like to have a accident."

Mister JayMac laddered back to Bebout, put an arm around him, and eventually got him quieted down.

"What a walking Looney Toon," Curriden said. "I think he's snapped."

Bebout rested easy the last thirty miles of our ride—but in Lanett, getting off the *Bomber*, he dumped a tin of Wedowee Snuff into Lamar Knowles's shirt pocket and patted it, like a mama giving her son a fresh handkerchief. Lamar took it as a joke, thank God, and the incident blew over.

Still, a lot of us worried Bebout would have one of his spells during a game. Thank goodness, though, a ballpark and playing ball seemed to calm and invigorate him at the same time—and, except for Henry, he played as well as any of the rest of us against the Linenmakers.

On Thursday and Friday evenings, despite a lot of noisy support from the Lanett crowds, the Linenmakers couldn't stay with us. We beat them seven to two and thirteen to zip. Henry had three home runs in the series—his concentration during this road trip rarely faltered—and twelve RBIs. He now had thirty-nine homers on the year and led his nearest competitor in that department—Lon Musselwhite, who had a solo shot on Friday—by a dozen and a half.

Given that the CVL season had only half the number of games played by the majors, Henry had a better home-run percentage than Ruth'd had in his top three seasons with the Yankees. In the bigs, with the same homer percentage he'd had in Highbridge, Henry would've hit *eighty-two*! Even Lanett's fans cheered when the third of his blasts sailed over the right-field wall into an egret-lined branch of the Chattahoochee.

In the same series, I did okay myself—seven hits in eight at bats. Every time Henry walloped a fence-clearer, I trotted home ahead of him. In fact, all of us feasted on Linenmaker pitching, and when we left on Saturday morning for Opelika, we rolled out with a certain greedy regret. Our second victory in Lanett, coupled with a rare Gendarme loss to the Boll Weevils, had lifted us into another first-place tie.

Lou Ed Dew, the manager of the Orphans, had his team loaded for Hellbender. They'd dropped six games back and could finish in a tie for first only if they won all six of their remaining games while we and the Gendarmes booted ours. In other words, the Orphans had *no* chance—we concluded our season with three home games against LaGrange. Either the Hellbenders or the Gendarmes would win the pennant. The Orphans still had a shot at second, though, and a chance to scuttle our dreams before we returned home. Lou Ed Dew meant to scuttle em.

That weekend series—a doubleheader on Saturday and a singleton on Sunday afternoon—turned prickly as soon as the Orphans' ace, Smiley Clough, took the mound. He threw high and tight at least once a batsman, a whistling low-bridger loosed with an oops-I-didn't-mean-to-do-that smirk. You didn't know whether to go after Clough with your bat or to sympathize with his control problems. Time we realized he needed his skull cracked and his smirk rubbed south, Clough had a deuce-to-zip lead and a breaking ball Nutter swore took its unhittable kink from a smear of KY jelly. Whatever, Clough went the full nine innings and shut us out.

The second game of the twin bill didn't go much better. Dew had scared up a gangleshanks kid from the Florida pan-handle to pitch for him, a kid named Marion Root. Root threw a sidearm speedball that shrunk a fraction of an inch for every foot it covered to the plate. By the time it reached us, it looked like a petrified hummingbird's egg.

ROOT FOR ROOT said a banner in the outfield. Orphan fans did, and he carried a two-hitter into the ninth.

Luckily, so'd our own sodbuster ace, Fadeaway Ankers, and in our last bat before extra innings, Henry polewhacked a Root hummingbird egg all the way to Sea Island, scoring himself and Worthy Bebout, who'd taken a sidearm fastball in the ribs swinging for the bleachers. We held on in the bottom half of the inning for a two-to-goose-egg win. The split kept us in a tie for first with LaGrange.

That night Henry told me Marion Root'd go up to the bigs. Not only that, Henry said, but Root would make a reputation for himself the equal of Bob Feller's or Johnny Vander Meer's. Not long after he'd pitched against us, though, Root reported for induction into the Army and spent the next seventeen weeks at the Infantry Replacement Center at Camp Wheeler near Augusta. He died the next winter at Anzio with the U.S. 45th Division, two weeks after going overseas.

Sunday's game against Opelika deserves no commemoration. We lost it. The score was sixteen to three, and none of our runs was earned. No excuses— the Orphans wrapped, waxed, and shellacked us.

One truly screwy thing did happen in the bottom of the eighth. On an easy liner to center, Bebout cried, "Woodrow! Woodrow, you take it!" and dropped to his knees. The ball carried over Bebout's head, allowing two runners to score and the hitter to reach third as Skinny hurried to chase it down.

"What the hell was that?" Curriden yelled at Bebout.

"He missed it!" Bebout shouted. "My sorry brother flat-out missed it!"

Amazingly, the Gendarmes lost to the Eufaula Mudcats in the Prefecture. The entire season, then, boiled down to our final three games against them at McKissic Field.

54

Almost every day the *Herald* featured the Hellbenders in the right-hand column on its sports page. Once they ran a photo of me—my bleached-out face and chest above the inky smudge of my knickerbockers—under the headline "Tenkiller Speedster Hopes to Help / Our Hellbenders Lug the Bunting."

A husky spinster lady who used the byline O. A. Drummond had written the piece, with more appeal to front-office press releases than to interviews or personal reporting. You often saw Miz Drummond at the stadium, dressed, even in the dog-days humidity and glare, like a fox-hunting freak: knee-high boots, tweed skirt, puff-sleeved blouse, snap-brim tweed hat. She never visited the clubhouse—the Hellbenders would've hooted her out in a skink's eyeblink—but always sat at a typewriter in the press box, three chairs from Milt Frye.

Anyway, I'd sent a copy of Miz Drummond's story to Mama and folded another copy into my wallet as a pick-me-up after a poor performance. Not long after getting my vocal cords back, I'd gone to Double Dunnagin with my ratty clipping and showed it to him.

"Whattuz l-l-lug the b-b-bunting m-mean?"

"To win the pennant, kid."

"So why d-didn't sh-she say s-s-so?"

"Cause she's a writer and lug the bunting's more poetic You oughta be asking Sloan."

By the end of August, though, we'd put ourselves in a place to lug the bunting, for real, and Miz Drummond's daily squib for the *Herald* was plugging the final LaGrange series like the next Joe Louis bout—twice on the front page, next to wire reports about U. S. naval operations around New Guinea and the Solomons. Highbridge had pennant fever. If FDR wanted the CVL and Mister JayMac's club to boost the morale of our locals, well, we were doing a bang-up job. Even a runt like Trapdoor Evans—speaking talentwise—couldn't walk through the farmer's market without drawing autograph hounds.

Henry didn't borrow Mister JayMac's Caddy on any of our off days leading up to Friday's game. Far as I could tell, he didn't once rendezvous in the victory garden or in Darius's old room with Miss Giselle. He slept in his own bed, getting six or seven hours of shuteye a night. He read two very brainy books Anatole Maguin's *The Pariah* and Victor-René Durastante's *Self-Evolution and Self-Extinguishment*. (I jotted the titles down in my notebook.) He'd focus on two pages at once, close his eyes like a camera shutter, and then page forward again—a method I hadn't seen him use before, like maybe he wanted to speed up his reading to beat the end of the season.

"Those any g-good?" I asked him about his books.

"Provocative. I wish I had them in the original French, but Mrs. Hocking could get them only in these somewhat clumsy translations." He finished the shorter book—the Maguin—in an hour, but spent most of one afternoon on the Durastante.

What Henry did Thursday and Friday, I don't know. I took Phoebe to a matinee at the Exotic on Thursday (*Above Suspicion* with Joan Crawford and Fred MacMurray) and spent my entire Friday—until going to the ballpark—clerking with her at Hitch & Shirleen's.

We didn't moon over each other, or try to smooch, or even spend much time holding hands. We just hung around and talked, or hung around and didn't talk, and that horrible morning in her house over to Cotton Creek fell further into our pasts, like it'd happened in 1938 to somebody else. When Phoebe had to wait on a customer or ring up a sale, I sat on a stool behind the counter and struggled to read *The Pariah*.

"That any good, Ichabod?"

"I d-dunno. Not much happens. This Frenchie in Senegal lives for a year in the basement of a government b-b-building, and nobody knows he's there. Or'd c-care if they did."

"Sounds a lot like Mr. Bebout."

"Henry l-liked it."

"Well, Henry's a genius. A certified aigghead."

What could I say to that?

"He's the nicest ugly man I ever knew," Phoebe said. "But put up that stupid book and talk to me."

So I did.

*

No one could say Buck Hoey had fueled a late-season surge by the Gendarmes because they'd played well all season. On the other hand, Hoey almost singlehandedly kept the 'Darmes' juices flowing in August—by his bullyragging, drive, and sheer revengeful orneriness. He wanted his new club to beat his old club so bad Emmett Strock would've had to shoot him to keep him off the field. In fact, the Hoey-for-Fortenberry-plus-cash trade quickly began to look like the worst player swap Mister JayMac had ever engineered.

You see, Strock put Hoey on third base, for Binkie Lister, where he didn't have to cover so much infield as he did at short. That move, along with Hoey's natural grit and his ill will towards his former boss, gave him the energy to raise his batting average sixty points. He also began using what he knew about the windups and body talk of CVL pitchers to steal bases (not really like him) and his Durocherlike talent for hurling insults to gig rival batters from his spot at third (exactly his style). He got under the skin of hitters, who rewarded his obnoxiousness by losing their cool and wasting their at bats. As a result (we heard), the same Buck Hoey who'd once launched a barrage of Burma-Shave jars in the Prefecture had become the darling of LaGrange. Even Binkie Lister, reduced to a backup role, liked Hoey; and Cliff Nugent, the 'Darmes' biggest star, recognized Hoey's value and didn't begrudge him his popularity.

Luckily, we had the Gendarmes at McKissic Field, where, what with the neck-to-neckness of the pennant race and all the rabble-rousing feature stories about us in the *Herald*, we also had a sellout. An oversell, in fact.

I dressed out in a stock room at Hitch & Shirleen's, across the shady street from the ballpark. Fans began to arrive four or five hours before the game's scheduled 7:30 P.M. starting time. Whites and coloreds, GIs and civs, occupied the stadium like a celebrating army.

Some of these folks spilled into Hitch & Shirleen's looking for Co-Colas, sweet cakes, chewing gum, tater chips, you name it, at cheaper prices than they'd get them for at the stadium's concession stands. Phoebe's daddy's folks returned to help her handle the extra customers, and I walked across the busy street on my spikes for our pregame meeting at six-thirty. Autograph seekers and advice givers orbited me like gnats. It took fifteen minutes to cover a hundred yards, and I heard some fans from LaGrange grousing that ticketsellers at a couple of gates had turned them away.

"F yall want to see this one," a man said, "we may have to buy some nigger seats, it's all that's left."

Inside, the stadium seemed to have inflated like a balloon. It creaked and wobbled and bulged. And our het-up Hellbender crowd carried us through that killer series' opener, boosting us to a foot-stamping win. Nutter hurled a tidy five-hitter, and Henry blasted a seventh-inning home run that may've come down in the Himalayas, with Yours Truly on board by way of a bunt single. Hoey didn't do diddly in the game. On my trot towards third base, I didn't even look at him.

"Nother pissant hit," I heard him say. He meant my bunt, not Henry's homer, but I said, "Too bad it cleared the fence," and jogged home with the only score that really mattered in that game. Behind me, Hoey chewed his vinegary cud.

An inning and a half later, when I stabbed a liner to my right for the game's final out, fans poured onto the field, and a brigade of GIs marched to Penticuff Strip singing "Take Me Out to the Ballgame" and so many off-color jody chants that fistfights with offended Good Ol Boys broke out.

The win put us a full game up, with only two to play.

In the clubhouse, Mister JayMac said, "Win tomorrow, and that's it. Except for our honor, I wouldn't much care if yall shanked Sunday's game. The 'Darmes could take their cheap win and ride home crying."

"Amen!" said Jerry Wayne Sosebee.

"So win tomorrow and wrap er all up."

"Win tomorry!" everybody shouted. "Win tomorry!"

Mister JayMac collared me on my way to the showers and dragged me over to Henry. "Yall meet me out to the gazebo exactly an hour from now, hear?"

"Yessir," we both said. Mister JayMac vanished into the echoey pandemonium of the understands. Henry and I looked at each other. Then Henry ducked out of the locker room in his uniform—to walk back to McKissic House.

"Gentlemen, jes a few minutes of your time." Mister JayMac paced the springy flooring of his gazebo on Hellbender Pond while Henry and I rode a bench against one of its walls. Mosquitoes whined, and ghostly patches of steam rose from the smoky mirror of the water, the stars overhead as sharp as buffed-up fork tines. "Does either of yall have any idea what I'm about to say?"

"Sir—" Henry began.

"Hold on now. Actually, you see, *I'd* prefer to break the news, even if you have a hunch about it, Mr. Clerval."

Henry'd gone stiff as a cigar-store Indian. His hip next to mine felt like a curved plank of hickory. He feared, I suddenly realized, Mister JayMac had heard from Miss Giselle's own mouth the damnable story of their *affaire de coeur*, and other body parts. Henry had a hand on one knee, and that hand began to twitch—the only movement except for his breathing I'd noticed so far. Me, I suspected a different reason for our interview with Mister JayMac.

"Few would admit you fellas are a sight for sore eyes," he said, "but yall've been that to me—even if sometimes I rode you damnably hard and put you up wet."

"Kizzy keeps us in fresh towels," Henry said.

Mister JayMac raised an eyebrow. "Listen. The Phils want yall for the rest of this season. Freddy Fitzsimmons prevailed upon Mr. Cox to get him some top-notch help from the minors, and the help he wanted was a coupla fellas from this lowly Class C organization. Yall'll catch a train out of Highbridge on Tuesday and report to the Phillies soon as you get there, likely for some serious playing time."

"Hot dog!" I said. "Hot diggety dog!"

"Great joy." Henry gripped his knee to keep his hand from twitching. "Great, unexpected joy."

"Unexpected? Henry, a man with forty-plus homers should be asking what kept him stuck at this level until now."

Henry said, "Very well. What did?"

"I did. The Phils weren't going nowhere, but we looked to be. God forgive me, Mr. Clerval, but *I* kept you here. I made Fitzsimmons cool his heels."

"Then God forgive you indeed."

"Yall could even start. Jimmy Wasdell, Philly's first baseman, has only two or three homers all year, and Gabby Stewart's hitting about .200 and trading out at shortstop with Charlie Brewster, no Ruth himself. In other words, yall could actually claim those starting spots."

"*Hot dog!*" I got up and did a jig. When I'd finished, Mister JayMac looked out across the pond.

"Don't know what *I'll* do to replace you next year, but yall're on your way. The Phillies may be too. Jes don't forget who gave you your shot when you start exercising the scoreboard riggers at Shibe Park." Mister JayMac stumped down the steps, as if to hike across the lawn to his bungalow.

"Sir!" Henry said.

Mister JayMac turned around.

"Why did you apprise us of our promotions tonight?"

Mister JayMac said, "You mean, before we've clinched? I guess it's because I can never deny myself any small pleasure. I like my dessert first. I flip to the back of murder stories to see who done it. A long-standing vice."

"If we don't clinch tomorrow," Henry said, "you will berate yourself for breaking the news so soon."

"Probably. Almost certainly."

"Then make no general announcement until the pennant is in our grasp. Danny and I will remain discreet as well."

"Excellent," Mister JayMac said. "Yall get some sleep." He angled away from us, a shadow in rumpled seersucker. Frogs croaked, fireflies blinked, and the smell of scorched peanuts drifted through the gazebo, oiling the hot night and the steamy surface of the water.

"A dream fulfilled," Henry said. "A chance to prove myself against the best."

I pulled Henry off the bench by his shirt front. He had to duck his head to keep from bumping it. "B-big leaguers," I said. "You and me."

Henry lifted me to his chest, squeezed my puny bones. In that cockeyed bandbox, he solemnly waltzed me around, swinging me a foot or so off the floor, wagging me like the bob in a grandfather clock. He smelled of soap, rubbed baseballs, and wet clay. I let him drag-waltz me, step-step, step-step, frogs and cicadas chorusing like bullroarers and pennywhistles. At last Henry put me down.

"He'd have t-to admit I could p-pl-play," I said.

"Who?" Then Henry understood and laid his hand on my head like a priest giving a blessing.

Miss Giselle stood at the foot of the gazebo's steps, a phantom in a pale organdy gown, white or trout-fin blue. Maybe it was a dressing-gown, maybe her thirty-year-old ballroom getup. Anyway, I sort of boggled. A damped-down glowworm sheen seeped from her. The helmet of her silvery hair shone dully too. She looked old, Miss Giselle did—not old-old, in face and body, but like she'd been shipped forward to us from a temple in Thebes, say.

"Congratulations, Henry."

Henry nodded a wary thank-you.

"Up to Philadelphia, away from Highbridge."

"I'm g-g-goin. Good night."

"Stay here, Daniel," Miss Giselle said. "Who knows what I'll do if you leave?"

"Go in, Giselle," Henry said. "It's late. The air feels humid and plaguey."

"Plaguey. Only you'd say plaguey and mean what you mean, but the air's just fine. I like it."

"Giselle, this charade must not persist."

"If you leave, I leave too. I see no charade, but a union that only days ago you also believed in."

"Woman, please, we do ourselves no glory, protracting this deception, indulging what cannot be."

"Ha." Miss Giselle quoted from a book that Henry knew: "*Everywhere I see bliss, from which I alone am irrevocably excluded.*"

"You say a lie, as once I ignorantly lied to myself. The truth is that bliss eludes the mass of us. Go back in."

"Get me to a nunnery, eh? And how have you come to regard yourself as one of 'us'? The 'mass of us'? You're a murderer, Henry. Hell's tortures are too mild for this . . . *sniveling* rejection you shy at me, you wretched devil!"

Henry sat down again. "Don't," he said, so softly it was almost a message to himself. "Whence did I come? What is my destination?"

"Philadelphia," Miss Giselle mocked. "Say we're finished—mince no words—and I'll go inside. You'll never lay eyes on me again. Just look me in the face and say it."

"That painful act I've already accomplished."

"If you meant it, you can do it again."

Henry sadly shook his head. "Our furtive meetings must cease. You may not accompany me when I leave."

"Then you've slain me, Henry. Slain me."

Henry's face was so moony white it seemed to reflect the trout-fin blue of Miss Giselle's gown. Miss Giselle sent him a bitter kiss off the back of her hand and pivoted in the shadowy grass. Henry watched her stride away.

"Fornication—filth and incest." Henry didn't mean to be funny, and I couldn't laugh at him because his whole body had shaken with the blurting of those curses.

"What'll she do?" I asked him.

His very skin sagged on him. "Forget me. Devote herself anew to the licensed desiderata of her husband."

I didn't know what that meant, but the grief in Henry's voice was plain enough. It quirked my own upbeat mood about our call-up. When we returned to McKissic House, his slumped shoulders vexed me every step of the way. I wanted to do a maypole dance around him. Instead I dragged myself to bed, in a house already dark and snore-riven. And Henry paid no heed to Christ's advice to set all anxiety aside.

On Saturday, the Gendarmes humiliated us. I don't remember the score, and I've struggled for years to forget my two muffs at shortstop. Buck Hoey led the charge against us, with four hits in five tries and an incredible catch in the eighth of a real stinger off the bat of Worthy Bebout. Hoey's catch killed our only feeble whack at a rally.

"Tied," Mister JayMac told us, like we didn't know we'd bungled our chance to coast. "Any need to explain what yall'll have to do tomorrow, gentlemen?"

"Excel or expire," Manani said. "Put up or perish."

"Cripes," Turkey Sloan said. "Knock it off, Vito."

"Suck it in or succumb." Manani caught Sloan's gaze and held it like a carrier gunner lining up a Zero in his cross hairs. "*Do or die.*"

Suddenly, "Do or die" no longer struck even our poet Turkey Sloan as the hackneyed saw of a low-grade dago brain.

55

On Sunday afternoon, the Gendarmes played us tough again. Their ace, Sundog Billy Wallace, dueled our rookie star, Fadeaway Ankers. Neither had his best stuff, but Wallace was always a scrapper and Fadeaway'd learned from Dunnagin how to pitch when his speedball had taken a holiday. By the middle of the fourth, the scoreboard read three to three.

Buck Hoey had picked up right where he'd finished yesterday's game. Nothing existed for him but himself, the ball, the bases, and the base paths. He didn't bullyrag or chatter, he just centered himself and played.

In the top of the fifth, at first again on his third single of the day, Hoey took a crouching lead, broke on Fadeaway's move to the plate, and geysered up out of his slide, after hooking around my tag, in a swirl of red dust. He called time to brush himself off, and when he did, I touched him on the hip with the web of my glove, a half-hearted effort to get the base ump to throw a thumb at him. No go. Because of the timeout, the fact Hoey stood off the bag slapping red-orange dust from his pants didn't mean cracklin bread.

My meaningless tag got Hoey's attention, though. He cocked awake and jabbed me in the gut with his finger.

"Uh-uh-uh," said the base ump, Little Cuke Gordon. "Hands to yoresef, Hoey."

"S just a love poke. Only one Dumbo's gotten all season. Less, of course, Jumbo's buggering him."

"Put a lid on it, Hoey, or clean it up."

"Christ, Gordon, you sound like a bluenose." Hoey returned to second. "And, Dumbo, you poor gazoonie," he said, kicking some dirt at me with the side of his shoe, "tell Mister JayMac he lost Highbridge a pennant the day he dealt me. Tell him it was a damned stupid thing to do."

I flipped the ball back to Fadeaway and returned to my spot at short. The only way to deal with an asshole, I thought, was to wipe it—which us

Hellbenders intended to do on the field. Hoey, meanwhile, tunneled into himself again, taking his lead, daring Fadeaway to pick him off. No need. The next hitter up fouled out to Curriden, ending the inning.

Later, during the seventh-inning stretch, with our organist playing a medley of show tunes and Cokesbury hymns, Milt Frye spoke out over the PA system: "S a great time to visit our concession stands. Slaw dogs, nickel Co-Cola, boiled peanuts, and, one of yall's favorites, Cracker Jacks. *Patriotic* Cracker Jacks—a prize in ever box, not a one made in Japan. . . .

"I've jes got some big news for immediate release. Namely, two of our worthiest 'Benders—though I don't mean Mr. Bebout—have earned train tickets to Canaan. Yessir. Come Tuesday, Jumbo Hank Clerval and Battlin Danny Boles will be bona fide big leaguers. The Phils need help, and these fellas're gonna go up to provide it. We know what they can do. Now them pitiful long-sufferers in the City of Brotherly Love're gonna find out too.

"Whadda. Yall. Think. Bout. That?"

Nearly everybody on hand went loopy. Cowbells. Hooting. Clapping. Ooga horns. You'd've thought FDR'd just announced the unconditional surrender of Hitler and Tojo.

In our dugout, Henry peered gloomily down the bench at Mister JayMac. "Who chose this ill-timed moment to divulge our good fortune?"

"It wasn't I," Mister JayMac said.

"Atta way a go!" Lamar Knowles told Henry and me. "I knew it. Didn't I tell you, Danny? Didn't I?"

Several other guys, including even Sosebee and Evans, came over to congratulate us.

The crowd rioted in place. Pretty soon we could hear it chanting, "Jumbo and Dumbo! Send em out PRONTO!"

Henry waved his arm in disgust. The crowd'd seemed to've forgotten the game in the hullabaloo of Frye's announcement, and the Gendarmes had another reason, like they needed it, to come after us like rabid badgers.

"Hush em up!" Mister JayMac shouted down the bench at Henry and me. "Get out there and tip your caps!"

Henry and I, the Mutt and Jeff of the CVL, clambered onto the field to greet the misplaced huzzas of our fans. We tipped our caps. The fans stamped their feet, whistled, or stood to cheer. From their own dugout or their places on the field, the Gendarmes squinted and frowned.

Henry raised his arms. *"ENOUGH!"* His bellow silenced the crowd. "We have work yet to do! This display bids fair to undo our enterprise!" He put his cap back on and galumphed grimly back to our dugout, with me more or less in tow and the crowd stunned into mass catatonia.

"Great," Mister JayMac said, scowling. "Jes great."

"Loose lips sink ships," Henry said. "But no one in this organization could see that prophylactic slogan's application to the situation here."

"I didn't authorize the announcement," Mister JayMac said. He called Euclid over. "Go up there and ask Mr. Frye who told him about the call-up. You got me?"

"Yessuh." Euclid shot out of the dugout and hustled up the steps to the press box.

"Cmon!" Mister JayMac yelled. "Draw a line under what Milt Frye jes blabbed to the world! Grab the flag!"

So happened, Henry had the lead-off spot against Sundog Billy in the bottom of the seventh. First pitch, he smacked it like a Bobby Jones tee shot. The snap of his bat was like a molar cracking on a jawbreaker. Everybody rose, even us guys in the dugout. If this was a balata ball, a big league cull, Henry'd just launched it into low earth orbit, a pre-Sputnik Sputnik.

The score stood four to three, Hellbenders.

Curriden fanned, as Wallace bore down. Heggie one-hopped a nubber to the second baseman for our second out. Euclid came back into the dugout. Henry buttonholed him even before Mister JayMac could get over to him.

"And what did you discover?"

"What did Mr. Frye say?" Mister JayMac chimed in.

Euclid stood dwarfed by the two men. He kept his eyes on the tobacco-stained concrete floor.

"Speak up, Euclid!" Mister JayMac said.

"Say Miz Giselle tol him," Euclid whispered.

"Holy fire! How'd she even know?"

"She overheard," Henry said. "And this is my recompense."

"Your what?"

Henry waved off the question and sat back down next to me as Euclid slunk back to his own roost next to Bebout. Dunnagin ended the inning by skying a hard-hit but shallow fly to Nugent in center. We had a one-run lead and two more Gendarme at-bats to survive. We survived the first un, but couldn't up our lead in our own trip to town.

In the top of the ninth, Fadeaway suckered Jim Keating, a pinch hitter for

Wallace, on a third-strike sinker into the dirt. Dunnagin trapped it with his mitt and swiped it across Keating's backside for a quick-thinking assist on the putout. One down. Two outs to the CVL championship. The crowd sounded like the ocean in a hurricane swell.

Buck Hoey came to the plate. *Bingo!* A blue darter into left center, right over my head. Hoey rounded first like he had it in mind to keep on coming. Musselwhite rifled the ball in to me, though, and Hoey retreated to first, mumbling something that got a weird grin from Henry, a half-innocent, half-psycho grin.

Nugent came up. He hadn't had a good night, but he led Strock's boys in hitting, with an average approaching .330. I expected Mister JayMac to signal Fadeaway to walk him, to get to the slumping Jed Balmore, LaGrange's second baseman, but Mister JayMac refused to put the go-ahead run on base this late in the game. He wristed a paint-brushing gesture at Fadeaway, a sign to paint the plate's corners—to give Nugent nothing in the fat of the strike zone.

Craftily, Nugent worked the count to three and two. He fouled off four pitches that plate umpire Grayson Dover—Mister JayMac'd pulled strings to keep Polidori out of this series—might have retired Nugent on, otherwise. Then, Fadeaway's tenth pitch, Nugent hit a low, twisting shot at Junior between first and second, almost on the outfield grass.

On the pitch, Hoey'd broken for second. He had to leap Nugent's ground-hugger to avoid putting himself out, but his skip step didn't slow him. As I ran to cover second, Junior bobbled the roller, got his grip again, and whipped a sidearm throw towards second in the hope, the near certainty, I'd get there in time to catch it, toe-kick the bag, and fire to Henry for a game-ending double-play.

Junior-to-Dumbo-to-Jumbo. A riff on the famous Dumbo-to-Junior-to-Jumbo combo.

Hoey was barreling. I picked off Junior's stinger at belt height. Hoey slammed the dirt and slid towards me feet first, cleats high. His spikes looked *big*, a grizzly's fangs ready to tear. When I kicked second, one of Hoey's shoes bit me in the groin and ripped into my left inner thigh. I began to fall. Little Cuke Gordon'd planted himself to see the force, and he twisted his face as he thumbed Hoey out. Falling, I sidearmed the ball to Henry as hard as I could and watched in agony as his glove hand reached damn-near halfway down the base path to meet it. His right leg strained back towards first to close the double-play circuit.

An instant before Nugent's foot hit the bag, the ball went *thwack!* in Henry's mitt, and Little Cuke threw his arm up in another show-boaty *gotcha!* Even face-down in the clay, I had to admire the guy's dramatic flair.

The game was over. The Hellbenders—my Hellbenders—had won. Our fans bounced up and down, do-si-do'd in the aisles, yodeled rebel yells, howled like wolves.

Then I stopped noticing because every part of me below my waist on my left leg seemed to've caught fire. I rolled to my back. It wasn't quite five in the afternoon, but the sky looked black and I saw stadium's lights blazing against that blackness, two dozen or so tall fuzzy haloes, shrinking and bloating. Stars swam into the blackness between the haloes, and my head bloated along with them, like someone had jammed a hissing air hose into my ear. The fire in my leg got hotter, my skin crisped like a burning paper sack, a mayhem of fluids seeped into the clay.

Buck Hoey's face blocked the haloes and the stars. "Nice play, Dumbo." A pair of baseball shoes fell out of the sky and bounced on my stomach. "Wear these in the bigs, kid. If you ever really get there."

Hoey vanished.

Where Hoey'd stood, the sky ran afternoon blue again. I pushed the shoes off my belly and doubled over, clutching my leg and making a noise that opened into a scream. Or maybe I didn't scream, for some of our fans—GIs, teenagers, feisty little boys—had scrambled onto the field to run about waving caps and souvenir pennants. They swung one another around like square dancers. None of them seemed to hear me. The National Anthem played scratchily, blaring through the PA system, but I guess nobody could hear it either. Junior Heggie knelt beside me, with Henry right behind him, and then, better late than never, Mister JayMac showed—dogged, I imagine, by memories of Charlie Snow's last day.

"Daniel!" Mister JayMac cried. "Daniel, can you stand?"

Nope. I thought maybe I was screaming again—a scream ricocheted between my ears—but Henry waved his arm at somebody near the clubhouse.

"A canvas litter for Daniel!" he shouted. "Immediately!"

I passed out—into dry-ice fog and a field of parka-clad ballplayers frozen against the brittle light pulsing without letup through the grayness.

5 6

Not until the next morning did I come around.

I lay flat-out in bed in a private room in the Hothlepoya County Hospital. A private room meant Mister JayMac, using his political clout and the full power of his checkbook, had sprung for my treatment with almost everything he had to spring with. Charlie Snow had died on him. Danny Boles wouldn't.

A bearded man in a white coat introduced himself to me as Dr. Nesheim. He straddled a chair next to my bed, his arms on the chair back and his chin on his clasped hands.

"Woozy? Take your time. You've got beaucoups of time."

Buck Hoey, I learned, had done for me. With one set of spikes, he'd shattered my right kneecap; with the other, torn the muscles of my left inner thigh. Then, throwing to Henry, I'd fallen, and fallen wrong, and done something very, very bad to my hip.

"Want me to sweeten the news for you, son, or would you rather take it all in one nasty gulp?"

One nasty gulp? How much more nastiness did this man want me to gag down? Even so, I said, "One nasty gulp."

"The orthopedic details of your injuries probably don't matter much to you right now," Dr. Nesheim said. "But they're severe."

"How severe?"

"You won't be able to play ball again."

"Our season's over. What about next year?"

"Not likely, Danny. That fella who spiked you, he's pretty much undercut your hopes of fame in the majors. Rehabilitation is going to be long, painful, and ... well, incomplete."

"I'm a ballplayer! A shortstop! That's what I am!"

"That was something you *did*, son. Now you're going to have to redefine yourself in quite different terms."

"I'm a ballplayer," I said.

Dr. Nesheim said, "The only consolation I can give you—if it will console—is, you won't have to worry about the draft or going off to war. Not as a dogface or swabbie, anyway. Uncle Sam won't want you any more than the Phillies do."

I was two and a half months shy of eighteen. I put my arm over my face and cried. Dr. Nesheim patted me on the arm and left. I didn't fault him. He seemed a decent enough joe—he'd given it to me in one nasty gulp, a dose of Epsom salts for the only life plan I'd ever made for myself. I didn't believe I couldn't use that plan anymore . . . and I *did* believe. The way my lower body felt like a sack full of broken glass told me all I needed to know about the reliability of Dr. Nesheim's prognosis.

Hoey'd gotten back at me for beating him out at shortstop, for taking away a pair of his baseball shoes, for my role in his ejection from a big game in LaGrange, and for greasing the duckboards of his late-season trade to the Gendarmes. Yessir, he'd decommissioned my wagon.

I spent the last two days of August and most of September in the Hothlepoya County Hospital. Between them, the Hellbenders and the Phillies paid for my stay. Mama and I could have never managed the bills. Deck Glider, Inc., had no medical plan for its line workers and mid-level managers, and even with a bonus for helping Mister JayMac's club to the CVL pennant, I hadn't cleared half a grand that summer.

During my first two days in the hospital, everyone on the team, except Henry and Mister JayMac, visited me. Even Trapdoor Evans and Turkey Sloan came by—with Sosebee, Ankers, and Sudikoff—to wish me a fast recovery and to laud me for turning the last double play of the year. Henry hadn't come, I figured, because he'd had to report to the Phillies, and their front office'd wired him money for a train ticket, probably in a first-class Pullman. No one else told me different—not at first anyways.

The visitor I most appreciated on Monday, though, was Phoebe. She came late in the day with Miss LaRaina, bringing a small box of Baby Ruth candy bars, a bouquet of crape myrtle and hydrangeas, and several tattered *Saturday Evening Posts*. Miss LaRaina sat subdued—almost prim—by my bed, but Phoebe twirled a finger in a stray lock on my forehead and smoothed back the hair at my temples.

"How you feelin, Ichabod?"

"Rotten. Howm I sposed to feel?"

"With yore fingers, or yore toes, or yore nose. Or yore . . . whatever."

"Phoebe," Miss LaRaina said tiredly.

"Mama's doing better, guy. She's seeing this really sweet Army nutpick out to the camp."

Nutpick?

"Phoebe," Miss LaRaina said again.

"Well, he's helped, yore kindly dome doctor has. He's got you to relax, to think some bout Daddy n me, to spend a little time to home."

"I never didn't think about yall, Phoebe. But I suppose I did think about myself more, and the terrible unfairness of my place in this dreadful war."

Terrible unfairness.

"But Danny doesn't want to hear this," Miss LaRaina said. "We came to be mood lifters, angels of mercy, not a tear-jerker episode of *Captain Pharram's Family*." She tapped a cigarette from a pack of Luckies. "Mind if I smoke, Danny? Keeps my hands busy and sort of rebraids my frazzled nerves."

"Not if I can have one too," I told her.

Phoebe took a cigarette from her mother, stuck it between my lips, lit me up. I bathed my lungs in smoke and blew out a whole stack of wobbly airborne doughnuts. The quick high the smoke gave me—the sensation of floating—lifted my mind away from the throb in my hip, the burn in my groin. Tobacco, the opium of the people.

"How come Mister JayMac aint been by?"

The silence spilling from Phoebe and her mama came down in deafening Niagara Falls torrents.

"How many top-heavy nurses been in here to jab needles in yore butt?" Phoebe suddenly asked me.

"Five or six. They can't stay away. I lose count."

"Phoebe," Miss LaRaina said tiredly.

"Oh, cmon, Mama. Yore doctor said to behave responsibly, not to chain yoresef to a church pew."

"Phoebe, I'd appreciate it if—"

I blew a smoke ring and cut Miss LaRaina off. "How come Mister JayMac hasn't visited me?"

Phoebe and her mama did that hurry-not-to-answer thing they'd already done once. Like Mariani coiling a spaghetti strand around a fork tine, Phoebe spiraled my forelock around her finger. The ash on Miss LaRaina's cigarette, meanwhile, grew like Pinocchio's nose. This time I waited.

"We've all suffered an unexpected loss," Miss LaRaina said. "You see, Miss Giselle is dead. She died either quite late last night or very early this morning."

"Cripes. Did Mister JayMac shoot her?" (For telling Frye to announce our call-up? For going the carnal hanky-panky route with Henry? And, if the second, how had Mister JayMac found out?)

"Uh-uh," Phoebe said. "Miss Giselle kilt herself."

"How? Why?" I may have known the answer to at least one of those questions, but I needed to hear it said. No, I needed a denial, a lie that didn't impeach my roommate. Now, too, I began to understand the bouts of dumbness that'd fallen on Phoebe and Miss LaRaina when I mentioned Miss Giselle or asked about Mister JayMac. Someone'd told them not to drop any more bad news on me than Dr. Nesheim already had.

"What about Henry? Is Henry all right?"

Another uh-oh look between Phoebe and her mama.

"What's happened to him?" I demanded.

"He's fine," Miss LaRaina said quickly. "He's just . . . fine."

"Uh-uh," I said. "I'm owed some truth. Let's have it."

"Listen to him, Mama," Phoebe said. "He's done got shut of his stutter. Completely, nearlybout."

"Phoebe, it's either completely or it aint," I said.

"Why, you're right," Miss LaRaina said. "He's become a regular Demosthenian." They marveled over me.

"Tell me what's happened to Henry, blast it."

Miss LaRaina said, "Once he knew how bad Buck Hoey'd hurt you, he left and got just sloppy drunk over it."

"Yesterday was Sunday," I said. "And Henry don't drink."

"Ordinarily, no," Miss LaRaina said, "but this spiking business unnerved him, and I've never known a Hellbender who wanted a bottle not to find one. Reese—Mr. Curriden—always had two or three hidden in his room. He'd distribute too. Hoarding's not his way, even in a whiskey drought."

"Mama," Phoebe said, looking at her feet.

"It's all right, child. Major Blumlein said to own up to my trespasses, not to cache them under a lampstand."

"He didn't tell you to parade em in front of Daddy."

"Your daddy isn't here." Miss LaRaina surveyed my room. "That young man there answers to Danny, not Daddy, and I assume him chivalrous enough to keep his own counsel." She blew smoke sidelong, holding her cigarette Bette Davis style. "Are you?" she asked me.

"Yessum."

"Well, then. Henry sends his regrets."

"Will he visit me before he leaves for Philly?"

"That's probably up to him and the railway timetable." Miss LaRaina smiled and took another sexy drag on the nub of her Lucky. She caught a knuckle's length of falling ash in one palm and dumped it in the terra-cotta pot of crape myrtle and hydrangea blossoms at her feet.

We talked another ten or fifteen minutes, mostly about Miss Giselle—her generosity, her lovingkindness, her sacrifices for Mister JayMac and the Hellbenders. Then Miss LaRaina said I looked peakéd. She and Phoebe had better go. The staff didn't want me overtaxed.

"Then tell em to write their congressmen," I said. "Look, I'm strong enough for yall to stay."

"Not if we fuss," Miss LaRaina said. "Fussin'll lay you down faster than a mile-long footrace."

Phoebe kissed me on the forehead. "I'll be back. Ever day till yo're out."

I held Phoebe's hand briefly before she slipped away, over to the door. "Miss LaRaina, leave me those cigarettes, okay? You can get some more."

Miss LaRaina walked over and laid her pack on my stomach.

"When's the funeral?" I asked her. When she just stared at me, like she'd forgotten an earlier part of our talk, I added, "Miss Giselle's?"

"Oh. Tomorrow, at Alligator Park. A memorial service. No burial. The body's being cremated."

"I can't go," I said. "I'd like to, but I—" I dropped my cigarette butt in the water glass on my bedside table and watched it fizzle and saturate. Miss Giselle dead. Henry not accounted for. My career an injury-blasted memory. The weight of all this wreckage squeezed tears from me. "Okay. Yall go on. Leave me be." I fumbled another cigarette out and got Phoebe to light it—to keep her from planting another wet sympathy buss over my eye. She and Miss LaRaina went to the door.

"Matches!" I called after them. "Please."

Phoebe tossed them onto the bed, not really within easy reach, and then I was alone again.

*

During September, every day until my release on the twenty-seventh, Phoebe kept her word and came to see me, usually in the afternoon after school. With the end of the CVL season, though, visits from other Hellbenders dwindled to one or two a week, for most of my teammates left Highbridge for their own hometowns or farms, or rode away to take winter-long defense jobs in shipyards, munitions factories, and bomber plants. Nutter, Hay, Sloan, Sudikoff, and Fanning stayed, with jobs at Foremost Forge or Highbridge Box & Crate—but only Nutter ever actually dropped by, usually with newspapers, his motor-mouthed five-year-old Carl, and a fresh—to me, anyway—anecdote about his days with the St. Louis Browns.

Mister JayMac visited me on Sunday afternoons at three o'clock and stayed fifteen minutes, tops. He never mentioned Miss Giselle, Darius, or Henry, but concentrated on asking how I seemed to be healing up and second-guessing Allied command decisions in Italy and the Solomons. By telephone, of course, he'd told Mama Laurel of my injuries, and of their severity, without trying to soft-pedal the truth or to weasel out of the club's financial obligations—even though my contract didn't say a word about insuring me for game-acquired or aggravated hurts. He would've paid Mama Laurel's way to Highbridge, but Mama told him tearfully in one call that coming to see me might make her lose her job. Colonel Elshtain had helped Deck Glider get its military conversion contract, but he didn't seem to have any leftover pull with the management at the Tenkiller factory, and Mama couldn't put her job up for grabs by asking for an emergency leave of absence.

"Then don't come, Mrs. Boles," Mister JayMac told me he'd told Mama. "I'll take care of Danny jes like he was my own."

Imagine my gratitude.

Anyway, Mama and I also talked occasionally. I told her to stay on the job and to pray for me. Ordinarily, we talked on Sundays, after Mister JayMac's humdrum visits, when he sat in a chair near the door, a black arm band on one sleeve and a look of heavy confusion on his booze-swollen face. Sometimes we'd talk, Mama and I, while Mister JayMac, who'd had the phone brought in, sat nearby in his widower's weeds and his deep-purple heartache.

"Yessum, they're treating me just fine," I'd say. "Yessum, he is." What else could I say—though it did pretty much tally with the truth—with Mister JayMac sharing my room?

Nobody brought me a copy of the *Highbridge Herald* until the Friday of my first week in the hospital. And when Nutter came in with it, he brought me only the sports page, which had a few major-league box scores and a whole section about a GI track meet at Camp Penticuff. I'd already read my *Saturday Evening Posts* from cover to cover.

"Where's the rest of this rag? Nobody here'll give me a copy and you come in with a piddlin snippet."

"Didn't think you'd care about anything but the sports," Nutter said. "After ball season, nothing worth preserving in type happens in this burg."

"What happened at Miss Giselle's funeral?"

"Memorial service. The usual. Blather, tears, you know. Remember Charlie Snow's. Only difference? Afterwards, Mister JayMac took his lady's ashes home in an urn."

"Oh." I changed the subject. "Where's Henry? He never came to see me, but I look in these here box scores for the Phillies"—I snapped the sports page with my knuckles—"and his name aint here. Where is he?"

"I don't know."

"He didn't go up to the Phillies?"

"Maybe he's sitting on the bench. Not finding his name in a box score only means he didn't play in that game."

I tacked about. "Why doesn't Hoey come visit me? He owes me that much, the jerk."

"Cripes, Boles, you're a pigheaded case. Hoey didn't—*doesn't*—like you. Plus he's ashamed."

"I bet."

"Anyway, he's not the sort to come creeping in here, hat in hand, to ask forgiveness. Which you already knew."

On Saturday, I got hold of a newspaper. It had a story clipped from the front page. I asked the nurse on assignment to my room why. She said a staff doctor with a cousin in the Ninth Air Force, headquartered in England, had clipped it for a scrapbook he planned to give his cousin on his return from overseas. Nobody else had a paper to loan either—the hospital tried to keep its premises litter free and to recycle paper products immediately. I believed the hussy. She lied like a front-office flack, and in those days I didn't know enough to see through the prevaricators the way I do now.

Two days later, about five in the afternoon, another nurse came by and looked in. "Nigger boy out here says he wants to see you. You want to see him?"

Euclid, I thought. "Yessum. Let me see him."

Euclid came in, eyes cast down, head respectfully hang-dog. He looked dirtier than usual, sweatier—as ragamuffinish in his clothes as anybody could look and still get in the door. The nurse—I could tell—figured she'd just done her unpaid good deed of the day.

"What's going on, Euclid?"

"Hey, Danbo. Braugh yoo ledder."

"Where?" I saw no letter. Euclid had his hands clasped in front of him like a recaptured escapee wearing cuffs.

"Heah." Euclid pulled a manila packet from under his stained muslin shirt and nearly poked me in the eye with it. I took it from him. He glanced away—at the ceiling, into a corner, at the foot of my bed.

"Who's it from?" I studied the handwriting on the front of the packet: *Daniel Boles*. And just that quick, I knew who'd written the letter. "Henry," I said.

"Yessa. Mister Jumbo say gib it yoo. Now I gots to go. Bye."

Euclid hustled out of the room. I opened the packet and spread out the pages inside it in my lap.

57

I write to you with considerable difficulty, Daniel, for I must labour both to express myself in an apposite idiom and to justify actions which might otherwise seem grotesque, if not monstrous. What I have done, however, I own as products, albeit misshapen and disfigured ones, of my finer sentiments—kindness, regard, love—rather than of mere destructive egotism. In allowing outrage to *deform my nobler affections in one case, I grievously erred. But in the other I sought only to reaffirm justice and the existing social order, not to instigate ruin and spiritual desolation.*

In the wake of your departure via ambulance to the county hospital, Daniel, I repaired on foot to McKissic House and took a shower. From Musselwhite I learned that your injuries would debar you from accompanying me to Philadelphia; would, indeed, prevent you from playing baseball at any professional level again. This news induced in me a bleak lethargy—the blues, Darius would baptise my psychological complaint—and likewise a vehement choler akin to the fury I had so often known as Victor Frankenstein's foresworn handiwork.

For two hours, my lassitude held my wrath in check; then, thinking on your love of our sport and your cruel abstraction from it, I recalled that just as Michelangelo had said, "It is only well with me when I have a chisel in my hand," you had once averred that you felt most alive when wearing a fielder's glove or gripping a bat.

This recollection goaded me from bed. I believe I may have howled. I forsook the still, hot rooms of McKissic House. I quitted the equivocal revelry of my teammates (men somewhat more enkindled by our victory than abashed by your ill fortune) and directed myself through the twilight to Cotton Creek Street and the clapboard dwelling of Linda Jane Hoey and her four children. It had occurred to me that Ligonier Hoey, unlike other Gendarmes, had a local home to which to retire. There his wife and helpmeet would welcome him, commiserate over his season-ending loss, and absolve him with laughter and kisses of any complicity in your becripplement. This conjectural domestic scene, so tender and so unjust, heaped faggots on my rage.

As I strode, dogs—spaniels, blueticks, rodent-faced mongrels—left their porches to defend their shabby fiefdoms and harry my passage. Heedless, I strode on, preparing myself for a head-to-head affray with the miscreant I had once counted teammate and friend. When a hound of umber eye summoned the brass to bite my heel, I twisted it up from the walk by its hackles, and flung it simpering into a pack of like-minded dogs trailing me along a holly row. The cur landed amidst its kindred, scattering them in girning panic. At length it scrambled lamely away into the shrubbery. I continued, impervious to the cruelty of my act and the mayhemic dimensions of my humour.

In the spacious confines of Alligator Park, I slowed my step, intuitively detecting a hint of what could lie in wait not only for my prey but also for me. I spoke one word aloud: "Atonement." The silhouetted planks of some teeter-totters, primitive machines for the fabrication of joy, calmed me with their offset diagonals. I must bank the coals of my anger, I reasoned, and confront Hoey as one sane and well-

intentioned being to another. When I knocked on his door, his youngest son—your fortuitous namesake, Daniel—opened it and gazed up at me as if from a trench.

"Jumbo's here!" he shouted. "The biggest man in the world! The mostest homers in a season!"

Linda Jane Hoey appeared behind young Daniel, wearing a look of commingled charity and exasperation, as if a black-sheep uncle had intruded on a private celebration. I was not beloved of Mrs. Hoey; my size and mien discomfited her. At every home game, she had held herself and her children frostily aloof, fearing perhaps that, if vexed, I would treat of her offspring as I had just treated of that vile dog. Before I could ask for her spouse, exasperation decided Mrs. Hoey's rejoinder to my unsolicited appearance.

"Buck's family needs him tonight, Mr. Clerval, and he needs us. What do you want?"

"Only a word or two. Let me see your husband and I will quit your neighbourhood as soon as we settle between us a certain important matter."

"What matter?"

Whereupon, quite like an immaterial phantom, Ligonier Hoey disclosed himself and pulled both Linda Jane and young Daniel from the door. Barefooted, he stood before me, his chin outthrust—how must I put this?—gladitorially.

"Do for you, Clerval? Pretty late to drop by on a social call. I'm not much in the mood."

"I scarcely wonder," I said. "In trying to thwart our final double play, you acted with undue aggression. I fear you meant to inflict injury."

"Didn't!" young Daniel said loudly. "Didn't either!"

Hoey commanded his wife to withdraw along with young Daniel. When she had obeyed, be said, "Screw you, Jumbo. My motto's play full out and don't cry in your beer if you draw to a busted flush."

"To date, playing full out hasn't resulted in your utter incapacitation," I observed.

"Look, what do you want? Crocodile tears? A written apology?"

"Buck, your dinner's getting cold!" Mrs. Hoey called. "Can't you discuss your problem later?" The brunt of this plaintive inquiry was meant, I felt, for me.

"I have no later here in Highbridge," I told him. "On Tuesday I leave for Philadelphia."

"Congratulations," Hoey said churlishly. "Rub it in."

"What I want includes not only an acknowledgement to your hapless victim—"

"Hey, Dumbo was hopeless—I mean, hapless*—long before I got to him."*

"—*of your crime against him, but, yes, a written apology for the* Herald, *and monetary reparations for his blasted career.*"

"Buck! Buck, come onnn!"

The miscreant shouted over his shoulder: "For God's sake, woman, let us talk! We're going for a walk to hash it out!" *He stepped onto the porch with me and pulled the door to with an emphatic bang. I could not determine if he harboured more asperity for me or for his wife.*

We walked side by side into Alligator Park. The dogs that had beset me earlier shunned us now, barking only tentatively. Hoey and I ended in the playground where the shadows of teeter-totters still laid an incongruous calm upon me. For an instant I believed that Hoey and I would discover not only an accord about his guilt but also a cure, Daniel, for your disability. We stood beside a metal children's slide—recreational equipment that had escaped scrap-metal requisitioning— weighing our provisional arguments,

"*In any championship game, a real competitor goes for broke,*" *Hoey said.* "*He brawls for every advantage. I won't apologise for that, Jumbo. You've got no right to ask me to.*"

"*Limits exist,*" *I said.* "*Today, however, to salve your lacerated pride, you robbed Daniel Boles of any chance of realising the most important goal of his life.*"

"*Jesus, I didn't notice you dogging it. You powdered one off Sundog Billy. You stretched like fucking Plastic Man to take Dumbo's last throw.*"

"*In neither case did I cripple a rival. Or strive to inflict any wound more distressing than defeat.*"

"*Horseshit.*"

"*I beg your pardon.*"

"*I said, Horseshit.*"

"*Your dogged refusal to admit culpability pisses me off. Continue thus and I may well have cause to thrash you an inch shy of extinction.*"

"*You'd like to beat the shit out of me?*"

"*You've proved yourself conscienceless.*"

"*Listen at you. Hank Clerval, the pacifist, wants to whip my brains into a meringue.*"

"*I do. I do indeed.*"

Hoey regaled me with a contemptuous fleer. "*Well, try it, you highfalutin tower of Jell-O. You hypocrite. You're no better than me, Jumbo—not deep down anyways, where the stinking rats of envy screw.*"

"*I ache for Daniel, for all the acne-ridden soldiers. I despair of their futures.*"

"Worry about your own. Them guys in the bigs'll eat a lummox like you alive. And you're so ugly, even success up there won't guarantee you any nookie. Zat why you're upset I put my spikes in Dumbo's jewels? Fraid you're gonna have to get you a new little gal-boy?"

"Have a care."

"Or is it the other way round? You're a real pirate's chest of secrets. The crap we don't know about you, why, it'd fill an encyclopedia."

Hoey anticipated neither the fury of my outrage nor my lunge. My left hand encircled his neck, compressed his topmost vertebrae towards his Adam's apple, and dragged him over to a pair of shaggy sycamores on a far margin of the playground. Hoey fought, but I had effected a one-handed cloture of his windpipe, which muffled his protests and vitiated his exertions. A leopard caching a springbok—so imagine me as I clambered into the larger of the sycamores and wedged Hoey between two of its branches. My conscience had left me, nor did it soon return.

"You sonuva b-b-bitch." Hoey's hiccoughing speech prompted first a remembrance of your stammer, Daniel, and then a brilliant inner movie of Hoey's hateful slide. So much the better for the indemnification I meant to extract, so much the more agonising for your petty tormentor.

Bracing Hoey in place, I removed his belt and secured his hands behind him. Because he strove to curse and bite me, I wedged his own soiled handkerchief into his mouth. We swayed together, sixteen feet above the indurate swell of earth from which the tree columned and spread. I hooked one leg about a stout upper branch, seized Hoey by the shoulders, and hurled him downwards with the same authority and force that Jehovah God launched Lucifer and his minions from Heaven.

The bones in Hoey's legs splintered with a firelike crackling. He writhed on the ground like a broken-backed squirrel. With a great eructation of wind and blood, Hoey expelled the gag I had fashioned for him and began both to curse me and to cry for help.

Not to have killed him pleased me. I brachiated from one bough to a lower one, released it, and struck the ground astraddle the man who had hectored you all season, the jerk who, just that afternoon, had gratuitously ended your career. "You s-sonuva," he continued to curse. "You s-s-sonuva . . ." His lips were foam-flecked; his eyes, like glowing dimes. My fury had not yet expended itself, nor, listening to Hoey's unrepentant curses, did I feel that I had yet satisfactorily avenged you. I took Hoey's tongue between two fingers and wrenched it bleeding from his mouth. His eyeballs started from his head, his back arched, and an uncouth groan broke from his larynx. I retrieved the handkerchief that he had spit from his mouth and pushed it back into that unlovely cavity—to stanch the flows of blood and wordless bawling vituperation.

Your nemesis's tongue in hand, I stood up and gloated over his devastation. "Fuck you," I told his writhing form. "Fuck you sempiternally." The jaundiced sclera of Hoey's eyes circumvolved back so that the veins in them seemed a macabre reflection of the veins in the dead-calm leaves of our sycamore canopy. A pang of doubt spasmed in me, and I withdrew from that place, abandoning him, as in my first life I had fled the scenes of crimes now freshly brilliant in memory.

Leaving Alligator Park, Daniel, I saw the hound that, earlier, I had pitched into its pack fellows. Recognising me, it nevertheless paced me along the walk. Its hackles bristled. Its eyes flashed like the beacon of a lighthouse in the Orkneys. Even in my agitation, I admired the animal for its doggedness. As a memento of my regard, I tossed it the tongue in my hand, and it fell to.

Behind McKissic House, I found that in my absence, albeit within the past ten or fifteen minutes, chaos had erupted. Mister JayMac's boarders clustered vigilantly on the grassy skirt of Hellbender Pond as Reese Curriden and Lon Musselwhite paddled a wooden johnboat towards what appeared to be a floating hearth log ablaze in the middle distance.

"Don't go too close!" somebody cried.

"What in hell're they planning to do?" someone else said. "Slap water at her with their paddles?"

"What is it? What happened?" I whispered.

"It's Miss Giselle in your leather canoe," Dunnagin said. "She took it out for a little jaunt, then—WHOOSH!—it burst into flames."

"She drenched it with gasoline," Trapdoor Evans said. "Rationed gasoline."

I shed my boots and ran into the blood-warm water. The flames from my kayak—indeed, from Giselle McKissic's shriveling upper body—leapt skywards like a wind-riven wall of marigolds, salvia, azaleas, and red clover. I swam towards that wall. Like the albumen of a thousand bloody egg yolks beaten to a swirl, the reflection of the flames jittered through the water. Daniel, I swam thoughtlessly, insensible to anything that was not my burning kayak, empty of any notion of what I must do when I reached the vessel. At length—quite rapidly, in fact—I overtook the johnboat oared by Muscles and Curriden.

Curriden shouted, "Henry, don't go out there!"

I continued my obsessive Australian crawl. Curriden thrust a paddle into my flank, hoping thereby to dissuade me from my purpose (whatever it might be). When he nudged me again, gouging me in the ribs, I grabbed and twisted the oar blade, drawing him with a prodigious splash into the water. He flailed and gasped, but finally dragged himself back into the johnboat without capsizing it, while I swam on my own headlong way.

Soon I dropped my legs and dog-paddled, for the heat streaming from the self-immolated Giselle's funeral barge struck me fully; it threatened to scald even those parts of me ostensibly safe under water.

"Giselle!" I cried for all but the newborn corpse herself to hear.

Muscles and Curriden—and my teammates ashore—shouted through the tumult for me to turn aside. Despite the heat and my growing exhaustion, I swam nearer the kayak, trod in place the tepid water, and slapped gout after gout at the horrific sight before me. Giselle piloted my canoe like a dead bride imperfectly cremated, then toppled forward like a released marionette, and, as the flames consumed the last of their fuel, submersed with the kayak. Down she went, resting on a seat of already-burnt woven grass, towards the silt and muck of the pond's stygian floor.

Daniel, I took a great breath, and dove. The vacuum established by the flooded hull of the kayak, as it plunged slowly into darkness, imparted itself to my body through the water. I was tugged after, like a fly in the paltry maelstrom of a shower drain. To what dread terminus would that watery engine deliver me?

Blessedly, I had filled my lungs before going under, and my capacity in this regard eclipses that of human beings conventionally propagated. The night above and the murkiness of the medium through which I swam conspired to blind me; and yet I saw not only filamentous pondwrack and slime-fouled cypress roots, but also the charcoaled body of my erstwhile paramour and the whalebone frame of my kayak. Indeed, descending, I saw the blackened monkey face and the brittle limbs of Giselle McKissic woven into the pond's liquid papyrus. Or believed I saw them.

How to extricate the woman from the sinking kayak? I could think of no way. Therefore, I spoke an abashed farewell and faced away from her watery grave to find the world again.

The instant I did so the tenebrous vision I had had of that scene, a tableau mayhap illuminated by pond phosphor, ichthyoidal incandescence, and my own remorseful longings, flashed into blackness.

Why not commit myself forever, I wondered, to that extinguishing medium and die with Giselle? She had taken her life to punish herself for crediting even a transitory happiness, but also to punish Mister JayMac for denying her a permanent one, and me for yielding to her blandishments only to forswear my desperate surrender when conscience unpunctually reasserted itself. (Indeed, in yielding to her appeals, I may have sought to cuckold, belatedly, my creator, for in each union with Giselle I always saw the visage of Elizabeth Lavenza, my creator's bride, whom I cruelly murdered.) I did not deserve to die with Giselle. She was not my wife, and I had loved her, whether carnally or reverentially, for too brief a time to sleep beside her forever in her aqueous mausoleum.

I surfaced and swam back to shore. Muscles and Curriden had preceded me. No one had any notion where Mister JayMac had gone or what we should do. Evans averred that Mister JayMac, to celebrate our pennant and also to benumb himself to the burden of Hoey's crippling assault on you, Daniel, had repaired to the arms of a fancy woman in the Oglethorpe Hotel. Several acceded to the probability of this last speculation.

Muscles said, "To hell with that. Heggie, call the cops, fire department too. To help bring the body up."

"Tomorrow," Lamar Knowles said. "It's too blamed dark to grapple for a corpse."

"Yeah, well, if Mister JayMac was here," Muscles said, "he'd set up floodlights and have her out in a hour, tops."

"He isn't here," Lamar Knowles said.

Euclid came down from the boardinghouse. He wriggled through the men on the edge of the pond and halted before me, daunted, I think, by my fell and waterlogged aspect.

"Miz Hoey say you wen ouw wi Mr. Hoey. Say Mr. Hoey ain come back. Say, do you know wha hopn to him?"

"No. I don't." I pushed through the crowd, all too aware that soon Linda Jane Hoey and the local gendarmerie would discover the injured Hoey and deduce correctly that I had broken his legs and torn his tongue from his mouth. It seemed, Daniel, that the span of my ill-fated liberty among your own kind was ending; likewise, my hopes of finding an accomplishment and thus a meaning in my second life through the instrumentality of baseball. A welter of perplexities gripped me as I entered McKissic House, climbed the stairs, and burst into our garret.

First, Daniel, through wrath and violence I had nullified all my efforts to atone for the nefariousness of my first life. My brutal treatment of Hoey and my wicked incognizance of the depths of Giselle's melancholia had evicted me from an unchartered society of human saints in which I had always assumed myself a member. Second, by these acts I had wronged my benefactor, Jordan McKissic, repaying trust with deviltry and throwing down by a type of roundabout homicide his marriage. Third, I had recklessly annulled the investments of both the Hellbenders and the Phillies, for my only choices now were giving up to the civil authorities or fleeing into the night.

Looking about my portion of our room, I found that Giselle had purloined some of my belongings: notebooks, letters, clothes, souvenirs of the Oongpekmut, etc. "Part of you I take with me" *read a note on my bed. Indeed, these items she had perversely—aye, and poignantly—included in her self-immolation and her submersion. All were destroyed; their char drifted through the trash and bacteria in the pond, or lay sodden and lost in its ebony bottom ooze. I recalled the grinding wretchedness of my worst days, whether as Frankenstein's bewildered get or as the heartsick widower of Kariak.*

I wept, Daniel. Weeping, I folded into a bag those clothes that Giselle had not taken. I advanced upon the stairs. I heard the downstairs telephone ring. I heard someone seize the instrument and speak. Momentarily, this person—Vito Mariani?—cried out to the Hellbenders in the parlor, "They found Hoey in Alligator Park, but he's dead, you guys! Poor ol Bucko's dead!"

I hurried down both flights of stairs and quietly let myself out. Then I betook myself through the most sparsely populated regions of town—school yards, alleyways, pine copses—until it seemed unlikely that either my teammates or the police would catch me and remand me to prison.

For all these reasons, Daniel, I have not visited you, nor reported to the club in Philadelphia. In my fugitive state, several agonies continually plague me, chief among them the murder—or murders—that I have committed. Also of scourging primacy are the heinous crimes inflicted upon the Hoeys and upon you, Daniel, as my comrade in hope. I might better have avenged you, I see now, by acquitting myself well in the major leagues than by savaging the man who debarred your own elevation there.

I am on the lam. This self-concealing style of life is not unfamiliar to me. Many years ago, I practiced it in the waste tracts of Alaska, becoming a creature of legend to the whites who journeyed through. Thus, the Oongpekmut called me Inyookootuk, the Hiding Man. I am again become Inyookootuk. In this role, my size notwithstanding, I have twice returned to Highbridge to befriend Linda Jane Hoey and her children, as I befriended the cottagers De Lacey in my first life. I leave canned food items on her threshold and chopped wood for her stove or fire grates in a box out back. These pathetic kindnesses do not redeem my crime or return the Hoeys' dead provider; I draw from them, however, a selfish consolation.

In our minds, as well as in our acts, we struggle for self-absolution. I do not believe in my maker, Daniel, for he did not believe in me. The God you worship seems at an unbridgeable remove. I would ask his forgiveness, but, as much as I wish to, I cannot regard myself as either his child or his ward. Therefore, sireless and alone, I devise salvific mental stratagems for myself, arcane apologia to justify and remit my sins. In the case of Hoey's murder, I have settled upon two mitigating circumstances, the second more compelling than the first. How, you may ask, have I slipped the bonds of the Sixth Commandment?

—I had no intent to kill Ligonier Hoey.

—Retribution is a portentous duty, but a more noble one than vengeance.

You see, Daniel, in doing what I did, I sought less to injure Hoey (although harm was required) than to uphold you. Unhappily, the mechanism of this advocacy converted deliberate harm to unexpected death. Never, though, did I seek to extract it.

Does my argument appear a self-deluding sophistry? Perhaps it is. But oh! Daniel, I know that the murders of my original incarnation were but the fleeting aberrancies of a gentle nature twisted by others—chiefly, my hedging maker—into an alien cruelty. Then, rejected and despised, I killed five times for revenge. In this much longer incarnation, by many accepted and by many others acclaimed, I have killed but once, Daniel, and then, unintentionally, for love. Does this not prove that I have undergone an evolution worthy of your regard? Am I not your friend?

Faithfully,
Henry

P. S. This message comes to you by my evangel Euclid, whom, on my most recent visit to Highbridge, I found at his mother's house. When you have read it, and digested all its implications, I beseech you to destroy it, preferably by flame. Fear not, however. We will meet again.

58

Like a rescue worker scratching through tornado wreckage, I reread
Henry's letter. Although Miss LaRaina'd left me some matches, and
a wastebasket sat near enough to drop the packet in and burn it without
setting the whole hospital afire, I put the letter back in its envelope and slid
it under my mattress. What lies I'd been spoonfed, what mealy-mouthed
crapola.

"Nurse!" I yelled. *"NURSE!"*

By the luck of the shift, I got the same slick honey who'd told me a
doctor'd scissor-clipped the Saturday *Herald* so his Army Air Corps cousin
could read the clip. Baloney. Bohunk Choctaw. Anyway, she came in with
her boyish perky flip-do and her creamy butt-hugger of a uniform—looking
cute, looking put upon—and eyeballed me like I was a bedrid stink beetle.

"You don't have to shout, Danny. Push yore call button."

"Miss Giselle burnt herself up. Henry threw Buck Hoey out of a tree.
Hoey croaked. Henry's scrammed. The *Herald*'s run it all, but yall've pulled a
damn ol hush-it-up on me."

"Darlin, who you been talkin to?"

"Why in hell'd you try to keep it from me?"

"Talk that way, I'll have to fetch some FiSoHex and scrub yore naughty
mouf out."

"Hells and damns you scrub. Flat-out lies you suck like Life Savers."

That raised her dander. "I do as I'm told." She flounced back to corridor
headquarters. When Phoebe came in, I waylaid her the same way. I stormed
and bellyached. She drank in my rant as much through her eyes as her ears
and squinted with tomboy skepticism.

"Well?"

"I liked you better tongue-tied."

"I liked you better on the up and up, playing straight and letting the
chips—"

"You mean the ch-ch-chips." She ratcheted like a slipped bicycle chain. "Look, relax.

"Uncle JayMac, grief-struck like he was, and still is, didn't want to dump any more on you than you'd awready got. Is that a crime?"

"But yall *lied!*"

"Who squealed, Ichabod? Who told you?"

Well, I knew enough to shut up. Standing on the burning foredeck loudly denouncing liars, I knew enough to lie. "I ast this guy limping past my door with Saturday's paper if I could see it. He let me s-s-see it."

During September, I had two follow-up operations, physical therapy with support bars and crutches (reminding me of Henry's reconditioning efforts in Missouri, after his self-directed height-reduction surgery), several sessions with an imported Camp Penticuff nutpick, and more time to brood and dismalize than a stalled front-line regiment with trench foot. I filled in the time by writing Mama Laurel letters and reading a long downbeat novel about a young British doctor with a clubfoot.

When I could hobble about on crutches, Dr. Nesheim released me. I spent my last two days in Highbridge in my old attic room at McKissic House. Everything Henry'd brought to furnish or decorate it was gone: the bed with its plywood bracing, the homemade bookcase, the woven-grass divider, the matted photo of a William Blake drawing, everything. Mister JayMac had wanted to stick me in a downstairs room until my departure for Tenkiller, to spare me the pain of climbing and descending, but I wanted no other room, even when I saw how changed—how naked, emptied out, and *big*—its stripping had left it. I said my struggles up and down the stairs would be therapeutic.

"Clerval snuck in to get the smaller items, we think," Mister JayMac told me on Monday. "They were gone when Curriden and I dismantled the bed and the book shelves." (Once gone, I noticed, Hellbenders ceased to qualify as misters.)

"Henry stole his own stuff?"

"That's a contradiction in terms, Mr. Boles. However, as a fugitive from justice and a lodger in arrears, he trespassed to retrieve it—a trick he may've learned from Darius."

"He didn't mean to kill Hoey," I said. "I mean, killing just wasn't Henry's way."

"Well, I wouldn't've blamed him if he had. What I find hardest to take is him forsaking the near-accomplished dream—the stupidity that compelled it."

"He loved me," I said.

A muscle beside Mister JayMac's eye twitched. "Neither Clerval nor anyone else has touched your notebooks. Your gear is all jes as you left it. Cept Kizzy washed and flat-ironed your Hellbender blouse and a whole pancake stack of skivvies."

How did Mister JayMac even know about my notebooks—there in my knife-gouged school desk, with its inked-in scratches and doodles—if they hadn't been touched?

And, I understood, my notebooks now probably contained the only copy of *From Remorse to Self-Respect: My Second Life* in existence anywhere. Henry's original had gone to carbon during Miss Giselle's suicide. I ran my fingers over the desk's oaken lid, but didn't try to peek inside its book compartment.

Mister JayMac went to the window by the fire stairs. He gazed out over the victory garden and down the hand-mowed slope past his gazebo to Hellbender Pond. It had been a rain-starved September; the corn'd turned to brown-paper spindles, and the grass had yellowish heat circles of different sizes—accursed fairy rings—singed into it in overlaps and stand-alone compass loops.

"Why do you suppose Giselle did that, Danny?" He had his back to me. "Had I hurt her that bad?"

Well, I could only stare.

"Cat got your tongue again, Mr. Boles?"

"Nosir. It's a hard question."

"She really did care for me. I wouldn't see it."

"She probably cared a lot," I said. "Caring too much can chase you furious."

Mister JayMac turned around. "As if you knew jackshit about it." His gaze drifted to the faded place where Henry's only matted picture had hung.

"Jackshit, jillshit—I thought you hated potty talk, sir."

"I'll have Euclid bring you up a fan, this hotbox could use one." He left, shutting me up in that hotbox alone. I could hear him clippity-clopping to the landing below.

Twenty or so minutes later, Euclid came up with a fan about five years older than Henry's old model.

"Where'd Henry go after he gave you that letter, Euclid? How'd he look? Have you told anybody else you saw him?"

"Nobody buh you."

"Okay, okay. Answer my other questions."

Euclid was sneaking into puberty. His jaw had widened, his chest had a new fullness. In his threadbare linen shirt, glossy hardware-store britches, and floppy-soled shoes, he set the fan on the floor and plugged it in.

"Come like a robber when Detta Rae honky-tonkin," he said. "Tol me gib you the ledder. Took off same way he come. Look big n scairy, thass how he look."

"Where'd he come from? Where'd he go?"

"How you spec *me* to know? Come from hell, Danbo. Went the same place Darius done gone."

"The same place Darius . . . ?" But Euclid just switched on the fan, which bumped around the floor like a wind-up frog, and left. Henry's midnight visit had scared the Georgia bejabbers out of him.

I crutched over to my bed and sat down. I had a ticket back to Oklahoma in my pocket. I'd leave on Friday, first day of October. What would I do in Tenkiller when I got there, though? It crossed my mind my most profitable option might be standing in front of the Cherokee Feed Store cadging dimes from home folks who mistook me for a wounded soldier. . . .

59

One night later, rain. It wet the grass, the victory garden, the crazy whirr of the crickets. Earlier in the evening, I'd moved my fan to the window, and a fresh breeze a little after midnight made me reach down and rumble for a sheet—a first for me that summer (unless, of course, the sheet had already been soaked in cold water). Then the fan spun moisture into the room, spitting icy droplets at my face and pillow.

The rain sharpened and picked up. It rattled the tin on the attic gables and cascaded down the fire stairs like some sort of stepping-stone waterfall. The gutters under the eaves clattered and gushed.

I sat up. A pitchfork of lightning jabbed down on the house's Alabama side. Through the window I could see, just for a sec, the thrashing corn in the victory garden, the thrashing magnolias and sycamores near the pond, and the skeleton of the gazebo. Then, noisy blackness. Then another many-fingered electric claw—right behind a coal-chute judder of thunder—grabbed for the corn, the trees, the gazebo, the pond. I saw a figure in a canoe on the rain-whipped water, Miss Giselle's ghost, or maybe just a floating pecan bough torn off its trunk by the storm.

My fan stopped prowling on the windowsill, its propellers creaked to a stall. The storm'd knocked our power out. To make sure, I reached up, shivering, and groped for the switch on the pole lamp beside my bed.

Thwick!

The dark dragged itself out like an endless roll of funeral bunting. McKissic House, probably half of Highbridge, was kilowattless. Yow. In town, you could usually get light with a finger flip, but now—torrents washing the factory district's cobblestones, the peanut fields outside town, and the barracks at Camp Penticuff—nothing but clattering blackness. I huddled on my bed, scairt numb.

Thunder grumbled, more lightning cracked: God Himself homering to the seats over the universe's edge. The crowd—which existed the way the dead exist—roared. The rain and the noise shook me; twinges beset my rebuilt knee, my jammed hip, the scars on my thigh. I prayed to Almighty God, and to my not quite so omnipotent mother.

A shape hovered into view on the topmost landing of the fire stairs; it filled the square of my window and bent there in silhouette like a shadow on a black-plastic movie screen. A horror movie. When the figure poked its head in the window and accidentally knocked my fan to the floor, I recognized it as Henry. A whole series of branching lightning strokes—like phosphorescent tuber roots, or a sky-size X-ray of nerve cells—lit up his crooked face from the sides. He grinned in his glum, turned-funny way.

Henry's greasy hair lay plastered to his skull like Johnny Weissmuller's after a fierce swim through a jungle lagoon. His eyes blinked yellow. His skin shone yellow. His teeth had the nicotine gleam of tobacco-stained store-boughts.

Maybe, I thought, our palship and his long letter aside, he'd come back to kill *me*—my reward for beating out Buck Hoey at short, getting Hoey traded, and setting up the conditions that had prodded Henry into throwing Hoey out of a tree and then yanking his tongue out. I'd snarled the long comeback Henry'd engineered after his nightmare march through Europe, over a century and a half ago.

"Daniel"—whispering—"Daniel, may I come in?"

"Sure. Where've you been? What're you doing?"

Henry's Sunday shirt and his muddy coveralls were sodden, but he climbed over the sill anyway and stepped on the fan he'd already knocked to the floor. In the middle of the room, he held his arms out and let the water drenching his sleeves drip in shimmery membranes to the floor.

"Didn't I promise we'd meet again?" The emptiness of our room—or his half of the room—quieted him, even though he'd helped to empty it.

"Henry, they'll catch you here, you'll end up in the pokey."

"No jail in Highbridge can hold me."

"Why'd you have to kill Hoey? It was bad enough, what Hoey did to me."

"My letter . . . I didn't mean to kill him, but to avenge you. In the end, I left him speechless."

"A funny word for dead, Henry."

"Come away with me . . . not for long. A few days only. To see where I've sequestered myself."

"I'm going home. I've got a ticket."

"Some possess tickets for that destination. Some do not."

These words lit up the inside of my skull. Henry'd left Hoey "speechless" out of regard for Daniel Boles, a pissed-off sense of abraded justice. He'd been my roommate. I could barely see him, a rain-soaked thing in the dark, but I used my crutches to stump over to him to give him a hug. My hands around his back got no closer than the rock-hard dimples on either side of his spine. He was too lean for love handles and too knurled for comfort, but I clove to him anyway, my crutches tumbled to the floor.

The bulb in my pole lamp pinged on, stinging our eyes. The fan Henry'd knocked to the floor began bumbling around. Henry looked twice as big in the light, and the fan sounded ten times as loud. Henry, still hugging me, pulled the fan's plug and switched off the lamp.

"Come, Daniel. Escape with me."

"I don't need to. This aint my prison, and I haven't done anything to run from the police for."

My reasoning didn't impress Henry. Even in the dark, he found my duffel and slapped it into my hands. "Pack." He helped me, piling clothes from my cardboard chifforobe onto the bed. Neatly. It made me realize he had owl eyes, two built-in nightscopes. I began to pack. "Don't forget your notebooks. They belong at the bottom, shielded and snug." So I dug them out of the school desk beside my bed. Henry took them and put them at the bottom of my bag with one easy plunge of his arm. I piled my clothes in on top, and my ball gear in on top of my duds, and faced Henry with my duffel slung GI- or maybe Santa-style over my shoulder, a crutch in one armpit.

"Out the window, Daniel. Into the rain and the bemusing tangles of the night."

I couldn't reply to such poppycock. I did a one-footed crutch-supported hop to the window. To my amazement, Euclid stood drenched on the fire-exit landing, waiting to take my bag and tote it down the slick wet stairs.

"Euclid!"

"Shoo," he said. "Shoo-shoo. Keep yo mouf shuh n gid on ouw. Me, I gots to come on back fo dawk."

We tip-toed—or, in my case, crutch-stumped—down the fire stairs in straggly single file, hurrying like the stoop-backed targets of a stoning. Down, we piled into a blue Studebaker Euclid said belonged to his mama, Detta Rae Satterfield. It had a "C" gas-rationing sticker on the windshield (like Colonel Elshtain's Hudson Terraplane), but I couldn't figure why, and didn't have the sand to ask. Henry scrambled into the back seat with my duffel. I arranged myself up front, on the wide divan-like seat with Euclid. He'd propped himself on a cushion as near the steering wheel as he could get.

Believe me, a fourteen-year-old chauffeur did nothing to boost my confidence in Henry's getaway plan.

Euclid backed us around McKissic House—not past the buggy house, but the other way—then drove straight through downtown Highbridge to the steel and concrete span that had given the town its name. To my surprise, Euclid did fine, weaving only a bit. He let Henry tell him where to turn and how fast to go, and we never made more than thirty miles per hour on our entire seventy-some-odd-mile trip into eastern Alabama.

Because of the downpour and wartime speed limits, our destination—not home, but Henry's hideaway and shrine—lay almost three hours away. It'd take Euclid that long again to return the Studebaker to his mama's. If the highway patrol—an irritable crew, what with all the restrictions on driving—stopped him for a license check, he'd probably catch a hiding mean enough to turn his skinny brown butt eggplant-purple.

"There!" Henry barked after our spooky, kidney-jouncing ride. "Halt there, Euclid!"

Euclid halted. All I could see in the 3:30 A.M. drizzle was wet pasturage, some forlorn pines, and a rugged grid of reddish gulleys between the road and one weedy field.

"Nigh." Euclid dropped us off at this unpromising-looking bump in the blacktop. "Yall behay, heah?"

60

Henry led me into the roadside brush: the blackberry vines, the pokeweed, the mimosa seedlings, the no-name stickery shrubs that snagged your cuffs and sent macelike burrs to hitchhike your socks. The rain'd slackened, thank God, but our shoes sank—often with sucking PLOOPs—both in the jumbled vegetable mulch and Alabama's oozy pasta-sauce clay. I began to think I'd gone off my nut to ride to this muddy natural chessboard of weedy rubbish and cut-bank arroyos, especially with a set of crutches. I had a train ticket back to Oklahoma—so why'd I let Henry pied-piper me to the redneck boonies?

"Where we goin, Henry? *Henry!*"

He just forged ahead, a driven upright bundle of backwoods energy—like a bear, or a Sasquatch, or a mad semi-human spawn of the land. The rain, more drizzle now than gullywasher, held all nasty winged insects out of the air, but the fight to keep up without sinking kept me from relishing their absence.

"*HENRY!*"

He looked back. "A dry side-channel of Tholocco Creek—our destination. We're nearly there."

The "dry" side-channel, when we reached it, had water in it—not a full beck's worth, but enough to put a cold squelch under your toes.

Anyway, squelching along in this tall gully, Henry led me to his hideaway: an earthen house tunneled into the bank of a drought-emptied creek. This shelter may've begun as a small cave, but, if so, Henry'd dug it out deeper and wider over the past two years, honeycombing the red earth with chambers. He'd also covered the creekbed doors with wild azalea, Allegheny hawthorne, and pine boughs. Nutlets from the hawthorne floated in the runoff sluicing down the cut. We waded into the earth house's flooded entrance, then replaced the damp foliage that had hidden it. A second chamber lodged higher and drier, and in that room, with coffee-can lanterns to see by, we spent most of the rest of the night.

Henry sat braced against one wall with his knees drawn up to his chin. I sat shivering on my duffel, my crutches stacked in front of me.

"Why have I brought you to this dank retreat?" Henry said. "I don't doubt you must wonder."

After looking around—at the coffee tins, the mats, the baseball equipment used for ornament—I said, "You could've given Worthy Bebout some decorating tips."

"I did."

"Well, he must not've listened." Why'd Henry brought me here? Despite its homey touches, it would have been a fine place for him to crack open my skull with a rock and feast on my brains with his fingers—if he'd been a meat-eater. Even in his eighteenth-century reign of error, though, he'd liked nuts and berries better than animal flesh, and his time among the Oongpekmut had corrupted his vegetarianism only a bit. But for the chill on my body, the clammy damp of my clothes, I might've enjoyed the coziness of Henry's Tholocco Creek warren, his coffee-can lanterns throwing shadows around, the mizzle outside hardly even hearable.

"Your father deserted you, Daniel, as mine did me. He fled from and forgot you, as my maker fled from and sought to forget me. Your sire—as did mine—renounced any part in your making and defaulted on his obligation to educate you."

"Dick Boles taught me how to play ball."

Henry shut up. He'd caught himself up in a riff of jazzy comparisons, though, and my tribute stunned him. He shook off the stun: "No small thing. No inconsequential pedagogy."

"But what were you driving at?"

"Recently, your father died. You may have smoldered these past several years with unspoken anger, but you have not yet mourned your father—as I, early in my second life, grudgingly mourned Victor Frankenstein."

"So?"

"So the process must eventually occur in you too, Daniel, or much of what hereafter befalls you, or occurs as a result of your own enterprise, will curdle on your palate."

"All right. How do you do it?"

The question caught him off-guard. "Do what?"

"Mourn."

"Oh," he said. "Oh." He crawled away from the wall and nodded into a farther chamber. "Follow." And he led me on a duck-walking tour that took us to a kind of dug-out viewing room. Here, when he set down the candle holder he'd brought, I saw a peculiar human shadow—like a straitjacketed Egyptian king—stretched out on the chopped-down shipping crate of an upright piano.

When Henry lifted his candle to show me the makeshift bier, I saw these words stenciled on the crate: *MENDELSSON / Ship to 486 Mims Street / Opp, Ala.* The letters danced in the candle flicker. The figure atop the crate resembled a mummy. It was a mummy. And it would've been the strangest mummy I'd ever seen, even if I'd never seen one before—which, as any fool could guess, I hadn't. And forget that that mummy embodied the remains of a whacko Swiss chemist a century and a half dead.

I leaned into my crutches and reached out to touch the corpse—it looked barely five and a half feet from soles to crown—of Henry's creator. The wrapper encasing it was a patchwork of smooth white pieces of horsehide— beaucoups of scraps stitched together with thousands of S-shaped seams. Henry'd made the sleeping jacket from the scrubbed, rubbed, and flattened skins of discarded CVL baseballs. Some of these horsehides were smudged with infield dirt, or pocked with bat marks, or roughened like old suede—but the shroud as a whole, under Henry's lantern, shone ivory.

The lovely weirdness of it made my nape hairs tingle.

"Out of Alaska, Daniel, I trekked into Washington with my dead creator (newly retrieved from a volcanic cave miles from Oongpek) slung over my shoulders. I bore him much as Aeneas bore his aged father, Anchises, out of the burning shell of Troy." Henry closed his eyes. "Sang that hero,

> 'Come then, dear father, up onto my back.
> I will bear you on my shoulders—you will be
> No burden to me at all, and whatever befall us,
> One and the same peril will face us both,
> And there will be one and the same salvation!'"

Henry opened his eyes. "Of course, as I came southward through the American Northwest, a thaw set in. Limbs once as firm as stone lost their durity, tending towards a malleable and aromatic decay. I confined them in the skins of animals—a dead elk the vultures had not yet begun to pick, a bison felled by drought—and remade Frankenstein's protective case each time I moved. During my last off-season with the Hellbenders, I made the sheath you see here. Denuding each ball and laying out its leathern wings wanted tedious labor. The needle-hooks I broke were virtually uncountable."

Henry gave his father an admiring look. "Don't you think he makes a handsome long pig, even though we feast on him only through our eyes?" He seemed to expect an "Amen!"

"Sure," I said. And Henry's stitched-up daddy definitely was a sight.

"Kneel here, Daniel."

I obeyed, mostly because the ceiling pressed so low that kneeling under it, even with my injuries, came easy. I propped my crutch against the piano crate.

"Take my father as your own. Revile him for his paternal failings, or grieve in silence for your heretofore unwept loss. Or do both together. Sometimes we must rage in order to reflect, inveigh in order to vindicate."

As I knelt there, Henry blundered softly out. In a way, taking Henry's daddy for my own and treating him to a prayer of curses may have helped some. In another way, it didn't seem to help at all. After a while, my brain'd turned into a shifting globe of axle grease. I leaned my head against the crate and tried to let go of the whole sad jam-up inside me.

Nothing came.

Out of politeness, or maybe pity, I stayed with Henry for two more days. Sleeping in a bunker a couple of dozen feet from his horsehide-jacketed daddy gave me an even creepier feeling than rooming with Henry had. It worried me I had a train ticket home, but Henry had only this creek-bank hole in the ground, fancy as it was, and no real prospects for a better life.

"What're you gonna do?" I asked him on Wednesday night.

"I continue to owe Buck Hoey's widow and children a debt."

"You can't creep around Highbridge trying to do them daily good turns. You'll get caught."

"I wish to redeem the crime—nay, the condign retribution—that befell Hoey and prompted his family's current suffering."

"But you never meant to kill him."

"Perhaps I did. I meant to do . . . great harm."

"Well, you're a big son of a gun, and trying to fix broken glider chains, or drop off bags of groceries, or cut wood for em—Henry, it just aint gonna do."

"My recidivism condemns me utterly."

That remark—the way he sat, his head in his hands—worried me. I could see him quitting, flinging himself off a cliff, even if the act maimed rather than croaked him. What a cross. He was suicidal, but couldn't die.

I rummaged in my bag and found the letter he'd written me.

I quoted from it: "*In this much longer incarnation, by many accepted and by many others acclaimed, I have killed but once, Daniel, and then for love.*" Henry didn't even look up. "Not for revenge, you said. For love. Evolution you call it here."

"Sophistries. Carrion comfort."

"So what're you gonna do?"

"What I must." Henry lifted his head. "Continue. Begin anew and continue."

"Turn yourself in. Then maybe you'll see justice done."

"Justice? I came to consciousness, Daniel, in its cynical and selfish abrogation."

"You've seen it done. We won the pennant, didn't we? You and I got called up."

Henry stared at me like I'd just proposed to end the war by sending the Japs my mama's favorite oatmeal-cooky recipe. Then he smiled—I think—and shook his head.

"Daniel, the electric chair would merely recharge me. Your species cursed and harassed me during my first career on this earth. It owes me one, I think."

Henry ate hawthorne nuts from a stoneware cereal bowl. I cracked some early wild pecans we'd gathered. Outside, the call of a shivering Alabama screech owl echoed over the empty channel of the Tholocco. Henry pulled off his left shoe and turned it upside down next to his cereal bowl.

I raised my eyebrows.

"To ward off ills otherwise sure to follow," Henry said. "I am entitled to my superstition."

On Friday morning, I stood on the blacktop on my crutches, my duffel at my feet and Henry hidden in a nearby pine copse. It wouldn't have done for him to ogre around in broad daylight. I was waiting for a chance to thumb a ride into Troy. In Troy, I planned to connect with my train out of Highbridge and to ride it to Memphis, where another carrier would pick me up and haul me across Arkansas to Oklahoma.

I had a pasteboard sign—TROY OR BUST—around my neck, and a stoic look on my farm-boy face. The ban on pleasure driving and the absence of cars made me begin to think I'd do better to set off crutching it, but finally a truck—loaded down, as my luck required, with dozens of stacked crates of live chickens—came grinding towards me from the southeast. The middle-aged driver pulled over and waved me towards his passenger side. He saw my crutches and got down to help me.

"You a wounded sojer, kiddo?"

His hair—the color of fresh-made doughnuts—rose in a greasy pompadour from his forehead, and his ratty pin-striped shirt lacked its top two buttons. He'd rolled its sleeves up to his elbows, where the twisted-over cuffs gave it a funny space-suitish look. I didn't want to lie so I lied not to lie, if you can follow my logic. I tapped my throat with one finger and lifted one of my crutches.

"Awright then. Climb on up."

We stuttered off, the reek of doomed chickens hanging over that truck like a moving canopy. The driver told me his name, who he worked for, how many kids he had, how much he admired and respected young fellas like myself who'd sacrificed life and limb to fight the Nips and the Huns. By the time we hit Troy, he'd invented an Army unit for me, a romantic battle or two, five or six heroic wounds, and a faithful sweetheart back home in . . . well, wherever I was from.

He drove me straight to the train station. He helped me down, carried my bag inside, and, at the ticket counter, shook my hand with a solemn, prime-the-pump rhythm. When he let go, I found a dollar in my palm.

"Nothin can repay yall for yore wounds, kiddo, but that's, well, that's a . . . a *token*. Okay?"

I nodded.

The trains from Troy to Memphis and from Memphis to Oklahoma teemed with young guys in uniform. I was dressed in civvies, and everybody aboard naturally assumed—correctly—I'd hurt myself in a frivolous schoolboy game, not in the training camps of Georgia or on the battlefields of Europe. So the dogfaces ignored me, and I felt lucky, privileged even, to be ignored.

Mama Laurel, Miss Tulipa, and Colonel Elshtain met me at the station in Tahlequah. On first catching sight of me, Mama commenced to cry her eyes out. She grabbed me and pulled me to her, my crutches be damned. She clung to me like a burr, then shoved me out to arm's length and gave me a sappy smile.

"At least you won't have to go off to war," she said. "At least you won't have to die."

"Mama, I done already done both."

Colonel Elshtain sniffed, but Mama and Miss Tulipa hugged me, flooding me with the stinks of woman sweat, prairie grime, and drugstore gardenia water.

I liked it.

61

The CVL shut down at the end of the 1943 season. Mister JayMac hadn't wanted it to, but only three of the league's eight teams had turned a profit that summer—the Hellbenders, the Gendarmes, and the Orphans. The other five clubs had taken a bath. Mister JayMac might still've willed the loop to go on, but the loss of Hank Clerval and myself, along with Darius's vamoosement and Miss Giselle's self-pyrotechnics, had yanked the heart right out of him. When the owners met in Highbridge after the Yankee-Card World Series, they voted five to three to suspend the CVL until the war ended and able-bodied prospects again came into the talent pool. Mister JayMac's vote counted twice—maybe three times—as much as any other owner's, but you can't force five smart men to bleed themselves bankrupt and so he had to bow to majority rule.

Over the winter, the Phillies, the Hellbenders' big-league holding company, tried to spruce up their image—the elite of Philadelphia's professional losers?—by sponsoring a contest to change their nickname. (What the hell was a Phillie anyway?) Thousands of people sent in entries, and Mrs. John L. Crooks, a caretaker along with her husband of the local Odd Fellows Grand Lodge, won. Her suggestion was Blue Jays. This was more than thirty years before Toronto organized an American League club with that name, and the Phillies played under it for only a season. They also lost their young, wise-ass owner that winter when Commissioner Landis kicked William Cox out of baseball for betting cold cash on his own team.

Anyway, when Mister JayMac learned of the name change, he told Miss Tulipa in a letter he thanked God for the CVL's decision to pack it in. "A blue jay isn't a ballplayer," he wrote. "It's a defecating, marauding, squawking pest in a fowl's deceitful glad rags, and I wouldn't want a player of mine to have to bear that epithet, not to mention the tatty costume they're like to design for it." Phillies, though, he could live with, even if it meant something squishy like, well, humanitarian.

When I got home, Tenkiller seemed downright boring. I passed most of one day studying a pair of prewar Texaco road maps and underlining names—Muskogee, Eufaula, Cherokee—with sound-alikes back among the counties and towns of the CVL. Trail of Tears connections. Well, I had some links to it of my own. Mostly, that fall, I laid or limped about, taking in *Life Can Be Beautiful*, *Stella Dallas*, and other suchlike day-time crap on the radio.

Eventually, I tossed my crutches, but when I walked, I hitched around like a man with a fresh load in his drawers. No one hired me to bale hay, dehorn cattle, or set up wildcat rigs over in Stillwell. To Mama Laurel's disgust, and even my own, I loafed. Tenkillerites knew I was loafing too; the town was too small for anybody local to suppose I was a poor wounded GI wrestling with the afterclaps of combat. I didn't pretend to that condition either. Some of my Red Stix pals had entered the services, and I respected their sacrifice too much to try to siphon off any of their glory, potential or real.

By December, a family friend had helped me get a position as a clerk at Funderburke's Penny & Nickel Emporium, a notions and stationery shop where I could move at my own pace and had no heavy lifting to do. Deck Glider, Inc., ran full tilt, of course, but every job there had someone in it and a whole queue of applicants standing by. My salary at Funderburke's fell ten or twelve bucks a week shy of the minimum janitorial salary at Deck Glider, but at least I had a job and folks stopped looking at me with pity or contempt.

I got a couple of letters from Phoebe that fall and a homemade Christmas card at Christmas. (She'd made the card out of construction paper and carefully scissored magazine photos—Santa Claus standing outside the Bethlehem stable with Oveta Gulp Hobby of the WACs, Alan Ladd, Franklin Delano Roosevelt, and the starting lineup of the '43 Yankees.) The second of her two letters read this way:

> Dear Ichabody Beautiful (alias Daniel Boles),
>
> How are things in Oklahoma. OK, I hope. I'd tell you to keep an eye out for injuns but you ARE one, sort of—an injun not a eye, but we're all eyes to ourselves, aren't we? (Eye = I, if you can't shred my wheat without a scorecard.) Sorry. School's started here, and I hate it. I'm blinkng away sand ten seconds after Mrs. Camson opens her mouth. My I's turn to ZZZZZ's.
>
> Mama keeps on improvng. It helps the Hellbender players have almost all gone home. It also helps Daddy writes more often—I suggested he shd. Letters seem to arrive every week now, even if some cutup in the S.O.S. or whatever has censored parts of them all with scissors.
>
> A senior boy here named Hal Frank Kimball thinks he likes me. He has one eyebrow and hormone hickeys. My girlfriend Sunny Ruth Grimes says he's AWOL—A Wolf On the Loose. When he comes paddng around, I ice up or shove in my clutch. Now don't get yr ego or yr dander up, Daniel, but I am waitng for YOU.
>
> No jump the gun panic, please. I'm NOT in a family surcumstance. No rabbit died. On the other hand, I never want to do the aweful thing we illeegly did until we do it again together—licensed and sanctified. That wld have to be better, wldn't it? God, I hope so. In the meantime, keep the tool cool, OK?
>
> Uncle Jay has been in a 2 maybe a 3 month mope. You shd drop him a line. You shd drop ME a letter. I promise to catch it.
>
> Yr patient little BB, Phoebe
>
> P.S. If you buy every word in my billydoo, yr a real smack. Read between the lines and hit the ones that count.
>
> P.P.S. Homer says hello.

Phoebe and I married in the early summer of 1947, the year the CVL started back up. (Her daddy, long home from the war, gave her away.) The Blakely Turpentiners replaced the Marble Springs Seminoles in Georgia, and the Roanoke Rebs took over for the Cottonton Boll Weevils in Alabama.

But I jump ahead of myself.

In the spring of '44, I'd hobble out of Funderburke's every afternoon and watch the Red Stix play or practice. I watched the players who came into town as closely as I did my ex-high school teammates. I noticed things—sneaky foot speed, an unhittable specialty pitch, hidden room for improvement— that other baseball folks, not exempting Coach Brandon and Miss Tulipa, couldn't see, and I wrote letters to Mister JayMac recommending a half dozen players—a couple of locals and four unscouted visitors—as guys to watch. Mister JayMac followed up, and after the war three of my first six picks wound up playing full- or part-time in the National League, two with the Phillies and one with Brooklyn.

Early in May, Coach Brandon got word a barnstorming team of Negro all-stars called the American-Afrique Something-or-Others had an official invitation to play an infantry team at Camp Gruber, a training post eighteen miles southeast of Muskogee. Coach Brandon had a drill instructor friend who could get us a pass onto the post to see the game, if we wanted it. A memory clip of the Splendid Dominican Touristers ran in my head— old Turtlemouth Clark pitching, Tommy Christmas chasing down long flies in center, our own Charlie Snow falling over the fence and fatally hemorrhaging, with Oscar Wall's game-winning drive in his glove—and I told Coach Brandon, Yep, I'd go, especially since it was a Sunday contest and I didn't have to work.

The game itself was the damndest exhibition I ever saw. The American-Afrique Zanies—that was their nickname—came out onto the field in clown costumes, all tricked out with pompons, face paint, big shoes, and fright wigs. They warmed up in these outfits, they even played the Army squad in them. They pranced and tomfooled around like circus performers. But despite their shenanigans, they still managed to rap the Army boys something like sixteen to zip. A walkover. The only thing making it bearable for us fans was the GIs' realization that the Freakies (as a few guys started calling them) could've beaten them in suits of armor. These decent dogfaces saved the game. They acknowledged the Zanies' talents without giving up on themselves or letting the coloreds push their lead up into the twenties or thirties.

I also got a kick out of the PFC announcing the game: "Now pitching for the Zanies, Whim-Wham? Dinkum-Do to center? And taking over at shortstop, Gumbo Giddyup?"

Three innings into the game, I figured out the Zany playing right field and going by the name Cuffy was none other than Darius Satterfield. His clown suit couldn't hide his muscular lankiness. The greasy white makeup melting on his cheek bones and the green and purple wig raying out from his head like a crown of vat-dyed yarn—well, that crap kept me from making a positive ID for an inning or three, but it couldn't blind me forever to the smoothness of Cuffy's play or the whiplash grace of his hitting.

I wanted to wade down the bleacher tier and pull Darius aside for a chat, but I never got within a hundred feet of him till the game ended and he sat under an awning of the barracks building provided as the Zanies' locker room. While Coach Brandon talked to his DI buddy, I limped into Darius's line of sight. When he saw me, his eyeballs gave me a bounce and his hand snapped up like it meant to hold me at bay.

"Danl Boles. Sweet gentle Jesus."

"What happened to the Splendid Dominicans, Darius?"

He studied me real good. "You look kinda puny, hoss. What happened to you?"

I gave him the short version and pressed my own question.

"Us Dominicans ran out of gas. Coupons. Working capital. Also goodwill. Mister Cozy got us all back to KayCee with him, but we had creditors galore and jes dropped apart. So I'm here today and mebbe tomorry as"—spreading the balloon sleeves of his arms—"a damn ol American-Afrique Zany."

"Mister JayMac'd love to see you back in Highbridge."

"Well, he aint big enough to beat me no mo, and I aint big enough to let him try." He pulled off his wig and used it to daub at the sweat-runneled grease on his face. "Sorry bout yo setback, Danl. Real, real sorry."

"He's your daddy. At least you got one. Miss Giselle's dead and he needs you."

"I heard that, bout po Miss Giselle. But Mister JayMac needs me like a hound needs another tic."

"You gonna stay with these . . . Zanies?"

"Nosir. Gonna quit em and join up. A man cain't play ball in wartime. I guess his duty lies elsewhere, but the war angles gainst you and it's a sorry style ball that gits played anyway. Take this turkey strut today."

"The wrong team was wearing the clown suits."

"Amen."

"Still, you should go home. You should let Mister JayMac help you get into a decent unit. You should probably—"

"Danl, put yo cumulated wisdom in a croker sack with a cow flop and burn it fo a night light. Nice to see you again."

Darius strolled around the corner and into the building. I tried to follow him. An MP with a billy and a .45 pistol in an unsnapped leather holster blocked my way: "Zanies only. You a Zany, kiddo?"

I tried to wait, to meet Darius when he came back out in his civvies with his teammates, but Coach Brandon found me, and took me home, and I never saw Darius again. So far as I know, he never played integrated pro ball, and I sometimes think he died overseas after enlisting—maybe right there at Camp Gruber—under a phony name.

62

Three years later I received a registered letter from Seattle, Washington. It contained round-trip airline tickets to Seattle from Tulsa, with stopovers in Denver, Salt Lake City, and Spokane. From Seattle, I had other tickets to Juneau, Alaska, from Juneau to Anchorage, and from Anchorage to Kodiak Island. The packet also contained a money order for two hundred dollars and a note:

Dear Daniel,

I have found your father's grave on Attu Island, at the westernmost extremity of the Aleutian archipelago. Allow yourself two weeks and embark upon a pilgrimage to your sire's final resting place. I enclose money and tickets to return you to Oklahoma at the conclusion of your valedictory journey. I will meet you at the airfield at Kodiak. You may recognise me by the stalk of wild celery I wear as a boutonniere.

Faithfully, "J." H. C.

Like I'd need a corny sign. Unless he'd cut himself down to a Munchkin's height or had plastic surgery on his ugly mug.

Anyway, the idea of a trip scared me. I'd never flown before, and the distance and the layovers terrified me. I broke the news to Mama, though, and told her both who'd sent the tickets and that I planned to go. She knew Henry from a creased team photo as "that big ugly-gawky fella m the back," and from my letters home as a decent roommate, and from stories out of Highbridge at the end of the '43 season as an on-the-lam murder suspect.

It'd crossed my mind Mama might take this news and pass it on to Miss Tulipa, or Mayor Stone, or our county sheriff, but I couldn't fly off thousands of miles without taking that chance and trusting Mama to trust me.

"Dick Boles don't deserve a graveside visitor," Mama Laurel said.

"I'm still going, Mama."

"Take the Brownie then. Take some pictures."

On my trip, I must have smoked a carton—*two* cartons—of cigarettes in all those different airports and on the flights themselves. I was twenty years old, almost legally an adult, but because of all my travel, bad meals, and missed sleep, I had an outbreak of schoolboy acne that upped my dependence on tobacco. By the time my umpteenth flight—this one aboard a small Electra prop plane—came down through the gray tattered fog and landed on Kodiak's airstrip, I had a lung-crumping cough.

Henry stood on the edge of the field near the parking lot. No one could miss him, even though he'd separated himself from the other two parties there to greet the plane. As a sure ID, though, he clutched a pale yellow stalk of wild celery in one hand. It also struck me, as I wobbled towards him, his face looked awfully ugly and fearsome that afternoon—most likely because of the ivory labrets, carven like polar bears, he'd inserted in the cheek holes (in Highbridge, mere scar-tissue welts) at the corners of his mouth.

"Roomy," I said.

Henry glanced about him, at the overarching sky and the nearby mountains visible through cloud or fog wisps. "Yes," he said, "but on clear days it seems even moreso."

*

A Russian Aleut by the name of Dorofey Golodoff—Henry called him Fego—flew us in a beat-up light aircraft to Nikolski, an Aleut village on Umnak, where my father had been stationed during the war. Fego lived near Nikolski in a *barabara*, or dugout sod house, that put me in mind of Henry's underground hideaway in a branch of Tholocco Creek in Alabama. We spent the night with Fego, a burly Asiatic-looking man with a broad squashed nose and long jet-black hair. I had a couple of inches of height on him, but he outweighed me by forty pounds or more, even though he moved from room to room in his house with the speed and agility of an otter. For supper, he fed us steamed clams, batter-fried octopus, and a salad of kelp, wild onions, and Fox Islands celery.

As we ate, Fego told us, "When the tide goes out, the table is set." Beyond repeating this comment, he said little else, and all I recall of what he did say is that Aleut folk saying, which explains how this hardy people could subsist in such a forbidding place. Fego, however, also received pay from the United States government as a surveyor and a backup mail pilot, and the next day he flew us to Attu, the remotest island in the chain, with a single delivery and refueling stopover at the naval station airfield on Adak Island, not quite midway between Umnak and Attu.

Luckily, or we wouldn't have flown, the day broke and stayed clear, with no fogs or willawaws arising from the collision of Bering Sea waters and the warmer flow of the Kurishio or Japan current, and an easy pewter chop moving along beneath the high whine of Fego's prop plane.

On Attu, Henry led me inland on foot from Massacre Bay towards the island's western mountains. Fego didn't accompany us. Through most of this trek, it drizzled on us. Towards late afternoon, the drizzle thickened into a light snow, and my injuries put an extra hitch and a gnawing round of lesser and greater pains into my limp.

We took shelter from the snow, the day's chronic gauziness, and the ache that had settled in my legs in a Japanese hut not demolished during the U.S. invasion four springs earlier. In the hut's litter, I found an empty sake bottle, a half-burnt diary in Japanese characters, and two sets of weather-warped snow skis. We ate from tins we'd backpacked in.

"Henry, what're you doing in this godforsaken place?" I asked between spoonfuls of lumpy pork and beans.

"Escorting you to your father's grave."

"I mean, besides that. Did you come back up here to live, to be the Eskimo Hiding Man—?"

"Inyookootuk."

"Yeah, Inyookootuk. To be the Hiding Man forever?"

"I am not an Aleut. I would hide forever among the Innuit of the mainland, but not in this storm-wracked island chain."

"Is that what you plan to do? Hide forever?"

"This is a temporary exile, Daniel, a mere sabbatical. I wish to re-create myself. As Wordsworth wrote, 'So build we up the Being that we are.' But I despair of the authenticity of my materials." He removed and pocketed his labrets, so as not to be distracted by them on our hike tomorrow, and refused to say another word that night.

The next day we reached a peak called Sarana Nose. The snow had stopped. The drizzle had stopped. Sunlight dropped through the whirling fog like lamplight through an aquarium full of seaweed. We reached an embankment on the mountain, a tierlike balcony on its flank, where several small stone cairns and a group of flat-nailed wooden crosses jutted up out of the muddy soil to mark burial plots. One cross boasted a round Japanese grave marker with Oriental paint-brush characters on it. I stood next to Henry in the chill, sweeping wind, dwarfed by him on a big volcanic sea rock at the top or maybe the end of the world.

"Here your father lies," Henry said.

"How do you know?"

"A party of Eleventh Air Force personnel came out here during the Army's mopping-up exercises—as hunters, not merely observers. They were shot or hand-grenaded by snipers. The snipers buried them here and memorialized their sacrifice."

"How do you know?" I said again.

Henry read the hand-lettered inscription: "'*Sleeping here, five brave soldier heroes who forfeited youth and happiness for their motherland.*'"

"A Jap wrote that?"

Henry said nothing.

"A Jap my daddy and his pals had come out here to hunt down and kill?"

Henry still said nothing.

"How do you know it's the graves of Dick Boles and his friends? Does the inscription list names?"

"I fear it doesn't."

"Then how do you know?"

"*Sleeping here, five brave soldier heroes who forfeited youth and happiness for their motherland,*'" Henry read again.

"That doesn't answer my—"

"Shhhh," Henry said, a mittened finger to his lips, exactly between the ugly labret holes at each mouth corner. "In this place, Daniel, before your father's grave, and in the presence of his enemy's uncommon integrity, you should stand speechless, humbly mute."

"B-B-But I—"

"Shhhh."

I bowed my head. Memories welled. When next I looked up, a bald eagle had caught a towering updraft. It wheeled in the high Aleutian gauze. Its talons seemed to spiral through my feelings like the threads of a screw. Finally, I looked at Henry, almost blinded by the sting of the wind and the thin wax of grief in my eyes.

Henry reached into his pack and rummaged out a brand-new National League baseball. He flipped it to me. I caught it with both hands, like an amateur. I stood there for a minute turning that ivory ball in my gloves before it occurred to me to wedge it into the natural cup of the stone cairn supposedly marking my daddy's grave. In that cup, the ball glinted like a lighthouse beacon and focused the whole of Attu Island around it, a pivot for the world to turn on.

I got out Mama's Brownie and took a picture.

As evening drew on, Henry and I walked back to the hut where we'd spent the night. The ache in my knee had let up, and my limp seemed less pronounced. I asked Henry what he'd done with *his* old man. He didn't answer.

"Come on, Henry. You didn't leave him in 'Bama, did you?"

He shook his head, still striding, still thoughtful.

"Then what? What'd you do?"

"He lies among a host of ancient Aleut mummies, fur- and grass-wrapped carcasses in a cave on one of the Islands of Four Mountains southwest of Umnak. His traveling days are over. There he will rest until the generative vulcanism of this archipelago drowns its islands, Daniel, or until the world expires in either fire or ice. I am resigned."

*

Henry refused to fly back to Kodiak with Fego and me aboard Fego's battered prop plane. He said he'd eventually return for a look-see to Oongpek, on Alaska's Seward Peninsula, but in the meantime wanted solitude and a chance to sort through his options. He paid Fego with a small stack of U. S. bills of various denominations for flying us to Attu and for returning me to Kodiak to pick up a commercial flight to Anchorage. Then he hugged me and stood clear as Fego and I taxied for takeoff, under a streaky sky, in a moderate crosswind.

"Whachu thinka that Henry fella?" Fego asked me when were up and rippling over the ashy chop of the Bering Sea.

His question startled me because he didn't talk all that much. I said, "Why do you ask?"

"Sumfin funny bout him. Not joos how beeg he is— sumfin else. Lak mebbe summa his feelins been cut loose. Lak beeg as he is, you know, sum parta him's missin."

"Which part?"

"Dunno. Soul mebbe. The spirit part,"

"How long've you known Henry, Fego?"

"Hey, I *don't* know him. Joos met him lass winter. I work for him sumtimes since, thass it."

"Oh."

"He tol me you roomed with him. Gude. Cause I lak to know the pipple I fly bettern I know this beeg ol Henry guy."

"Oh."

"So whatchu thinka him?"

"I think he's working hard on his soul," I said. "I think he's becoming a real person."

Editor's Note

Danny Boles, a long-time scout for the Philadelphia Phillies who began working for the Atlanta Braves in 1978, died on opening day of the 1991 baseball season. He was 66. In the early 1980s, he had his vocal cords removed to halt the advance of a throat cancer whose recurrence in 1989 led to his death.

Always a famous raconteur. Boles learned to talk with the aid of a microphone-like amplifier that he held to his throat. The amplifier gave him a mechanical-sounding "robot" voice that he was still able to infuse with personality. To obtain the material assembled in his memoir *Brittle Innings*, I conducted nearly forty interviews with Mr. Boles. They ranged in length from twenty minutes to nearly three hours. He also gave me access to his longhand transcriptions of the journals of "Henry Clerval." From these sources, I distilled the remarkable text now in your hands.

Look next year for my sports biography *The Good Scout*, in which I chronicle Mr. Boles's career as one of the most able major league scouts in post-war America. It will not stretch your credulity quite so far as *Brittle Innings* has likely done, and I immodestly regard it as the best book on this topic since Mark Winegardner's *Prophet of the Sandlots*.

——GABRIEL STEWART
Columbus, Georgia

Acknowledgements

In addition to my family, I must thank these people: Howard Morhaim, my indefatigable agent; Lou Aronica, an editor and publisher who likes baseball as much as I do; Jennifer Hershey, who edited the ms. with intelligence and care; Eddie Hall, who sent me a little book about baseball in the nineteenth century; Diane Hughes, who told me about her hemophiliac father; Joel Gotler, who saw the film possibilities in this material; John Kostmayer, who did a screenplay based on an early novella-length version of this story; Mark Winegardner, author of *Prophet of the Sandlots*, a masterpiece of sports writing; Michael Hutchins, the originator and operator of a website devoted to my work, who helped me secure a revisable electronic file of the novel and also caught an error in my early-season CVL standings; Patrick Swenson, editor and publisher of Fairwood Press, for this new edition of a work dear to me; Elizabeth Hand, a masterful writer, for her kind introduction to this edition; and, of course, Mary Wollstonecraft Shelley and the makers of Universal Pictures' *Frankenstein* films of the 1930s.

ABOUT THE AUTHOR

Michael Bishop is the author of the Nebula Award-winning novel *No Enemy But Time*, the Mythopoeic Fantasy Award-winning novel *Unicorn Mountain*, the Shirley Jackson Award-winning short story, "The Pile" (based on notes left behind on his late son Jamie's computer), and several other novels and story collections, including *The Door Gunner and Other Perilous Flights of Fancy: A Retrospective*, edited by Michael H. Hutchins. He also writes poetry and criticism, and has edited the acclaimed anthologies *Light Years and Dark*, three volumes of the annual Nebula Awards collections, and, more recently, *A Cross of Centuries: Twenty-Five Imaginative Tales About the Christ*, and, with Steven Utley, *Passing for Human*. He is currently working on a Young Adult novel, *Joel-Brock the Brave*, dedicated to his exemplary grandchildren, Annabel English Loftin and Joel Bridger Loftin. Michael Bishop lives in Pine Mountain, Georgia, with his wife, Jeri, an elementary-school counselor. He followed the Atlanta Braves even in the 1980s . . . when they were losing.

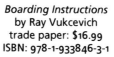

CPSIA information can be obtained at www.ICGtesting.com
Printed in the USA
LVOW08s0005180214

374067LV00004B/76/P